1918

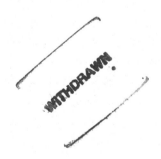

DAVID CORNISH, MD

To Mom, Dad, William, David, Madison, and my wife Dr. Dianne Dukette, the best editor an author ever had.

"If the epidemic continues its mathematical rate of acceleration, civilization could easily disappear from the face of the earth."

COLONEL VICTOR C. VAUGHN
CHIEF, DIVISION OF COMMUNICABLE
DISEASES, U.S. ARMY 1918

CHAPTER 1

The big ship sliced through the cold North Atlantic water with only a slight splashing sound at the bow, and a low rumbling of her reciprocating engines. Aside from the occasional creaking noise of a big ship, there were no other sounds. She was the steel-hulled Troop Transport *USS Madawaska*, named for the most Northeastern town in the United States. She displaced 15,000 tons, was over 500 feet long, and carried a beam of 55 feet.

Madawaska was originally a German ocean liner christened *Konig Wilhelm II*. Like many German passenger ships, she had been voluntarily docked at Hoboken, New Jersey in 1914 at the beginning of The War. This was done to avoid capture by the British Royal Navy that had a commanding presence in the Atlantic. However, *Wilhelm II* was seized by the United States military following America's entrance into The War in April, 1917. She was refitted by the navy with four 6 inch deck guns and two machine guns. She was also painted in the British camouflage "dazzle" pattern of seemingly random stripes and blocks of olive green and gray shades. This paint design actually made big ships harder to see at a distance.

The ship was commissioned *USS Madawaska* in August, 1917, and assigned to the Cruiser and Transport Force of the Atlantic Fleet. Her usual crew consisted of 39 officers and 550 sailors, and she could carry up to 2,400 troops.

Major Edward Noble stood on *Madawaska's* stern deck. It was early morning, and the gray sky and the gray sea met at a horizon that made the two barely distinguishable from one another. Noble had not been able to sleep. He had been topside for over an hour before any daylight appeared, and was still mostly alone on the deck. Although this was the beginning of the fourth day of a twelve day Atlantic crossing from France, it seemed as though they had been out for weeks. He watched the smoke from the ship's single funnel meander toward the stern as she sailed at the relatively slow speed of 15 knots.

It was very cold on this Monday, January 14, 1918. This was the coldest winter on record for the eastern United States and the North Atlantic. Small collections of clear blue ice could be seen on the wood decks and metal deck railings. The ocean breeze sometimes blew tiny flecks of ice against those who were topside, which could be painful. Noble turned up the lapels of his heavy army coat against his neck, and pulled down the brim of his cap against the cold.

The Major climbed the starboard ladder to the mid-ship top deck and walked slowly forward amidships. Along the ship's decks, from bow to stern, were hundreds of stacked oval life rafts. No one even dared think about their use.

Early in 1917, believing that America would eventually enter The War against her, Germany adopted a policy of unrestricted submarine warfare. Germany sought to strangle Allied Atlantic sea lanes before the U.S. could transport a large army to Europe. However, Germany was only able to maintain five long-range submarine U-boats on the lanes, so their effect was limited. Nevertheless, Allied Naval ships still took zigzag courses across the Atlantic to avoid German submarines.

Allied Destroyers and Armored Cruisers began accompanying Troop Transport ships in 1917, making kills for the U-boats even harder. A Destroyer, *USS Rowan*, and an Armored Cruiser, *USS San Diego*, could be seen 500 yards to the *Madawaska* port and starboard sides during this voyage. Both warships carried the new technologies of passive sonar hydrophones and depth charges that gave some hope of destroying stalking submarines. In addition, Troop Transport ships were too fast for the U-boats. The Transports also no longer travelled in convoys, which further decreased U-boat pack hunting. Still, there was always reason for concern, and everyone aboard *Madawaska* knew it. U-boats had sunk over 5,000 Allied ships, with a loss of only 178 U-boats.

Noble stopped his walk along the deck near the ship's bow, placed his elbows on the side rail, and leaned slightly forward as the overcast sky lightened. He thought about the last nine months since America had entered The War, and how long ago that seemed. The War had actually begun three-and-a-half years earlier with very little initial impact on the U.S. Historians were already debating what to all it. Some called it "The Great War". Others called it "The War to End All Wars", "The Kaiser's War", "The War of the Nations", and "The European War". In France it sometimes was called "La Guerre du Droit" (The War for Justice) or "La Guerre pour la Civilisation" (The War to Preserve Civilization). In America it was frequently known as "The War for Democracy". In 1914, the German philosopher Ernst Haeckel wrote, "There is no doubt that the course and character of the feared 'European War'...will become the First World War in the full sense of the word." "The First World War" term implied other world wars would follow. This thought was too horrible for Major Noble to even consider. So, he just called it "The War".

European countries had maintained a balance of political and military power for over 85 years. However, there had been a slow and steady rise in expansionist polices among many European states. An arms race had been underway between Germany and Britain since the 1890's. Significant resources were used to enlarge and improve the Imperial German Navy and the British Royal Navy. The military build-up eventually spread to the rest of Europe. Concurrently, a complex network of political and military alliances throughout the continent developed. Multi-government maneuvering for influence and dominance in geo-political, financial, and military arenas created a precarious situation known as the "Powder Keg of Europe".

On June 28, 1914, Gavrio Princip, a Bosnian-Serb student, assassinated the heir to the Austro-Hungarian throne, Archduke Franz Ferdinand of Austria in Sarajevo, Bosnia. The alliance dominos began to fall, as one country after another declared war on opposition alliances. At different times, the Allied Powers (Russia, France, Britain, Italy, Serbia, Belgium, Japan, Romania, Portugal, Greece, and several others) declared war on the Central Powers (Austria-Hungary, Germany, The Ottoman Empire, and Bulgaria). With many of the involved countries having distant global colonies, the conflict soon spread around the world.

The War eventually mobilized over 70 million military personnel worldwide. Campaigns were engage in Europe, Africa, Asia, India, and on the Atlantic and Pacific oceans.

The Germans planned a quick and early victory against the French and the Russians. However, with help from British forces, the Germans were halted east of Paris by September, 1914. This established the "Western Front" whose geography changed little until 1917. The Russians were defeated in a series of battles on their western frontier. But, German advances were slowed by stronger resistance than the German military leaders had anticipated. Nevertheless, Germany achieved a good defensive position within France and incapacitated 230,000 more Allied troops than it had lost.

The stalemate on the Western Front contained 5,965 miles of troop trenches. At any given time, over a three year period, 1.2 million soldiers fought in these trenches. The troops came to call the Western Front "The Sausage Factory" because of the outdated Napoleonic military tactic of massive frontal assaults on the enemy. Earlier in The War, generals threw millions of men to their deaths against new technologies for which they were not ready. For example, on July 1, 1916, the British Army endured the bloodiest day in its long history, suffering 57,470 casualties in about one hour. That particular offensive would eventually cost the British nearly half a million men.

On May 7, 1915, a German U-boat sank the passenger ship *RMS Lusitania*. The sinking killed 1,198 people, including 128 Americans. The American President Woodrow Wilson demanded an end to attacks on passenger ships, and would not tolerate unrestricted submarine warfare. Germany complied with these demands and thus thwarted, for a time, an American entry into The War. President Wilson later made unsuccessful attempts to negotiate a settlement between the Allies and the Central Powers.

At the start of The War, Germany had cruisers scattered across the globe. The cruisers were later used to attack Allied merchant shipping. From February to July, 1917, German U-boats sank 500,000 Allied tons per month, reaching a peak of 860,000 tons in April. However, the British naval blockade of German ports, and their mining of international waters, began to take its toll on German sea power and its industrial output. Britain eventually asserted its control of the sea, and the bulk of the German surface fleet remained confined to port for the duration of The War.

After ten brutal months of the Battle of Verdun, the Germans attempted to negotiate a peace with the Allies in December, 1916. Effectively and unilaterally, Germany tried to declare itself the victor. This peace offer was completely ignored by the Allies, even as President Wilson once again tried to intervene as peacemaker. The well-intentioned effort came to nothing.

Germany became convinced it was only a matter of time before the U.S entered The War on the side of the Allies. Acting on this belief in January, 1917, Germany resumed unrestricted submarine warfare. The Americans were outraged. Suddenly, Britain's secret Royal Navy cryptana-lytic group, known as Room 40, broke the German diplomatic code. Britain intercepted a proposal from Berlin to Mexico (the Zimmerman Telegram) to join The War as Germany's ally against the United States. The telegram was designed to delay America's deployment of troops to Europe, and buy Germany time. Germany planned to use the additional time for its previously successful unrestricted submarine warfare program. The submarines were essential in the effort to stran-gle Britain's vital war supplies quietly coming from America.

President Wilson was under great political pressure to act. The very popular former President, Theodore Roosevelt, spoke passionately about the continued and outrageous sink-ing of neutral country ships by German U-boats. Wilson's own deep religious convictions caused him to see The War as a confrontation between democracy and tyranny; between good and evil. Although President Wilson won reelection in 1916 by keeping America out of The War, he released the Zimmerman telegram to the press as a way of building sup-port for the U.S. entry into the conflict. On February 3, 1917, he announced to Congress he was ceasing official diplomatic relations with Germany. Then, U-boats sank seven addition-al U.S merchant ships. On April 6, 1917, President Wilson asked Congress for a declaration of war against Germany. The Congress granted his request. The United States did not become a formal member of the Allies, but considered itself an "Associate Power".

When Congress declared war, the U.S. maintained a very small army. However, following the passage of the Selective Service Act, four million men were drafted into military ser-vice. Provost Marshal Enoch Crowder, who oversaw the draft, planned to expand the spring call-up to all men between the ages of eighteen and forty-five. Any man not employed in an essential industry could be drafted. Crowder said, "All men within the enlarged age range would be called within a year". Not since the Civil War would such a large percentage of the nation be in military uniform.

Sizable numbers of American troops did not arrive in Europe until the fall of 1917. General John J. Pershing was made commander of the American forces, which were called the American Expeditionary Force, or AEF. Government censorship completely insulated the nation from knowing America's involvement in The War was disastrous in the early days. Antiquated doctrine called for the use of large blunt frontal enemy assaults. Such military tactics had no realistic chance of success in an age of barbed wire, machine guns, and more precise indirect artillery fire. Huge casualties quickly taught the Americans to abandon this 19th century military approach, just as the British and French had done years earlier.

To make matters worse for the Allies, things were not going well in Russia. Nicholas II, the Russian Tsar, was leading his country's defense on the Eastern Front. Matters of government were left to his wife, Empress Alexandra, who was increasingly seen as incompetent. Street protests grew as war shortages took their toll. The Empress's adviser, Rasputin, was even murdered by royal opponents in 1916. By February, 1917 (per the Russian calendar), demonstrations in Petrograd culminated in the abdication of Tsar Nicholas II. A weak Provisional Government was appointed and shared power with the Petrograd Soviet Socialists. The lack of governmental authority led to extreme confusion and chaos within the nation as well as in the military. The army became ever more ineffective, and both The War and the Russian government became increasingly unpopular with the citizens. This discontent led to a rise in popularity of the Bolshevik party and its leader, Vladimir Lenin.

Lenin promised to pull Russia out of The War. With this promise, the Bolshevik party won a historic victory in the November election. In December, 1917, Russia made an armistice with Germany and began peace negotiations. As Major Noble left port in Brest, France, it was widely believed Russia would cede vast territories to the Central Powers in exchange for a peace agreement. These territories included Finland, the Baltic provinces, and parts of Poland and Ukraine. The Allies knew all-too-well the meaning of this armistice. Very large Central Power forces would be moving from the Eastern to the Western Front. At the same time, America would also be sending large troop forces to that same Western Front. The War was about to heat up.

The world conflict had seen a host of new technologies emerge. Telephones and wireless communication were completely changing the art of war. Field telephones and radios were used for more accurate spotting and ranging of indirect fire with mortars and machine guns. Aircraft helped with spotting and reconnaissance. Sound detection technology was used to locate enemy batteries. Germans were using large 150 and 210 mm howitzers and Austrian 305 and 420 mm guns. Artillery was responsible for the largest number of casualties including many head wounds. As a result, combatant nations developed the steel helmet, led by the French and their Adrian helmet in 1915. Light automatic weapons were introduced, such as the Browning automatic rifle. The most powerful land-based weapons were railway guns weighing hundreds of tons each. Germany developed the Paris Gun that was able to bombard Paris from over 60 miles with shells weighing 210 lbs.

Flamethrowers were first used by the Germans. These weapons were of little tactical value, but were powerful demoralizing weapons that caused terror on the battlefield. Similarly, widespread use of chemical weapons such as chlorine gas, mustard gas, and phosgene terrified Allied troops. When the British naval blockade deprived Central Powers with many raw materials, the new Haber process of nitrogen fixation provided German forces with a constant supply of gunpowder.

Much of the European campaign involved trench warfare. Railway systems built inside the trenches were used to supply enormous quantities of food, water, and ammunition required to support the millions of troops living in them. Later, vehicles with internal combustion engines and improved traction systems replaced the railways.

The stalemate of trench warfare, and tens of thousands of miles of barbed wire, spurred the creation of new offensive weapon: the tank. Britain and France were prime users of a technology that came from California farms in its great Central Valley. Benjamin Holt, and his two rotating steel tread Caterpillar, showed how a vehicle could travel in most any terrain. Put a large gun on the vehicle, and you have a formable land weapon. The British Mark II tank was a major advance for the Allies.

Manned observation balloons floating high above the trenches were used as stationary reconnaissance platforms. The balloons made the undetected movement of large numbers of troops impossible. The balloons usually had a crew of two, who carried parachutes. This was essential, since the balloons were easy targets for ground and aircraft fire.

Fixed-wing aircraft were first used for military reconnaissance during the Italo-Turkish War. The Italians employed airplanes for this purpose in Libya on October 23, 1911. By the following year, aircraft were used to drop grenades and to take aerial photographs. The Allies and Central Powers later took full advantage of airplanes. Both sides used the new art of air war to perform ground attacks against troops. Defensive anti-aircraft guns were invented to protect ground forces. The combatants also began to experiment with air-to-air rockets.

Strategic bombers were developed principally by the Germans and British, though the former used Zeppelins as well. The Germans conducted raids with Zeppelin airships against England during 1915 and 1916, hoping to damage British moral and cause aircraft to be diverted from the Western Front. This plan worked well, as panic took several fighter squadrons from France to England. It was rumored that the British were actually building a ship from which Sopwith Camel biplanes could take off and land. The secret *HMS Furious* was called an "aircraft carrier", and would be used to raid Zeppelin hangers later in the year.

Major Noble picked his elbows up off the bow deck railing and moved several yards up wind from three soldiers who had stopped near by him. The soldiers were huddled together as they attempted to strike a match in the cold breeze and light cigarettes. Noble did not want to inhale their exhaled smoke. He had seen too many lungs of smokers at necropsy to believe the habit was a healthy one.

Major Edward Noble had seen many necropsies, because he was a physician. In the United States, he was a new type of physician called a Doctor of Internal Medicine. The term "Internal Medicine" came from the German term "Innere Medizin". In the last two decades of the 19th century, Innere Medizin became a discipline popularized in Germany that described physicians who combined laboratory sciences with the care of adult patients. Many American physicians seeking to improve their clinical skills, and U.S. medical training in general, studied in Germany and other European countries. Some of these doctors were establishing Innere Medizin in America, and gave it the English term Internal Medicine. They began to refer to themselves as Internists. Since the patients of Internists were usually seriously ill, or required complex investigations, much of their work was in hospitals. Some Internists were beginning to focus on disorders of specific organ systems. These doctors were now being called Internal Medicine subspecialists.

The gray sky continued to lighten with the new day. Noble looked at his watch and noted it was nearly time for an early breakfast. He began experiencing abdominal gnawing that all hungry humans know from birth, and this actually made him happy. Much of his time in France was spent dining on army rations that were at best cold, and at worst putrid. He had lost nearly twenty pounds with war cuisine. Meals aboard *Madawaska* were, in comparison, heaven sent. Each one was to be savored and appreciated for the sheer delight of eating wholesome food again.

Noble walked onto the upper decks of the superstructure. He went through one of the sea lock doors, down a few corridors painted the ubiquitous olive green, and into the officer's mess hall. Since the ship was a passenger liner in its former life, the navel mess halls were uncharacteristically large with high ceilings. The thick wall-to-wall dark blue carpet was amazingly clean for the traffic it had seen over many months. Noble knew this was due to the navy's strict adherence to tight ship maintenance. The room was lined with port holes, each with dark blue curtains drawn to the sides. Long tables with white tablecloths filled the mess hall, and both high-back wicker and brass chairs with red cushions lined the tables. Porcelain flatware and crystal glasses were on the tables, and there was real silverware. All the furnishings were also leftovers from the ship's past. Noble loved all of it, even as he felt somewhat guilty for doing so. He hung up his hat and heavy brown army officer service overcoat with three sleeve braids, and found a chair. Only a few other officers were seated in the room at this early hour. Noble guessed they were also colleague insomniacs. A short stocky Seaman with a small pad of paper and pencil walked up to Noble as he sat down on one of the long tables alone. "Good morning, sir," said the Seaman. "How do you like your eggs?"

Eggs, thought Noble. Who would have ever thought I would dream of fresh eggs? "Gee…scrambled. Thank you. Do you think I can have a double helping?" asked Noble, thinking that this was perhaps not allowed.

"No problem, sir. It'll just be a minute." The Seaman did an about face and headed to the officer's galley.

More officers were gradually entering the mess hall and ordering breakfast. There were relatively few naval officers aboard. However, scores of army officers were traveling back to the U.S. and were now streaming into the mess hall. Noble thought it would be some time before his order arrived, given the number of meals to be prepared. However, naval efficiency was again evident when Noble's breakfast was delivered by the same Seaman who had taken his order.

"Here you go, sir," said the Seaman.

"Wow, that smells good," said Noble. "Thank you so much." A large plate of scrambled eggs with sausage, hash brown potatoes, pancakes, a biscuit, butter, and raspberry preserve was placed before him. Another Seaman then brought a cup of hot coffee and freshly squeezed orange juice. Noble felt as though he was about to have the best meal of his life. And, he was.

As Noble thoroughly enjoyed his breakfast, the Captain of *Madawaska* entered the room and removed his cap. The officers all stood and saluted in good military form, and the Captain said with a smile, "At ease." As the officers sat down to resume eating, Captain Richard Baker walked over to Noble's table and sat down beside him. The Captain, sporting a thick slightly graying black mustache with similar hair, was a handsome muscular man with a Mediterranean look to him. He wore the navy blue service blouse with a high round collar and silver devices of the anchor and eagle. His sleeves had the traditional four gold rings and a gold star.

"You're Major Noble, right?" asked the Captain. A nearby Seaman waved at the Captain, and he nodded back as if to say, "Same breakfast as always".

"Yes, sir," said Noble. He thought it remarkable the Captain knew he even existed. This was a Captain who wanted to know everything about his ship, and who was aboard her.

"Sorry I haven't had a chance to welcome you aboard the *Madawaska* until now," said the Captain. "I try to greet all the officers if I can. If I recall, you were put on the ship's passenger manifest not long before we departed Brest."

"That's right, Captain," said Noble. "It was on pretty short notice."

"Did you join the army right before going to France?" asked the Captain.

Noble smiled. "Just about like everyone else, sir. Like tens of thousands of Americans, I felt it was my patriotic duty. I was commissioned as an army Captain two months after the declaration of war. My wife was very upset, but knew I had to do what I had to do. Ultimately, she completely supported my decision. Still, she has had to manage the domestic front with our three small children, along with some help from our two older children. After just a few weeks of basic training, I set sail for France in early September last year. Just by chance, that voyage was also on the *Madawaska*. I think that was before you were given command of her."

"You're a Major now," said the Captain. "That's a pretty fast promotion. You must have really impressed your superiors." A Seaman delivered the Captain's meal, and he began to eat as he listened to the Major.

Noble blushed with some embarrassment as he said, "Well, they were very kind and gave me gold leafs in two months time."

"What did you do in France, Major?" asked the Captain. As he asked the question, he noticed a brass caduceus on Noble's collar.

Again with a smile, Noble said, "Well, there were less than 800 physicians in the entire U.S. Army and Navy at the beginning of the war, with about 140,000 doctors in the country. Now, almost 30% of all American physicians are in the military. And, I'm one of them. I was sent to St. Denis near Paris to assist in the formation of Base Hospital No. 36. With the great help of the American Red Cross, and a terrific group of army nurses, we used available supplies to convert school dormitories into hospital wards. Eventually, the hospital had the capacity to care for 600 patients. We then constructed tent wards to accommodate another 2,200 patients. It was a pretty big operation, and kept us very busy."

"I'll bet there were a lot of really sick boys, there," said the Captain in a lowered voice.

"Sorry to say that's very true," said Noble. "I'm an Infectious Disease subspecialist, and I saw everything from cholera to yellow fever in the troops. At times it seemed that microbes were a much bigger threat than the Germans. I'm an Internist, but it was necessary for me to learn a lot of surgical skills as the war injuries came in. Of course, there were plenty of those."

"Looks like you have been called back now," said the Captain.

"Well," said Noble, "on January 7th I received orders to promptly return home to Boston and await further orders. That was it. There was no explanation given for my departure, or even a word as to who was ordering me to do so. Three days later I was on the dock at Brest and sailed off with the *Madawaska*. Perplexing, to say the least. We most certainly had not completed our mission at Base Hospital No. 36. But, those were my orders."

Both men were now finished with breakfast. The Captain wished Noble well with his unusual army orders, and the Major thanked the Captain for taking a moment to speak with him. Each man admired the other for the hard work and sacrifices they had made for their country.

Since his orders were simply to return home, Noble had no specific duties aboard ship. Nevertheless, he had volunteered his expertise to help the ship surgeons, and they indeed needed it. Most of the nearly 500 troops aboard suffered from war inflicted injuries. The injuries ran the full range between amputations, large healing wounds, and psychiatric illness. With hundreds of thousands of Americans leaving for Europe each month, war casualties were mounting in very large numbers. Noble was not a surgeon. But, as he mentioned to the Captain, Noble had learned valuable wound management skills from surgeons at Base Hospital No. 36. Those skills were surely needed on the *Madawaska* as she brought wounded back to America.

Noble thanked the Seaman for the best meal he ever had, and he meant it. He carried his coat and hat as he left the mess hall. He used the stairs to walk down two amidships decks to Sickbay No. 2, which was converted from large meeting rooms and cabins. As he walked into the sickbay, he saw a number of six foot high polished stainless steel sterilization chambers. Numerous trays of surgical instruments were either in the process of being sterilized, or being packaged following sterilization. The walls of the bay were painted off-white. Along most walls were numerous double rows of patient cots that could be folded up against the bulkhead if not in use. However, most of the cots were occupied today. The room was thick with the odor of wood alcohol and iodine.

Noble hung up his coat and hat on a coat rack, and took a stethoscope from his overcoat pocket. He had a strong emotional attachment to this instrument, for it was once his father's stethoscope. Noble had used it almost every day since medical school. He put on a long white coat, and a wave of contentment came over him. He was much more a physician than he was a soldier, and he was now in his true element.

"Hello, Dr. Noble," said a hospital Corpsman. "Good to see you again."

"Thank you," said Noble. "Is Lieutenant Commander John Mullen around?"

"Yes, sir," Said the Corpsman. "He is in the next ward. He's expecting you."

Noble walked into the next room where a very young appearing man with blond hair was dressing a patient's leg wound. Noble wondered how such a fresh-faced enthusiastic "boy" could be such an accomplished general naval surgeon, but he was.

"Edward! Good morning!" said Mullen." "Have you eaten?"

"Hi, John. Yes, I have." said Noble. "After St. Denis, and army 'bully', that meal was saintly."

Mullen said, "I hate to rub it in, but as we make our transatlantic crossings, we eat like that every day."

"Don't let the army troops know that, John," said Noble. "If they catch wind of how 'easy' you have it, they'll mutiny." Noble knew very well that no one on *Madawaska* had it easy. Still, the opportunity to rib a navy man was irresistible.

"Eat your heart out, Major," Mullen said laughing.

Noble asked, "How can I help you today, John?"

"Plenty to do, Edward. Lots of 'blighty' aboard *Madawaska*. I wonder if you could help with debridement of a mustard gas victim?"

Mustard gas. Noble felt a deep chill grip him. Just thinking the words caused terror in anyone that ever remotely thought of coming in contact with it. Noble had seen a lot as a physician, but he felt twinges of nausea even hearing the name of the substance. Still, there was work to do.

"I'll do what I can, John," said Noble. "In Base Hospital No. 36, I cared for many patients exposed to mustard gas."

Noble would never forget those effected soldiers. Mustard gas (a group of bases known as *mustards*) in its impure form, or 1, 5-dichloro-3-thiapentane, is yellow-brown in color with a distinctive odor like mustard plants, garlic, or horseradish. It is a viscous liquid at normal temperatures. It is not very soluble in water, but is very soluble in fat. It was sprayed by aircraft, or dispersed in munitions such as land mines, mortar shells, and rockets. More typically the gas was delivered by means of air-dropped bombs or artillery shells.

People exposed to mustard gas rarely suffer immediate symptoms. Mustard contaminated areas may appear completely normal, and victims can receive very high doses and not know it. However, within 24 hours of exposure, victims begin to experience intense itching. Their skin gradually formed large blisters filled with yellow fluid. Exposed eyes caused a severe conjunctivitis with eyelid swelling and temporary blindness. If inhaled at high concentrations, the agent caused bleeding and blistering within the respiratory system, damaged mucous membranes, and caused pulmonary edema.

Skin blistering usually caused first or second degree chemical burns. But, occasionally there could be disfiguring third degree burns that were often fatal. Mild to moderate exposures were unlikely to kill, as it was lethal only about 1% of the time. But, victims often still needed lengthy periods of medical treatment and convalescence. This had the effect of removing large numbers of opposition troops from the battle theater by rendering them incapacitated.

Mustard gas remained in the environment for several days, and could cause injury to troops entering the area after its application. It could also contaminate a soldier's clothing and equipment and cause injury to others when the soldier returned after an exposure. It was an ideal area-denial weapon which forced soldiers to abandon afflicted areas. Gas masks did not protect soldiers from the chemical weapon's effects. In The War, the Germans first used the agent against the British near Ypres in 1917, and later against the French Second Army. Allies did not use the gas until they captured a German stock of it in November, 1917.

Noble knew that skin damage could be reduced if povidone-iodine in a base of glycofurol was applied before there was evident skin irritation. However, since few soldiers knew they were exposed until there were skin symptoms, it was rare that a victim was treated in time. The vesicant property of mustard gas could be neutralized by oxidation or chlorination with household bleach, or by applying 2% NaOH, 70% diethylenetriamine, and 28% ethylene glycol monomethyl ether. Patient's wounds would be decontaminated by these agents. The resulting lesions were then treated like any other burns. Mustard gas wounds healed slowly. The risk of infection from *Staphylococcus aureus* and *Pseudomonas aeruginosa* was a constant threat, and Dr. Noble dreaded those complications.

Mullen led Noble to yet another sickbay ward, where a young Corporal was lying prone on a bulkhead foldout cot. "The Corporal's company at The Front was hit by a series of artillery shells laced with mustard gas," said Mullen. "He was the only survivor of the 'bonk'. Fortunately, his only contamination with mustard came as small shards of shrapnel tore away parts of the uniform on his back. The rest of his body was spared." Mullen lifted up a white sheet with pink-yellow serous stains covering the Corporal's back. Noble saw the soldier's extensive third degree burns. There was obviously a considerable amount of necrotic tissue on the wounds. "As you can see," said Mullen, "this morning it became apparent we will need to do some debridement."

"I'll get right on it, John," said Noble. He could smell the unmistakable odor of necrotic flesh and knew there was no time to lose.

Since the procedure to help the Corporal's wounds heal would be painful, he was given IV morphine sulfate as well as inhaled chloroform. He became very restful and relaxed with the procedural sedation. Two hospital Corpsmen lifted the Corporal to a surgical table so that there would be more room to work. Noble put on a face mask, a white surgical gown, and gloves. A Corpsman assisted Noble by handing him instruments and gauze.

Noble was aware that irrigation is the most important means of decreasing the incidence of wound infection. This is because soil or tiny foreign bodies remaining in a wound increase the inoculum of bacteria. He drew up in a large syringe a dilute solution of 1:10 of povidone/iodine solution in isotonic (normal) saline for irrigation, and for antiseptic activity. The most recent literature was clear on this point. The extent of the patient's posterior thoracic wounds required several applications of 500 ml of the solution. Runoff solution was captured in a steel basin.

To the extent he could, Noble then determined the depth of the wounds on his patient's back. He was confident that the patient could have a good result, because he did not have any risk factors associated with bad outcomes (i.e. diabetes, obesity, malnutrition, chronic renal failure, known retained foreign bodies such as glass, or extremity involvement).

The doctor then began the tedious procedure of debridement. First, mechanical debridement was performed with a wet-to-dry dressing to remove thick exudates, slough, or loose necrotic tissue. Then, using a scalpel and tweezers, he gently and methodically resected permanently devitalized tissue with the technique known as sharp debridement. If not removed, this tissue impairs the wound's ability to resist infection. Fat, muscle, and skin are therefore removed. The procedure continued for the better part of an hour. If bones, joints, or tendons are exposed, biosurgery with maggots could be an effective method of debridement. The larvae produce enzymes to break down dead tissue without harming healthy tissue. Larvae of the *Lucilia sericata* fly are utilized, but none were available on *Madawaska*.

When the debridement was completed, gauze strips moistened with saline were placed on the wounds. Noble knew it would be many weeks before the Corporal would be out of danger of wound infection. It would take meticulous nursing care, perhaps more debridement sessions, and a fair amount of luck for him to fully recover. However, for the time being, the Corporal had a fighting chance. The pain would be substantial, and Noble shuttered to think what that would be like for the young man.

Mullen walked over to the Corporal as he was lifted back on to his foldout cot by the hospital Corpsmen. "Pretty good job, Major," said Mullen. "Well, make you a surgeon yet."

"Thanks," said Noble. "However, I'll pass." Noble liked the Lieutenant Commander. He was extremely competent, and a very pleasant surgeon with whom to work. He was also of the new generation of American physicians that wanted to base decisions on science rather than opinion. This approach was refreshing for Noble, since it was not yet universally accepted in the U.S., or even in Boston.

Noble spent the rest of the morning assisting the naval medical and surgical staff with a variety of problems. The work was extremely tiring and stressful, but Noble knew his talents were greatly needed. He realized each future eastern *Madawaska* voyage would take 2,400 fresh troops to Europe. Larger and larger groups of severely wounded troops would be sailing westward to the U.S. with her. Ever greater numbers of physicians, hospital Corpsmen, and nurses would be needed for these mounting casualties. However, The War had already depleted the supply of competent American health care workers. There were now only a marginal number of such workers to serve the American civilian population.

The physicians and staff in the ship's sickbays staggered their lunches, as they did with all meals. This way, there was always enough attending staff to ensure prompt care for the ailing troops. Noble left for a quick lunch in the mess hall, and requested a cheese sandwich with potato salad and a large very crisp dill pickle. It was a luxury to have lettuce, mayonnaise, and catsup with the sandwich, and salt with the potato salad. He rushed back to Sickbay No. 2 after lunch.

Noble had dressed a number of superficial wounds that afternoon, and tried to ensure patients were all receiving enough pain control. Later a Petty Officer First Class with a hospital Corpsman rating walked over to him. "Major, I wonder if I can ask for some help. Lieutenant Commander Mullen is in surgery and isn't available right now."

"Sure. What can I do for you?" said Noble.

"Well, there is a Seaman who seems pretty sick," said the Petty Officer.

Without any more discussion, the two men walked to an adjoining room with walls lined with attached folded cots containing sickbay patients.

The Petty Officer stopped by the cot of a man who was diaphoretic and in a great deal of pain.

"Major, Seaman McCarthy fell from a ladder yesterday, and landed on his right anterior thigh. He had some minor pain with a bruise until about four hours ago. The pain then greatly increased very suddenly. He has marked tenderness of his right thigh, has a temperature of 101° F, and has a blood pressure of 95/65. But, other than a bruise and some minor swelling, I really don't see anything else. I've given him some codeine, but it hasn't helped much."

Noble walked closer to the patient and put his right hand on the man's forehead. He also placed his left hand first and second fingers on the Seaman's left radial pulse. His heart rate was 110. "How are you feeling, Son?" Noble asked.

"Not...not very good, sir. My leg really hurts", said the Seaman.

"Can you bend your right knee?" asked Noble, as he palpated the patient's right thigh.

"No, I can't. It's stiff."

Noble looked closely at the man's right leg. He felt the skin along the length of the leg, and palpated its muscles as well as the right knee. Beyond a small lower right thigh bruise and some modest swelling, the Petty Officer was right. There was no other visible abnormality.

Noble said to the Seaman, "I need to take a small needle and place it into your lower thigh. Is that all right, sailor?"

"Sure, doc. Do what you got to do."

The Petty Officer left for a few minutes, and returned with a syringe, an eighteen gauge needle, and some sterile saline. Noble cleaned off the man's skin in an area about four inches from the superior aspect of the sailor's right knee. He drew up a few milliliters of saline into the syringe. He then quickly inserted the needle about an inch into the man's thigh, while drawing back on the syringe plunger. A small amount of yellow-pink fluid was drawn into the syringe. The sailor grimaced with the procedure, but did not make a sound.

Noble took the syringe to a small table located at the side of the room. On the table were a number of bottles of different sizes that contained various colored liquids within them. There was also a microscope. Right next to the table was a sink.

Noble placed a sample of the syringe yellow-pink fluid onto a glass slide with a tiny wire loop with a long handle. He allowed the sample to air-dry for a few minutes, and then used a flame from a candle on the table to heat fix the specimen onto the glass slide. From a bottle marked "Crystal Violet", he placed a drop of blue liquid onto the glass slide for one minute. This was washed gently with tap water from a small dropper. Gram's iodine (named for the inventor, Dr. Christian Gram) was applied to the slide for one minute. This was again washed with tap water. A dropper was then used to add 95% alcohol until drippings from the slide were clear. A tap water rinse was placed on the slide. A counterstain with Safranin was applied for 45 seconds. A final rinse with tap water was used a fourth time. To complete the process of gram staining, the glass slide was dried with bibulous paper.

Noble sat upon a stool at the small table, placed the prepared glass slide onto the microscope stage, applied a drop of oil onto the slide with a cover slip, and began to study the specimen. He saw a few polymorphonuclear blood cells and very large numbers of gram-positive cocci in chains. The sadness that comes from a bad diagnosis came over Noble, as he stood up and walked back to the Petty Officer and his patient.

"Please have general surgery prepare this patient for an aggressive debridement of the right quadriceps muscle immediately", said Noble.

"Major, what's happening?" asked the Petty Officer.

Noble put his right arm around the back of the Corpsman, and walked a few steps away from the patient. Noble whispered, "The sailor has developed spontaneous gangrenous myositis of his right quadriceps that is likely due to *Streptococcus pyogenes*. Very rare, and associated with nearly a 100% mortality. His only hope is surgical debridement as soon as possible. The only good sign is that we have caught this before any dermal signs have appeared. Please act quickly."

The Petty Officer hurried off to contact general surgery. Noble walked slowly back to the Seaman. He held his hand as he told him of the pending surgery. He did not tell him of the likely outcome.

The Seaman looked straight away into Nobles eyes and said, "Thank you, doc. I know you've done your best for me. I want you to know that I really appreciate it."

Noble just smiled, patted the man's hand, and left the room. As he did so, tears welled up in Noble's eyes. Seaman McCarthy had his whole life ahead of him. He was strong and brave. He was without any chronic medical problems whatsoever, and had done nothing to deserve what was coming. Yet, the young man now faced the battle of his life. This was so unfair and unjust. However, microbes do not know or care about fairness and justice. Noble walked out onto one of the lower level decks, watched the sea, and waited to gain enough composure to return to an omnipresent battle with the microbes.

CHAPTER 2

For the rest of that afternoon, and much of the evening, Noble was back in the world of wounds and infections. In addition, he had dozens of new symptoms to sift through on the sickbay. Despite the broken bodies and dreams from war, he tried to take satisfaction from knowing that through his efforts some degree of reduced suffering was achieved. There was hope of partial, and even full, recovery for some of the young men he treated. Even at times when hope was tenuous at best, he was always amazed at the appreciation soldiers felt for work of the doctors and staff. Sometimes appreciation was all that was left in the lives of the patients aboard *Madawaska*.

At 8 PM, John Mullen walked over to his new friend of four days and commanded, "Edward, go get something to eat and head back to your cabin. That's an order, soldier."

Noble had just finished cleaning and dressing a wound. Seated, he looked up at Mullen with a grin and said, "You don't out rank me, Lieutenant Commander."

Mullen replied, "Navy always outranks army. Didn't they teach you anything in Basic?"

"I guess I missed that seminar," said Noble. "Are you sure you don't need any help now, John?"

"Nope," said Mullen. "I will be leaving as soon as I make some quick post-op rounds in Sickbay No. 2. I mean it, soldier. Get out of here. We'll see you tomorrow?"

"I'll be back bright and early, John." Noble continued, "How did it go with Seamen McCarthy? I know you did the debridement."

Mullen's forehead furrowed. "That was an amazing call, Edward. He had extensive necrosis of his right quadriceps down to the femur. At the very best, I doubt he will keep his leg. That is if things go well. Take off, now. See ya' tomorrow."

Noble saluted his colleague, put his very soiled white coat in a laundry hamper, carefully put his treasured stethoscope in his army overcoat, and headed off to the mess hall for supper.

Noble was served dinner by the same stocky Seaman who had given him breakfast so many hours earlier. Once again, navy cuisine was a delightful experience. Simple meat loaf (with no detectable insects), Boston baked beans, corn on the cob, mashed potatoes with butter and gravy, and great black coffee. The meal was topped off with a large warm chocolate chip cookie.

After dinner, Noble went below to his cabin. Under normal circumstances, he would have had to share accommodations with at least one other officer. However, with less than a full complement of personnel aboard this westbound voyage, he had a small cabin all to himself. Aside from his clothes and duffle bag, the only other personal items in view were a small framed photograph of his family on a narrow night stand, an alarm clock, a pad of paper with a pencil and pen, and two medical textbooks: *Preventative Medicine and Hygiene* by Dr. Milton J. Rosenau, and *The Principles and Practice of Medicine* by Sir William Osler, MD. Noble had planned to read for a time after retiring for the evening, but he was sound asleep within minutes of hitting the pillow.

Four days later, on Friday, January 18, 1918, Noble had established a routine for himself aboard *Madawaska*. Routines can help accomplish two positive things for people. First, they help people to be on time when they are most tired. Anyone readying for work or school in the morning knows how routines can be helpful. Second, routines can give purpose to lives that are in transition. Both situations were occurring at the same time for Edward Noble.

Noble awoke early each morning and spent time topside walking and thinking in solitude. During these times he thought most deeply about his wife and best friend, Lillian. He thought about his five children, his long-time friends, and his plethora of experiences in Europe. He wondered how much longer The War would continue to destroy the best of humanity. He dreamed returning to his medical practice at 852 Harrison Avenue, across the street from Boston City Hospital.

The Major had the same early breakfast each morning. He called it "comfort food", and that is how the stocky Seaman referred to it when Noble entered the mess hall. ("Comfort food' again, sir?") At lunch, he had a quick cheese sandwich. Dinner was taken between 8 and 9 PM. He would read late at night until fatigue would overtake him.

Noble put in nearly twelve hours each day as another "hand" in Sickbay No. 2. His broad knowledge of science-based Internal Medicine, his newly acquired basic surgical skills, and his Infectious Disease expertise, made him invaluable to the other physicians. His colleagues did not look forward to the day Dr. Noble would leave *Madawaska*. And that day was coming soon.

Including his experience at Base Hospital No. 36 at St. Denis, Noble had seen more Infectious Disease diversity in 4 months than he could have seen in Boston over a decade.

Noble diagnosed and treated measles, diphtheria, tetanus, osteomyelitis, dengue fever, endocarditis, scarlet fever, erysipelas, other streptococcal infections, staphylococcal infections, scores of abscesses, amebiasis, leishmaniasis, trichinosis, schistosomiasis, enterobiasis, hookworm, trichuriasis, trichomoniasis, stongylodiasis, mumps, rubella, varicella-zoster, and many many more.

This Friday morning Noble went to Sickbay No. 2, put on his white coat, put his stethoscope around his neck, and went to work as usual. He checked on his Corporal with mustard gas third degree burns. It had been four days since Noble performed extensive debridement of the soldier's wounds. A hospital Corpsman was redressing the Corporal's back wounds with sterile saline soaked gauze strips. Noble picked up a clip board hanging next to the soldier's bulkhead foldout cot.

"How are you doing, Son?" Noble asked the Corporal. "Are you hanging in there?" Noble knew the patient was heavily sedated with opiates, so his answers would necessarily be brief.

"OK, sir," said the Corporal. "The pain medication really helps. I'm pretty constipated though, sir."

Noble read the patient's vital signs: heart rate 85, blood pressure 132/76, respiratory rate 19, and temperature 100.0° F. He watched as the Corpsman changed the dressings. The back wounds were moist, and with less swelling. There was also less bleeding. In addition, there were now areas of light pink tissue at the base of some wounds. This was a new finding.

"Corporal," said Noble, "things are looking really good. You seem to be without any new infections, and your wounds show signs of healing nicely." Noble motioned toward the light pink areas and said to the Corpsman, "Granulation tissue." Both men nodded with slight smiles and marked approval. Noble continued, "The morphine is likely causing the constipation. We'll try a new semi-synthetic opioid called oxycodone that causes less constipation."

Noble once again said to the Corporal, "You're not out of the woods yet, Son. You have a long way to go. But, with the great help of the hospital Corpsmen while you are aboard ship, and the help of the army nurses in New York, you now have a great chance of healing up fine. It's just going to take some time."

"Thank you so much, sir," said the Corporal. "I'll never forget you".

Noble smiled, brushed a lock of hair from the boy's forehead, and walked to his next patient. He would never forget the Corporal, either.

Later in the morning, Noble saw Lieutenant Commander Mullen in one of the adjoining patient wards. He waved to Mullen and walked over to him as the surgeon removed sutures from a healing surgical wound. "Good morning, John. How did you sleep last night?"

"Like a baby, Edward," said Mullen. "Although this has been a very cold Atlantic crossing, the sea conditions have been very mild. My cabin is near the bow, and it can be pretty hard to sleep in rough seas. It gets really dicey in the sickbays, as well. Try performing surgery in a gale! Not only is the surgical suite moving all over the place, but your patient occasionally and unexpectedly jumps off the surgical table! We have the sickbays and surgical suites amidships for a reason. In rough waters, as the ship's bow and stern move up and down, the movement is minimized at the ship's fulcrum. That is, amidships. By the way, how are things with the mustard gas patient?"

"Good, John," said Noble. "He's healing at a quick rate. I think he is going to make it, although he'll need good nursing care for a couple of months. By the way, how is Seaman McCarthy with the quadriceps gangrenous myositis?"

Dr. Mullen suddenly stopped cleaning the wound from which he had just removed sutures. His usual happy demeanor vanished. He put his hand on Noble's shoulder. "Edward, Seaman McCarthy died last night."

Noble's heart skipped a beat, and he suddenly felt dizzy. He put his right hand to his forehead. He thought about how brave and appreciative the young man had been during his physical examination. His left hand went to his abdomen. After a few moments, Noble said, "That was fast, John. Sepsis?"

"Yes," said Mullen. "He went into septic shock late last night. He was unconscious, so it came peacefully for him."

Noble sat down on a nearby stool, without speaking.

"Edward," said Mullen, "you did say the prognosis was grave. You made a tough diagnosis, and gave the boy the only shot he had. I can tell you are taking this one pretty hard."

After a few minutes, Noble said softly, "McCarthy was about the same age as my oldest son. Countertransference in patient care is very powerful, John. At times it is simply unavoidable, as Sigmund Freud wrote a few years ago."

Noble strolled for a time on the same deck where he had walked and worried about Seaman McCarthy three-and-a-half days earlier. He thought to himself that no matter how many times one loses the fight for a patient, it never gets easier. Regaining composure, he returned to Sickbay No. 2 and continued the battle.

That evening, Noble walked into the officer's mess hall at about 9 PM and found it nearly empty. He was specially tired and hungry. He requested a dinner meal that had become as standard as his breakfasts and lunches now were. As he waited for the meal to be delivered, Captain Richard Baker walked into the mess hall. He motioned to the Seaman taking meal requests. It was clear everyone knew exactly what the Captain's meal choices were. His diet appeared to be as unchanging as Noble's. The Captain came over to Noble's table and sat in a seat facing him.

"Major Noble," said the Captain, "Do you mind if I sit here?"

"Not at all, Captain," said Noble quietly. "Please, have a seat." Noble was actually happy to have some company. People may not realize the work of a physician can frequently be very lonely. Patients often are too sick to communicate much. In such circumstances, physical and laboratory diagnosis can be a one-sided endeavor.

"Lieutenant Commander Mullen told me that you took the passing of Seaman McCarthy pretty hard today," said the Captain.

Noble just nodded slightly. He did not really want to talk about the boy's passing.

The Captain went on, "The least pleasant job a Captain has is writing notification letters to families. I will need to write a letter before we dock, and post it in Hoboken. May I add anything in the letter from you?"

Noble felt a sudden sense of relief. He dropped his eyes toward the dinner table and thought about the question for a few moments. He looked back up to the Captain, and said, "Mention he was a brave kid who appreciated everything that everyone did for him. I saw in his eyes the love he held for his country, and that he was a truly honest young man." Noble noted to himself these were also qualities he admired in his own eldest son.

"Thank you, Major," said the Captain. "I will most certainly add your comments."

Both of the men's meals arrived at the same time, and they began to eat. Noble continued to be impressed by this Captain who not only made it his business to know everyone on his ship, but sincerely cared about his crew and "guests".

"How old are you, Major?" asked the Captain. "You look so young, but you have white hair."

Noble did have a full head of nearly white hair that parted on the left, and was combed to the right as it fell slightly over his forehead. "I was born in 1873. I'm forty-five. I started turning grey when I was twenty."

"How did you come to chose medicine, Major?" asked the Captain.

"Well," said Noble, "my father, Charles, was a general practitioner who was fascinated with the great puzzle known as the "differential diagnosis". His passion was the assemblages of these puzzle pieces into the correct diagnosis. Of course, the pieces of the puzzle in medicine are the history, physical exam, and laboratory data. As a child I often went on rounds with my father in the hospital. I also accompanied him to the homes of patients when he looked in on them. I suppose his passion for the differential diagnosis rubbed off on me to some degree. My father also impressed upon me the need to have a solid background in the sciences if one is interested in medicine. I dreamed of being a great physician like my father. So, I worked in school to assure myself, and him, that I had an aptitude in the sciences."

Noble did not want to tell the Captain what his father actually thought of American medicine in the 1880's and 1890's. As late as 1900, the only U.S. medical school that even required a college degree, let alone any training in the sciences, was Johns Hopkins. Only recently had the American Medical Association begun to push for the use of the scientific method by physicians. Until the 20th century, the decision to use the scientific method or not was left up to individual physician's discretion. By 1901, Harvard, Pennsylvania University, and Columbia University also required college degrees for medical school entrance.

By the end of the 19th century, most U.S. medical school students received no training in anatomy, laboratory work, or even saw a patient until they began practice right out of school. Medical or surgical residencies were optional. Even though Charles Noble attended medical school when many did not believe in the germ theory, he was of the "new school" that raised the quality standards of medical education. Charles wanted his son Edward to model any future medical training after those seeking to make American medicine the best in the world. This was distinctly different than what U.S. medical education was at the end of the 19th century: at best, mediocre, and at worst, medieval.

The visionary American physicians who were demanding much more of American medical training were often found within the new medical school at Johns Hopkins. These physicians included the world renowned microbiologist William Welch, the world famous Internist William Osler, and the first director of the Rockefeller Institute Hospital, Rufus Cole. Cole wanted doctors to do research in hospitals using "control" patients. That is, patients who were not given a study intervention and did not know it. This was the only way, using the scientific method, to know what works and what does not work. Random chance would determine who would enter study treatments and who would not. Many had a problem with this approach. However, Cole and many others knew this was the only way for medicine to sort out truth from mysticism. Here began the corner stone of the "new" medicine; the prospective randomized blinded controlled clinical study.

Early in the new 20th century the American Medical Association and the Council of Medical Education began to rate medical schools. Class A schools were "Fully Satisfactory", Class B "Redeemable", and Class C "Needing Complete Reorganization". Within four years of the group's report, thirty-one States had denied licensure to Class C schools. Large numbers of American medical schools closed. American medicine was on a new road to excellence.

Noble continued about his own road toward a medical career. "With my father's guidance and encouragement, I graduated from college at Boston University in 1895, where I majored in chemistry. I entered the Boston University School of Medicine that year."

"Why did you go to that particular medical school," asked the Captain?

Noble explained, "My father liked the school for its foundation in the sciences, superb clinical training, and its social mission. It was founded in 1848 as the New England Female Medical College. The school has the unique distinction of being the first institution in the world to formally educate women physicians, and award them a medical degree. It is also notable for being the first medical school in the U.S. to award an MD degree to an African-American man, and an African-American woman, in 1864. The school has had a long tradition in the study of Infectious Diseases, which was another of my father's interests. Dr. Rebecca Lee Dorsey, who graduated in 1886, was at Louis Pasture's side when he administered the first rabies vaccine to Joseph Meister in July,

1886. She was also the first woman physician in Los Angeles, California, that same year."

"Sounds like a medical school with a proud tradition," said the Captain. "What did you do then?"

Noble said, "I married my darling wife in 1898, and I graduated from medical school in 1899." Noble was too modest to say he graduated summa cum laude. "My father had insisted that I do a formal residency, so I chose a three year Internal Medicine residency at the Massachusetts General Hospital. I was very fortunate to be chosen for a fourth year as Chief Resident. Since I shared my father's strong interest in Infectious Diseases, I did a two year Fellowship in "ID" at both Massachusetts General Hospital and Boston City Hospital. The latter is administered by Harvard University. In 1905 I began a practice of Internal Medicine and Infectious Disease at Boston City Hospital, and opened an office nearby."

"You have a lot to return to after The War, Major," said the Captain.

"But, there are a lot of 'ifs' and 'whens', Captain," said Noble. "'When' The War ends, and 'if' my new orders take me somewhere else. I'm not sure at all what the future holds for me."

"I'll hope the best for you, Major," said the Captain. I guess you'll have a better idea when we arrive, in less than four days."

Both men had finished their dinners, and parted with a salute. Captain Baker came away with a deeper sense of admiration for the Major, and the personal journey that had brought him to the *Madawaska*. In turn, Dr. Noble both appreciated the opportunity to talk about his life, and the caring that the Captain displayed for him. Noble went promptly to his cabin for much needed sleep. There was still much to do in the remaining days.

Over the next three days, Noble kept to his strict routine. If he did not keep busy, he would begin to dwell on how much he missed his family and the full life he had before leaving all of it for France. On the other hand, and with few exceptions, most of the ill troops on *Madawaska* were either holding their own, or improving. The generally positive clinical outcomes Noble had seen over the past eleven days were definitely a comfort for him. In an odd sort of way, he would miss the ship when it docked the next day. He surely would miss its wonderful crew and passengers.

On Monday, January 21st, at about 8:45 PM, Noble finished up dinner after his final full day working in Sickbay No. 2. He had a double helping of meat loaf and mashed potatoes, and was pretty sure he had put on about 5 lbs since they set sail from Brest. He felt a new sense of excitement, and he could feel the same emotion throughout the ship. He knew that the people aboard *Madawaska* must experience the same elation each time they make the east-to-west transatlantic crossing. There was likely less of that particular emotion on the west-to-east leg of its journeys.

As Noble left the officer mess hall, someone ten yards behind him called out his name.

"Major...Major Noble!"

Noble turned quickly around to see a young Petty Officer Third Class walking toward him. He looked as if he was of American Indian heritage. Above his single shoulder chevron and below the navy eagle was the four "lightning bolts" of a Radio Operator.

"Are you Major Edward Noble, sir?" asked the slightly out-of-breath Petty Officer.

"Yes...yes, I am."

"They told me to look for a tall wiry army Major with white hair and wire rim glasses with round lenses," explained the Petty Officer.

That was Noble's description, but he did not care for it. His wife, Lillian, always referred to him as "wiry" because she could tease him with the term. Yet, at 5 feet 11 inches tall, and 155 lbs, he did fit the term. He knew he was even more "wiry" now since his significant weight loss at St. Denis.

The Petty Officer continued, "I'm glad I located you, sir. This evening we came across a cable that had arrived in Brest, France for you the day we set sail. It was brought aboard, and unfortunately misplaced…until now. I found it in a mail cubby hole where it shouldn't have been sorted. The Petty Officer took a small brown sealed envelope from his coat pocket and handed it to Noble. Noble saw that it had his name on it, and also "*USS Madawaska*".

"Thank you very much," said Noble, who took the envelope and saluted.

"You're welcome, sir," said the Petty Officer as he turned and rushed away.

Noble stood looking at the envelope for some time. Since leaving for France, he had come to expect the worst in most things, since that is what war usually delivers. He dreaded opening it. He finally turned slowly, and made his way back to his small cabin.

Sitting on the bottom bunk of a bunk bed, Noble slowly opened the envelope and read the cable.

Major Edward Noble, AEF.
Brest, France
USS Madawaska

Thursday, January 10, 1918
From: Base Hospital No. 5

Camiers, France

Hello, old boy! I heard you had been ordered back to Boston. Guess they have had enough of you in St. Denis! Putting all humor aside, I'm envious. Although it has been a comfort to know you were in France too, I am so happy for your good fortune! Please have a safe voyage. Say hi to Lillian for me, and please say hi to my dearest Katherine if you get over to Brookline.

Your good friend,
Colonel Harvey Cushing, BEF.

Noble's pulse rate immediately decreased. His face grew a toothy grin. He thought of the defense mechanism humans have evolved that prods them to assume the worst. He folded the cable and carefully put it between the pages of Sir William Osler's text book. Just before departing for France, Noble had added Cushing's new 1917 book to his own collection: *Tumors of Nervus Acusticus.*

Patient suffering, the cruelness of war, the cold, the endless Atlantic, and the longing for his wife and children, were taking its toll on Noble's usually positive disposition. However, at least for the moment, Noble beamed. It was light shown on his soul to hear from his old friend, Harvey.

Dr. Harvey Williams Cushing was a pioneer neurosurgeon, and was one of the most famous physicians in the new 20th century. He had attended Yale College, and graduated cum laude from Harvard Medical School in 1895. He was a surgical house officer at the Massachusetts General Hospital in Boston when he came across Edward Noble by chance in the autumn of 1895. Noble had just started his first year at the BU School of Medicine when the two met on a tennis court one Saturday afternoon. Noble won the match, and never let Cushing forget it. They became fast friends. Noble's wife also became good friends with Cushing's bride, Katherine Stone Crowell, when the two were wed in 1902.

When Cushing lived in Boston, and even later, he and Noble enjoyed reading books from each other's medical book collections. Cushing's collection included the 1543 large leather-bound folio of anatomist Andreas Vesalius, called *De Humani Corporis Fabrici.* Cushing was also an excellent illustrator. He gave many of his illustrations of people he had known to others. Many times, resting upon his cot at Base Hospital No. 36, Noble envisioned his wife's illustrated Cushing portrait framed in his parlor.

In 1896, Cushing became an assistant resident at the newly founded Johns Hopkins Hospital in Baltimore. There he had the opportunity to work under the pre-eminent surgeon, William Halstead. Halstead introduced the use of rubber gloves in surgery, and broke convention by insisting on the formation of detailed plans prior to any surgical procedure. Harvey Cushing lived right next door to William Osler, who was considered by most to be the world's most famous Internist. They also developed a life-long friendship. In 1900, Cushing spent one year in Germany experimenting on the relationship of blood and cranial pressure. Osler was in England that summer, and Cushing visited him there. Olser, like Cushing and Noble, loved old books. Osler called Vesalius's anatomy book "the greatest medical text ever written".

As Professor of Medicine at Johns Hopkins University, and Physician-in-Chief of Hopkins Hospital, Dr. William Osler spent a week in 1903 as a guest attending physician at the Massachusetts General Hospital in Boston. Dr. Noble was Chief Resident at the time, and rounded hours with the Professor. At the end of the week, Dr. Osler was so impressed with young Noble's clinical skills that he offered him a position on his staff at Hopkins for the next year. Noble had to decline, since he had two small children and needed to concentrate on them. He also knew that his wife, Lillian, would never leave Boston. Dr. Osler was pleased to autograph Noble's prized 1892 first printing of the Professor's text *The Principles and Practice of Medicine*. It had been one of Noble's treasures ever since.

In March, 1909, Dr. Cushing carried out his first operation for acromegaly, an insidious chronic debilitating disease associated with bony and soft tissue overgrowth. The patient was a 38 year old farmer referred by Charles Mayo. The approach to the pituitary gland was via a frontal flap opening the frontal sinuses. The patient made a remarkable recovery, which was only the second successful operation of its kind. Between 1909 and 1911, Cushing collected 43 patients with lesions involving the pituitary gland. He reported his findings in 1912. Glucocorticoid excess from pituitary hypersecretion of adrenocorticotrophic hormone became known as Cushing's syndrome. Cushing's transphenoidal method of surgery for brain tumors reduced mortality from 90% to 8%, and changed neurosurgery forever.

Cushing collaborated with Ernest Codman on the clinical use of Roentgenograms in 1896. The application of X-rays to make pictures inside the body had only been made in November of the previous year by Wilhelm Roentgen. Cushing also collaborated with the physicist Dr. William Bovie on the use of electrical coagulation during surgery to reduce bleeding. Cushing introduced America to the 1896 Scipione Riva-Rocci mercury sphygmomanometer for the non-invasive measurement of arterial systolic blood pressure. This introduction made blood pressure a vital sign and revolutionized the western world approach to hypertension. Cushing had a number of eponyms associated with his research and discoveries, including Cushing's ulcers: the gastrointestinal hemorrhagic complication arising after head injury or neurosurgery.

In 1912, Dr. Cushing moved his family to Brookline, Massachusetts, and became Professor of Surgery at Harvard Medical School. Later he became the Moseley Professor of Surgery, and surgeon-in-chief at the Peter Bent Brigham Hospital. The Cushing and Noble families became very close during those years. Dr. and Mrs. Cushing had five children: William Harvey, Mary Benedict, Betsey, Henry Kirke, and Barbara. The Cushing children were about the same ages as the five Noble children, which made for a wild time when they were all together.

In the fall of 1917, at the age of 48, Cushing joined the army and was sent with a group of Massachusetts General Hospital physicians to Base Hospital No. 5, in Camiers, France. This group came to be known as the Harvard Unit which was part of the British Expeditionary Force (BEF). Noble and Cushing frequently communicated with one another since Noble's time at Base Hospital No. 36 in September. Along with messages from his family, letters and wires from Cushing were always a high point in Noble's day.

The majority of competent and productive U.S. medical researchers were now in France, or at least in the military. The

Rockefeller Institute had temporarily given up its civilian status, and was now known as U.S. Army Auxiliary Laboratory No. 1. Its entire medical staff was now commissioned army officers. In the same way, the Johns Hopkins staff was sent as an AEF Unit to "Hopkins" Base Hospital No. 18, in Bazoilles, France.

To colleagues and fellow workers, Harvey Cushing could be extremely exasperating and a hard task master. He was a perfectionist, and his sarcasm and stormy outbursts could be acid-like. This was particularly true in the operating theater. However, he would often apologize for the outbursts. His extreme and rigid dominance over his assistants during his operations came from his caring for the welfare of his patients. Throughout the course of his patients' illnesses, Cushing was devoted to their every comfort and gave attention to their slightest needs for the sake of their successful recovery. With his patients, Cushing was most charming, friendly, and compassionate. With them, he never seemed rushed in any way. He was also adored by his student physicians. His surgical clinics were considered the Mecca of the art. Many resident house officers and medical students remembered the warm hospitality of a friendly Cushing family. Dr. and Mrs. Cushing were very gracious hosts for those who were learning from the famous surgeon.

Cushing engaged in correspondence with colleagues all over the world, and the communications were often intense. Noble treasured his letters and wires from "Harvey". After reading his friend's cable, Noble slept soundly during his last night aboard *Madawaska*.

Early the next morning, Tuesday, January 22nd, Noble noticed a great many people topside. Groups of sailors and soldiers could be seen on all decks. Loud talking and laughing was heard everywhere. Arms and hands were motioning in all directions. Everyone was very excited to be coming home. While it was still dark, there was a tiny light on the western horizon, as the ship sailed west-south-west. Noble thought the light might be Montauk, New York, on the eastern tip of Long Island. If so, it would be another nine hours before they would reach the mouth of the Hudson River. The idea of home was yet more real.

The Major ate his usual, and last, mess hall breakfast. Captain Baker was there to say goodbye to the passengers disembarking that day. Noble made it a point to thank Baker for his considerate discussions over the last twelve days, with special thanks for last night's chat. Baker told Noble to be sure to look him up if ever he sailed on *Madawaska* again, although he knew such a repeat voyage was unlikely. Noble said very sincerely that if he had to sail on a Troop Transport again, he hoped it was on Captain Baker's ship.

Noble went to Sickbay No. 2 for his final rounds through the wards. The Corporal with mustard gas burns continued to do well, and was even sitting up on a chair for short periods each day. After docking, the Corporal, along with several hundred of his fellow patients, would be transported to Army hospitals on Long Island for further treatment and convalescence. Scores of other wounds were also gradually healing. Noble changed some wound dressing and adjusted some pain mediation doses, and then prepared to go to his cabin and pack for departure.

As Noble took off his white coat and stored his sentimental stethoscope, Lieutenant Commander Mullen came up behind him. "Edward," said Mullen. "I guess this is it."

Noble looked around with a sad smile, and then hugged Dr. Mullen...something he rarely did.

"Edward," started Mullen, "I just want you to know that I think you are the best physician I have ever met. You are forever going to be missed on this ship, sir."

"Gee, John," exclaimed Noble. "You're not going to get mushy on me all of a sudden, are you?" Noble said those words as his own eyes moistened.

"Naa," said Mullen, who was also tearing up. "Not you, ya' ol' army goat. I will need to stay on board until tomorrow, so I wanted to say goodbye before you took off. I won't have any shore leave until then. When I do go ashore, I usually go to Manhattan and just sit around in Central Park until we leave for Europe again. We will be packed with troops on the eastward voyage, but we'll have many fewer cases in the sickbays. It's the voyages west that keep us busy."

"John," said Noble, "Doctor, I have the utmost respect for you. If my family ever needed a general surgeon, you would be my first choice. If you're ever in Boston, please look us up."

"Same here," said Mullen. "If you're ever in Spokane, Washington, I'll punch you if you don't visit. OK?"

The two men shook hands as real friends do, saluted one another one last time, and then went back to their tasks at hand.

Noble collected his few personal effects from his cabin into his duffle bag, and decided to spend the rest of his journey topside. It was cold and breezy even for January, but it was very clear and rather dry. It would be a sunny day. Even more people were now on the decks as the sun rose behind them. Patients in wheel chairs, who could handle the cold and the ships movement, were on the decks as well. Some Corpsmen had positioned a few supine patients upon gurneys on outside decks. As tiny land formations and lights could be seen far in the distance, one could hear whispers of people explaining to others what they were: Hampton Bays, East Patchogue, Freeport, Long Beach.

Lunch time came, and most of the army officers grabbed their lunches from the mess hall plates and went back out to watch the horizon. Noble thought the dashing off to be somewhat rude, but the Seamen did not seem to care. The navy personnel's job was the safe transport of hundreds of troops back to the U.S. Their work was not yet complete, and they were going to do it professionally until their "cargo" was repatriated. Besides, they all made these trips every few weeks.

There were other passengers aboard that no one spoke about. They were the Americans who had lost their lives in Europe and were coming home forever. No one knew their numbers, since the Government kept that secret. The coffins would be surreptitiously removed from the ship's holds, so that foreign agents, and the American public, would not know how The War was going.

At about 3:30 PM, the ship reached Lower Bay and turned a hard port side to the north. Aside from the nearly imperceptible zigzag motion of the ship over the last twelve days, this was the first time a big turn was noticeable since they left Brest. They all knew they only had about an hour left of the voyage. It was not long before the taller buildings in Brighton Beach and Borough Park could be seen.

A little later, Noble looked up and suddenly caught his breath. He heard soft gasps from all about the ship, as everyone aboard became silent. Noble put his right hand to his forehead in a salute. He straightened his posture, and saw everyone around him do the same. Even some of the wheelchair bound patients where helped to stand briefly by Corpsmen and other soldiers. On the port side was Governor's Island and the Manhattan skyline beyond it. Somewhat closer, and off the starboard bow, was Ellis Island. And, also off the starboard side, was the Statue of Liberty with the Stars and Stripes flowing gracefully near her. She stood with her famous torch against a brilliant blue sky. Suddenly, the ships extreme quiet was broken by a spontaneous roar of cheering and shouting. It was a scene that Major Noble would never forget.

The troops were now, clearly, ready to return home.

CHAPTER 3

The skyline of Manhattan showed a few ten and twelve story buildings along the Hudson River. After crossing the Atlantic for twelve days, this view seemed like something from another world. But, the troops dearly wanted to be part of this world as soon as possible. *USS Madawaska* slowed as she prepared to make her starboard turn toward the Hoboken, New Jersey docks. In the distance, the troops could see the three to five story masonry row houses that were the dominant architecture of the city.

Hoboken, New Jersey, on the west bank of the Hudson River, was an integral part of the New York Harbor shipping industry. A city of about 70,000 people, it was nicknamed "Mile Square City" because of its 48 streets laid out in a gridiron. Two of the world's biggest shipping companies, the Hamburg-American Steamship Company and the North German Lloyd Shipping Company, shared Hoboken's German liner piers. Eight to ten passenger liners could be seen docked at the piers at a time. Slender "finger" piers extended 900 feet into the Hudson River, and each had two story dock buildings along its full length. A sign, with one huge word atop each dock building, could be seen from the Hudson: "Hamburg – American – Steamship – Co.". Five other Troop Transports were docked at Hoboken as the *Madawaska* was met by four tug boats. They were the *USS President Grant*, the *USS Mount Vernon*, the *USS Agamemnon*, the *USS President Lincoln*, and the *USS Mercury*.

At the beginning of The War in 1914, Germany purposely stored many of its passenger liners at neutral U.S. docks in order to avoid capture by the Allies. Some of the liners were docked at Hoboken, and one of them would later become the *USS Madawaska*. When the U.S. entered The War in 1917, the Hamburg-American Line piers and the docked passenger liners were seized by the government under eminent domain. Hoboken then became the major point of embarkation for the more than two million American soldiers ("doughboys") destined for Europe. The soldiers hope for an early return led to General John Pershing's slogan, "Heaven, Hell, or Hoboken…by Christmas".

Madawaska went to minimum screw, and the port tugs positioned themselves along side in order to put her into dock. This was only the third time Noble had seen this elegant large ship choreography, and he found the dance to be most beautiful. Barely a bump was noticed during the process. Noble reminded himself that several of the troop transports were docking or departing every day from Hoboken.

The dock was on the ship's starboard side as she was nudged into position, ropes were thrown to the dock crews, and then securely tied up. Gangways were quickly wheeled into place, and departures of troops and crew began immediately. The docks were now a military base, and the navy and army worked twenty-four hours a day receiving Troop Transports and readying them for the voyages back to Brest. Dozens of injured troops were now being carried off *Madawaska* and taken to awaiting hospital buses. Tons of new supplies, and 2,400 fresh troops, would be aboard *Madawaska* soon. She would again set sail between seventy-two and ninety-six hours from now.

Carrying his duffle bag, Noble went down the gangway and walked into the 900 foot long two story dock building. Thousands of military personal were present, as the *USS President Grant* was being loaded on its port side along the same dock. There were so many people that it was impossible to walk a straight line. Noble began the trek to the large pier building along the coast line of Hoboken.

Noble was very tired as he reached the pier building, but was happy to be once again on American soil. His duffle bag seemed to gain weight as he walked to one end of the building. He eventually saw a sign that read, "General Office – 37 Broadway, N.Y.". At the office he asked where the "Victory Hotel" was, and was directed to the intersection of Washington and 11th Streets. This meant another four city blocks to carrying his duffle, with its seemingly increasing mass.

Army troops were everywhere in a sea of brown uniforms. Outside the pier building were scores of horse drawn carts, motor trucks, and automobiles, with all sorts of military and transatlantic voyage supplies. Signs for boat clubs and public baths were common, as the buildings around the pier were originally for civilian passengers. Noble wondered if these establishments were doing less business now, or more. As the air was cooling, Noble noticed it was already 6 PM and dark. But, the winter sky was clear, and the stars were very bright without the Moon present.

Noble finally reached his destination. At the corner of Washington and 11th was a historic plaque commemorating the first officially recorded baseball game in U.S. history. At this site, in 1846, the Knickerbocker Club and the New York Nine played the historic game at Elysian Fields. Noble smiled and knew he would have to recount this moment for his three sons who loved baseball. Noble entered the front office of the Victory Hotel, again showed his orders, and was given a key to a second story suite. He was too tired to eat or do anything but prepare for bed. In what appeared to be one motion, he brushed his teeth, set his alarm clock, took off his clothes, and fell fast asleep.

Very early the next morning, Wednesday, January 23rd, Noble awoke to his alarm, showered, dressed, and checked out of the hotel. A small delicatessen across 11th Street served him two bagels with cream cheese. When he stepped back out onto the street, an army bus was idling and taking on passengers. Noble showed the driver his orders, boarded, and found a seat. When the bus was full of brown uniforms, the driver took off south down Washington Street to Observer Way, turned left on Hudson Place, and proceeded to the Hoboken Terminal in the southeastern corner of the city. As was the case the evening before, there were thousands of army personnel everywhere. Multiple trains were coming and going, and it took some time to figure out which train went where, and when.

Noble finally found his train, and walked down yet another very long corridor to it. A blue uniformed conductor showed him where to stow his duffle bag, among dozens of others, and he found an empty seat in the train car. The train was full of army and navy personnel, but Noble was desensitized to them. In about seven hours he would arrive back in Boston, and there was little else on his mind. He had brought along Dr. Olser's text book in case he thought of a topic he wanted to study along the way. It was hard for him to believe that only thirteen days earlier, he had been in France.

The train made only five minute stops along its journey. With each stop, there was mass confusion as huge numbers of military boarded and departed. As they traveled along the Long Island Sound, the train passed Bridgeport, New Haven, and Providence. But Noble paid little attention. He was only focused on home. When the train reached New England, the weather was overcast and colder than ever. There was little heating on the train, and Noble found himself thinking about the nicer accommodations on *Madawaska*.

As the hours crawled by, all Noble thought about was Lillian. She had written him nearly every day while he was in St. Denis, and the letters helped him retain his sanity as the world of wounds and disease attempted to consume him.

Noble first met Lillian Alexander at Radcliff College in Cambridge, Massachusetts. She had chosen the school for its academic reputation. The "Harvard Annex" was a private program for the instruction of woman by Harvard faculty that had been founded in 1879. Woman had previously tried to gain access to Harvard without success, so a banker by the name of Arthur Gilman gave the "Annex" its start. In 1882 the Annex was incorporated as the Society for the Collegiate Instruction of Women, in a small house on Appian Way near Brattle Street in Cambridge. The bathroom of the little house was pressed into service as a laboratory for physics, among numerous other inconveniences. Because the institution was housed with a private family, generous "mothering" was given to the girls when they needed it.

In 1894, the "Society" was chartered by the Commonwealth of Massachusetts as Radcliffe College, and that was the year Lillian entered the school. It was named for Lady Ann Mowlson (born Radcliffe) who established the first scholarship at Harvard in 1643. While Lillian attended Radcliffe, the school began building a new campus near Harvard College. In 1896, the Boston Globe wrote of the "Sweet Girls" of Radcliffe, and that "the percentage of graduates with distinction is much higher at Radcliffe than at Harvard".

In 1896, Lillian briefly dated a Boston University School of Medicine sophomore by the name of Richard Cunard. However, at a Harvard campus lecture on the new science of epidemiology, Lillian saw a young man named Edward Noble and decided that she had to meet him. After the lecture, she went over to the young Noble, introduced herself, and asked him if he would have coffee with her and discuss the talk they had just heard. One hour later, she went home to her boarding house and told the other girls that she had just met her future husband. Her "fiancé" was also a Boston University School of Medicine sophomore. It was not important that Noble did not yet know he was destined to be engaged to her.

But, that is the way Lillian was. Her mind was made up, and that was that.

Needless to say, Edward fell head-over-heels for Lillian. The poor boy had no chance against Lillian's perseverance, intelligence, and beauty. They were married in 1898; the year Lillian graduated from Radcliffe, and one year before Edward graduated from medical school. She was twenty-two, and he was twenty-five.

Lillian graduated with a degree in epidemiology before there was even a department of that discipline in America. She designed her own curriculum within the Radcliff departments of biology and statistics. Even as she became a mother and homemaker, Lillian continued her study of epidemiology. She became aware in 1906 of the work of Wade Hampton Frost of Johns Hopkins. Frost participated in the mosquito-control and quarantine efforts in New Orleans, which became the first successful arrest of a yellow fever epidemic in the United States. Frost's application of the "index case", the use of life-table methodology to express incidence in person-years to estimate secondary attack rates, and the representation of epidemics in mathematical terms thrilled Lillian.

Lillian thought like Frost. She loved concepts such as *correlation does not imply causation*. She learned from Frost that most outcomes, whether disease or death, are caused by a chain or web of events consisting of many component causes. Unlike many epidemiologists, Lillian and Frost realized there needed to be a deeper understanding of the science in order to discover *causal* relationships. This required new approaches to investigation, such as the case series, case control studies, cohort studies, and prospective studies. Lillian corresponded with Frost many times over the years, and they had lively discussions about random error, systematic error, internal and external validity, odds ratios, relative risk, and selection bias. These were the tools the epidemiologist used to find the truth. And Lillian adored the truth.

Lillian could be stubborn. Very stubborn. Once she had a direction, it became a mission. Noble learned early to give Lillian ample space for her missions. She had the fortitude of a railroad engine, and was nearly as hard to stop. However, as resolute as she could be, she was equally dedicated to her family. Her husband and her children were the center of her life, even as she avidly pursued her missions.

At lunch time, a boy ran through Noble's railroad car selling sandwiches for 20¢. Noble bought a cheese sandwich that was stale and barely palatable. They were now only an hour from Boston, and Noble stared blankly out onto the New England winter scenery as it went by. He eventually dozed off to sleep with the rocking of the railroad car.

At 1 PM, Noble was jarred awake as the train finally pulled into the Boston and Main Railroad Station. The wheels squealed, the breaks hissed with rushing steam, and the train came to a full stop. A conductor yelled, "Boston and Main!" and the usual chaos at train stops began. Hundreds of military personnel departed from the train as hundreds climbed on to it. Many of the stops in the last seven hours had been in small towns, so the rush of people had been less at those stations. But, this was Boston, and the traffic now was nearly as busy as Hoboken had been.

Noble climbed down the railroad car ladder as a conductor was pulling out luggage from the hold beneath the car. Since there were dozens of duffle bags, and they all were identical, the conductor yelled out names of bag owners. After a few minutes, the conductor yelled, "Noble!" and the Major put the bag strap onto his right shoulder and started out of the boarding area.

Noble walked through the large station that had an exterior reminiscent of the Greek Parthenon. The station was in the northeast end of the city between Canal Street and Haverhill Street, and just north of Haymarket Square. He hoped to catch a trolley that would take him close to his home. He walked out of the front of the building and started toward the street curb. Suddenly, behind him, he heard a deep voice yell out, "Major! Major Noble!" Noble turned around and saw a very tall Staff Sergeant standing fifty feet away. As the Sergeant walked toward him, Noble guessed the lean young man stood about 6 feet 4 inches. His dark hair was crew cut, and he had very broad shoulders. His specialty uniform mark was that of a Wagoner.

"Major Noble!" yelled the Sergeant again. "Over here!" The Sergeant was now standing next to Noble. "I'll take your bag, sir."

Noble was confused. Why was an army Wagoner here to pick him up? "I'm very sorry, Sergeant, but there must be some mistake. I'll just catch a trolley."

"You are Major Edward Noble, sir?" asked the Sergeant.

"Yes, but…"

"My orders are to pick you up and take you to your house, sir. I have a staff motor car at the curb, over there," as the Sergeant motioned to an olive green Ford military automobile off to the right.

"I really appreciate it, Sergeant, but I'm just a Major. No one would send an army staff car for me."

"Someone did, sir," said the Sergeant.

Noble was now very curious. "Who sent the car, Sergeant?"

"I thought you knew, sir. It was Colonel Victor Vaughn," exclaimed the Sergeant.

A rush of childhood memories ran through Noble like a moving picture show at a nickelodeon. He smiled with one side of his mouth, and dropped his gaze slightly as he shook his head slowly. Very quietly, so that the Sergeant could not hear him, Noble whispered, "Uncle Victor."

"Here, let me take your duffle, sir, and I'll get you home," said the Sergeant. He placed the bag in the back of the staff car, and then opened the back door for the Major. He went to the front of the vehicle, turned the starter crank, and the engine turned over and began to idle. As he pulled closed the driver's door, he said, "I'm Staff Sergeant Campbell, sir." The Sergeant was accustomed to driving soldiers who had just returned from Europe. He knew it was best to let them bring up their experiences rather than ask.

"Nice to meet you, Sergeant," responded Noble as the car left the curb. Noble became quiet as he thought of his old family friend, Colonel Vaughn.

Born in 1851, the Civil War swirled around Victor Clarence Vaughn during his early years of life. Vaughan would later write that his youth had taught him to "hate war and to love peace so dearly that I have been willing to do my small bit in fighting for it". He learned fluent Latin during college and taught himself chemistry. He earned a PhD in chemistry at the University of Michigan, and also earned minors in geology and biology. While a professor of physiologic and pathological chemistry, and associate professor of therapeutics and material medica, he entered medical school in 1876. In 1878 he spent a year at the University of Berlin in Germany studying bacteriologic technique under Dr. Robert Koch, who would go on to discover the tuberculin bacillus. While in Berlin, Vaughn met Edward's father, Charles Noble, who also spent four months under the tutelage of Dr. Koch. The two Americans became fast and life-long friends. Vaughan was appointed dean of the University of Michigan Medical School in 1891, and remained at that post even now.

As a young man, Vaughan was diagnosed with Tuberculosis. But many years later, only a small apical lung lesion was seen on a Roentgenogram. He also contracted malaria as a youth. In 1898, during the Spanish-American war, he also contracted yellow fever. Perhaps these illnesses prompted Vaughan to focus his intellect on Infectious Diseases. He read the epidemiological literature on the spread of typhoid fever through food and water, and discovered that the common housefly served as a vector for the disease. His numerous sanitary measures were responsible for reducing the annual troop death rate from 879 per 100,000 in 1898, to 107 per 100,000 in 1899. He was instrumental in making the typhoid vaccine compulsory for the military in 1912, and deaths from that disease greatly decreased.

In 1916, President Wilson's administration began to make military plans in case the U.S. entered The War. The

Council of National Defense was created, and the Secretary of War presided over it. Other Council members included the Secretaries of the Army, the Navy, the Interior, Agriculture, Commerce, and Labor. The Wilson administration asked Dr. Vaughn to serve on the Medical Division of the Council while he remained dean at the Michigan Medical School.

The sixty-seven year old Dr. Vaughn, and his five sons, obtained their commissions in the U.S. Army immediately after the Congressional Declaration of War. His sons eventually became a Lieutenant, a Captain, a Major, and two Lieutenant Colonels. Vaughn had been a lieutenant in the Army Reserves and was promoted to Major. Very soon, he was promoted to Colonel. President Wilson then established the Executive Committee of the Medical Division of the Council of National Defense. The Executive Committee consisted of the Surgeon General of the Army (Dr. William Gorgas), the Surgeon General of the Navy, (Dr. William Braisted), the Surgeon General in charge of the U.S. Public Health Service (Dr. Rupert Blue), and five physicians that included Dr. William Mayo, Dr. William Welch, and Dr. Victor Vaughn. In no uncertain terms, Dr. Vaughn was one of the most famous and powerful physicians in America.

The Surgeon General of the Army, Dr. Gorgas, rightfully put Colonel Vaughn in charge of the Division of Communicable Diseases in the U.S. Army. For Vaughn, the conservation of the health of the troops was a matter of prime importance.

Now, it appeared as though Colonel Vaughn had sent a staff car to pick up Noble. Even though Vaughn had known Edward since he was five years old, there was more to it than that. Was the Colonel involved in Noble's orders to return to Boston?

The sky was overcast and the air very cold. There was still ice and some snow on the ground from a storm that passed through New England a few days earlier. Horse drawn carts, along with motor cars and trolleys, mixed dirt and snow on Boston streets. This mixture became the brown slush that adorns all big cities after winter storms. Army and navy uniforms were everywhere among civilians, and this was a big change from Noble's departure four months earlier.

The Sergeant drove the staff car to Stanford Street, to Bowdoin Street, and then right on Beacon Street. On the left they passed the Boston Common with its Frog Pond and Swan Boat pond, where Noble had played as a boy. As they passed the cross street Hereford in Back Bay, Noble asked Sergeant Campbell to pull the car over to the side of Beacon Street.

"Major, I can take you to your house," said the Sergeant.

"Thank you, Sergeant," said Noble. "But we're less than a block from my house, which is almost on the corner of Beacon and 'Mass Ave'. I would like to walk the rest of the way."

Sergeant Campbell knew coming home from war was an emotionally turbulent experience. Everyone must find their own way to deal with it. He said, "No problem, sir," as he stepped out of the idling car, opened up the left back door for the Major, and took his duffle from the back of the vehicle.

"Again, thank you, Sergeant. This has made the last leg of my trip very pleasant."

"You're welcome, sir," said the Sergeant. "Oh, yes. One more thing. My orders are to be available to take you anywhere you need to go in Boston, sir. If I am off, then I will be sure to have one of the other Wagoners available. We are stationed at Camp Devens, so just call the motor pool there, tell them who you are, and we'll go where you are."

"That's…that's great, Sergeant," said Noble. "Then, I'll see you again." The two saluted, and the staff car drove on down Beacon Street and turned right on Massachusetts Avenue. Noble considered how odd it was to have an army staff car, and driver, available for his use whenever he needed it. This is a service Generals are privileged to have. Not a Major.

Noble walked west, on the north side of Beacon Street. The familiar pink brick houses lined the street, one right next to the other. Many leafless trees were along the curb, with some snow on the soil of the tree wells cut into the sidewalk. There were few pedestrians because of the cold. He thought it strange to know a place so well, but feel as though it is new to you.

He finally walked up to his home at 468 Beacon Street. The five story bow-front pink brick building had a mansard roof, and drapes pulled over the numerous windows. He stood for a short time looking at the large dark green front door to the left of the building's front, and a garage door off to the right. Noble had bought a new 1917 Ford, and converted a first floor storage area into a small garage. He looked forward to driving the Ford again soon, since he had left for the army shortly after its purchase.

Noble climbed three stone stairs, reached into his army coat pocket for his house keys, unlocked the front door, and entered his house. Facing the front door, immediately beyond an indoor receiving area, was a small sideboard against a flight of stairs. The stairs climbed left-to-right, onto the second story. The sideboard had family photographs, a vase with flowers, and a porcelain tray the family used for keys, coins, and other pocket items. To the right, beyond open French doors, was Noble's library. Large inset bookcases from the floor to the ceiling could be seen in the library. To the left was a large parlor with a fireplace, sofas, and numerous chairs. The walls were furnished with evergreen floral wallpaper, along with numerous paintings and family photographs. Thick Indian carpets were thrown upon a hard wood floor.

Noble put down his duffle bag, and walked off to the left through the parlor. He passed the Dr. Cushing drawing of Lillian as he made his way to the kitchen. As he came up to the open French doors to the kitchen, a petit woman 5 feet 6 inches tall stood at the sink with her back to him. Her shoulder-length light brown hair had a barrette upon each temple. She wore a white blouse and a light tan skirt measuring eight inches from the floor. She was quite busy washing vegetables.

Noble's heart seemed it would beat out of his chest as he laid his eyes on her. His face flushed, and he felt his hands trembling. From the kitchen door he said, "Lilly."

Lillian Noble stopped her task at the sink, and raised her head to the level of a window just above it. Her arms fell to her side, as she slowly turned around to face her husband who had returned to her. Her blue eyes were already filling with tears which began to stream down her pink cheeks.

"Oh...Edward," Lillian said softly as she slowly walked toward him, arms rising to hold him.

They embraced in a way that only two people who feel as one do. Lillian buried her face in the right side of his chest. Several minutes went by before any other words were said, with Noble gently rocking her from side-to-side. She then pulled his face to hers with her hands and kissed him for a very long time.

Lillian finally said through her sobs, "We all thought you were coming home yesterday. We thought something terrible had happened. The navy couldn't, or wouldn't, give us any information. We've been so worried."

"I'm so sorry, Lilly," said Noble. "Once I found out that the ship would leave Brest a day later than I was originally told, I knew a letter would not get here in time. I had no access to a cable office, and only the ships commanding officers have use of the radio."

"We worried about the U-boats..." said Lillian.

"That's all done now," said Noble. "Put it out of your mind as I have. I don't know why I am here, but here I am. Is anyone else here?"

Lillian smiled for the first time since her husband's arrival. She said, "Arthur is in the guest room. He's been staying there since the accident, with his upstairs bedroom too hard to reach. He's dying to see you."

From Lillian's letters, and letters from his other children, Noble knew all about Arthur's accident. At nineteen, Arthur was Noble's oldest child. He had entered Boston University in the fall of 1917, but joined the Student Army Training Corps at about the same time. The draft had been expanded to include all men between the ages of eighteen and forty-five, and college students were to start military training as soon as possible. Arthur was commissioned in September as an army Second Lieutenant, and was sent to Camp Devens to begin training. However, while helping to build a barrack at Devens in October, Arthur fell off a ladder and suffered a right femur fracture. This required a cast to his hip. The medical officers at Devens allowed Arthur to convalesce at home, since he lived relatively close to the camp. "I'll go and see him," said Noble.

Noble walked back through the parlor, passed the library, and on to the guest room toward the back of the first floor. He reached the bedroom where his 6 foot tall son, weighing 170 lbs, was sitting in a wheel chair with his fully-casted right leg stretched out in front of him. Baseball, tennis, football, and crew, had sculptured Arthur into a muscular young man. With kindly handsome facial features like his grandfather's, and closely cut brown hair, Arthur had always been very popular with the girls. Noble said, "Doesn't the army teach you to stand when a commanding officer enters the room?"

Arthur looked up from an anatomy textbook, took a double-take, and shouted, "Dad!"

Noble walked over to Arthur and gave him a bear hug. Noble said with a smile, "At ease, Lieutenant! Arthur! It's so good to see you!"

"Mom was really worried about you, Dad!" said Arthur. "Gee, we were all really worried! How was the Troop Transport trip, Dad?"

"Nothing to it," said Noble. "I didn't do a thing across the whole Atlantic. How's the leg?"

"Yeah, right, Dad." Arthur knew his father could not just sit around for twelve days and do "nothing". "The orthopedist said I can get the cast off in March, with some rehabilitation in Boston after that. One of the physicians at Devens, Dr. Roy Grist, said he can help me with rehab on the days I'm at the camp. I'll be back to active duty in no time. I can get around now OK with crutches, and I have been exercising my left leg with stretching and bending. I need to be in the best condition possible when I get the cast off. Then I can make the most of rehabilitation exercises with my right leg."

Lillian came into the guest room, and put her right arm around her husband while putting her left arm around the neck of her son. Squeezing Noble she said, "You know, darling, you have lost a lot of weight."

"Yeah, Dad. You look like one of the skeletons at the medical school," said Arthur chuckling.

"I've lost some weight, I know," said Noble. "But, it's not quite that bad."

"How about some pizza, guys?" said Lillian. "We need to put some pounds on our Major here."

The thought of pizza topped off Noble's day. It was his favorite food, aside from cheese sandwiches, and it was not something that one found in France or on troop transports. Lillian and Edward held hands as they walked back to the kitchen. Arthur got up on his crutches to prove to his father that "I can do it". Noble and his son sat at the kitchen table as Lillian began to knead the dough for a Chicago style pizza. For the first time since arriving at Base Hospital No. 36 months earlier, Noble was beginning to feel a tad normal.

Arthur explained to his father that the Secretary of War, Newton Baker, had recently written presidents of all U.S. colleges with more than one hundred students. College presidents were informed that army officers and non-commissioned officers would be providing instruction from this time forward. Effectively, the teaching of academic courses in U.S. colleges had ended, and was replaced with military training. Military officers had taken virtual command of each of the country's centers of higher education. Some essential non-military training with strategic value continued, as was the case with medical education. However, most academic pursuits had simply gone into hibernation for the foreseeable future.

By now it was nearly 4 PM this Wednesday. The three Noble grade school children would be returning home soon. It was not long before the three adults in the kitchen heard the gradual increase of laughter, shrieking, and arguing that is the rule among young siblings. The noise became deafening as the "crowd" came through the front door. A young woman ushered the three children upstairs to put their things away and to begin homework. From the kitchen, Lillian called out, "Akeema, can you bring the children down to the kitchen? I have someone for them to meet."

"Yes, Mrs. Noble. They will be right down," said a voice from upstairs.

A few minutes later, the same noise level was heard rumbling down the stairway to the sitting room. Three children entered the kitchen, and abruptly stopped. There is nothing like the great surprise of children as they become completely motionless and silent. The three processed the wonderful new situation before them, like encountering gifts under a Christmas tree on Christmas day. Noble sat smiling at the three child "statues". Then, there was a huge collective scream from the three as they threw themselves at their father, nearly knocking over his chair. A mass of arms, legs, torsos, and heads slammed and pressed against Noble with the hope of getting closer to him. There came a succession of multiple questions and requests from children of different ages, such as: Where have you been? Tell us about France! What is The War like? How big was the ship you were on? Did you meet General Pershing? Did you have a good time, Daddy?

Noble laughed, "Wait! Wait a minute! We can get to all of that later. First, *you* tell me about the things you have been doing!" Noble was, most definitely, a very happy man. All at once, and for the next half-hour, the three children told their father every thought they had saved up for him over the last four months. And, Noble loved every minute of it.

During this whole affair, the young woman who had brought the children home stood off to the side of the kitchen and laughed along with them all. The woman was Akeema Ayuluk. At twenty years old, she was the Noble family nanny who was now as much a part of the family as anyone. She was of the Unalirmiut group of Yup`ik people in Alaska.

Yup`ik means literally in English "real people". She was born in the tiny village of Golovin. Her village sat on a peninsula only 1,500 feet wide that jutted into Golovnin Lagoon, one hundred miles east of Nome, Alaska.

At the age of seventeen, Akeema decided to pursue her dream of becoming a registered nurse. She made her way aboard ships, trains, and buses from Golovin to Boston by working as a cook, maid, and a stewardess. The journey took many months, but she finally arrived in Boston where she enlisted the help of an employment agency. The agency staff immediately appreciated her intelligence, self-sufficiency, reliability, and her kindness with people. She spoke five languages fluently: English, French, Russian, German, and the Unaliq sub-dialect of Yup`ik. Being a great cook and organizer, the agency felt she would be perfect for the Nobles who were seeking a nanny. Akeema fit instantly into the Noble family as though she had been born into it.

Akeema was 5 feet 9 inches tall, which was unusually tall for the Yup`ik, and weighed 120 lbs. She had Asian coal black eyes with high cheek bones. Her smooth chocolate skin provided a stunning contrast to her brilliant white sclera and teeth. Her hair was such a thick jet black color that it almost appeared as a shimmering dark blue. She wore her hair in a long ponytail that nearly reached her waist.

Akeema was dressed much like Lillian, with a light blue blouse and a light brown skirt. Since the U.S. had entered The War, women's clothing had become very simple for lack of cloth. Even the colorful dyes of women's clothes a year earlier were no longer available. Therefore, ladies were wearing mostly pastels. The knee-high leather boots popular in 1917 were now crafted into military boots. Presently, women wore either ankle-high shoes or "flats" with very low heals. Even when ladies had fashionable clothes and shoes from previous years, it was patriotic to dress simply.

Eventually, Akeema came over to Edward, gave him a hug, and said, "It is wonderful to have you back, Dr. Noble! I cannot tell you how much your children missed you!"

Thank you, Akeema," said Noble. He admired her qualities of deep religious conviction, loyalty, resourcefulness, and a unique special quiet reserve common among the Yup`ik. "You do such a great job with Bernard, Michael, and Rabbit." "Rabbit" was Noble's nickname for his five year old, Marguerite. He called her that because, since she was a toddler, she bounced and hopped when she was excited and happy. And, Marguerite was excited and happy most of time.

"Thank you, Dr. Noble," said Akeema. "I love them so."

For an hour the seven people in the Noble kitchen talked non-stop about everything from the rising cost of groceries to the outlook for the upcoming Boston Red Sox baseball season. Noble had not received much news over the last two weeks. Arthur told him that, as expected, the Central Powers had signed an armistice with Russia. Russia was no longer a player in The War. With millions of Russian troops returning home, the Germans and other Central Power nations were now free to send huge numbers of troops and resources to the Western Front. At the same time, thousands of Americans were arriving in France every day. Both the Central Powers and the Allies now realized the outcome of The War would be decided on the Western Front.

It was now dark, and one additional Noble family member was expected to arrive momentarily.

"I hope she arrives soon, Edward," said Lillian. "I don't like it when she is out when it is dark."

Noble began to say, "Well, will go for her if it is much more..." He stopped short of finishing his sentence when all heard keys opening the front door.

Florence Noble walked inside and closed the door. She was wearing her dark blue Navy Reserve uniform, which consisted of a navy-blue serge skirt and high black leather boots. There was a white blouse buttoned around her neck, and a navy-blue serge coat with a waist belt that ran under two plaits in the front and back. She wore a round straight brimmed navy-blue hat that was flat on the top, and had a circular ribbon around it that read "Naval Reserve". Since she was a nursing student, she had the rank of Ensign.

Florence saw her father, dropped a bag with books, and ran to him in the kitchen yelling, "Daddy!"

"Oh, Daddy, we were so worried about you! How come you're late? Oh, I don't care!" She hugged her father and actually made it somewhat hard for him to breathe. However, he did not tell her to stop, either.

"Florence!" said her father smiling. "I leave for a few months, and you go from being my teenage girl to an Ensign! No one let this cat-out-of-the-bag at all. When did you join?"

"I wanted it to be a surprise, Daddy," said Florence. I joined in November. They're eager to have nursing students join the Reserves, since they need nurses in the regular navy as soon as they graduate. I could even be a Lieutenant-Junior Grade by graduation!" Florence so wanted her father to be proud of her. Of course, he was.

"Well, at least for now, I'm still the ranking officer around here," Noble joked.

Arthur jumped in, "I don't know dad. I think Mom out ranks you in this house!" Everyone laughed, but thought it was likely true.

At this point, Lillian had finished baking two large diameter cheese pizzas. She had some bottles of Coca Cola in the kitchen ice box, and everyone had a marvelous time with the celebration feast.

Noble watched his oldest daughter as she giggled with Akeema about a new handsome movie star in the very popular movie tabloids. She was young, but he had said of her since she was a little girl that she had an "old soul". Florence was eighteen years old, and a nursing student at Boston City Hospital. Boston City had one of the most respected nursing education programs in New England, and Noble was very proud of his daughter for sticking with the challenging curriculum. Just like Akeema, Florence was 5 feet 9 inches tall and weighed 120 lbs. She had gold-blond hair that was usually pulled into a pony tail, and was nearly waist length. When she was not in her Navy Reserve or nursing student uniforms, she wore brightly colored ribbons in her hair. Her pale green eyes seemed to have a light of their own.

Florence had almost the same build, perfect posture, and flattering figure as Akeema. Since they wore their hair in nearly the same style, from a distance they almost looked like twins. However, the two women showed the full range of feminine beauty found in that fair gender. When the two walked about Boston streets, all eyes were on them.

After the feast, Edward and Lillian went upstairs to tuck the three younger children in bed. Arthur went to his down stairs room to read an army manual for new officers. Florence went to Akeema's room ostensibly to talk about today's nursing lesson, although Lillian said they would likely read tabloids.

Noble was exhausted. He and his wife prepared for bed, when Lillian suddenly said, "Oh, Edward. I almost forgot. A telegram came for you yesterday. It's in the library." She ran downstairs to get the telegram for him. Returning upstairs to their bedroom, she handed him the sealed envelope.

Noble was now apprehensive. Perhaps these were his orders that had been purposely kept from him when he left St. Denis. He carefully opened the envelope and read the contents.

Major Edward Noble, AEF.
468 Beacon St., Boston, USA

Tuesday, January 22, 1918
From: Undisclosed

Major Noble. You are hereby ordered to report to the Army Intelligence Cable Office, 2nd floor, South Department, Boston City Hospital, Boston, Massachusetts, USA, at 0900, January 24, 1918.

"Edward, what does it say?" asked Lillian. "Who is it from?"

"I...I don't really know, Lilly," said Noble. He read the cable out loud to her. "It's in the usual army format, for sure. But, it doesn't say who sent it."

"Lillian exclaimed, "Well, at least you know what the 'South Department' is, at BCH."

Noble knew the Department well, since he had worked there since 1905. In fact, he was the Department's Medical Director. Infectious diseases patients were treated in the "South Department" pavilions within Boston City Hospital. These wards were not chosen by chance. The South Department was located on the farthest hospital campus corner from downtown Boston, in order to minimize contagious risk.

"Lilly, of course I know where the South Department is. But what is the 'Army Intelligence Cable Office'? There is no such place in the Department, or at Boston City Hospital."

There were now more questions than answers. In any case, Noble was likely to find out the answers to those questions tomorrow. While pondering these events, Noble fell asleep in Lillian's arms while she stroked his white hair. She turned out the lamp, and worried what lay in store for her husband.

CHAPTER 4

E arly the next morning, Thursday, January 24th, Lillian arose before the rest of her family. She wanted to ensure her husband had a good breakfast before his trip to Boston City Hospital. She asked him what he wanted to eat, and not surprisingly his request was much like his standard aboard *Madawaska*.

"What do you think you'll find at BCH, darling?" asked Lillian.

"Lilly, I have no idea," said Noble. "I didn't tell you that Victor Vaughn had a staff car sent for me at the Boston and Main Terminal."

"Uncle Victor!" said Lillian. "Do you think he had you sent home?"

"I'm pretty sure he had something to do with it," said Noble. "But, I guess I'll have a clearer idea about all of this around 0900 this morning. I'm going to arrive there pretty early so that I can size up the situation."

Just before Noble was to leave, Arthur, Florence, and Akeema came into the kitchen to wish him well. Arthur was going to Boston University for classes, Florence had lectures at Boston City, and Akeema would be preparing the children for school. Lillian told him how handsome he was in his officer's uniform, and Noble flashed her a fake smile showing all his teeth. Noble kissed Lillian, and took off for BCH.

Noble reenacted his usual routine for the day's commute to work. He walked west on Beacon Street to Massachusetts Avenue, and caught a trolley southwest to the corner of Mass Ave. and Albany Street. That was the location of the South Department.

Boston City Hospital was built during the Civil War as the Union was gearing up for anticipated causalities. A central domed administrative building was constructed that looked like a miniature Washington D.C. Capital Building. This building was located directly east of Worcester Square, and was called the Rotunda. Stretching out from the Rotunda were four expansive patient pavilions. Over the years, the numbers of pavilions had greatly expanded. Now, the large square area between Harrison Avenue on the northwest, Concord Avenue on the northeast, Massachusetts Avenue on the southwest, and Albany Avenue on the southeast, was nearly packed with patient pavilions.

Noble departed the familiar Mass Ave. trolley and walked across the street to the Boston City Hospital campus. Entering a door at the end of one of the large buildings, he walked to a nursing office on the first floor. He asked where the "Army Intelligence Cable Office" was, and the secretary in the office directed him to an area on the second floor. Noble followed the directions as he climbed stairs to the second floor, and walked to the southernmost end of the building.

In an area that had previously been administrative offices, there was now a single door. No sign stated where the door led. Stationed at the door was a very large army Sergeant sentry with an "MP" arm band for "Military Police", and a rifle. Next to the Sergeant was a very small table with a note pad and a telephone, and a small chair. Noble stood for a time in front of the door and sentry. Finally, he asked, "Sergeant, is this the Army Intelligence Cable Office?"

"Major, sir, please state your name." asked the Sergeant.

"I'm Major Edward Noble, Sergeant."

"Do you have your orders and identification, sir?" the Sergeant asked. Noble showed him the relevant documents. "We have been expecting you, sir. You're early, sir. However, you can enter if you choose, sir."

"Thank you, Sergeant."

"You'll need these from now on, sir," as the Sergeant handed the Major keys to the door. "Please do not lose these, sir. That would be very unfortunate, sir."

Noble thanked the Sergeant again. With some trepidation, he unlocked the three foot wide heavy oak door, and opened it.

The Major walked into a rectangular office that was about twelve by fifteen feet in floor space. To the left was an oak roll top desk with pencils, pens, writing paper, a desk lamp, and a telephone. The desk had a matching oak chair on coasters. Next to the desk was a small stand with a typewriter on it, and a coat rack. To the right were a hunter green leather sofa and a matching wingback chair, along with a floor reading light. Straight ahead was another three foot wide heavy oak door. On all other wall surfaces were built-in ceiling-to-floor book cases full of medical text books, atlases, military strategy books, phone books, and a complete new set of the Encyclopedia Britannica. Above was a ceiling fan with lamps attached to it. There were no windows. The hard wood floor was brand new. The ceiling had been freshly painted and the room smelled of new paint. Everything in the room was also new, and it looked as though no one had ever used any of it.

Looking at the desk, Noble noticed all the pencils had been sharpened but never used. The typewriter was a state-of-the-art Remington.

Noble took off his heavy army overcoat and hung it on the coat rack. The temperature in the office was very comfortable without it. He wondered what was behind the next door in the office. He tried the door knob, but it was locked. Since there were two different keys on the small ring given to him by the Sergeant, he wondered if the second key unlocked the second door. It did, and he opened it.

The Major entered a room that was at least four times the size of the office he had just left. The ceiling was about 12 feet high, and also had a fan with lamps. The much larger office was on the corner of the building, so there were very tall windows on each of the corner walls off to the left. There was a second similar window to the right, on the longer wall he faced. In the center of the room was a four foot square oak table with thick legs. There was nothing on the large table. Against the wall to the right sat a roll top desk with a chair, and two identical desks against the longer wall straight ahead. All the desks and chairs were identical to the ones in the first smaller office. Each desk was set up as the first, and each had a telephone. There were also eight-foot high built-in book cases wherever there was space. Each bookcase was also filled with new text books on a full range of sciences. Two hunter green leather wingback chairs were in the room with floor reading lamps next to them. The hard wood floor was new, and the smell of fresh paint was also apparent in this second office. As before, everything was new.

The most amazing finding of all was seen against the wall to the left. A large horizontal desk piece was attached to a five foot high backboard. The desk piece had numerous columns of keys, little lights, and cords with male jacks. The high backboard had rows of female jacks that were associated with little lights. Each jack represented an incoming or outgoing trunk line. This was a state-of-the-art manual exchange, or telephone switchboard. Next to the switchboard was another large oak table with a telegraph key pad, a printing machine, a radio, and another new Remington typewriter. Large cables ran from these devices and into output/input ports in the walls. Noble had never seen anything like this before.

Seated before the switchboard, in another oak chair with coasters, was a young woman. She wore the usual brown army tunic with a high collar, but with a matching skirt. She had a small brown cap without a brim that army soldiers sometimes wore. Her blond hair was worn up under the cap. Acting as a long distance operator, she connected a trunk line for a caller. As Noble walked into the room, the woman looked over her left shoulder towards him, smiled, put up one finger to say 'just one minute', and completed the connected call. She then promptly stood up at attention, saluted, and said, "Good morning Major Noble! You're a bit early!"

Noble noticed the single gold bars on her shoulder straps, her bronze "U.S." on her right front collar, and a bronze pair of flags with a center staff on her left front collar. This meant she was a Second Lieutenant in the Regular Army, and was a member of the Signal Corps. He was in awe of the office, and perplexed by the young officer in it. He saluted back.

"Major," said the Lieutenant, "is there something wrong? You look confused."

Noble smiled. "Well, I guess I am, to a degree. This office...the other office...they're really something. Also, except for nurses, I didn't know there were women officers in the regular army."

"They mentioned that you wouldn't know of our work here," said the Lieutenant. "There are 300 of us in the U.S. Army Signal Corps, sir. Many of us are even in France. General Pershing himself asked for us."

Noble was likely hearing top secret information, and his mouth fell open slightly.

The Lieutenant continued, "The General wanted women who were at least twenty-five years old, fluent in French, and had extensive experience as Bell Telephone operators. Two of the three of us picked for the Army Intelligence Cable Office at Boston City worked for the New England Telephone Company, and one of us worked for the Boston Telephone Dispatch Company. For this work, the three of us also had to be expert at sending and receiving Morse code."

"This is simply amazing", said Noble. "What is all of this for?"

"Sir," said the Lieutenant, "they call this a telecommunications center. We can act as local telephone operators, long distance civilian telephone operators, or long distance operators between military facilities." Pointing to her consul in front of her, the Lieutenant said, "See, here is our cordboard that connects us to anywhere in America. These lines are secure for all military intelligence. If there is secret information to encrypt, we can use the telegraph," as she pointed to her right. "We can also use the telegraph to send and receive messages to areas that are not well served with long distance telephone connections. Although there are 10 million telephones in the U.S., most of them are in large cities. As you know, calling outside of Boston can be hit-and-miss. Our radio has a range of 500 miles, if there is a receiver to pick up the signal. Of course, we must use the telegraph for our transatlantic cable connection."

"You have a direct transatlantic cable connection…here?" asked Noble.

"Yes. But, you know what?" she said with excitement.

"No, what?" said Noble, who was still not sure if he believed whether all of this was real.

The Lieutenant continued, "Our telegraphy has Edison Quadraplex capability, so the transatlantic cable can send and receive two messages at once. On top of that, the speed is really fast. It can send or receive up to 120 words a minute to and from Europe."

Noble had not known all this was possible, and he had no idea why it was at Boston City Hospital. Even more of a mystery was the reason why he was here looking at it in the first place. "What is that over there?" Noble asked as he pointed to a type of printer to the right of the Lieutenant's cordboard.

"This is really neat, Major," said the Lieutenant. "This is the newest model of a Buckingham Machine Telegraph that can print some Morse code messages in plain Roman letters. All you need to do is put a regular telegram message blank in the machine and it prints out the message quickly, legibly, and ready-to-read. Someday no one will even need to learn Morse code."

"Lieutenant," said Noble, "you mentioned there are three of you here?"

"Yes, three of us are assigned to Boston City." said the Lieutenant. "All 300 women in the Signal Corps are supposed to be at least twenty-five years old, but many of us aren't. It was too hard for the army to find women with all the criteria they sought. So, the age minimum was stretched a bit. I'm twenty-one, Claudette is twenty, and Marié is nineteen. Our orders are to staff the Army Intelligence Cable Office... we call it the A.I. Office for short...in twelve hour shifts, twenty-four hours a day. We are attached to Camp Devens. However, the Signal Corps put the three of us up in an apartment on Worcester Square, across Harrison Avenue from Boston City."

"Where did you learn French?" asked Noble.

"I'm American, but my family lived in Quebec, Canada for many years when I was little. I picked up French there."

"What's your name, Lieutenant," said Noble, sensing he was going to work with her for a long time.

"I'm Karen; Lieutenant Karen Pecknold, sir."

"Glad to meet you, Lieutenant Pecknold. Can you send and receive cables here...to anywhere?"

"Major," said the Lieutenant in a matter-of-fact way, "why, this is your office, sir. Do you want to send one?"

Noble could think of no reason why he was there, why he could send or receive messages to anyone he wanted at any time, or why this "A.I. Office" was his. However, like a kid with a new bicycle, Noble asked to send a message to Colonel Harvey Cushing, BEF, at Base Hospital No. 5, Camiers, France. He wanted to tell Harvey that he arrived safely, and that for the time being he would be at Boston City Hospital. Noble half thought he would be told "no", but Lieutenant Pecknold said, "Yes, sir," and proceeded to tap out the message on the telegraph key. "The message will be in France in a few minutes, sir," said the Lieutenant. Noble just shook his head in complete amazement.

The Major spent some time studying the new marvelous equipment, and asking many questions about its use and capabilities. At one point the Lieutenant asked the Major if he wanted her and the other Signal Corps officers to use the "Telegraphic Code" book when U.S. Public Health Service information came by cable. This was designed to keep telegraph operators from learning potentially sensitive information about infectious diseases among troops, or the rest of the nation. Noble said that was not necessary, since the Signal Corps officers were already military, and so was the Public Health Service. He was fascinated to learn that the A.I. Office could also receive airmail delivered directly from the nearby Aviation Section of the U.S. Army airfield.

Noble began to thumb through the huge library of brand new books in the A.I. Office, when the phone near the cordboard rang. The Lieutenant said, "Sir, there is a visitor here to see you."

"Who is it?" asked Noble with a great deal of anticipation.

"Colonel Victor Vaughn, sir. He'll meet you in the small office."

Noble was full of questions. However, perhaps he would finally be given some answers. He went into the small office and sat in the oak desk chair, with his right food slightly twitching. Soon the second door opened and Colonel Vaughn, one of the most famous physicians in America, entered. He was 5 foot 7 inches tall, and weighed 275 lbs. He looked very out of place in his U.S. Army uniform. He had gray hair cut short on the sides, long on the top, and had a gray mustache. He had a very kindly round face that could flash an impish smile.

"Colonel Vaughn!" shouted Noble, as he stood to shake both Vaughn's hands. He quickly halted after hand shaking, and saluted. "It is so good to see you, Colonel!"

"Aren't you going to call me 'Uncle Victor', Edward?" asked Vaughn.

"That was thirty-five years ago, sir," said Noble, laughing. "Now, you are 'Colonel'."

Vaughn sat down on the hunter green sofa, sat back, and crossed his legs. "You've lost weight, Edward. How was the crossing?"

"OK, Colonel. I kept myself busy in sickbay."

"I trust the family is well; Lillian and the children?"

"They're all fine, sir. Arthur is mending a broken femur from a fall at Devens, and is a Second Lieutenant. Florence is a nursing student, and an Ensign in the Reserves. Lillian is as beautiful and brilliant as ever, and of course is active in the Red Cross and a zillion other things. Bernard, Michael, and Marguerite are all doing grand."

"That's great, Edward. Just great."

A few moments of silence passed, and then Noble could no longer contain himself. "Colonel, I'm sorry to be abrupt, but why exactly am I here? Why is this incredible office here? The Signal Corps officer in the large room refers to this place as 'my office'. Why is that?"

A few more moments passed as Vaughn's expression became very serious. He took a deep breath as he began. "Edward, since last fall, the U.S. has constructed thirty-two huge Army cantonments that are designed to turn a few million boys into soldiers. The camps each hold 30,000 to 40,000 troops or more at a time. As training camps, there are thousands of troops arriving and leaving every day. The great majority of the camps were built in just a few weeks, and many of the troops still remain in tents. Gorgas, Welch, Cole, and I surveyed many of the camps last fall, and we are very concerned."

Noble thought to himself how impressive the four surveyors were. Major General William Gorgas, Army Surgeon General, had controlled the mosquito population in Florida, Havana, and the Panama Canal, and abated the transmission of yellow fever and malaria. Rufus Cole had made the Rockefeller Institute Hospital a model of how clinical research should be conducted. Colonel William Welch, Dean of the Johns Hopkins University School of Medicine, was a driving force in the restructuring of American Medicine.

Vaughn continued. "We are already seeing problems in the camps with pneumonia and cerebrospinal meningitis. At Camp Wheeler in Georgia, hundreds of troops were coming down with measles every day. As you know, measles in adults can be quite severe."

"Edward, in the Crimean War, British, French, and Russian troops spread cholera. In the American Civil War, troops spread typhoid, dysentery, and small pox. In the Franco-Prussian War, Prussian troops also spread small pox. In the Spanish-American War, troops spread typhoid. With this in mind, General Gorgas has expressed to us his *nightmare*."

"His *nightmare*?" asked Noble.

"Yes," answered Vaughn. "His nightmare is that of an epidemic sweeping through the cantonments. Given the traffic through the camps, an epidemic outbreak in one camp would be extraordinarily difficult to isolate from the others. The results could be catastrophic. Such an epidemic could spread to the civilian population as well. The General intends to do all he can in his position to stop any of this from happening."

"Edward, did you know that General Gorgas has made me in charge of the Army Division of Communicable Diseases?"

"Yes, I heard that Colonel," said Noble. "He definitely picked the best man for the job."

"Well, Edward," said Vaughn, "my measure of success with infectious diseases is a pretty high bar when one considers the health of a military organization. One is successful when the morbidity and mortality rates from these diseases are no higher among soldiers than they are in the same civilian age groups. Edward, this high standard has seldom been reached in military history, much less maintained for a long period of time. This goal will take extra special resources, tools, skills, and extraordinary people. This is where you come in, Major."

Vaughn's eyes narrowed. "In the calendar year of 1917, among the troops who contacted pneumonia, the mortality rate was an astounding 11.2%. That is way too high. However, so far in 1918, the same mortality rate is now 23.1%. This is absolutely not acceptable."

"Edward, I need a superb, objective, specially trained, and seasoned clinician to monitor infectious disease conditions throughout the nation, and the world. This clinician needs to be able to correlate this data with current events, so future projections and predictions can be made. These predictions can assist me in my charge to avoid the General's *nightmare*."

Vaughn then stated directly, "Instead of huge numbers of doctors in the field performing this work without your skills or experience, I want to try and stretch the reach of your expertise with the latest technology in telecommunications. We also have top-notch army personnel to assist you with this new work. You will be able to participate as an attending physician at Boston City Hospital while we make all of this information available to you. I thought that would be pleasing for you, as you contribute to The War effort in a very exceptional way."

Noble ran his right hand through his hair, and exclaimed, "Colonel, thank you for the vote of confidence, but are you sure I'm the right man for the job? With all of this technology, I'm not sure where to..."

Vaughn interrupted, "Know where to begin? You'll figure it out. By the way, is Lillian still a U.S. Public Health Officer? Does she still do some work with Milton Rosenau?"

"Yes on both counts, Colonel," said Noble. "When she is able, she does some epidemiologic work for Milton. He works out of the Naval Hospital in Chelsea, Massachusetts, and has a small satellite office and lab here in the South Department of Boston City. As a professor of medicine at Harvard School of Medicine, they give him pretty much what he needs."

"That's just great, Edward," said Vaughn. The A.I. Office has a very high security clearance level, but I will be sure to give clearance to both Lillian and Milton. Milton's a good man. And, Lillian is the best epidemiologist I know, and smart as a whip. Why, then, did she ever marry you?" Vaughn said, as he had many times, with his usual sly grin.

"Just bum-luck, Colonel," joked Noble.

"Edward, I want you to go home and relax until Monday, and that's an order. You deserve it. Between cables, the telephone, and radio, we'll be in touch a lot. Say hi to the family for me." Vaughn then stopped and stood still for a moment. After a time, he said, "Edward, as you get older, you remind me of your father more and more."

Both men saluted, shook hands, and Vaughn left the office to return to Washington D.C. Vaughn's visit had stirred great emotions in Noble. His comments about his father caused Noble to sit for a time on the office hunter green sofa and think about that most important man. Events in his Noble's life were beginning to mirror the life of his father, in unanticipated ways.

Charles Noble was born in 1828 in Brookline, Massachusetts. As a child, he loved to study all things biological, including rotten apples and moldy bread. His mother put up with these "delights" around the house because the boy enjoyed them so. He was also an avid reader and learned as much as he could about these biological processes. In later years he taught himself to read German and French, since those were the languages of science.

Charles attended medical school at Harvard, and then arranged on his own for a two year general medical mentorship at a local hospital. Since there was no salary associated with this additional training, he lived in the hospital and assisted in the hospital laboratory for small sums of money. His physician mentors nicknamed him "the sponge", because he soaked up knowledge just like one.

The Civil War began in 1861, and at thirty-three, Charles Noble became a commissioned officer in the Army of the Potomac Medical Corps. At the time, disinfectants were unknown, the relation of dirt to infection was generally not understood, anesthesia was just coming into general use, and most treatments were wholly inadequate. Hospitalization was often considered a death sentence. During the war, there were 204,000 deaths from battle, but 416,000 additional deaths from disease. About half of the disease deaths were from typhoid fever and dysentery, and the rest were from pneumonia and tuberculosis. Outbreaks of measles, chickenpox, mumps, whooping cough, and malaria were very common.

In 1862, several army physicians, including Charles Noble, requested the creation of a commission that would work to decrease war deaths associated with disease and infection. The acting Surgeon General finally agreed and appointed "a commission of inquiry and advice in respect to the sanitary interests of the United States forces". The U.S. Sanitary Commission was born, and Charles became one of the field physicians associated with it.

Commission field officers began to inspect Federal troop camps and hospitals. What they found was revolting. Most of these facilities were littered with refuse, rotting food, and other rubbish that was in as state of decomposition. Slops were deposited in pits within camp limits or thrown out of buildings. Heaps of manure were set right next to camps. There was often no fresh water, even for hospitals. The use of iodine, bichloride of mercury, and sodium hypochlorite were not empirically used to quell infection until wounds became a raging inferno. Cleanliness and adequate clothing were a low priority.

Field officers inspected cooking areas and cooking methods, available clothing and bedding, and toured camp grounds. They considered the location of camps, drainage from them, ventilation of tents and quarters, the quality of rations, and general living condition. Importantly, they had the authority to tell commanding officers what needed to be fixed in the camps, and were able to report commanding officers who did not heed their advice. The commission persuaded highly respected doctors, like Noble, to write widely distributed pamphlets on sanitation and hygiene.

The Sanitary Commission promoted the distribution of condensed milk, beef-stock, sterile bandages, and the use of sterile conditions in medical facilities. They stressed troop diet and cleanliness. Car loads of fresh fruits and vegetables were sent to troops to discourage scurvy. They organized Union woman groups to send tons of quilts, blankets, pin-cushions, butter, eggs, sauerkraut, cider, and chickens to the troops. The fitting of hospital ships was strongly recommended by field officers in order to speed treatment of casualties. Therefore, hospital ships like *USS Daniel Webster* No. 2 came into being.

Charles read the new scientific literature in three languages whenever it was available, and applied it to his work. He became enthralled with experiments performed by a young Frenchman by the name of Luis Pasteur. In 1862, Pasture used a glass flask with a long downward curved neck ("swan neck" flask) to conclusively show that germs did not spontaneously generate in broth. Passage of germs through the long flask neck was slowed, which decreased the growth of bacteria in the flask broth. This experiment was responsible for the firm establishment of the germ theory in Europe.

Also in 1862, Pasteur theorized that milk, wine, and beer spoiled because of the presence of microbes. He showed he could decrease or stop some foods from spoiling by heating them. This process became known as pasteurization, and greatly improved the safety of milk. With these results, using the scientific method, Charles began to make the same connections others were making in Europe. Microbes can cause disease, and physicians must learn to deal with microbes if they want to battle disorders caused by them.

Charles Noble was promoted to Colonel, and worked among several field hospitals near Washington, D.C. between 1862 and 1864. President Abraham Lincoln once toured one of these hospitals and was shown typical improvements for which the Colonel was responsible. Charles was deeply moved when the President personally thanked him for his many efforts to better the lot of the Federal troops.

After the war, Charles returned to Brookline and resumed his thriving, growing, and very successful general practice. Much of what he learned in the army was applied to the care of patients in the greater Boston area.

In 1867, the British surgeon Joseph Lister began to wonder if the growth of microbes in broth flasks, and the spoiling of milk, could be related to infections in surgical wounds. He started using carbolic acid to clean surgical instruments, and even used the chemical directly on wounds. He found that instruments cleaned with the chemical were associated with fewer infections, and wounds treated with carbolic acid became less infected as well. He theorized the chemical was a disinfectant against microbes.

The Pasteur flask experiment also caused Lister to wonder about the transmission of microbes. He noticed that birthing by midwives was associated with fewer infections than birthing by surgeons. Since midwives were washing their hands more often, he believed infections were spread by hand contact. He insisted that his surgeons wash their hands thoroughly before surgery, and that they wear gloves. Charles incorporated these evidence-based observations into his own medical practice. He began to see positive results quickly. The scientific method was making his practice of medicine better.

In 1870, Charles married Elizabeth Marks, and three years later they had their only child, Edward. In 1878, Dr. Noble had an opportunity to study with the world famous microbiologist Dr. Robert Koch in Germany. Just two years earlier, Dr. Koch had found *Bacillus anthracis* endospores in soil and determined they were the cause of "spontaneous" outbreaks of anthrax. During his four months in Berlin, Charles met Dr. Victor Vaughn. During that stay, Charles traveled with Dr. Koch to Paris and briefly met Louis Pasteur. With Charles' broken French, and Pasteur's broken English, the two talked for hours about the field of microbiology. Pasteur was very impressed with the general practitioner's fund of knowledge. This was especially noteworthy because Dr. Noble was an American, and the United States was considered scientifically backward by Europeans.

Charles and Pasteur wrote one another many times over the years. In fact, Charles provided significant help to Louis at a critical point in his research. In 1885, Pasteur produced the first vaccine for rabies by growing the virus in rabbits, and then weakening it by drying the affected nerve tissue. Just as the vaccine was produced, a nine year old boy was mauled by a rabid dog. Pasteur was not a physician and could have faced prosecution for treating the boy with his new vaccine. Pasteur cabled Charles Noble in Boston, and consulted with him concerning this ethical dilemma. Charles cabled back, "Louis, you need only do the right thing". On this advice, Pasteur administered the vaccine to the boy, who did not contract rabies. Pasteur became world famous, and his success laid the foundation for the manufacture of many other vaccines.

During his long career, Charles experimented with the formulation of his own vaccines. He used a Chamberland-Pasteur filter made of unglazed porcelain that filtered out bacteria from a pure culture. This left a bacterial toxin that could be used as a vaccine. Charles introduced in Boston the autoclave invented by Charles Chamberland for sterilization. He also introduced to New England an invention by Dr. Koch's assistant, Julius Richard Petri. This invention allowed for the efficient growth of bacterial cultures; the Petri dish.

When Edward was fourteen years old, Charles Noble suddenly died of influenza pneumonia in 1889. This was a horrible experience for Edward, who stayed with his father during his short but devastating ordeal. However, the influenza pandemic of 1889-1890 was not yet finished with the Noble family. Only four months after Charles' passing, Edward's mother Elizabeth also died of influenza. Since that time, the word "influenza" was carried in a special dark place within Edward. The word itself came from medieval language meaning "influence of the stars". In this case, the influence mentioned was not a positive one.

Charles Noble was a shrewd investor who made a fortune in Boston real estate in the 1870's and 1880's. With the passing of Elizabeth, Edward received a sizable inheritance. These financial resources allowed him to treat many of the poor for free at Boston City Hospital. In his office on Harrison Avenue, Edward saw many patients who were unable to afford health care.

Major Edward Noble again composed himself. He was emotionally and physically exhausted from the events of the last few weeks. He resolved to follow Colonel Vaughn's order and take the next four days off. He thanked Lieutenant Pecknold for the office tour, told her he would return on Monday, and left the A.I. Office.

As Noble made his way to the stairs on the second floor, he passed one of the long patient wards. Eighty feet away, at the end of a central walkway, stood a man in a starched and pressed white Navy officer uniform. Standing 5 foot 7 inches, and weighing 170 lbs, the man was stout in stature. But, he displayed a straight and determined posture. The navy officer had a dark complexion, small dark brown eyes, and black hair neatly combed and slicked with hair dressing. He sported a thin black mustache. As he watched Noble walk to the end of the pavilion, his stance stiffened. He remained expressionless as his eyes tracked Noble. His name was Commander Richard Cunard.

CHAPTER 5

The sun began to warm the frozen Kansas prairie on the morning of Friday, January 25th. The temperature had dipped to the seasonal average of 19° F the night before, but it was expected to reach a warm high of 41° F in the afternoon. Overall, the winter had been much colder than usual, with night lows of -30° F to -35° F. Winds made it even colder.

This was Haskell County in Southwest Kansas, which is part of the U.S. Great Plains. The land was flat, and trees were encountered only occasionally. The landscape was dotted with small wood and earthen sod houses, barns, corrals, and grain storage silos. Windmills were a common sight on the prairie, and a major source of power. Few homes had electrical lines or telephones. Most of the county had less than one person per square mile. The largest city in the county, Dodge City, had a population density of about fifty per square mile. Only forty years earlier, Wyatt Earp and Bat Masterson had been lawmen in Dodge.

Haskell County's economy was based wholly on agricultural products, such as wheat, sorghum, soybeans, cotton, and corn. However, livestock were everywhere, and humans lived closely with large numbers of fowl, cattle, pigs, and dogs. Late in the 19th century, as many as 8 million cattle a year were run from Texas along the Santa Fe Trail to Dodge City. In Dodge they were loaded onto trains bound for the East. Livestock remained a major industry in southwestern Kansas in 1918.

Nearly sixty years old, Dr. Loring Miner was a large robust man with a handle bar mustache and a personality that filled the open land in which he had lived since 1885. He was also a man of contradictions. He drank hard and often, ate ferociously, and drove automobiles too fast. He was an active county political party leader who fully expected his patients to use his own grocery and drugstores. However, there was another side to Dr. Miner. He had attended medical school at Ohio University and was part of the scientific movement in American medicine. In this regard he was very much like Charles Noble and Victor Vaughn. He read the classics in Greek, and prided himself on his medical knowledge. He even built a laboratory in his medical office near Copland and performed state-of-the-art medical tests there. His practice ranged over hundreds of square miles. He used his horse, horse and buggy, his automobile, and occasionally trains to reach his patients on isolated farms. He even contemplated learning how to fly, buying an airplane, and using it to reach distant patients. Air travel was attractive, since there were few paved roads in Haskell County.

Late in the morning, after a busy day seeing patients in his office, Dr. Miner prepared for his usual huge lunch with a beer. He was heading for the ice box when there was a knock on the office door. Miner never refused patients, even when they came between him and his beloved lunch. He opened the door, and a young woman entered. "Good morning, Dr. Miner. I'm sorry to bother you, but could you look at my husband and tell me if he is alright?"

"Sure, Susan. Bring Doug in," said Miner.

The woman helped her husband, who was twenty-three years old, into the office. "He was fine early this morning, doctor. But he just...just turned sick."

"Doug," started Miner, "How were you last night?"

The man was so fatigued that he was not paying complete attention. "I was fine, doc."

Miner took a medical history from the patient's wife. Over just an hour, the man had gone from feeling perfectly well, to seriously ill. He had a horrible headache, a hacking non-productive cough, feverish feelings with chills, and body aches that made him moan. Completing his review of symptoms, Dr. Miner checked vital signs: heart rate 112, respiratory rate 25, blood pressure 121/71, and temperature 105° F. Minor then performed his exam of the eyes, nose, and ears, the mouth, the skin, the lymph nodes, and the neck. He examined the pulmonary, cardiovascular, gastrointestinal, urinary, musculoskeletal, and neurological systems. He took a urine sample, checked it for glucose and bilirubin, and viewed it under his microscope. He drew a sample of blood, viewed a prepared blood smear under the microscope, spun it down in a centrifuge, and plated it for culture.

Having completed his preliminary examination, Miner turned to the man's wife and said, "Susan, at this point it looks like Doug has influenza."

"What's that, doctor?" asked the woman."

"The grippe," said Miner.

"Oh, yes," she said. "The grippe."

"It comes through Haskell County most years," said Miner, "and usually in the winter. For now, give him two of these aspirin every 6 hours for the muscle aches and the fever, and make sure he takes in a lot of fluid. If things get worse or change, bring him over if you can. I'm sure he'll be fine.

The woman thanked Miner for his help, told him she would pay his fee of $2.00 at the beginning of the month, and left.

Dr. Miner was unsettled about this particular case of influenza. He had diagnosed influenza many times, but there was something different about this man. The symptoms were more violent than usual, there was a very high fever, and the onset was much more rapid than any prior case he had seen in his practice.

Miner put the influenza patient out of his mind as he saw other patients, until late in the afternoon. A fifteen year old boy was brought to his office with a horrible headache, a hacking non-productive cough, feverish feelings with chills, and severe body aches.

The next day, Saturday, Miner planned to stock his grocery store. However, he diagnosed three cases of influenza in patients brought to him by worried families. And, these patients were very ill.

On Sunday, which was usually a day off for Miner, the doctor diagnosed four cases of severe influenza.

Over the next week, Miner was called to the towns of Copland, Santa Fe, Jean, Sublette, Satanta, and to distant farms and ranches, to see very ill patients he diagnosed with influenza. But this was unlike any influenza that he had ever seen, even considering the 1889-1890 pandemic. It was severe in its symptoms and rapid in onset. But, it was now also lethal. Some of Miner's patients, who had started out with severe influenza symptoms, had quickly died of pneumonia. What also puzzled Miner was the fact the mortalities were not babies, toddlers, the elderly, or infirmed. Rather than the typical influenza fatalities, those stricken were the strongest and previously healthy young men and women. Miner continued to take blood, urine, and sputum samples which gave him no clues. He read his journals and textbooks, and talked to colleagues around the state. He even tried to boost the immune systems of victims with diphtheria and tetanus antitoxins without effect.

The rising number of influenza cases and fatalities frightened even the burly Dr. Miner. On Sunday, February 3rd, Miner road his horse to Copland and sent a cable to the U.S. Public Health Service about his clinical observations.

CHAPTER 6

On Saturday, January 26th, Edward Noble was enjoying the third day of a four day vacation. These were his first days off since leaving for France, and he loved every minute of them. It was very cold this Saturday, so the family decided to drive downtown and go roller skating in an indoor rink.

Noble opened up the Beacon Street garage door, and cranked up his 1917 Ford. The vehicle was a Model-T Woody Wagon truck with a one-ton capacity and a stronger frame than the standard Model-T. It had a worm-gear differential along with solid rubber rear tires. Its hood, radiator, and fenders were black, but the body was made of yellow wood paneling. It had a wood roof and two rows of bench seats. Behind the second seat was a large storage area. Noble, Lillian, Florence, Akeema, and the three smaller children crammed into the bench seats, while Arthur and his leg cast were loaded into the back storage area. Away they all went, as Edward happily drove his Ford to 148 Franklin Street, at the corner of Franklin and Congress Streets.

Roller skating was all the rage. In 1902 the Coliseum in Chicago had promoted indoor skating popularity by opening a large roller rink. In 1908, even Madison Square Garden featured roller skating on certain days of the week. Most cities in American now had roller rinks, and the Noble family made full use of Boston's.

The family rented skates for each individual, and began to skate in the large oval rink. Loud music came from both a pipe organ and a Victor V phonograph that played ten inch disk records. When not skating, family members snacked on popcorn, sandwiches, and root beer. Florence was the best skater of the lot, and seemed to float on the rink. She skated forwards, backwards, and sometimes on one foot with her opposite leg stretched out behind her. Today Florence spent much of her time teaching the art to Bernard, Michael, and Marguerite. Akeema was new to the sport, and was still trying to stand without falling. Edward and Lillian liked to skate together slowly, as young children whizzed around them. Arthur had to be content to watch the whole affair from the side lines. However, he enjoyed watching all the young women skate, and all of them enjoyed his watching them as well.

Roller skating is a wonderful family activity, because it combines physical exercise with the ability to speak with family members as they skate on and off the rink. This is especially nice on a cold weekend afternoon. Noble was sitting, drinking a root beer, and watching Florence give Lillian a lesson in elegant roller skating. Bernard and Michael rolled off the rink to take a breather. Both were becoming fairly good skaters. As they sat down to eat popcorn, their father asked them "So, boys, we didn't get a chance to finish our discussion a few nights ago about the Boston Red Sox. How are they shaping up for the 1918 season?"

Bernard, ten years old with black short hair, was built like a baseball catcher. He was somewhat short for his age, but with a solid thick physique. Bernard was outgoing like his mother and older brother, and unlike his father in that regard.

He was more attentive to sports than he was to school, and spent most of his allowance money on baseball cards.

"Dad, the Red Sox are looking pretty good" said Bernard." As you know, they finished second in the American League in 1917, behind the Chicago White Sox." Actually, his father had forgotten that fact, since he left for France at the end of the last baseball season. Bernard continued, "The Red Sox had 90 wins and 62 losses, with a win percentage of .592. But, the White Sox had a percentage of .649, which was considerably better than the second place Red Sox."

Bernard's younger brother, Michael, was seven years old. He had light brown hair that was like his father had been before he went gray. Michael had a physique more like his father's, which was slighter than both his brothers. He was more studious than Bernard, and school work came easily to him. Even though he was only in first grade, he excelled in reading, math, and the sciences. Michael was also fearless. At the age of six, he once jumped into the Charles River to save a floundering four year old girl. For his age, he was a fine swimmer. Michael also followed baseball closely, since his revered older brother Bernard lived and breathed the sport.

"Actually, Dad," said Michael, "the Red Sox led the League in batting, pitching, and fielding. They made use of sacrifice hitting with 310, which was 75 more than second place White Sox. They had a good strike-out-to-walk ratio of 1.23, which was slightly less than the Yankees and White Sox. Their defensive efficiency, or the percent of balls-in-play-converted-to-outs, was the best at .724. Their field percentage, or put-outs + assists divided by put-outs + assists + errors, was the best at .972."

Noble marveled at the boys' mastery of their favorite team's statistics. If they could master all these numbers, then he was not worried about their future scholastic endeavors.

Bernard added, "Based on win percentages, I don't think the Red Sox have anything to worry about from the St. Louis Browns, the Philadelphia Athletics, the Washington Senators, or the New York Yankees. But their percentages were very similar to the Chicago White Sox, the Cleveland Indians, and the Detroit Tigers. The White Sox were second place in batting, pitching, and hitting. Cleveland was third place in those areas. Therefore, those are the teams the Red Sox must beat this year in order to reach the World Series."

Bernard and Michael then skated back onto the rink to race. The boys' father just shook his head. He thought to himself what the human mind can remember, if only it is motivated to do so.

Akeema needed a rest from her skating trials, and Marguerite followed her. Marguerite was five years old, had curly auburn hair cut to a few inches long, and was in constant motion. She enjoyed everything and everyone. The little girl was still having some difficulty standing on her skates and required a hand to hold during her trial-and-error attempts. Akeema drank a root beer, and Marguerite munched on a sandwich.

Noble called out, "Rabbit, how's it going with the skating?"

"It's <u>hard</u>, Daddy!" yelled back Marguerite. "I fell down on my knee!"

Her father went through a mock examination of his daughter's knee, which was part of the routine they had for various bumps, scrapes, and hurts. "It's OK, Rabbit!" Her father's diagnosis seemed to melt away any previous afflictions.

"Akeema," said Marguerite, quickly moving to a new topic as young children often do, "can you tell me again about the houses you live in at your place?"

Akeema smiled and said, "Sure, Marguerite. Remember, I told you my people live in Alaska which is very far from here. In my village of Golovin, the men have a center called the *qasgiq* where they sing, dance, and tell stories. It is round dome-shaped building. During the winter months, the *qasgiq* is where men teach boys survival and hunting skills, as well as other life lessons. They also teach tool making and how to make qayaqs, or kayaks. The women's house is called the *ena*, which is right next door to the *qasgiq*. Women teach the girls how to sew, cook, and weave. Boys live with their mothers until they are your age, and then go to live in the *qasgiq*. Each winter, for about six weeks, the young boys and girls switch living places. The men teach the girls survival and hunting skills, and the women teach the boys how to sew and cook."

"Akeema," said Marguerite, "I like that we live with our Mommy and daddy in the same house."

Akeema again smiled, "Well, Marguerite, during the spring, summer, and fall, our Yup`ik families travel all together as we search for food. That means hunting seal and salmon, mostly."

"Tell me again about some of the very special animals, Akeema," said Marguerite.

"OK, Marguerite. My people believe that some animals have special spirits. The orca, wolf, raven, spider, and whale, are revered animals to my people. We wear special amulets of animals, or little necklaces, which can protect us and our families."

"Spiders are <u>good</u>, Akeema?"

"My people think so. Our folklore says, for example, that a spider has a benevolent spirit that can save people from peril with its web, or lift them to the sky in danger." Akeema looked over at Edward and smiled.

"I could have used a spider amulet in St. Denis, Akeema," said Noble with some seriousness. Noble realized that Akeema was of two cultures. She stood with one foot in Yup`ik mysticism, and the other in American scientific method. She was very comfortable in both.

Akeema took Marguerite to skate with her mother and big sister. Noble walked over to Arthur who was being attended by three pretty girls. Edward waited for them to leave, and then said quite sarcastically, "It's tough putting up with all the 'help', wouldn't you say, Son?"

Arthur smiled, and said, "Yeah, dad, it's a dirty job...but someone's got to do it. There are fringe benefits to serious injury."

"I'll bet," said his father. "I hope you can get over it somehow." Edward was glad that there was something positive to his son's femur fracture. The last three months had not been much fun for Arthur.

"Dad, I am really looking forward to getting the cast off and starting rehab. I have a wager with the orthopedic surgeon that I can be 'normal' again in half the time it takes most guys. If I win, he must let me use his box seats this spring at Fenway Park to see the Red Sox...with a date."

"Sounds like something to really work toward," said Noble.

"Yeah. Dr. Cunard also said he could get me some Red Sox tickets."

Noble felt that his heart skipped a beat. He turned his head straight toward his son and wondered if he had heard correctly. Noble questioned, "Did you say Dr. Cunard? Where did you meet him, Arthur?"

"Dad, Dr. Cunard has been over at the house a few times when you were in Europe. Didn't Mom tell you?"

Noble answered slowly, as if to disguise his emotions. "No, Arthur. She didn't."

On a sunny Monday morning, January 28th, Noble took the Massachusetts Avenue trolley to the Boston City Hospital South Department and went directly to the Army Intelligence Cable Office. He saluted the Sergeant sentry at the door, and hung up his coat. Entering the large office, he saw a very petit Second Lieutenant sitting at the cordboard. She had short curly black hair under a brimless Army cap and ebony skin. She took off her headset, and while saluting said, "Good morning, Major! I'm Lieutenant Claudette Pierre-Louis of the U.S. Army Signal Corps, sir."

"Nice to meet you, Lieutenant," said Noble, who liked to try to place accents with countries of origin. "Judging from your accent, you're from Haiti, right? That's where you came to speak French?"

"Correct, sir," said the Lieutenant. "I'm of Mulatres ancestry. I also speak Spanish. Major, I know that Lieutenant

Pecknold already showed you around the office. Let me show you how the three of us will prepare materials for your review each day. In the center large table, we will sort incoming reports into six stacks. One stack will be for urgent messages. A second will be for infectious disease general reports from around the world. A third will deal with domestic military infectious disease reports, while a forth will have domestic civilian ID reports. A fifth will have items on European troop movements and other battle information. Finally, a sixth stack will be for any personal messages you have received. We will try and sort the more interesting or important items at the top of the stacks, but that may not always be correct."

"Thank you, Lieutenant", said Noble. "That will be very helpful. The three of you are so efficient! I hope that you will bear with me as I catch up to you all. I need to learn how to use all of this wonderful information you collect here."

"Just let us know what you need, Major, and we'll do our best to obtain it for you. You will note that there are some reports already sorted and awaiting your review on the center table."

Noble walked to the table and saw a collection of cables, as well as transcribed telephone and radio messages. The "world" stack mentioned sporadic cases of seasonal influenza in various parts of France. There was nothing unusual about these outbreaks. The local and regional influenza epidemics discussed in domestic communications were common for this time of year. In the "domestic military" stack were reports of scattered pneumonias and measles outbreaks in the cantonments that were also not out of the ordinary. Among the other communications was a copy of the weekly *Public Health Reports* published by the U.S. Public Health Service. It contained information on domestic and world communicable diseases such as yellow fever, plague, mumps, measles, chickenpox, and many others. For the most part, things were pretty quiet in the world of infectious diseases.

In the "personal" stack was a cable from Camiers, France.

Friday, January 25, 1918
From: Base Hospital No. 5

Edward, Old bean, it was so good to hear from you! Glad you are back at BCH, and your old haunt, the South Department. There is a lot of talk here about the Russians signing an armistice with the Germans, and Central Powers troop movements to the Western Front. This may not be as beneficial for the Germans as they first thought. The armistice seceded so much Russian territory that the Germans have had to divert many troops east just to maintain control of it. This will help the allies, as Americans increase their numbers on the Front. Hope Lillian and the kids are fine.

Your good friend,
Colonel Harvey Cushing, BEF.

Noble left the A.I. Office feeling very positive. Communicable diseases were quiet worldwide, there was positive war news, and his friend at Base Hospital No. 5 was well. Before going to the Boston City wards for the first time in four months, he decided to see if his friend Milton Rosenau was at his BCH satellite lab.

Milton Rosenau was forty-nine years old, with a very distinguished medical career. He earned his medical degree from the University of Pennsylvania, and received postgraduate training in Europe in the areas of sanitation and public health. He later joined the U.S. Marine Hospital Service (MHS). He served as a quarantine officer in San Francisco and Cuba, and then became the director of the MHS Hygienic Laboratory where he transformed a one-person operation into a bustling institution with divisions in bacteriology, chemistry, pathology, pharmacology, zoology, and biology. He had been a pioneer in the study of anaphylaxis, and conducted research on yellow fever, malaria, typhoid fever, poliomyelitis, and disinfectants. One of the two textbooks that Noble had taken to France was Rosenau's *Preventative Medicine and Hygiene*.

Rosenau had made his biggest contribution in the area of pasteurization. Outbreaks of numerous diseases, including tuberculosis, had been linked to raw milk. Louis Pasteur had developed pasteurization many years earlier, and the process was known to make milk consumption safe. But the public continued to prefer raw milk because the high-temperature process imparted an unpopular "cooked milk" taste. In 1906, Rosenau established that low temperature, slow pasteurization (140° F for twenty minutes) killed pathogens without spoiling the taste. This could remove a key obstacle to public acceptance of pasteurized milk. Edward Noble met Rosenau in 1913, when Rosenau became a Harvard University Medical School professor and co-founder of the Harvard and Massachusetts Institute of Technology School for Health Officers. This is also when Lillian Noble took up the cause of milk pasteurization.

Following the declaration of war, Rosenau joined the navy and was both an attending physician and researcher at the Naval Hospital in Chelsea, Massachusetts. The Harvard affiliate satellite lab at Boston City Hospital gave Dr. Rosenau added subjects for his studies.

Noble left the building with the A.I. Office and walked to a different pavilion on the South Department campus. There, also on a second floor, was a small laboratory with a sign on the door that read "Harvard and Massachusetts Institute of Technology Laboratory". Noble opened the door and saw a man sitting at a lab bench, hunched over a microscope. There was no one else present. Milton Rosenau was a tall athletic man with a long face and piercing eyes behind silver wire rim glasses. He had dark wavy hair and a very thick dark mustache. Everything about Rosenau's demeanor suggested kindness, and he was known as a very easy person with whom to work.

"Hey, Lieutenant Commander," said Noble entering the lab, "is there a doctor in the house?"

"Edward!" yelled Rosenau in a deep voice, "Edward!" Rosenau leaped up from his lab bench and hugged the shorter Noble. "Lillian told me you would likely drop by today! Gee, it's great seeing you! Lillian has been telling everyone about the St. Denis hospital and your trip back to Hoboken. Quite the traveler, Major!"

"Yeah, Milton," said Noble. "A real cruise vacation. Everyone should try it."

Both men laughed. They traded family tales and caught up on military matters. Noble asked about Rosenau's medical work over the last few months.

"The Chelsea Naval Hospital is a pretty busy place these days, Edward." said Rosenau. "It serves large numbers of naval personnel that come and go through Boston Harbor every day. It also serves numerous nearby naval installations, as well as the Commonwealth Pier in Boston. John Keegan and I have been working on a special antiserum for patients with severe pneumonia associated with measles, but so far we haven't had much luck with it. Lillian has just been great with her epidemiologic studies of the New England measles outbreaks. We asked her specifically to track and study measles complicated by pneumonia, with the hope that we can find clues to this particularly devastating problem with young men. She is a real jewel, Edward."

"Thanks, Milton," said Noble. "She thinks the world of you and John. Lillian is so thankful she has had an opportunity to apply her skills toward your work, and contribute to the work of the Harvard Technology Lab."

Noble stopped for a moment, and then continued. "Milton, I hope you don't mind if I ask you something?"

"Not at all, Edward," said Rosenau. "What's the problem, my friend?"

"Milton," said Edward, in a hushed voice, "did you know that Richard Cunard has been over to my house a few times while I was away? My son, Arthur, told me."

Rosenau frowned slightly, with his lips pressed together in a half-smile. "Lillian told me that Cunard had been over a few times to discuss the most recent milk pasteurization campaign here in New England. Lillian has been helping me with that effort for five years now, as you know. She has taken that project on with a vengeance, as she does with everything she cares about. Do I catch a little bit of jealousy here, Edward?"

"It's just that she didn't tell me about it, and you know Cunard's past interest in her," exclaimed Noble.

Rosenau let out a deep laugh. "Edward, you old fool. You are the <u>love</u> of Lillian's life, and I can attest to that one-thousand percent. Every other sentence out of her mouth is about you, and her love for you, and your family. As far as she is concerned, Cunard's visits are only to further her goal of total public acceptance of milk pasteurization. Cunard has his own extensive experience in public health, and Lillian will take any help she can get."

"Thank you, Milton," said Noble, with a more relaxed voice. As an understatement, Noble added, "I guess being off to war can warp one's judgment somewhat."

"However," cautioned Rosenau, "I don't trust Cunard. He has been unusually interested in the milk pasteurization campaign since you left. His sudden attraction to philanthropy is out of character for him. I'm sure that Lillian is oblivious to anything Cunard might be up to, but he bears watching. I'll keep an eye on him as well, Edward."

Noble thanked Rosenau for his kind thoughts, his confirmation of Lillian's devotion, and the fact that his good friend would watch out for Lillian at Boston City. Noble then left to start work as an Internal Medicine attending physician on the BCH wards.

The first week back at Boston City hospital was a busy one. Noble was welcomed by many of his long time colleagues and workmates, including the charge nurse for the South Department, Terry Tomlinson. The new Boston City

Hospital Internal Medicine residency had a number of first year residents, called interns, and many other second and third year residents. All three years of medical residents had rotations through the South Department, since it provided excellent infectious diseases training. Noble began to familiarize himself with the various knowledge and skill levels of each resident on his service, so he might help each one reach full potential on the ID rotation.

Each day Noble checked in frequently with the A.I. Office in order to learn how to make daily assessments of worldwide communicable diseases. He had instructed the army Signal Corps officers to have him contacted anytime they felt a report was urgent. He gave them his home number on Beacon Street and told them to call him anytime, twenty-four hours a day, seven days a week. Things were heating up on the Western Front, but all was quiet on the infectious disease front.

On Sunday, February 3rd, Noble was at home with his family. They all attended early morning Mass at the Cathedral of the Holy Cross on the corner of Washington and Union Park Streets. The Nobles loved the cathedral's Gothic Revival style of variegated Roxbury puddingstone with limestone trim, and the huge round stained glass window facing Washington Street.

It was very cold, overcast, and it had snowed on Saturday. After Mass, Lillian made a large breakfast for the whole crew. Following the meal, Lillian and Edward sat at the kitchen table drinking coffee and enjoying a very relaxed weekend morning. Edward casually asked Lillian, "How's the NWP?"

Lillian instantly developed a sparkling smile. "Darling, the National Woman's Party is doing very well! As you know, unlike the National American Woman Suffrage Party that stresses individual state action, the NWP has put its priority on the passage of a constitutional amendment! As I wrote you last October, I asked Akeema to watch the children for a few days so that I could go to New York. While there, I was fortunate to march with thousands of suffragettes and deliver a petition with over one million names in support of our cause! Since the U.S. entered The War, President Wilson has been travelling the nation telling us "The War is for democracy". The NWP has been carrying banners at the President's rallies stating that America is <u>not</u> a democracy. How can it be, if half the population can't vote?"

Sensing that Lillian was getting very worked up, Noble said, "Lilly, remember, I'm on <u>your</u> side."

"I know that, dear," said Lillian. "However, I'm not sure if you heard the great news! The House passed a bill on the day you left France, with two thirds majority, for a constitutional amendment offering women's suffrage! Now it goes to the U.S. Senate."

"That's wonderful, Lillian!"

"Thank you, dear. I know that we have always had your support. We now have to put more pressure on Congress than ever before! Unfortunately, many oppose women's suffrage for fear that women will press for a prohibition constitutional amendment."

Edward added, "Well, you know Lilly, women back the prohibition movement by a wide majority. This doesn't sit well with many, including a lot of women."

"We can't let that deter us, Edward. That is a separate question altogether. I know that many are trying to link the two arguments, but we have to keep a clear and precise goal here."

Edward completely agreed with his wife on suffrage. However, he knew when it was time to change the subject. Just then, his daughter Florence came into the kitchen, followed by Akeema. Florence carried a nursing textbook, and both she and Akeema sat down at the kitchen table. Florence asked, "Dad, can I ask you about something?"

"Sure, honey, what is it?" replied her father.

"I'm just having some problems working out IV fluid flow rates. Can you take a second to help me with this?"

"It really is easy, honey," said Edward. "Let me show you." Her father gave her an easy way to time IV fluid drips per minute and convert that number into milliliters per minute. All the while, Akeema sat listening to the conversation. She hoped to someday apply to nursing school at Boston City Hospital. Shortly after her employment with them, the Nobles had offered to give her the money for the tuition. However, Akeema was steadfast in her determination to earn all of it herself. Whenever she had the chance to listen to Dr. Noble or Florence talk about medicine, she always took it.

The family played games, listened to music on the phonograph, and read into the afternoon. Suddenly, at 3 PM the front door bell rang. "Who can that be in this weather?" asked Lillian, as she answered the door.

A very tall young Sergeant took off his hat as Lillian opened the door. An army staff car idled at the curb. "Ma'am, is Major Noble at home?" asked the Sergeant.

"Yes, just a minute," Lillian said, with a new look of concern.

Edward came to the door, hearing the visitor was for him. Standing at the door was Sergeant Campbell of the army Wagoners. "Sorry to bother you, sir," as the Sergeant saluted. "But, Lieutenant Pecknold said you would want this. She asked me to deliver it to you in person."

The Sergeant handed Edward a sealed cable envelope. "Thank you Sergeant," said Edward, as the Sergeant quickly re-entered the staff car and departed.

Edward opened the envelope, read the cable, and felt as though he were sinking into an abyss. He took a very deep breath and carried the message over to Lillian. While clenching his teeth, he handed the message to her without comment. She read the cable.

Sunday, February 3, 1918
From: Army Division of Communicable Diseases

Washington, D.C.

Major Edward Noble. On February 4, travel by rail to Camp Funston, Kansas. Gather information on public health conditions in the camp. Return to the A.I. Office for debriefing no later than February 13.

Colonel Victor Vaughn

Lillian began to softly weep. Edward had only been home for eleven days, and now would be off again to a far away place. She walked over to hold her husband for a long time.

Edward arose very early on Monday, February 4th to pack his duffle bag and prepare for his long trip. The night before, he called the Camp Devens motor pool and asked for a ride to the train station. Lillian arose with him, made him a hot breakfast, and gave him a Thermos of hot black coffee. Neither one of them spoke much. This surprise trip was taxing, and each of them did not want the other to feel their pain over it. While it was still dark, the army staff car with Sergeant Campbell arrived on time. Edward carried his bag outside to the curb. Lillian followed him into the cold dark February morning.

"Darling, try to contact us if you can. I can't bear not hearing from you. I love you," said Lillian fighting back the tears.

"I love you too, Lilly. I'll be back before you know it." Noble kissed his wife, turned, and hurried into the staff car before he would become any more emotional than he already was. He asked the Sergeant to quickly drive to the A.I. Office first, so that he could have a final look at its messages before he left.

Noble entered the office and saw the third of the Signal Corps officers at her cordboard. She was Second Lieutenant Marié Lafayette from New Orleans, Louisiana. Her accent was neither Southern nor Cajun, for she had the authentic dialect of the region. Noble noted her deletion of the post-vocalic "r" was not unlike New York "Brooklynese". However, this was the real native New Orleans English. Her hair, tied up under her Army cap, was the most fire-red color that Noble had ever seen. She had an almost white complexion along with stunning deep blue eyes.

"Oh, hello Major. I didn't expect you here today," said the Lieutenant.

"Good morning, Lieutenant Lafayette. I just wanted to get the latest reports to review on my trip to Kansas. Anything pressing that you have seen?"

"All of it seems routine, Major...except for one," said the Lieutenant. Look in the domestic civilian stack, sir."

There was a single cable in the designated stack. Noble picked it up.

Sunday, February 3, 1918
From: U.S. Public Health Service

Copland, Haskell County, Kansas. Report from local physician of unusual influenza epidemic. Large number of cases. Severe nature. Many fatalities among young men/women. Physician has asked for Public Health Service to post this information, and give recommendations.

Original cable from: Loring Miner, MD

Noble thought the message very odd, and disturbing. Why was this epidemic not being covered by any other source, including the *Public Health Reports*? Noble suddenly had an idea. "Lieutenant, can you quickly find out for me how far Camp Funston is from Copland, Kansas?"

"Sure, right away, sir." The Lieutenant picked an atlas off a nearby bookshelf and thumbed through it. "Let's see. It's nearly 300 miles away. Are their some arrangements you would like to make, sir?"

"Yes, yes I would," said Noble. "Please make arrangements for me to travel to Copland after my tour of Funston, and let Dr. Miner know ahead of time that I'm coming, if that is possible. I think I can stretch my trip to include this second sojourn, and still be back in time."

"I'll get right on it, sir. If I can't send a message to you by radio on your train, I'll send a cable to Camp Funston with the schedules. We can send a currier to Dr. Miner's residence if we must, sir."

Noble thanked the Lieutenant and hurried back to the waiting staff car.

CHAPTER 7

S ergeant Campbell drove Noble to the Boston and Main Railroad Station where they had first met less than two weeks earlier. The station was very busy as usual, with hundreds of military personnel coming and going during all hours. Noble rushed to his train and stowed his duffle in a storage area outside his two bunk cabin. He thought to himself that he would have to buy some flowers for Lieutenant Lafayette, who on short notice had secured for him one of the best accommodations on the train. Noble arranged his belongings in preparation for the two day journey to Northeastern Kansas. Lillian had prepared some small meals for him so he did not have to rely on the inconsistent cuisine aboard the train. Just before departure, Noble was joined by his cabin partner, a 300 lb Brigadier General who was close to retirement and promptly began a nap in his bunk.

The train took Noble across the lower elevations of the Appalachian and Allegheny Mountains through New York, and then on to Cleveland, Ohio. It passed through Indianapolis, Indiana, St. Louis, Missouri, and across the

Mississippi River. It stopped in Kansas City as it traveled through the expanse of the Great Plains. Three-fourths of the journey was on the flattest terrain imaginable. Noble received an appreciation of America's size, given that his destination was only half-way across it.

The trip was very boring, and extraordinarily lonely. At least aboard USS Madawaska there was plenty to do, and many wonderful people with whom to interact. Noble's Brigadier General cabin mate slept most of the time, as did most everyone on the train. For most of the trip the landscape was covered with snow or frost, and the sky was a featureless gray. It was cold. Noble kept a blanket on most of the time since heating on the train was at best inadequate, and at times nonexistent. At least he had hot coffee in his Thermos for much of the first day.

It was very late on Wednesday, February 6th, when the train reached Camp Funston on the southern rim of the vast expanse of Fort Riley. Wild Bill Hickok had been a deputy marshal at Fort Riley only forty years earlier. The fort was one-hundred miles west of Kansas City. Tracks ran along the northern edge of Camp Funston, so Noble was essentially at the camp upon arrival. Noble gathered up his things, and left the train as it stopped along 1st Street. A Corporal, with the camp's Motor Convoy Service of the Quartermaster Corps, called out to him as he departed the train. Noble thought to himself he must be the most easily recognizable person on the planet. People were forever picking him out of crowd, based on a physical description.

"Major...Major Edward Noble!" yelled the Corporal. "I'll drive you to your room, sir."

"Thank you, Corporal," said Noble. "I'm really tired."

"It will only be a few minute's drive, sir." As the Corporal loaded Noble's bag into the Ford Model-T army staff car, he said, "I guess you won't have time to go to 'The Zone'? It's just one block north of here. That's where we go to relax.

It has theaters, bowling alleys, restaurants, clothing stores, a bank, a barbershop, drug store, and even a pool hall."

"Thanks, Corporal, but I think I'll pass. I have a busy day tomorrow."

The Corporal handed Noble a cable envelope that had his name on it, and also "A.I. Office, BCH". Noble opened it and found a complete listing of dates, times, and contacts for him between now and his arrival back in Boston. Noble thought he now definitely had to buy some flowers for Lieutenant Lafayette. The staff car drove to the Camp Funston corner of 7th and H Streets, where an officer's barrack was located. Noble thanked the Corporal and found his small room on the first floor. It was bitterly cold in his room, and the bed blanket was nearly as thin as a bed sheet. Fortunately, Lillian had sent him with an extra blanket. Noble promptly went to bed and fell asleep.

Noble awoke early Thursday morning, February 7th. He enjoyed his first shower in two days, and then followed his cable directions to an officer's mess hall for a very quick breakfast. He then walked along H Street to the camp Headquarters.

On the first floor was the office of the Commanding Officer. Noble entered the office and introduced himself to a woman at the front desk who told him the Major General was waiting for him.

Entering the office, a short rotund man stood from his desk and said, "Major Noble. I'm Major General C. G. Ballou. Welcome to Camp Funston. Colonel Vaughn of the Army Surgeon General's office told us to expect you. I trust you had a good journey?"

"Thank you, General," Noble said as saluting. "It was fine."

"Well, then, shall we get to the camp inspection?"

"Sir, it's really not an inspection. General Gorgas and Colonel Vaughn just want to get a better idea of what resources you all need in regards to public health. I think I am here to help you, sir."

"We need all the help we can get, Major. As we walk, I'll give you some background. Camp Funston was built in a large meadow on the Fort Riley government reservation in order to draw trainees from all the Great Plains states. Construction began in July, 1917, and amazingly was completed on December 1st. This meant completing construction of several troop barracks every day. The camp is huge. It covers over two square miles. With an average of 56,000 troops in camp at any given time, it's the second largest of the thirty-two American cantonments. You can imagine running a medium size city that appeared 'almost overnight', and where the citizens only stay a short time before they leave. It's a challenge, for sure."

The weather was very cold, but billowy clouds let intermittent sunshine in against a blue sky. The two men began to walk around, and through, many camp buildings that had a light snow about them. The tour lasted all day and into the evening. At times, various Colonels took over the tour, as the camp commander had other duties that needed his attention.

Noble found that the two story wood barracks, each over one-hundred and fifty feet long, overcrowded with troops. Construction of barracks had not kept up with the numbers of incoming recruits, so numerous huge tents were erected throughout the camp. Ventilation was poor in all the tents and buildings. In addition, the layout of the camp did not take advantage of natural ventilation, and the barracks had been built too close together. There was also virtually no space between the men's beds and cots.

Heating for this kind of weather was completely inadequate. There was wholly insufficient warm clothing, blankets, or bedding. At night, the men huddled at the barracks' stoves even more closely than their cots were arranged.

Noble noted Camp Funston was designed like many other cantonments. The last building completed was the hospital and its laboratory. In addition, medical facilities were far too small for the numbers of troops they were to serve.

Noble was reminded of his father's tour of Civil War camps. It was truly sad that not much had changed in fifty-five years. Little concern for public hygiene was given when these present day cantonments were built. There were few places for men to wash their hands, and there were too few lavatory facilities. There was also not enough clean water for the huge number of men. Raw sewage was seen in many areas. Garbage was piled in places which encouraged the growth of vectors.

Reviewing camp records, Noble found Funston's death rate for pneumonia was twelve times greater than similar age groups in the civilian population. Unfortunately, all the nation's cantonments had about the same pneumonia mortality rates. Young recruits were transported on over-crowed trains directly to the camps, and then kept in close quarters as they went through the stages of enlistment. Colonel Vaughn had pointed out to the government the dangers associated with the army's mobilization procedures. This was documented long before there were any men assembled in cantonments. However, the official government answer to Vaughn was the following: "The purpose of mobilization is to convert civilians into trained soldiers as quickly as possible, and not to make a demonstration in preventative medicine." Records also showed that Wilson administration appointees believed camp hospitals were not necessary. They reasoned the troops would not be in the camps very long before they were shipped overseas.

It was late in the evening when Noble completed his tour. It had been a firsthand eye-opener for him. He now had a much better grasp of the problems the U.S. military faced as it geared up for war. He also understood why Colonel Vaughn had sent him to Funston. Noble came away from the camp with a wealth of information, and a better appreciation for the work that lay ahead. He thanked Major General Ballou for his hospitality, and promised to do all he could to secure more resources for Funston. The General was sincerely grateful that someone might help his troops.

Noble walked to his small room, gathered up his things again, and was met by the Motor Convoy Service Corporal who took him back to the Funston train station. "Are you sure you don't want to go to 'The Zone' tonight, Major? Your train won't be here for awhile. There will be some very lovely ladies there tonight, I'll bet ya'," said the Corporal.

Noble laughed. "No thanks, Corporal. I have the loveliest lady in the world back home. Do take care, and thank you for your help." The Corporal drove off, and Noble waited an hour in the dark for the train. This was the second-to-last leg of his westward train journey. He was going to Haskell County, Kansas, to find out why Dr. Loring Miner took the trouble to send a cable to the Public Health Service.

The train finally stopped briefly in Camp Funston, picked up a few passengers, and ran all night with numerous stops. Noble was only able to sleep in small segments, so the night was a series of train whistles, stops, starts, and railroad station lights. He had a simple train bench on which to sit, and this did not help matters. Still, there was one positive about the trip. The train was only half full. They were traveling into the very sparsely populated area that was Western Kansas.

At 5 AM on Friday, February 8th, Noble's train stopped at a concrete pad along McBride Street in Copland, Kansas. Noble and his bag were nearly thrown off the train, which immediately started up again and soon disappeared. Aside from some street lights on the other side of the road, it was pitch dark and overcast. And, it was very very cold. Noble hoped that Lieutenant Lafayette's planning continued to work perfectly, because he was in the middle of the United States, and was completely alone. Right across the highway was a U.S. Post Office on Santa Fe Street. That was the extent of civilization the Major could now see.

An hour and a half went by before Noble heard a horse drawn carriage in the distance. Slowly, a large older army Sergeant with a dusty uniform drove a carriage up onto the train concrete pad. Noble noticed the small horse head symbol below his shoulder chevrons that meant he was a Stable

Sergeant. The Sergeant laughed as he jumped off the carriage, and said, "Major Noble, I presume. Good morning, sir, and welcome to Haskell County. Sorry about the wait. I'm out of Dodge City and only found out about your arrival yesterday afternoon. Apparently, someone really wants you here. My orders came directly from the Army Surgeon General's office in Washington."

Noble again thought about the great scheduling job Lieutenant Lafayette had done. "I can't tell you how much I appreciate this, Sergeant."

"Here to serve, sir," said the Sergeant. "I'm to take you to a Dr. Miner's office. I think it's actually his house on his ranch. It's about ten or twelve miles from here, and the roads are pretty rough. That's why we have horse drawn carriage instead of an automobile. Cars don't do very well our here, Major."

"I'm just glad to be here, Sergeant. Shall we go?" said Noble.

Noble placed his bags in the carriage, and off they went. It was very dry, so the carriage wheels tossed up clouds of dust. In no time, Noble was as dusty as the Sergeant. In any case, the sun peeking through clouds was still low in the sky. It felt wonderful on Nobles face.

As they drove on, the Sergeant told Noble of the bad "grippe" that was moving through Haskell County. It seemed that just about everyone was getting it, and it was laying up people for several days. He said he felt fortunate not to have caught it.

It was now mid-morning as the carriage turned onto a dirt side road. In the distance was a white clapboard house with a porch and several shade trees around it. The rest of the property was like the rest of this part of Kansas; flat, with low scrub growth. There was a nearby large red barn, a garage, a stable with horses, a carriage, a windmill, and various pieces of farming equipment. The farm seemed to be an unlikely origin for a U.S. Public Health Service alert notice.

The carriage drew up to the house porch as the Sergeant said, "Major, this is it. I'll wait until someone answers the front door, and then I'll be on my way. My orders are to take you back to the Copland train stop, so I will pick you up here at 2000 hours, sir."

"I'll be here, Sergeant. And, thank you so much for all your help."

Noble climbed the stairs to the front porch, opened a screen door, and knocked. He heard noise from within the house that sounded like items being thrown or dropped. Eventually, the door opened and a barrel-chested older man in a white coat opened the front door. "Well, you actually do exist! You must be the Major Noble mentioned in the cable. Come in, come in! I'm Dr. Miner. Please call me Loring. My wife is with her sister working on a Red Cross fundraiser in Wichita, so I'm a 'lone rancher' right now."

Noble stepped into the house, and Miner shook his hand. Noble noticed that the man's hand was huge, and that he could not get his whole hand around it. The inside of the house was very different than the unassuming exterior. The house was very clean, elegant, and had classically painted oils on the walls. This was the home of a sophisticated, educated, and civilized man. "Thank you, Loring. Yes, I'm Major Edward Noble, and please call me Edward."

Miner remarked, "You know, two days ago a military currier from Dodge City delivered a telegram here, which said you were coming. It also said you were a physician, but didn't say why you were coming way out here. Is this because of the cable I sent last weekend to the U.S. Public Health Service? Are you with the USPHS, Edward?"

No," said Noble, "I'm not. I'm attached with Army Division of Communicable Diseases. The only reason I'm here is because we monitor all sorts of communications concerning public health. I was given notice of your USPHS cable just before I was to leave for a tour of Camp Funston. Your message concerned me. By the way, I'm an Internist with a special interest with infectious disease."

"Well, no one has contacted me yet about the cable, except you, Edward. I'm glad, because I am perplexed and worried."

"What about, Loring?" asked Noble.

"I think it's better if I show you," said Miner. "I have some patients to see. Do you mind if we take my horse n' buggy? It's faster than an automobile when we have a ways to drive."

"Not at all," said Noble. "I've already had some experience with the roads.

The two men rode off in Miner's buggy. Miner wanted to check on some patients in whom he had diagnosed influenza. He also wanted to see some new patients with similar symptoms. Each of the houses they were to visit were situated miles apart on the flat terrain. In between ranches and farms were endless fields of grain and grazing cattle.

They arrived at the house where the first patient Miner had encountered with the grippe lived. Miner had made that diagnosis about fifteen days earlier. A young man opened the door as the two physicians arrived, and Miner introduced Noble.

"Hi, Doug," said Miner. "How are you feeling?"

"I'm feeling fine now, doc."

"Doug, how long were you ill?" asked Miner.

"Oh, about three days, I recon'", said the man. "Doc, I've never been so sick in my life. It came on so sudden-like. Really, I thought I was going to die. But, after about three days, it left me as quickly as it come. But, the problem now is Susan, doc. She's really sick."

The man and the two physicians walked into a bedroom where a young woman was lying. She was barely able to talk, so her husband answered the historical questions posed. The man said, "She was fine, I mean really herself, until yesterday afternoon. She was talking to me, and then just stopped. She put down on the bed, told me of a terrible headache, terrible body aches, and she started coughing." Miner took her vital signs. The only abnormal vital sign was an alarming temperature of 104° F. She was also very diaphoretic. The only remarkable part of her physical exam, aside from her marked fatigue, was a few scattered rales upon lung auscultation. Both physicians took turns examining her.

"Doug, do you mind if we collect some blood and urine samples for examination at my place?" asked Miner. "If she coughs up any sputum before we leave, that would be important to study as well."

"Go ahead, doc. Do what you can. Is she going to be alright?"

"I think so, Doug. But, as you know, the grippe going around is a bad one. You will need to help her the way she helped you. Here is some aspirin to take as you did, and be sure she gets enough water. Let me know if something changes."

The physicians collected their samples, which included some scant white sputum. Then, the two rode of in the buggy to see the next patient.

"Edward," Miner said as they drove along the dirt road, "I've seen two basic patterns with this influenza. Most of the patients have the most abrupt onset of symptoms I have ever seen. They have extreme fatigue and myalgias that can cause strong stoical young men and women to cry, and even scream, with pain. Their fevers are all very high, at 104° to 105° F. One patient had a temperature of 106° F for a time. But, then in about 72 hours or so, it leaves as fast as it arrived. However, there is a significant minority of patients that just continue to get worse. They seem to develop a pneumonia that is very severe. Some of these patients die quickly; in just a few additional days. I've seen more influenza deaths than usual, and that includes the 1889 pandemic. Of course, it's impossible for me to know the attack rate, or real mortality rate, because it's just me out here."

Noble listened very intently.

"There's one more thing, Edward," said Miner. "Almost all the victims are young men and woman in their twenties. Fewer of them are really young children, or the elderly. This is also very different than the 1889 pandemic."

The two doctors visited three more homes where one, two, or even three family members were afflicted with essentially the same symptoms. In those homes were also family members who had completely convalesced from apparent influenza. Most of the courses lasted less than three days.

Noble thought how fortunate he was to have an opportunity to see these patients in the field, and was glad he had made the extra effort. Actually hearing the first hand histories, and examining the patients directly, was of great benefit. Noble also had a profound respect for Dr. Miner. Here was a scientific-method physician practicing evidence-based medicine on the very front lines. Even with his incredible disadvantages of large distances between patients, and no new devices like Roentgenograms, he was putting the differential diagnosis pieces together in the best tradition of medicine. Many physicians in Boston could not hold a candle to Dr. Miner's skills. Noble thought he was much like his father. He was also a lot like Dr. Victor Vaughn.

The two men rode back to Miner's ranch to study the specimens they had collected. Miner showed Noble his laboratory in his house, and Noble just shook his head in amazement. Except for some very exotic tests, Miner's laboratory was as good as the lab at Boston City Hospital.

Miner motioned Noble over to one of his lab's work benches. "Edward, look at this urinalysis under the microscope." Noble looked at all the specimens collected that day.

"They're all normal, Loring."

"That's right, Edward. Now, look at the blood smears that we have collected."

Noble examined all the CBDs collected. He also used gram staining to look at the sputum specimens with oil emersion. "Loring, they're all normal. There's some variation in lymphocyte counts, but for the most part, they're normal."

"Correct," said Miner. "This is influenza, but I have no idea what the agent is. I've cultured patient's blood, and it seems that only contaminants are present. I've plated sputum cultures, and I have obtained a full list of organisms that can cause disease. There are species of streptococcus, staphylococcus, pneumococcus, and *Streptococcus hemolyticus*. On the other hand, these organisms are also normal flora of the respiratory tract. I've read that Richard Pfeiffer, the director of the Institute for Infectious Disease in Berlin, found the agent responsible for the 1889 pandemic, called "Pfeiffer's bacillus". The bacterium is now referred to as *Bacillus influenzae*. Pfeiffer wrote he had found *B. influenzae* 'in astounding numbers'. I've plated sputum onto chocolate agar plates for 48 hours, as is suggested for this organism. I think I have seen some *B. influenzae* show up, because of the characteristic small, round, convex colonies that are strongly iridescent. They even show the 'satellite phenomenon' by growing bigger colonies around staphylococcal colonies and other bacteria. In culture, they have the correct gram negative coccobaciliary morphology, and tend to lose their capsules over time. In fresh sputum samples, I have seen the short 1.5 μm coccoid bacilli occurring sometimes in short chains, with occasional long rods and large spherical bodies."

"That's wonderful work, Loring," said Noble. "You have found *B. influenzae* in the specimens?"

"Yes, I have," stated Miner. "The problem is, they're no more 'astounding in number' than any of the other organisms. In fact, there are very few in number...even in the fatal cases. In some fatal and non-fatal cases, I haven't found any at all. Many, or all, of these organisms might just be normal flora in these patients."

"Loring, I'm astonished at the observations you have made in just a couple of weeks," said Noble. "You have accomplished by yourself what takes some well-staffed labs and large clinics months to do."

It was now precisely 8 PM and Noble heard a horse and wagon draw up near the house. "Well, Loring, the Stable Sergeant is here, right on time. Army punctuality. I want you know what a pleasure it has been to accompany you today on your patient rounds. When I round on patients, I go from bed-to-bed in the hospital. You must go miles using horses to get to most of your patients. Your careful observations here in Haskell County are extremely valuable, and I can assure you that even the Army Surgeon General will hear about your work."

"Thank you so much for your very kind words, Edward. It is so nice to talk to a fellow physician who knows the science of the art. No chance you might take up a practice here?" Miner laughed. "I'm sure we can set you up in Copland."

"I doubt my wife would go for it," said Noble, knowing that he was being teased. "But, seriously Loring, please keep in touch with me. You can send a cable to Boston City Hospital, mail me letters there, or even just drop notes off at the Army depot in Dodge City. They'll get to me."

"Will do, Edward," said Loring. "It's been a true pleasure."

The two men shook hands in earnest, and Miner went outside with Noble as he loaded his bag on the army carriage. As Noble drove off, Miner saluted. Noble saluted back.

Back on the train concrete pad in Copland, Noble again waited in the cold and dark. He reflected on his two days in Kansas, and realized the wealth of information he had obtained in such a short period of time. Much had to be done with Camp Funston, and the other cantonments. Noble felt the same unsetting feeling about a local endemic that Dr. Miner felt. Perhaps it was just a contained communicable disease phenomenon that happens all the time. Perhaps the only reason Noble knew about it was because of the new information technology available to him. Then again, perhaps not.

The train finally arrived and picked up Noble as fast as he had been dropped off. It was another difficult night as the train charged back to Camp Funston.

Very early Saturday morning, February 9th, Noble was dropped off on Funston's 1st Street. He had only a little time to shower in one of the officer's barracks. The water was freezing, but Noble could not stand the idea of arriving in Boston without showering for three days. The shower was so cold that he actually felt warmer leaving the barracks in the cold Kansas February morning air. After eating an English muffin and having a cup of black coffee, the east-bound train arrived.

The next two days were not an improvement over the trip west. In fact, they were much worse. The train was packed with military. The train cars were colder than they had been on the first trip. Noble had no prepared meals from Lillian, and he was forced to buy whatever food venders brought aboard the train at stops. He had no hot black coffee. But, the worst part was that he did not have a cabin this trip. In order to accommodate the Haskell County leg of the journey, Lieutenant Lafayette could not arrange a cabin for Noble. So, for two days, he sat in a train seat along with hundreds of other men. Noble tried to convince himself he was atoning for sins he had committed by having the luxury of a cabin on the way west. But, that didn't make him feel any better.

There was also much more snow in the Eastern U.S. than there had been during the first train trip. This meant a slower journey, with many more stops for clearing off the tracks. All of the enlisted men were very subdued during the long trip, and Noble understood this was due to their destination. Almost all of the young men wore brand new uniforms and had just completed their brief basic training. They were destined for U.S. ports, Troop Transports, the Atlantic, and then The Western Front.

February 9th and 10th melted into one large unpleasant day for Noble. If the first trip had been boring, this trip was mind-numbing. The train was too full to allow any reading or study. Besides, Noble was too tired to do any of that anyway.

When the train finally pulled into Boston and Main Train Station on Monday morning, February 11th, Noble felt as though an archangel had taken him to heaven. His leg muscles ached, and his hip, knee, and ankle joints felt fused together as he carried his duffle through the terminal to the street outside. Sergeant Campbell was waiting dutifully at the curb with an army staff car.

"Sergeant," said Noble, "I think you are the most beautiful thing I have ever seen."

"Must have been a very long trip, Major," the Sergeant said laughing. "I take it you want to go straight home?"

Noble only smiled back, since the answer to that rhetorical question was obvious. "This time, Sergeant, I don't mind if you take me to my front door on Beacon Street. In fact, you can carry me inside if you want." The Sergeant let out a loud belly laugh with that imagined scene.

Walking into his house, he saw Lillian turn in the kitchen and run to him. She kissed him long and hard. She then said, "I could just hit you, Edward! I waited and waited for a message from you. I worried the whole time you were away." She kissed him again and hugged him around both of his arms.

"Lilly," said Noble, "if there had been a way, I would have even sent a carrier pigeon to Beacon Street. Unlike the A.I. Office at BCH, there's not much interest in sending personal cables from the cantonments. As far as Haskell County goes, there was no long distance service at all. I'm sorry, Lilly."

"I'm just giving you a hard time, Edward. By the way, you're kind of smelly. You smell like you have been on a train for days, around hundreds of other smelly smoking soldiers, and haven't taken a shower for about a week."

"I'm that irresistible, am I?"

"Take a shower," said Lillian, "and we'll see how irresistible you are. Akeema has taken the children to school, Arthur is at Camp Devens for lectures, and Florence is at Boston City Hospital. Got the picture, big guy?"

Noble smiled and said, "I'll be finished with my shower faster than you can say 'irresistible'".

After resting a day after his trip, Noble took the trolley to Boston City, Wednesday morning, February 13th. He first went to a small flower shop on Harrison Avenue and purchased a pretty bouquet. Entering the Army Intelligence Cable Office, he waited for Lieutenant Lafayette to turn around from her cordboard. Holding out the bouquet, Noble then said, "This is for the great, quick, and incredibly punctual scheduling you did for my Kansas trip, Lieutenant!"

"Good morning, sir! Thank you, sir! That was so thought-ful! I'm glad the trip went well, Major!"

"Lieutenant, I was picked up and dropped off with such precision, and so many times, that I think you should be a Colonel in charge of army logistics," said Noble.

The Lieutenant chuckled at the idea. She stood to find a vase for her bouquet. "There is a cable from Dr. Miner for you, sir. Also, Colonel Vaughn will be arriving soon to talk with you." Noble picked a telegram up from the center office table and read it.

Tuesday, February 12, 1918
From: Haskell County

Hope your trip home was a safe one, Edward. New cases of influenza are occurring every day here in Haskell. The affliction has really taken over my practice. The local news-paper is only mentioning 'the grippe' in the back pages, but there are a lot of people ill in the county. I hear they have closed some schools in Copland, Jean, Santa Fe, Satanta, and Sublette. I think they have closed schools even in Dodge. Many severe cases. The sparsely populated county is not allowing the spread as fast as it could be. Thank God. Will keep you posted.

Your friend,
Dr. Loring Miner

Noble thought how fortunate the army was to have a "sen-sor" like Dr. Miner in the field. He is a good man, Noble said to himself. He then set out to catch up on local, national, and world reports on infectious diseases until Colonel Vaughn arrived.

About two hours later, the Colonel walked into the A.I. Office. Vaughn and Noble sat in the smaller front room.

"I'm sorry, Edward, that I sent you so soon, and on such short notice to Funston," said Vaughn. "But, we really do need to get a better handle on the public health issues at the cantonments. What did you see?"

Noble went into great detail about his tour of the camp. He listed out the problems as he had seen them.

"What do you think we should do, Edward?"

"Colonel," said Noble, "these are my recommendations. There isn't much we can do about the hundreds of barracks that are already built. But, the camp tents need to be placed farther apart, and spaced farther from the wood barracks. Future wood barracks need to be built to replace the tents, and they need to be properly spaced as well. When possible, adequate window space should be constructed toward the prevailing winds. This will take full advantage of natural ventilation. More efficient heating is essential. The minimum barrack cubic feet per soldier, as recommended by the army, should be followed. Right now, the recommendation isn't adhered to at all."

Noble continued, "The government must ask industry to speed up production of blankets and warm clothing. Perhaps women's axillaries can help with this effort, as they did so well during the Civil War. I'm sure the Red Cross can act as an excellent distribution system for these much needed items. Camp planners must place a high priority on construction of proper plumbing for fresh water and sewage disposal. Garbage must be carried away, or buried, as soon as it is produced."

"The hospital at Funston would not even be adequate for a camp population one quarter its present size. There needs to be a tripling of the number of physicians and nurses, at the very least. The lab must be also able to handle the load of 56,000 troops. It can't now. It goes without saying there aren't enough medical supplies on hand. I'm not even sure if there is a system in place to ensure the troops are all adequately vaccinated."

"Colonel, no time is gained by hurrying sick men, or the bearers of infections, into the camps. They simply fill the hospitals, and lower the effective strength of the fighting force. I recommend drafted men should be assembled in groups, no greater than thirty, in places near their homes. There, they should be cleaned, bathed, barbered, clothed in clean garments, subjected to their vaccinations, and held in isolation for ten to fourteen days. They should be examined for disease, tagged with the infectious diseases they have had, and sent to the cantonments in locked cars. At the camps, they must be restricted to barracks holding no more than thirty men for some days. During all this time, they can be exercised and drilled by officers. In this way, we can achieve your goal of military infectious disease mortality similar to the civilian population. This is how we avoid the General Gorgas 'nightmare'."

"Every year, thousands of young men are assembled without suffering from infectious diseases on campuses of our great universities. I know you know this, Colonel, since you are still dean of the medical school at the University of Michigan while you serve in the army. With some effort, planning, and attention to public health details, we can accomplish the same thing with the draftees."

Vaughn listened carefully to all that Noble reported. When Noble was finished, Vaughn said, "Edward, can you have your report typed up and sent to me via cable by tomorrow?"

"Of course, Colonel. I'll get right on it."

"This is really important, Edward. I am going to give your report to General Gorgas. I know he will discuss it in detail with the Civilian Surgeon General, Rupert Blue, who is also chief of the U.S. Public Health Service. General Gorgas will also be discussing this directly with the Secretary of War, Newton Baker."

"Oh, one more thing." Noble said. Noble described the original cable he received from Dr. Miner and his trip to Haskell County. He went into great detail about his findings there.

"Edward, keep an eye on the situation in Kansas, and keep me informed. I hope you can stay in touch with Dr. Miner. Sounds like a great physician."

Noble bid the Colonel farewell as he prepared to travel back to Washington D.C. Noble was very gratified that the information from his trip, and his subsequent report, would have an audience with the highest levels of government.

Over the following week, Noble re-established his new routine of frequent A.I. Office visits and ward attending. During the week, a high-speed motor vehicle accident occurred involving a small bus and a Boston municipal fire truck. Numerous compound bone fractures and other lacerations followed. Several of the injured now had wound infections, so Noble, the hospital staff, and his residents, were busy serving these ward patients as well as the others.

The "big day", Thursday, February 21st, finally arrived. Arthur had been dreaming of it four months running. Recent Roentgenograms showed a good femur union within Arthur's large cast. Such fractures can take up to five or six months to heal. However, it looked like Arthur was going to finish up with the cast in four months. His orthopedic surgeon said it was "due to the blessing of young strong bones, allowing things to turn out as well as they have". Arthur had also done all he could to expedite the healing process. He had eaten a protein and calcium rich diet, and had been lifting weights with his other three limbs. He had kept his weight down, which can be a problem when young very active people are suddenly semi-confined to a wheel chair. He was in excellent physical condition.

Noble had been seeing patients on the wards, when he dropped by the A.I. Office late in the morning. He expected Arthur to come by the office any time. Lillian had driven him in the Ford to see his orthopedic surgeon at Boston City Hospital. Noble hoped the cast would come off, since he knew how disappointed Arthur would be if the process was delayed.

Noble was reading some reports when Second Lieutenant Pecknold answered the internal telephone. "Major, it's the sentry. Your wife and son are here."

"Great!" exclaimed Noble. He ran through the small office and into the outside hallway. There stood Lillian with Arthur, who had a grin as wide as the building.

"Well, dad, it's a go! I got the cast off!" Arthur was on crutches, with a sock on his right foot. "Dad, I know you said I needed to be prepared for what I would see when the cast came off. But, I didn't know it would look like <u>this</u>." Arthur pulled up his right pant leg. Exposed was an entire leg that appeared as if no muscle was attached to it at all. It looked like a right femur, patella, tibia, and fibula, with skin stretched around them.

Lillian said, "Just goes to show what happens without exercise. Pretty impressive."

"Mom...impressive? What you mean is de-pressive! This is awful!"

"Son, you have a lot of work ahead of you," said his father. This is why it takes months of reconditioning and rehabilitation to return to normal."

"Arthur, look at it this way," said his mother. "For the next several months, you can have a number of your girl friends help you with leg exercises."

Arthur had not thought of that, but was intrigued with the idea. "Well," said Arthur, "the orthopedist said the cast would be on four to six months, and I did it in four. Now he says rehab will take four to six months, and I am going to do it in four...or less. I guarantee that; with or without the girls." Arthur smiled, and both his father and mother knew how that was going to play out.

"If anyone can do it, Son, you can," said Noble. "You'll have to work at it every day, but I know you will be diligent. Thanks for coming by. I need to work for awhile in the A.I. Office, but I'll be home at the usual time this evening." Noble kissed Lillian, and put his arm around his son, congratulating him for reaching a new stage on the road to a full recovery.

Noble re-entered the office. Lieutenant Pecknold mentioned to him as he walked by, "Major, there is a new navy secure message for you on the table. It just came in."

Noble picked up the cable from the table and studied it. It was a combination of naval ship surgeons' reports from the last week. Small influenza outbreaks were reported on the *USS Minneapolis*, and *USS Madawaska*. There was a similar outbreak at the Naval Radio School in Cambridge, Massachusetts. But, the clinical descriptions of the outbreaks were ones of a mild form of influenza, and not like the type witnessed by Noble in Haskell County. Perhaps these were different strains than the Kansas type?

Today, Thursday, February 21st, Private Dean Nelson left on-leave from Camp Funston in Northeastern Kansas. He travelled 300 miles southwest to the town of Jean, Kansas, in Haskell County. Nelson stayed with his family in Jean. His army leave was a short one, and he soon returned to Camp Funston. On that same day, Ernest Elliot left Sublette, Kansas, in Haskell County, to visit his brother at Camp Funston. When Elliot left his home in Sublette, his son had just come down with influenza.

CHAPTER 8

On Friday, February 22nd, Noble was back at Boston City Hospital. A quick check of hospital admission records for the last month had not shown an increase in influenza cases. In fact, there were fewer admissions with influenza than were usually seen in the winter. This somewhat eased Noble's mind. Noble hoped it was true he had just seen, partly by chance, a small epidemic of particularly virulent influenza localized to the nation's midsection.

After briefly passing by the A.I. Office, Noble went by the Harvard satellite lab to see his friend Milton. As he often was found to be, Rosenau was hunched over a microscope. Lillian was in the lab as well, seated at a desk with numerous ledgers and log books before her. Lillian looked up as Noble walked through the door and said, "Hi, darling. I didn't know that you were going to drop by today."

Noble came in and touched Lillian lightly on the shoulder. Rosenau looked up from the microscope, smiled, and said, "Well, look what the cat dragged in! I hear you had quite a trip. Lillian told me all about Camp Funston. I understand the information is classified. However, both Lillian and I received letters from Colonel Vaughn stating that we have security clearances in your little office on the other side of the South Department. Seems we have tickets to the prom over there."

"The Colonel did say he would arrange for both your security clearances," said Noble. "I could use all the help I can get in the A.I. Office. And, you're right, Milton. The trip really gave me a great introduction to the cantonments and public health. It's safe to say, Milton, that we have a long way to go with troop health during military training."

Noble discussed his Haskell County trip with Rosenau and added many of the details. Rosenau was very interested in that information, and commented, "Sounds like we don't have a lot of epidemiologic data to study with this outbreak, Edward."

"And, it's not likely to get any better," said Noble. "As you know, influenza is not a reportable disease. This might be due to the influence of people who believe influenza is not a disease at all."

"Right," said Rosenau. "You're talking about the miasma theorists who believe environmental factors, such as imbalances in the weather or atmosphere, cause these disorders."

"So, for the time being," said Noble, "we'll have to rely on the keen observations made by astute physician-scientists like Dr. Miner. By the way, what are you two working on?"

Lillian said from her desk, "Recently we've been looking at the epidemiology of cantonment pneumonias. A lot is being done on the topic as we speak, darling. Rufus Cole and his group at the Rockefeller Institute have been using a vaccine against pneumococci Types I, II, and III. They have twelve thousand study subjects, and nineteen thousand controls, at Camp Upton on Long Island. The study is ongoing, but early results are promising. There are no study pneumococcal pneumonias so far, but several dozen control pneumonias. On the epidemiological side of the fence, we are preparing a report for the Pneumonia Commission regarding measles related pneumonias."

"Oh, yes," said Noble. "That is the commission chaired by Cole, with Oswald Avery, Lieutenants Thomas Rivers and Francis Blake, and Captain Eugene Opie. Very prestigious group. Can you give me a hint about the report's conclusions?"

"Well, darling, eventually the Commission will hear that measles cross-contamination kills, and that the associated pneumonias are secondary infections. Our recommendations will sound familiar to you. There is an imperative to have disease-specific contagious disease wards in the cantonment hospitals, hospital cubicles for individual patients to segregate them, and detention camps to hold new recruits for up to ten or fourteen days."

"Sounds like all of us are making similar requests of the military," said Noble. "I hope someone is listening."

Noble and Rosenau then talked at length about various processes used for the manufacture of antitoxins. Antitoxins for tetanus and meningitis were now common, and similar techniques were now being tried for other infections. Horses were injected with gradually increasing doses of some virulent bacteria, and the bacteria in turn produced a toxin. The horse's immune system then generated antibodies that bound to the toxin molecules and neutralized them. The horse was then bled without harm to the animal, solids removed from the blood, and the remaining serum purified. This purified substrate contained the antitoxin.

Noble found this research exciting. He marveled at how much physicians in 1918 could do to help avoid, or attenuate, communicable diseases. Only forty or fewer years ago, humankind was virtually helpless against the majority of microbes. But, now there were antitoxins for diphtheria, meningitis, and tetanus. There were vaccines against cholera, typhoid, typhus, rabies, and anthrax. A vaccine for smallpox had been around even longer than that. New sera, vaccines, and antitoxins were on the horizon. There was so much more that medicine could do to avoid infection. The prospects for the future were very bright.

Over the weekend, Noble was on-call for the infectious dis-ease service at BCH. Because telephone service widely avail-able in large metropolitan areas, it was possible to be accessible for medical residents' questions in the off-hours. The problem was that an attending physician had to stay at home. However, the weather had been cold and overcast, so the Noble family remained at their house over the weekend anyway.

On Monday, February 25th, Noble first rounded on the sickest patients on the South Department's wards, and later checked in with the A.I. Office. After about forty-five min-utes, Lieutenant Pierre-Louis received an internal phone call. After a few minutes, she turned to Noble and said, "Major, we seem to have some kind of problem."

"What's the matter, Lieutenant?" said Noble.

"Well," answered the Lieutenant, "there seems to be… well…there's some kind of commotion at the A.I Office door. The sentry says that someone is demanding entrance into the office."

"What's the person's name, Lieutenant?" asked a bewil-dered Noble.

The Lieutenant asked the sentry for the name of the per-son demanding entrance. There was a moment of silence as the Lieutenant's dark eyes darted from side to side, as though she were trying to follow a conversation partially out of ear-shot of the telephone receiver. Finally, she said, "The sentry says…he says…the person's name is…Commander Richard Cunard."

Noble's lips pursed together, and his pulse quickened. He folded his arms against his chest, and thought to himself this was completely within character. A thousand thoughts raced through Noble's mind as he tried to analyze the odd situation before him.

Richard Cunard had been in Noble's Boston University School of Medicine class of 1899. He had been interested in Lillian Alexander, and dated her for a short time in 1896. But,

Lillian fell in love with Edward Noble, and they were married in 1898.

Cunard had a distinguished career in public health. He served as an intern in the Marine Hospital Service (MHS) from 1899 to 1900. Cunard became an assistant surgeon in 1900, and met Dr. Rupert Blue at the MHS. Blue asked Cunard to help him with the San Francisco bubonic plague epidemic in 1902, where he performed admirably. Cunard helped again with the epidemics following the San Francisco earthquake and fire in 1906. Cunard showed himself to be skilled at diplomacy, when he wanted to be.

Cunard helped to set up public health programs in Hawaii in preparation for increased international traffic following the opening of the Panama Canal. He helped with the New Orleans yellow fever outbreak of 1908, but made enemies when he forced the city to pay for Public Health Service expenses to fight the epidemic. It was perceived by some in New Orleans that a portion of these expenses had been incurred by Cunard personally.

In 1912, President William Howard Taft nominated Rufus Blue to be the civilian Surgeon General. Blue appointed Cunard to a regional New England U.S. Public Health Service post, where he became a champion for public health research. Cunard also helped disseminate public health information, which included pamphlets on Rosenau's milk pasteurization campaigns. Cunard's political clout increased when Blue became the president of the American Medical Association from 1916 to 1917.

Cunard was already in the Naval Reserves when the U.S. entered The War, so he became a Commander when he began active duty in the regular navy. Rupert Blue had him assigned to Boston where he was in charge of a number of projects. He assisted the Red Cross in venereal disease programs. He oversaw industrial hygiene and health services for tens of thousands of workers laboring in war plants, and the communities around them. Cunard was put in command of all Quarantine Officers stationed on the Boston area piers. He was to give administrative support for the application of vaccines for tetanus, diphtheria, typhoid, and smallpox. Because of his political connections, Boston officials appointed Cunard to the Boston City Hospital Board of Trustees. As such, he helped with the administration of the hospital, and was given an office in the central BCH Rotunda.

Despite Cunard's accomplishments, he was a brooding man who was unimaginative and was known to hold grudges. He had not married. Whereas Noble had been a stellar medical student, and was summa cum laude in his class as well as valedictorian, Cunard was an average student who was envious of Noble. Noble was a very quiet and somewhat introverted student, but was very popular and respected by his peers and medical school faculty. Cunard, on the other hand, was not very popular and was not trusted by his fellow students. On more than one occasion, Cunard had been accused of cheating, although this was never proven.

Many appreciated Cunard's administrative skills. However, Noble was universally known as a far superior clinician and diagnostician. Noble's friends were not Cunard fans. Harvey Cushing thought Cunard boring. Victor Vaughn did not believe Cunard was a good evaluator of new data, and lacked the critical thinking required to integrate new research into clinical practice. Milton Rosenau questioned Cunard's morals.

So, Noble was now confronted with Commander Richard Cunard's demanding entrance into an area for which he had no security clearance. In addition, the two men had personal issues with one another that were over two decades old. Noble already knew this was not going to go well.

Noble went into the little A.I. office and closed the door to the larger room. He sat down at his desk and picked up the telephone. "Lieutenant?" asked Noble. "Please ask the sentry to let Commander Cunard in."

Noble put down the phone onto the desk and waited. He could hear muffled voices outside the small office door. Finally, the door slowly opened and Cunard entered the room.

Noble spoke first, thinking that he could defuse this awkward situation. He decided to take an informal friendly approach. "Good morning, Richard. Good to see you again. Please make yourself comfortable, and have a seat."

Cunard was dressed in his usual starched and pressed white naval uniform. He removed his cap, sat down on the hunter green sofa, and took a deep breath. "That is 'Commander Cunard'."

Noble smiled slightly and said, "Oh, come on Richard. Old classmates of '99 don't have to use all the military ranks, and all of that."

"This is not a personal visit, Major," said Cunard. "This is an official enquiry."

Noble was now concerned. Not only was this not going to be a friendly exchange, it was taking on an air of open hostility. "Ok...Commander. What can I do for you?" asked Noble.

"To what service are you assigned here, Major?" demanded Cunard.

"I am assigned to the Army Division of Communicable Diseases...Commander." Noble was trying to control his tendency toward sarcasm.

"Who is your commanding officer, Major?" demanded Cunard.

"Colonel Victor Vaughn, head of this Army Division," said Noble, in a matter-of-fact tone. "You might already know that he was appointed to that position by the Army Surgeon General himself."

"What is the purpose of this army installation in Boston City Hospital, Major?" asked Cunard in a louder voice.

"Commander, that is classified information," said Noble.

"I am not asking for this information, Major," said Cunard. "I'm ordering you to tell me."

"I cannot give out that information, Commander, unless you can produce the proper security clearance," said Noble. "Do you have that with you?" Noble couldn't resist, knowing that he had no such document.

"Major, let me make something abundantly clear to you," Cunard said, almost shouting. "This operation must be clearly under a formal command structure. If I find out that it is not, I will see to it that you are placed under a court-martial."

"Commander, be assured that I will pass on your thoughts directly to Colonel Vaughn and General Gorgas." Noble actually meant that statement completely.

"By the way, Commander," added Noble. "I posted an advisory by cable with the U.S. Public Health Service concerning an influenza endemic in Kansas. Did you see it?"

As Cunard opened the outside door to the A.I. Office, he said in almost a sneer, "I haven't read it yet." With that, he closed the door and was gone.

Noble could not believe Cunard had taken this approach. Making such a threat when there was clearly a 'command structure' with the A.I. Office did not make any sense. It was a fight that Cunard could not win. Noble knew the presence of the office, and Noble's lead in it, was getting under Cunard's already thin skin. Noble was certain Cunard felt he should be in charge of such an operation. In addition, the fact that Noble had returned safely from France may have derailed other plans held by Cunard.

Noble left the small office for the bigger one, and asked Lieutenant Pierre-Louis to send a cable to Colonel Vaughn. He wanted to be sure the Colonel read his version of the Cunard visit before he read any other.

Over the next week, the work of the South Department was fairly routine. Patients were moved constantly in and out of the various wards without much notice. This movement was concealed largely because there was an extensive series of underground tunnels linking many of the Boston City Hospital pavilions. This fact was not commonly known outside the hospital. The tunnels were constructed during the Civil War and were made to withstand bombardments, if Confederates ever attacked Boston. The tunnels were made of concrete and were 8 feet wide and 7 feet high in most places. Medical and surgical residents used the tunnels frequently to quickly move about the BCH complex. Patients were moved within the tunnels on gurneys in the same manner. However, in the winter cold, many of the city's homeless moved into the tunnel system. The homeless sought comfort from the steam heating within the tunnels. This meant residents and attendings traveled in groups within the tunnels to ensure their safety. The hospital staff did not have the heart to require the indigents removed, since New England winters can be lethal without shelter. Sadly, health care providers often put their own safety at some risk, for the benefit of others.

On Monday, March 4th, in the early afternoon, a Private in one of the kitchens at Camp Funston was beginning to prepare dinner for hundreds of soldiers. In civilian life he worked in a large restaurant as a cook. His military meals were simple, but he prided himself on preparing wholesome food.

The Private first noticed a headache that grew quickly with intensity. In less than an hour, he began suffering severe body aches, a non-productive cough, shortness of breath, feverish feelings, and pronounced sweating. Looking very pale, the kitchen Sergeant First Class sent the Private to sick call. The physician Captain in the camp clinic diagnosed influenza. However, the doctor was concerned about the Private's fever of 104° F, and bibasilar pulmonary rales. He feared this was becoming pneumonia and admitted the patient to the camp hospital for further observation and evaluation. By that evening, the Private had bilateral basilar lung consolidation by auscultation and percussion. He had in fact developed a bilateral pneumonia. The Private was very ill.

On Tuesday, March 5th, three enlisted troops were admitted to the camp hospital with headaches, severe body aches, a cough, and a high fever.

On Wednesday, March 6th, ten soldiers at Camp Funston were admitted to the hospital with diagnoses of influenza.

In the afternoon of Friday, March 8th, per his routine, Noble dropped by the A.I. Office. The communicable disease world seemed unusually calm around the globe. Aside from Noble's U.S. Public Health Service advisory concerning Haskell County, there had been no other mention of unusual influenza activity by any agency, including Public Health itself. Noble entered the office and said, "Good afternoon, Lieutenant Pecknold. Looks like its a little warmer today."

"Good morning, Major. Yes, it is. Very pleasant."

Noble read a cable from Harvey Cushing which was the first he had seen in awhile.

Thursday, March 7, 1918
From: Hospital Base No. 5

Good to hear from you, old friend! Sorry I haven't written, but we have been very busy with illness and wounded here. Things are definitely warming up on The Front. Lots of doughboys arriving every day. Very interesting trip to Kansas! But it sounds like a small outbreak in an out-of-the-way part of the country. Keep in touch.

Your friend,
Colonel Harvey Cushing, BEF.

As Noble went through the domestic military message stack, he came across a series of reports from Camp Funston: Influenza admissions at camp hospital: 3/4/18 – One; 3/5/18 – Three; 3/6/18 – Ten; 3/7/18 – Thirty. Noble's eyes grew wide, and his respiration rate increased. He put his right thumb and 2nd finger to his jaw. He was seeing information that no one in the world outside of Camp Funston had seen. And, no one in the world could put this together with Haskell County...except Noble.

"Lieutenant, please send this information, in this order, to Colonel Vaughn," said Noble, as he handed the Lieutenant a group of cables. "Also, send a cable immediately to the Camp Funston Medical Corps and request that they send me daily hospital admission numbers for influenza."

"Consider it done, Major," said the Lieutenant.

"Also, Lieutenant, send a cable to Copland, Kansas. The cable is for Dr. Loring Miner, and ask him how things are with influenza in Haskell County. I haven't heard from him in bit. It will be necessary to have an army currier bring the cable out to his house. Can you arrange that, Lieutenant?"

"Done, sir."

Noble worried about the situation over the weekend. He spoke to both Lillian and Rosenau about Camp Funston. However, Lillian said it was hard to make any epidemiologic projections without any real data, and Rosenau reminded Noble the clinical data was anecdotal at best. Noble conceded the view of the problem at this point was subjective. But, one must use what information one has to make a hypothesis. Right now, it looked like a serious form of influenza was spreading.

It wasn't until Tuesday, March 12th, that Noble received word from Dr. Miner. Entering the A.I. Office in the afternoon, Lieutenant Lafayette told Noble of the cable from Copland. Noble read it quickly.

Tuesday, March 12, 1918
From: Haskell County

Hi, Edward. Got your message. It's really quite remarkable. The county influenza just suddenly disappeared. It happened virtually overnight. Thank God for that! I have to say I am still frightened by what I saw these last six weeks. It was unlike anything I have ever seen before. Hope all is great on your end, Edward. Come and see us anytime in Copland!

Your friend,
Dr. Loring Miner

After reading this good news, Noble turned to his domestic military stack. The stack combined an up-to-date assessment of the situation in Camp Funston. Influenza admissions at camp hospital were as follows: 3/8/18 – Forty-two; 3/9/18 – Sixty-three; 3/10/18 – Eighty-seven; 3/11/18 – Ninety-eight.

In the civilian domestic stack was a *Public Health Reports* message stating that a modest increase in influenza had been seen in New York State. The Ford Motor Company, with a very good health insurance plan for its workers and accurate records, had seen an increase in influenza related absenteeism. There was nothing, however, out of the ordinary with these observations.

Noble sat down and wrote out a cable message to be sent to Colonel Vaughn, who had not yet commented on his message from March 8th.

Tuesday, March 12, 1918
From: A.I. Cable Office, BCH

Hello, Colonel. This is an update on the information sent to you on the 8th. On one hand, it appears that the Haskell County influenza endemic has passed. On the other hand, the number of influenza cases in Camp Funston is showing an alarming increase. Please keep in mind that a huge number of troops are brought into, and shipped out of, Camp Funston every day. A flood of new recruits are sent constantly from Funston to other Army camps, onto Troop Transports, and eventually to Europe. As you know, the U.S. is presently sending 10,000 troops a day to Europe. Will keep you advised.

Major Edward Noble

Noble knew Colonel Vaughn was a great advocate for troop public health concerns. Vaughn had literally written the military book on the subject. Convincing Army Surgeon General Gorgas of the problem was easy, since he was also a physician who had been on the front lines against disease. However, Noble also knew there were many forces to deal with when it came to such matters. It would be an uphill battle to convince the Under Secretaries of War, the Secretary of War, and even the President himself, there might be an influenza problem. Noble decided he had to continue monitoring the situation and give as accurate of an assessment as possible, to anyone who would listen.

Over the next week, Rosenau and Lillian sent their measles report to the Pneumonia Commission. It was well received. What the military would do with the information, or Noble's recommendations for that matter, remained to be seen. Lillian told her husband of the results of another pneumococcal vaccine tested in Camp Gordon outside of Atlanta. One hundred men with measles were selected for the study. Fifty received the vaccine, and fifty acted as controls. Fourteen controls contracted measles related pneumonia, while only one study subject fell ill. Lillian was forlorn that no statistical analyses of the results were performed. However, at least this showed a positive study trend.

Rosenau told Noble about some of the recent findings concerning pneumococci, the organism most associate with pneumonia. Some pneumococci are virulent and lethal, while some are not. Oswald Avery and Alphonse Dochez focused their research on the fact that some pneumococci were surrounded by a capsule made of physacharides, or sugar. Perhaps this capsule was involved in virulence, and could be exploited in developing vaccines or antisera. As always, Noble was eager to hear any and all developments that could help him in his own war with microbes.

By Monday, March 18th, Noble remained disquieted by the incoming news. The Signal Corps officers were beginning to understand Noble's requests more each day, and anticipate them. Noble entered the A.I Office, and Lieutenant Pierre-Louis said, "Hi, Major. It's on the desk."

Noble went to the top messages on the stack of interest: Influenza admissions at Camp Funston hospital; 3/14/18 – Seventy-two; 3/15/18 – Sixty-four; 3/16/18 – Eighty-seven; 3/17/18 – Eighty-one.

Below the Camp Funston reports were others: Influenza diagnosed in the Georgia camps of Forrest and Greenleaf. Ten percent of the troops in each camp reported ill. Few deaths.

Two-thirds of large U.S. camps were now reporting influenza. Thirty of the largest U.S. cities were also reporting influenza, with most of these cities adjacent to military facilities. The *Public Health Reports* estimated a spike in influenza mortality cases, but this was only preliminary.

"Lieutenant," asked Noble, "when you go to Devens, do you see many with the grippe there?"

"Yes, sir. Just in the last week to ten days. There is not a lot, and most of them are confined to barracks. A few are in the camp hospital. Everyone says the sick have the grippe... that is what they say. Also, around the Worcester Square apartment the three of us share, there have been some families with the grippe. Is that what you mean, sir?"

"Yes, Lieutenant, that is actually very helpful," said Noble.

Noble took the trolley home that evening along Massachusetts Avenue, and relayed the new influenza information to Lillian over dinner.

Later at the dining room table, Lillian requested, "Marguerite, you need to eat more of your corn."

"I don't like corn, Mommy."

Florence interjected, "Marguerite, did you know that I like corn?"

"Really?" said Marguerite."

"And, I do to," said Akeema.

"Well, I'll try, Mommy," said Marguerite.

Florence leaned over to her mother and said quietly, "It works every time."

Lillian smiled the smile parents have when they have outwitted their children. She realized it was only a matter of time before Marguerite figured out the tag-team operation used on her. Lillian then returned to the topic of influenza with her husband. "Darling, I think you have the influenza sequence of events worked out pretty well."

"Thanks, Lilly," said Noble. "The distances between camps and cities, the time courses, and the known incubation periods for influenza all fit perfectly. The endemic in Haskell County has become epidemic and has spread to Camp Funston. It's now in much of the eastern United States. But, from the reports coming in at the A.I Office, the original influenza has attenuated. It is just as infective, but it is not as virulent. I realize there is more data to come in, but the epidemic has changed."

"Again, I think you have a very plausible scenario, Edward," said Lillian. "We know from studies of past epidemics and pandemics, including the one from 1889-1890, that the infection changes with time. Perhaps the very virulent form you witnessed in Haskell County is now less threatening. It will be interesting to see what happens over the next seven to fourteen days in Camp Funston."

Noble changed the subject, turned to Bernard and Michael, and asked them about their days at school. Both of them stuck their tongues and said, "Blaaaa!"

"Oh, come on you guys," said their father. "It's not that bad."

Michael said, "We're just waiting for the first game at Fenway, Dad. Do you think we can go to an early home game?"

"Boys, the first opportunity we have, we'll go," said their father. "We'll bring the whole family."

"Yay!" said Marguerite.

Noble then turned to Arthur, who was eating his corn on the cob. "Arthur, how's the ol' leg?"

"Pretty good, Dad," said Arthur. I still can't walk on it, but it's getting stronger. There's a pool at the rehab center where I do exercises and flexibility work-outs. It really helps."

Florence again interjected, "Yeah, Arthur, tell Dad who is helping you with the exercises in the pool."

"Well, Dad...Gail is helping me keep flexibility in my right leg joints," said Arthur.

"I'll bet she is, Arthur," said his father, with a quick wink to Lillian. Lillian just frowned.

Arthur said, "I'll be out on the Charles River with the crew in no time."

"Florence," asked her father, "how is nursing school going?"

"Well, Dad, I didn't do as well on this term's exam in physiology as I had hoped. I got a B+. In any case, we're all looking forward to your lecture with us, Dad. "

"That's not a bad grade," said her father. "I hope the group will get something out of my talk that's coming up."

Noble then turned to Akeema, who was finishing up with some green beans. "Are you starting to get used to some of these foods, Akeema? I know that you struggled with many of them early on."

"Dr. Noble," said Akeema, "I want you to know that I appreciate all the food that I am so kindly given. They are different than our diets in Golovin, but I have found most of them delicious. I especially like 'corn on the cob'. It tastes so good, and is so funny to eat. I've even become used to beets. They make your tongue purple. We don't eat a lot of vegetables back home."

Lillian then said, "It's a school night, everyone. Let's all get up stairs, brush your teeth, and get ready for bed."

The Noble family picked up their plates from the dinner table, and prepared for the day's completion. As Noble drifted off to sleep that night, he hoped he had seen the end of this early influenza season.

Monday, March 25ᵗʰ, Noble arrived in the A.I Office and went straight to the center table. The Camp Funston report today was a summary, since influenza activity had greatly subsided. Over a three week period, 1,100 young recruits had been ill enough with influenza to be hospitalized. Twenty percent of them developed pneumonia. However, there had been only thirty-eight deaths, which was only slightly more than the average.

Noble continued to study the Camp Funston summary, and the other collected ID documents for the day. At one point, Lieutenant Pecknold took off her headset and turned to Noble. "Major, we just received a cable from Washington. Colonel Vaughn would like to talk to you by telephone at 1100 hours. I will try to establish a good long distance line for you at that time, sir. Is that OK, sir?"

"That would be fine, Lieutenant. Do you think you'll have a good line then?"

"Well, we'll see, sir. We'll give it a try."

At 11 AM, Noble was seated at one of the roll top desks in the large A.I. Office waiting for the Colonel's call. Lieutenant Pecknold saw one of the lamps on the cordboard light up, and put in a cord jack to establish a connection with an incoming call. "Yes, Washington. This is A.I., BCH. We hear you. Major, do you want to pick up this call in your office?"

"Yes, Lieutenant. Thank you."

Noble went into the small office and closed the door. The telephone on the desk rang, and he put the earpiece to his ear. The reception was good, but Noble had to speak somewhat louder to be heard. The usual static with long distance calls was minimal. "Colonel Vaughn…is that you, sir?"

"Yes, Edward," Vaughn said, speaking somewhat louder himself. "I still find it amazing that you can be in Boston, and I am in Washington D.C., and we can talk. Anyway, I received your messages about Camp Funston, and have been keeping General Gorgas appraised of the situation. What is your take on it now, Edward?"

"Yes, sir, it is always strange to talk long distance. In any case, it appears that the influenza outbreak in Haskell County did become epidemic and spread into Camp Funston, sir. From Funston, the majority of the other camps in the eastern U.S. have experienced the infection. In fact, the largest cities in the nation have witnessed the extension of influenza as well. All the time courses and geography fit perfectly."

Noble continued, "My concern with this problem, though, came from my first-hand observation of the epidemic in Southwestern Kansas, sir. The aggressiveness of the influenza outbreak there was truly remarkable. I have been going over the domestic and international influenza data for the military and civilian populations, and it appears that the infection attenuated beyond Haskell. The data will require refinement as more municipal and military records are available, but it seems there was only a minor increase in mortality overall."

"So, at this point you think influenza is not a serious issue?" asked Vaughn

"That's a relative question, Colonel. There is no evidence that this seasonal epidemic in the United States is serious. We also have no evidence yet of a spread of the epidemic beyond our shores. Still, we can use this event as a study of our ability to contain a highly contagious communicable disease. I would have to say, Colonel, we would get an "F" in school with this performance. The majority of the 1,100 hospitalizations for influenza at Funston can most certainly be avoided in the future if we follow my recommendations, sir. I realize the Pneumonia Commission received similar recommendations from Milton Rosenau and Lillian. But, I know that you know these things already, sir. You have taught the rest of us these principles."

Noble could hear the Colonel chuckle through the earpiece. "You sounded like your father just then, Edward. You know, he taught me so much. He was like you are now; trying to make sense of diseases in large military camps by using the scientific method. He would be so proud of you."

"Thank you, Colonel. What is especially sad is we continue to make the same mistakes that were being made during the Civil War."

"Very true, Edward," said Vaughn. "There are many in the military who don't understand communicable diseases, and don't realize their cost to our fighting forces. Even worse, our civilian leadership understands these concepts less than the military. They view preventative measures against infectious diseases as a waste of resources. They want all efforts and materials to go directly to fighting the enemy. They just don't realize the microbial enemy can be many times more treacherous than the human enemy. You cannot know how often these topics are pressed by General Gorgas and me. We can't even get the civilian Surgeon General many times to listen to us."

"Colonel," said Noble, "Lillian and her fellow epidemiologists have modeled these problems before. They have conclusively shown that preventative health measures save not only lives, but money. A lot of money. I guess our job is to teach these lessons to those who are in power."

"Correct," said Vaughn. "Influenza can be deadly, Edward. But, for many years the infection that has taken many more lives is measles. The infection reeks havoc in two ways. First, it lowers the ability of the host to fend off other secondary infections that can be very lethal, especially pneumonia. Secondly, it can strike so many at once that hospital and other medical facilities are overwhelmed. This breaks down the most ample provision for the care of the sick, and renders successful isolation impossible. My work on the epidemiology of measles showed that every one thousand men with measles will progress to forty-four cases of pneumonia...and fourteen will die."

"I've read your treatise on measles, sir," said Noble, "and it is the foundation of many studies that have come after it. It seems to me the preventative proactive steps against measles are the same for influenza. Following the recommendations by Rosenau, Lillian, and me, will accomplish much against both disorders."

"I completely agree with you, Edward," said Vaughn. "But, the problem is that very few see it that way, including those in the medical profession. Many...if not most... people in the military, government, medicine, and in the general population, do not view influenza as a serious disease. Everyone sees 'the grippe' come through their communities every fall and winter, and do not understand the dangers associated with it."

"Well, Colonel," said Noble, "if there is anything I can do on the public relations end of this, let me know and I will do all I can."

"I know you will, Edward," said Vaughn. "We must all keep up the pressure with government and military planners on all levels. For now, Edward, keep doing what you are. Information, and the correct interpretation of it, is critical for the health and safety of our fighting men. We'll talk again soon, Major."

"Thank you for your call, Colonel." And with that, Colonel Vaughn hung up.

Noble re-entered the large office. Lieutenant Pecknold mentioned to him as he came through the door, "Major, there is a cable from Colonel Cushing on the table." Noble picked up the message.

Monday, March 25, 1918
From: Base Hospital No. 5

Hello, Edward. Things are not looking good here. A major 'Jerry' operation has made an unprecedented advance of 40 miles, and pushed The Front to within 75 miles of Paris. We may need to evacuate. Keep us in your prayers.

Your friend,
Colonel Harvey Cushing, BEF.

Noble looked up from the cable and said, "Lieutenant, I have been so involved with monitoring Camp Funston and the other camps that I have not been keeping up with The War news."

"Very understandable, sir," said the Lieutenant. "There's a confidential war assessment in the stack from today, Major."

Noble found the day's summary from The War Department on the table, and took it into the small office to read. The Germans had drawn up spring offensive plans, code named "Operation Michael". Their plan was to divide the British and French forces with a series of attacks and advances before significant U.S. forces arrived in Europe. The operation had commenced on March 21st with an attack on British forces near Amiens. Allied trenches were penetrated using novel infiltration tactics, called *Hutier* tactics, after Oskar von Hutier. Instead of long artillery bombardments and massed assaults, Germany used brief artillery and infiltrated small groups of infantry at weak points. Meanwhile, three heavy Krupp railway guns fired 183 shells on Paris, causing panic and many Parisians to flee.

Many Germans, and some Allies, believed a German victory was near. The offensive was so successful that Kaiser Wilhelm II had declared yesterday, March 24th, a national holiday.

When Noble finished the summary, He returned to the large office and said to Lieutenant Pecknold, "Well, this isn't very good."

The Lieutenant looked over at Noble and said, "Major, I don't mean to make things worse, but your wife just called. I took a message, since you were engrossed with The War summary."

"What did she want, Lieutenant?"

"She would like you to try and come home a little early today, if you can," said the Lieutenant. "Seems that someone is ill at home."

Noble called his house immediately, and found out from Lillian that Florence and Akeema were both sick. Noble had additional rounding to do on the wards, and went about that task as quickly as possible. He told his resident team that he was sorry, but he would need to leave a little early today.

Noble arrived at his home on Beacon Street at about 4:30 PM. He was met at the door by Lillian, who began to fill him in on the details as they went upstairs to the bedrooms.

"Edward," said Lillian, "both of the girls were fine this morning and ate a normal breakfast. Florence had a Naval Reserve meeting, and put on her uniform. Akeema walked the children to school as always, and they both looked fine. However, Akeema began to complain of a headache shortly after she returned from the children's school. Not long thereafter, she felt very hot, developed a cough, and complained of severe body aches. Florence returned early from her Reserves meeting less than an hour after Akeema went to bed. She described the same symptoms, Edward, and actually cried with the aching pain she experienced."

Edward and Lillian reached the two rooms where the young women were now in bed. Edward asked Lillian a number of other pertinent questions, and received a further negative review of systems. Edward then examined the two women, who looked very ill. Akeema had a temperature of 102° F, and Florence had a temperature of 103° F.

Finally, outside of the womens' rooms, Noble told Lillian, "Most likely influenza, Lilly. They look like they are otherwise doing well. All we can do now is give aspirin for the pain, and plenty of fluids. Let's be sure to keep the other children away from them, as well as their utensils, etc. You and I must wash our hands frequently, since this has been shown to decrease the spread of influenza."

"Ok, Edward," said Lillian. "I feel better now that you have seen them. I was pretty worried about them both."

"If this goes like the rest of the seasonal influenza we have seen in the last few weeks, they should bounce back in about 72 hours. We'll watch them closely."

Over the next three days, the Noble family did all they could to help the two women with influenza, and to keep everyone else in the family healthy. Lillian pushed oral hydration and gave aspirin as needed for the severe, almost unearthly, myalgias that were one of the hallmarks of this influenza strain. The two women did nothing except sleep. On the afternoon of Thursday, March 28th, Lillian went up stairs to give the women some juice, and found both of them sitting up for the first time in their rooms. Their temperatures were near-normal and both of them said one thing: "I'm hungry".

Florence and Akeema's influenza course was nearly identical to cases in Funston, and the other cantonments. They were also the same as reported influenza cases in much of the United States. However, what was not being reported to the Army Intelligance Cable Office, or anywhere else, was that the same symptoms were present with a number of troops now bound for Europe.

CHAPTER 9

On Monday, April 1st, Dr. Edward Noble was scheduled to give a talk to a group of hospital nursing students. The talk would be at bedside, so necessarily the tutorial would be performed right on the hospital wards.

The Boston City Hospital wards were considered to be a state-of-the-art design. They were of the pavilion style that included fifteen foot high ceilings and twelve foot high windows. This plan ensured adequate natural lighting and ventilation. Some of the South Department wards had single bed isolation suites. The original pavilions had two stories, with twenty-four beds to a ward. More contemporary pavilions had three stories with larger bed capacities. Each pavilion was up to one hundred and sixty feet in length.

Ward beds were lined up perpendicular to the walls, with the head of beds against the walls. Each ward had a wide central walkway. Two foot high oak cabinets with marble tops were located at the foot of some of the beds, and held personal patient items along with some hospital supplies. Set on the cabinets were slender one-foot high electric lamps with small glass shades. At the end of each ward was a four foot wide and ten foot high wood door. On either side of each door were floor-to-ceiling one foot diameter white Ionic columns that hid the heating and ventilation system. They gave the wards a "Greek" or "Roman" look. The floors were hardwood covered with terrazzo pavement, and were without carpets or rugs. This was easy to keep clean, but made for a lot of noise as people walked on them. South Department pavilions had the added measures of glazed brick walls. These features made the communicable disease wards easier to clean. Overall, the ward interiors were very neat and esthetically pleasing.

At the pre-designated time, on one of the large South Department patient wards, fourteen Boston City Hospital nursing students gathered along with their Nursing Supervisor. Since all the women were dressed in white dresses, white stockings, white shoes, and white nursing caps, the gathering looked much like a snow drift in the middle of the ward. Promptly at 9 AM, Dr. Noble arrived and walked up to the group.

The Supervisor began, "Good morning, ladies. We are very fortunate to have Dr. Edward Noble back from France, and attending again at Boston City. As you all know, Dr. Noble is a renowned Internist and Infectious Disease consultant. He will speak to you about pressure ulcers today."

Florence Noble stood toward the back of the circle of nursing students. She did not want to appear as though she would receive any preferential treatment from her father. Nevertheless, her ear-to-ear grin gave her away as supremely proud of him.

Dr. Noble addressed the group. "Good morning, ladies, and good morning Mrs. Tomlinson. I am honored to have the opportunity to talk to you about a significant problem in institutionalized and critically ill patients. This problem causes much pain, decreased quality of life, and leads to significant patient morbidity and mortality. What is most important is that <u>nurses</u> play an important role in decreasing the severity of this problem. The problem is pressure ulcers in the infirmed. Pressure ulcers are ischemic soft tissue injuries resulting from pressure, usually over bony prominences. They can also occur with poorly fitting casts or appliances. The external appearance of a pressure ulcer may underestimate the extent of the underlying injury."

"I have chosen this part of the South Department today because there are several examples of the different stages of pressure ulcers you will encounter. All the patients have already agreed to have you see their wounds, and we greatly appreciate their help in this regard."

Noble walked over to the first patient and said, "As we look at our patients today, please gather around each bed in a circle so all can see." He then showed the patient's sacral area. "This is a good example of a Stage 1 pressure ulcer. The skin is intact with non-blanchable redness in a localized area. This stage is a warning of more serious lesions to follow if appropriate measures are not taken promptly. 'Overlays' are what we call additional ulcer support surfaces designed to be placed on top of one another. In this way, the patient can assume a variety of positions without bearing weight on the ulcer. The patient should be repositioned every two hours."

Noble walked to the second patient and showed a left heel. "Here is a Stage 2 ulcer with a partial thickness loss of the dermis, which represents a shallow open ulcer with a red-pink wound bed. You will note there is no tissue sloughing. These ulcers can also present with an intact or ruptured serum-filled blister. Stage 2 ulcers usually require an occlusive or semi-permeable dressing that will maintain a moist environment. Wet-to-dry dressings are avoided since these wounds generally require little debridement. Are there any questions at this point?"

Florence could no longer contain herself. She raised her hand, and her father called on her by saying, "Yes, Miss?" There was a barely perceivable smile that came over the senior Noble's face. Florence knew he had betrayed his pride for his daughter, and this made her even more proud of him.

Florence asked, "Doctor, how can we tell if there is a true wound infection?" Now she felt embarrassment for the question.

"Good question, Miss," answered Noble. "This is not always easy to determine, because the patient may not have a fever or leukocytosis. Look for local tissue involvement, such as warmth, erythema, local tenderness, purulent discharge, and the presence of a foul odor. Sometimes the only manifestation of an infection is delayed wound healing. The best treatment for a wound infection is to avoid it in the first place. That is why early nursing care is critical."

Noble moved to the third patient and said, "This is a Stage 3 ulcer," as he displayed a right elbow. "There is a full thickness tissue loss, with subcutaneous fat visible. Sloughing is present but does not obscure the depth of the tissue loss. At this stage, there can be tissue undermining and tunneling deeper into the soft tissues. Let's look at the patient just to our left so that we can compare a Stage 3 ulcer to a Stage 4." Noble showed the group another heel, and said, "This is a Stage 4 ulcer. There is a full thickness skin loss with exposed bone, tendon, and muscle. Sloughing, or an eschar, may be present on some parts of the wound bed. Stage 3 and 4 ulcers require treatment for infection, debridement of necrotic tissue, and appropriate dressings so that healing can be accelerated. Surgery is necessary for some of these ulcers, using skin or musculocutaneous flaps."

"Just a couple more comments about these serious lesions," said Noble. "Patients need to be encouraged to take in proper nutrition if they are to heal these ulcers. For pain control, we usually use aspirin, and occasionally morphine sulfate, or codeine. Ulcers with heavy exudates need an absorptive dressing. Desiccated ulcers lack wound fluids, which provide tissue growth factors to facilitate reepithelialization. Thus, pressure ulcer healing is promoted by dressings that maintain a moist wound environment while keeping the surrounding intact skin dry. Saline moistened gauze is a good choice."

"Finally," Noble concluded, "there are five parameters of care that should be monitored and documented in the medical record daily. These are: Evaluation of the ulcer, status of the dressing, status of the area surrounding the ulcer, the presence of pain and the adequacy of pain control, and the presence of possible complications, such as infection. This information is invaluable for both nursing and attending physicians to monitor the success or failure of treatment."

"Perhaps in a few days we can check on the nursing progress with these various pressure ulcers. I need to go for now. In any case, thank you ladies for the chance to speak on this very important topic," said Noble.

The Supervisor said, "Thank you very much for your clinical pearls, Dr. Noble."

As Dr. Noble walked out of the patient ward, he subtly looked behind him. There, still grinning ear-to-ear, was his daughter. He felt, again, great pride in her.

Noble walked to a different pavilion where the A.I. Office was located. He saluted the ever-present army Military Police sentry, and entered the large room. "Good morning, Lieutenant Lafayette. Got anything interesting today?"

"Hi, Major. You sound like you're in a good mood today, sir. There is a cable from Colonel Cushing." Noble read his friend's latest cable.

Monday, April 1, 1918
From: Base Hospital No. 5

Things are better, Edward. The latest German advance has been halted. No need to evacuate, at least this time. Say hi to everyone for me.

Your friend,
Colonel Harvey Cushing, BEF.

The most recent War Department summary had validated Cushing's assessment. After heavy fighting, "Operation Michael" had been halted. Lacking tanks or motorized artillery, the Germans were unable to consolidate their gains from the original advance. Their supply lines had also been stretched beyond capacity. The sudden stop was also due to the fierce fighting of the four Australian Imperial Force divisions that had done what the other armies could not. That is, stop the German advance in its tracks. With a second German breakthrough of Allied lines, the Australians were again able to stop them.

American forces were being used to bolster the depleted French and British commands, and this began in earnest on March 28th. Another important development was the appointment of General Foch as supreme commander of the Allied forces. Foch was to take a coordinating role rather than a directing one. This meant that the British, French, and U.S. commands (with the latter under General Pershing) would now operate largely independently.

As Noble left the office for the hospital wards, he said to Lieutenant Lafayette, "I'll see you later, Lieutenant. You are correct. I am in a good mood today." Noble thought to himself that he had a lot to be in a good mood about. The War was going better, his family was now healthy, and there were no serious problems on the infectious disease horizon. Things were looking up.

The Noble family had not had a real holiday in a long time. Noble's responsibilities at the A.I. Office precluded a long holiday, but a shorter one was overdue. The spring weather was warming up Boston, and everyone was ready to end the winter "hibernation" that can be common in New England. So, the family decided to take a two-day holiday on Cape Cod.

Very early on the morning of Saturday, April 6th, the Noble family readied for their outing. Lillian, Florence, and

Akeema, had prepared a number of meals for everyone over the next two days. All the usual picnic favorites were included, and there were plenty of cakes, pies, cookies, as well as Edward's favorite...double chocolate brownies. Suitcases and bags were packed, and the whole entourage was loaded into the Ford, which included a rooftop storage rack.

The Nobles drove east on Commonwealth Avenue to the Boston Harbor piers to board a ferry for the Cape. The mornings were cold and frosty in early April, but the days became very pleasant by mid-morning. The forecast for the weekend called for afternoons in the high '70s, with mild breezes, and calm seas.

The truck was parked and unloaded near the ferry pier, and the group started out for the waiting boat. This operation took two trips, given the amount of material to move and the fact that Arthur was limited in the help he could give. Noble thought to himself that loading the USS Madawaska was less of an ordeal.

Everyone had their own particular plans and desires for the trip as they went aboard the Ferry. Edward and Lillian just sought a degree of normalcy in their lives, and to spend it with their family. Arthur saw it as chance to practice swimming and strengthening his right leg. Florence saw it as a break from the challenge of school, and perhaps an opportunity to flirt with boys on the beach. Bernard and Michael looked forward to playing catch and scouting the upcoming Red Sox season. Marguerite wanted to play in the warm sand, and be with her father, who she had missed so terribly. Akeema looked forward to being by the sea again, where her ancestors had lived for thousands of years. The trip was a meaningful one for all.

The ferry had the capacity to carry up to one hundred people. However, it was still early in the tourist season and the boat was barley one-quarter full. Florence, Akeema, and the younger children climbed the ferry stairs to the second level in order to experience the full effect of the voyage. This meant braving a brisk breeze as the ferry sailed on. Edward and

Lillian preferred to watch the passing sea from the lower deck that was mostly enclosed by large glass windows. Arthur sat beside them, still saddled with his crutch issues.

"It's such a wonderful day, darling," said Lillian.

"Perfect," replied Noble. "We couldn't have ordered up better weather. We won't need our light coats later on."

"Dad," said Arthur, "there are a lot of small islands out here. I don't remember that."

"Well, Arthur," said his father, "we haven't been out here since you were much younger. Those are the Harbor Islands. We sail out east beyond them, and then head southeast for about fifty miles. We'll be there in a little over two hours."

Marguerite had climbed downstairs from the second level, and ran up to her mother. "Mommy, can I buy a soda?"

"Gee, Marguerite, why don't you wait until we get off the ferry?"

"Lilly, we're on a holiday," said Noble. "Let's splurge. Rabbit, here is a nickel. Give it to the man in the white coat over there and buy a soda. But, you have to drink it here, alright?"

"Thank you, Daddy!" as Marguerite ran off for her purchase.

"Edward! You're spoiling that child," said Lillian.

"Oh, Lilly. Rabbit knows it's a special occasion. Look how happy she is!"

"She sure does love her father," exclaimed Lillian. She asked about you every day you were gone at the 'bad place', Edward."

The ferry passed Black Rock Channel, Massachusetts Bay, and on toward the tip of Cape Cod. The Cape is shaped like a giant "U" that forms Cape Cod Bay. On the east tip of the "U" is the small picturesque Provincetown. Since Provincetown is on the southern side of the "U" tip, the ferry would turn abruptly north in order to enter Provincetown Harbor.

The ferry docked at the Provincetown pier, and the Nobles carried their bags onto shore. They walked a short distance to a bicycle rental shop that had just opened for the Saturday tourists. This also took two trips. The group rented seven bicycles and a cart. Noble would have the extra duty of pulling Arthur around with crutches in-hand. All in the party knew how to ride bicycles, although Marguerite was still fairly slow at it. Akeema learned how to ride during her first summer in Boston, since she had never even heard of bicycles before traveling to the continental United States. As she was with all things, Akeema was determined to master the skill. She was now quite good at it.

The Nobles rented bikes with the newest developments, including derailleur gears and hand cable-pull brakes. However, Cape Cod is very flat, so cycling would not be very taxing.

With some difficulty, the Nobles took all their belongings with them on the bicycles to a nearby small hotel on Commercial Street. They already had reservations for their two-day stay, and simply needed to drop off the things they did not immediately need.

The group first went to a small restaurant at the corner of Pearl and Commercial Streets. Noble had never seen eight people eat so much food...even in a naval mess hall. Pancakes, waffles, maple syrup, sausage, hash brown potatoes, eggs in all styles, muffins, bagels, coffee, orange juice, butter, preserves...and more. At the completion of this feast, everyone had completely cleaned off their plates, including seconds. Noble joked with his wife that if this kept up, he would have to get another job just to pay for it all.

The Nobles then rode their bikes south on Commercial Street, north on Cornwell Street, and then north onto Race Point Road. Their journey would only be two miles long, but they traveled slowly with five year old "Rabbit" taking her time.

Noble told Lillian and Arthur, "We'll ride through some beautiful groves of trees after leaving the town itself. We'll pass Blackwater Pond after about one-half mile. In the last thousand feet or so, we'll take Race Point Road through the sand dunes. We'll park our bikes and walk the last 250 feet or so to the beach.

Noble knew the area well. His parents brought him to the north side beach beyond Provincetown in the summers as a child. Some of Noble's fondest memories were of this place.

Cape Cod is known for its sand dunes. The north side of the Cape "U" had an extensive system of dunes that jutted up against the north shore beach. Today, the area was simply gorgeous. The white sand dunes, and the white sand of the beach, formed a striking border with the Cape's green trees and low lying foliage. The deep blue water, punctuated with emerald green areas, shimmered below a blue sky with occasional white clouds. Noble thought it was God's country.

Noble was somewhat winded after hauling his son in the small cart. However, Arthur was smiling like King Arthur while he was drawn by his father. When the "royal" procession ended, it was time for Arthur to go it alone with crutches on the sand. The party of eight set out for the beach.

Out came the beach blankets, umbrellas, beach chairs, and picnic baskets. All within eyeshot of their parents, the younger children headed for the water's edge and the mild surf. Akeema followed the children, but had a look in her eyes as though she was thousands of miles away. Arthur hobbled to the water and began his exercises. Florence wore the newest and smallest style tank top bathing suit, and hoped some boys would see her in it. Today, each of these eight people was in the place they wanted to be.

Over the next hours, Bernard, Michael, and Marguerite were quite industrious. The trio dug holes in sand that quickly filled with seawater, built elaborate sand castles, and waded in the waves. The brothers later played catch on the beach. Arthur took shifts at exercising his right leg and working on a tan. Florence and Akeema took a long walk on the beach.

"Any news on the suffrage issue, Lillian?" asked Noble, while watching his children.

"Well, I keep in touch with the National Woman's Party frequently, as you know. Things are not looking good in the Senate, where opposition to the Nineteenth Amendment is gaining strength. At least the President has seen the error of his ways and now supports the Amendment. I guess he finally believes women can contribute to the country, and therefore can have a say in how its run."

"Do I hear a bit of sarcasm in your voice, Lilly?" said Noble.

"Yes, darling," replied Lillian, "but that, of course, is your forté."

Noble smiled, because he knew it was true. "But, you know, Lilly, I have to say that I am concerned about directions the government has taken this last year. I realize we are at war and that special provisions must be taken. Certainly, even President Lincoln had to make stern measures to keep the Union intact. Still, it is a question of degree."

Noble continued, "The administration's new Sedition Act permits placement of a citizen in prison for twenty years if he or she 'utters, prints, writes or publishes any disloyal, profane, scurrilous, or abusive language about the government of the United States'. Just a simple criticism could land a citizen in jail for a very long time."

"I share your concerns, Edward," said Lillian. "Even our conversion now is contraband. There is no room for any dissention in the government, even if it helps The War effort."

"There are other areas of concern as well," said Noble. "The country is mobilizing in ways that have not been seen since the Civil War. Nearly all Americans would agree the Allies must be victorious in the present confrontation. But, as we seek to protect our free society, we must be careful what follows such a mobilization. The federal government has taken control over much of the lives of citizens for this effort. For example, the War Industries Board tells companies which raw materials they will receive, and how much. It controls all production and prices. The National War Labor Board also tells workers how much they will be paid. The Railroad Administration now dictates every aspect of the railroad industry, and therefore much of the distribution of goods. The Fuel Administration strictly directs all fuel distribution. The Food Administration now governs all pricing, production, and distribution of food. Therefore, at every step in the production of goods and services, and their distribution, the government is in complete control."

Lillian added, "Those of us in the National Woman's Party are also concerned about Wilson's Committee on Public Information. It feeds government-written press releases and stories to the newspapers. It oversees civilian censorship. It has also enlisted the aid of over one hundred thousand people to give government-approved speeches at the beginning of meetings, vaudeville shows, and even movies. We've witnessed such speeches at Boston area nickelodeons."

Noble said, "I just hope the America we knew, and now fight for, returns after this 'Great War'."

"I hope so, too, darling," said Lillian.

Noble replied, "The President has made it clear nothing will stand in his way in The War effort. Wilson has demanded, 'Force! Force to the utmost! Force without stint or limit! The righteous and triumphant Force which shall make Right the law of the world, and cast every selfish dominion down in the dust'. I just hope we don't end up destroying the very thing we hope to preserve."

Noble continued, "But, for now, three of us in this family are in the military. Four million Americans have either been drafted, have joined the armed services, or are about to be drafted. All of us must do what we can to finish this fight and return our nation to the republic we love."

Just then, Marguerite ran up to her parents and said loudly, "Is it lunch time yet?"

Lillian looked at her watch and was surprised at the time. "Why, yes it is, dear." As if the other members of the family were wired together, all of them walked up to the Noble beach "base" and asked the same question. Noble could not believe any of them could be hungry after that huge breakfast, but this was apparently the case.

The picnic baskets were opened, and a second feast began. Sandwiches of every description were consumed. A snack gaining popularity from a New England firm, the Tri-Sum Potato Chip Company, was eaten voraciously from a tin. Potato salad, coleslaw, pickles, pork and beans, cookies, cakes, brownies, and sodas were ingested like there was no tomorrow. Afterwards, the group just lay on their beach blankets "stuffed to the gills", as Arthur said.

Later, Marguerite walked up to Arthur and began to rub his gradually enlarging right leg. "I'm sorry you broke your leg, Arthur," she told her oldest brother. "Does it hurt?"

"Thank you, Marguerite," said Arthur. "Not much now. It did right after the accident, and then again after the cast came off. But, it doesn't that hurt much now. It's just weak from no exercise."

"It doesn't look as much like bones now, Arthur," said Marguerite. "I'll rub it for you." Marguerite's massage actually felt very good, and Arthur gave his sister a big brother hug. Next to her father, the little girl most looked up to Arthur. He was the one that assumed the paternal role when her father went off to war. Arthur hoped she would not be too upset when it was time for him to return to military duties. And that day was coming soon.

Arthur said with a broad smile, "Marguerite, it won't be long before I'll be able to carry you on my shoulders, like I used to. Won't that be great?"

Marguerite let out a big scream in reply, "Yay!" The thought of being carried again on her big brother's shoulders brought on her signature jumping like a rabbit.

Later in the afternoon, the Nobles loaded up their bikes with empty picnic baskets, and rode back to their hotel rooms. They took an evening walk along Commercial Street and watched the sun set to the west. The evening was cool, but only light jackets were required to remain very comfortable. Everyone remarked on how bright the stars were out on the Cape. The group even saw some shooting stars, which made Marguerite scream with delight.

Noble had planned on a light dinner, but that would not be the case. He could not figure out where the hamburgers, hotdogs, relish, ketchup, mustard, root beer floats, and milk shakes all went.

Bedtime neared, and the Nobles returned to the hotel once again. Edward and Lillian had one room, Florence and Akeema a second, and Arthur and the three smaller children a third. After lights were declared out, Arthur secretly told ghost stories to his brothers and little sister. They loved them, and Arthur swore them to secrecy about the after-bedtime tales. He knew Marguerite would tell their parents anyway.

The next morning, the Nobles tried their hands at fishing off one of the Provincetown piers. They rented poles, lines, and bait from a nearby vender, and marched far to the end of the pier. Noble thought perhaps his family was not cut out to be fishermen, since none of them caught anything. However, Akeema did. Noble felt it fitting that a representative of the Yup`ik people in Massachusetts should be the one to catch a 12 lb striped bass with a wire line and worm. Akeema was very solemn about the catch. She handled the fish with grace and care. At one point she bowed her head, closed her eyes, and whispered something in Unaliq.

"Akeema," asked Marguerite, "what's the matter? Is something wrong? Aren't you happy?"

Akeema took some time to answer. Finally, she knelt on her knees with the little girl and said, "Marguerite, my people be-lieve that spirits live within the animals we catch and eat. We must honor them, and respect them, for good fortune to follow us. My ancestors have shown me great honor by permitting this fish spirit to come to me, even in this far away place."

"Are you going to eat the fish?" asked Marguerite.

"Yes," said Akeema, "if your father can help me bring it home correctly. I will make a traditional Yup`ik meal with it. I hope all of you, my wonderful Massachusetts family, will bestow honor by dining with me. I will make a necklace with the fish bones to honor the animal's spirit, and the sign my ancestors have sent me."

Noble said, "Akeema, your explanation is one of the most beautiful things anyone could possibly have said about my family. We'll have the bass packed in ice, wrapped carefully, and we'll carry it in one of the picnic baskets for safe journey." Everyone was moved by Akeema's discussion. Lillian, Florence, and the three small children hugged her. Arthur and Edward shook her hands. They went to the bait and tackle vender to properly pack the bass for transport back to Boston.

By early afternoon, it was time to return home. The rented fishing materials and bicycles were all returned, the bags again packed, and the ferry boarded for Boston Harbor. The three small children slept during the entire return trip, while the five adults watched the sea from the boat. At one point, Akeema sat down beside Noble and said quietly, "Dr. Noble, I want you to know how much it means to me that you and Mrs. Noble have helped me catch, and bring back, this animal. I know it is different from your customs, but it is very meaningful to me. You have shown me and my ancestors great honor. I will say a special prayer for you and your wife every day from now on."

Noble could only smile and pat Akeema gently on the arm. He also felt honored to have participated in a custom that meant so much to the newest member of his family.

On the morning of Monday, April 8th, Noble came by the A.I. Office with his usual rounds. Just as he was about to enter the office, Milton Rosenau dropped by. "Milton," said Noble, "this is a surprise. What's up?"

"Edward, I haven't talked to you in a while, and just wanted to say 'hi'." Rosenau followed Noble into the office."

"Good morning, Major," said Lieutenant Pierre-Louis. "And, good morning Lieutenant Commander. I haven't seen you in some time."

The two men greeted the Lieutenant, and then both went to the center table. Noble read a few of the cables very carefully. After a few moments, he said, "Very interesting."

"What's that, Edward," asked Rosenau.

"Brest, France, has just started to witness an outbreak of influenza," said Noble. "Milton, it's right on schedule."

"What do you mean, Edward?"

"This is exactly what we would expect, Milton, and fits perfectly," said Noble. "We have a specific movement of the infection, proper incubation times, and predicable time courses: From Haskell County, to Camp Funston. From Funston, to several other cantonments. From the cantonments, to adjacent large cities. Also from the camps, to points beyond the United States. So, where would you expect the first epidemic outbreaks in Europe to be?"

"Brest, France?" asked Rosenau.

"Exactly," said Noble. "And, right on time. I have been following small contained influenza endemics in France since I arrived in January. But, this fits perfectly. The French port of entry for American troops is Brest. "

"Any idea about the severity of the infections?" said Rosenau.

"The disease seems to be just like the attenuated form we saw in most of the United States. For the most part, it is pretty mild. In France they are calling it the 'three day grippe'. One of the cables described a French command in Brest that has been incapacitated by influenza. But there are very few reported deaths from it."

"Edward, it is amazing that you have so much information available to you, and so fast. Just amazing."

"No kidding. The other 'amazing' parts of this office are the three Lieutenants that essentially live here, or close to it. They are the heart of the place." Lieutenant Pierre-Louis just looked up and smiled. She was busily translating a French transatlantic telegraph communication.

Noble then went off to the wards, and Rosenau set out for the naval hospital in Chelsea.

On the afternoon of Friday, April 19th, Noble was already in the A.I. Office when the internal phone rang. "Major," said

Lieutenant Pecknold, "It's your wife. She's at the exterior door."

"Great, Lieutenant, have her come in."

Lillian entered the larger office, and said, "Hi, darling. I was on my way to the Harvard satellite laboratory and thought I would drop by. I take it that I still have a security clearance?"

"Still do, Lilly," said her husband. "Lots of interesting things have come into the office today, and in the last few days. Some good, and some less good. First, things were looking good at The Front for a time. The Germans launched another offensive recently, called Operation Georgette. Their aim was to neutralize, or capture, the northern English Channel ports in France, and deny the Allies use of them. However, the Allies halted the German offensive with limited gains by the Central Powers."

"That's a blessing," said Lillian.

"Yes," said Noble, "but the Germans just launched another offensive in the last week, led by Erich von Ludendorff. It has been very successful. They broke through the Allied lines and our troops have been making a quick and serious retreat. Listen to one of the communications from an Allied General to the troops: 'With our backs to the wall, and believing in the justice of our cause, each one of us must fight to the end. The safety of our homes and the freedom of mankind depend alike upon the conduct of every one at this moment'."

"Edward, that sounds positively awful," said Lillian.

"Things do sound bleak, Lillian," said Noble. "But, then one of the twists and turns of fate occurred. Just as the Germans were making great gains against the Allies, they too were hit with influenza. Listen to this intercepted communication from Ludendorff to Berlin: 'It was a grievous business having to listen every morning to the chiefs of staff's recital of the number of influenza cases, and their complaints about the weakness of their troops'. There is independent confirmation of the effect of influenza on German fighting readiness from, guess who? "

"Who," asked Lillian, completely engrossed in the discussion.

"None-other than our friend Harvey Cushing," said Noble. "Listen to his cable to me from yesterday:"

> *Thursday, April 18, 1918*
> From: Base Hospital No. 5
>
> Edward. The expected third phase of the great German offensive gets put off from day to day. I gather that the epidemic of grippe which hit us rather hard in Flanders hit the Germans even worse, and this may have caused the delay. Keep us all in your prayers, good friend.
>
> Colonel Harvey Cushing, BEF.

"You know, Edward," said Lillian, "Harvey never talks this way in his letters with his wife, Katharine. She has read to me many of his letters, and they don't go into any of the dangers."

"Lilly," said Noble, "I'm sure he wants to spare her any pain. Also, he knows I have a security clearance, and we can write freely. The things he talks about with me would never pass the military censors to his home in Brookline with Katharine. Nevertheless, the German offensive in France has stalled, and that may be due in part to the epidemic. It would appear that both the Central Powers and Allied forces are affected."

"That brings us to the other 'front'," said Noble. "There are interesting developments in that regard. On April 10th, the rank-and-file regular French army was hit with the influenza epidemic. Only shortly thereafter, the British army was hit hard by the infection. Within the last few days, Paris itself has seen the epidemic."

"Truly interesting, Edward," said Lillian. "I have to use a mental picture of my high school geography, but it sounds like the epidemic is spreading in concentric circles."

"Very astute of you, my dear," said Noble. "Now I know why I married you," he said with a grin. Lillian played like she hit his shoulder.

"I married you, and don't forget it," laughed Lillian. Lieutenant Pecknold laughed with her.

"Lillian, you might be interested to know that the Allied press has now taken a new name for the epidemic," said Noble. "They call it the 'Spanish flu'."

Lillian, the epidemiologist, had to interject her thoughts at this point. "Looking at the influenza epidemic information that you have synthesized, one can see how the name 'Spanish flu' would be created. However, Spain is officially neutral in The War, correct?"

"Yes, Lillian," said Noble. "Correct."

"So," Lillian continued, "the Spanish press doesn't have the same censorship that the French, German, and British governments have imposed on their newspapers."

"Correct again, Lilly," said Noble. "You can add American government censorship of the press, also. As far as I can see, in A.I. Office communications regarding The War, there is no Spanish press censorship at all. There was even wide press coverage in the last week of Spanish King Alphonse XIII and his family's serious illnesses with the grippe."

"Both the Allies and the Central Powers don't want to let on there has been any reduction in fighting capacity. So, very little appears in their respective newspapers. The Spanish, however, are free to report all the various details of the influenza epidemic. It would be simple wrong to conclude the epidemic is 'Spanish' in origin. I'm sure there are those in the Allied military and governments that are not discouraging this perception."

"As always, Lilly," said her husband, "you're analysis is right-on-the-money. 'Spanish flu' is a misnomer, and few want to change that name given to this epidemic. Well, I must be off to the wards, darling. I'll see you later."

"Don't forget about tomorrow," said Lillian. "Tomorrow is the 'big day'."

"How could I possibly forget, Lillian," said Noble. "Tomorrow is Red Sox day."

CHAPTER 10

Saturday, April 20th, was the first opportunity Noble had to take his family to the new season's Boston Red Sox baseball game. Normally, they would have taken the subway to Fenway Park. But this year, with Arthur's debility, the family Ford was once again pressed into service.

It was a pleasant clear New England spring afternoon, with an expected high of 75° F. After the long winters in the northeast, Boston always came alive in the spring. New Englanders hid away in their homes four to five months a year, and then showed an explosion of human activity in the spring. Everyone was looking forward to the sights, sounds, and smells of the ballpark.

Noble drove the Ford to the Fenway-Kenmore neighborhood on Yawkey Way, where Fenway Park was located. Bernard and Michael always referred to the park as "The Fens". The family parked the car and walked to the front of the park. The long two story high brick structure at The Fens entrance always looked like a warehouse to Noble. However, long brightly colored American League flags hanging on the facade gave the structure away as a real major league ballpark.

The family made its way to their favorite seats. The Nobles always sat along the left foul line at third base, and a few rows up from field level. Edward, Marguerite, Lillian, and Florence sat in a row immediately in front of the row where Bernard, Akeema, Michael, and Arthur were seated. Bernard and Michael had strategically placed Akeema between them. Akeema was still learning about this game called baseball, and the two brothers were going to be her tutors today.

Noble asked his youngest child next to him, "Can you see alright, Rabbit? What is your favorite part of the baseball games?"

Smiling and laughing all the while, Marguerite said, "I can see OK, Daddy. I like the hotdogs, and when they hit the ball really high."

"Me too, Rabbit," said her father.

Lillian motioned to a vendor selling the usual hotdogs, pretzels, Cracker Jacks, popcorn, and sodas, and began to empty his inventory. It would be another feast for the Nobles.

Noble turned over his right shoulder and said, "Arthur, it looks like you're really coming along with your rehab."

"You're right, Dad," said Arthur. "I weight-bear on my right leg now for several minutes at a time. I can walk short distances, too. It just tires quickly, so it really is an endurance issue at this point. But, my calf circumference is nearly fifty percent larger since February, and I have full extension and flexion of my right knee. The orthopedist says I will be able to return to full duty in about a month."

"That's great, Arthur," said his father. "You really have done a marvelous job of rehabilitation. It will be wonderful to see you 'normal' again, if you can ever be called normal." Both Noble and his son laughed. Arthur played like he was going to punch his father in the head.

Bernard then called out to all eight people in the party, "OK, everyone. For those of you who don't follow the game as Michael and Arthur do, we are going to help you all during the game."

"Oh, great," whispered Florence to her mother, seated to her left.

Bernard continued, "Opening day for the Red Sox was just five days ago, here at The Fens. The Red Sox played a three game series with Philadelphia, and won all three games. They have played two games of a five game series with New York, and have won both of them. So, the Red Sox are five-for-five, this season. We are off to a great season, ladies and gentlemen!"

Michael said, "Bernard, I think you should be an announcer for the team!"

Noble turned around to his seat and asked Bernard and Michael, "Boys, who is your favorite player this year?"

Bernard and Michael looked at each other in amazement. Michael said, "You're kidding, right, Dad? Are you serious?"

"Really. Who is your favorite player?" asked Noble again.

Bernard said, "The pitcher, Dad. Look out there at the team warming up."

Noble saw a young man who he estimated to be 6 feet 2 inches tall, and weighing perhaps 220 lbs. He had a fast ball that made a zipping sound in the air, and a sharp crack as it slammed into the catcher's mitt. "Who's that," asked Noble.

Both boys just shook their heads; appalled at the lack of knowledge their father displayed. "Dad," said Bernard, "it's the 'Bambino'. 'The Colossus'. The 'Sultan of Swing'. The 'Babe'. He's Babe Ruth, dad."

"He sure has a great arm, guys," said Noble.

"He's great, Dad," said Bernard. "In the 1916 season he had the third most wins in the American League, threw the most shutouts with a total of six, and was the earned-runs-per-innings-pitched leader. And, he was only twenty years old. Last year he had the second most wins in the league and was the complete game leader. He's a 'whizz-bang' player!"

"Wait until he gets a chance to bat, Dad," said Michael. He had the best batting average on the team last year, with an average of .325. The team average was .246, and only two other players were even in the three-hundreds. He led the major leagues with a .555 slugging percentage, and tied for the American League lead with eleven home runs. The Babe tied for second in doubles, and tied for third in runs batted in. And, he accomplished all of that with seventy-five to one hundred fifty fewer plate appearances than his opponents."

"He's our <u>favorite</u>, dad," said Bernard. "He's A-1, and he is going places!"

Akeema asked, "I really don't know what all those numbers mean. Do I need to know all of that to know who wins the game?"

"No," said Michael. "The stats just help you to know who is doing the best job. Knowing who wins is easier, and we'll help you with that." The brothers were pleased they could teach something to a woman who spoke five languages fluently.

Everyone said the Pledge of Allegiance to the American flag at the beginning of the game, and listened to a short speech about The War. The boys helped Akeema with the rules of the game, and by the 6th inning she was screaming for the "Sox" like everyone else at The Fens. During the 7th inning stretch, another round of baseball cuisine was ordered and consumed in the fullest measure. Also, everyone sang along to a song by Jack Norworth called *Take Me Out to the Ballgame* that had become very popular amoung fans.

During the game, Florence enjoyed a break from nursing school, and talked to a number of boys from Westchester who were as interested in her as they were with the game. Edward and Lillian held hands during most of the game, and felt so blessed to have another weekend with their whole family. Arthur felt a new sense of vitality as the end of his convalescence was in sight. He would soon be as active as the Red Sox and Yankees had been today. The Red Sox won the 6th game of the season with the Yankees, 4-2. The Sox were now six-for-six, and the Noble boys sang *Take Me Out to the Ballgame* all the way back to Beacon Street. Akeema sang right along with them, being a new baseball fan.

On Wednesday, May 1ˢᵗ, Noble was scheduled to round with his South Department team. The most senior member of the team, aside from Dr. Noble, was Dr. David Schafer who was a second year medical resident at Boston City Hospital. Schafer was a smart and affable young man with neatly combed blond hair and an intense interest in golf. He was raised in Stockton, California, located in the Great Central Valley. He had graduated with honors from the Medical Department of the University of California in San Francisco, and had decided to continue his medical education in Boston. Like most physicians in training, Shafer had joined the military and was a Second Lieutenant in the Army. Noble had seen talent in Schafer when he was an intern, and had taken an immediate liking to him.

Noble met his team on the South Department, at the designated place, and at the designated time. "Good morning, lady and gentlemen. What do you have for me today?" said Noble.

The group consisted of Dr. Schafer, an intern, and two medical students. One medical student was from Harvard, and the other was from Boston University (BU). Dr. Schafer had chosen one of the medical students to present the team's case. All four were dressed smartly with waist length white coats, name tags, and stethoscopes around their shoulders. Noble had a white coat that was mid-thigh length. In Boston City, only attending physicians and third year residents wore the longer coats. This was a sign of their stature in the hospital hierarchy.

The chosen young woman from BU stepped forward and said, "Doctor, our patient is the third bed from the back, on the left side of the ward." She walked swiftly to the bedside, with the rest following. The student picked up the chart at the foot of the bed, and began to speak.

"Good morning, Mrs. Spistosky. I would like you to meet our attending physician, Dr. Noble." The student then addressed the group surrounding the woman's hospital bed. "Mrs. Spistosky is a 22 year old woman who has intermittent severe fatigue, as well as severe joint pain of the small joints of the hands and wrists. This includes swelling, tenderness, and occasionally joint effusions. She was admitted to Boston City yesterday morning because of severe pleuritic chest pain. Physical examination shows normal vital signs, some swelling of her hand joints, and a clear chest. Her white blood cell count is 3.5 K/μL, platelet count is 95 K/μL, and the blood hemoglobin is 35 g/dL. The urinalysis is normal. Blood cultures are so far negative, and a gram stain of the blood was negative. Roentgenograms of the hands only show some soft tissue swelling, and those of the chest show very small bilateral pleural effusions."

"What do you think is going on?" said Noble.

"Well, sir, we aren't really sure. We think that she may have an occult infection, or perhaps rheumatoid arthritis. She feels better with the codeine we have given her."

"What are you planning to do next?"

The student replied, "We are thinking of performing a thoracentesis, in order to remove fluid from the pleural lung space for culture.

Noble said, "I'm glad you are treating her pain. Remember what Ambrose Pare said about the true mission of the physician: 'To cure occasionally, to relieve often, and to comfort always'." Noble turned to the patient and said, "Hello, Mrs. Spistosky. How are you feeling today?"

"I feel better, Doctor. The medicine they are giving to me is helping."

Listening to the patient speak, and knowing her name, Noble asked, "Are you from Russia?"

"Yes. My parents brought us to America when we were children."

Noble noted to himself that she was not of European descent.

"Mrs. Spistosky, how often do you have these episodes of joint pain, swelling, and chest pain?"

"Every couple of months, doctor. It's pretty painful."

"Do you ever have any rashes?"

"Why, yes. If I am in the sun, I sometimes get a rash on my face. Then it goes away."

Noble motioned with his hand on his own face about his checks and the bridge of his nose. The patient nodded yes.

Noble continued, "Do you ever have any mouth sores?"

"Yes, doctor. In fact, I have a small one now."

"Any headaches?"

"All the time, doctor."

The medical students and residents looked at one another. They had forgotten to ask these questions of the patient.

Dr. Noble then quickly examined the patient. He looked at her skin, her eyes, and saw a small aphthous ulcer on the inside of her left check. He listened to her chest, palpated her abdomen, and noted some slight swelling of the bilateral hand joints and wrists. He did a neurological examination. He then looked at her Roentgenograms, and noticed the normal hand joints and the slight soft tissue swelling about them. The chest roentgenogram was in fact normal, accept for the small pleural effusions.

"Well, the patient most likely does not have an infection. Please do a Wassermann Test. This is a test devised to see if blood antibodies to syphilis will react to bovine muscle cardiolipin. I predict the test will be either negative or very weakly positive."

The chief resident asked, "Dr. Noble, what do you think the patient's disorder is?"

"The patient most likely has lupus erythematosus. This is most consistent with the findings of repeated non-destructive arthritis, photosensitivity, a malar "butterfly" rash upon her face by history, bucal mucosal aphthous ulcers, headaches, fatigue, pancytopenia, pleurisy, and pleural effusions. Given the lack of cardiac, renal, and serious neurologic findings, her disease involvement at this point is only moderate. That, plus her gender, gives her a better prognosis."

"What should we do now, Dr. Noble?" asked Dr. Schafer.

"The literature shows from 24 years ago that quinine, when used with a disease flair, can be effective therapy. Twenty years ago, salicylates used with quinine was shown to help calm the symptoms. Please start therapy as soon as you can."

Noble excused himself from the team after completing rounds, and went off to the A.I. Office. Second Lieutenant Pecknold was on duty at the time. Noble said, "Hi, Lieutenant, how are things?"

"Pretty good, sir. Can I help you with something?"

"Lieutenant," said Noble, "I realize this is not official Army business, but I wonder if you could send a cable message to the Boston City Hospital Administration?"

"No problem, sir. What's the message?"

"Please remind the administration that the South Department has an allocation of money in the annual budget for new equipment. The hospital doesn't have an Einthoven electrocardiographic device that is now common in the Netherlands. Even many New England hospitals have the device. In order to better diagnose heart ailments, using Einthoven's P, Q, R, S, and T deflection scheme, we need the "ECG" to interpret heart electrical activity of specific patients. The cost is relatively modest, and the cardiac examination only requires a patient to put his or her arms, and left leg, into containers with salt solutions. The literature is clear that much can be learned about symptoms of chest pain and syncope with this device. I simply want to add this modest request to the budget. Since we have far more allocated to us than we have yet spent in 1918, this is a minimal request."

"Major, I'll send this via cable right now," said the Lieutenant.

On Saturday, May 25th, the Nobles decided to take in a cinema matinee. Movies were extremely popular. The War had only intensified the desire to spend time in a darkened room with moving pictures, and an accompanying piano or organ. Hollywood was producing over 800 silent movies a year, so the selection for the public was immense. Entrepreneurs were creating movie theaters out of vacant buildings, placing chairs in them, and showing motion pictures for a nickel per person. These establishments were called nickelodeons. Young men and women followed a new group of actors called "movie stars" in tabloids, like *Photoplay*, closer than they did the President of the United States.

The Nobles loaded the clan into the Ford once again, and drove from Back Bay to the downtown area. There were several nickelodeons in operation, but the Nobles preferred one with a large pipe organ and "feature length" films that could last two hours or more. Their favorite nickelodeon sold popcorn, sodas, and small sandwiches during the show which were irresistible to the whole crew. On the drive along Commonwealth Avenue, all five Noble children, and Akeema, discussed in detail the personal lives of movies stars that "everyone" knew. The stars included Mary Pickford, Douglas Fairbanks, Charlie Chaplin, and D.W. Griffith. Edward and Lillian had not even heard of most of them. Arthur, Florence, and Akeema wanted to see the 1917 film *Bathing Beauties*, with a young actress named Gloria Swanson. But, this was felt to be too much for the younger children.

The group parked the car and met Harvey Cushing's wife Katharine, and her three youngest children, for the cinema. The group paid to enter the theater, and found seats near the front row. First, there was a political speech by a local "Minute Man". This was followed by sing-along songs and comedian jokes from actors who also performed vaudeville in the downtown area. Then, there was an eleven minute film called *The Bond*, starring Charlie Chaplin and Edna Purviance. Edward, Lillian, and Katharine all knew it was a propaganda film produced for the Liberty Load Committee to help sell U.S. Liberty Bonds for The War. The story was a series of sketches humorously illustrating various bonds in life: the bond of friendship, the bone of marriage, and Liberty Bonds to knock out the Kaiser. Charlie Chaplin "knocked out" the Kaiser in the film.

With the short film completed, the Nobles watched a double feature. The first very popular 1918 film was a western called *Squaw Man*. The second was also a 1917 favorite called *The Immigrant*, with Charlie Chaplin. The family hissed and booed the bad guys, and cheered and applauded the good guys. They all had a marvelous time.

After the films, the Cushing family went to the Noble Beacon Street home to visit for a few hours. In the sitting room, with glasses of California wine, Katharine Cushing mentioned to Noble, "Harvey tells me you have been conversing with him very regularly since you arrived in France."

"Yes," said Noble, "we have kept in good contact. Harvey sounds good, and of course, always mentions you and the children. I know he is very eager to return to Brookline."

"You know," said Katharine, "Harvey thinks the world of you. He hopes you will come to Harvard with him after The War."

"That is so kind, Katharine," said Noble. "However, I so much look forward to resuming my practice in Boston and continuing my long association with Boston City Hospital. Besides, with Harvard running the clinical aspects of the hospital, I can see Harvey all the time anyway."

Just then, Marguerite ran up to the adults with her stereo photo viewer. "Look at the Grand Canyon!" she exclaimed while jumping. Each adult in turn looked at a marvelous colorized 3-dimentional view of the canyon through Marguerite's stereo picture viewer.

"That's beautiful, Marguerite!" said Katharine. "Do you have a favorite stereo picture?"

"I think my favorite is the Pyramids of Egypt," said Marguerite, as she showed the canyon to Betsey and Barbara Cushing.

In the sitting room corner, Bernard, Michael, and Henry Cushing played marbles. They also talked of the Red Sox 3 to 2 win over the Chicago White Sox that day. This gave the Red Sox a 21 to 12 record for the season, and put them three games ahead in the American League. The Boys were quite pleased.

In another corner of the large room, Florence and Arthur discussed various political questions of the day. They considered the direction of The War, and whether America entered The War too soon or too late. Topics like child labor and women's suffrage were not controversial, since both of them agreed on those points. Akeema listened intently to their discussion. She thought to herself that men and women in her own tribe had similar open political deliberations. Yup`ik women were very vocal about important tribal issues, and were unrestricted in their views.

A little later, Arthur played a few chess games with Akeema. She had learned the game quickly, and never made the same strategic mistake twice. He was resigned to the fact that she would soon be able to beat him without much effort. However, this did not concern him that much, because Akeema was "family". The Nobles kept completion amoung family members within a healthy perspective.

On Friday, May 31st, Noble relaxed in the A.I. Office during an unusually slow day at the South Department. The wards were uncharacteristically flush with empty beds, so he had told his residents and medical students to take a walk outside and enjoy the warm spring sunshine. Noble had become very accustomed to the A.I. Office, and it seemed in many ways like his second home. He was reading a few new medical journals delivered that day to the office, when Lieutenant Lafayette said, "Major, the sentry called. There is a carrier here with a message for you."

"Have the carrier bring it into the small office, Lieutenant," said Noble. A boy brought an envelope to Noble, who was at his desk. He opened it, and found it was a response to his request for an Einthoven ECG heart machine. The application for the funds was a formality, since Noble had the authority to purchase some needed South Department equipment. Very little of the discretionary funds had even been spent. Noble's eyes widened. His request had been denied. Why? By whom? At the bottom of the message was the signature of the denying Trustee member: Commander Richard Cunard.

Noble was a controlled man, and rarely deviated from restraints on his own language. But, this time he removed restraints and said loudly, "Damn!" Noble walked into the larger office.

"Major...are you alright?" asked the Lieutenant. She had never heard the Major swear before.

"I'm fine Lieutenant," said Noble. "But of all the petty, little, and malicious things... This was not really a denial of the ECG machine purchase. This was a slap at me."

"Sir?" said the Lieutenant.

"Never mind, Lieutenant," said Noble. "I'm just venting." Noble walked over to the large central table and began to read newly arrived messages to take his mind off Cunard's latest rebuff of him. What he read on the top military world stack made him forget all about the ECG machine.

Friday, May 31, 1918
From: French Command

1,018 French Army recruits in small French station. 688 hospitalized with Spanish flu. Forty-nine dead in few days.

US Army Intelligence.

Noble thought to himself that nearly sixty-eight percent of an army company was hospitalized. More importantly, five percent of an entire population, consisting of healthy vibrant young men, suddenly died. And, they died of influenza in a very short period of time. This was unusual. But what did it mean? Was the communication correct? Was this really influenza? Was it really in days? He filed this away in his mind for future review and analysis. But the next message caused him to pause as well.

Friday, May 31, 1918
From: British First Army

Summary of May British First Army Spanish flu: 36,473 soldiers hospitalized, tens of thousands sickened.

British Expeditionary Force

This was an unusually large number of very ill influenza patients. It was even more unusual to have such late seasonal influenza. Not impossible, but unusual. And the patients were so young. This is why the next cable was even more worrisome.

Friday, May 31, 1918
From: U.S. Public Health Service

Analysis of recent March/April influenza epidemic in Louisville, Kentucky. Higher than average deaths. Forty percent of deaths were in ages between 20 and 35.

USPHS

Noble would have to wait for details in order to ask Lillian to do statistical analyses of this Louisville observation. However, a quick calculation showed these findings to be a statistical extraordinary. Or were they simply an anomaly? Were these isolated events Noble could read because of his remarkable access to information? Or was there a connection? He thought back to his visit with Dr Miner in Haskell County. What he saw in Haskell was similar to Louisville, only earlier. Was there more to the recent U.S. epidemic than even Noble had deduced?

Noble read conflicting army intelligence cables on May 31st. The mild form of influenza arrived in Bombay, India, by way of a British troop transport. It had then spread along railroad lines to Calcutta, Madras, and Rangoon. Another transport delivered it to Karachi. It also reached Shanghai, China, at about the same time. Similar reports were coming in from Algeria, Egypt, and Tunisia. These places described the epidemic as "the three day fever", as it was called in similar ways in the United States during the spring. What did this mean?

That Saturday, June 1st, Noble told Lillian of the recent cables. As any good epidemiologist and statistician would say, she would need more data before meaningful projections could be made. Nevertheless, they talked about possible implications for the United States. Noble told his wife, "Lilly, if there was a public health emergency in America, we are completely unprepared for it."

"Do you really think so, Edward?" said Lillian sounding worried.

"In about one year, the military has grown from less than 800 physicians in the army and navy, to over 30,000. Virtually all of the medical school graduates from 1914, 1915, and 1916 are now in the military, and most are in Europe. These are some of America's finest doctors. In fact, nearly all the physicians left in civilian life are elderly, and trained before medical education reforms were put into place. Many of them are not even competent."

"The situation sounds dire," said Lillian.

"There's more bad news, Lilly," said Noble. Many of our best medical schools have sent their entire faculties under uniform as intact units to France. Johns Hopkins did this, and so has Harvard. That is why Harvey Cushing is at the 'Harvard Unit', Base Hospital No. 5, in Camiers, France. Many of our best medical researchers are no longer in the country. American medical research capacity has been cut to the bone."

"We still have nurses available, right?" said Lillian,

"Actually," said Noble, "the situation with nursing in the U.S. is worse still. Even the large medical centers, like Boston City Hospital, have barely enough nurses to fill needed shifts. Conditions in the general community are much worse than that. The War has gutted the availability of U.S. Public Health Service nursing. As if these circumstances aren't bad enough, The War effort has depleted the nation's reserves of medical supplies and equipment. Everything from bandages to morphine are in short supply."

"We'll just have to pray for an end to The War, and soon," said Lillian.

Noble added, "And, we need to pray for peace with the microbes." It sounded like a joke, but he was never more serious.

CHAPTER 11

Noble arrived at early Boston City Hospital on Friday, June 7th. The census in the South Department had increased markedly, and he desired an early start on the day's work. In addition, his son Arthur was now deemed officially rehabilitated and fit for duty. Noble wanted to spend Friday evening with his family, since Arthur would be leaving for Camp Devens the next morning.

When Noble entered the first ward for rounds, his usual team was waiting for him. "Good morning, Dr. Noble," said Dr. David Schafer.

"Good morning, Dr. Schafer," said Noble. Lowering his voice slightly, Noble said, "David, you only have three weeks left as a second year resident. On July 1st you start your third year. Are you ready for the 'long coat'?" Noble was referring to the mid-thigh length white coats worn by third year medical residents and attending physicians. It was a mark of authority, but also of increased responsibility.

"Well, sir," said Schafer, "I'm as ready as I'll ever be. I have to admit that it's a little scary…being a senior resident,

I mean. But, I promise to do the very best job I can. I only hope that I can finish most of the third year before I am sent to Europe."

"You'll do great, David," said Noble. "You are ready." Noble didn't comment further on the issue of completing the third medical residency year. That was because he felt it was very likely Second Lieutenant Schafer would be in France by the end of the year, or earlier.

"So, what's our first case, lady and gentlemen?" asked Noble.

"Dr. Noble," said the team's intern, "Do you have a minute to see one of my outpatient clinic patients before we round on the wards? I think I need some help with him."

"Sure," said Noble, who was always eager to help, and eager for a clinical challenge. Noble walked with the whole team down a short first floor hallway and into one of Boston City Hospital's outpatient clinics. The intern led them to one of several small exam rooms. Two medical students were already interviewing the patient as the team entered.

"Mr. Olson," said the intern, "This is Dr. Noble. Do you mind if he takes a peak at you?"

"No, not at all".

The intern then recounted the patient's history for the group. "Mr. Olson is a 42 year old man who has had a chronic cough productive of yellow sputum for a couple of months, a slight decrease in his appetite, and a tendency to fatigue very easily. He has no other medical history. He denies any fevers, chills, or night sweats. He has had no fevers during his clinic visits. His hemoglobin is only low-normal at 11 g/dL. His other blood tests, urinalysis, blood cultures, and a chest Roentgenogram are all normal."

Noble approached the patient while saying, "Hello, Mr. Olson. I'm Doctor Noble. Pleased to meet you. I can tell from your hands that you work with abrasives?"

"Yes, sir. I'm a mason."

"Have you lost any weight?"

"I've lost seven or eight pounds over the last couple of months."

"Have you coughed up any blood?"

"No, sir."

" In the last few months have you had any headaches, loss of consciousness, visual changes, shortness of breath, chest pain, abdominal pain, nausea, vomiting, diarrhea, constipation, or blood in your stool?"

No, sir."

Dr. Noble looked at the patient's eyes and mouth, felt for lymph nodes, auscultated and percussed the man's chest, palpated his abdomen, checked his genitals, felt his muscles and joints, and looked all about his skin. He then looked at the man's Roentgenogram.

Noble noticed a spittoon on the floor near the patient. "Did you cough up that sputum recently?" pointing to the spittoon.

"Yes, sir. Just a few minutes ago."

"Can you cough up some more deeply?"

"I'll try, Doctor." The patient proceeded to forcefully cough several times, and deposited the sputum into the spittoon.

Noble picked up the spittoon and told the students and residents, "This is going to take some time, people. Why don't you attend to other patients on the ward for now. I'll call you back when I'm finished."

Noble walked out of the exam room, down the hall, and stopped at a small room with a "Clinical Laboratory" sign on the door. Inside the room was a small table with a microscope and several colored bottles. The table was very similar to the one Noble used on the USS Madawaska. He used an inoculating loop to spread sputum on four glass slides, applied carbol fuchsin, and placed them over a beaker of water. He set the beaker on a hot plate resting on the table, and brought the water to a boil for five minutes. He let the slides cool, and washed off the stain with tap water. Drops of acid-alcohol were applied until the alcohol ran clear, and the slides were once again rinsed with tap water. He applied the methylene blue counterstain for two minutes, and rinsed with tap water a final time. The slides were then blotted with bibulous paper.

Noble then methodically examined the slides under the microscope with oil emersion and cover slips. He spent nearly thirty-five minutes on the examination.

The two students and resident were speaking to a clinic patient when Dr. Noble popped his head into the exam room. "When you are able, come down to the Clinical Lab. I have something I want to show you."

A few minutes later, the team and the two clinic medical students joined Noble in the little lab room. Noble asked one of the students to look into the microscope viewer and tell the group what she saw. "Well...I...really don't see anything, Dr. Noble," said the student.

"Look closer," said Noble. "Tell me exactly what you see."

After a few moments of intense study, the student said. "Well, the microscope field is blue, with a few blue clumps."

"Anything else?" asked Noble.

"Well...there are two tiny specks of red. Elongated specks."

"Very good," said Noble. Those are bacillus. Acid-fast bacillus, using the Ziehl-Neelsen stain. The bacilli have a thick lipoidal wall that resists staining. However, once a stain penetrates the wall, it cannot be removed even with vigorous use of acid-alcohol. Hence the name 'acid-fast'. There are sometimes so few bacilli that it takes some study to find them. Nevertheless, the patient has tuberculosis.

"But the patient has very few classical signs or symptoms of TB, Dr. Noble," stated the intern.

"Very true, doctor," said Noble. But, there were enough positive and negative clues in his history, physical examination, and lab data, to make TB a possibility. Remember that pertinent negatives in your inquisition are as important as positives. One interesting historical item is the fact that the patient is a mason. He may have a sub-clinical degree of pulmonary silicosis that is profession-related. Pre-existing silicosis is associated with a thirty-fold increase in TB."

Noble went on, "Two researchers, Albert Calmette and Camille Guérin, successfully immunized cows against an attenuated bovine-strain of tuberculosis in 1906. I had the pleasure to meet them once at an Internal Medicine meeting in New York. The vaccine is called "BCG" for "Bacillus of Calmette and Guérin". I hear they plan to test the vaccine in humans in a few years in France."

The resident sincerely thanked Noble for his help. Noble then excused himself from the group. Although he was pleased that he could assist in the care of the patient, Noble felt no joy. In fact, he felt depressed. He knew that there was no adequate treatment for tuberculosis. Surgically induced pneumothorax, or the plombage technique that collapse an infected lung to "rest" it, were of little value. Mr. Olson would likely be committed for months or even years to a sanitarium for tuberculosis. Even if he received the best care available, he still had a 50% chance of dying of his infection. There was little to celebrate with the diagnosis.

Later in the morning, Noble made his usual stop at the A.I. Office and greeted Lieutenant Pierre-Louis. Noble had been studying cables for some time when Lieutenant Commander Milton Rosenau and Lillian dropped by. Rosenau and Lillian entered the office smiling, but found a very serious Noble poring over messages. Noble's mood could even be described as dark. "Hi, Edward," said Rosenau, "is something wrong?"

"Hi, Milton," said Noble with a slight frown. "Hi, dear," Noble said to his wife, as he gave her a small hug. "Have a seat." The three went into the small office. Rosenau and Lillian sat on the sofa. Noble sat at the small desk facing them.

"The epidemic influenza we saw this spring in the U.S. continues to spread in Europe. Most of the reports speak of the mild 'grippe' experienced in most of the United States. In the 'concentric circles' you mentioned before, Lilly, the epidemic has reached Portugal, England, Scotland, Wales, Germany, and Greece. An identical disease has now been described in parts of China. But there are new reports that I have been seeing over the last week. These reports are sketchy, poorly verified, and incomplete at best. But the troubling thing is that there are now several of them."

"What kind of reports?" asked Rosenau.

"Well, there are intelligence reports of a 'curious epidemic resembling influenza'. However, it is violent. Very violent, and is similar to descriptions given to me in Kansas by Dr. Loring Miner. They talk of an illness with an extreme cyanosis, very high fevers, and intense 'air-hunger' by its victims. And it kills. It kills fast. People are dead in twenty-four to forty-eight hours."

"Where is this happening, Edward?" asked Lillian.

"I mentioned to you the outbreak less than two weeks ago in a French new recruit camp. But, on June 3rd, sporadic reports mentioned a very similar 'strange illness' in Spain. Then, just two days ago, there was a report from Copenhagen about 'women dropping in the streets'. Some of these reports have even made their way into the back pages of the *New York Times*. But the *Times* ascribed these serious illnesses to 'undernourishment' in the affected populations. One article was entitled 'German Hunger Spreads Disease'. In view of classified army intelligence briefs I've read, I believe the military media censors are using propaganda to lessen public concern and avoid harm to moral."

Noble continued, "Highly classified cables today referred to 'the mysterious sickness now prevalent in Spain, comes from Germany, and will doubtless soon reach other countries'. The report describes German workers dying at their tasks 'from lack of nourishment'. Army cables have mentioned the German construction of multiple new hospitals east of The Front solely to deal with the 'new' disease. Intelligance reports have also stated that a 'mysterious' disease is decimating the Romanian civilian population. I must conclude that there is more to these reports than rumor."

"What do you think is happening, Edward?" said Rosenau.

"No one can be sure, Milton," said Noble. "There is almost no hard data on which to study. It's not known how the army is obtaining this information, and if it these reports are simply local occurrences or something more generalized. At this point, I only have sets of symptoms together with more precise epidemiological observations on the present influenza epidemic in Europe."

"Any theories, Edward?" said Lillian.

"Yes, I have a theory. I saw a violent form of influenza in Haskell County three months ago. Additional detailed observations were made by a very competent physician there. I have no idea if this disorder actually started there, or came from somewhere else. However, with all the information at my disposal through the A.I. Office, there were no similar reports before Haskell."

Noble went on, "We know that influenza does change over time. Such changes have been witnessed with seasonal influenza, and pandemics, as occurred in 1889-1890. My theory is that an attenuated and less lethal form of influenza made its way from Haskell to Camp Funston, and then quickly spread to the rest of the United States. In short order, the attenuated form traveled to Europe along with hundreds of thousands of American troops. Three months after Haskell County, the attenuated form is epidemic in Europe and now Asia."

"But, something has changed," said Noble. "Something dramatic and alarming. This is just a theory, but I believe the attenuated influenza form has mutated back to a more virulent type. Unlike Haskell County, with one of the lowest population densities in the eastern half of the United States, the new virulent form is in the very densely populated European continent. And, it is spreading."

"My God, Edward," said Lillian. "My God. And, if you are correct...it's coming back."

There was silence amoung the three in the small office. Noble could see tears forming in his wife's eyes. He saw Rosenau's jaw muscles clench as he began to process what he was hearing. Noble's own pulse rose as he felt his heart beating against the inner wall of his chest. He held tightly onto a pencil with his right hand as his knuckles turned white. The pencil snapped into two pieces. He hadn't felt the impact of his theory until he actually heard himself say it.

"Edward," said Rosenau, "what are you going to do?"

"First," exclaimed Noble, "I am going to pray that I am damn wrong. This theory is based on the most minimal data, and even those aren't well substantiated. However, if I am correct, it is likely there are only three people in the world who are seeing the full picture here. And, those three people are sitting in this little army intelligence office right now."

Noble persisted, "I need to raise the issue of United States port quarantine to the highest levels of both the military and the government. Since we really don't know what we are dealing with here, this is our only hope. It just happens to be the same recommendation that I made after my Camp Funston trip, and that both of you made to the Pneumonia Commission. However, there is now a new sense of extreme urgency. There is no time to lose."

The three discussed the need to keep today's discussion highly confidential, and the proper channels would be used to make their case for strict quarantines. Rosenau and Lillian left for the Harvard satellite laboratory, and Noble walked back into the large office.

"Lieutenant," said Noble, "I have a cable to send to Colonel Victor Vaughn, and it is of the highest priority and security."

"Yes, sir," said Lieutenant Pierre-Louis. "I'm ready when you are, sir." Noble then began to dictate a long and detailed cable to his commanding officer. As she transcribed his words, Noble could see a gradually deepening fear on the Lieutenant's face. But, as a dedicated Signal Corps Army officer, she did not miss a word to be sent.

That evening at the Noble home, Arthur was given a going-away party. Katharine Cushing and her five children were there, along with several of Arthur's friends from school. His mother, Florence, and Akeema made a ham dinner with several courses and a large double-fudge cake. Lillian had saved food and sugar ration coupons for just such an occasion.

After dinner, the partiers went through a number of childhood photograph albums starring Arthur, complete with pictures of him naked in a bassinet. Arthur's Eagle Scout merit badges were on display, as well as several trophies in multiple sports. Every party member shared many stories about the Second Lieutenant, and most of them poked fun at him. But, Arthur loved the entire affair, and the group loved him. He had always been gregarious, and he was fully in his element. At one point, Arthur did a long series of deep-knee bends to prove the success of his rehabilitation. While lying on the floor, he also lifted a sofa with his legs. All were impressed.

Very early the next morning, while it was still dark, Edward and Lillian helped Arthur pack his duffle bag and loaded it into the Ford. They drove their son to a bus station not far from Cambridge and New Sudbury Streets. Lieutenant Arthur took his duffle from the back of the family truck, and then stood especially tall. "I'm ready to go back to active duty, Mom and Dad."

Lillian hugged her son outside the bus station, as she softly sobbed. "Arthur, please call and write whenever you're able. Ok?" she said.

"Mom," said Arthur, "Camp Devens is only thirty-five miles northwest of Boston. When I get a leave, I'll come home. I'll call and write too, Mom."

"Please do, Arthur. I will miss you so. It doesn't matter if your thirty-five miles away, or thirty feet away. I will still miss you." Arthur took a handkerchief and dried his Mom's eyes.

"Take care, Son...especially while climbing ladders," said Noble. All three laughed. "No joking though. Your country needs you. Your country needs a lot more men like you. We know you will make us proud, Son."

With that, Lieutenant Noble saluted Major Noble. His father experienced a combination of love, pride, sadness, and worry; emotions so often felt as sons leave for the military.

His mother hugged Arthur again, and the Lieutenant turned and entered the bus station. Noble stood with an arm around his sobbing wife for a very long time before leaving in the Ford.

On Monday, June 17th, Noble traveled to the A.I. Office with the hope there was a reply from Colonel Vaughn concerning his high priority cable ten days earlier. He had not yet heard from the Colonel, and was considering sending a second message. However, Lieutenant Pecknold informed him that Colonel Vaughn would attempt a long distance call from Washington D.C. later in the morning. Noble decided to wait for the call, given the importance attached to it.

While Noble waited, a cable arrived for him from France.

Monday, June 17, 1918
From: Base Hospital No. 5

Edward, I remember your telling me of epidemic influenza in the States some months back. Influenza, as you described, made the rounds here too. But, there has recently been a terrible grippe here as well. Many men are very sick. Many deaths. They say civilian grippe casualties in Paris are also marked, and that it is coming from the Germans and their malnutrition. I hope the grippe, and The War, pass soon.

Your friend,
Colonel Harvey Cushing, BEF.

Noble wondered how Cushing's cable had gone though military censors in France. It was likely an error on some Lieutenant's part. Nevertheless, it was more evidence that something with communicable disease had changed for the worse in Europe.

It was near noon when Lieutenant Pecknold awakened a napping Noble on his small office sofa. "Major, I have Colonel Vaughn on the line."

"I'll take it in here, Lieutenant. Please close the office door behind you." Noble picked up the telephone on the office desk.

"Edward! Can you hear me?" shouted Vaughn.

"Yes, sir, but just barely," shouted back Noble. The connection was tenuous at best. "Did you get my message on the 7th?"

"Yes, Edward, I did," said Vaughn, with a slight improvement in the quality of their phone call. "I'm sorry that it has taken me some time to acknowledge your cable, Edward. It took days for me to communicate with Colonel Welch, Rufus Cole, and General Gorgas. I have made them aware of your analysis of available data, and your concerns."

"What do they think, Colonel?" asked Noble.

"First, let me say, Edward, that I have full confidence in you and your recommendations. In my view, and in the view of General Gorgas, we should adopt strict quarantine protocols for all military ships docking in American ports."

"So, the quarantines will actually begin?" said Noble

"It's not that easy, Edward. You must remember that we have 10,000 American troops departing for Europe every day. A smaller, but substantial, number of troops returns each day from Europe, and also depart for American ports as well. In addition, thousands of civilian transport and cargo ships enter and leave American ports every day. This is a huge amount of maritime traffic, Edward. To quarantine even some of these ships would be a major undertaking. Besides, the Secretary of War, and the President himself, want to ramp up The War effort as fast as humanly possible. Anything that will slow this process has an uphill battle to implement through the government."

"Colonel," said Noble, "with all due respect, we need to concentrate only on ships arriving from Europe at this time. If we quarantined passengers from Europe for only seven days, we would slow the troop oversees deployment for only... seven days. It would be a one-time small 'hit' to deployment, and could mean the difference between a full scale European assault with a healthy military and civilian population...or disaster."

"Edward," said Vaughn, "what you say makes perfect sense on every level. But, as you know, just two days ago the *Public Health Reports* stated that June had the lowest pneumonia mortality in the U.S. for the year. And, influenza activity is practically non-existent. The Secretary of War, Newton Baker, and the civilian Surgeon General, Rupert Blue, also read these reports. It will be a hard to convince them to do anything different as we challenge the Central Powers."

"Colonel," said Noble, "I know you agree with me on these points. But, please try to bring this argument to them: The way to preserve the present low level of national infectious disease is to quarantine inbound European ships. I know the intelligence on the matter is very preliminary. However, I believe you have asked me to monitor world events in the A.I. Office for this very reason."

"Edward, I will continue to make your case in Washington. But, this is no simple task. Keep monitoring events, and keep me informed. We'll talk again soon." With that, Vaughn hung up.

Noble sat for a long time alone in his office with both elbows on his desk, and both hands on his jaw. He thought about his next steps. He could only gather information that might later sway opinion at the highest levels of authority. However, Noble's impression was he had failed. He had failed to make a good enough argument for a comprehensive quarantine. In this regard, he failed the entire nation.

On Thursday, June 27th, Noble had lunch with his wife in a small restaurant on Harrison Avenue near the hospital. The weather was warm, and was becoming more humid every day. Lillian filled her husband in on the family news. The three small Noble children were now out of school, and Akeema had taken them to the Boston Common to play. Florence was looking forward to a few weeks off from nursing school soon. Arthur had written recently and said he was enjoying the physical exercise and officer training at Camp Devens. Everyone was gratified with the new summer except Noble, for he was worried about ominous things.

As the two walked back toward the South Department and entered the A.I. Office, Noble expressed his hope that the government would act soon on his recommendations.

Lillian greeted the Lieutenant on duty, "Hi, Marié."

"Hello, Mrs. Noble. Did you try that Cajun recipe I gave you?"

"Yes!" Lillian said. "It was a big hit at home. Even Edward loved it."

"Major," said Lieutenant Lafayette, "there is a broad distribution cable from the army you might want to see."

Noble went to the central desk and picked up a world military stack cable.

Thursday, June 27, 1918
From: U.S. Army, Washington D.C.

No Influenza in our army. No notices have reached the War Department about the influenza amoung the German troops on the Western Front. The reported epidemic is not regarded here as having serious proportions. It is clear the soldier who has it is incapacitated for duty, and thousands may be down with the disease at once, so that military movements may be delayed. The American troops have at no time shown any form of the disease. Precautions have already been ordered, however, to meet any emergency.

Noble sat down on a roll top desk chair, and handed the cable to Lillian. As she finished reading it, Noble said, "The propagandists at least feel the need to say something. That probably says volumes by itself. Looks like there won't be any push for port quarantines, however. I guess Victor hasn't been all that successful in Washington." Noble rested his head on one elbow propped on the desk top.

"Edward, you'll just have to wait for an event that will crystallize public opinion. The government may not respond to anything else, given the situation in Europe. Perhaps that is your only recourse."

"Perhaps," said Noble.

Later in the day, as Noble was working on one of the wards, a nurse quickly approached him. "Dr. Noble," the nurse said somewhat out of breath, "Lieutenant Lafayette in the A.I. Office said she needs to talk with you immediately."

Noble excused himself, and walked quickly to the office. Opening the door, he said, "What is it Lieutenant?"

"Major, the navy directed us to pick up a radio transmission from a ship right off the coast of New Jersey. It's about 350 miles away from Boston, near Cape May, at the mouth of Delaware Bay. She's a 9,400 gross ton British freighter called *The City of Exeter*, sir, and she's coming from Europe."

"What is the transmission, Lieutenant?" said Noble.

"Well, the radio reception is very poor, and keeps cutting in and out. However, before I lost contact, I was able to make out the following: 'This is *The City of Exeter*. Many crew members ill. Ship's medic believes it is the grippe. Please assist us in docking...'"

Noble's back stiffened and his fists clenched. He quickly realized that the first known U.S. encounter with the mutated influenza was about to occur. "Lieutenant, there is no time to lose. Do the best you can to contact the *Exeter*, and tell her to proceed to a maritime quarantine pier at the Philadelphia Naval Complex. I heard of it when I was in Brest. Then send a message to Colonel Vaughn, the civilian Surgeon General Blue, and the Navy Surgeon General Braisted. Let them know why this is action is being taken. The navy in Philadelphia also needs to know about the quarantine, and to expect the ship today. If they can't raise her by radio, tugs may need to meet her with directions."

"Will do, sir," said the Lieutenant.

Over the next two days, with the *Exeter* in quarantine, Noble kept close contact with the Philadelphia quarantine pier. He would have preferred a seven day quarantine, but the navy released the ship after just two. The situation aboard the *Exeter* seemed to have stabilized, so on Sunday, June 30th, she set sail north on Delaware Bay. She was once again destined for a Philadelphia dock.

That morning after Mass, the Noble home telephone rang. Michael answered it, and called out to his father. "Dad, it's for you. It's Lieutenant Pierre-Louis."

Noble came to the telephone and said, "Hi, Lieutenant. Anything new?"

"Sir, I think I need to read to you a radio message I received from *Exeter* a few minutes ago. It reads: 'This is *The City of Exeter* approaching Philadelphia. Critically ill aboard. Frightening situation. Dozens of crew in desperate condition. Please give assistance immediately.' Major, what should we do?"

"Lieutenant," said Noble, "listen to me very carefully. First, call a friend of mine, Dr. Alfred Stengel, at Philadelphia Hospital and tell him to arrange for ambulances to meet the *Exeter* at the dock upon arrival. No one else can be present. All personnel must have surgical masks, and the ill must be taken to a quarantine area in the hospital. Dr. Stengel is an infectious disease expert and will know what to do. Second, call the British consulate and tell them of the quarantine. They will need to make their own arrangements. Third, Colonel Vaughn must be told of the action, as well as the civilian Surgeon General and the Surgeon General of the Navy. I cannot tell you how important this is, Lieutenant."

In view of the very early release of *Exeter* from quarantine, Noble was reminded of saying his father sometimes told him:

"Edward, take care that you don't step over dollars to pick up pennies".

"You can count on me, sir," said Lieutenant Pierre-Louis. The Lieutenant transmitted the message immediately.

However, for the next week, the A.I. Office could not confirm *Exeter* had even reached Philadelphia. Noble eagerly awaited word on the disposition of *The City of Exeter* crew. But the navy kept the entire affair secret, and even the A.I. Office was having difficulty obtaining information. It was crystal clear to Noble that the military, and the government, did not want any news available that might decrease American morale. Of course, secrecy made fighting epidemics much harder.

Arriving in the office early on Monday, June 8th, Noble asked Lieutenant Pecknold, "What do you have this morning, Lieutenant? Something interesting?"

"Lots, Major. It's all on the table, as usual, sir."

In the stacks, Noble found a message concerning the *Exeter*.

Friday, June 5, 1918
From: Philadelphia Hospital

Hi, Edward. I have to say that the city owes you a lot. It's still early, but it looks like your quick quarantine of the *Exeter*, and the arrangement for special handling of the ill, may have saved Philadelphia from a horrible epidemic. We think it was influenza. Many of the crew have died. Death seemed to be due to pneumonia. But, accompanying the pneumonia was an unearthly cyanosis, and bleeding from nostrils. Edward, I have never seen anything like it before. Take care my friend. Hope this is the end of it.

Dr. Alfred Stengel

Noble felt relief with the message. But, that relief was
short lived. Other messages in the stacks caused him to return to a state closer to anxiety.

Monday, June 8, 1918
From: BEF, London

287 people died of influenza in the last week in London.
126 died in Birmingham. Statement by physician performing necropsies on these patients: "The lung lesions, complex
or variable, struck me as being quite different in character
to anything I have met with in the thousands of autopsies I
have performed during the last twenty years. It was not like
the common broncho-pneumonia of ordinary years."

German Kaiser and family reported to be
very ill with Spanish Flu.
Army Intelligence

Monday, June 8, 1918
From: USPHS

Outbreak of epidemic influenza, Birmingham, England.
The disease is stated to be spreading rapidly and to be present in other locations. Fatal cases reported.

Public Health Reports

Noble turned to Lieutenant Pecknold and said, "Lieutenant,
I have asked you and the other Signal Corps Lieutenants to
send a total of three messages to Commander Cunard this last
week. Have there been any responses to them?"

"No, sir. None."

"That's it," said Noble, as he slammed his fist on the central table. Noble walked briskly out the office, out of the South Department pavilion, and out onto the Boston City Hospital campus. He walked in a near straight line in the warm summer sun to the central hospital administrative building called the Rotunda.

The first floor of the Rotunda was an open space, with marble floors and natural sunlight entering from numerous windows. Paintings of past BCH administrators lined the inside walls of the Rotunda. A large dome with fresco paintings of New England's past was prominent overhead. Lining the second floor of the Rotunda was a walkway that circled the inside of the dome. Doorways to administrative offices were situated all along the dome's inner perimeter.

Noble climbed the stairs to the second floor walkway, and came to a door that read, "Dr. Richard Cunard. Board of Trustees." He opened the door, and entered a large office with thick tan colored carpeting and impressive mahogany furniture. The walls were covered with photographs of Dr. Cunard posed with people such as Presidents Theodore Roosevelt, William Taft, and Woodrow Wilson. Below a large painting of Commander Cunard in his white navy uniform, was a woman at a desk in a white dress. The woman asked, "Hello, do you have an appointment?"

Noble asked, "Is Commander Cunard in?"

Yes," the woman said, "but do you have an..."

Noble did not stop walking, opened a second door, and closed it behind him. He entered an even larger office that was better appointed than the first. More photographs of Dr. Cunard with dignitaries adorned the walls, and a number of detailed sailing ship models were located about the room. Large picture windows along a curved outer Rotunda wall let in the morning sun. Cunard was seated at a huge mahogany desk in the center of the room, dressed as always in a starched and pressed white navy uniform. This was a stark contrast to the field army uniform Noble wore daily.

Cunard looked up from his desk, and said calmly without expression, "Well, well, well. Major Noble. As rude as always."

"Commander, "said Noble firmly, "I have sent you three messages this week and you have answered none of them."

Cunard replied, "If this is about the Einthoven ECG heart machine, then get out of here right..."

Noble cut Cunard off mid-sentence. "This has nothing to do with the ECG machine, Commander. I know you have some communicable disease information available to you from the U.S Public Health Service. I also know you don't have all the information acquired by the military. But, you are in charge of Boston Harbor's quarantine program through the navy and the USPHS. That's why I need to speak with you urgently about critical issues that will influence the health and safety of the New England military and civilian populations."

Cunard interrupted Noble and said, "I don't have time for this now."

Noble persisted. "You had better make time, Richard. I'm sure you are aware of *Public Health Reports* from as late as today that mention a severe influenza epidemic in England. Richard, it's worse than that. An extremely virulent form of influenza is spreading throughout Europe. And, it is lethal. What is worse, it will come to our shores in short order if we don't do something to stop it. <u>Now</u>." Noble related the story of *The City of Exeter*, the descriptions by Dr. Stengel, and the findings of recent necropsies in London.

"Why don't you tell all of this to Victor Vaughn?" Cunard said casually. "Why bother me with this?"

"Richard, I have told <u>several</u> peoples at many levels about the epidemic," said Noble. "The military doesn't want to slow troop deployments. The government, along with the U.S. Public Health Service, doesn't want to affect national moral. So, nothing is happening on a large scale because no one wants to acknowledge the problem exists. However, you could impose a short quarantine of ships from Europe. Since Boston Harbor is a major port for shipping and troop movements, you could substantially decrease the risk of spreading the epidemic in the Northeastern U.S."

Cunard paused for some time at his desk, looking down at some papers. He slowly closed a file on his desk, and took off a pair of reading glasses. He looked up at Noble and said, "Major, this is the most ridiculous story I have ever heard. Everyone knows there is an epidemic of Spanish grippe in Europe. It's even in the papers. It's influenza. Just influenza." Cunard continued, "In case you haven't heard, there is a war going on, and people actually die in wars. There are no advisories for port quarantines. There has been nothing from Surgeon General Blue, nothing from Army Surgeon General Gorgas, nothing from Navy Surgeon General Braisted, and nothing from War Secretary Baker. Hell, there hasn't even been anything from your pal Victor Vaughn, who's the head of Army Communicable Diseases. So, I am supposed to order a Harbor quarantine because you heard about some sick people on a Philadelphia ship?"

"Richard," said Noble, "I know we have had our differences over the years. But, this is much bigger than any of that now. I realize this requires you to act on information that is still within a strict security clearance and not common knowledge. However, a brief ship quarantine program for Boston Harbor could save numerous lives. If you can just trust..."

Cunard again interrupted. "Get out of here, Noble. I have no time to 'chew the rag'. If you don't leave now, I will have military police arrest you where you stand."

Noble looked Cunard straight in the eyes. He did not have to speak to transmit his thoughts. Cunard knew that he was being told he was making the biggest mistake of his life. But, Cunard did not like Noble. He enjoyed denying Noble his request. Any request.

Noble took a deep breath, turned, and left the room. He again had failed to convince an influential person of the extreme dangers ahead. Only this time, the risks had increased by a log.

CHAPTER 12

Nearly three weeks later, on Saturday, July 27th, the Nobles invited Milton Rosenau and his wife for a family afternoon dinner. The weather was very warm and clear, but not as humid as New England summers can be.

The Noble Beacon Street home had a small yard behind it. The yard had a green lawn, with lush plants and flowers along a high wood fence. A large maple tree provided abundant shade. Beneath the tree was a large picnic table with a floral table cloth. Lawn chairs were set around the table. The Nobles cooked outside, and served hamburgers, hot dogs, a lettuce salad, potato chips, pork and beans, potato salad, lemonade, and sodas. The adults had a Lodi, California chardonnay. Apple pie a la mode was served for desert. It was a wonderful time.

After dinner, Bernard and Michael filled Rosenau in on the Red Sox baseball season. That day the Red Sox had played their ninety-second game, and had beaten the Chicago White Sox 6-4 in Chicago. The Red Sox were now five games ahead in the American League, and the boys spoke so fast in their excitement that Rosenau had difficulty following them.

Florence conversed at length with Rosenau's wife about her nursing studies, the Naval Reserves, and her likely transition to active duty in the fall. Florence was asked if active duty troubled her. Florence answered, "Not at all. I'm grateful that I will have a skill that my country needs, and can use immediately. I know my brother, and my father, think exactly as I do."

Lillian told the Rosenaus about Arthur and his ongoing officer training at Camp Devens. Arthur was enjoying both artillery school and radio school. He had commented on how The War was re-writing U.S. military strategy. For exercise, Arthur had convinced his commanding officer to allow him to form a crew with fellow Second Lieutenants. They had been able to row a couple of times on the Charles River, and this was a great delight for the Boston University crew enthusiast.

Akeema read a story about Alaskan bears to a gleeful Marguerite, who jumped up and down in her chair with every paragraph. The bear was sacred to the Yup`ik, and Akeema enjoyed relating stories about them to her bubbly little friend with curly auburn hair.

After dinner, as Mrs. Rosenau was speaking with Florence, the Nobles and Rosenau talked about various topics over Chardonnay. Since Mrs. Rosenau did not have an A.I. Office security clearance, the three spoke softly. Rosenau asked, "Edward, has there been any news from The Front?"

"Actually," said Noble, "there has been a lot of news. Two German assaults in June and early July were aimed at Paris. The assaults were code named Operations Blucher and Yorck. But, both offensives were turned back by the Allies. On July 15th, the Germans launched Operation Marne in an attempt to encircle a large part of Allied forces on The Front. However, the Allies mounted a counter offensive a week ago and pushed the Germans back across the Marne to their Kaiserschlacht lines. So, the Central Powers have achieved nothing in months. This Allied counterattack represents our first successful offensive of The War."

"Really!" said Rosenau. "That's wonderful! Everyone has been concerned that America's entry into The War had not yet made a difference. Perhaps that is now beginning to change?"

"I think so, Milton," said Noble. "One of the problems for the Allies so far has been holding the Western Front, and maintaining supply lines at the same time. There just haven't been enough troops or supplies left to mount adequate offensives against the Germans. For this reason, the Western Front has remained essentially the same since 1914. But, since last fall, U.S. troops have been streaming into Europe. As everyone knows, the U.S. is pouring hundreds of thousands of fresh troops into the fight. Until now, the Americans have been improving and fortifying supply lines while adding their own supplies to The War effort. This has freed up some Allied troops to engage in an offensive strategy."

Noble continued, "For the first time, I am reading some optimism in Allied intelligence reports. Things are not going well for the Germans on the Western Front, or in the homeland. Between March and April, there were 270,000 German casualties, including many highly trained storm troopers. German industrial output is now at 53% of 1913 levels. In addition, the Germans are as affected by influenza as the Allies are. Neither side is admitting it, but influenza has stalled many Central Power and Allied military plans this summer. I did see one July U.S. Army Intelligence estimate that over 200,000 British troops were hit hard enough with influenza that they could not report for duty during a fierce battle."

"Maybe there will actually be an end to this thing," said Lillian.

"The whole world wishes for that, dear, and is impatient to get back to 'normal', said Noble."

"Edward, what about the other 'front'…the battle with influenza?" asked Rosenau.

"Well, Milton," said Noble, "I have less positive news on that war. Colonel Vaughn has received multiple cables and telephone calls from me about universal American port quarantines. If there's a man on this planet that understands the problem, and completely agrees with the only solution, he is Victor Vaughn."

"He's a good man, Edward," said Rosenau. "Of course, you know better than anyone. You have known him your whole life."

"And," said Noble, "my father would have trusted Victor with anything. The Colonel has had numerous conversations with another outstanding individual in public health, namely Army Surgeon General Gorgas. The General is known and respected by everyone in both the military and the government. Former President Theodore Roosevelt called Gorgas the single most important 'machine' on the Panama Canal project, and thinks highly of him to this day. I know that the General has discussed the issue with the Navy Surgeon General, the civilian Surgeon General, Rupert Blue, and the Secretary of War himself. I also know that the Colonel has personally conveyed your recommendations concerning measles to these authorities as well. But, as respected as Vaughn and Gorgas are, the military and government do not want to divert one second from the deployment of troops or supplies to Europe. So, nothing has happened."

"Do you think further monitoring of the epidemic will eventually change their minds...make a difference?" asked Rosenau?

"Well, Milton," said Noble, "there are two issues here. First, no one in authority will slow military deployments unless there is hard evidence that the epidemic will do one of three things: alter American industrial output, slow troop preparations, or lower civilian moral enough to adversely affect The War effort. The second issue is this; it's getting harder all the time to obtain information one can use. Even the A.I. Office is not getting the amount or quality of intelligence it was earlier in the year. I think the military is withholding its own intelligence from the people who are supposed to study it. I just happen to be one of the people asked to be a student of the data. In other words, the first issue can't be addressed unless the second issue permits it. Frankly, I'm stuck here."

"What are you going to do?" said Rosenau.

"I am going to continue to do the job that my commanding officer ordered me to do. That is, give the army my analysis of world communicative diseases. Some of the news out of Europe, and now Asia, is actually coming from the civilian newspapers. I might eventually find those sources as important, or more important, than intelligence I receive from the army."

"Edward, what exactly do the Europeans think is the cause of the influenza epidemic?" said Rosenau.

"That is an excellent question, Milton," said Noble. "There is very little information in that regard coming out of Europe. I'm sure they are thinking wildly about it, and have accumulated some useful clinical, microbiologic, and pathologic information. On the other hand, Europe is in shambles after four years of war. Even the brightest of European research groups may no longer have the facilities or personnel to tackle an issue like influenza in earnest. Even if there is some meaningful study of the epidemic, which may not be happening, we are not hearing about it."

Noble went on, "The information I have seen is that most physicians and researchers still hold true to Richard Pfeiffer's work."

"Oh, yes," said Rosenau. "Germany's Pfeiffer and his isolation of the bacteria *Bacillus influenzae* from the 1889-1890 pandemic."

"Few in Europe are willing to offer alternative hypotheses, in view of the prestige and reputation of Pfeiffer," said Noble. "As I mentioned to you in February, Dr. Loring Miner in Kansas saw very few *B. influenzae* in sputum specimens. There are those in Europe that say, 'if no *B. influenzae*, it is not influenza'. The organism seems to be involved in human deaths. But, animals infected with *B. influenzae* do not have the same disease as humans do. This is contrary to one of Koch's Postulates, as you know. However, perhaps not all organisms that cause human disease fulfill Koch's Postulates. I don't know, Milton. I'm not sure we know what causes influenza. To me, it remains a medical mystery."

"You are not alone in your skepticism," said Rosenau. "There are plenty in medicine who are not as sure as Pfeiffer is about 'Pfeiffer's bacillus'."

"On that note, Milton and Lillian, do you want some more chardonnay?" asked Noble.

Both Rosenau and Lillian said yes, and Noble walked into the house to pour two glasses of wine. On his way back from the kitchen, Noble noticed a card and envelope on a small table next to French doors leading to the back yard. He put down the wine glasses, and read the card which said, "Wed., July 24. Lillian. Thank you so much for helping me with the recent milk pasteurization promotion in the *Boston Globe*. You are such a dear. Richard Cunard." Noble read the envelope for the card, which was addressed to "Lillian Alexander".

Noble walked to the shaded picnic table in the back yard, gave the wine glasses to Rosenau and Lillian, and sat down. A few minutes passed, as the three all agreed that the chardonnay was excellent. Noble then said, "Lilly, I saw that you received a card from Richard Cunard. It's interesting that he addressed it to 'Lillian Alexander.'"

Lillian laughed, "Isn't Richard funny?" She turned to Milton and remarked, "'Alexander' is my maiden name. Richard can be so silly. It was sweet of him to send me a card, though. I worked pretty hard on that pasteurization promotion."

Both Noble and Rosenau looked at each other without verbal comment. "Sweet" was not the word they would use to describe Commander Richard Cunard.

On Monday, August 12th, the day started out routinely in the A.I. Office for Noble. After greeting Lieutenant Lafayette in the morning, he read a summary of the findings from the

Pneumonia Commission that had investigated a small July outbreak of pneumonia at Fort Riley, Kansas. The Commission determined that typical lobar pneumonia with pneumococci types II, III, and IV were responsible. There was nothing unusual about the localized and contained outbreak. There was little else in the message stacks, so Noble went off to the hospital wards.

Shortly after lunch, Noble returned to the office with his wife. All the ceiling fans were at full speed, since the day was hot and humid. Lillian asked Lieutenant Lafayette if she could wear a lighter uniform in this weather. The Lieutenant said, "The Major already said that we could wear lighter uniforms, Mrs. Noble. However, we have been given strict Devens command orders to wear our tunics while at Boston City Hospital. I guess they want us to look 'military' all the time we are here."

The Lieutenant gave Lillian the most recent epidemiologic journal received at the office, and she began to read it at a roll top desk chair. Noble began to thumb through cables that had arrived earlier in the day. He stopped mid-breath, and bit the inside of his cheek. He brought a series of cables closer to his face, and adjusted his wire rim glasses in order to read them more closely. After a short time, Noble said to his wife, "Lilly, this is not good."

"What is it, Edward?" said Lillian. Edward read her the first cable.

Sunday, August 3, 1918
From: U.S. Navy Intelligence

Secret. Confidential. We are confidentially advised that a disease of a very severe nature is sweeping Switzerland. Many affected. Many deaths. Reliable sources have designated the disease as the Spanish sickness: the grippe.

Naval Intelligence Officer.

When Noble had finished, Lillian's expression was of sadness and internal contemplation. She said, "It's spreading." Noble then said, "Lilly, there's more." He proceeded to read her the next two cables.

Thursday, August 8, 1918
From: U.S. Army Intelligence

The steamship *Bordeaux* heading from France to New York was struck by influenza. Virtually the entire crew was incapacitated. The steamship had to put into Halifax, Nova Scotia. The crew remained on board for several days until they were able to make way again.

Office of the U.S. Army Surgeon General.

Monday, August 12, 1918
From: U.S. Navy Intelligence

The Norwegian freighter *Bergensfjord* arrived in Brooklyn, New York, after burying four crew members at sea. Very reliable information states that the crew members died of influenza. After docking, two hundred crew members were taken to a quarantine ward at a Brooklyn hospital. Many in critical condition.

Naval Intelligence Officer.

Lillian was silent for a few moments, and then said, "The number of potential contacts with the disease is increasing. This is happening just at a time when policies and procedures should be in place to decrease them. Darling, I know that you have been trying to raise the level of concern since late June. I know that you have done everything possible in this regard."

"Lilly," said Noble, "to date, the numbers of potential influenza contacts at American ports has been small enough to allow good people to do the right thing...successfully. In the case of the steamship *Bordeaux*, the crew had the good sense to put into port and simply wait. It appears that the crew may have passed the contagious stage of the disease by the time they put into port in Brooklyn. In the case of the Norwegian freighter *Bergensfjord*, quick action by port authorities may have averted a major breach in confinement of influenza in New York. In the same way, we were fortunate with the *Exeter*. But, without a uniform policy, there will come a time when the number of potential contacts overwhelms the good intentions of vigilant people. We are getting closer to that time."

Noble continued, "This is what we are up against, Lillian." He read another cable.

Monday, August 12, 1918
From: New York City Health Department, New York Port Authority

There has been recent concern over the grippe that could involve New York. There is not the slightest danger of an influenza epidemic in our city. The disease seldom attacks well-nourished people. It is also decidedly uncommon to have serious complications with influenza, as we have seen for many years each fall and winter.

Royal Copeland, NYHD.

"I can understand the lack of concern with seasonal influenza," said Lillian, after listening to her husband. "But, the experience of New York City in the last week should be enough to further engage the New York Health Department. People are not looking at the problem critically. Many do not take the present influenza seriously, because others are not taking it seriously. Everyone begins to look to others to do the critical analysis, instead of thinking it through themselves."

Noble said, "The Chief Army Surgeon of the New York port of embarkation, Colonel J. M. Kennedy, has assured newspaper reporters that this disease is not at all dangerous unless pneumonia develops."

Lillian replied, "By the time pneumonia develops, from what you have said, a person has been contagious for many hours or a few days. There is no way to contain this disease with that approach."

"You're exactly right, Lilly," said Noble. "And, the recent U.S. Public Health Service bulletin on the topic suffers from a similar misconception." Noble read to Lillian a portion of the circular.

Monday, August 5, 1918
From: U.S. Public Health Service

...Medical officers in charge of quarantine stations should be on the alert for the so-called Spanish influenza. The disease is apparently caused by *B. influenzae* with a predilection for pulmonary involvement, and fumigation procedures should be used against it. However, this circular does not contemplate consideration of cases of ordinary pneumonia or respiratory infections, but only those infections involving a considerable number of the crew and which appear to be highly communicable and suggestive of epidemic influenza.

U.S. Public Health Service Bulletin.

Lillian shook her head. "Although this is the first time the USPHS has publicly suggested any measures against the epidemic, it is hardly enough. First, singling out only sailing vessels with 'a considerable number' of crew affected will miss many cases of influenza. Second, how are field quarantine medical officers supposed to know the difference between ordinary and extraordinary pneumonia in the earliest stages? I can't say this is much above doing nothing at all."

"Again," said Noble, "you're right on target. There is one bright note, though. In the August 10th edition of the *Journal of the American Medical Association*, the Chief of Medical Service at Camp Grant, Illinois, made some useful suggestions. Dr. Joe Capps stated that during a three week experiment, he found gauze masks are effective against influenza. I understand that Rufus Cole of the Rockefeller Institute agrees. Dr. Capps also suggested that in cases of influenza, sheet tents should be placed between hospital beds. In army hospitals, soldier's heads should be alternated with the feet of nearby soldiers so as to decrease contamination by coughing. Also, curtains should be placed down the center of mess hall tables. Any measures that can slow the spread of the disease are surely welcome."

Lillian said to her husband, "There are no epidemiologic data on which to make hard calculations and projections. National, military, and logistical concerns have made that impossible for the moment. However, based on subjective data only, I would estimate that the potential port contacts would plot out on a logarithmic scale as a straight line. In other words, the beginning of the new influenza epidemic in the United States is about to begin, if it hasn't already."

Lillian wanted to be home for dinner preparation, so she kissed her husband, bid Lieutenant Lafayette good bye, and departed. As she left, Noble noted that there were two cables in the personal stack. Interestingly, the two cables were transcribed three days apart, but not sent until today. He read both of them.

Sunday, August 3, 1918
From: Base Hospital No. 5

Hello, Edward. I hope that you are well. I am not. I have been ill the last couple of days with severe myalgias, a high fever, and a form of fatigue that has not been previously known to me. My legs are extremely painful, and I have been unable to get off my cot since the illness began. I wonder if this is the Spanish grippe? I do hope I feel better soon. If not, I may need to consult one of my Internist friends here in Camiers. Please say hi to Katharine and the children for me.

Your friend,
Colonel Harvey Cushing, BEF.

Tuesday, August 6, 1918
From: Base Hospital No. 5

To: Major Edward Noble.

Colonel Harvey Cushing has asked me to send you a cable, since he is unable to do so. Colonel Cushing has been extremely ill these last three days. He is very weak. He is having difficulties with his gait, and is unable to stand. I am his attending physician, and I will suggest that he be sent to Paris presently for a time. He has asked me to request that you get word to his wife and family.

Sincerely,
Captain Ronald Savona, BEF.

Noble's own legs felt weak after reading the cables, and he also felt great fatigue. He wondered if these symptoms might simply be in sympathy for his friend. He sat down at an office roll top desk, picked up a telephone, and the Lieutenant connected him with his home. He left a message with Akeema to have Lillian call him the moment she arrived. He wanted her to be the one who called Katharine Cushing.

Noble arose on the morning of Tuesday, August 20th, and gave his farewells to Bernard, Michael, and Marguerite as they went off for their first day of 6th, 3rd, and 1st grade, respectively. Their mother had made them a "Noble" breakfast of scrambled eggs, oatmeal, sausage, orange juice, marmalade, and toast. The children wore new light-weight school clothes from the J.C. Penney's department store, since the weather was still hot and humid.

It was hard for the children to contain their excitement over seeing their friends after summer vacation. Bernard and Michael wanted to compare baseball notes with all their buddies. The day before, the Red Sox had beaten the Cleveland Indians 6-0 in Boston. With only two weeks left in the regular season, the Red Sox were ahead by four games in the American League. Things were looking hopeful for a pennant win. Marguerite wanted to show her friends how well she could play marbles, just as her brothers had taught her. She compared notes with friends about roller skating, which was now her favorite sport. Akeema and Lillian had Marguerite trace with a pencil the outline of her hand on a sheet of paper. On the paper was written, "Marguerite Noble; First Day of First Grade; August 20, 1918". Lillian planed to frame and display the sheet on the family photograph wall. The wall contained traced hands of the other four children from their first days of first grade.

Before Noble left the family house, Lillian reminded him that Katharine Cushing was very appreciative when given news about her husband. She had not heard anything yet from the army. Noble was receiving more information, and faster, than Katharine was from France. Lillian relayed the message that Katharine would like to hear everything and anything sent to the A.I. Office concerning Harvey. Noble assured his wife he would be more than happy to do so.

This morning, Noble took the Massachusetts Avenue trolley along with his daughter to Boston City Hospital. He was dressed in his usual field uniform, and she was dressed in her white nursing student clothes. Noble knew it was likely his two oldest children would be going to Europe soon. Although he was so proud of both of them, he was also full of concern. He had been in France, and knew what awaited them. Florence spoke to her father over the noise of screeching trolley wheels, people shouting, and clanging trolley bells. "Dad, we were told our Naval Reserve nursing group will likely be placed on active duty on September 16th. They are frequently activating nursing students before graduation. Our officer training would be much abbreviated, and we would likely be going to France just a few weeks after that."

Noble wished he could sit down with this news, since he felt a heaviness come over him. However, there was only room to stand on the crowded trolley. Someone offered a seat to Florence, who sat next to her father. Noble said, "I knew this was coming, Florence. Of course, I am so proud of you and your brother. Still, your departure upsets me so."

"Dad," said Florence, "I'll be just fine. Not only can I help in The War effort, I can also learn a lot while I pitch in. We're told they really need nursing help in the base hospitals."

Noble knew that was an understatement, having seen the lack of nursing first hand. "Dear, I know that you will always do the right thing. But, please, just avoid unnecessary risks. I've told Arthur the very same thing."

"Don't worry, Dad," said Florence. "This war will be over soon, and I'll be home faster than you were!"

The trolley reached a stop near the corner of Massachusetts and Harrison Avenues, and the Nobles departed to enter the hospital campus. Noble kissed his daughter on the forehead, told her to learn all she could during her surgery rotation, and walked off toward the South Department.

Noble went directly to the A.I Office, and said hello to Lieutenant Pierre-Louis. "Looks like some pretty big stacks on the table, Lieutenant. You've been busy." Noble walked over to the central table and decided to look at war activity summaries first. There was much information to read, and it was very positive.

On August 8th, the Allied counteroffensive that had started nearly three weeks earlier was still raging. It was called The Battle of Amiens, and it found the III Corps Fourth British Army in the north, the First French Army in the south, and the Australian and Canadian Corps driving a spearhead in the center. This involved 414 Mark IV and Mark V tanks, and 120,000 men. They advanced seven miles into German-held territory in just seven hours. U.S. Army Intelligence reported that Germans referred to the battle as the "Black Day of the German Army". With successful Australian and Canadian campaigns, the British pushed even farther north, and the French advanced south.

On August 10th, the British maintained a fourteen mile advance into German territory. However, German resistance stiffened. By today, August 20th, the French Third Army captured two hundred huge German guns, as well as the Aisne heights overlooking the German position north of Vesle. Meanwhile, the Third British Army observed the German forces thinning on The Front. So, the British quickly attacked with two hundred tanks toward Bapaume.

Allied strategists realized that a continued battle line attack after enemy resistance hardens is a waste of lives. So, they changed tactics. The Allies had better success turning battle lines around the enemy, rather than rolling over them. Attacks were also undertaken quickly, in order to take advantage of successful advances on the flanks. Operations were quickly broken off as advancement stopped. This tactic minimized Allied losses, and maximized resources against the Germans.

U.S. Army Intelligence had intercepted some interesting German Communications in the last few weeks. After the impressive Allied advance on August 10ᵗʰ, the German High Command realized The War "was lost", or so said the intercepted message. They convinced the Kaiser that victory in the field was improbable. Austria and Hungry told Germany they could only continue The War until December. There were now indications that the Kaiser had asked the Queen of Holland to assist in mediation with the Allies. Noble could not tell how reliable this information was, or if the Allies were paying much attention to it.

Noble smiled widely as he read the war summaries. He was about to comment on them to Lieutenant Pierre-Louis. However, she finished a transcription and turned to him before he could speak. The Lieutenant said, "Major, sir, you better see some of the other cables right now before going off to the wards."

Noble's expression changed from a friendly smile to one of concern. He picked up some of the other neatly stacked cables on the central table, and took them to a roll top desk. Any hopes for a pleasant day were dashed immediately.

Sunday, August 10, 1918
From: Brest, France.

Confidential. Army reports soaring death rates from Spanish influenza amoung troops of multiple nationalities at the port of Brest. The reports come from army and navy physicians who are confident in their diagnosis. British declare epidemic over. However, so many French hospitalized in Brest with influenza that the naval hospital has been closed.

U.S. Army Intelligence.

Thursday, August 15, 1918
From: New York Harbor

Two Norwegian steamships, and a Swedish steamship, arrived in New York on the 14th and 15th with influenza. Many ill. Many taken to local hospitals.

U.S. Naval Bulletin.

Thursday, August 15, 1918
From: West African Coast

Freetown, Sierra Leone. Coaling station for steamers, serving Europe, South Africa, Orient. *HMS Mantua* arrived with crew of 200, majority suffering severely with influenza.

British Naval Intelligence, U.S. Naval Intelligance.

Sunday, August 18, 1918
From: New York Harbor

Influenza outbreaks on steamships *Rochambeau* and *Nieuw Amsterdam*. Many severely ill. Crew taken to St. Vincent's Hospital.

U.S. Navy Intelligence.

Monday, August 19, 1918
From: New York

Army describes some troop fatalities in Europe from Spanish influenza. Impact on troop strength and morale described as minimal.

New York Times.

Tuesday, August 20, 1918
From: New York City Health Department, New York Port
    Authority

Some influenza has been described in New York City. Cases minimal and mild.

Royal Copeland, NYHD.

Despite more reports to read, Noble paused. He put his palms flat on the desk before him, stiffened his elbows straight, and rolled slightly back on the oak chair with coasters. He took a very deep breath and let it out slowly. He thought long and hard about the cable reports. The demon that was this particular influenza was extending its invisible tentacles in all directions, while hiding aboard sailing vessels. The demon's reach was far, since it was clearly global in size. It was now probing the U.S. eastern seaboard ports, trying to find a wide-open door to the continent. Time was now short.

"Lieutenant," said Noble softly.

"Yes, sir."

"It is of the highest priority," said Noble, "that you find Colonel Vaughn, wherever he is, and arrange for me to speak with him. Hopefully, that can be via telephone. Lieutenant, this is a matter of national security, and requires your full skills for the moment."

"Yes...sir," said the Lieutenant. She had never been given an order like this before, and it scared her. "On the double, sir."

Noble returned to the cable stack. There was more bad news.

Tuesday, August 20, 1918
From: Paris, France

Hello my old friend. Things are not well with me. I have been in Paris for two weeks at the direction of Dr. Savona, who believes I have contracted the Spanish influenza. I am very feeble, and have been in bed most of the time. I do not have the strength to eat my meals in the mess, so I dine in my room. I have great difficulty focusing my eyes, and am trying to get used to wearing glasses. (I guess I am going to look like you, from now on.) I have also severe bilateral leg cluadication that allows me to walk no more than one or two short blocks. Edward, I am not getting better, and this troubles me. I wonder what effect these maladies will have, if they are truly chronic, on my future surgical endeavors. Please tell Katharine where I am, and that I love her dearly.

Your good friend,
Colonel Harvey Cushing, BEF.

Now, Noble's best friend was severely affected by this strange new microbial adversary. At that moment, Lieutenant Pierre-Louis called out to Noble. "Major, I have the Colonel on long distance. He is in Asheville, North Carolina. He left Camp Macon in Georgia just a few days ago. Major, the connection is not very good, and it may not hold long."

Noble went into the small office to take the call. There was so much static on the line that Noble had to hold the receiver a few centimeters from his right ear. "Colonel Vaughn...are you there, sir?"

"Yes, Edward," came the voice of Vaughn that sounded every bit of 500 miles away. "Welch, Cole, Russell, and I are relaxing after a tour of southern cantonments. The Lieutenant said this was urgent."

"It is, Colonel," said Noble. "I cannot speak about all of the cables I have read in the last several days, since I don't know how long we have this telephone line. But, severe influenza is appearing at multiple ports around the world, and aboard multiple ships bound for the United States. Sir, I realize at this point that we can't stop the epidemic from reaching our shores. However, strict port quarantines can <u>slow</u> its progress. If we can slow it, we can better isolate the groups that contract it. This could, in the long run, save many many lives. But, time is very short. If seven day quarantines are not possible, then perhaps five days would suffice, Colonel. Anything is better than what we are doing now, which is virtually nothing."

"Edward," said the Colonel over the loud static, "you know I trust completely both your assessments and your intuition in these matters. With each of your detailed and specific reports over the last several weeks, General Gorgas, and the Colonels Welch, Cole, and Russell, have become very concerned indeed. The fatalities of U.S. troops in Europe from influenza have been worse than even you know. Much of that information remains classified and highly censored. Edward, I promise that all of us will contact the highest military and government authorities and ask them to..."

"Colonel?" said Noble. "Colonel?" Noble only heard static over the telephone.

The Lieutenant came on the line and said, "Major, I am so sorry. We have lost the connection. Do you want me to try and reestablish it?"

No," said Noble. "I got the gist of the Colonel's comments. Lieutenant, please contact my resident team on the ward and let them know I will be late. I have something I must do."

Noble left the A.I. Office and walked in the hot sun toward the Boston City Hospital Rotunda. On his way he thought about his phone call with Vaughn. He knew that Vaughn, and the other great men, understood completely the present danger. He knew they continued to do all that was possible to affect port quarantines. He also realized all of them were fighting an incredibly difficult political battle. And, it was a battle they were presently losing.

Noble reached the Rotunda, climbed the stairs to the second administrative level, and opened the door to Commander Richard Cunard's office. The office receptionist raised her head from her paper work, and stared at the man who had just closed the door behind him. "Mmm...Major Noble. Major, the Commander has instructed me to call military police if you barge in here again. I don't believe you have an appointment."

"Miss," said Noble, "I am not going to barge in, and no, I do not have an appointment. I wonder if you could ask the Commander if I might speak with him briefly."

The woman seemed as though she was caught off guard by the civil request. "Well...I will ask the Commander if he will see you or not. Stay here." The woman left her desk and went into Cunard's office for a few minutes. The woman reappeared, sat at her desk again, and said, "The Commander will speak with you for a few minutes. You may enter."

"Thank you," said Noble, as he walked through the main office door and closed it behind him. Cunard was seated at his desk, in his white navy uniform, reading numerous accounting logs. He looked up over his reading glasses and pursed his lips as he saw Noble stand near his desk.

"Major, what do you want?" said Cunard.

"Commander, I am not here to demand that you impose a five or seven day quarantine of Boston Harbor. I am here to <u>plead</u> for the quarantine. Please know that I have spoken with the Colonel Victor Vaughn, who completely agrees with my assessment. The Colonel has also spoken at length with General Gorgas, Colonel Fredrick Russell, Colonel William Welch, and Colonel Rufus Cole. You are aware of the prestige of these men in American medicine. All agree that port quarantines are essential as the so-called Spanish influenza reaches the U.S. Even the U.S. Public Health Service has put out a bulletin suggesting quarantines of effected ships. You and I both know the only really effective action is to quarantine all in-bound ships for a time."

Noble continued. "If you could also use your influence to have Surgeon General Rupert Blue quarantine all eastern seaboard ports, we might substantially weaken the coming epidemic. Richard, I know you have heard some reports from Europe concerning influenza. It has even been in the *New York Times*. The fatality rates seem to be extraordinarily high."

Cunard listened to Noble without expression. When Noble was finished, Cunard slowly removed his reading glasses and placed them carefully on his desk. He placed both his forearms on his desk top, and folded his hands together.

Cunard said, "Major, I have read the USPHS bulletin that you speak of, and it makes no suggestion of a general quarantine. I have my officers in Boston Harbor looking for ships with crew members suffering with severe pneumonia-related influenza. They are very capable and diligent. I have heard nothing else from USPHS, the navy, the army, or anything from the office of the Secretary of War. Just like I told you the last time you were here, I haven't even heard a word from the Army Surgeon General...the one you say who 'agrees' with you. I am not going to do anything that impedes this country's deployment of men and materials for The War effort."

"I completely understand the position that you are in, Richard. Believe me, I do. But, even a slowing of the epidemic here in Boston might convince other port cities to follow suit. You might be able to..."

Cunard interrupted Noble. "I am not going to do anything, Major. Do you hear me?"

After a pause, Cunard began to raise his voice. Noble saw his face turn red, as he bared his teeth when he spoke. Cunard continued, "You know what, Noble? I am so tired hearing you tell everyone you are so 'right' all the time. You became an expert at it while we were at BU. But, you know what? There is no epidemic in the U.S. There is very little influenza. If it comes, we will see the same thing we saw last spring. Nothing but a three day grippe. I am going to enjoy watching everyone as they discover you have been 'crying wolf' for all these weeks. Needless alarmism; that is all you have been spreading. I will never understand what Lillian ever saw in you."

Noble could handle Cunard's criticism, until he mentioned Lillian. Noble's pulse raised, and he clenched his fists. He also felt blood rush to his face. But, then he took an instant to rationally consider Cunard's attacks. He thought of the problems that would ensue if he acted on his present feelings. He let his hands relax, as he took a deep breath and exhaled calmly.

As Noble turned and walked to the office door, he looked back behind him and said, "Cunard, you are pitiful." He left the office and felt great sadness. Great sadness for Boston, and great sadness for the entire country.

That night at the family home, Noble described in detail to his wife the A.I. Office cables, and the conversation with Vaughn. Lillian commented, "This influenza is obviously very infectious, and there is definitely serious disease associated with the infection. It is spreading through the human population very quickly. By your intelligence accounts, it is extending in a global manner. It appears that the infection is unstable in terms of the number of people becoming sick with it. Endemic and epidemic infections need not be virulent, or associated with mortality, for their definitions to be changed to the next level. It just so happens this infection is both virulent and lethal. In any case, Edward, this epidemic fulfills the definition of a 'pandemic'."

Lillian and her husband stared at one another for a few moments silently. In all of the communications through the Army Intelligence Cable Office over the last seven months, no one had ever used the word "pandemic". If one adds the word "severe", the pandemic classification takes on a whole new meaning.

"Lilly," said Noble, "you are still very much involved with the American Red Cross as a regional director, the Women's Auxiliary, and as an official with the U.S. Public Health Service. Right?"

"Yes," said Lillian, "of course."

"Then, you must work through these agencies to begin a project they won't initially understand," said Noble. "Boston must begin to make thousands of gauze masks in anticipation of the coming...pandemic. It has been suggested the masks be made of a half-yard of gauze, folded as a triangular bandage covering the mouth, nose, and chin. It will take many volunteers hundreds of hours to produce enough masks for the population. Do you think it is possible? The medical literature available has suggested mask efficacy against influenza."

"Darling, if you think it is valuable, we will do it. I will start tomorrow promoting the project," said Lillian. Noble then described the serious situation with Harvey Cushing, and asked that she contact his wife. Lillian said she would call her by telephone that evening.

Lillian expressed her disappointment with Cunard and his refusal to quarantine Boston Harbor. "Richard has never had the moral and ethical posture that you have, daring," she said to her husband. "Among a million other characteristics, these are the reasons you stand head-and-shoulders above Richard Cunard."

Noble could not describe in words his gratitude over these words from his wife. Perhaps it was the tension of the A.I. Office memos. Perhaps it was the knowledge of the demon at the Atlantic doorstep to America. Perhaps it was his time in France. Perhaps it was four years of world war. In any case, Noble had felt a degree of insecurity concerning his relationship with his wife since his return in January. He walked over to her, and embraced her. For the first time in 1918, he felt he was really home.

CHAPTER 13

Noble was not in a particularly good mood on the morning of Tuesday, August 27th. But, his mood was to get decidedly worse after greeting Lieutenant Pecknold at the A.I. Office. The cable stacks were deeper than ever.

Tuesday, August 27, 1918
From: London

HMS Africa stopped at the Freetown, Sierra Leone coaling station. The steamer was in port longer than expected because five hundred of the six hundred laborers of the Sierra Leone Coaling Company were too sick to report to work. *Africa's* crew and remaining company workers helped coal her. Reportedly, seven percent of the *Africa* crew now dead.

British Naval Intelligence, U.S. Naval Intelligence.

Tuesday, August 27, 1918
From: New Zealand

HMS Chepstow Castle carried New Zealand troops to The Front. The ship stopped at the Freetown, Sierra Leone coaling station. Nine hundred men aboard now reported severely ill with influenza. Thirty-eight buried at sea.

British Naval Intelligence, U.S. Naval Intelligence.

Tuesday, August 27, 1918
From: London

HMS Tahiti coaled at Freetown, Sierra Leone coaling station. Before reaching England, sixty-eight were buried at sea.

British Naval Intelligence, U.S. Naval Intelligence.

Tuesday, August 27, 1918
From: West African Coast

Secret. Confidential. Sierra Leone. Intelligance estimates that six percent of the county's African population has died over the last few weeks. That percentage is still climbing.

British Naval Intelligence, U.S. Naval Intelligence.

Noble sat at one of the roll top desks, and recalled from Greek mythology the story of Cassandra. Cassandra was the daughter of King Priam and Queen Hecuba in Homer's Iliad.

The god Apollo granted Cassandra the gift of prophecy. But, Cassandra then rejected Apollo's romantic advances toward her. Cassandra was then cursed by Apollo to have the power to tell the truth about the future, but never to be believed.

Noble felt as though he was a present day Cassandra. The future was revealed to Noble via technology, rather than through special powers granted by the gods. However, like Cassandra, Noble spoke the truth about the future and was not believed. There was nothing more he could do but try to prepare for the coming demon. The ultimate dark irony was that Noble did not know where, or what, the demon was. But, it was coming nevertheless. Of this he could be certain.

Major Noble instructed Lieutenant Pecknold to forward today's cables on to Colonel Vaughn in North Carolina, and to title them "Top Secret. Highest Priority. For Colonel Victor Vaughn's Eyes Only." Noble sent no commentary, since he had sent those innumerable times before.

About two miles east of Boston City Hospital was the Commonwealth Pier. The pier was along the northern side of a huge channel extending west from Boston Harbor. The channel was over four thousand feet long and five hundred feet wide. The navy on Commonwealth Pier operated a "receiving ship". Actually, this was not a ship at all. The "receiving ship" was a gigantic dock barrack where seven thousand sailors ate and slept before they travelled to and from Boston. Navy ships arrived and departed every day from the pier, and from the many nearby piers. Each sailor had little more space in the "receiving ship" than what his body took up. "Crowded" was considered a gross understatement.

This day, August 27th, two sailors on Commonwealth Pier reported to sickbay. They suffered from severe fatigue, excruciating global muscle aches, severe headaches, hacking coughs, and high fevers. The young navy Lieutenant physician who saw the men diagnosed influenza, and had them return to their bunks in the receiving ship.

At almost the same time as the two sailors were seen in sickbay, Lieutenant Pecknold in the A.I. Office prepared a cable for Major Noble, and set it on his center table.

Tuesday, August 27, 1918
From: Boston Commonwealth Pier

The steamer *Harold Walker* departed Boston, headed for New Orleans. Severely ill crew members aboard. The steamer is scheduled to depart for Mexico after undocking in New Orleans.

U.S. Navy Intelligence.

The next day, August 28th, eight sailors on Commonwealth Pier reported to sickbay. They suffered from the same symptoms as the men who presented to sickbay the day before. Again, the young Lieutenant physician diagnosed influenza. The men returned to their bunks in the receiving ship.

Late in the morning on Thursday, August 29th, the young Lieutenant at the Commonwealth Pier sickbay telephoned Chelsea Naval Hospital. The hospital was four miles north of the pier, as the crow flies. The Lieutenant asked to speak to Lieutenant Commander Milton Rosenau. A medical Corpsman walked up to Rosenau as he studied a blood culture, and told him of the call. Rosenau went to a nearby telephone.

"Lieutenant Commander Rosenau here."

"Sir, I'm Lieutenant Hegemier at the Commonwealth Pier sickbay. I think we have a problem, sir."

"What's the problem, Lieutenant?" asked Rosenau.

"Sir, two days ago I saw two sailors with influenza. Yesterday there were nine sailors with influenza. Today, sir, there are fifty-eight. The thing is…well…"

"What is it, Lieutenant?" said Rosenau forcefully.

"Well...sir...they are very ill. I have never seen anything like this before. Some of them are critical, sir."

"Lieutenant, listen to me very carefully," said Rosenau. "Segregate the ill men from the others immediately. I don't mean soon. I mean now. I will arrange to have army ambulances pick them up and bring them here to Chelsea. If you have any surgical masks, place them on the men. Keep as few personnel with them as necessary, and have them also wear masks. Everyone is ordered to wash their hands frequently."

As soon as Rosenau hung up the telephone, he instructed navy hospital personnel to create a quarantine ward for the fifty plus men that would soon arrive. He then placed a call to the A.I. Office and asked Lieutenant Lafayette to find Major Noble.

"Sir," asked the Lieutenant, as the Major consulted a medical textbook, "I have Lieutenant Commander Rosenau on the line. He says it is urgent."

Lieutenant Lafayette studied Noble's face as he spoke to Rosenau. She saw him turn decidedly pale as a frown came over his forehead. Noble put his left hand over his eyes, and held the receiver with his right hand. Several minutes passed before he said, "Fine. Yes. I will be there as soon as possible."

Noble hung up the telephone. With his left hand still covering his eyes, he said softly to the Lieutenant, "Please contact Colonel Vaughn. As soon as possible, ask him to authorize at least twenty-five army ambulances to go to Commonwealth Pier and pick up quarantined patients. They are to be taken to the Chelsea Naval Hospital. Then, call Sergeant Campbell at Camp Devens and ask him to take me immediately to Chelsea."

"Yes sir," said the Lieutenant. "Is anything wrong, sir?"

Noble paused before answering. He finally removed his left hand from his eyes. "Yes, Lieutenant. There is a lot wrong."

"May I ask what, sir?"

"Lieutenant. It's here. It's in Boston." Noble then turned and walked quickly out the office door.

Sergeant Campbell drove from Camp Devens and picked up Noble in an army staff car. The drive to Chelsea was through the greater Boston metropolitan area, and across the Mystic River. For this reason, the trip took some time. Chelsea Naval Hospital was located on a southwestern hill that rose from the Mystic River. The eighty-eight acre compound had been commissioned as a navy hospital in 1836. Former President John Quincy Adams had been a patient there in his later years. But, a new state-of-the-art naval hospital had been built just three years earlier. It was thought to be prepared for most medical emergencies.

Noble thanked the Sergeant for his help, and proceeded to the main hospital building. He noticed a number of army ambulances near the hospital, along with masked medical personnel and masked patients on gurneys. Upon entering the building, Noble asked the whereabouts of Lieutenant Commander Rosenau. With navy efficiency, he was told where to go, given a white linen smock, rubber gloves, and gauze mask to wear.

Noble walked up stairs to a large ward with numerous white wrought iron hospital beds. Masked staff were busily erecting linen tents about the beds, and stacks of clean linen were placed on small stands around the room. Noble counted sixty beds, and about a third of them held patients. A frequent dry hacking cough arose from the patients. Their frequency reminded Noble of popping popcorn. The coughing was also loud, and made it hard to hear others speak. At the other end of the room was a gowned and masked Rosenau at a bedside. He walked over to Rosenau, who saw him approaching. "I'm really glad to see you, Edward. As you can see, we still have about thirty more in transit. I guess this is the main event, my friend."

"Yeah," said Noble. "Show time. Do you mind if I jump right in and start examining some patients? It's time we start learning firsthand about this foe."

"You're the best man for the job, Edward," said Rosenau.

Wearing his smock, gloves, and mask, Noble arbitrarily walked over to a bed with a man in his early twenties. He looked very ill. "Hi, sailor. I'm Dr. Noble. How are you feeling?"

"Not...very...very good, sir [cough]."

"Can you tell me what's been going on with you the last few days," said Noble.

"Well...Doc...I tell 'ya...I felt just fine [cough]... until this morning. Fine." The man's eyes closed as he appeared to drift off to sleep. Noble saw a certain dullness in the man's affect that he had not seen before with influenza. It was obvious that any additional history must come from the Commonwealth Pier documents. He picked up a clipboard at the foot of the patient's bed. Fortunately, a Corpsman at the pier had written some historical notes which showed the young man had developed sever prostration and headache over just a few hours. Later the patient noted the onset of chills, increasing feverish feelings, and extreme limb pain. By the time he was seen at the pier sickbay, he had a frequent hacking cough that was productive of blood-streaked sputum. He complained of pleuritic chest pain under his sternum, epistaxis, photophobia, and severe pain with eye movement.

The man already had vital signs taken on admission to Chelsea: temperature 104° F, respiratory rate 21 per minute, pulse 85 per minute, normal blood pressure. Noble began to examine the patient. His skin was hot, diaphoretic, and turbid. His face, neck, and trunk had an erythemic flush. When Noble gently brushed the man's skin, the patient winced as though he was experiencing pain. Noble took from his coat his stethoscope. He listened to the man's chest, and heard scattered course rales.

A Corpsman walked up to Noble and said, "Sir, if you are looking after this man, here is the result of the WBC drawn as he arrived. He also had blood cultures taken, along with cultures of sputum and his nasopharynx. There is also a urine sample. When we can, as Dr. Rosenau has ordered, we will perform roentgenograms on all the patients."

"Thank you," said Noble. He read the WBC report which said 2.5 K/μL. "Mild leukopenia," Noble said to himself.

Noble took a cursory look at many of the patients on the quarantine ward, and found the histories, physical examinations, and available laboratory data remarkably the same. What was also the same were their ages: all were in their late teens and early twenties.

Noble gave a sigh of relief as he walked over to Rosenau, who was drawing a blood sample from a patient. Rosenau said as he saw Noble approach, "What do you think, Edward?"

"Well, Milton," said Noble, "they definitely have influenza. It is very similar to the moderate form I saw in Kansas, and it is very similar to the moderate form described in Europe. These boys are very sick. But, from what I can see, the devastating influenza in the reports from Brest and Sierra Leone has not made its presence known here. These sailors look like they are going to make it. We'll know more with the results of blood tests, cultures, Roentgenograms...and time."

"Any suggestions on treatment until we have a better grasp on the infection?" said Rosenau.

"I would assess the hydration status of each patient, and then start up IVs of normal saline and isotonic glucose at a rate of 100cc an hour. This can be titrated to each patient after a few hours. Use caffeine and benzyl benzoate for their coughing, and sodium salicylate or acetylsalicylic acid for the fevers, myalgias, and pleuritic chest pain. Cool compresses can be given to the ones with the higher temperatures. Hopefully, they have the 'three day grippe'."

"Thanks, Edward," said Rosenau, "for arranging for the ambulances, and coming up here at such short notice. With the specimens we obtain from the patients, Lieutenant John Keegan and I will see if we can identify a pathogen. Perhaps from that study we can prepare a vaccine or serum. Do you think that Lillian could give us some logistical help with that, Edward?"

"I'm sure she will do all she can, Milton."

"Edward, I hope you don't mind if we keep in touch."

Noble just laughed, and patted his friend on his back. He turned, left the hospital, and found Sergeant Campbell waiting for him outside. He was much more relaxed on the return trip to Boston City Hospital, given what he had seen in Chelsea. Arriving at BCH, he instructed Charge Nurse Terry Tomlinson to begin clearing as many patients from one South Department pavilion as possible. He ordered the creation of a quarantine ward, much like the one established at the Chelsea Naval Hospital. Noble was going to make his stand against the demon in the final line available to him. He knew it was only a matter of time before that battle would begin.

Camp Devens sat on five thousand acres, thirty-five miles northwest of Boston. Like other cantonments, Devens had been thrown together for speed, and not with consideration of containing infectious disease. At the height of construction, over ten huge barracks a day were completed. It was designed to hold 36,000 troops. It now held 45,000 troops. The camp also suffered from most of the deficiencies that Major Noble had witnessed at Camp Funston in Kansas.

Many excellent physicians were working at Camp Devens. Frederick Russell was preparing to study the existence of streptococci in the mouths of healthy soldiers. Major Andrew Sellards had just passed infectious material through a porcelain filter to isolate measles virus. On August 29th, he inoculated human volunteers to see if he was successful.

On Sunday, September 1st, four soldiers reported to the Devens medical clinic with chills, severe headaches, extreme muscle aches, high fevers, epistaxis, severe eye pain with movement, and coughing productive of pink blood-tinged sputum. The men were dyspneic and in some distress. They were admitted to the camp hospital with a diagnosis of pneumonia. None of the pneumonia patients were quarantined. Concurrently, the camp continued to receive recruits and send newly trained troops to points beyond. They travelled by rail to other towns, other camps, and to ports of departure for Europe. They also went on leave into nearby cities. This Devens traffic involved thousands of troops every day.

That Sunday morning, Noble was at home enjoying a day of rest. Lillian had prepared a large early breakfast for everyone, and Noble's mood had lifted from the previous week. He reflected on the patients he had examined in Chelsea thirty-six hours earlier. Perhaps the pandemic was only going to give Boston a glancing blow, instead of the blunt insult it had given European and African cities so far. Perhaps.

The Noble family attended morning Mass, and then returned home to resume a leisurely Sunday. Noble played on the parlor floor with Marguerite, even though they were still dressed in their church clothes. "Daddy, do like this one?"

His daughter handed Noble a stereo photograph, and he placed it in the viewer. "Oh, Rabbit, it's a picture of the White House. It's very pretty."

"I like this one, too, Daddy," said Marguerite. She handed her father another stereo colored photograph.

"I really like this one of the Capital building in Washington D.C.," said Noble. "Rabbit, the pink cherry blossom trees around are beautiful, don't you think?"

Every time her father approved of one of the stereos, Marguerite would bounce in excitement as she knelt on her knees in her bright red Sunday dress. Her auburn hair curls bounced with her. After awhile, Noble assisted Marguerite with a tea party for her favorite doll, "Lucy". This consisted of setting up tiny cups, saucers, flatware, spoons, and a tea pot for "Lucy" and several invited guests: a worn teddy bear from President Roosevelt's 1904 election, a homemade Yup`ik girl doll constructed by Akeema in her people's tradition, and a large stuffed green toad with green glass eyes. Fun was had by all, but Noble felt that he was the recipient of the most pleasure.

Bernard and Michael could barely contain there excitement over tomorrow's coming events. September 2nd was the final day of the regular baseball season for the Red Sox. The Sox had recently won, and lost, double headers against Philadelphia.

But, they still maintained a three game lead in the American League. The final two games of the season would be played on Monday against the Yankees in New York. Bernard and Michael spent a full hour explaining the strategies that Red Sox manager, Ed Barrow, would use to defeat the Yankees and clinch the pennant. Noble loved baseball, but did not delve into the detail of the game like his boys did. Although he did not know all the statistics, he was fascinated by the fact that Bernard and Michael had such a command of them. He felt this was excellent training of the mind, encouraged it enthusiastically, and believed that the learning of such detail and organization would serve both boys well later in life. Noble listened intently to his children's baseball management theories as both boys wore their Red Sox caps and shirts.

During tea parties with a diverse guest list, and the dissection of baseball facts into the tiniest of minutia, Florence and Akeema sat in the library. They were also dressed in their Sunday clothes, which were different than in previous years. It was felt that somber pastel colors were a matter of good taste and patriotism, given the number of families that had lost loved ones in Europe. Few wore extravagant jewelry for the same reason. Still, young women liked to be stylish. Military influences were popular in women's clothing, but both ladies liked to stay as far from that as possible. Instead, they wore soft V-neck light colored blouses. Their skirts were now at a scandalous mid-calf length, and they wore heeled shoes along with flesh toned silk stockings. Some of the older women at Mass raised eyebrows at such fashions, but most young women wore them. In the library, the women were reading copies of Zane Gray's *The U.P. Trail*, which was the number one best seller of the year.

Later in the morning, Arthur called from Camp Devens. He spoke for some time with his mother, who missed him terribly. She needed to know what her son was eating, if he was warm at night, and if he was keeping clean enough. She wanted to know all about his friends, commanding officers, and if there were any women in the camp. To the last question, Arthur said there were very few, but that they were all "very popular" with the troops. Lillian commented that she bet they were.

Lillian finally turned over the telephone to her husband when she was satisfied with her loving interrogation of her son. "Hi, Dad," said Arthur, "or should I say Major, sir."

"Very funny...Second Lieutenant," said Noble. "How are you, Son?"

"I'm doing great, Dad," said Arthur. "My commanding officers say I'm doing extremely well with my officer training. They think I could be made a First Lieutenant soon if I keep up the pace. They think I may be Captain material in short order."

Noble replied, "Keep this up, Son, and I'll soon be calling you 'sir'. How's the leg?"

"No problem, Dad," said Arthur. "I don't even think about the accident anymore, and no one here can tell I was ever injured. I run through the obstacle courses like everyone else...actually better. We go on runs with the squad all the time, and I can beat everyone anytime. We have only been able to row a few times on the Charles River, but I'm stronger now than I was on the Boston University crew."

"You have such determination, Arthur," said Noble. "Whether it was mastering a new sport, or earning your ranks toward Eagle Scout, you have always met and exceeded all expectations. The U.S. Army is darn lucky to have a young officer like you."

"Thanks, Dad," said Arthur. "I really do like the army. However, when The War is over, I want to resume my pre-medical studies at Boston University. I want to be like you, the physician, and not you, the Major...if you know what I mean."

"Got 'ya, Son," said Noble. "And, you will be a wonderful physician, Arthur. I wish your grandfather could have known you. He would have been so proud of the medical tradition he set in place for our family. I don't think it will be that long before you can resume your studies, Arthur. The War is going well for the Allies."

"It sure sounds that way, Dad," said Arthur. "We hear that we likely will be sent to France before, or shortly after, the first of October."

Noble didn't comment on that statement. He knew it was only a matter of time before both his oldest children would be part of the "War for Democracy".

"Dad, I also really enjoy my radio class. We can already contact ships at sea that are more than seven hundred miles away. It won't be long before we will be able to do that on land as well. The new army field radios are quite good, and are very clear for some distance."

Noble replied, "I know the field commanders at The Front are re-writing battle strategies with radio. You have also mentioned that fact."

"You know, Dad," said Arthur, our instructors tell us that in the not-too-distant future, very tall radio broadcasting towers will be built all over America. Eventually, people may be able to afford radios in their own homes. Can you imagine that, Dad? Families could listen to music as it is actually being played in another city. A person could listen to theater... radio theater. One could hear lectures, speeches...even the news as events actually occur. I might even like to do something like that in the future, Dad."

Noble had not thought of radio in that way, since he was introduced to the device as a medium for war communication. However, he could instantly see the civilian value of radio. Noble said, "Arthur, maybe in the future, as a physician, you could speak to tens of thousands of people about health-related topics...all at once. Wow, would <u>that</u> be something!"

"That would be <u>really</u> neat, dad!" said Arthur. "Dad, I have already been on the telephone too long, so I need to get off. I'm due at religious services held for the troops on Sundays. Please tell Marguerite, Florence, and Akeema that I will see them in just a few weeks. Tell Bernard and Michael,

'Go, Red Sox!' for me. Give Mom all my love. And Dad, I love you too."

"I love you too, Son. Take care, and call again soon when you can." Arthur hung up the telephone. His father also missed him terribly. He hoped that his son would not be placed too close to The Front. In fact, the farther from it the better.

A short time later, Lillian came into the parlor, kissed her husband on the forehead, and asked him about his conversation with Arthur. Noble filled in his wife, who was always eager to hear more about her oldest child. Later, Noble asked her, "Dear, how are the gauze masks coming?"

"Pretty good," answered Lillian. "The Women's Auxiliary and the Red Cross volunteers have already made a few thousand masks. You know they are all eager to help. Most of the women have been engaged with war-related projects this last year. So, many of them were not exactly sure why I asked them to participate in this particular project. But, Edward, there are very strong rumors in Boston of Spanish influenza cases among the military. The ladies put two-plus-two together, and have figured out what the masks are for. So far, no one seems worried about it, but I want you to know that the word is at least partially out there."

"Well, Lillian," said Noble, "please keep me informed about what the populace is saying. We want preparation, not pandemonium. Also, I wonder if you can expand somewhat the scope of the work of the volunteers?"

"Sure, dear, what do you need?"

Noble replied, "The city's medical system is going to be in desperate need of linen and blankets, whether it is for the military or others. Collecting these items, and making them from unfinished materials, would be extremely important. For example, Boston City Hospital has barely enough linen and blankets now to meet the needs of existing patients. The War has siphoned off much of the available hospital supplies, and these are in very short stock. Do you think it's possible for your groups to gather some of these items?"

"Well," said Lillian, "most of the excess linen and blankets in the general population were donated many months ago. People are hanging on to the items they have. The last time I was at the J.C. Penney department store to buy school clothes, there was not much of a selection. In any case, I will see what the ladies can dig up. I'll make sure they know it is for a good cause."

Following a light lunch, Noble was reading from the *Boston Globe* in his "college" style light brown suit when the phone rang. Lillian answered it. "Oh, hi, Milton. [pause] Why...yes. He's right here. Edward, its Milton. He says it's urgent."

CHAPTER 14

"Hi, Milton," said Noble, in his cheery mood. "How's it going?"

"Edward," said Rosenau, "five of the men with influenza at the Chelsea Naval Hospital died last night."

Noble was taking a sip of black coffee when Rosenau began to speak. Noble startled so abruptly that he nearly spilled the entire contents of the cup. He felt the blood in his face run out as though there was a drain attached to it. He slumped back into his chair in the kitchen. "What happened, Milton?"

"All the men were as they were when you left them, until about 11:00 PM last night. Suddenly, within less than thirty minutes of each other, five of the men displayed a marked rise in their respiratory rates. They began to struggle with breathing, which increased with each passing minute. We applied O2 by masks, but it had no effect. Soon, bloody froth gushed from their nostrils and mouths in huge quantities. Then, Edward, something happened that I have never seen before. It was horrible. The men's faces first turned cherry-red. But, later their faces gradually turned a cyanotic indigo-blue color that I will never ever forget. It was so deep, so profound…it looked unearthly. The men fought for every breath, struggling to clear themselves of the seemingly endless amount of red fluid that flowed from their respiratory passages. Suddenly, they became very quiet, and showed no further struggle. They breathed as if their bodies knew it was the end. Quietly, one by one, they died. Edward, they all died a horrible hideous death. The staff is very shaken on the quarantine ward. They were all just young men."

Noble was motionless, and speechless. He had heard a similar clinical description of a few patients six months earlier. That account came from Dr. Loring Minor. Since then, no similar signs and symptoms had been described in the United States. Until now. But, this time it was much worse.

After a long pause, Rosenau continued. "Edward, the situation appears to be critical. Four more men are now beginning to show similar signs as the five who died. What is even worse is the fact that ambulances brought us fifty two more patients with influenza from Commonwealth Pier. The Chelsea Naval Hospital is already beyond full capacity."

Noble thought for several moments before he responded to his friend. Finally, he said slowly, "Milton, I will contact army brass to see if some of the sailors can be taken to Devens. We're preparing an influenza quarantine pavilion at Boston City, and perhaps we can take some of the ill there. The only other thing I can suggest is that you ask the navy for some large spare tents that could be erected on the Chelsea Naval Hospital campus."

"The other problem," started Rosenau, "is the availability of staff and medical supplies. We are at bare-bones now, Edward. Everything has been sent to Europe. We might be able to get a few tents, but that's about it."

"I'll see what I can do, my friend," said Noble. "I think we need your work on a vaccine or antiserum sooner rather than later. I'll contact the army right away." The two physicians hung up the telephones. Noble called the A.I. Office and asked for high priority messages to be sent to Colonel

Vaughn, but he was not sure what his commanding officer could do.

For a time Noble sat alone in his kitchen chair and thought about his invisible foe. The demon had not attenuated. In fact, it was stronger than ever. Noble wondered if it was simply flexing its muscles, and preparing for a full-force blow.

On Tuesday, September 3rd, Noble arrived early at the A.I. Office. In the past few days, as a stream of influenza patients came from the Commonwealth Pier, the Chelsea Naval Hospital had tried to send patients wherever it could. A few of the Chelsea patients had been transferred to the quarantine pavilion at Boston City. There had also been more deaths in Chelsea. Colonel Vaughn had been touring more of the nation's cantonments, and had not yet been reached.

As Noble waited for his latest attempt to communicate with Vaughn, he read through some of the stacked cables in the office. News from Europe was positive. The British Third Army battled northward beyond Arras. Bapaume finally fell to the New Zealand Division of the Third Army on August 29th. The Allied pressure along a 70 mile front was heavy and unrelenting. Intelligence intercepted a German communication that told the story: 'Each day was spent in bloody fighting against an ever on-coming enemy, and nights passed without sleep in retirements to new lines.' In nearly four weeks of fighting, over 100,000 German prisoners were taken.

On September 2nd, the Canadian Corps outflanked the Hindenburg Line, making it possible for the French Third Army to advance deeply. This sent repercussions along the entire Western Front. The Germans had no choice but to order six of their armies to withdraw behind the Hindenburg Line. This meant the Germans withdrew the entire Western Front, all at once.

The next cable brought a smile to the troubled face of Major Noble.

Monday, September 2, 1918
From: New York City

Today, the Boston Red Sox baseball club won the first of two games against the New York Yankees, 3 to 2. The Red Sox lost the second game, 3 to 4. However, at the end of the regular season's 126th game, the Red Sox were 2.5 games ahead in the League. Therefore, the Boston Red Sox are the American League pennant winners for 1918. They will face the National League pennant winners, the Chicago Cubs, in Chicago, for the first game of the World Series on September 5th.

New York Times.

Noble knew his sons would already have heard the results of the game by the time he returned home. Still, he folded the cable and put it in his coat pocket. One of the boys would surely want it for a scrapbook.

The next cable was not so well received.

Tuesday, September 3, 1918
From: Camp Devens, Massachusetts

Twenty–two cases of severe pneumonia reported at Camp Devens over the last three days. Dr. Roy Grist, army physician, has diagnosed the cases as influenza.

Army Intelligence.

Instantly, Noble made the connection between the Commonwealth Pier and Devens. He felt a wave of abdominal cramps come over him, and for a moment he was sure he would vomit. Noble sat down at one of the office's roll top desks, put both of his elbows upon it, and rested his face in his open hands. The picture was now much clearer. The demon had not only extended one of its tentacles from Boston's port. It now had found a tightly packed concentration of human beings on which to feed. Noble again thought of the tragic Greek story of Cassandra.

After he had collected himself, Noble said softly to Lieutenant Pierre-Louis, "Lieutenant, please send a message to Dr. Roy Grist at Camp Devens. This is highest priority; urgent. The influenza patients at Devens must be quarantined as soon as possible, if they haven't been already. Ask for a return message stating this cable was received. I have heard about Dr. Grist, and he is a good man. I know he will take this advice and quickly comply. Be sure this message comes from me."

"Yes, sir," said the Lieutenant. "It will be sent in just a few minutes."

Noble put on his white coat, and walked over to a nearly empty South Department pavilion that had been designated as the influenza quarantine ward. He put on a mask, gloves, and a white linen smock. A few Commonwealth Pier sailors were there, and were presently stable. Charge nurse Tomlinson saw Noble walk in, and quickly walked over to him. She said, "Dr. Noble, Dr. Schafer asked me if you could speak to him as soon as you arrived."

"Where is he, Terry?"

"He's in the outpatient clinic. He said it was very important."

Noble thought to himself that he was tired of "important" news. Lately, "important" meant "bad". Nevertheless, he left the pavilion and walked to the hospital's outpatient clinic. He found the third year resident, Dr. Shafer, an intern, and two medical students in an exam room. All of them, as well as a young man on an examining table, had gauze masks on. Upon entering the room, Noble asked, "Lieutenant, you wanted to see me?"

"I'm glad you're here, Dr. Noble. This is a 24 year old man who was brought to the clinic by fellow employees. He was feeling well until just a few hours ago. While he was working, he suddenly developed a pounding headache behind his eyes, a severe dry cough, chills, chest pain with breathing, a feverish feeling, severe bilateral arm and leg pain, and epistaxis."

Noble already knew where this was going. "What else, David?"

"Well, his respirations, pulse, and blood pressure are all normal. His temperature is 104° F. He is very lethargic and diaphoretic. He has fine bilateral rales, but no labored breathing. The rest of his exam is normal. All we have back from the clinical lab so far is a WBC of 2.1 K/μL. We've already obtained sputum and blood cultures, as well as a urine sample. We'll get a Roentgenogram when we can."

"What does the man do in his job?" asked Noble.

"He's a dock worker, sir," said Schafer.

"Where does he work?" again asked Noble.

"Let's see...he works at...eh...the Commonwealth Pier, sir," said Schafer. Do you think this is the Spanish grippe, sir?"

If Noble had said what he was thinking at that moment, it would have surprised Dr. Shafer. Noble knew the demon had now placed a small tentacle into the civilian population of Boston. The first known civilian with pandemic influenza had emerged in the city. But, the tentacle would not be small for long. No, this was just the beginning.

Noble instructed the group to move this new patient to the quarantine ward immediately. He walked with them to insure that the process was a rapid one. The patient's gurney was wheeled onto the ward, and the man placed into a bed. White linen hung from brackets placed in the walls, forming triangular barricades between the beds. An IV was started by a nurse, and he was given medication for his cough, pain, and fever.

David Cornish, MD

After tending to the new patient, Noble happened to glance up and see a short stout man in a white uniform standing at one end of the large ward. It was Commander Richard Cunard. Noble ignored him for a time, until Cunard finally yelled out, "Major, I want to speak to you immediately!" Noble was finished with the patient anyway, and walked over to Cunard.

"Yes, Commander. What can I do for you?"

"What is the meaning of this?" yelled Cunard. "What is this place?"

"What does it look like, Cunard?" said Noble calmly. "It's a quarantine ward. Do you have difficulty reading signs?" as Noble pointed over to a door with a sign that said "Quarantine Ward. Stay Out".

"Don't get funny with me, Noble," yelled Cunard. "Under whose authority was this ward established?"

"My authority, Cunard," said Noble. "Let me remind you that I am the Clinical Director of the South Department. And, in my clinical opinion, the hospital requires an influenza quarantine ward."

"So, you misuse BCH resources based on rumors floating around in the city?" said Cunard. "I'm going to have you brought before a court martial, Noble! In addition, I'm going to report you to the Massachusetts Medical Board!"

"Cunard," said Noble, "I don't have time for you or this foolishness. You are violating the established rules of this quarantine ward by not wearing the proper protective clothing. You can also report me to anyone you want. But, if we do not quarantine these patients now, there may not be anyone around to try me for my 'crimes'. If you do not leave this ward immediately, I will have you forcibly removed by the Military Police for your own safety."

Cunard knew he had lost this round with Noble. But, before he turned and left the pavilion, he said, "Noble, I am going to make it impossible for you to even work as an orderly in this State."

Noble was not concerned about Cunard's threats. He had other things on his mind.

By Saturday, September 8th, Noble could see from A.I. Office intelligence the rapid spread of the infection. As if watching a Greek tragedy where the ending is pre-ordained, he read the flurry of intelligence cables documenting the pandemic progression. Four days earlier, several students at the Harvard Naval Radio School had taken ill with influenza. More than one hundred men were reported ill with the infection at the Newport Naval Base. The Chelsea Naval Hospital was beyond capacity, even with the use of tents. Just five days ago, there were only eighty-four patients in the 1,200 bed hospital at Camp Devens. Now, Devens had hundreds of hospitalized patients, and nearly all of them had influenza. Boston City Hospital now had several dozen civilian influenza patients, with more arriving every day.

Cables also told an alarming story beyond the city limits of Boston. A few days earlier, several hundred soldiers had left Boston for the Philadelphia Naval Yard. By the time they arrived, three hundred of them had to be hospitalized with influenza. Similar troop transports from Boston had now arrived at the Puget Sound Naval Station in Washington State, and at the Great Lakes Naval Station near Chicago. In both places, hundreds of troops were hospitalized upon arrival with influenza.

The demon had encircled Boston, and was now riding the military trains and ships to other parts of the country. When the demon killed, even seasoned clinicians like Dr. Minor and Dr. Rosenau were shocked by it. Still, Noble maintained a degree of hope. The numbers of deaths after the initial Chelsea fatalities had been small so far. If local military physicians could adequately quarantine the ill, maybe the demon could be caged. Just maybe.

Americans in the eastern U.S. were beginning to be concerned over reports of the recent introduction of "Spanish Influenza" in the country. Attendance at public functions had begun to drop. For example, the Boston Red Sox had won the first game of the World Series, 1 to 0, with Babe Ruth pitching a shutout in Chicago. However, one-third fewer fans attended the game, compared to the previous year. The next two games, of which Boston was victorious in one, had the same greatly decreased attendance. But, there was also evidence that the populace still didn't see the pandemic as a great threat. The *Boston Globe* had reported that over one thousand local naval personnel had been hospitalized with influenza. But they dismissed the problem by saying it was due to Boston women "kissing" sailors. Noble wished it were that simple.

On Tuesday, September 10th, Noble arrived at the A.I. Office at his usual time. As soon as he opened the office door, Lieutenant Pecknold said, "Major, they need you on the quarantine ward right away."

Noble walked to the ward, put on the protective garments, and entered the large pavilion room. He could see several more beds were now filled with patients from the evening before. However, Noble heard loud gasping sounds coming from a far corner of the ward. A group of nurses and residents huddled around patients in that area. Noble walked over to the site of the activity, but was not prepared for what he would see.

One of the patients was a young man in extreme respiratory distress. He arched his back as he struggled with every breath. His face and bare trunk were a brilliant red color. But, there were very distinctive mahogany colored areas over both check bones, and over his ears. Bloody frothy fluid poured from his mouth and nose, covered his body and bed, and spilled all around the floor. In some places the fluid was a half-inch thick. The man made a terrible moaning sound as he exhaled. Bubbling pulmonary rales with each breath were so loud that one could hear them some feet from the bed. With his writhing, the patient had pulled out his IV.

Dr. David Shafer and a nurse were standing over the man. The nurse was trying to restart the IV, and the third year resident was attempting to replace an oxygen mask that had also been pulled off by the patient.

In the next bed was something Noble had heard about, but had never seen before. A young man lay motionless. There was also bloody frothy fluid about his body, bed linen, and the floor. An orderly was attempting to clean up the area. The appearance of the man was horrifying. His entire face and trunk were a deep indigo-blue. This made the man so dark that it was difficult to know to which race he belonged. The man's respiratory rate was low, and shallow, despite the oxygen mask. There was no apparent struggling from the man. The patient's lack of fighting was also very terrifying, in that there was a sense of resignation. Resignation from life.

Schafer looked up from his work with the writhing patient. "Dr. Noble. Glad you're here, sir."

"Can you bring me up to date, David?" said Noble.

"The cyanotic man in the next bed was stable until just about two hours ago. He had been receiving cinnamon in oil and milk for his cough. He was also given salicin for his pain and fever, which rose to 106° F. We applied cool compresses to his face and trunk. Then, his respiratory rate gradually began to rise and became increasingly labored. I felt he was possibly becoming acidotic from infection and was trying to compensate with a respiratory alkalosis. Per your instructions, I administered sodium bicarbonate by IV along with epinephrine. We also gave O2 by mask at the fastest flow we could. I know that some have given quinine to influenza patients. But, I didn't because you have not been convinced from the medical literature that it works. Is that OK, sir?"

"Lieutenant," said Noble, "you have done a marvelous job. Don't worry about that. What happened then?"

"The man only became more agitated as his respirations became more labored," said Schafer. "After about forty-five minutes, things really started to change."

"How so," asked Noble.

"Look at the man before us, as he labors for every breath. Do you see the deep red-blue areas confined to his cheeks and ears? That is how the man in the next bed looked a little over an hour ago. Gradually, this localized coloring spread over his entire face and chest, and greatly deepened in shade."

Noble commented, "So, what we are seeing is essentially the same process, but in different stages of evolution. One patient is an hour ahead of the other. In fact, since I arrived, I can see that the man with an initial slight cyanotic change has already had an extension of it."

"What else can we do, Dr. Noble?" asked Schafer.

Noble stood between the two beds and looked at the gravely ill men in them. He gritted his teeth, and pursed his lips together. So, this is what the demon has been performing on humanity far away. He hoped it could be stopped, or at least kept away. But, now it is here. Right here. Right before him. Daring him to try anything to stop it.

"I don't know, David," said Noble quietly. I don't know. As soon as you have another IV in place, treat the second man as admirably you did the first. Maybe it will make a difference with him."

Dr. Shafer walked over to the first cyanotic man, felt his pulses, and listened to his chest with his stethoscope. "Dr. Noble," said Schafer. "This man is dead."

About one hour later, the second man was also dead.

CHAPTER 15

The next day, Wednesday, September 11th, Bernard and Michael Noble were somewhat disappointed. Many weeks earlier, it looked like the Boston Red Sox had a good chance of a World Series appearance. At that time, their father had said he would try to secure tickets to one of the Series home games. However, Noble had changed his mind as the threat of pandemic influenza grew greater. Limiting potential exposure was prudent, and one does not do that while attending a World Series baseball game. Apparently, many others felt the same way. Over 27,000 fans watched the third game in Chicago. However, only slightly more than 15,000 fans came to the sixth and final game. What was even more telling was the fact this was a home game at Fenway Park. Bostonians were becoming fearful. They had good reason to be.

Despite their protests, Bernard and Michael were required to go to school that warm fall day. Fortunately, the final game started at 1:46 PM. Akeema rushed the Noble children home to Beacon Street, when they were joined by Katharine

Cushing, her three younger children, as well as Lillian, Florence, Marguerite. All ten fans began to follow the game in a most unusual way.

During the game, someone passed notes out to a compatriot on Yawkey Way. Based on the note, a short descriptive flyer about recent inning plays was quickly typeset and printed. Thousands of flyer copies were printed in this way. Then, several automobile vans fanned out around the city to distribute flyers to eagerly waiting fans...for 5¢ a flyer. The vans then returned to Fenway and repeated the distribution process. All ten Sox fans at the Noble house waited for a Ford Model-T van to drive by their house every ten to fifteen minutes. One of the Noble boys would hand a boy in the van a nickel in exchange for the latest flyer update.

For the next several hours, Bernard and Michael took turns running into the house screaming the latest news. Bulletins sounded like this: "Top of the 1st inning; No runs!" "Bottom of the 2nd inning: No runs!" "Bottom of the 3rd inning; Max Flack committed a third inning error, allowing two Red Sox runs!" "Babe Ruth replaced George Whiteman in Left Field!" "Top of the 4th inning; Cubs with one run!"

Edward Noble made it a point to return early for the festivities at his home. He was not in a pleasant mood, as he watched more and more influenza patients fill his quarantine pavilion. And deaths were becoming more common every day. Still, Noble felt he had an obligation to his sons, the rest of his family, and himself. That obligation was to put all of the worry and sadness aside for a few hours, and try to enjoy a special baseball game. Noble knew his upbeat demeanor would be an act for the most part. But, his family and friends deserved that act today. Therefore, Noble was able to yell and scream right along with the other Red Sox fans.

The whole party ate hot dogs, hamburgers, pickles, and potato chips, while drinking liters of Coca Cola. Milton Rosenau was even able to join in the revelry in the early evening. Finally, the last flyer arrived by a Ford van. Michael screamed at the top of his lungs as he ran into the house. "Top of the 9th inning; No Cubs runs! Finale score, 2 to 1! BOSTON RED SOX 1918 WORLD SERIES CHAMPIONS! Carl Mays winning pitcher!"

Noble had never seen his family so energized and happy. Even though it was a school night, everyone continued to celebrate until 10:00 PM. Bernard and Michael danced for hours. Marguerite bounced all over the first floor of the house. Arthur briefly called home, adding his exclamations to all the others. Akeema did a series of traditional Yup'ik dances, which consisted of an individual remaining stationary while moving the upper body and arms rhythmically. The limited motion by no means limited the expressiveness of the dances, which could be gracefully flowing, bursting with energy, or wryly humorous. Everyone enjoyed her dances, and Marguerite laughed and laughed as she bounced about.

Joyful noises could be heard all over the city that evening. Noble knew that Boston would have to store up all the joy it could for what was coming.

Any small hope Noble maintained of holding the demon at military gates were dashed over the next seven days. Every day, more civilian influenza cases arrived at Boston City Hospital than the day before. The Quarantine pavilion had been filled to capacity, and now cases were filling the other pavilions. In fact, no longer was the South Department the infectious disease area of the hospital campus. The entire hospital was beginning to serve only one entity: the demon. It was no longer possible to quarantine the influenza patients. There were just too many of them.

On Wednesday, September 18th, Rosenau and Lillian came by the O.I Office. They showed their identification and were allowed by the sentry to enter. With the fall weather cooling, and with increasingly overcast days, the ceiling fans were all turned off. One could now hear steam within the hospital heating elements along the office walls. Lieutenant Lafayette looked up from her cordboard and said, "Hi, Commander. Hi, Mrs. Noble."

"Good morning, Marié," said Lillian. "Will the Major be in soon?"

"He should be here any minute, Mrs. Noble," said the Lieutenant. "He's not in the best of moods. BCH is at capacity with influenza, and more patients are arriving every day. He's trying to find ways to deal with this problem." Just then, Noble entered the office, wearing no particular expression.

"Hi, Milton, Lilly," said Noble. "I didn't expect you here today."

Rosenau said, "Lillian and I are going to meet John Keegan at the satellite Harvard lab today to begin the initial planning for our influenza studies. Edward, as you and I have discussed in the past, I continue to wonder if influenza might actually be a filterable virus. If so, we need to be able to predictably pass it and see the same infection in others."

"One of the Koch Postulates," said Noble.

"Yes," said Rosenau. "I already have navy permission to offer some Boston navy brig sailors amnesty if they participate in such an experiment. We have to work out carefully the details, and we are so fortunate Lillian has agreed to help us in that regard. Somehow, we will collect sputum and blood samples from living influenza victims. We will also emulsify lung tissue from dead victims. We'll find the right proportions for diluting the samples in saline, centrifuge them, drain off the fluid, and pass it through porcelain filters. We will then try to infect volunteers with the filtrate. This will all take some time to do in the proper way."

"If anyone can do it," said Noble, "you three can." Noble and the other two sat down on the office oak coaster chairs. Noble gave a deep sigh, and leaned back in his chair. "Milton, I know I'm not telling you anything you don't already know, but things are going from bad to worse. I received an army cable this morning that said 1,543 Devens troops were hospitalized...just today. The camp is turning some of the larger barracks into hospital annex wards. This means hundreds of carpenters must shell in dozens of verandas to hold additional troops. All the tents that are available are also being employed."

Noble continued. "Boston City Hospital is beyond full. The hallways, corridors, and even the tunnels are packed with severely ill patients. We are beginning to place patients in the Rotunda, but that will be full by the afternoon. The army has provided us with several large tents, and we are going to erect them in some of the Brookline parks. This is an attempt to accommodate the western suburbs and perhaps decompress pressures on BCH. However, Milton, we are running out of everything. We only have a few days' supply left of IV solutions, compressed oxygen, analgesics, epinephrine, gloves, linen, smocks...everything."

"The Chelsea Naval Hospital has been over capacity for some time," said Rosenau. I understand that Massachusetts General is now over capacity, as are the rest of the other Harvard hospitals."

Noble said, "The military has a stream of railroad cars full of aspirin, digitalis, atropine, glacial acetic acid disinfectant, paper bags, sputum cups, thermometers, linen, etc., in various parts of the country. Colonel Vaughn cabled me and said these supplies can be shared with civilian health care institutions. But, it's not going to be nearly enough. Other cities in the country with nearby military bases are beginning to experience the same problems that we are. We're just farther down the pandemic evolutionary road. Of course, the other competing entity for resources is The War."

Rosenau added, "There is one positive note, Edward. I saw the U.S. Public Health Service telegram about influenza. Six million pamphlets are being distributed by the U.S. Mail, Boy Scouts, Red Cross, and other groups. The pamphlet information is pretty sound: Go to bed if ill, use handkerchiefs, avoid crowds, stagger work week hours to decrease personal contacts, use personal cars instead of public transportation. Even Surgeon General Rupert Blue is promoting this public health initiative."

"This is great," said Noble, "but I only wish this were all done a couple of months ago. Frankly, the demon is loose, Milton. All of these efforts are too late." Noble rose from his chair and put on his white coat. He put his stethoscope around his shoulders. As he walked toward the office door, he said, "There are other emerging problems. The BCH staff is starting to contract influenza. We have five nurses and a resident who are very ill right now. As the numbers of ill increase, the number of caregivers is decreasing."

"I can't think of a worse combination of simultaneous health care effects," said Lillian.

"It's worse than that, Lilly," said Noble. "Today hospital administration informed me that several funeral directors are refusing to pick up the dead, for fear of infection. Also, Boston area grave diggers are not reporting for work. This is likely due to a combination of fear, and of illness." Then, abruptly, Noble stated matter-of-factly, "Sorry, but I have to run." Noble remained expressionless as he bid Rosenau and his wife goodbye, and walked off to the hospital wards. Noble had a growing sense of hopelessness with the work ahead. For the first time in his life, he was not sure if he wanted to be a physician.

Both Noble and his wife were now working seven days a week at their respective tasks at Boston City Hospital. Whenever possible, they drove the Ford together in order to avoid public transportation. When that was not possible, Noble insisted that his wife and Florence use the Ford. He took the trolley. Since Akeema did not drive, Lillian used the Ford for family errands that would have required trolleys in the past.

On Sunday, September 22nd, Lillian came by the A.I. Office to ask her husband if he would like to have lunch with her. Noble welcomed the break, and the two walked across Harrison Avenue to a small delicatessen. Noble ordered his favorite sandwich, which was an assortment of cheeses, with lettuce and tomato on whole wheat bread. Lillian had a Caesar salad with croutons. They both drank water. "You seem especially quiet today, Edward," said Lillian. "What's the matter?"

Noble finished chewing a bit of his sandwich and took a drink of water. He said, "There were a number of distressing cables today, Lillian." Noble took a folded piece of paper out of his uniform tunic. "Officers from Devens were recently sent to Officer Training School at Camp Grant in Illinois. Three days later, there were 194 influenza admissions at the camp hospital. The next day, 371 admissions. The next day, 492 admissions. Four days after the first influenza admissions, they began to have their first deaths. In six days, the hospital went from a census of 610 to 4,102."

"That's a faster progression than at Devens," said Lillian.

Noble replied, "There were too few ambulances at Camp Grant to carry the ill to the camp hospital. So, they began to use mules to drag carts full of influenza victims. But, the mules became exhausted from the exertion, and stopped working."

"Things are very serious at Devens, Lillian," continued Noble, who again began to read from his folded paper. "Today, 19.6 percent of the entire Camp is on sick report. 75 percent of the sick report troops are hospitalized". Both Noble and his wife fully recognized the meaning of those statistics to them as parents. But, neither one of them wanted to discuss further those implications.

Noble went on, "Lilly, if military planners would only have listened to their Communicable Disease Division, the U.S. Public Health Service officers, and their own physicians. If they did, any adverse effects on The War effort would be insignificant compared to the resources saved. But, no one in authority could see the incredible profits from the modest investment in quarantines. And, they still don't."

"Did something else happen, Edward?" asked Lillian.

"As an epidemiologist," said Noble, "you're not going to take this easily, Lilly. A few days ago, a train crammed with 3,108 troops left Camp Grant. Its destination was Camp

Hancock, near Augusta, Georgia. Several Camp Grant physicians pleaded with the camp commanders to hold the train for a few more days. They asked to quarantine the men to ensure they were fit for the journey. This plea was ignored. Some of the men were already febrile as they boarded the troop train, and productive coughing was everywhere. On the way, hundreds of men became violently ill. Hemoptysis was common in every one of the troop cars. When they finally arrived at Camp Hancock, one-quarter of the men required hospitalization. Lilly, as of now, ten percent of the troops on that train are dead."

Lillian sat for a moment before saying, "It's a nightmare, Edward. A nightmare."

"There is another chilling aspect, Lilly," said Noble. "During the trip from Illinois to Georgia, the troop train stopped many times. Boys boarded the trains to sell food and snacks, and then returned to the small towns along the train tracks where they lived. This happened all the time during my train trip to Kansas in January. Troops also stepped off the train at quick stops in order to get some fresh air and stretch their legs. This went on for over five hundred miles."

"So," said Lillian, "the train effectively inoculated large areas of Illinois, Kentucky, Tennessee, and Georgia."

"You were right, Lilly," said Noble. "It's a nightmare... come true."

Early in the morning of Monday, September 23rd, the weather was cold and raining. It was obvious to all that fall had arrived in New England. The browns, reds, yellows, and oranges of autumn's leaves were already being matted on the ground by the rain. Noble checked in with the A.I. Office to get a sense of the progression of the pandemic. In his personal cable stack was the first message from Colonel Cushing that Noble had seen in weeks.

Sunday, September 22, 1918
From: Base Hospital No. 5

Camiers, France

Hi, my old friend. Sorry that I have not written is awhile. It seems that I was in a bit of "hot water" with the British Expeditionary Force, to which I have been attached this last year. I wrote a letter that was critical of one of the British physicians here, and it seems he has friends in high places. Well, the BEF censors forwarded it to the British Command, and they threatened to give me a court martial. Fortunately, I also have friends in high places. I'm not naming any names; Gen. William Gorgas, and the Secretary of War are a few of them. In any case, this whole dumb matter was fixed when I was transferred from the BEF command to the American Expeditionary Force. (You really don't have to mention this to Katharine, since she worries about everything.)

I'm back at Base Hospital No. 5, and trying to do the best I can with my new situation. Since the grippe many weeks ago, I tire very easily, and must rest a large part of the day. My legs are very wobbly, and I cannot stand for long periods of time. I can't feel the floor beneath my feet, and I have uncomfortable paresthesia on my soles. My bilateral cluadication is no better, and I still can't walk more than a few blocks before I must rest. My vision remains blurry, despite of my new glasses. It's hard for me to focus my vision on things. I work on improving my strength every day.

I hear the Boston Red Sox are World Series Champions! I'll bet "bean town" was a sight to behold that day!

I get depressed with my new situation, but I try to keep a positive outlook. I long to return to Brookline and resume my life. Please give my love to Katharine and the children, and say hi to everyone for me.

Your friend,
Colonel Harvey Cushing, AEF.

Noble wrote a quick message on a note pad, and asked Lieutenant Pierre-Louis to send it to Colonel Cushing. In his message he wished his friend success with his convalescence, told him he would surely pass on his love to his family, and purposely down-played the pandemic in Boston. The last thing Cushing needed now was alarm over his family's safety. However, Noble pondered something as he wrote his note: Were survivors of the pandemic destined for other chronic ailments, as his friend was experiencing?

Just as Noble was about to leave the office for the wards, Lieutenant Pierre-Louis called to him. "Major...wait...an urgent message is coming from the Army Communicable Disease Division in Washington D.C." She paused for a moment as she translated verbally a message coming in traditional Morse code. "Major...the message says, 'Urgent. Secret. Major Edward Noble to meet Pneumonia Commission...immediately...at the Camp Devens hospital, Massachusetts by 1200 hours. Signed, Colonel Victor Vaughn.' That's it, sir."

Noble suddenly felt flushed. He now realized there was more going on at Devens than even he knew, and he was left with a sense of panic. He tried to disguise this emotion while he planned his next move. In this weather, the train would be the fastest mode of transportation to Devens. Noble waited a moment before replying, and then said quietly, "Thank you, Lieutenant. Please call Sergeant Campbell at Devens and ask him to pick me up at the train station in Ayers. Tell him this is highest priority. I'll leave for the Boston station right now, so he can gauge the time. Let the ward clinic team know that I won't be able to meet with them today."

"Yes, sir. Right away, sir."

Noble concluded the situation must be much worse than even Army Intelligence was reporting. The Pneumonia Commission consisted of some of the most influential physicians in the United States. William Welch, Rufus Cole, Fredrick Russell, and Victor Vaughn. If all of them were traveling to Devens on such short notice, something important was happening. Something ominous.

Noble took the trolley up Massachusetts Avenue, and caught the subway to the downtown Boston and Main train depot. The Fitchburg line ran a commuter rail service to the small town of Ayer, which was located at the northeast tip of Camp Devens. Ayer had become a major north-south-east-west commercial railroad junction, and the large railroads to it were out of proportion to its population. In July, 1917, the Devens military "city" of 50,000 sprang up nearly overnight right next to Ayer. With Devens at its doorstep, Ayer's importance increased even more.

It was unlikely Noble would see his son during this unplanned trip. Still, as the train sped thirty-five miles to Ayer, he hoped he might. His last conversation with Arthur had revealed the strong, thoughtful, and intelligent young man he had become. He wanted to tell Arthur that, in person. He wanted to tell him just how proud he was of his son.

With only a few quick interruptions along the way, the train pulled up to the two train station buildings along Ayer's East Main Street. The engine slowly hissed to a full stop, and Noble began to depart his car. As Noble stepped into the rain with his umbrella, he noticed an odd sight off to the side of the station buildings. Many dozens of long wood boxes were stacked in rows. Several men were beginning to load the boxes onto the train cargo cars. There were both automobiles and horse drawn carriages with more long boxes on East Main Street. Men were carrying the boxes from the street vehicles and stacking them with the others. For a time, Noble could not make sense of this work. But, then he knew.

The boxes were pine boxes. Coffins. Dozens and dozens of coffins. And, the automobiles and carriages were hearses.

Noble stared at the spectacle as he stood at the little train station. There were so many coffins. Were these war dead? No, that could not be. The dead from Europe arrive at U.S. port cities. They are taken off trains at their home towns, not put on trains in small towns.

From behind him, Noble heard a familiar voice. "Awful, isn't it, Major..." said Sergeant Campbell."

Noble turned around with a perplexed expression that caused Campbell to stop mid sentence. "Oh. I thought you knew, sir, being with the Communicable Disease Division and all."

"Hi, Sergeant," said Noble. "I'm here to meet with some authorities from Washington today. What's going on here, Sergeant?"

"Sir, I guess you're here to see it for yourself." Campbell motioned to the army staff car. Both men stepped into the automobile, and drove east on Main Street toward the camp.

By now, Sergeant Campbell and Major Noble were old friends. But, Noble did not make many comments, nor did he pose any questions, on the way to Camp Devens. The Sergeant could tell the Major was deep in thought. It was the kind of thought that forces people into motionless, as they stared off into nothingness. They drove onto the mammoth 5,000 square acre camp that was a heavily wooded area at one time. However, the only remnants of that forest were thousands of low-cut stumps. Noble could see the numerous lengthy troop barracks in the distance. Even though it was raining, the camp seemed oddly quiet. Very few soldiers were seen about the barracks, which was not common in any weather. The car drove along Sherman Avenue and made its way to the camp's field hospital. The hospital consisted of a series of parallel buildings, each one hundred and sixty feet long, which looked exactly like troop barracks from the outside. The building closest to the Avenue had a sign on it that read simply "Base Hospital".

Then, Campbell abruptly stopped the car. Both men in the army staff car looked silently at the sight before them.

Lined up at the entrance to the field hospital were hundreds and hundreds of men. All the soldiers were coughing constantly and were very pale, or even gray in color. All looked dreadfully ill as they stood in a non-moving immense procession. Most of the troops had only blankets to shield them from the rain. Along the course of the line were men who had fallen to the ground, motionless. Some of the fallen were now covered with mud.

It took Noble a moment to gather up words. "Sergeant, thank you for picking me up at the Ayer station. Could you be ready to take me back to the station later? I don't know when that will be."

"Just let me know, sir," said the Sergeant. "Good luck, sir,"

With that, Noble left the car and walked through the front entrance of the hospital. Inside, in a large patient receiving station, there was total confusion. Dozens of very ill appearing men, continuously coughing, stood or sat on the floor waiting for someone to help them. But, there were no attendants to be seen. Noble decided to go onto a ward and ask if members of the Pneumonia Commission had arrived. He wondered if there were any medical personnel in the hospital at all.

Noble walked through what was likely an outpatient clinic packed with soldiers. He headed toward a door that read "Hospital Ward No. 1". As he approached the huge room, the stench coming from it brought on a wave of nausea. It was the stench of decomposing organic material. The huge ward was completely open, without any partitions between patients. The ceiling was made only of rafters twenty-five feet high, and the walls were painted a very light military green. The floor was made of bare wood slats. At one end of the ward was a large American Flag fastened to the wall.

Standing at the other end of the room were four men in officer field uniforms, and a fifth with a thigh-length white coat. One of the officers was Colonel Victor Vaughn. In spite of gauze masks, Noble knew who the other three officers were. He had seen them lecture at medical meetings many times.

As Noble walked up to the officers, the man with the white coat handed him a mask. Noble put it on. Colonel Vaughn glanced at Noble, and his eyes squinted slightly to show he briefly smiled behind his mask. "Edward, I'm glad you got my message." Vaughn turned to the other Colonels and said, "Gentlemen, I want to introduce to you Dr. Edward

Noble from Boston City Hospital. He's the subspecialist who has been assigned to the Army Intelligence Cable Office since January."

A short man in his sixties, weighing about three hundred pounds, reached over to shake Noble's hand. "Glad to meet you, Major. I'm William Welch of Johns Hopkins. Victor has told me so much about you. I understand you are both an Internist and an Infectious Disease clinical specialist." Welch's gauze mask hid his famous white mustache and goatee.

"Yes sir, I am," said Noble. "It's an honor to finally meet you, sir."

A tall athletic looking man stepped forward to shake hands and said, "I've also heard a lot of very good things about you, Dr. Noble. My name is Rufus Cole, and I'm from the Rockefeller Institute in New York."

Noble thought it odd that these men were telling him who they were. Everyone in American medicine knew who they were. "The pleasure is all mine, sir," said Noble.

Vaughn then said, "Edward, this is Frederick Russell, who is General Gorgas's deputy on scientific matters. The General is in France presently, so the Army Surgeon General Deputy is directing the influenza effort."

"Dr. Noble, how do you do?" said Russell.

"Fine, sir. I am somewhat overwhelmed, however, with… this," said Noble, motioning to the room with his hand.

"Edward," said Vaughn, "the four of us just arrived following an eight hour train trip from Washington. You only followed us by a few minutes. The deputy Army Surgeon General, Charles Richard, requested that we go to Devens immediately and see firsthand the emerging crisis." Vaughn turned to the man in the white coat. "This is one of the field hospital physicians, Captain Roy Grist. He was beginning to brief us on the situation at hand."

"Excuse me, sir," Grist said, as he turned to Noble. "Do you by chance have a son by the name of Arthur. Arthur Noble…the young Second Lieutenant with a femur fracture?"

"Why, yes," said Noble. "Do you know him?"

"Yes, yes," said Grist. "What a great kid! I arranged for some of his rehabilitation at the camp in the months he visited here with his full leg cast. We now often eat meals together in the officer's mess. Great kid."

"Thank you, Dr. Grist," said Noble. "I know he appreciated all the medical help at Devens."

Dr. Grist was a slender and fit appearing man in his early 30's, with thick bushy black hair. Noble could not see his full face because of the gauze mask, but his eyes seemed both kind and very tired. Dark circles formed beneath both eyes in the way severe fatigue can manifest itself. Noble thought this is a caring army physician who has had too little sleep in many days, and has seen way too much misery.

Noble turned his attention back to the task at hand. The smell on the ward was moderately better with the gauze mask, but Noble still found it hard to tolerate. The ward probably had two hundred and fifty percent more patients in it than it had been designed to hold. A quick look about room showed hundreds of men in ten rows who were coughing to such a degree that the sound was like a continuous roar. Blood tinged sputum was all about the beds, the cots, the linen, on the patients, and on the floor. Some of the patients writhed as Noble had seen at Boston City Hospital. Some were very quiet, as he also had recently witnessed. And, some were in various stages of a bluish-purple transformation. Noble thought to himself this transformation was the most flagrant and audacious sign of the demon in its full furry.

Dr. Grist said to the group, "Devens has a maximum hospital bed capacity of 1,200. Right now, we have more than 6,000 patients. As you have seen, hundreds more ill men show up every hour. We have converted several troop barracks into hospital wards, and have over 5,000 men in tents. But, there still is not enough space. Men are in hallways, corridors, offices, porches, exam rooms, and even in closets. In about two weeks, we have had over 12,600 cases of influenza."

Grist continued, "As you can also see, we have very few attendants for the sick and dying. We usually have twenty-five physicians in the entire camp. The army has now sent us two hundred and fifty doctors, and this is still not enough. Dozens of our doctors are also ill, and thirty percent of our nursing staff is severely ill. I don't know how many doctors and nurses have died in the last few days. There's no one around to count them. I do that know, just two days ago, twelve Red Cross nurses arrived to assist us. Eight of the twelve collapsed with influenza today, and two are already dead. Sixty-three men have died so far this morning. This count is completely inaccurate, since men are dying where they stand in line outside. At first we tried to promptly pick up their bodies. But, that work took attendants away from the living on the wards. For now, we'll just have to retrieve the bodies when we can."

The Pneumonia Commission, and Dr. Noble, stood helpless on the ward and could only struggle to comprehend what they were seeing. Dr. Vaughn said, "This ward is so crammed that there is barely room for a person to walk between the beds, cots, and men on the floor. And this is just one ward." The Commission noticed that interspersed among pale coughing soldiers were men with bluish cast faces. Others had the indigo-blue color that was ghoulish and terrifying.

Dozens of men had copious amounts of bloody frothy fluid streaming from their mouths and noses. Linen soaked with blood, sputum, vomit, urine, and feces, was everywhere. Many men were incontinent and laying in their excrement, surrounded by flies. In addition to the other odors, one could smell formalin that had been added to sputum cups to keep flies away. The few attendants on the ward were going about the task of carrying off the dead. As soon as a body was removed, another patient took the departed soldier's exact place; be it in a bed, cot, or on the floor.

Dr. Grist commented, "It starts out as an ordinary attack of influenza. However, two hours after admission they begin to show mahogany-colored spots over the cheek bones. The lips, ears, nose, cheeks, tongue, conjunctivae, fingers, and sometimes the entire body take on a dusky, laden hue. A few hours later you begin to see the cyanosis extending from their ears and spreading all over the face. They fight for air as they suffocate. Death comes only a few hours later. It's horrible."

Noble asked, "What is the time course of the illness, Dr. Grist?"

"It depends," said Grist. "Some have a course that takes three to four days to death. Not uncommonly, we see young men who feel perfectly well, then die a hideous death in less than twelve hours. Some men have been working normally... and just drop dead. But, the marked cyanosis is the striking phenomenon. Many patients exhibit even on admission an incredible intense cyanosis, especially about the lips. This is not the dusky pallid blueness that one is accustomed to seeing in a failing pneumonia. Rather, it is a deep blueness...an indigo-blue color. None of us has ever seen anything like it before. Have you, Dr. Noble?"

"Yes," said Noble, slowly. "Regrettably, we have been seeing it at Boston City Hospital frequently over the last thirteen days...in influenza patients."

"When doctors or nurses see the cyanosis," said Grist, "they begin to treat these patients as terminal. When they walk in this way, they are the walking dead. They have them lay or sit in places where it will be easier to carry their bodies away later. I cannot tell you how terrible it is to treat these dying young men this way. However, what else can we do?"

Grist continued, "The other striking phenomenon is the hemorrhaging. Patients begin to bleed from everywhere, even their eyes. Blood can spurt from their nose and mouth with enough power to travel several feet. The pain they encounter seems to be immeasurable and indescribable. Their coughing can be so forceful that it tears apart the muscles and cartilage of their chests. Their headaches are discussed as though sledgehammers have split open their skulls. Many have had both their ear drums blown open by the infection, and they scream with agony with the pain of it. When they are able to speak, many of them pray to die. I have had men ask me to shoot them."

"There is no doubt in my mind," said Grist, "that there is a new mixed infection here. But what, I don't know. Nevertheless, my total time is taken up hunting respiratory rales. Rales dry or moist, sibilant or crepitant, or any other of the hundred things that one may find in the chest. They all mean the same thing here...pneumonia. And, that means in so many cases, death."

Grist then asked, "Gentlemen, is there any hope of getting more supplies to Devens? We're just about out of everything. We don't even have any more gauze masks. We need more nurses, doctors, and people to collect, cook, and distribute food. We also need people to clean linen, make beds, and deal with the dead."

"Well," said Vaughn, "the army has hundreds of tons of supplies coming by rail right now to New England. But the problem is obvious. Not only do cantonments need desperate help, but so do the civilian communities near them. Boston is a perfect example, as Dr. Noble has just mentioned. It's hard to believe there will be enough to go around. Of course, the War Department will insist on its large share."

"Colonel, I do understand," said Grist. "But, as you can plainly see, things are critical here. To give you a better appreciation of that critical nature, I need to show you something." Grist motioned the group to follow him to another building. Noble shared his umbrella with Vaughn, and the other five men shared two umbrellas found near the exit door. Devens had turned into a giant mud flat with the long and heavy rain. This was not making the business of caring for the ill any easier. It also made walking on the grounds very difficult indeed. Noble looked at the dark gray sky, and felt it matched the overall mood of the camp.

Grist brought the Commission and guest into another large barrack that was dark and very quiet. Shades had been drawn on the lower row of double windows that lined the length of the building. As soon as Noble's eyes adjusted to the lower light, he could see why the barracks was adorned this way. It was a chilling sight. The barracks was a giant morgue. Dozens of long rows of young men were laid out on the floor. Hundreds and hundreds of men. They had all been dressed in their field uniforms, including their boots. Many of them wore their doughboy hats. The group simply stood quietly as they looked at the most disturbing scene.

"This is how we started out dealing with the dead," said Grist. "At first, we had the time to prepare the men's bodies correctly, respectfully, and with great reverence. Men would place each body carefully into a coffin, and ready it for transportation to the Ayer train station. From there, the boys would be placed on trains for their final journey home. But, the numbers of dead grew and grew. More and more workers fell ill, so there were fewer and fewer around to do this work. The supply of coffins was exhausted, and there was no one around to make more of them. The hearses could not keep up with the increasing numbers of dead, either. So, things have gone to hell. Here, let me show you.

Grist led the group to another building near by the first makeshift morgue. As they entered this next building, the smell of decomposing organic tissue mixed with the odor of formaldehyde became stronger and stronger. Grist opened a door to a large darkened room. Once again, Noble's eyes had to adjust to dim light within the room. When they had adjusted, Noble understood how things "have gone to hell", as Dr. Grist had mentioned.

The true horror that was now Devens became crystal clear. Stacked in row after row, from the floor to the ceiling like cord wood, were bodies. Hundreds and hundreds of bodies. Many of them had necropsies performed on them, so numerous torsos and craniums were partially open, or completely open. Some still had their scalps pulled over their faces after having their brains removed. Most of the bodies had a bluish mottled cast that was hard to reconcile as being in any way human. Dried pinkish fluid was everywhere. On the bodies. On the floors. On everything.

"We're running out of places to put them," said Grist.

Noble had seen many terrible sights in France, but nothing like this. He turned away from the view of the room. As an internist, he preferred the study of the living to the dead. However, Colonel William Welch was both a microbiologist and a pathologist, and he wanted to see more. "Is the necropsy room in operation?" asked Welch.

"Yes," said Grist. "It's in the adjoining building. Come with me."

As the group walked to the camp hospital postmortem laboratory, they found conditions no better. Bodies littered the hallways surrounding the lab. Colonel Rufus Cole commented, "It appears that bodies are now placed on the floor without any order or system." He and the rest of the group had to step among the bodies to get into the necropsy room.

The postmortem laboratory had a cement floor, and white tiles that went half-way up the walls. The rest of the walls and ceiling were painted white. Various charts and anatomic poster diagrams were hung on the walls. About ten stainless steel necropsy tables lined the middle of the room. Over each table were very bright electric lamps and weighing scales that hung from the ceiling. Each table had a draped body on it, and each body was in various stages of autopsy. Dozens of buckets with organs in them were lining the walls and placed on the floor. At one end of the room were tables used to dissect organs. On the other end of the room was a row of microscopes and tools used to make microscopic slides.

Grist led the group to a table where a young pathologist was busy at work. Grist said, "Everyone, I want you to meet Captain Timothy Caron, one of the camp's pathologists. Captain, this is the Pneumonia Commission from Washington I told you about this morning. And, this is Colonel William Welch." Welch nodded at the young pathologist.

"Well...eh...gee," said Caron. "Excuse me for my appearance. As you can see, we have our hands full these days."

Noble thought to himself that he had never heard a greater understatement in his life.

Welch said, "Please, please. Don't worry about it. We're just here to assess the situation, Captain."

"Well," said Caron, "it isn't everyday that the world's most famous pathologist walks into one's lab. If you're here to assess the situation, I guess seeing is better than telling." On the table before the doctors was the body of a soldier who had likely been in his late teens. When the body was moved even a slight amount, pink fluid poured from the mouth and nostrils. His chest was open and his lungs had been removed. At the side of the stainless steel table was a bucket with the man's lungs in them.

Welch leaned over the bucket and exclaimed, "The soldier's lungs are not floating."

"No," said Caron. "The lungs are filled with enormous quantities of bloody, frothy fluid, as are the bronchioles, bronchi, and the trachea. All the alveoli are also filled to the brim with this serous fluid. There is barely any air left in them. The usual pneumonia also has fluid in the alveoli. But in these influenza patients, the spaces between the alveoli are also extremely congested with huge quantities of serous fluid, alveolar cellular debris, fibrin, red blood cells, and white blood cells. The quantity of material in the lungs is extraordinary. Some of the lung specimens don't even have pneumonia, per se. Instead, they just have these very unusual intra-alveolar space changes."

Welch asked, "May I see some of the lung microscopic slides, Captain?"

"Sure," said Caron. "The six microscopes over there have lung specimen slides on them right now, and there is a stack of additional pulmonary slides next to each microscope. Incidentally, we are taking extensive cultures of all the lung specimens. We are doing all we can to try and understand this." The Commission and Noble went to the microscopes and spent the next thirty minutes reviewing pulmonary histology.

Welch finally raised his head from the microscope, paused, and then said, "The pathological pictures are striking. The pneumonia in the specimens is unlike any I have seen. I am struck by how different in character they are to anything I have seen in the tens of thousands of autopsies I have performed during my career."

Noble realized this statement was coming from one of the world's most renowned pathologists. Welch had been reading the medical literature in many languages since Noble was in diapers. Noble looked over at Colonel Rufus Cole, who was a long-time protégé of Colonel Welch. Few anywhere knew the great pathologist better. It was apparent that Cole was disturbed because <u>Welch</u> was disturbed. This only added to the tension Noble felt.

"Captain," asked Welch, "are you able to give us a summary of the findings in the other organ tissues you have examined thus far?"

"Yes, sir," said Caron. "At least I'll try, sir. Starting at the top, the brain shows marked hyperemia, and the convolutions of the brain are flattened. Brain tissues are notably dry. In the cases accompanied by delirium, the meninges of the brain are richly infiltrated by serous fluid, and the capillaries are injected. There are islands of edema in the cortical substance surrounding greatly dilated small vessels. In addition, there are hemorrhages into gray matter of the spinal cord along with edema."

Caron said, "Moving now to the trunk, the pericardium and heart muscle are inflamed. The heart muscle itself is often soft and hypertrophied. The kidneys are almost always affected with inflammation. The liver is occasionally affected to a moderate degree. The adrenal glands show necrotic areas, frank hemorrhages, and occasionally abscess. The adrenals can also show considerable congestion and inflammation. Muscles of the thorax can be torn apart by the internal toxic process and by the stress of extreme coughing. Other muscles have shown necrosis or 'waxy' degeneration. The testes usually show very striking changes in nearly every case."

Caron continued. "But, it is the lungs. The lungs set this disease apart from all others."

The group spent the next two hours looking at gross anatomy preparations and histological slides. They looked at stained lung specimens that sometimes showed *Streptococcus hemolyticus*, *Streptococcus pneumoniae*, and *Staphylococcus aureus*. These bacteria were sometimes in small quantities, sometimes in large quantities, and sometimes not seen at all. Meningeal specimens rarely showed *Streptococcus pneumoniae* or meningococcus. Most of the time there were no bacteria seen in meningeal specimens. These results were confusing.

The Devens visitors thanked Dr. Caron for his great help and preliminary work on the pandemic. The group continued to tour the camp with Dr. Grist and gain as much information as possible. While at Devens, the visitors noticed the line to the hospital grew in length, the number of hospitalized patients grew, and the number of bodies stacked in the morgue increased.

Late in the afternoon, Colonel Welch excused himself to make a few telephone calls. When he returned, he said to the group, "Based on some new kind of infection or plague we have seen today, I just made a few requests. First, I called the renowned Brigham Hospital pathologist, Burt Wolbach, to come to Devens and assist in the investigations here. Second, I called Rockefeller Institute's talented molecular biologist, Oswald Avery, to travel here and work in his area of expertise. Finally, I placed a call to the deputy Army Surgeon General and asked him to help in the immediate and rapid expansion of hospital space in all U.S. camps. I have also asked him to order a quarantine of all cases, and to eliminate the transfer of personnel from one camp to the other. Deputy General Charles Richard said he would speak to the army chief of staff about these issues immediately."

The Pneumonia Commission thanked Noble for his work, and left to catch the train that would take them back to Washington. Sergeant Campbell picked up Noble at Devens and took him to the Ayer train station. On the way back to Boston, Noble hoped the deputy Surgeon General could initiate the recommendations Colonel Welch had made. He only wished those same recommendations had been enacted months earlier.

As the autumn sun set that evening on the train, Noble recalled one of his favorite novels. In 1898, while still in medical school, Noble was captivated with a new novel by H.G. Wells called *The War of the Worlds*. In it, Martians invaded the Earth and begin the extermination of humanity. At the time, Noble loved the book, but thought the premise preposterous. Now, the idea of extermination did not seem so far-fetched. Only this time, the enemy was invisible.

CHAPTER 16

Revelry at Camp Devens, on Wednesday, September 25th, was before sunrise at the traditional hour of 0500. Lieutenant Arthur Noble had been sound asleep, as were the rest of the men in his company, when the bugle played its usual tune. The difference now was that Noble was sleeping outside on a barrack porch cot, and not actually in a barrack. So many camp barracks had been turned into medical facilities that healthy troops were more crowded than ever. In addition, the New England autumn nights were dipping into the low 30's° F. The thin army blankets issued to the troops were completely ineffective. To make matters worse, barrack porches leaked when it rained. Still, Arthur was trying to make the best of the poor conditions at Devens. He figured that even these dismal living quarters were better than those experienced at The Front.

Every morning Arthur and his company began the day with a run along part of the perimeter of the camp. This is when Arthur would think about his army training and the coming day's events. He had completed the early Basic

Officer Training (BOT) instruction in military customs and courtesies, military history, leadership, officership, small arms training, combatives, drills and ceremonies, physical training, and field exercises. Arthur was now considered an upperclassmen, and his final weeks of training were concentrating on specific field training exercises, building team skills by overcoming challenges, and simulated deployment environments. There were also courses in intelligence, weather, machine maintenance, logistics, large and small munitions, military strategy, and communications.

When he joined the army, Arthur had scored highly on the Officer Qualifying Test that covered math, verbal, and analytical skills. The military needed so many officers quickly that the baccalaureate degree requirement had been waived back in 1917. Therefore, advancement for those who qualified came quickly. Just a few days earlier, Arthur had been informed that he was promoted to a First Lieutenant. It looked as though he would soon be able to pick his full duty assignment.

The company run ended as dawn showed itself. It was now time for a shower, and this was not a pleasant experience. The showers were outdoors, and without any barricades against the wind. There was also no warm water. As one might expect, showers were kept very brief.

With their uniforms on, the young officers met with their drill Sergeant for morning inspection and military review. By now, the company was polished and fully within army discipline. They all knew European deployment was near.

It was time for breakfast, and this is where the term "basic" in "basic training" was best understood. On each officer's tin was placed one large spoonful of cold scrambled eggs, two thick strips of cold hard bacon (which chewed more like jerky), and a cold biscuit with butter. Their tin cups were filled with lukewarm black coffee which the troops nicknamed "Diesel No. 2". The camp medical officers had told everyone to space themselves four feet from others during meals. Troops were to be situated so that no one faced another person directly.

But the need for more hospital buildings had made this order impossible to follow. In fact, the troops were now closer than ever before. The mess halls were so full, even with staggered meal schedules, that everyone's shoulders touched the shoulders of the troops beside them. The men were ordered to cover their mouths with coughing, but this was not consistently performed.

After breakfast, the men briefly assembled again for the raising of the Stars and Stripes. The troops then went about their morning assignments. As an upperclassman, and now as a First Lieutenant, one of Arthur's duties was to be a leader and mentor to the new group of underclassmen. Just ten days earlier, a new class of Second Lieutenants had entered Camp Devens. Arthur was now junior commanding officer for a new company. In his new role he was very involved with their early officer training. He walked over to the nearby new recruit barrack and assembled them for their morning inspection. It was hard for Arthur not to laugh out loud at his new company's improperly worn hats, ruffled uniforms, and poorly polished boots. Still, only three months earlier, it was Arthur's company that looked exactly the same way. Arthur tried to strike a balance with them between disapproval and encouragement, as good officers should.

After morning inspection, Arthur's company of underclassmen was scheduled for rifle practice. Normally, a Battalion Sergeant Major with Target Excellence would train the new officers. However, so many army specialists were ill that many of the upperclassmen were required to do this training. Arthur had been a company star with the rifle, so he was a logical choice as a temporary instructor.

Arthur lined up his company and handed them the two most used rifles in the U.S. Army. They were the 30.06 Springfield (M1903) short barrel bolt-action magazine rifles, and the 0.303-inch American Enfield (M1917). Troops liked both weapons because of their reliability in the field. The company had already practiced disassembling and reassembling the rifles in daylight and in the dark. Now it was time for target practice.

The new officers were to practice firing the weapons while in the prone position. The targets were set up, the rifle magazines filled, and the firing began. There was a light rain, and Arthur thought the weather was similar to how French autumns were described. This was a good training simulation.

It was 0730, and about 30 minutes into the target practice, when Arthur noticed a change. It was barely perceptible; hardly noticeable. It was not really a pain, or even a discomfort. It was more like an itch. Only the itch was located right behind his eyes.

Within twenty minutes the retro-orbital itch became a discomfort. Hundreds of rifle rounds had been fired, and Arthur dismissed the discomfort as a necessary complication of target practice. Within another twenty minutes the discomfort became a pain. He asked the company to switch to the second type of rifle issued to them, and sat down on the damp grass for a moment to rest. Arthur thought to himself that near freezing night temperatures, while in the rain, were taking their toll.

Twenty minutes later the pain had become a throbbing. Arthur had believed resting would give him back the energy he needed for his company's rifle practice. Instead, he now found it difficult to stand. His shoulders, neck, and arms felt heavy, and they had a strange ache inside them. Arthur could not understand it, because it was only in the low 40's° F outside. But, he felt hot. He noticed his forehead was sweaty. He noticed he was sweating inside his uniform as well.

Arthur rose from the ground with some difficulty and walked over to Joseph, who was another upper classmen. He asked Joe if he would watch his company for just a little while. He needed to lie down for a short time. Arthur offered to pay back this effort by watching Joseph's company in the afternoon. Joseph accepted the request, and Arthur walked back to his barrack. His legs were becoming heavy with simple slow strides, and they ached. Strangely, Arthur now felt cold.

And, there was a new sensation. It started out as a slight full-ness in his chest. Soon it felt as though something was caught in his lungs, and that he would feel so much better if he could just cough it out. However, coughing did nothing to relieve him of this sensation. Arthur finally reached his cot on the barrack porch. He pulled his blanket up over him, and fell asleep.

At 0930, a deep cough rattled Arthur awake from an un-comfortable sleep. The pounding behind his eyes had be-come a stabbing. He found it difficult to focus his vision, and all his extremities ached in a way he had never experienced before. The fullness in his chest had become a heaviness, and his coughing nearly constant. Now, with each cough, his chest hurt. And there was another new symptom. Arthur had to think about it for a moment, because it was very subtle. It was difficult for him to even describe to himself. It seemed, in some odd way, there was not quite enough air on the porch where he lay. This, of course, was ridicules because he was outside. Still, there just wasn't quite as much air as he was used to.

The stabbing behind Arthur's eyes was now a splitting. It was difficult for Arthur to think. And, he again felt hot. Very hot. He looked at his uniform and saw it was sopping wet under his arms and along the middle of his chest. Sweat now dripped from his forehead and down his back. Arthur began to think the unthinkable. He dare not say it for fear the words would make it real; make it stick. When he could finally deny it no longer, Arthur said quietly out loud, "The grippe."

Arthur wanted help. But, he still had enough of his facul-ties to realize help would be hard to find. Everyone had seen the long lines of sick men. Hundreds and hundreds of men. What to do? Perhaps his friend Dr. Roy Grist could help. Yes. He needed to find his friend Dr. Grist.

Arthur found it more and more difficult to put thoughts together in a cohesive way. The splitting behind his eyes made the simplest thought a monumental task. He forced himself to formulate a plan by carefully stringing one action onto another. He struggled to his feet and began the work of producing steps. He knew his barrack was near the hospital ward where Dr. Grist usually could be found. Hospital Ward No. 1. To avoid the long line of men at the hospital, Arthur circled around the building and entered through a service door in the back. Avoiding any eye contact with staff members, he moved through a storage room, a supply room, and into the ward itself.

Standing became more arduous for Arthur. Also, the sensation of too little air in the room had turned into frank shortness of breath. The light on the ward was blinding, and opening his eyes made his splitting headache much worse. He leaned against a wall and squinted his eyes to look for a slender man with thick bushy black hair. It seemed to Arthur that hours went by as he waited for someone to match that description. Or, was it seconds?

At the far end of the giant room, one hundred and sixty feet long, Arthur saw a man who could possibly be Grist. There was almost no room between the hundreds of ward patients lying on the cots and floor. So, Arthur edged along the wall of the room while leaning against it. In the process, he stepped on dozens of patients who didn't seem to notice. When Arthur was about fifteen feet from the man with black hair, Dr. Grist looked up and said, "Why, Arthur. I didn't know you were here. You had better put on a mask..." Grist stopped mid-sentence. He could see the young man was barely able to stand. He was a grayish color, diaphoretic, had labored breathing, and had a very bad dry cough. Grist thought to himself, "Oh, no. He has it."

Grist quickly surveyed the ward. A cot had just become available in one of the ward's four corners. The previous cot inhabitant had just been carried away by two corpsmen. Not to lose the chance, Grist quickly moved toward Arthur, put his right arm around his back, and guided him to the vacant cot. At least Arthur would not have to lie on the floor.

"Arthur," said Grist, "Tell me how you feel."

"Dr. Grist," said Arthur. "I...I...my head...I have a bad headache [cough]. I...I'm having trouble breathing."

Grist had seen enough in the last several days to know what was happening. He reached into his white coat pockets and brought out a thermometer cleaned with alcohol, a sphygmomanometer, and a stethoscope. Arthurs' vitals were: blood pressure 110/71, pulse 72 and regular, respiratory rate 22, temperature 102° F. Grist performed a heart and lung exam, and heard course rales and a few wheezes bilaterally. His mucus membranes were dry, he was very diaphoretic, and his skin turgor poor. Grist realized that Arthur had influenza with early bronchitis. Whether there was an early pneumonia present or not was not yet clear. Grist knew Devens was out of most supplies. There was also no one to attend to the young man with newly placed single silver bars on his shoulder epaulets. But, he knew someone that could provide both supplies and expert attention.

It was 10:30 AM, and Dr. Noble stood at the A.I. Office center table reading war news. All through September the Germans had put up strong rear guard actions and had launched a number of counter attacks. However, only a few of these attacks had succeeded, and then only temporarily. Towns, villages, outposts, high terrain, and trenches along the Hindenburg Line continued to fall to the Allies. The Allied Third Army was victorious at Ivincourt on September 12th. The Allied Fourth Army was victorious at Epheny six days later. Just yesterday, on September 24th, a combined assault by the British and French along a four mile front brought them within two miles of St. Quentin. With the outposts and preliminary defensive lines of the Siegfried and Alberich positions eliminated, the Germans were now completely back behind the Hindenburg Line.

More U.S. Army Intelligence interceptions seemed to indicate that Germany asked Emperor Charles of Austria to urge for peace on September 10th. Austria had sent a message on September 12th to all Central Powers, Allies, and neutrals, suggesting a meeting for peace talks on neutral soil.

Germany made a peace offer to Belgium on September 15th. Both peace offers were rejected on September 24th. In any case, the German High Command had reportedly told leaders in Berlin that armistice talks were inevitable.

"Major," said Lieutenant Pecknold, "there are some new transmissions that you might want to see."

"Sure, Lieutenant," said Noble. "What's there?" The Lieutenant handed Noble a two freshly printed messages, and he read them.

Wednesday, September 25, 1918
From: Camp Mead, Maryland

1,500 ill with Spanish influenza.

Army Intelligence.

Tuesday, September 24, 1918
From: Camp Pike, Arkansas: Francis Blake, Army
Pneumonia Commission

8,000 cases of Influenza in four days. Every corridor, and there are miles of them, with double rows of cots. Nearly every ward with an extra row down the middle with influenza patients. Many barracks about the camp turned into emergency infirmaries. Camp closed. Death is now the Commanding Officer.

Army Intelligence.

Noble stood with his arms braced on the center office desk top, and elbows locked. He closed his eyes and felt hopelessness wash over him. Multiple camps in the U.S. now looked just like Devens. Even the army's own Pneumonia Commission was describing the situation as "death is the Commanding Officer". Of course, Noble hoped promises of camp quarantines would actually happen. But, he also knew it was all too late. All of it was useless. Noble could do little more than watch the reports print in the intelligence office. The demon was now free to extend its tentacles wherever humans would take it. It preyed on the very species that desperately tried to avoid it. The demon had new strength and vigor. To Noble, it seemed to delight in its dance with death. And it seemed to love the dance most with the youngest, and the strongest.

Noble remained motionless with these thoughts for some time. After a long silence in the A.I Office, Lieutenant Pecknold saw a call light brighten on her cord board. She plugged a connector cord into the proper socket and established the line. After a few moments, she said, "Major, you have a call from Captain Roy Grist at Camp Devens. He says it's urgent."

"Thank you, Lieutenant," said Noble. "I'll take it in the small office." Noble walked into the adjoining room, closed the door, and sat at his desk. The phone rang, and Noble answered it. "Yes, Roy. How can I help you?"

"Major Noble, sir...it's your son...Arthur. He's very ill."

Noble felt the equivalent of a twenty pound two-by-four strike him squarely in the face. He dropped the phone receiver, and his forehead actually hit the table top. For an instant, he did not know where he was or that he had been on the telephone just seconds earlier. He sat looking at the phone now on its side on the table. He did not want to pick it up again, because the sound coming out of it might repeat itself.

Through the receiver on the desk, Noble could hear faintly, "Major...are you there, Major? Major?"

Noble put the receiver to his ear and said, "Roy...what did you say?"

"Major, Arthur is very ill," repeated Grist. "I'm calling because Devens is out of all supplies as we care for the ever increasing influenza casualties. There is no more help here for them. Major, perhaps you can bring some items and care for him yourself? He's a good kid, sir. I just thought you might want to know. If you are able, he is in the far northwest corner of Base Hospital Ward No. 1."

"Thank you, Roy," chocked Noble. "I will be there right away." Noble hung up the phone.

Noble did not stop to tell Lieutenant Pecknold that he was leaving. He put on his coat and rapidly walked to one of the South Department pavilion supply rooms. He found three large laundry sacks and began taking various supplies he would need to battle the demon himself. "Hand-to-hand combat", Noble thought to himself. Only this time, the battle was over his own son. Medicines, syringes, IV bottles, needles, various containers, linen, and towels. Lots of towels. Noble told himself that he would pay back the hospital quadruple the supply's value at some future time. He then nearly ran to the Harvard satellite clinic.

Noble and his wife had driven to BCH in the Ford truck that day. Lillian was setting up the experiment design that Dr. Rosenau and Dr. Keegan would use with the influenza serum they were developing. Noble burst into the laboratory and saw Lillian at one of the desks. "Lilly," he said, partially out of breath.

Lillian looked up from her note book. "Oh, hi dear. I didn't think you were going to drop by so soon." As she finished her sentence, she could see in her husband's face that something was wrong. Dreadfully wrong.

"Arthur is very ill with influenza," said Noble, as calmly as he could. "We must go to Devens right now to help him. I have supplies outside the lab door, and will need to leave with them in the Ford immediately."

In one motion, Lillian closed the note book and stood to get her coat. There was no time to tell Rosenau where she was going. After putting on her coat and starting for the door,

Lillian's eyes met Edward's. Both of them had tears forming as they communicated in the non-verbal way of all parents. They knew the job that lay before them.

Outside the lab, Noble grabbed two of the laundry bags recruited for the mission, and Lillian picked up one. They ran to the small automobile parking area near the South Department, loaded the bags in the back, and started their journey to Camp Devens. The first leg of the trip would be surprisingly quick. As influenza made its presence known with each passing day, lighter and lighter traffic was encountered on Boston streets. At times within the city of Boston, the Noble Ford was the only car on the roads.

Unfortunately, the trip outside of Boston was nowhere as easy. Very few highways outside of large cities were paved. It had also been raining in New England for a few days. The dirt roads to Camp Devens were muddy, and large pools of water were encountered in many areas. Noble prayed that his extra strong Ford truck chassis, motor train, suspension, and tires were up to the challenge. The thirty-five mile drive to Devens took over three hours.

At about 3 PM, the Nobles drove the mud-caked Ford along Sherman Avenue in Camp Devens. They took the Ford off the avenue, passed the huge line of ill men, and drove to the back of the building where Base Hospital Ward No. 1 was housed. The two parents carried off their life-sustaining supply bags, and swiftly walked through the rear building storage and supply rooms while wearing gauze masks. Even though Noble had told his wife what to expect on the ward, she put her hand to her mouth and began to cry with the sights and smells of it. It was still overwhelming for Noble, as well. They immediately made a dash for the ward northwest corner by following the perimeter Arthur had stumbled along some hours earlier. There on a cot, in the extreme corner of the room, was their son.

Arthur's parents found him with violent paroxysms of coughing productive of copious white sputum. Kneeling by her him, Lillian said softly, "Arthur. Arthur. We're here, Son."

Arthur opened his sunken eyes, and between coughs, said, "Mom...Dad? You're...here?"

"Yes, Arthur," said Lillian. "We're here. Everything is going to be alright, Son." She placed her hand on her son's damp flushed forehead.

Noble instantly went about the task of assessing his son's condition. "Are you having trouble breathing, Son? Are you having any pain?"

[cough] Yes, Dad...it's hard to catch my breath. It hurts to breath. My arms and legs...ach. My head...Dad. It hurts... so bad."

Noble took vital signs using devices he had with him. Blood pressure 105/65, pulse 81 and regular, respiratory rate 25, temperature 104° F. Arthur had turbid diaphoretic skin with a crimson color to his lips, injected conjunctiva, coryza with slight epistaxis, moderately labored breathing, scattered course bilateral rales with rhonchi, prostration, severe fatigue, and a somewhat dulled affect. "Son, I think you'll feel better very soon."

"He's very dehydrated, Lillian. We need an IV access."

Noble placed an IV needle in one of Arthur's left forearm veins, attached a rubber line to a bottle of normal saline with dextrose, and added sodium bicarbonate to the IV solution. He hung the IV bottle from a shade cord on a nearby window. He began to give morphine IV, as well as epinephrine. By mouth, he gave Arthur a caffeine pill, benzyl benzoate, and sodium salicylate.

Lillian lightly brushed Arthur's short hair, placed cool damp cloths on his forehead, and held his hand. Within about ten minutes, Arthur's coughing greatly decreased, his wheezing eased, and he began to sleep. "At least he is much more comfortable now," said Noble. "He looks in need of several liters of fluid. I hope we have enough."

Over the next several hours, Noble titrated the medications for pain, coughing paroxysms, wheezing, and fever. His vital signs remained stable, and his temperature was 102° F. Arthur slept continuously.

Sunset came. Aside from a few electric lamps at either end of the large room, the ward was black. The noise of the hospital remained deafening and terrifying. Coughing on the ward sounded like a giant grinding machine in need of oil. Dozens of men at any given time gasped for every breath. Periodically, someone would scream with intense unremitting pain, and then fall silent. If ever there was a hell on earth, thought Noble, Base Hospital Ward No. 1 was now in it.

At about 1 AM on Thursday, September 26th, Noble checked Arthur's vitals, as he did every half-hour. Blood pressure 110/65, pulse 84 and regular, respiratory rate 25, temperature 102° F. Arthur had received five liters of IV fluid. His respirations were nearly normal, and his rales and rhonchi had actually improved. He continued to sleep comfortably. Even with the chaos all around, Noble and Lillian eventually fell asleep with their son between them.

It was 4 AM when Noble and his wife were jarred awake by a sudden and violent jerking motion from Arthur on his cot. The young man was struggling to breath. With each breath, he arched his back and spread his arms off to his sides. His father had fallen backward onto the floor with his son's movement. He quickly sat up and knelt again at the side of the cot. Copious amounts of bloody frothy fluid spewed from Arthur's mouth and nose. Arthurs' eyes were wide open and stared motionless at the ceiling. Blood trickled from the corner of one eye. There was now a heliotrope lavender hue covering his son's face. He gasped with every inhalation, and moaned with each exhalation.

Noble quickly took a set of vitals. Blood pressure 85/45, pulse 86 and irregularly irregular, respiratory rate 30 and very labored, temperature 106° F. Chest auscultation revealed impaired bilateral pulmonary resonance, severe course bubbling rales, severe rhonchi, and greatly decreased heart sounds. As Noble touched his son's chest and neck, he could hear and even feel a horrid sensation. Both the sound and touch reminded him of the crackling of Rice Krispies in milk. Arthur's eyes were open, but he was not responsive to voice or stimuli.

"What's happening?" screamed Lillian.

"Lilly...Lilly," Noble said firmly. "You must calm down. I need your help. You need to try and keep all the fluid coming from his mouth from choking him further. Keep his head to the side, and collect the fluid on the towels and the basin."

Noble's exam showed Arthur now had extreme bilateral pulmonary consolidation to the extent he had never observed before. Before their very eyes, their son was suffocating. The crackling noise about Arthur's torso was crepitus from subcutaneous emphysema. With every tortured breath, bursting pulmonary bronchioli were pumping air through his mediastinum and under his skin.

Arthur's rigors had pulled out his IV needle. Noble worked to replace it, even as his son flailed his extremities. Once IV access was reestablished, Noble again administered drugs to help Arthur improve ventilation and respiration, and attempt to halt the progression of hypoxia. From his exam, Noble could not tell if his patient was having atrial fibrillation or numerous premature atrial contractions. The heart beats seemed to be conducting peripheral pulses, so paroxysms of ventricular fibrillation contractions were less likely. Therefore, he chose to add digitalis to his treatment regimen.

Their son's writhing continued over the next forty-five minutes. Arthur's color rapidly changed from lavender to a deep indigo-blue. His respirations gradually slowed, as did his pulse. At one point, his appearance caused his mother to fall against an adjoining wall and shriek in panic over the process enfolding before her. Noble went to her and did his best to console his wife. He had no further treatments to offer his son.

At 5 AM, Arthur had stopped his struggling movements and was actually quite peaceful. His father took vital signs once again. Blood pressure 55/35, pulse 45 and regular, respiratory rate 15 and very labored, temperature 106° F. Almost no breath sounds were audible in his chest. Noble administered more epinephrine and a large fluid bolus from the final IV bottle from the laundry bag. Lillian sat on her knees at her son's side, held his hand, and said a quiet prayer that Noble could not hear. She took from her pocket a rosary, and said, "Hail Mary, full of grace…"

Noble looked at his wristwatch which read 5:32 AM. He put his hand on Arthur's chest and felt no struggle against it. He placed his second and third right hand fingers just anterior to his son's sternocleidomastoideus muscle. Then, to his radial artery. Then to his femoral artery. Noble listened to Arthur's anterior chest with his stethoscope. He then sat on the floor against the corner wall.

"How is he doing, Edward?" asked Lillian as she was also sitting on the floor with her back against the corner wall.

CHAPTER 17

Noble felt as though his own soul had left his body. He had no more energy to even speak. And he no longer cared. He had devoted his life to the nonsense he called modern medicine, and the scientific method. But, in the end, the demon had stolen his son away. Right in front of him. And it was easy. Effortless.

"Edward, what's wrong?" said Lillian.

Noble knew that his next four words would be the hardest for him to say in his life. He did not want to say them, because that would be admitting their truth. He was having trouble even forming the words in his mind. Now, how do you say them to a boy's mother?

After a very long hesitation, Noble wiped tears from his eyes and looked up from the floor. "Lilly. Lilly…Arthur… is gone."

Time stood still for Noble. He heard nothing. It was though the universe just stopped. He could only see his wife, who did not move. Noble felt that he had just shot Lillian through the heart with his words. Finally, her head dropped parallel with the floor. She put her hands to her face. Her whole body moved with each coming sob. Noble moved to her and put his arms around her. She put her head to his chest.

While holding Lillian, Noble looked up at the cyanotic body with blood stained linen laying on the army cot. Gone was the boy who loved baseball. Gone was the boy who had earned the rank of Eagle Scout in record time. Gone was the Boston University crew member who was revered by his classmates and adored by coeds. Gone was the patriotic new First Lieutenant who was thrilled with the idea of serving his country. And, gone was the boy who so wanted to be just like his father. Both of his parents cried, holding each other, for a very long time.

By 6:30 AM, army doctors were circulating the ward and pronouncing the dead from the night before. Soldiers followed the doctors and were collecting the bodies.

"Lilly," said Noble in a whisper. "If we don't do something, the army will collect Arthur and stack his body with hundreds of others. Not only can I not stand the idea of that, but we may never know what happens to his body. We need to do...something."

Lillian looked up with tears dried on her checks, and more being produced. "What can we do, Edward?"

"Stay here," Noble said. "I'm going to call Sergeant Campbell for some help." Noble stood up, and eventually made his way to a reception area telephone at the other end of the ward. He spoke for a few minutes, and then quickly returned to Lillian. "The Sergeant is going to help us. We need to unobtrusively wrap Arthur in clean linen sheets. Then we'll wait."

Arthur's parents had a new mission. They wrapped the body and waited as the army doctors drew closer in their duties. Noble was certain they would lose Arthur's body forever if his death was discovered. However, with true army efficiency, Sergeant Campbell arrived in only minutes. He liked Noble. The Major always treated him with the respect that many officers did not. He wanted to return the favor. Built like a lumberjack, Campbell picked up Arthur's body by himself. The party of three, with their precious cargo, then quietly departed the ward.

Once outside in the cold overcast morning, Campbell put Arthur's body in the idling army staff car. With the Nobles in their Ford truck, and the Sergeant in the staff car, the group hastily drove off for Boston. The road was somewhat dryer than the day before, but the trip still took two hours. Lillian sat close to her husband, with her hand on his right thigh. However, neither of them spoke during the entire trip.

It was 9 AM when the two cars reached the Noble Beacon Street home. Campbell stayed with the body, and the Nobles went inside. Lillian began to call funeral homes as she tried desperately to stay focused. After 45 minutes, she walked into the library where Noble sat staring into space. Lillian was again crying as she said, "Edward, I've called every funeral home in Boston and surrounding cities. All of them are refusing funeral arrangements for fear of the grippe. They also said grave diggers are not reporting for work out of fear, and because many are ill. What are we going to do?"

Noble put his fingers through his white hair, and then wiped tears from his eyelids. The last thing he wanted now was another challenge. He thought for some time. He finally said, "Lilly, we can't wait for the funeral homes to open up again. Who knows how long that will be. We need to bury Arthur in the Chestnut Hill family plot, and consider other arrangements later."

Lillian, who was already exhausted, dropped to her knees and cried loudly. "Oh, Edward! How much more of this can we take? When will this ever end?" Noble did not know the answer to that question. He was beginning to think it would never end.

Noble placed a call to Milton Rosenau, informed him of the situation, and asked him if he could help. Rosenau said he would leave for Brookline immediately. He placed a call to Boston City Hospital and spoke to Florence. He told her the news, and said they would soon pick her up on their way to Brookline. Meanwhile, Lillian drove the Ford to the three younger children's school. She planned to pick the children up, and also pick up Akeema who was reading in the school library that day. Noble placed a call to the Cathedral of the Holy Cross. He asked if he might take one of the priests for the trip to Chestnut Hill, which is just west of Brookline. Having secured a priest, Noble gathered up a bible and three shovels and left with Sergeant Campbell and his son.

At nearly noon, the army staff car pulled up to the Chestnut Hill Cemetery along Heath Street. Set on a rolling green hill, the cemetery overlooked Hammond Pond to its north. The family Ford was waiting for them. Lillian had been trying to comfort three distraught children who were crying when Noble arrived. The priest from Holy Cross had given solace to both Noble and his daughter during their journey. Only moments later, Rosenau arrived in a navy staff car.

The party of ten, with Sergeant Campbell carrying Arthur's body, walked up a hill with a very gentle slope. Atop the hill were the graves of Charles and Elizabeth Noble. Lillian had brought blankets along, and she spread them out around the new grave site. The grass was still damp from the cold morning. Campbell gently placed Arthur's body near his grandfather's grave. The priest gave Last Rites. Then, Noble, Campbell, and Rosenau began a macabre task that none of them even vaguely contemplated only a few hours earlier. They began to dig a grave for Arthur.

The digging took about two hours to complete. During this time, the funeral procession spoke of the young man whose body lay draped in sheets before them. They cried often. Arthur's siblings occasionally rested their heads on Arthur's chest and spoke to him. Florence spoke of missing her big brother who always protected her at school. Bernard and Michael told him of the upcoming baseball season, on how much they would miss him at Fenway Park. Marguerite told him how much she loved him, and how much she loved looking at stereo pictures with him. The youngest Noble lamented that she would never again be carried upon her big brother's shoulders. Lillian held his hands, and just cried. She cried until she could not sit up any longer, and lay down next to him. Akeema said many prayers in Unaliq.

When the grave was finished, the priest performed a brief funeral service. Noble and his wife read a few of their favorite passages from scripture. Noble's choice was one of Christ's ethical admonitions in the Sermon on the Mount, found in Matthew 6:19-21:

"Do not store up for yourselves treasures on earth, where moth and rust destroy, and where thieves break in and steal. But, store up for yourselves treasures in heaven, where moth and rust do not destroy, and where thieves do not break in and steal. For where you treasure is, there your heart will be also."

Some of Arthur's favorites were also read. This included I Corinthians 13:7:

"[As for love] It always protects, always trusts, always hopes, always perseveres".

In their own ways, each in the procession said a little prayer. Then, Noble, Campbell, and Rosenau, used rolled sheets to lower Arthur's body into the grave. The men filled in the hole with their shovels, with tears streaming down everyone's faces. Akeema had fashioned a cross with some branches and rope found in the back of the Ford. After some individual reflection, the group left.

On the way down the grassy hill, Noble felt as though the demon was daring him to come after it again.

On the morning of Friday, September 27th, Lillian arose early to help prepare the children for the day. She felt it necessary to reestablish a routine quickly as part of the healing process. After breakfast, she drove the children and Akeema to school. Akeema came along to stay at the library and resume a personal study program she had formed for herself. Florence had taken the trolley to Boston City Hospital, where nurses were desperately needed.

Noble remained in bed. He had slept very little the night before. His thoughts had whisked him away to many different places in time, and had left little room for sleep. But, Noble was more than tired. He was giving up. Science and medicine had failed him at the very time he needed them most. Many people now hung small garlic amulets around their necks to stave off influenza. Noble's battle for Arthur's life would have been just as effective if he had given him one of these necklace tokens. The outcome would have been the same.

Pulling the bed blanket over his head, Noble thought of resigning as Medical Director of the South Department. Perhaps he would quit medicine altogether. Maybe he would go AWOL and just leave New England. Or, he could stay in the army, find a useless desk job somewhere, and be as productive then as he felt now. Maybe he would move to Provincetown on Cape Cod, and sell snacks to the tourists. For now, he did not want to do anything or go anywhere.

Lillian parked the Ford in the first floor garage, entered the house, and began the thousand chores a family needs done. Occasionally, she would go into the darkened bedroom to check on her husband. At 10:30 AM, she halted her tasks, went into the bedroom, and opened up the drapes. She sat down on the bed and said, "Edward?" There was no answer or any movement from Noble. "Edward," she repeated more sternly. No response. She pulled the blanket from his head and turned his face toward hers, even as he kept his eyes closed.

"Dr. Edward Noble," Lillian said loudly. "I know what you are doing, and I completely understand it. You feel you failed Arthur. You feel you failed as a physician. You may feel you have even failed as a father and a husband. I know you, Dr. Noble, and I know you are thinking of giving up.

Maybe you have already decided on giving up. But, you know what?"

Noble opened his eyes to the question, but did not speak.

"I'll tell you what, Dr. Noble," said Lillian, with her lips pulled back to expose her front teeth. "I am not going to let you give up. Do you know why?"

Noble didn't answer, but his eyes widened.

"Because, first, you are a great physician. You are the best clinician in this city, and everyone knows it. I will not let you give up and deprive the good people in Boston of your talents. Second, I will not let you give up and abandon your children when they need you so completely. Thirdly, I will not let you give up when I need you. I need the strong man I married twenty years ago. All of him. Finally, I will not let you give up and dishonor the memory of our fine young man, Arthur. What would he say to you, Edward?" With that, Lillian pulled the bed covers completely off her husband, and promptly left the room.

Lillian was angry. She stood at the kitchen sink stirring soup for the evening dinner. She stirred so quickly that the bowl contents sloshed up over the sides and into the sink. It was bad enough watching your son die before you. But, now she was forced to watch her husband go through a different kind of death.

Forty minutes later Lillian heard a small noise behind her as she worked in the kitchen. She turned around quickly. Before her was her husband, showered, shaved, and with his army field uniform on. She set the bowl into the sink, and through her arms around her husband. He held her tightly.

"Lilly," said Noble. "I will not abandon you. I will not abandon our children, or medicine. And, I will do everything to honor the memory of Arthur. You are completely right. Arthur would say to me, 'Dad...come on! Fight this thing! You can't do everything, but you can do what you can do!' I can hear those words as clearly as if Arthur were standing here now."

Lillian looked up at her husband, smiled, and said, "That's my doctor!" She prepared a breakfast for Noble, and later kissed him as he drove off to Boston City Hospital.

Lieutenant Lafayette gave her sincere condolences to Noble when he arrived at the A.I. Office. As he began to catch up on cables from the last two days, he again thought of the words he believed his son would tell him repeatedly: "You can't do everything, but you can do what you can do!" Noble dove into the work with new vigor. He began to read the stack of cables awaiting him.

Thursday, September 26, 1918
From: USS Olympic; Cruiser and Transport Force,
     Atlantic Fleet

USS Olympic on route to Southampton. 383 influenza cases immediately after departure. Sailors and soldiers on guard dropped where they stood with fevers of 105° F. 1,900 ill, 119 dead so far.

U.S. Navy Intelligence.

Thursday, September 26, 1918
From: USS President Grant; Cruiser and Transport Force,
     Atlantic Fleet

USS President Grant sailing with six other transports on route to St. Nazaire, France. On route, 2,600 fall ill with influenza. 246 buried at sea. Not known how many died after docking in France.

U.S. Navy Intelligence.

Thursday, September 26, 1918
From: Great Lakes Base, Chicago

According to an intern physician, Lieutenant James Wallace, there are so many staff physicians ill or dead that he is now in charge of the hospital medical operation. The 3,000 bed hospital is at overflow capacity. More than 100 dead per day. Among other things, they need more aspirin and whiskey.

U.S. Navy Intelligence.

Friday, September 27, 1918
From: Philadelphia Naval Yard

1,400 hospitalized with influenza. Sept. 19th – Two deaths. Sept. 20th – Fourteen deaths. Sept. 21st – Twenty deaths. Deaths mounting daily.

U.S. Navy Intelligence.

Noble read that the first civilian influenza case had been diagnosed in Washington D.C. two days ago. Since the U.S. Public Health Service had designated influenza as a reportable disease on September 21st, more reliable data was forthcoming. Twenty-six states in the country were now reporting influenza. Acting Army Surgeon General Charles Richard had followed Colonel Welsh's advice and ordered strict quarantine of all ill troops in US cantonments. However, Noble knew this was now largely symbolic. Trying to quarantine the huge number of influenza cases presently in the camps was impossible.

Thursday, September 26, 1918
From: Boston, Massachusetts.

In view of more than 1,000 deaths from influenza in New England in the last ten days, the Commonwealth of Massachusetts is ordering the closing of all schools, churches, theaters, pubs, bars, salons, parades, and other public meetings until further notice. Fines are imposed for those who do not protect others from coughing, and also for spitting publicly.

U.S. Public Health Service.

Noble wondered if his children would be sent home early from school today. But, there was a bigger concern. Tens of thousands of New England workers would now be out of jobs, and out of money. Just when the populace needed more resources with the advancing pandemic, there would be substantially fewer resources with the loss of work. This would quickly have a negative ripple effect in the economy. "Lieutenant, could you call my house for me? I need to talk to my wife."

"Of course, sir." In a few moments Lillian was on the line.

"Hi, dear," answered Lillian, in a sad voice. "What's happening?"

"Lilly," said Noble, "I'll tell you more about it tonight. But, the city and state governments are closing institutions where influenza can easily spread. This is a good thing. However, there is going to be a huge number of people out of work, beginning today. I think it is time for you to mobilize every and all social services as quickly as possible. You are part of so many great institutions: The Red Cross, the U.S. Public Health Services, the Bureau of Child Hygiene, Family Social Services, to name a few. They will all need to be operating at two hundred per cent efficiency to avoid social disaster."

"I'll get right on it, darling," said Lillian. "I have to get the kids early today. They have closed their school."

"I heard," said Noble. "One other thing, Lillian. Everyday items are likely to get pretty scarce. You need to go to the stores today and pick up enough supplies for the family to use for several weeks. Canned foods, water, etc. Tonight I will give you prescriptions for several medications and medical supplies we may also need. Those items are already in short supply, and will likely be completely unavailable soon."

"I'll have everything we need by tomorrow, Edward," said Lillian. And, one more thing."

"What's that," asked Noble.

"That's my doctor!" said Lillian, as she hung up the telephone.

Noble smiled at his wife's approval. He felt a new sense of purpose as he saw the many tasks that lay ahead. He also held a responsibility to honor his son's memory. When he thought of the demon, Noble drew an analogy with The Western Front in France. If the enemy cannot be defeated with a frontal assault, then one must out flank it.

Noble read of at least one victory against the demon:

Thursday, September 26, 1918
From: Provost Marshal Enoch Crowder

The next scheduled military draft round has been cancelled.

Department of War, Washington D.C.

This was more evidence that Dr. Welsh's recommendations to Charles Richard had a positive effect. At least for now, there would be fewer fresh victims pumped into the cantonments. However, at the same time, there was a major setback.

Friday, September 27, 1918
From: Philadelphia Public Health Director, Wilmer Krusen

The Liberty Loan Parade in Philadelphia, which will raise millions of dollars in War Bonds, will be held as planned on September 28th. The parade is expected to be the largest in Philadelphia history.

U.S. Public Health Service.

Noble could not believe what he had just read. A naval yard near Philadelphia developed hundreds of severely ill personnel with deadly pandemic influenza. At the very same time, Philadelphia planed to purposely mix thousands of sailors and soldiers with the civilian population. Noble knew this must not happen. "Lieutenant, please cable an urgent message to Dr. Wilmer Krusen, the Philadelphia Public Health Director." Noble dictated to the Lieutenant a plea to stop the parade at all cost. "When you are finished with the cable, please try to reach by telephone Dr. Howard Anders in Philadelphia through the medical school there. Please tell him it's urgent. I'll wait for the connection."

It was some time before Lieutenant Lafayette was able to reach anyone in Philadelphia at all. Finally she called out to Noble, "Major, I have Dr. Howard Anders on the line."

Noble took the call in the small office. "Howard. Is that you, Howard?"

As usual, the connection was poor and the voice barely audible over the static. "Edward? Edward Noble?"

"Yes, Howard, it's me, Edward. I haven't seen you since the Philadelphia public health conference at the University of Pennsylvania School of Medicine two years ago."

"It's great to hear from you, Edward," said Anders. "But, why the urgent call? Is it about influenza?"

"Yes, Howard, it is. My guess is that you have been beating the drums about this 'Liberty Loan Parade'?"

"Gee!" said Anders. "Edward, everyone in the public health community...including me...have been yelling for days to postpone the parade. I've talked to Health Director Krusen about it many times. I even talked to several city newspapers reporters. Still, Krusen refuses to budge. There is intense pressure by the federal government to hold this parade. They are expecting huge donations. You know, I do have an idea, though. You're in the army, right Edward?"

"Yes," said Edward. "I'm presently attached with the Army Division of Communicable Diseases, which is headed by Dr. Victor Vaughn."

"Everyone knows Vaughn," said Anders. "You know, if we can't have the parade postponed, maybe we can have the army attempt to screen for early symptoms in troops going to the parade? If so, we could limit the contagion on the parade route."

"If you know anyone in the army," said Noble, "I could try and reach them."

"Well," said Anders, "I do know a young man that has been temporarily assigned to organize troop involvement in the parade. He is particularly talented in large-scale organization efforts."

"That's great, Howard. Stay on the line and give my assistant that contact information. I will do my best to work on your great idea. It's been a pleasure, and I hope to see you at next year's U of Penn conference."

Noble turned the call back to Lieutenant Lafayette. She was told how to contact the officer arranging for army troops to march in the Philadelphia parade.

It took nearly two hours for the Lieutenant to reach the officer in question. "Major," said the Lieutenant, "I have the officer on the line. He's a Lieutenant Colonel."

"Colonel, sir," said Noble. "I am so sorry to bother you, sir. I am Major Edward Noble with the Army Division of Communicable Diseases here in Boston. My commanding officer is Colonel Victor Vaughn, who has asked me to monitor communicable diseases in the military. Sir, I'm sure you are aware of the present danger influenza poses."

"Yes...yes I am, Major. I've heard of the problems in many of the cantonments and navy bases. How can I help you?" Noble noted how young the Lieutenant Colonel sounded for his rank.

"Well, sir," said Noble. "I was told by Dr. Howard Anders that you are organizing the soldiers who will be marching in tomorrow's parade?"

"Yes, Major. My usual assignment is training tank crews at Gettysburg. But, for just a few days, I am helping to place troops in the parade."

"Sir," said Noble, "I wonder if you could simply ask some of the army physicians to screen the troops for early symptoms of influenza? This could significantly decrease the spread of the disease."

"Major, I'll do whatever I can to safeguard both military personnel and civilians. You can count on me, sir."

Noble was puzzled. Why had the officer called him "sir"? "Colonel, you don't need to call me 'sir'. I'm just a Major."

The officer laughed. "Well, Major, I was actually brevetted to Lieutenant Colonel temporarily in the National Army. My real rank is Captain. So, I guess it's habit to call Majors 'sir'."

"In any case, Colonel," said Noble, "it's been a pleasure. Thank you for considering the safety of our troops. By the way, I didn't catch your name, Colonel."

"It's Dwight. Dwight Eisenhower."

Noble hung up the telephone knowing he had done what he could for the people of Philadelphia. He also realized this was not enough.

The next day, Saturday, September 28th, Noble read the reports of Philadelphia's Liberty Loan Parade. It was the city's greatest parade ever. Tens of thousands of soldiers, sailors, and marines marched with thousands of flags and banners. Civilian groups, from women's auxiliaries to the Boy Scouts, marched alongside the military. Several hundred thousand people attended the parade, with people standing nine and ten rows deep on the sidewalks.

Noble knew the incubation period for influenza was twenty-four to seventy-two hours. He could now only wait for the inevitable.

Sunday, September 29th, Noble was at the A.I. Office to see if there were any reports of infectious diseases, other than influenza, coming in. There was not a single report of other communicable diseases in the world. That was not to say there was only influenza. It just meant the entire world was consumed with the disease, and was thinking of little else. Noble thought it ironic that when influenza was not killing people, people were busy killing themselves around the world.

Lieutenant Commander Rosenau was putting the final touches on his experiments with influenza. He was close to using the experimental design that he, Lieutenant John Keegan, and Lillian, had developed for their first trial. Rosenau dropped by the A.I. Office, and found Noble in a poor disposition. Aside from the obvious, Rosenau enquired about Noble's mood. "How are things going my friend?"

"Milton," asked Noble, "are you familiar with the *USS Leviathan*?"

"I've heard of her," said Rosenau. "She's the biggest ship in the world, right?"

Yes," said Noble. "That she is. She has a length of 950 feet, and a beam of 100 feet. That makes her nearly twice the length and width of the ship I was on in January. Just like *USS Madawaska*, she was a German ocean liner seized in Hoboken when the U.S. entered The War. It was President Wilson himself who changed her name from *SS Vaterland* to *USS Leviathan*. As a troop transport, she can carry more than 14,000 troops at a single Atlantic crossing. She is also very fast. She has an amazing cruising speed of 26 knots."

"So, what's the problem, Edward?" asked Rosenau.

Noble explained. "Just two weeks ago, *Leviathan* arrived from France and had buried several crew and troops at sea due to influenza. Even the Secretary of the Navy, Franklin Roosevelt, had to be carried off the ship in New York because of influenza. Everyone in the Army Communicable Disease Division, and General Gorgas himself, have been pleading with the Secretary of War to simply quarantine the ill before these Atlantic crossings."

"I know," said Rosenau. "You have been beating that drum for months."

"Well, the army did perform quarantines before this latest *Leviathan* voyage to France, and segregated ill troops within her. However, the onshore quarantines were very short and not carefully administrated. In addition, ill troops were allowed to eat with everyone else once she sailed. Forty-eight hours after leaving New York, thousands of men were already ill. *Leviathan's* sickbays were quickly overwhelmed. As more sleeping quarters were converted into sickbays, more and more troops were required to bunk outdoors on the ship decks. They had to endure freezing nights and storm waves that soaked their blankets. Then, the fatal version of influenza began to show itself. Hundreds of men throughout the ship began to suffer from bloody serous fluid flowing from their mouths and nostrils. On the decks, this mixed with urine, feces, and vomit, to make a slippery bloody soup everywhere."

Noble continued. "So many aboard were dying that the ship's officers could not record their names fast enough. At night troops would here soldiers scream out, 'I've got it!' Next morning, those same soldiers would be found dead. They began to bury the dead at sea. Scores of sheet-wrapped bodies floated in the wake of *USS Leviathan*. By the time she docked in Brest, several thousand men needed to be hospitalized. We don't know how many more died once in France."

"Maybe this will cause the War Department to look closer at its policies?" asked Rosenau.

"I don't know, Milton. I just don't know."

Rosenau knew Noble was distraught, and in a very tenuous emotional state. He sought to bring up something positive. "Just to let you know, with the help of Lillian and Keegan, I will soon be attempting to infect volunteers on Gallops Island in Boston Harbor with influenza. These volunteers have not been in the Boston area for months, and have no history of influenza. We hope this will help us with an antiserum or vaccine, eventually."

Noble acknowledged the ground-breaking work by his friend, Keegan, and his wife. It would be these efforts that would eventually conquer the demon. He wished his friend Godspeed in the research.

Rosenau left the A.I. Office for the Harvard satellite lab feeling optimistic about his upcoming work. Noble left the office for the wards, and was feeling pessimistic about his.

Monday, September 30th came. It was forty-eight hours since the Philadelphia Liberty Loan Parade. On the cable stacks was a message from Health Director Krusen.

Monday, September 30, 1918
From: Philadelphia Public Health Director, Wilmer Krusen

The influenza epidemic is now present in the civilian population and is assuming the type found in naval stations and cantonments.

U.S. Public Health Service.

Noble was so angry that he threw his pencil against the office wall, tore up the telegram, threw its pieces on the floor, and yelled, "Damn it!" He sat down in a chair, rested his elbows on the desk before him, took off his glasses, and buried his face into his hands. "The stupidity! The utter foolishness!" muttered Noble. Quoting Krusen, "'...assuming the type found in naval stations and cantonments.' Has he seen what <u>that</u> really means? Does he even know what he is saying?"

Over the next few hours, Noble read about the new situation in Philadelphia. In just two days, nearly every hospital bed in the city was filled with influenza patients. One hundred and seventeen people died of influenza...that day. Now, the city government was closing all schools, churches, theaters, and banning all public gatherings...after the parade. Even public funerals were now illegal.

And, this was just the beginning.

Noble sat with his hands on his face for a very long time. It seemed that ignorance was aiding and abetting the demon at every turn. After awhile, Lieutenant Pierre-Louis gently asked, "Major...are you alright?"

Noble slowly took his hands from his head, and replaced his round lens wire-rimmed glasses. He slowly turned to the Lieutenant, and said matter-of-factly, "No...no, Lieutenant, I'm not alright." She was then frightened by what Noble said next. "Lieutenant...watch with me the commencement of the richest, and most abundant, horror that humankind has ever seen."

There was complete silence in the A.I. Office, as Noble left for the South Department wards.

CHAPTER 18

Noble arose on the morning of Tuesday, October 1st, ate breakfast, and prepared to drive once again to Boston City Hospital. Lillian went with him to help complete Rosenau's study design. However, as soon as the experiment protocol was underway, she planned to spend all her time organizing the various social services Boston seriously required.

Akeema Ayuluk had turned Noble's library into a school room for Bernard, Michael, and Marguerite. Since all Boston student classes were cancelled for an uncertain amount of time, Lillian did not want them to fall behind in their studies. The Noble parlor was now a storage room for stacks of linen, canned foods, dried foods, water bottles, medicines, and medical supplies of all descriptions. Arthurs' bedroom had become a shrine to him. Everything was exactly as it had been the last time he was there.

The day before, Florence was offered a $100 bribe to assist in the care of an influenza patient at home. As a Navy Reserve officer, this was not possible. Still, it demonstrated the lengths some were taking to try to survive. Florence had also recently been told she would not be put on active duty quite yet. Instead, the Navy Reserve had agreed to let Reserve nurses stay in Boston and render the care desperately needed by the community. Florence's father had told her influenza nursing care was often just as important as medical care.

Noble, and his wife and daughter, drove to BCH in the Ford truck. Boston was now a very different place. There were almost no pedestrians. Many shops and small businesses were not open. There were very few cars, trucks, buses, or horse-drawn carts on the streets. Because of too few passengers, and large numbers of ill public transportation employees, the trolleys and subway were not running.

The car was parked in the small hospital parking lot, and the three family members went off to their various tasks. There were now dozens of large tents jammed with the city's most infirmed about the BCH campus. Lines of ill people twisted and turned about the grounds, as numerous clinics tried to triage them. Noble entered one of the South Department pavilions to find patients on cots and on the floor. Reminiscent of Camp Devens, patients could be found in the hallways, the verandas, the offices, meeting rooms, exam rooms, and outside door entrances. As Noble surveyed his workplace, he recalled the story of the Dutch boy and his finger in the dike hole.

Noble entered the main ward and put on his gauze mask. He realized that small studies some months ago had suggested such masks held a benefit. But, he was now questioning those studies. Only adequately powered, high quality prospective randomized controlled studies could conclusively answer this question. Those studies were forthcoming. But, anecdotally, he now believed gauze masks offered no protection from influenza at all. The masks provided care givers a false sense of safety. However, since hope was all the medical establishment had to offer at this point, he saw no need to have people stop wearing them. Besides, Boston and many other cities were passing ordinances requiring people to wear masks.

The pavilion ward now looked just like Camp Devens Base Hospital Ward No. 1. And it smelled just the same. Deceased patients whose bodies had long since been removed had left layers of bloody bodily fluids on the floor. The fluids had dried into a proteinaceous goo that stuck to one's shoes. This made a crinkling noise with every step. Dried bloody linen was stacked in every corner, along with spent IV bottles, tubing, needles, and syringes. The sounds of the ward were like Devens, as well. The coughing was deafening. At any given time, several patients were gasping for any air they could get into their ruined lungs. Constantly, one could see groups of deep indigo lavender-blue patients awaiting their fate.

To the side of the room stood Lieutenant David Schafer, who was trying to rescue yet another patient from the demon. Noble walked over to him and noticed how different the young man looked compared to the first time they met. As a second year medical resident, Schafer had the youthful blush of enthusiasm that made teaching medicine fun again. That was all gone now. Dr. Schafer, the third year resident on an infectious disease ward in 1918, had changed. He had lost a lot of weight. His long white coat now drooped about his shoulders as if it were on a thin wire hanger. His hair was unkempt. His complexion was sallow and his eyes sunken into his head. Lost also was the speech of the exuberant student eager for the next fact to learn. He now spoke in the monotone of someone that had seen too much for his years. Noble had heard the term "burned out" used to describe some physicians on The Front. To him, Schafer fit that description. Nevertheless, he wanted to somehow sound upbeat as he addressed his young resident in charge of the ward. "How are things going, Lieutenant?" asked Noble.

"Fine," said Schafer without emotion. "This patient is likely a Type I, so I'm going to see if I can save him."

"Type I?" said Noble. "I'm not familiar with that category."

"It's something the residents have come up with, sir," said Schafer. "We wanted to see if we could triage the influenza patients into groups, so we could concentrate on the ones most likely to survive."

"Fascinating," said Noble, hoping to elicit some visible interest in the resident. "Tell me about it."

"We group them into three categories," said Schafer, showing no particular interest in the conversation. "Type I patients are moderately ill clinically and gradually worsen over three to five days. Type II patients appear to improve gradually over three to five days, and then suddenly and quickly worsen. Type III patients arrive with severe symptoms the moment they hit the ward."

"How do you triage these groups?" asked Noble.

"Well, Type I patients seem to have the best chance of survival if we play close attention early on to pain control, pulmonary toilet, hydration, and control of the signs of infection such as coughing, wheezing, and arrhythmias. We try to jump on Type I patients as soon as we have identified them. Type II patients usually don't need much more than nursing care at first, since they are gradually getting better. They either do get better, or they quickly die later. So, we don't spend much extra time with them. Type III patients really don't have much chance at all. In fact, when they come in, nurses attach identifying cards with a string on their great toes right away. Since they are going to die anyway, it saves them time later. For the same reason, they put new patients on the floor right next to the Type III patient cots. When the Type IIIs die, it's easier to put new patient in their place quickly."

Noble thought the residents should be commended for applying new clinical learnings to their patients so quickly. However, it was sad that their triage system had become so mechanical. On the other hand, they were simply trying to do the most good for the most patients, with ever decreasing resources. The residents actually lived at the hospital. They were around the pandemic twenty-four hours a day, seven days a week. One had to take that into consideration before being too critical of them.

"At the resident morning report," said Schafer, "we try to let all the medical residents and students know where the Type I patients are, so we can look in on them during the day. Morning report otherwise has become very easy. There are more and more Type II and III patients relative to the Type I patients. So, we are rounding on the same number of patients during the day even as more patients are admitted. Also, all the patients on the critical list in the evening are dead the next morning. Our triage system has been surprisingly successful."

Noble felt it was hard to attach the word "successful" to anything that was related to the pandemic. Still, he tried to remain understanding and objective. "How is the staff holding up, Lieutenant?"

"Not all that well, sir," said Schafer. "First, we are running out of most supplies. Within just a few days, we will no longer be able to adequately care for even the Type I patients. Influenza has taken its toll on the staff, also. Everyone is very tired. Eight physicians are hospitalized right now and some of them are Type IIIs. Two resident doctors have died. Fifty-four nurses are also hospitalized, with many Type IIIs in their ranks. Ten nurses have died over the last week. A number of nurses have not been reporting for their shifts. Naturally, everyone worries they will be next on the triage list. Nevertheless, we are very grateful the army Medical Corpsmen are helping to collect the dead in the mornings."

As Noble and Schafer spoke, Medical Corpsmen were systematically removing patients who had died the night before, and replacing them with new patients. Noble had not seen the BCH morgue lately. However, based on the hospital scene before him, he was certain it closely replicated the Devens experience.

"We're all looking forward to your talk tomorrow, Dr. Noble," said Schafer. "Will that be at the noon hour?"

"Yes, Lieutenant," replied Noble. "Actually, it's at 12:30 PM. It's only a brief overview. But, I'll try to make it a meaningful summary." Dr. Schafer then went off to hunt for Type I patients on the wards.

Noble pondered his conversation with the young resident. Some would have reprimanded him for his cavalier attitude toward the death surrounding Boston City Hospital. However, Noble knew the entire hospital staff was near a breaking point. He had seen similar dulled facial expressions in St. Denis staff. For the physicians and nurses at BCH, time had ceased to have the meaning humans usually attach to it. Now, every minute was like every other minute. All hours were like all other hours. Every day was more horrible than the last. Existence for them equaled endlessness. Medicine was no longer a discussion about individual patients. Now, there were only discussions about types and groups of patients. There were just too many of the sick and dying for any one person to fully grasp the suffering of individuals. At some point, people give up trying to embrace the impact on single patients. Boston City Hospital was at that point. One had to add to the equation the very real fear you might be next with an ID tag on your toe.

Noble walked off to another pavilion to see if he could identify any Type I patients.

On Wednesday, October 2nd, BCH residents and medical students assembled for the 12:30 PM lecture by Dr. Noble. Hospital attending physicians, and faculty from Harvard and Boston University medical schools, usually held noon hour lectures for the house staff. However, over the last several weeks the lectures had become few in number. A combination of overwhelming ward work and illness had made the lectures difficult to hold or attend. However, every house staff member was making an extra effort to make this particular lecture. The reason was abundantly obvious.

Nearly every hospital room of any type or size was filled with very sick and dying patients. The only area available for the Noble lecture was a storage room in the Boston City Hospital underground tunnel labyrinth. The reason this room had not been recruited into ward service was because it was too difficult to get gurneys through its narrow door. The windowless room with concrete walls and floor had numerous empty wood crates strewn around. Wood shaving and sawdust packing material was strewn about the floor. Few of the crates contained the supplies they originally held, since the hospital was nearly depleted of everything. The house staff sat on the crates and balanced their sack lunches on their laps.

At the scheduled hour, Noble promptly arrived in the storage room. He stood very erect at the front of the large audience who were eager to hear his thoughts on today's topic. He wore a clean white coat over his field uniform, and had shined his army officer boots for the occasion. Noble was not in a happy frame of mind. However, he put on a pleasant smile for the house staff, who very much deserved it.

"Good afternoon," began Noble, who had several three-by-five cards in his hand. "For the medical students who may not know me, I am Dr. Edward Noble. I am the Medical Director of the Infectious Disease South Department here at Boston City Hospital. Welcome all of you."

"Today I am going to speak on the broad topic of influenza treatment. If you have been at BCH more than just a few days, you are aware of the gold standard with which we measure all clinical research. I am referring to *prospective randomized controlled clinical trials*, or RCTs for short. However, before beginning, I need to make an important disclaimer. There have been no RCTs performed for any of the treatments we will discuss today. That's right, none...except for one I will mention later. At best, all of this information is reported as case studies. At worst, it is anecdotal and professional opinion. However, ladies and gentlemen, that is all we have.

"I have divided the talk into two parts. First, I will discuss specific treatments for specific influenza symptoms and complications. Second, I will discuss general treatments and influenza prophylaxis. When I can, I will mention how likely a particular intervention is to be successful, in my opinion. The last three words are critically important to remember. That is, 'in my opinion' should be taken with the same skepticism as you would any personal opinion. I will grade the interventions as 'likely to work' (A), 'probably work' (B), 'possibly work' (C), 'unlikely to work' (D), and 'dangerous' (F)."

"We will not be talking today about direct manipulation of immunity with antisera and vaccines. Much work in this area is underway as we speak. But, there just is too little information to discuss right now. This will most certainly be a future noon hour lecture."

"I have just a few comments before I begin. First, I want you all to know what a great job you are doing for the patients of BCH. Your dedication, and personal sacrifice, for the wellbeing of the people of Boston can never be overstated. Second, some of the interventions we will discuss today may seem odd, or even stupid. However, before passing judgment, remember that physicians throughout the country and world are desperate to help their patients. Desperate situations often require desperate measures. You must consider how you would approach some of these desperate clinical problems in your own practices."

"On the other hand, I need you to consider the other side of the debate around desperate medical measures. Please remember one of the first medical school lessons you learned at Harvard, Tufts, Boston University, or the school you attended. That is, *Primum non nocere*; the Latin for "First, do no harm". *Primum non nocere* means that, given a clinical problem, it may be better to do nothing than to do something that risks causing more harm than good. The phrase reminds each of us to think of the possible harm any intervention might cause. The words require us to momentarily pause before applying therapies with obvious risk of harm, but a less certain chance of benefit. *Primum non nocere* for all physicians is an expression of hope, intention, humility, and recognition that human acts with good intentions may have unwanted consequences."

Noble poured a glass of water from a pitcher on a small table, drank it, and continued his lecture. "Now, onto the issue of influenza symptoms and complications. The pain associated with influenza, which includes severe headache, myalgias, earache, pleurisy, and chest pain from coughing, is well cared for with opiates, (A). This is probably the most important treatment we can provide for patients…too comfort always. Hypodermal morphine is effective, as are opium, heroin, and codeine. Relieving fevers is also a comfort, and acetylsalicylic acid, sodium salicylate, and cinchonidin salicylates are helpful, (A)."

"Coughing can be so severe as to tear chest respiratory musculature. Caffeine and benzyl benzoate can help reduce coughing. Dyspnea can be eased by compressed oxygen delivered by mask, if the patient is moderately ill, (A). However, it is obvious that severe influenza pneumonia does not respond to O2. A trial of O2 might be reasonable, but if it does not have an effect in just a few minutes, it is best to save this valuable treatment for others. Respiratory wheezing is properly treated with IV epinephrine, (A)."

"Patient agitation must be viewed with caution. We want to relieve the type of perturbation that makes other care for a patient difficult, and is terrifying for the victim. However, too much sedation can reduce the respiratory drive required by a moderately ill patient to maintain proper ventilation. Therefore, great care must be given with opiates, and also bromide, (B), that is used to calm agitation. Cardiac arrhythmias originating from the atria are best controlled with digitalis by mouth, hypodermic, or IV, (B). There is some evidence that strychnine, (C), can be used, but its side effects are worse than digitalis. A decreased cardiac output, referred to in the past as a 'weak heart', has been treated with camphorated oil, (C)."

"There are far more treatments that fall under the categories of general measures and prophylaxis. Quarantine is the best weapon we have against influenza. However, to be effective, quarantine must be immediate and complete. For these reasons, it is very hard to do. Obviously, in the midst of a pandemic, quarantine becomes impossible." Noble paused for an instant, as he briefly remembered a time when quarantine was not impossible.

Noble continued, "There has been much discussion of the use of gauze masks. Earlier this year, there were a few small case studies that suggested masks were successful against influenza. Boston, and many other municipalities, now have laws requiring the wearing of masks in public places. I believe all of you have heard the rhyme concerning mask use:

Obey the laws
And wear the gauze
Protect your jaws
From Septic Paws

However, I mentioned earlier we do have one influenza-related RCT, and it deals with gauze masks. In a recent *Journal of the American Medical Association* paper, a RCT was reported from the Great Lakes Naval Station. 8% of those using masks (the study group) developed influenza, while 7.75% of non-mask wearers (the control group) fell ill with influenza. Therefore, the gauze masks gave no clinical benefit. Of course, I am not advocating that you break the law, or that you urge others to do so."

A resident called out from the audience, "If we do, maybe we'll go to jail and not have to come to Boston City Hospital." Everyone in the room laughed loudly.

Noble realized that a little humor from the house officers was a good thing. He decided to play along with it. "Believe me, I've had similar thoughts myself." The room again erupted in laughter that was even louder.

Noble returned to the topic. "Many in the U.S. are using quinine as prophylaxis against influenza pneumonia. However, there is no adequate proof for its use. I give it a (C). Urea hydrocolloid is used for the same reason, and I give it a (D). Many advocate sunlit rooms, plenty of fresh air, 'light' diet, liberal amounts of fluid, and avoidance of constipation. These items receive a (C), except for the last two. Adequate hydration is critical, and dehydration is a very common cause of death in this infection. I give it an (A). From what I have seen, constipation associated with influenza comes from dehydration. So, the former is treated with the latter.

For septicemia, many have used sodium bicarbonate IV, bicarbonate of soda orally, and sodium chloride. I give all of them a (B). Dr. CC Barrows wrote an interesting paper in the January 19, 1903, *New York County Medical Society* journal. It involved a 17 oz. formaldehyde 1:5000 solution given IV to patients suffering from culture positive streptococcal septicemia. Some have used his treatment for influenza septicemia. I give it an (F). I give the same grading for the administration of arsenic as grippe prophylaxis."

"A very popular medical treatment is a 'mustard plaster'. There are numerous recipes for the plasters, but the most commonly used among physicians is the following: A skin irritant is applied to the skin, which creates blisters. The blisters are opened, and the affluent mixed with morphine, strychnine, and caffeine. The mixture is then injected into the patient. I give this treatment an (F). Some also treat influenza with hydrogen peroxide IV (F), typhoid vaccine, (D), or the homeopathic herbal drug gelsemium, (C)."

"One researcher gave anecdotal evidence for turning the entire body alkaline in an attempt to rid it of influenza. This is done with very large doses of potassium citrate and sodium bicarbonate given orally, by enema, and applied to the skin, (F). Venesection of one pint or more of blood has been suggested with the first sign of pulmonary edema or cyanosis, (F). Opiates as a cure, and not solely for pain, are employed, (D). Other medical treatments include methylene blue IV, (F), metallic solutions IM, (F), iodine in glycerin by mouth, (D), liquid abolene by mouth, (D), nasal Vaseline© with menthol, (D), syrup hydriotic acid, (F), syrup iron iodide, (D), oral weak izal antiseptic solution that is used to wash cars, (F), carbolic acid with quinine gargle, (F), nasal boric acid with sodium bicarbonate powder, (D), and warm water gargle with chlorinated soda, (D)."

"There are two other medical treatments that are extremely popular among physicians and the general population. The first is alcohol. The preferred form of alcohol is whiskey.

One recommendation is to take one pint of whiskey each day, for ten days. Many feel that this dose is too small, and the course not nearly long enough."

The house staff audience broke out in laughter, and applause.

"Very funny, ladies and gentlemen," smiled Noble. "However, this is being used as medical therapy, and is in great demand. The going rate for whiskey in Boston is $11 per half-pint. It's much more in other cities. When a Baltimore city ordinance closed public places recently, the Health Commissioner refused to close saloons for therapeutic reasons. Druggists are now selling whiskey for medicinal purposes, and making a tidy profit from it."

Another house officer called out, "I wonder how druggists feel about prohibition?" The audience, and Noble, laughed. Noble was glad to see the house staff taking a break from the pressures of recent patient care.

"In any case," said Noble, "I give alcohol a (D)." Noble only smiled with a few hisses and boos heard in the room. Noble said, "Another prominent U.S. physician recently stated cigarettes are 'good for all kinds of ailments', and prescribes them for influenza. I give that an (F)."

"There are two other physician treatment regimens on which I would like to comment. First, is the 'Dean of Medical School Treatment'. This consists of:

1. Bed rest.
2. 'Simple' diet.
3. Mustard plasters.
4. Mustard footbaths.

I give this regimen an (F)."

"The second regimen is found in the latest edition of Dr. William Osler's wonderful textbook, *The Principals and Practice of Medicine*. Here is what the prestigious Internist feels is the proper treatment of influenza:

1. Aspirin.
2. Bed rest.
3. Gargles.
4. 'Dover's powders' (Ipecac for vomiting induction, opium for pain and cough).
5. 'Diet'.
6. Fresh air.
7. Purgation.
8. Elimination.
9. Digitalis, large doses.
10. Caffeine salts.
11. Hypodermic strychnine for asthenia, large doses.

Ladies and gentlemen, there is no one in this room who has more respect for Dr. Osler than I do. I have met the great man, and he is an inspiration to all of us who seek the truth in modern medicine. It is in this spirit that I respectfully disagree with some points of this treatment regimen. I would raise the issue of the lack of RCTs, and other objective findings, that might substantiate the induction of vomiting and use of strychnine in influenza. I feel that Sir Osler would gratefully acknowledge the collegial disagreement, and even require it from us. I will most certainly stand completely corrected if future RCTs find this regimen sound in the treatment of influenza."

The room was completely silent. Dr. Noble had challenged the world's greatest authority in Internal Medicine. However, the audience collectively began to feel a sense of relief. Great men who seek the truth are made even greater when they are shown to be wrong, and yet welcome it. In this way, debates in medicine become objective and not personal in nature. With the present discussion, all in the audience felt Dr. Osler and Dr. Noble were truly great physicians. Their admiration of both men grew, rather than diminished.

Noble took another drink of water, pulled up a tall stool on which to sit, and continued on. "I would like to continue with general treatments for influenza. However, let's consider various popular folk remedies for it. It is safe to say that a majority of American citizens are using many of these remedies, and that many physicians also promote them."

"All of us have seen the thousands of people wearing camphor balls and garlic, usually within small amulets, around their necks. This is an extremely common folk influenza treatment, and I give it a (D). Many use home and industrial solvents as gargles to avoid the grippe, and all of them get an (F). For those who can afford them, kolynos gas masks are used for the same reason, (D)."

"Probably the most common folk remedy for influenza is homemade tea. There are dozens of popular recipes for grippe tea, but the most popular is a tea made of sassafras roots, leaves from a pokeweed plant, and elm tree bark. These plant products are put into a one-gallon kettle, boiled in water for several hours, and then cooled. A woman in Rogersville, Missouri, claims that no one has died of influenza who has partaken of this tea daily. I give all the tea recipes a (D)."

"Another popular treatment combines cough syrup with a liniment ointment. The cough syrup is made from boiled and strained cherry tree bark that is sweetened. 'White lightning' (moonshine) is added to the mixture. The ointments is made from hog lard, kerosene, and camphor, and is applied warm to the chest. This double treatment gets a (D)."

"There are many proponents of frigid air treatment along with brisk walks. Depending on the weather conditions, this would receive a (D) or (F). Others strongly urge overheated rooms, (D), and keeping feet dry, (D). Cod liver oil gets a (D)."

"There are nutritional regimens that include malt, the milk-and-egg treatment, and fruit. There is no evidence that these foods keep people from contracting influenza, or dying from it. However, keeping a diet adequate in kilocalories and other nutrients seems to be helpful in influenza convalescences. So, I give them a (C). Hot lemonade is a very popular treatment. Because it also encourages hydration, I also give it a (C). You might have noticed that the price of lemons has skyrocketed in the last few weeks, and this is because of its perceived medicinal qualities. I understand that a grocer in the North End was recently arrested for charging exorbitant prices for lemon."

"Let's talk about commercial products for a moment. Belladonna is sold in drug stores for colic and 'asthma influenza'. For the symptoms, I give it a (B), although I do not believe it prevents contracting influenza. Aconite, for fever and pain, also gets a (B). Some use Sozodont to keep mouths clean and avoid influenza, (D). Lysol© disinfectant used for the home gets a (D), and used orally gets an (F). Influ-BALM© receives a (D), as does benetol, and Vicks VapoRub©."

"Finally, there is the supernatural realm. Many people throughout the United States seek help from faith healers and charlatans. Some believe influenza is a curse that must be removed by professionals who deal with such maladies. Needless to say, I give these treatments a (D)."

Noble stood up from the stool. "Thank you very much for your attention, ladies and gentlemen. I am confident that we will have better clinical data in the future, and will have better treatments for this disease. Maybe we will even be able to prevent it someday. It is very safe to say that we will revisit this topic soon. Good afternoon." The audience applauded the summary, and slowly rose to return to the wards.

As Noble left the storage room, he wondered just when there would be better clinical data and better treatments. Right now, at Boston City Hospital, nearly twenty-five percent of the entire patient population was dying every day. As occurred aboard naval vessels, hospital employees were writing out so many death certificates that they were becoming illegible. The administration had to remind workers to write legibly so there could be some record of those who died in BCH. Somehow, it was hard to imagine that "better treatments" were anywhere in sight.

Noble had not yet been to the A.I. Office that day, and decided to make a later-than-usual check in. Because of illness, there were now times when no sentry was on guard at the A.I Office door. This was one of those times. Noble entered the large office from the small one, and was surprised by what he saw. Seated at the cordboard was Lieutenant Lafayette. But, something was wrong. Gone was the usual youthful smile as she turned to her left to greet her commanding officer. The conjunctivas of her blue eyes were reddened, and her eyelids appeared slightly swollen. Her fiery red hair was not combed neatly beneath her army cap, as it always had been. Her uniform was somewhat ruffled. She sat slumped in her oak chair.

"Oh, Lieutenant Lafayette," said Noble, trying to hide his apprehension. "I expected Lieutenant Pecknold, since this is usually her shift."

Lafayette did not answer right away. Instead, she began to cry. She quickly wiped tears from her eyes and straightened up her torso. She spoke slowly in her distinctive New Orleans accent. "I'm...sorry...Major," said Lafayette as she took short breaths in an attempt to stop her sobs. "I'm...sorry."

"Marié," said Noble, never having used her first name before, "what's wrong?"

Lafayette used her tunic sleeve to wipe her check. "It's Karen, sir. Lieutenant Pecknold. She took ill yesterday afternoon. I helped as much as I could, until I had to report for duty. Claudette...Lieutenant Pierre-Louis... then helped her as much as she could. She started up with terrible nose bleeds. She couldn't stop coughing. When she said she was having difficulty breathing, Claudette called the camp. There was an army ambulance in the Roxbury area, and it came to pick her up. They took her to the Devens hospital, sir."

Devens, thought Noble. Devens. Even though Boston City Hospital was only blocks away from the Lieutenant's Signal Corps apartment on Worcester Square, it really didn't matter to which hospital she was admitted. The conditions in all of them were the same. The care was the same. The disease was the same. Noble again felt the demon toying with him.

The Major walked over to the distraught Lafayette and put his hand on her shoulder. He knew that she had read, heard, and translated mountains of information about influenza for the past many months. He knew, that she knew, how serious this situation actually was. Still, Noble tried to console her. "I'm sure she is going to be OK, Marié. I know the doctors and nurses at Devens will provide the very best possible care they can for her." Noble knew his second sentence was very true. He was by no means certain of the first.

"I know she is in good hands, Major", as Lafayette dried an eye. "I'll be OK, too. Lieutenant Pierre-Louis and I will take over her shifts until she is better, sir. Twelve hours on, twelve hours off. You can count on us, sir."

"No," said Noble, forcefully. "That is just too much for you two. The office will just have to do with two-out-of-three shifts covered. I will take this up with Colonel Vaughn. In the mean time, just continue with your regular shifts."

Noble could tell Lieutenant Lafayette was eager to return to her work as a way to contain her emotions for awhile. He also could tell she was very thankful for his concern about Karen, and the wellbeing of the other two Signal Corps staff members of the A.I. Office. "There are messages for you on the table, sir," said the Lieutenant, returning to her normal army demeanor.

Noble thanked the Lieutenant, and walked over to the familiar central table. He read some of The War cables, and the news was good. The Germans were now completely back behind the Hindenburg Line following the major September Ally offensives. With the Wotan position of the Hindenburg Line breached, and the Siegfried position in danger of being turned from the north, the Allies felt it was time for an assault on the entire length of the enemy line.

The Allied attack on the Hindenburg Line had begun on September 26th, and included the Americans. The American troops were much greener than the English and French troops, who had been in battle for over four years. For example, the Americans encountered problems coping with long supply lines for large units in difficult terrain. Nevertheless, French and American units broke through enemy lines at Champagne, forcing the Germans off the commanding heights. As the Allies were closing in towards the Belgian frontier, Bulgaria signed a separate armistice on September 29th. When this happened, the Allies gained control of Serbia and Greece. Intelligence reports stated that on the 29th, Kaiser Wilhelm II was informed by the German Supreme Command that "the military situation was hopeless". The Allied noose about Germany was tightening.

Noble's mood was lightened somewhat as he turned to his personal stack of messages. In the stack was a U.S. Mail letter, from the Board of Registration in Medicine. He opened the letter.

Commonwealth of Massachusetts
Board of Registration in Medicine: Est. 1894
178 Albion Street
Wakefield, Massachusetts
September 16, 1918

Dear Dr. Edward Noble;

The mission of the Board of Registration is to serve the public by striving to ensure that physicians, and health care institutions in which they practice, provide to their patients a high standard of care, and to support an environment that maximizes the high quality of health care in Massachusetts.

The Board investigates complaints, holds hearings, and determines sanctions. These functions are critical to protecting the public by ensuring that only competent and ethical physicians are practicing in Massachusetts.

Dr. Noble, there has been a complaint lodged against you concerning the improper allocation and use of a Commonwealth city and county hospital ward facility. The complaint was filed on September 3, 1918. The Board considers such complaints from credible sources as very serious. The Board will convene a hearing on this matter at the Department of Public Health, 2nd Floor, 250 Washington Street, Boston, Massachusetts, on Tuesday, February 18, 1919. The Board respectfully requests your presence at 2:30 PM. You may have legal counsel present if you wish.

Very sincerely,
The Board of Registration in Medicine.

Remembering his establishment of a quarantine ward in the South Department, Noble had only one comment. He said very softly,
"Cunard."

CHAPTER 19

That evening in the Noble home, on Wednesday, October 2nd, Lillian and Akeema prepared the family meal. There were very few fresh vegetables, fruits, or meats on the menu. Boston area grocery markets were nearly empty. Most food was either baked that day with Peerless Minnesota flour, or came from cans or jars. The family was now using the reserves it had stored some weeks earlier.

Marguerite said grace, and asked God to take care of Arthur's soul. Following that request, each family member said "Amen". Although the meal was not what Lillian wanted for her family, she and the others were grateful to have any food at all. With war rationing, and now the pandemic, having something to eat was truly a privilege. Akeema reminded the three small children how fortunate they were.

"Milton and John are now ready for their clinical trial on Gallops Island," Lillian told Noble. "My work with it is finished, and now I can now spend all my time on community issues."

Noble finished chewing a bite of Hormel Cedar Cervelat dry sausage and took a drink of reconstituted dried milk.

"Lilly, that's great. The city really needs your help. Eight hundred and fifty of Boston's physicians are away in Europe, and more than twice that number of nurses are also gone. Now the pandemic is stretching health care resources beyond all limits."

Florence added, "Dad, did you know that right now forty-three percent of the Boston City Hospital staff is hospitalized? More and more doctors and nurses are becoming severely ill, and the number of deaths is climbing. It's pretty scary, dad."

"I hadn't heard it was that high, Florence," said Noble. "The three Boston medical schools, Harvard, BU, and Tufts, are trying to fill the huge physician gap left by The War and the pandemic. They have directed their medical school students to help in the local hospitals. The students have already taken on many roles left by ill BCH residents. They are also beginning to work in grade schools, and some empty buildings, as greater hospital ward capacity is sought. The local nursing schools are also releasing students to work in these same areas. Lilly, this is where I need to discuss some logistical matters that concern you."

"What sort of logistics are you talking about, dear?" asked Lillian.

Noble took a helping of canned corned beef, known as "Willie" by American troops, onto his plate. "Well," said Noble, "the medical and nursing students that will be out in the field providing medical care need at least occasional supervision. The faculties of the three medical schools have asked me to look in on them, when I can. Boston City Hospital has agreed to this, and so has the Army Communicable Diseases Division in Washington."

"They all know you are such a great clinician and teacher, dear," said Lillian. "But what does this have to do with me?"

"I knew you would be out in the field as well, as you organize community efforts in this evolving crisis," said Noble. "There's increasing lawlessness in the city, Lilly, as basic necessities run lower. I thought I could ask the Camp Devens Army Wagoner section to loan Sergeant Campbell out to you as an escort. However, there is not a single soldier to spare at Devens. So, there is only one person available to be your escort."

Lillian smiled, since she now understood the logistics her husband had mentioned. "You?" she asked.

"Yours truly," said Noble, who smiled back. "We'll take the Ford out when you have community tasks to complete. The army has offered to provide gasoline, since it is in short supply in the civilian sector. We'll also take Florence to the home health visits authorized by the Naval Reserve. This will give me an opportunity to drop by some of the established satellite hospital wards to assist the medical and nursing students."

Lillian was greatly relieved. She had not wanted to concern her husband about safety issues, since he had enough worries right now. Still, she was aware of rising crime in New England and elsewhere. She had also heard about armed kidnappings of nurses who were forced into health care slave labor. With Edward along, she would be less troubled over security for herself and Florence.

The family finished up their meal with dried pears, apples, and apricots, and cleaned their dishes. Noble read a story to the three small children, said prayers with them, and then tucked each in bed. Bernard, Michael, and Marguerite would all be up early the next day. Akeema was keeping the children on a strict home study regimen, while their own school remained closed. Noble, Lillian, and Florence were also going to turn in earlier than usual. Each was to begin new projects the next day, and they wanted to get an early start with them.

As Lillian left the kitchen for the bedroom, she passed through the parlor and found her husband standing before one of the walls. Lillian had framed Arthur's Eagle Scout medal, and mounted it along side Arthur's hand print from his first day of 1st grade. She stood beside Edward and put her left arm around his waist. Both stood silently for several minutes.

Finally, Edward said, "Lilly, I miss him so."
"So do I," Lillian said. "So do I."

Early the next morning, Thursday, October 3rd, the Noble family was up and busy. Breakfast was dried cereal with reconstituted milk, and toasted English muffins with berry preserve or peanut butter. Lillian saved dried bacon for Sundays only. The children went off to the Noble home library, which Akeema now called the "school room". Bernard and Michael had nicknamed it the "detention center". Noble put on his usual field uniform, and Florence put on her Naval Reserve uniform. Lillian wore a loose light blue blouse, a plain brown skirt, shoes with low heals, and a simple broad brimmed hat. The weather was unseasonably warm with cloudless blue skies, and Lillian wanted to be ready for the warm and sunny afternoon.

As Noble prepared to leave the house, he marveled at his wife's social connections. She was a Boston Women's Auxiliary chapter president, a U.S. Public Health Service officer, an American Red Cross local president, a local organizer in the National Women's Party and its suffrage movement, a leader in Dr. Rosenau's milk pasteurization initiative, active in the Radcliff Epidemiological Society and its other academic pursuits, and knew by first name many local and state government legislators.

Lillian had already helped plan the coordination of nearly eight percent of the American population as volunteer Red Cross production workers. She helped organize the U.S. into thirteen national Red Cross divisions in order to mobilize "Home Defense Nurses". The Red Cross national War Council then appropriated large sums of money to assist these divisions as the pandemic spread across the nation. Florence, as a Naval Reservist nursing student, would be helping one such Boston Home Defense Nursing group.

Lillian now wanted to see for herself how some of these programs were working, and what other services were needed. Made up almost completely of women, Lillian's organizations planned to act where government could not, or would not.

The Nobles put sack lunches and bottles of water in the Ford truck, opened the garage door, cranked up the engine, and drove off west on Beacon Street. They turned south on Massachusetts Avenue toward their first stop. A modest amount of medical supplies had been given by Camp Devens and the Chelsea Naval Hospital for the Noble community effort. In addition, Noble had purchased four times the value of the medical supplies he used for Arthur's care. The combined groups of medical supplies were stored at Boston City Hospital awaiting pick up by the Nobles.

On their way to BCH, in the lightest traffic they had ever seen, Lillian vented some frustration to her husband. "I just cannot understand it, Edward. I just don't."

"What's the matter, Lilly?" asked Noble.

"Congress," said Lillian, with clinched teeth.

"Oh," said Noble. "You're still burning over that, aren't you?"

"Of course I'm burning over 'that'," said Lillian. On Monday we were so close. So...close. Even President Wilson made personal appeals to the Senators. We were just two votes shy of the two-thirds majority we needed. Two votes, Edward!"

"Lilly," said Noble, "all of us advocating for the 19th Amendment are disappointed. The fact that the vote was only two Senatorial votes short is very upsetting. But, this is the closest so far to victory that women's federal suffrage has come. You might just make it on another vote."

"Great," Lillian said sarcastically. "The NWP doesn't think it will come up for a Senate vote again this year. Edward, women have died in Europe for our dear country, and some have even been buried at sea from troop transport carriers. Yet, women are not valued enough to be full citizens of the United States. I'm really angry, Edward."

Noble knew his wife well enough to allow her time to express herself. The women's suffrage movement in America was not about to go away, and he knew Lillian and her fellow suffragettes would redouble their efforts. But, for now, there was another sinister battle to fight.

They drove the Ford around to the back of one of the BCH South Department pavilions, parked, and went into the building. Some of the staff had volunteered the previous day to help carry out the stored supplies. Once loaded up, the Nobles were off to their first destination.

Southeast of the hospital, at the corner of Swett and Reed Streets, was an abandoned shoe factory warehouse. Cots and linen barriers had already been set up in the warehouse as a BCH satellite hospital. Harvard, BU, and Tufts medical students, as well as nursing students from schools all over Boston, had swept clean the building and were already filling it with the ill. The Nobles parked the truck and began to bring in their supplies. Several hundred people were standing and lying on the sidewalks outside the front of the building, as medical students tried to decide who should be admitted and who should remain on the street. When Noble entered the building, he saw Dr. David Schafer busily examining patients in the large open warehouse. Wide ceiling windows let in a large amount of sunlight that facilitated patient examinations. Feeling some relief in the knowledge that the third year resident was there, Noble called out to the young doctor. "Dr. Schafer. Good to see you."

"Dr. Noble! How are you sir?" said Shafer, who still looked as though he himself needed medical attention. "It is so great to see a familiar face!"

"Hi, David," said Noble, who felt the resident was one of his closest friends in at BCH. "I'm just coming buy to drop off what little supplies we have to spare. How is it going?"

"Well, sir, not so bad," said Schafer. "There are fewer Type III patients that show up at this hospital annex. We seem to get more Type I patients here. Maybe we'll have a better salvage rate than at the main hospital. Can you stay for awhile, sir?"

"Sorry, Lieutenant," said Noble. "We have a lot to do today and I can only stay a minute. I'm confident about this place, though, now that I know you are here to supervise. You're the ranking 'attending', it looks like."

Schafer laughed. "Yeah, who would have known. A third year resident in charge of a ward with three hundred patients. We'll do what we can, sir."

"I know you will, Lieutenant," Noble said smiling. "If you need help, have someone call and leave a message at the A.I. Office at BCH for me. I'll drop by when I can. There are a number of other satellite facilities around the city that I need to visit as well. At least you'll have some supplies for awhile. We'll bring more when they become available." Noble knew the meager supplies he brought to this satellite hospital would last only a few hours. The temporary facility would then have nothing with which to medically serve the influenza patients. All the students could really offer was a place off the streets, water, and kindness.

"We'll see you later," said Noble. He saluted the resident, who saluted back. In many ways, he felt that Dr. Shafer was the kind of resident Arthur would have been. He liked that thought. As Noble walked out of the building, he thought about how little his visit there would help anything. However, Arthur's words came back to him, almost as though he were whispering them in person: "You can't do everything, but you can do what you can do!"

Although the Red Cross had organized groups of former nurses and nursing students into "Home Defense Nurse" groups, ninety-three percent of calls for home health assistance went unanswered. The Naval Reserves had agreed to the Red Cross request for help in this regard. So, Ensign Florence Noble had been assigned to home health duties for a few apartment buildings in South Boston. This was the Nobles' next destination.

The Nobles were taking their first trip into Boston neighborhoods in several weeks. They drove east on Harrison Avenue, and then south on Dorchester Avenue. They observed many differences from the city they once knew. The most obvious difference was how empty the streets were of vehicles and pedestrians. When they did see people walking, they noticed they were never in groups. People walked quickly, individually, with their heads down. Most wore gauze masks. Noble mentioned, "I suspect people are avoiding any contact with others, if they can help it." In addition to the lack of people, the sidewalks had mounds of uncollected garbage. Garbage collection was another social service that had virtually disappeared.

As they drove on, the Nobles noticed numerous white and tan colored bags of varying lengths on the sidewalks. Sometimes there was just one bag. Sometimes there were many bags in stacks. Similar bags were often seen on house porches. As they drove along the streets, Florence said, "There sure is a lot of garbage out on the streets. What kind of garbage is in all these white bags, Mom?"

There was a long silent pause in the family car. Suddenly, Lillian gasped, and put her right hand across her mouth. Noble had been concentrating on driving and had not been watching the street sidewalks closely. However, when he heard Lillian, he looked at one side of the street and then the other. He experienced a wave of extreme nausea as his carotids pulsated against his uniform collar . He gradually slowed the truck to an idling stop in the middle of Old Colony Avenue. He took his hands off the steering wheel, and sat back in the front bench seat. He felt as though he might vomit. As tears came to his own eyes, he looked to his left to see tears running down his wife's cheeks. They could not believe it. Here. In Boston.

"Mom...Dad," said Florence, "what's wrong?"

"Dear," said Lillian through sobs. "The white bags... they're...they're bodies."

When Florence realized what her mother had said, and the meaning of the white bags, she also gasped and put her right forearm to her lower face.

"This is unbelievable," said Noble slowly. "Even with the office reports, I had no idea it was this bad...this fast."

"I...I don't have words for this," said Lillian, weeping. "People are now forced to put their loved ones out on the sidewalks...like the family garbage. Edward, it's horrible."

The three sat in the truck for some time, trying to comprehend what they were seeing. As Old Colony Avenue stretched south to the horizon, so did the linen and sackcloth bags on both sides of the street.

After several minutes, Noble refocused and realized they had a duty to the living. The little they could do, they would do. He put his foot on the throttle, accelerated the Ford, and drove onto Dorchester Street. He finally turned south on Gates Street, near Thomas Park, where Florence's apartment buildings were located. All along their route were linen bags.

For some time, Noble had noticed something odd about the houses during their journey. There was something on the doors. Something was on nearly all the doors.

"Lillian," said Noble, "can you tell what is on the house doors? Maybe I need new lenses on my glasses, but I can't make it out."

"I know exactly what it is, Edward," said Lillian, who was trying her best to look at the situation objectively. "It's crepe. Crepe for the dead."

"I see," said Noble. He deliberated his wife's words for a moment. "I see. Families are placing crepe on the doors of houses where loved ones have died?"

"Yes," said Lillian. "Per the custom, families place white crepe for someone young who has died. Black crepe is for the middle-aged recently deceased. Grey crepe is for the elderly."

"And, the crepe is on almost every door," said Florence. "And...most of the crepe is white."

Once again the Nobles fell silent. Nearly every door. All neighborhoods. Throughout the city. All the same. Linen bags everywhere. Crepe everywhere. Noble once again felt the demon taunting him. Laughing at him. Laughing at his knowledge, his science, his medicine, and everything he cared about.

The Nobles pulled up at their first nursing stop, which was an apartment building on Gates Street. As they carried some supplies out of the truck, they could see a group of small children playing jump rope about thirty yards north on the sidewalk. They could faintly hear their chant as they played:

I had a little bird,
Its name was Enza.
I opened the window,
And in-flu-enza.

The children said the chant over and over again. It was as though even children understood that the very air we breathe carried something else with it. Something unseen. Something deadly.

There were two families to visit in the building. The Nobles entered the old musty smelling structure and climbed the dark stairs to the second floor. There was garbage outside most of the doors in the hallway. The three walked to apartment No. 5, and knocked on a door with chipped dark brown paint. A boy about fourteen years old answered the door. "Hello," said Florence, "is this the McCracken family?"

"Yes...yes it is," said the boy. "Please come in. My name is Mark."

"The Red Cross received a call that your family needed some assistance?" said Florence.

"I...I think so," said the boy. "I'm here with my three little brothers and my little sister. My father worked at the harbor piers, but he...died at his work, about a week ago. My mother is very sick. She's over there."

The Nobles entered the single room apartment that smelled of urine. Drapes were drawn across the sole apartment window, and dishes were piled up in a sink that had not been cleaned in many days. Three young children sat on a worn carpet in the center of the room, and were nearly motionless. There was only one chair in the room, along with some mats and blankets on the floor. On the room's couch was a very ill appearing woman who was about forty years of age. Florence went to the woman's side to make a quick assessment.

Noble quickly examined the three children, who were pale and very thin. All had temporal wasting, decreased upper arm circumferences, and markedly decreased scapular and triceps fat folds. The fourteen year old boy was not much different.

"Dad," said Florence, "the mother's blood pressure is 95/48, heart rate 99, respirations 22, and temperature 104° F."

Noble went over to the mother and performed a quick heart and lung examination with his stethoscope, as well as a cursory neurologic exam. "She has a significant bronchitis, but no clinical pneumonia at this point. However, all five of the McCrackens are malnourished, and the mother is very dehydrated. She also has the non-violent form of influenza delirium. Unfortunately, we don't have any IV fluids. Boston City Hospital doesn't have any either."

"Mark," said Lillian, "your mother obviously can't care for you and the other children, and all of you need food. We can leave you with some things to eat, but you will need to do your very best to have your mother drink as much water as possible. If we drop by each day with some supplies, she will likely receive more attention from you than she would in a hospital. That is assuming there was even space in a hospital. Here is a suction tube that you can use to help her drink. Do you think you can do that, Mark?"

"Yes...I think so," said the boy. "Do you think she is going to live?"

"I don't know," said Lillian. "Her best hope right now... is you. We'll also leave some aspirin for your mother's fever. You can give her two tablets every four hours if she continues to feel as hot as she is now."

"I think...I can do it, Ma'am," said the boy.

Florence then asked, "Mark, you mentioned that you're here with three brothers and a sister. Where is your third brother?"

The boy turned toward one of the walls, and pointed to a corner. "He's in there."

The Nobles saw a box for ten pounds of macaroni in the room's corner. "He's in the box?" asked Florence.

"Yes," said the boy. "He's...dead. He's been dead for a couple of days."

Noble walked to the room corner and opened one of the ends of the macaroni box. In it he could see the head of a boy that was probably two or three years old. The body was nearly black, and in early stages of decomposition. Noble nodded to the others. Mark was correct.

"Mark," said Lillian, "I will be contacting the Bureau of Child Hygiene to also look in on you when they can. If your mother gets any sicker, or doesn't improve, they may need to take you and your siblings to a place where you can get more help."

Mark said he understood what he had been told, and was very grateful for the visit. The Nobles left small amounts of crackers, bread, dried fruit, and powdered milk with the boy and his family. Noble offered to carry his brother's makeshift coffin to the sidewalk. Mark was relieved by the offer, because he was afraid to even touch the box. While departing, they said they would try to visit again tomorrow.

The Nobles visited the second apartment with several more influenza victims and, thankfully, no dead bodies. The second group of people was also given instructions on hydration, nutrition, and left with one or two days of food.

There was a time, not long ago, when all of these people would have had places to go for a multitude of high quality social and medical services. But now, all such places and agencies were overwhelmed with people in need. Actually, many of these services no longer existed. All the Nobles could hope to do for was help these people in their homes and apartments, and hope for better days.

The Nobles reentered their truck and drove off to the next apartment building. As they left, Noble looked in the truck rearview mirror and saw a horse-drawn cart slowly moving along the street. Men in police and firemen's uniforms were loading the linen bags onto the cart by stacking one on top of another. It appeared that some services, like the Boston Sanitation, Fire, and Police Departments, were doing their best to help in the crisis. The cart stopped in front of the apartment building the Nobles had just left, loaded the macaroni box, and moved on.

As the Nobles drove north on Dorchester Avenue, two large steam shovels were at work just west of the road. Since there was virtually no one on the streets, Noble slowed the vehicle to get a better idea of the work at hand. The two steam shovels were digging a hole about one hundred feet long, fifty feet wide, and ten feet deep. The machines were digging at one end of the large hole. Stacked on the other end of the hole were hundreds of linen and sackcloth bags. Workers were attaching tags on the ends of some of the bags. Other workers were throwing the bags into the hole in rows.

Florence asked, "Dad, what are they doing? Are they burying the bodies?"

"Yes," said Noble. "They're digging a mass grave. It looks like they are trying to tag the bodies whose identities are known. Perhaps this is for some future attempt at identification. But, for now, something must be done with the dead."

Earlier in the pandemic, the poor and unknown were placed in mass graves like this one. However, there were no longer enough people to prepare and bury the dead fast enough. In an ultimate democratic process, everyone was now interred together.

It was growing dark as the Noble truck travelled north on Massachusetts Avenue toward Boston City Hospital. The day had been long. The Nobles had visited a number of satellite hospitals and apartment dwellings that day, and had distributed all the supplies they carried. Although they would pick up more supplies tomorrow, they knew the amount would be smaller. Unless something changed, the amount of supplies would dwindle each day until there was nothing left to distribute.

Noble wanted to check in for just a few minutes at the A.I. Office, since he had not been there in over 24 hours. When he entered the small office door, he was very surprised to see that Lieutenant Pierre-Louis was not at her usual cordboard.

Instead, she was lying on the office couch. As he closed the door behind him, he could see that the Lieutenant was crying heavily.

"Claudette," said Noble, "are you alright?"

The Lieutenant had both forearms over her face, as she lay with her head on one of the arms of the couch. Her army cap was on the floor. She was crying so hard that she could not answer Noble. He walked to the desk and wheeled the oak coaster chair over to the couch. He sat down and took one of the Lieutenant's hands. "Claudette," Noble said again, "please tell me what the problem is."

The Lieutenant was able to get a few words out in between sobs. "Major...its Karen...Karen Pecknold." She resumed crying for a time, and then started again. "She...she...died, sir. She's dead." The Lieutenant resumed crying.

Noble felt a sinking feeling in his chest. "Heart-sick", he thought to himself. Here we go again. Noble took off his glasses, set them on the nearby desk, and put both hands over his face. He ran his hands through his white hair. He put his elbows on the arms of the oak chair, and supported his head with his hands on either side of his face. He couldn't find a position that he could maintain comfortably for more than a few moments.

After several minutes, Noble said, "Claudette...I am so sorry. So sorry. I'm sorry for you. I'm sorry for Marié. I'm sorry for Karen's family. And...I'm sorry for me. Karen was the first person I met at Boston City Hospital after returning from France. I remember she was so excited about her job, and prepared to be great at it. She also was supremely proud of the technology as she gave me a grand tour of the office. She did everything possible that first day to make my own new job easier. She was such a joy."

The Lieutenant slowly sat up on the couch and brushed the tears from her eyes. Noble gave her a handkerchief. She dabbed the corners of her eyes as she gradually composed herself. Eventually, she sat up straight in her usual army posture and assumed a more official presence. "Marié and I will miss her so," the Lieutenant said. "The three of us have lived together at the Worcester Square apartment for nearly ten months, and we all became such great friends. As the oldest, she was sort of our leader. We looked up to her. She was so kind and caring...so wonderful."

Lieutenant Pierre-Louis cupped her face with her hands and resumed crying. Quickly, she once again put on the air of an army Lieutenant. "Major, we would like to have Karen's body shipped back to Quebec, where some of her family still lives. However, the trains are not running consistently anymore, and there are scores of coffins that are just sitting at the nearby train station. To make matters much worse, we don't know where Karen's body is. We may never know where it is. There are just so many. So many. Still, we are going to hold a very brief memorial service Monday morning at the Cathedral of the Holy Cross. Sir, we hope you can attend. The ceremony must only be fifteen minutes long, since the city has limited funerals to no longer than that. As you know, public gatherings are greatly discouraged. Do you think you can attend, sir?"

"I wouldn't miss it for the world," said Noble. "Just let me know when, and I'll be there." The Lieutenant told Noble the short service would start promptly at 0800 hours. He then told the Lieutenant to leave her office shift early. She picked up her cap and purse, put on her coat, and started for the door. She stopped for a moment, turned back to the Major, and kissed him on the cheek. "Thank you for caring, Major," said the Lieutenant. She then quickly left through the main office door. Noble for the first time felt a kernel of happiness in a truly awful day.

On both Friday and Saturday, the Nobles worked long hours traveling in the Ford truck. From satellite hospital, to satellite hospital, they drove. Some of the satellites were warehouses, some were schools, some were government office buildings or libraries, and some were just tents. At every location the situation was identical. Students were caring for the sickest population anyone had seen before. Sanitary conditions were meager. There were almost no supplies. And, there was ever-present death. Death everywhere. The sights and smells of death were not just everywhere. They were now everything.

In addition to the satellites, the Nobles continued to visit apartment buildings. The apartment scenarios were the same as the hospital satellites. And with each day, there were more white bags on the streets than the day before. Each day the death carts carried more bags than yesterday. Each day there was more crepe on house doors. Every day became more horrible than the day before. Everyone silently asked themselves as the hours passed, "Am I next?"

Death could come over several days. Or, it could come so suddenly that the afflicted dropped dead on the street where they walked. The Nobles occasionally drive past people dead on sidewalks with small bags of food still in their grips. A man in an apartment told them of his recent ride on one of the few running Boston trolleys. After boarding the trolley, six people promptly died. The dead included the driver. The Nobles asked what he did then. The man said the trolley came to a stop, he jumped off, and he walked home. People were becoming accustomed to the frightful.

On Sunday the Nobles took some much needed time to rest. In the early afternoon they drove to the Chestnut Hill cemetery to spend a few moments with Arthur. The family so wanted to have a proper tombstone for their loved one. However, everyone in Boston wanted tombstones. And, there was no one to cut them anyway. So, the cross fashioned by Akeema stood as the only marker of Arthur's grave.

The family sat around the graves of Edward's parents and the first Noble son. Although there were spontaneous talks about Arthur, most of the time at the cemetery was spent in quiet contemplation.

The Noble family noticed one change from past Chestnut Hill visits. Several small groups of people huddled over plots in the cemetery while others dug holes. Six feet in length, and six feet in depth...holes. White bags were next to newly dug holes everywhere. Families were now burying their loved ones themselves, as the Nobles had done.

Early Monday morning, October 7th, the Nobles boarded their truck and drove to the Cathedral of the Holy Cross. Boston was virtually a ghost town. However, scores of people were standing outside the Washington Street front of the cathedral. Noble had to park on the nearby Pelham side street because of the crowd at the church.

It was nearly 8 AM as the three Nobles entered through the four large red doors of the cathedral. In the narthex, people with large note pads asked those entering the church who's service they were attending. By city ordinance, public funeral services were now limited to fifteen minutes. The cathedral staff was trying to accommodate multiple memorial services at the same time. Therefore, small groups of grieving people were directed to an area in the church, given a brief service, and then quickly ushered out of the cathedral. No caskets were in the church since burials were performed beforehand.

A woman found the name "Pecknold, Karen, Second Lieutenant" alphabetically among dozens of yellow legal papers written on a pad. She directed the Nobles to the front left corner of the church nave. There, about a dozen people were assembling before a young priest with a white robe. Florence and Lillian Noble sat together, and Major Noble sat between his Second Lieutenants; Claudette Pierre-Louis and Marié Lafayette. Noble noticed the church was unusually quiet given the numbers of people that were walking in, walking out, standing, and sitting. There were sounds of shoes shuffling in a huge church, quiet words spoken by a dozen priests conducting a dozen memorials, and soft sobs from those attending the small services.

Claudette and Marié stood at attention when the Major arrived, but Noble quickly had them sit back down in the pew. Nearly all of the sobbing attendees at Karen's memorial were from the Army Signal Corps at Camp Devens. Noble knew they had all seen their share of death in the last weeks. The young priest also had a pad of paper with many names. He was probably performing thirty to forty memorials a day, and had done so for weeks. He was pale and had the posture of a very tired man. He went about his duty, as anyone would, who had done the same thing over and over again for a long period of time. Toward the end of the fifteen minute service, the priest flipped additional papers to find some written words specifically about Karen. He spoke of her energy, her devotion to God, country, her work in the army, and her inner and outer beauty as a person. Karen's fellow army comrades wiped tears away as the priest said a final prayer. Noble knew it was unlikely that anyone would ever find her body.

Noble stood from the pew and began to walk to the cathedral north aisle, beyond the rows of ogival white arches. He happened to glance toward the back of the church. There, some fifty rows of pews away, was a man sitting in the corner. He was a large man, and Noble could not make out his face. But, he thought his body proportions and seated posture were very familiar.

"You can see him, can't you Major?" said Lieutenant Lafayette, noticing Nobles stare toward the back of the church.

"I see someone... someone who seems familiar, Lieutenant," said Noble.

"You know him, Major," said the Lieutenant. "He's Sergeant Campbell, sir."

"Is he attending a service here, Lieutenant?" asked Noble.

The Lieutenant brushed some tears from her check. "Sort of, sir. He's here for Karen."

"Karen?" said Noble. "I didn't even know the Sergeant knew her."

"Oh, he knew her alright," said the Lieutenant. "Do you remember when I told you an army ambulance picked up Karen when she became ill, and took her to Devens?"

"Yes," said Noble. "I remember clearly you telling me that."

"Well, it wasn't really an ambulance, sir," said the Lieutenant. "Sergeant Campbell drove her to Devens in an army staff car. You see, the Sergeant has been secretly seeing Karen. They were lovers. In fact, they were planning to be married after The War. He met Karen through you, actually. During one of his trips for you, they met at Boston City Hospital. He was seeing Karen at our Worcester Square apartment for over eight months."

"And, they have been keeping it secret because of the officer fraternizing rule at Devens," said Noble.

"Yes," said the Lieutenant. "They truly loved each other, Major. The Sergeant is really broken up over it."

Noble bid the Lieutenants goodbye, and explained the situation to Lillian and Florence. He told them he would meet them at the car in a few minutes, but he had something to do first.

Noble walked along the north cathedral aisle to the back pew row. There, Sergeant Campbell sat sobbing with his hands over his face and his head bowed. Noble sat down beside him, and put his hand on his broad shoulder. The Sergeant lifted his head, saw it was Noble, and put his hands back onto his face. "I guess they told you, Major," said the Sergeant. "Are you going to tell my commanding officer at Devens, sir?"

Noble had been watching helplessly as the demon destroyed tens of thousands of families. He was not going to condemn an individual man who sought only to create a new loving family. He realized officers were required to report those who disobeyed the fraternizing rules. Noble himself could be punished for failing to report the Sergeant. However, he would not give the demon yet another indirect triumph. "Absolutely not, Sergeant," said Noble. "And, I am so...so sorry for your loss. Everyone who met Karen felt she was simply a wonderful person. If anyone in command ever finds out about your relationship, it won't be from me."

"Thank...thank you, Major," chocked Campbell.

Noble could tell that the Sergeant wanted time by himself in the cathedral. He left through the front of the church where additional mourners awaited their turns to honor loved ones, and say goodbye. By refusing to reveal Sergeant Campbell's secret, Noble felt there had been a tiny victory against the demon.

CHAPTER 20

O n this warm and humid Wednesday morning, October 9th, the Nobles set out early for a newly established Red Cross Center on Commonwealth Avenue near the Boston Common. Nearly one hundred volunteers were now helping to prepare large quantities of newly donated supplies from both the military and civilian sectors. Several train cars with army and navy supplies had arrived in Boston, and people were giving all they could from their own homes. Individual cities, and the entire country, were coming together during the pandemic. Volunteers cleaned laundry, prepared meals, and made gauze masks. Volunteers also were using their own vehicles to transport supplies to the infirmed, and to move patients to satellite hospitals. For the first time in many weeks, there were new supplies of drugs, syringes, IV fluids, and other medical supplies for the overflowing wards throughout Boston. It still was not nearly enough, but it would help.

In the evenings, Lillian enlisted the Women's Auxiliary and its existing War Bond drive structure to help the Red

Cross. Lillian and other Auxiliary leaders had already organized Boston down to the city block level for bond sales and
recycling of strategic materials. Now, the same organization
was assisting in the distribution of food, linen, and clothing.
The Auxiliary had established banks of telephones so people
could access these emergency services.

There was still plenty of bad news. In the past week, fifteen
more Red Cross nurses had arrived from other Massachusetts
cities to help in the Boston area. Ten of the nurses had already
been admitted to hospitals with influenza, and three had
died. Medical residents from Boston City and Massachusetts
General Hospitals were dying as they worked, as were many
medical students from BU, Tufts, and Harvard. Scores of
nursing students were also dead and dying. The number of
health care workers continued to decrease each day, as the
number of influenza victims soared.

The city began stricter measures to combat the pandemic.
Nonessential meetings were completely banned. Some cities banned all funerals, but Boston continued to allow fifteen
minute memorial gatherings. Influenza sufferers were to
be quarantined until all clinical manifestations of the illness
subsided. However, there were almost no personnel available to enforce the quarantines. The Boy Scouts and the Red
Cross continued to pass out US Public Health Service pamphlets with preventative guidelines. Like many other cities,
Phoenix, Arizona passed a law imposing jail sentences and
heavy fines for shaking hands.

After the United States entered The War, hundreds of
thousands of temporary workers streamed into large metropolitan areas for war-related work. The workers were usually
very young men and women who saw an opportunity to help
themselves and their families. They were new to the large cities, and had few friends or family nearby. The workers had
been crammed into crowed working conditions and shared
boarding house space with large numbers of other workers.
South Boston had many such workers holding jobs at the harbor piers, as well as other civilian positions with the military.

Subsequently, the Red Cross received reports that boarding houses in South Boston were experiencing severe health related problems. The Nobles were asked to survey the situation, and help who they could.

After parking the truck outside a large dilapidated boarding house on E 2nd Street, the Nobles found a woman about twenty years old dead on the curb. They entered through the front door, and found no one at the check-in desk. They walked down a hallway with a worn wood floor and garbage lying along the walls. They knocked at a door that said "No. 1". No one answered. They found the door unlocked and entered. Noble had thought he had seen all the horror the pandemic could present. He was wrong.

The Nobles entered a common living area that had five small bedrooms adjoining it. There was an old faded Indian rug on the floor. Garbage covered most of the horizontal surfaces in the apartment. The room had an overpowering smell of urine, feces, vomit, and decomposing flesh. The Nobles covered their noses, even though they already wore gauze masks. Three of the small adjoining rooms contained only small cots, dirty linen, and more garbage. But, there was more in the other two bedrooms.

One of the bedrooms had bodies of two young men stuffed in the corners. Each had been dead for several days, and they were very badly decomposed. One of the bodies was partially wrapped in a sheet covered with dried blood, and the other had no shirt. The other bedroom had a double bed in it, and two bodies of young men. One of the men appeared to have died within the last twenty-four hours. However, the other body in the bed had been dead for several days and was also far along in decomposition. The bed was covered in dry pink blood. One or both men had been incontinent of urine and feces before they died, and dried vomit was crusted on both their faces. Noble surmised that one of the young men must have been lying next to a corpse for several days, as he struggled to live.

Hell-on-earth. This was a term Noble applied to a lot of places these days. Lillian and Florence promptly left the second bedroom. The sights and smell of this experience overwhelmed Lillian, and she suddenly vomited. Noble began to escort his wife and daughter out of the apartment. Florence helped her mother outside to the truck since there was little more they could do there. As Noble was about to leave the boarding house, he noticed a young man sitting near the check-in desk. The man wore overalls with grease on them. His hair was oily and his hands were covered with grease.

"I heard someone in the house," said the man, "and came to see who would ever come in here."

"I'm Dr. Edward Noble with the Army Communicable Diseases Division. I'm working with the Red Cross right now. We heard some of the boarding houses in South Boston were distressed, and came to see if we could help."

The young man laughed loudly. "Thanks, doc, but nothing can help this hell-hole. I think I'm the only one that actually lives in this building now. Dozens have either gone to the hospital, died here, or ran away in fear. Me? I'm just waiting for it to get me too. I try to find work at the piers, when there is some."

"Where is the manager of the boarding house?" asked Noble.

The young man laughed even louder. "What a joke. Did you see the lady dead out on the curb?"

"Yes...yes we did," said Noble.

"That was Katie Collins," said the man. "Great, beautiful kid. Came here to Boston to earn enough money to open a store with her husband in Illinois. She came down with the grippe, and was pretty sick. She didn't have enough money for the rent, so the manager kicked her out onto the street a few nights ago. She had nothing to drink for a day when he threw her out. I think she died of a fever out there on the curb. Most of us were at work when it happened."

"That's appalling," said Noble.

"Yeah, everyone else thought so too," said the man. "When some of the guys found her dead, and learned what had happened, they took the manager out to the back yard and stabbed him. His body is still out there."

So, this is what it was all coming to, thought Noble. Greed, cruelty, and vigilantism. The best of humanity could be found at the Red Cross Center on Commonwealth Avenue, and all of the hospital wards about the city. The worst of humanity could be found here on E 2nd Street.

Noble told the man he would let the sanitation department know of the deaths in the building. All he could say otherwise was "good luck".

The Nobles visited all the boarding houses they were asked to survey. Many of the same conditions were found in each. They were able to treat a few who were only moderately ill. But, many of the buildings were now inhabited only by the dead.

The last stop for the evening was to look in on the four McCracken children on Gates Street. As of yesterday, the children's mother had remained stable and well hydrated with the good care provided by her son, Mark. Today they came with food, clean clothes, and hope that the family was on the mend. However, their hopes were not to be realized. Mrs. McCracken had died the night before. Mark had already wrapped his mother in a sheet. He and Noble carried the malnourished body out to the sidewalk for collection.

There were now three small children led by a fourth, who was all of fourteen. The disposition of the McCracken children was a serious remaining problem. Orphans of dead parents were now overwhelming the Bureau of Child Hygiene system. In spite of pleas for help, thousands of children had no place to go. There were reports of groups of Boston and Chelsea children scurrying about at night looking for food. One city block in Chelsea had sixteen orphaned children, and this was not an uncommon event. There were many more families with only one parent left from the pandemic, who was now ill. These children were being referred to as pre-orphans.

After moving the mother's body, Noble asked his wife, "Whatever are we going to do with the children, Lilly? They have no place to go, and there is no functioning service to help them."

"They have a place to go, Edward," said Lillian.

"Where?" asked Noble.

"Our home," said Lillian.

Noble frowned, and put his hand to his forehead. He knew this was coming. "Lilly, I want to help them as much as you do. However, we are running low on stocked food and other supplies. Without more deliveries to Boston planned anytime soon, we might not have enough for our own family."

Lillian looked at her husband with her blue eyes tearing. Her torso straitened, and she threw her shoulders back. She spoke slowly. "Dear, you need to listen again to Arthur speaking to you. He is speaking to me. 'You can't do everything, but, you can do what you can do!' We can't take in every orphan in Boston. However, we can take in these four children right now. We will need to ration our food for a time. But, we are going to do this, Edward."

Edward knew his wife's mind was made up, and that was that. Of course, she was also right. He began wondering what quarter-strength concentrated milk would be like.

The Nobles had the children bring a few of their belongings, and loaded them into the Ford. As they drove away, one of the small children said softly, "Bye bye, Mommy. I love you." Noble cursed the demon under his breath. Lillian cried softly.

It was dark when the Nobles pulled the truck into the Beacon Street house garage, closed the door, and walked inside. Bernard, Michael, and Marguerite stood motionless when the four McCracken children walked in with the rest of the Noble family. Akeema knew instantly what was happening, and she smiled at Dr. and Mrs. Noble. Akeema's employers were living up to her belief that they were among God's chosen people for our world. Lillian asked the Nobles to go into the parlor for a family "conference". When all were seated, Lillian began to speak.

"Everyone," said Lillian, "I need your full attention." She waited for everyone to be very still, especially the Noble children. "The Noble family is blessed in so many ways. We have a wonderful home, food, clothes, and even a truck. But, you all know that the world is having a very difficult time right now. There are many sick people, even here in Boston. And, there are children who do not have a place to stay because their parents have gone to heaven. This is what has happened to Mark, Brian, Joseph, and Helen. We have opened our home to these children, the McCrackens, so we can share with them our blessings. Can you do that for them...share with them your blessings?"

The Noble children all nodded strongly "yes", and began to clap. Bernard and Michael walked over to the three boys, and were widely excited when they learned they too were Red Sox fans. Marguerite asked young Helen if she wanted to play with her favorite doll "Lucy". Helen reacted as though this was the first time she had experienced happiness in an age. The two little girls ran off to play dolls. Akeema exclaimed she now had more than doubled the number of students in her "school". Noble, Lillian, and Florence felt they had finally accomplished some good during that awful Wednesday.

By Friday morning, October 11th, a new routine had already been established in the Noble home. There were now eleven people in the household, and everyone had jobs to do. All were expected to contribute to the common good by helping with meals, cleaning dishes and clothes, and ensuring the house remained clean and tidy. Meal portions were much smaller than before, and there was a greater reliance on grains and rice on each of the menus. During breaks from Akeema's scholastic instruction, the children were given playtime in the back yard. The weather remained very warm and humid, so the children could more easily "blow off steam" outside.

Today Edward, Lillian, and Florence set out for Chelsea and several hotels there. The Women's Auxiliary phone bank had received reports of a number of influenza sufferers that were unable to care for themselves, and their families. So, the Noble trio drove out to see what they could do for them.

They picked up a considerable quantity of food and medical supplies at the Commonwealth Avenue center, including some IV fluids. However, the increasing numbers of pandemic victims were already outstripping the higher level of supplies now available.

The situation in Chelsea was even worse than South Boston had been. Noble theorized this was simply a function of the worsening pandemic over time. Chelsea had more bodies wrapped in blood stained sheets on the curbs. More crepe on the doors. More bodies lying where they dropped. More bodies in hotel rooms with bloody fluid seeping from their nostrils and mouths. And, of course, indigo-blue mottled bodies were everywhere.

In one hotel room, the Nobles discovered an entire family of seven who had died within the past twelve hours. The family wore the all-too familiar hallmark of the disease; indigo-blue cyanosis. On the floor of the small hotel room was a layer of thick sputum with frothy blood. The combination made for a viscous mixture that sloshed as one walked through it. On top of this floor layer was another black layer. The black layer consisted of thousands of flies.

Some families simply locked up rooms where loved ones died, and stopped entering them altogether. The rooms became de facto tombs, where bodies began to mummify.

The Nobles began to notice an increasingly serious trend in all the Boston communities they visited. It was a huge issue that could dwarf all others, accept influenza itself. It was stealing the very life from more and more people every day. And it was growing. Growing quickly and fiercely. It was fear. Raw, uncontrolled, and pure, fear.

Type I patients described by the Boston City Hospital residents had a chance to survive the infection if they simply had enough food and water during their illness. Also, there were thousands of people who had other ailments other than influenza that needed modest amounts of care from others. But, now there was fear. Genuine and perfect fear. It was both fear of the known and the unknown. It was both real and imagined. But, the fear itself was real. And it was intense and swelling. It was everywhere. It was pervasive. It caused people to cross the street rather than pass someone on a sidewalk. It caused people to look away if someone spoke to them. It caused people to ignore cries and pleas for help. Fear caused the infirmed to simply slip away in death when only weeks before they would have been saved. Fear kills. And, fear was killing a lot.

As fear increased, the other major casualty was hope. Hope was fading in the population. Fading fast. For many, there seemed to be no end to the horror. In fact, there appeared to be a logarithmic increase in the death and destruction. Hopelessness bred apathy, and apathy bred inaction. Inaction, and its cousin inattentiveness, joined together with fear. And, the dying escalated.

As if things weren't bad enough, another serious problem was emerging. The majority of influenza survivors were taking several weeks to convalesce. In addition, the convalescence from this novel disease was not an easy one. The survivors were unable to care for themselves for a much longer period of time, compared to past influenza pandemics. Fortunate patients discharged from hospitals, or cared for at home, were now dying in the community for lack of custodial care. This newly emerging enigma threatened to cause as many deaths as the acute infection.

The Nobles did encounter occasional successes. They carried with them this day more medical supplies than on previous excursions, and they were putting them to good use. The seriously dehydrated patients, who Dr. Noble deemed Type I, were responding to IV fluid therapy. Signs and symptoms in this class of patients, such as cough, wheezing, fever, headache, and myalgias, were adequately treated with some of the medication now in the Ford. Control of these clinical maladies not only gave the patients an opportunity to rest, but helped them eat and drink on their own. This increased the chance of survival when no care givers were around. At times of discouragement, all three Nobles would repeat, "You do what you can do".

As the Nobles interacted with the healthy New England citizenry, they came to learn the populace had their own explanations for the carnage before them. A minority of people felt that curses from some unknown persons were causing the mortalities. It was not known why these curses were much more effective than past denunciations. However, many were convinced this was the cause.

Another larger group believed in the miasma theory of disease. This theory held that "pollution" (from the Greek *miasma*) or noxious "bad air" caused disease. Miasma was considered a mist or poisonous vapor filled with particles from decomposed matter (miasmata) that one could identify by a foul smell in the air. It was akin to changes in the atmosphere or the weather. Some actually felt it was the weather itself or changes in barometric pressure that caused the disease. The miasma theory had been in vogue since the first century AD, and survived to the 20th century.

The most popular theory amoung the populace held Germans ultimately responsible. Somehow, the Germans had created and spread the disease in an attempt to win The War. When Dr. Noble heard proponents of this theory, he could not divulge additional information he had about the matter. It was not commonly known that huge numbers of German troops had succumbed to the pandemic, along with an unknown number of Allied soldiers. Either the pandemic was a German experiment that had dreadfully gone wrong for the Central Powers, or it had nothing to do with them whatsoever. Nobles' experience in Haskell County clearly dispelled this notion.

With small increases in medical supplies and food, most Boston hospitals and their satellites were delivering slightly better care. The Nobles also saw some improvement in the communities. However, everyone knew these gains would be short lived without much more support. And no one knew when, or from where, that support would come.

On Monday, October 14th, Noble decided to spend the morning at Boston City Hospital. For the last two weeks, the great majority of his efforts were in the field with his wife and daughter. Noble had only dropped by BCH for short visits. But now, he felt the need to touch base with the "home office" as he continued to circulate about the satellite hospitals and help with home health. Noble first dropped off Lillian at the Commonwealth Avenue Red Cross center, and then drove with Florence to BCH. Florence would help on the wards until it was time to travel into the field once again.

Over the last few weeks, Noble had seen a real change in his daughter, Florence. She was increasingly confident in her nursing skills, and was becoming a first-rate nurse. Her assessments of patients were as good as nurses who were years ahead of her in tenure. She was building upon her knowledge base, and making solid additions to it every day. Noble was now certain that her career in nursing would be a stellar one.

After walking Florence to her ward, Noble went to the A.I. Office. It was now a strange place for him. There had not been an army sentry for many weeks. Since the death of Lieutenant Pecknold, every third shift of the office Signal Corps staff was empty. This morning was an empty shift, so no one was present in the office. It was odd to open the large office door and not see one of the Lieutenants busily transcribing an important new transmission.

During the shifts covered by Lieutenants Pierre-Louis and Lafayette, the young officers tried to keep up with the incoming work as best they could. However, there was too much for just two shifts to accomplish in the office. There were now stacks of messages on the roll top desks held together with rubber bands. None of these stacks had been translated, collated, or decoded. There was also dust on the office surfaces that would not have been allowed to accumulate before.

The young Signal Corps officers tried to put the most important processed messages in their proper stacks on the central table for the Major. They had learned what he both wanted to read, and also liked to read.

Noble went to the center table and began to skim confidential cables concerning The War. It was now evident the Germans were no longer able to mount a successful defense against the Allies. When the Balkans collapsed, Germany lost its main supply of oil and food. On October 3rd, the liberal Prince Maximilian of Baden was appointed Chancellor of Germany, instead of the more militant Georg von Hertling. Allied Intelligance felt this action was a preparation for an armistice. All this news was becoming common knowledge in the German military, and threats of mutiny and desertion were everywhere.

A telegram had been sent through the Swiss government to Washington D.C on October 5th. It read, "The German Government requests the President of the United States of America to take steps for the restoration of peace, to notify all belligerents of this request, and to invite them to delegate positions for the purpose of taking up negotiations. The German Government accepts, as a basis of peace negotiations, the program laid down by the President of the United States in his message to Congress of 8 January 1918..." "In order to avoid further bloodshed, the German Government requests to bring about the immediate conclusion of an armistice on land, on water, and in the air." Allied military intelligence believed the telegram was an attempt to arrange a better peace treaty with the Americans than was possible with the Allies.

In addition, there were now unimpeachable intelligence reports of one million German soldiers unfit to fight because of the Spanish Flu. Noble could only infer from this estimate the number of Allied troops infected with influenza.

Putting war news aside, Noble was overjoyed to receive a cable from Harvey Cushing.

Monday, October 7, 1918
From: Base Hospital No. 5

Camiers, France

I hope this message finds you in good health, my old friend. The news I hear from the States is not good. We hear daily of thousands of our dear countrymen dying of the Spanish Flu, and we can only wring our hands with each word. Please let me know if you, your family, and Katherine and the children, are alright. I lie awake at night worrying about you all.

Although I am doing no worse since recovering from the grippe, I am also doing no better. I still have difficulty focusing my vision, which makes surgery a challenge. I continue to walk with a cane, and can only go a few short blocks before I must take an extended rest. My legs are, well, wobbly. There is no better clinical term to describe them. I must go to bed early each evening in order to have the stamina to make it through the next physician day.

I am so saddened by the victims of the grippe in America and Europe. They are all doubly dead in that they died so young. I know the best minds are working on the problem; like Rosenau, Welch, Vaughn, Park, Williams, Avery, Russell, Cole, Flexner, Lewis, you, and Lillian. I hope that you all can discover why it is the young who must feel the full slamming force of the disease as they do.

Take care, Edward. I do hope I can see you all soon.

Your friend,
Colonel Harvey Cushing, AEF.

Noble quickly hand wrote a message for the next shift Lieutenant to send to Cushing as soon as possible. Cushing had not heard from Noble in the week since his message arrived at the A.I. Office. Cushing may not have received any mail at all, given the state of the U.S. Postal Service. He did not want to have his friend worry needlessly in France, as he tried to deal with his own health issues.

Also on the desk was another welcome cable from Colonel Vaughn.

Tuesday, October 8, 1918
From: From: Army Division of Communicable Diseases

Washington, D.C.

I'm sorry that I have not written or called you sooner, Edward. As you well know, things in the Communicable Diseases Division are, well, busy. I know you have your hands full, since Boston seems to have been the index U.S. city in the pandemic. Once again, please know how terribly sorry I am about Arthur. He was a fine soldier, a wonderful student, a great son and brother, and an all-around illustrious young man. He had a lot of his grandfather in him.

The influenza is remarkable. The susceptibility of the population seems to be of a very high percentage. When introduced, it strikes down so many at practically the same time that adequate care of the sick is impossible. The disease reduces to a minimum the resistance of the body to secondary infections, especially pneumonia. Cold, thirst, and hunger also take a heavy toll. In the second effect of influenza, the large number attacked simultaneously overwhelm hospital facilities, breaks down the most ample provision for the care of the sick, and renders successful isolation impossible. Among soldiers, it renders an efficient army helpless.

This infection, like war, kills young, vigorous, robust adults. The husky male either makes a recovery in extremely variable amounts of time, or likely dies. The most insane procedure carried out in 1918, from the viewpoint of an epidemiologist, was the sudden and complete mobilization of the students in our universities in the Students Training Corps. How many lives this procedure sacrificed I cannot estimate.

Keep at your important work, Edward. You have been a beacon of insight and truth in your interpretation of the Army Intelligence Office data. If authorities did not readily adopt your recommendations earlier, they do now. In my view, your work will save lives in the far reaches of the country. We are all indebted to you.

However, never again allow me to say that medical science is on the verge of conquering disease."

Colonel Victor Vaughn.

Victor Vaughn was very much like a father to Noble. For this reason, Vaughn's encouraging comments were more than appreciated. They were the most important words Noble had received since Lillian gave her stern lecture to him following Arthur's death. The words would give him much needed strength to continue his fight against the omnipresent demon. Noble was not at all sure any of his A.I. Office work had saved lives. But, there was still hope that it could. And hope was in exceptionally short supply everywhere right now.

Noble wrote another note for the Signal Corps officers to wire when they returned. This message was for Colonel Vaughn, and mostly said "Thank you".

Noble left the office for the South Department wards. At first glance, there seemed to be fewer patients on the wards than two weeks ago. There were also less bodily fluids on the floors and beds, and less bloody linen stuffed into corners. Noble saw one of the second year medical residents as she examined a patient who looked clinically stable, and walked over to her. She wore a simple skirt and blouse, a waist-length white coat, and her hair was tied up upon her head.

"Anna," said Noble.

The resident looked up from her patient, and said, "Oh, Dr. Noble. I didn't know you were here. Good to see you, sir!"

"How are things going, Anna?" asked Noble. "I've only been by the hospital a couple of times over the last two weeks. I thought I would drop by and see the great work the resident staff is doing."

"Thank you, sir," said the resident. "Well, I guess things are OK. I mean, they are pretty much the same."

"Are there fewer patients in the South Department wards now, Anna?" asked Noble.

Well, yes, in a way sir," said the resident. "There are several reasons for this appearance, and not all of them are good ones. First, the satellite hospitals have taken some of the pressure off BCH, for sure. However, we are seeing a great many more Type I and Type II patients now. This is good, since we have more of a chance to salvage these groups, as you know. But, we feel this phenomenon is mostly due to natural selection. From what the medical and nursing students tell us, there are simply a lot more Type III patients now in Boston. This proportionately decreases the number of other influenza types to hospitalize. It just looks like there are fewer patients overall, because so many of the Type III patients die at home and on the streets."

"From what I have seen in the field," said Noble, "I would have to completely agree with the student's assessment. However, I must say the hospital wards themselves look much better since the beginning of the month."

"When you have fewer Type III patients," said the resident, "you have less bleeding and incontinence. It's easier to keep up with the cleanups every day. Also, we have had more help from the army enlisted men from Devens. That has been a great help."

"How are the supplies holding up?" asked Noble.

"We have nearly exhausted the new supplies that arrived by train last week," said the resident. "BCH must share with the other hospitals, and there's only so much to go around. Without another shipment, we'll be out of most everything before the end of the week."

Noble did not want to mention that he was not aware of any new shipments coming to Boston. For the time being, he said he hoped there would be more soon.

"One other thing," said the resident. "We are running out of food. I don't mean just the hospital. I mean, everyone. The medical residents are sharing their rations. In fact, we have a weekly rotation where one resident is in charge of giving out rations to the others. But, the portions are getting smaller as the food stocks dwindle. I realize that all of New England is facing a similar dilemma. I'm just not sure what the solution is going to be."

"That's easy," said Noble. "More food." He smiled with the comment, and the resident laughed somewhat nervously. "Anna, have you seen Charge Nurse Tomlinson around? I wanted to check in before I left."

The resident's eyes open widely as she paused to answer. She then gazed at the floor. "Dr. Noble...I guess you haven't heard."

Heard about what, Anna?" asked Noble.

The resident again paused. "Dr. Noble...Mrs. Tomlinson died two days ago...sir."

Noble experienced a cramping feeling in his abdomen that was now painfully common. Actually, it was almost a normal feeling, since he had experienced it so often over the last many weeks. He sat down on a nearby wood chair. Noble thought to himself, the demon...again. He took off his glasses and covered his eyes with his right hand. "Not Terry," he said, as though saying it would make this new revelation untrue.

"I'm so sorry, sir... so sorry you had to hear about it this way," said the resident. "I didn't know you hadn't heard. She was at work on Sunday, and went from her usual self to gravely ill…in just two hours. It was quite clear she was a Type III. It was over in just eight hours, sir."

Type III. Terry Tomlinson would never be a "Type III" to Noble. But, he was not going to dwell on that. The resident, who had watched hundreds die over the last month, was simply giving a clinical description. But the thought of nurse Tomlinson as a Type III… It was unthinkable.

"You knew her a long time, Dr. Noble?" said the resident, who was seeking to comfort him somehow.

Noble sat staring into nothingness for several moments. Slowly, he began to briefly described his relationship with the departed nurse. "Yes, Anna. Yes, I knew Terry Tomlinson a very long time. She was a young nurse fresh out of school when I first took my attending position here at Boston City Hospital in 1905. She was the brightest and most enthusiastic RN in the hospital. Many could not understand why I chose her to be the Charge Nurse for the South Department here at BCH. She was so inexperienced, and knew nothing of communicable diseases. However, I wanted someone who had both the capacity and the desire to learn, and she overflowed with both. She was the best nurse I have ever known. And, she was a treasured friend. She will be irreplaceable." Noble continued to stare off in no particular direction after he finished.

The resident felt that Noble wanted to have his own thoughts right now, and excused herself. She left for another ward containing the full ravages of influenza. Noble returned to the A.I. Office briefly to write a third note for the Lieutenants to send. This time, it was a note of condolence for the family of Terry Tomlinson, RN, who lived in Brighton, Massachusetts.

It was now time for Noble to pick up his daughter and drive back to the Red Cross Center. However, as he was about to leave the South Department pavilion, Noble noticed someone at the end of the ward. The person looked familiar, but he could not readily identify him. After a few moments, Noble recognized the man, and quietly uttered his name.

"Cunard."

Noble did not recognize Dr. Richard Cunard at first because he looked almost like a completely different man. Gone was the freshly pressed white Commander navy uniform. Instead, Cunard wore a ship officer uniform with a wrinkled and stained knee-length white coat. Rather than slicked back hair with a seven day hair cut, Cunard's hair was longer and disheveled. He had lost weight, and his face was drawn and pale with a beard of a few days. Most notably, gone was the posture of a man with self-confidence and self-importance. As he viewed a patient's chest roentgenogram, by holding it up to the room's light, Cunard's back hunched forward and his shoulders drooped. His pose reminded Noble of a man who felt defeated.

Cunard finished studying the roentgenogram and lowered it to his side. As he did, he briefly glanced to his right and saw Noble looking at him. Very quickly, Cunard lowered his head and turned away to face the wall.

For a tenth of a second, as he glanced up, Cunard's eyes had met Noble's. In that tenth of a second, Noble knew that Cunard knew.

Cunard knew he could not have stopped the pandemic introduction completely in Boston. However, Cunard did know he could have listened to Noble months ago and taken his advice. If he had, he could have slowed the arrival of influenza long enough to apply adequate quarantines at critical entrance points. At best, many lives could have been saved by avoiding infection all together. At worst, the city could have been given more precious time to prepare for the infection. Either way, Cunard ignored Nobles pleas solely out of jealousy and pride. Now, he would live with that knowledge for the remainder of his life.

Noble turned to leave the pavilion. As he did, he recalled the overcrowding at Camp Grant near Rockford, Illinois that resulted in hundreds of camp deaths. At that same time, on September 25th, a train departed Camp Grant for Camp Hancock near Augusta, Georgia. Hundreds of soldiers died of influenza on that train. The officer, who refused to decrease the overcrowding and the train departure, was Colonel Charles Hagadorn. On October 8th, Colonel Hagadorn shot himself while in his command office. Noble wondered if Cunard felt a similar level of guilt.

CHAPTER 21

Florence was working in one of the original BCH western pavilions along Harrison Avenue when her father came for her. After she finished starting an IV, the two drove to the Red Cross Center in the Ford. Noble chose to wait for a later time to mention nurse Tomlinson, so they spoke of the day's duties instead.

Boston streets were becoming more deserted with every passing day. Ever greater quantities of refuse littered the streets, and weeds were now growing tall through cracks in the roads and sidewalks. Noble thought Boston was beginning to look like Hollywood depictions of western ghost towns. They drove north along an empty Massachusetts Avenue, and turned east on an equally empty Commonwealth Avenue. The new Red Cross Center was located on the corner of Commonwealth and Arlington Street, overlooking the Boston Common.

They parked the truck on Commonwealth, and Florence went into the center to let her mother know they had arrived. A few minutes later, Florence walked out of the building with her mother. Lillian carried a box of supplies destined for the stops they would make in South Boston, and Florence carried a newborn wrapped in a pink blanket. Behind his daughter and wife, Noble noticed a petit woman with short dark hair, fair skin, blue eyes, and a toothy grin. She appeared to be in her late 20's, and also carried a heavy cardboard box filled with supplies. Noble jumped out of the truck to assist them.

"Hi, dear," said Lillian. "How's Boston City Hospital?"

"The usual, Lilly," said Noble, knowing that she probably could tell something was not altogether usual.

"Dear, I want you to meet one of the ladies who volunteers at the center. This is Rose. Rose, this is my husband Edward."

"Glad to meet you, Rose," said Noble. Up until now, Noble hadn't noticed two small boys walking behind Rose. The older boy held the younger boy's hand.

"Rose and her husband have made sizable donations of supplies to the Red Cross Center. She has been such a wonderful help this morning."

Noble helped Rose put the heavy box in the truck. Rose then turned to keep the two small boys from running into the street. After she had collected them, she turned to Noble and said, "These are my two boys. Joe, Jr. is three years old, and John is one-and-a-half." The boys proudly marched over to Noble and shook his hand.

"I take it you have a new baby?" said Noble, motioning over to the newborn held by Florence.

Rose laughed. "That's Rosemary. She's just 4 weeks old."

"Even with her very young children, Rose has been such a help today," said Lillian.

"Do you live in Boston, Rose?" asked Noble.

"Actually," said Rose, "we live on Beal Street in Brookline. My husband, Joe, is an assistant general manager at Bethlehem Steel in Quincy. While he supervises the construction of transport and war ships, I thought I would help out during this awful pandemic. By the way, your last name is Noble, correct? Is that any relation to Dr. Charles Noble of Brookline?"

"Why...yes it is," said Noble. "He was my father."

"I hear his name all the time in Brookline. He is still so fondly remembered as such a compassionate and fine physician."

"Thank you, Rose," said Noble. Another thought suddenly crossed his mind. "Now, I have a question for you, Rose. Do you know the Cushings in Brookline, by chance?"

"You mean Harvey and Katherine Cushing?" said Rose.

"Yes, exactly," said Noble.

"We know them very well, Edward," said Rose. "I know Katherine Cushing from the Brookline Women's Auxiliary."

"Maybe we can all get together at our home on Beacon Street, Rose," said Lillian, who seemed thrilled with the idea. "The Cushings are some of our best friends. We're all looking forward to Harvey's return from France."

"That would be terrific," said Rose. "Katherine misses Harvey so much. Maybe all the boys will be able to come home soon."

Just then a girl ran from the building carrying a purse. She called out to Rose, "Mrs. Kennedy, you forgot this."

"Thank you so much! I would be in such a fix without my purse!" said Rose.

Rose and her three young children were to be driven back to Brookline by a member of her side of the family, the Fitzgeralds. So, she stayed behind at the Red Cross Center as the Nobles began their rounds for the day. The Nobles departed with the promise that their family, the Cushings, and the Kennedys, would get together someday soon.

As the Nobles drove south loaded with supplies, they passed two new huge pits being carved in the Boston landscape. Hundreds of white bags lay beside the pits. Instead of two steam shovels working feverishly, there were now four. The weather was still very warm and humid. There was no perceptible breeze. The smoke from the four steam shoves rose slowly up from each machine, forming a single column as high as the eye could see. Noble envisioned the column as an unearthly notice to humanity from the demon. The notice was "Whatever you do, I win."

On Wednesday, October 18th, the Nobles had numerous rounds to perform in Chelsea, Massachusetts. However, the night before, Lieutenant Commander Rosenau had called to see if the three Nobles could join him for lunch near the Chelsea Naval Hospital. Rosenau had a surprise for them, but would not say what it was. So, just before noon, the Nobles drove to a small office building on the Naval Hospital campus that looked over the Mystic River. Outside the two story clapboard military style building were a number of shade trees on a grassy hill. The hill sloped gently down to the river. Although humid, the sky was clear and there was a welcome slight breeze from the west. As directed, the Nobles walked to the west side of the building and found Rosenau seated at a picnic table. The table had a red checkered tablecloth, and there were also plates, flatware, and glasses present. In the center of the table was a small vase with a fresh carnation in it. The Nobles stopped and stared at the site. It had been many weeks since they had seen anything like this.

"Milton, it's so beautiful!" said Lillian. "How did you...?"

"I have a surprise for the three of you," Rosenau interrupted, with a big smile. "Please, sit down."

"This is such a pretty setting, Milton," said Florence, who was accustomed to stark accommodations at Naval Reserve functions.

"All of us have been working very hard, and doing things that make us heartsick," said Rosenau. "You need a break." With all three Nobles now seated, Rosenau brought out a large paper sack from under the table. He began to reach into the bag and bring out oblong objects wrapped in paper. Each had the name of one of the Nobles, and one said "Rosenau". He handed the objects to his guests, and invited them to open them.

In each of the paper wrapped objects was a very large sandwich. Some were rye bread, others wheat. Some were ham and cheese, some tuna, and one just cheese. There were also various types and quantities of mustard, catsup, relish, mayonnaise, and lettuce on each. Rosenau then pulled from below the table four bottles of ice cold Coca Cola. He opened each bottle with an opener, and then brought out a large bowl of potato salad. The Nobles sat speechless, motionless.

"Well, aren't you going to eat?" asked Rosenau, still with a big grin.

"Milton," said Noble, "where on earth did you get this food? And, it's fresh! Just the smell of it wants to make me cry with joy!"

Rosenau laughed. "The Armored Cruiser USS *San Diego* docked this morning in Boston Harbor. I know the head cook on board the *San Diego*, and made a deal with him. In exchange for three cartons of cigarettes, I had him make sandwiches I thought each of you would like. He threw in the sodas and potato salad just to be nice. Now, <u>eat</u>."

They all bit into the sandwiches, and closed their eyes as people do when they are eating something special. Lillian said, "I feel a little awkward eating such wonderful food, when there is so much starvation in New England."

Noble laughed. "Lilly, of course you said that with your mouth full of ham and cheese sandwich."

"Yeah, Mom," said Florence, chuckling. "A tad hypocritical, I'd say."

"Oh, stop it, you bunch of bleeding hearts," said Rosenau. This is a gift from me, and you all deserve it. So, eat."

And eat they did. No one spoke for fifteen minutes as the entire lunch was consumed. Florence giggled when her father licked the paper that had wrapped his cheese sandwich. Noble had not enjoyed such culinary delight since his voyage on the USS *Madawaska*, or his wife's pizza.

After finishing the wonderful meal, conversation turned to more serious topics. "What's the news from the A.I. Office, Edward?" asked Rosenau.

"The pandemic is spreading quickly in the U.S.," said Noble. "After its establishment in Boston, and then in Philadelphia and New York, the infection jumped to other large cities near military bases that are sometimes far away. Cities like Seattle near Puget Sound, the Great Lakes training station near Chicago, and New Orleans. The infection has then continued along rail and river transportation lines to other smaller areas. Cases sometimes sprout in cities many miles from other index cases, and then backtrack to towns in between. In this way, the pandemic has been moving south from Chicago, and north from New Orleans. You can follow the progression of the infection at each successive northward port-of-call along the Mississippi River. At the same time, the disease has been relentlessly marching west."

"How about the Pacific coast?" said Rosenau.

"This is interesting," said Noble. "Cities such as Los Angeles and San Francisco have had relatively light numbers of cases. One reason for this is because these cities have had advance warning of the pandemic. San Francisco has had a particularly good quarantine system. Its public health director, a guy named William Hassler, quarantined all naval installations as soon as he heard about outbreaks in the East. Public gatherings were banned, and he convinced the city to put together an infrastructure to deal with the coming influenza. This included drivers transporting medical supplies and food into the various city districts in preparation for the pandemic, and setting up telephone banks for communication. The Red Cross is making one hundred thousand gauze masks for the population. Volunteer doctors, nurses, and other health care providers are already assigned to specific duties if the pandemic worsens in specific city areas. So far, there have been relatively few cases in San Francisco. I guess we'll see what happens next."

Rosenau added, "I hear a researcher at Tufts School of Medicine is producing thousands of doses of a vaccine against influenza. The public health authorities in San Francisco are planning to have the vaccine shipped to them by train at the end of the month. We're all wondering how that will go."

"The situation is rightfully terrifying," said Noble. "People are hearing and reading about the approaching pandemic. First, it's a thousand miles away. Then, its five hundred miles away. Soon, its one hundred miles away. In no time, its ten miles away… Suddenly, one's neighbor dies a horrible death. One can see what is going on in the minds of our countrymen throughout America."

"That's right, Edward," said Rosenau. "I'm not sure which is worse; being in the middle of the death, or watching it come ever nearer to you."

Noble tipped up the bottle of Coca Cola and finished off every drop. "Milton, some of the reports coming into the office from around the country are disturbing in other ways."

"How so?" asked Rosenau.

"Well," said Noble, "society's functions are failing one by one. There are estimates that more than eighteen hundred telephone company employees are out; either severely ill, or dead. Phone companies in many places are allowing only emergency calls. Operators randomly listen to calls and cut off phone service to those who make routine calls. However, censoring phone calls has an unintended consequence; it's much harder for people to conduct essential economic business.

Thirty-eight hundred Pennsylvania Railroad workers are not working. Again, they are either incapacitated or dead. Some of the railroads have set up their own hospitals. The entire mid-Atlantic and New England transportation system is now malfunctioning. This jeopardizes most of the nation's industrial output."

Noble continued, "Other essential services are coming to a halt. Mail service, power generation, public transit, police and fire services, garbage collection, sanitation…they're all failing. For example, The War left the U.S. with only about seven hundred Public Health Service officers. Many of them are now sick or dead."

"And this is happening nationally?" asked Rosenau.

"Absolutely, Milton," replied Noble. "National industries are intertwined. Each is dependent on many others for proper functioning. Illness, and fear, have drastically decreased production in agriculture, horticulture, mining, manufacturing, and construction. This has radically decreased goods distribution, such as in rail services, ground transportation, and waterway shipping. What has followed is a huge negative impact on wholesale, retail, commodity dealers, and grocers. In turn, this has forced people out of work just when they need the income the most. There is now less money for people to spend or invest. So, production of goods and services will decrease even further. And with the loss of productivity at a certain economic step, the successive steps suffer even more. The progressive cycle continues its downhill swirl."

Noble finally summarized by saying, "We are looking at a complete collapse of the entire economic and financial system in the United States, and likely the entire world...at every level."

On that dark note, it was time for the four to once again battle influenza in the ways they could. Rosenau returned to the Naval Hospital and his labs in order to continue both clinical and experimental work. The Nobles pursued their combination of hospital, home health, and home relief efforts.

The Nobles sincerely thanked Rosenau for his little treat today. All of them were not sure when, or even if, they would have a similar meal again.

On Friday, October 18th, the trio was back on the streets of South Boston. The city was now experiencing intermittent power failures which added to the fear and isolation felt by the populace. Of course, the loss of electricity froze up businesses dependent on it, and exacerbated the economic burden on the area.

Noble estimated there were at least twice as many death carts meandering through the city now as there had been just fourteen days earlier. The horse drawn and motor powered carts, along with the mass grave steam shovels, were some of the only public services operating efficiently. The black market was also thriving. Alcohol had been at a premium for weeks. But now, food of all types was being traded at enormous prices. Some undertakers were charging $350 for a coffin, and home health nurses were being given over $300 a month for private assistance. If one considered that an average family of four made $3,000 a year, one could realize the relative sky-high prices being charged.

The Nobles came upon more apartments and hotel rooms where entire families could not feed themselves. Noble's original prediction for those recovering from influenza was sadly coming true. The very young, the very old, and those with other maladies, were vanishing. When the young and strong are struck down overnight, many times there is no one to help the others. In this way, the demon caused a "ripple effect" of death. Death gave death.

Before the family ventured out on their daily rounds, Noble dropped by the A.I. Office for a time. Lieutenant Pierre-Louis was hard at work at her cordboard, trying to keep up with the influx of information. Since many radio messages were not written down, and many cables were not transcribed, Noble found he would be given several communications in one format or one topic only. Today it was newspaper articles. And, Noble was very upset over them.

Later, Noble was driving the Ford quietly toward South Boston. Suddenly, he pulled the truck alongside the curb on Flaherty Way. "I just have to vent for a moment," said Noble to his wife and daughter as the truck idled. "Whoever is managing the news in the national papers believes they are doing a service to their communities. But, they're not."

"What do you mean, dear?" said Lillian, who was surprised by the abrupt stop.

Noble pulled from the truck back seat a leather carrying case, and took out several A.I. Office transcriptions. "When one reads newspaper comments about the pandemic, one understands why there is confusion in the population," said Noble. "Here is a series of recent comments in newspapers from all over the country: 'The reason there have been so many military hospital admissions for the grippe is not because troops are sick, but because military doctors order it.' 'There is not cause for alarm if precautions are observed.'

'The Spanish influenza is nothing more or less than old fashioned grippe.' 'When printing items about influenza, they should be confined to simple preventative measures.' 'Don't get scared to death.' 'Don't let flu frighten you to death.' 'Don't panic.'"

Noble continued, "One health care official in Illinois said, 'Nothing must be done to interfere with the morale of the community. It is our duty to keep the people from fear. Worry kills more people than the epidemic.' At the same time, Cook County Hospital in Chicago has published an influenza mortality rate of over 39 percent. Of course, I'm not even including the numerous newspaper additions that don't mention the pandemic at all. Do you see what I'm getting at <u>here</u>?"

Lillian set her jaw as she did when she was both thinking and concerned. "I see what you mean, Edward."

"Are they talking about some other planet, dad?" said Florence. "These statements don't sound like the planet I'm living on right now."

"None of us want people jumping off buildings," said Noble. "There must be a balance between reason and concern. However, there is no balance in this reporting. These newspaper articles are read throughout the United States, and they are performing a disservice in two ways. First, if readers take the statements literally, they will have very little need to plan ahead for themselves, their families, and their communities. Mounting community efforts with food, clothing, transportation, and medical care won't happen. No thought to comprehensive quarantines will be given. They will just go about their willy-nilly business as usual. Then comes the real disservice. Newspaper readers will begin to notice that people around them are suddenly dying. The white bags will pile up, and the dead buried in mass graves. Readers will then believe nothing the papers print. Even if rational steps are printed to avoid contracting influenza, they will be too late. Then, raw fear…the kind that does kill, will rear its ugly head. This is an outrage."

"What can be done, Edward?" asked Lillian.

"I will do all I can, with the technological A.I. Office 'megaphone' at my disposal, to get the message out to the rest of the nation. Maybe I will be shouting in the dark, but shout I will. I am not going to sit back and go through 'channels' as I did before the arrival of the pandemic. Even if I get into political hot water for the effort, it will be worth it in the long haul."

Lillian knew what a determined Dr. Edward Noble was like. His comments affirmed one of the reasons why she loved him. Yet, his remarks also worried her greatly. Her husband was already facing an unjust hearing with the Medical Board of Massachusetts. But, incurring the ire of military brass was a "whole new ballgame", as her sons would say.

This Friday would be one of the most distressing days yet for the Nobles. They expected more white bags on the sidewalks. They expected more crepe on the doors. They even expected more young people dead, alone, in hotel rooms. They anticipated more entire families gone without so much as a whimper. But, there were now quiet and sinister differences. The differences were the expressions on the faces of the living. The population had simply given up.

People were resigning themselves to imminent deaths. People sat on porches, sidewalks, and park benches; waiting for the demon. The Nobles no longer saw fight in the people. Only resignation. As the society they once loved fell apart around them, people were simply letting go. There was no food. No sanitation. Raw sewage ran in some streets. Rotting garbage was everywhere. Rotting people were everywhere. It seemed like the Nobles were witnessing the end of civilization itself.

The other change they noted about the streets was a moderate increase in the number of people on them. But, these were not people full of industry. They were homeless, and had nowhere else to go. There was an aimless wandering, sitting, standing, and lying with people dressed in rags about the city. They were all waiting for the inevitable. In the last few days there had been a sharp decline in donated goods that would have helped the homeless. This was not because of a lack of concern on the part of those who remained healthy. The lack of donations came from the rapidly falling amount of materials to donate. Boston was running out of everything.

That night the Ford returned to the Beacon Street home that was also running dangerously low on food. Eleven people dinned on a meal that would have been light for six. Everyone went to bed hungry, but there were no complaints. They all knew they were fortunate. Everyone was well, had a clean house, and had at least something to eat. They also had each other. Just before bed time, the power went off...again. The new large family lit candles and went off to bed knowing that the future was uncertain. Uncertain for everyone.

Over the weekend, several more railroad cars filled with military supplies arrived at the Boston and Main Train Station. Red Cross and Women's Auxiliary volunteers swarmed over the cars the instant the train had come to a full stop. Volunteers in automobiles, trucks, and horse drawn carts drove the supplies to collection centers in Boston, Brookline, Chelsea, Cambridge, Newton, Medford, and many points in between. Spread so thin, the supplies represented only a few days of relief. But, it raised the spirits of a New England population that surely needed it.

On Wednesday, October 23rd, the Nobles ventured once again to South Boston and their numerous stops at homes, hotels, and satellite hospitals. They carried with them supplies from the train, and were happy for it. Still, it was getting harder and harder to get out of bed every morning and face the decomposition of humanity.

The weather was finally beginning to cool into an average fall temperature. The sky was clear and blue, but the familiar brisk October wind spoke of colder weather to come. As the Nobles journeyed onward, they all began to notice a change in the scenery. It was subtle at first, but became more obvious as they drove through the South Boston neighborhoods. It was Noble who noticed it first.

"Lilly…Florence…something is really different today. Can you see it?"

Lillian answered, "Yes…yes…you're right. It's different. It's really different."

Florence weighed in, "Dad, at first I thought I was imagining things. I'm not?"

Noble paused for a few moments, as his eyes darted back and forth along both sides of streets bordering Thomas Park. Then, slowly, he said, "I can't…I can't really believe it. There are less of them. Aren't there?"

"Yes…yes, Edward," said Lillian. "It's not just less. It's a lot less. A lot."

Noble then said, "It's dramatic. There are a lot less white bags out here. I mean, a lot less."

Florence added, "Dad, your right. But, there are also a lot more people on the streets. They're not just sitting around. They look as though they are walking…walking somewhere. They look like they have places to go."

As they drove on, they noticed a few people with brooms sweeping the sidewalks in front of their homes and stores. Some were picking up garbage. Some actually had a few items out on sidewalks they wanted to sell.

The Nobles still found large numbers of people who urgently needed assistance. They started IVs, gave out oral fluids and some drugs, dispersed food, and handed out clean linen and clothes. But, the other amazing site was empty cots at some of the satellite hospitals. Dr. Schafer at the shoe warehouse actually had excess capacity for the first time since the facility opened. Lines outside the satellites were dozens…not hundreds.

On their way back home that evening, there were two steam shovels instead of four digging a large hole.

By Friday, October 25th, the change in Boston was palpable. For the first time in weeks, the Nobles found themselves waiting for traffic at large intersections. They had to stop for pedestrians. Stores were opening and so were some factories.

Although there were still numerous people with influenza, they were not dying at the rate seen just a week earlier. The number of home health referrals was rapidly decreasing. Because of fewer apartments to call on, the Nobles finished their rounds early for the first time. The Nobles drove back to Boston City Hospital. During their ride to BCH, they noted the white bags on the sidewalks were not only less in number. They were becoming rare.

Arriving at BCH, Florence went to the wards while Noble and Lillian went to the A.I. Office. For the first time in many weeks, there was an army sentry outside the office. Noble saluted the young soldier, and said, "It's good to see you back, Sergeant. How are things at Devens?"

"It's good to be back, sir," said the Sergeant. "I have to say that Camp Devens seems to be returning to a more stable state. Can't say it's normal. But, it's better than it was, sir." Noble gave a kindly smile that only partially hid some of the residual pain he felt about Camp Devens. Lillian could not muster any expression at all.

When Lieutenant Lafayette saw the Nobles enter the office, she uncharacteristically stood at her cordboard, saluted, and said, "It's so nice to see you, Major, and Mrs. Noble. I feel as though I haven't seen you much in the last few weeks."

Noble smiled again. "You haven't, Lieutenant. But, maybe that is about to change. I'm sure you've notice a huge change in the last few days in Boston."

"Yes sir," said the Lieutenant. "Camp Devens is really different, too. There's no longer a crowd outside the camp hospitals like there has been. Major, is the influenza over?"

"It just might be, Lieutenant. I have some tasks for you this afternoon. What we need to find out quickly is the present census at many of the larger hospitals, and their satellite facilities. We need to hear from some of the larger eastern cities, like New York and Philadelphia. A few census reports from the larger hospitals would be helpful, as would comments on influenza from their public health departments. Can you do that for me?"

"I'll get right on it, sir."

The Nobles went to several document storage boxes on the office book shelves, and began to collect influenza census data from a number of hospitals in the mid-Atlantic and New England states. From other boxes they pulled similar information from European cities. They brought up chairs to the center table, and began to tabulate the data. Meanwhile, Lieutenant Lafayette began calling numerous hospitals. As new data arrived in the office, the Lieutenant placed it on the table for assimilation.

For nearly three hours, the Nobles collected numbers. They added and subtracted long columns of numbers, and aligned other columns of numbers. They drew graphs and tables on graph paper, and found slopes of lines. Then, they performed the whole process again from information gathered from cities such as Chicago and New Orleans.

There was a flurry of paper, pencils, and phone calls. Suddenly, the Nobles looked up from their work and just stared at one another. Noble said, "That's it, isn't it? That's really it."

"Yep, dear," said Lillian. "That's really it."

"Sir," said the Lieutenant, "forgive me for asking, but what are you and Mrs. Noble doing?

"Well," said Noble, "with your help, Lieutenant, maybe we have just saved tens of thousands of lives."

The Lieutenant's expression, without words, was 'OK. What did we do?'

"Lieutenant," said Noble, "we now know what we are seeing in Boston is real. The pandemic is winding down in the east. Last week in Philadelphia, for example, there were 4,597 influenza deaths. But, this week, there is about a tenth that number. The same phenomenon is going on in New York, and in Boston. But, the pandemic continues to roll westward."

"How does this save lives, sir?" said the Lieutenant.

Lillian answered. "We have been able to accurately calculate that the pandemic predictably reaches a peak, in any given area, in about six weeks."

"Does that mean we stop it by then?" asked the Lieutenant.

"Absolutely not," said Noble. "We treat some patients and help them through their infections. But, we do nothing against influenza itself. It reaches a peak in six weeks because it burns up all the susceptible hosts in that area. Then, it just moves on to find new fresh victims."

"Lieutenant," said Lillian, "this is important because we now have a basic idea where a given area is in terms of the pandemic's evolution. With this information, we can suggest that an allocation of resources be provided ahead of the influenza 'wave'. As the pandemic is winding down in one area, we can move doctors, nurses, and supplies to areas that are just beginning to witness the infection. This has enormous implications."

Noble hand wrote a series of messages for the Lieutenant to begin sending to U.S. Public Health Service offices, as well as some newspapers, in areas destined to be hit with the pandemic soon. The messages stated there is a <u>real</u> danger with influenza. But, with the proper positioning of resources and personnel ahead of time, and planning strict quarantines, the impact of the pandemic can be lessened to a degree. He instructed the Lieutenant to begin wiring the messages as soon as possible.

"Edward," said Lillian, "you realize these wires are not going to sit well with some in high places." She reached for her husband's hand with the statement. Both of them recalled the recent newspaper editorials about the pandemic.

"Lilly," said Noble, "you know we can't just talk about this data. The 'nothing to fear' approaches with the pandemic just leads to needless deaths. We have to get this out. Now."

Lillian knew he was right. She just worried about the consequences for her husband.

As Noble handed the messages to Lieutenant Lafayette for transmission, she said, "Oh, Major. I almost forgot. This cable came for you...and Mrs. Noble...today. It says 'very urgent'." Noble took the telegram from the Lieutenant and read it carefully. After some time in contemplation, he set the message on the center table, and looked up at Lillian.

"It seems," said Noble, "that both you and I have been invited to speak at the first session of the new 'Influenza Commission', appointed by the Governor of New York, Charles Whitman. It's chaired by Herman Biggs, who is the New York State Commissioner of Health. I guess everyone is going to be there: Rufus Cole, William Park, Paul Lewis, Milton Rosenau, Victor Vaughn, and epidemiologists, microbiologists, biochemists, and pathologists from around the nation. It's on October 30th. Next Wednesday."

Lillian sat speechless, with her mouth wide open. Finally, she said, "They want us to speak at the first session? Wow! But, how can we do that with a house full of..."

Lieutenant Lafayette said, "I'm sorry to interrupt, Mrs. Noble, but perhaps you should read this." She handed Lillian another cable.

Lillian read the next cable, and said to her husband, "Now, that's interesting."

"What's that?" said Noble.

"It's a message from Victor Vaughn, dear," said Lillian. "He's already contacted the Navy Reserves. He made arrangements for Florence to stay at home and help Akeema with all seven children while we're in New York. Boy, he must really want us to go."

"Then, we'll take him up on it," said Noble. "We'll have to start working on our talks right away."

"I guess," said Lillian, slowly. Both she and her husband realized what an incredible privilege this was. They also both realized what an opportunity this could be to redirect the effort against the pandemic.

"Lieutenant," said Noble, "please let Commissioner Biggs know we are extremely honored to attend the Influenza Commission session."

As the Nobles drove home that cool evening, Edward thought long about the demon. He and Lillian, with their epidemiologic data survey, confirmed the influenza attack rate was about 25% to 50%. That is, 25% to 50% of people exposed to the demon would contract the disease.

However, influenza departed a community just as quickly as it entered. Although the demon could not be defeated with a direct assault, humanity had two indirect weapons against it: First, for the fortunate who have a chance to survive the demon, adequate nutritional, medical, and nursing care could help a victim through convalescence. Second, the demon could be deprived of victims and cause it to leave an area quicker. This deprivation is called quarantine.

The weapons of careful convalescence and quarantine could not be brought up against the demon instantly. Both need meticulous planning, preparation, and require a thorough understanding of the demon. This was perhaps Nobles' greatest challenge. He needed to foster a much better understanding of the demon among community leaders, and the public. Given information available to Americans, the challenge was not a simple one. But, it was one Noble had to assume.

The entire weekend of October 26th and 27th was used to prepare for the New York trip. Along with a drastic decrease in influenza deaths, there appeared a modest increase in grocery store food. Lillian restocked the Noble cupboards as best she could. She ensured there were enough clean clothes for the seven children during their three day trip. Noble filled the Ford gas tank at the Boston Army Depot, and made sure it was in fine running order. The Nobles knew that Florence and Akeema were extremely capable of caring for the children, so there was only slight parental worry. In any case, the Boston schools were reopening on Monday, so the children would have plenty to do. Noble and Lillian spent the rest of their time writing out their talks for the commission on 5X8 inch cards.

Early on the cold Tuesday morning of October 29th, the Nobles were picked up by an army staff car. The young man that helped them with their luggage was, as always, Sergeant Campbell. Opening the car door for Noble, the Sergeant snapped to attention, rose to his full 6 foot 4 inches height, saluted, and said, "Good morning Major...Mrs. Noble. It is a distinct pleasure and honor to serve you once again, sir."

"Thank you so much, Sergeant," said Noble. "It's great to see you to. How are you doing?"

"Well, sir," said the Sergeant, "as well as can be expected. I miss Karen a lot, sir. I miss her every minute of every day. I doubt that is ever going to change."

Noble knew the feeling all-to-well. He patted the young man on the shoulder, stepped into the staff car, and away the three went.

CHAPTER 22

The Nobles were driven to the Boston and Main station. Sergeant Campbell helped them again with their things, told them he would pick them up at the station on Thursday, and saw them off at the train.

Colonel Vaughn had once again worked his magic for the Nobles. In a train packed with military and civilians, he was able to arrange a small private Pullman room for the Nobles during their seven hour journey.

Although the New England and Atlantic state scenery wore its famous fall colors of reds, browns, yellows, and oranges, the Nobles did not see much of it. They had brought with them several books and journals required for their talks. Many of the best and brightest minds in American medicine were gathering to discuss the pandemic. The Nobles were honored, and humbled, to be invited to the Commission. They wanted to do their best to add meaningfully to the conversation. So, they were hurriedly researching talks that would usually take months to prepare. Their friend Milton Rosenau had left for the meeting the day before, and would be presenting preliminary findings from his Gallops Island study.

A little after noon, the train arrived in Manhattan and stopped at its famous 42nd Street destination. The Nobles gathered up their luggage, departed the train, and walked toward the terminal. As they entered the main concourse, the majesty of Grand Central Station was fully realized. The 470 foot long, 160 foot wide, and 150 foot high building was most impressive. The ceiling was painted with the zodiac constellations, but backwards. The stars were shown as seen by God, and not by humanity. As the Nobles walked in the enormous building, sunlight shown in bright columns through 75 foot high arched windows. Noble thought it looked like a cathedral, with a divine quality that lifted his spirits. He could almost hear Arthur whispering to him, "Dad, do what you can do".

The Grand Central exterior was as spectacular as the inside. Its beaux-arts design boasted large arches flanked by Corinthian columns. Atop the building was a fifty foot high sculpture depicting Mercury, the god of commerce, supported by Minerva and Hercules, representing mental and moral strength. Noble thought to himself that one needs both types of strength to battle the demon.

The Nobles caught a taxi outside of Grand Central Station, and were driven to the Lower East Side. Their hotel was located on East Broadway Street overlooking Seward Park. The first day of the Influenza Commission conference would be held at the New York City Academy of Sciences, just a few blocks away from their hotel.

The Nobles unpacked their belongings in their hotel room, and then took brief naps after their trip. They freshened up just before they had room service deliver the evening's dinner: eggplant parmesan, hot rolls, salad, chocolate cake, and a white wine. It was the best meal the two had tasted since Rosenau's *USS San Diego* Armored Cruiser sandwiches. After dinner, the Nobles worked on their talks until 11 PM. They slept soundly that evening.

Noble and his wife arose at 5 AM on Wednesday, October 30th, then showered, and dressed. Noble wore a pressed army field uniform, and Lillian wore a black skirt with matching jacket over a white blouse. Room service brought croissants, butter, preserves, and coffee, and they consumed all of it quickly. They spent the next two hours brushing up their talks, and then left their room to catch a taxi for the Academy of Sciences.

The Academy was another imposing 19th century building, with classical Greek limestone pediments supported by traditional tall marble columns. Once inside, the Nobles were given name tags to wear, and entrance tickets to the main conference room. The Commission meetings were to be held in a large conference room hosting several hundred people. The room floor had a thick burgundy colored rug covering it from wall-to-wall. Six huge Schonbeck chandeliers adorned with Swarovski/Strass crystal hung from the ceiling. Each chandelier crystal refracted rainbow spectrum light with an almost spiritual quality. Portraits of past Academy presidents decorated the room walls. Scores of Academy members were present, along with the new Commission members, invited speakers, and many other invited physicians and scientists. Colonel Vaughn, wearing his army uniform, saw the couple enter the room and quickly came over to them.

"You made it!" exclaimed Vaughn. "I am so glad you could, Edward. These people need to hear your practical experience and comments. Lillian, you are as beautiful as ever! This group must join the 20th century in their thinking, and you're just the person to really help them along!"

"Thank you, Victor," said Lillian. "I am so honored to be here, and I know Edward feels the same way. But, I have to say, this is all very intimidating. After all, I'm just a mom."

"Hardly," scolded Vaughn. "You're one of the best epidemiologists in the room, if not the best! You're going to do great." Vaughn accompanied the Nobles to their seats in the first row facing the podium. Lillian sat next to the bacteriologist Anna Wessel Williams of the New York City municipal laboratories. Noble sat between Victor Vaughn and Milton Rosenau, who wore his navy uniform. Others in the first row included Rufus Cole of the Rockefeller Institute, William Park who was director of the New York Laboratories, Oswald Avery of the Rockefeller Hospital in New York City, and Paul Lewis who had proved polio was caused by a virus.

As the audience prepared for the beginning of the session, Vaughn leaned over to Noble and whispered, "William Welch won't be coming, Edward. He has influenza."

"Is he alright?" asked Noble, with great concern.

"Yes, he's doing OK. He's been pretty sick, but he'll pull through. I hear General Pershing in France has it as well."

Herman Biggs, the New York Commissioner of Health, and Chairman of the Influenza Commission, stood at the podium and opened the meeting. After thanking the New York Academy of Sciences for hosting the session, and greeting the speakers and audience, Biggs spoke of the global pandemic. "There has never been anything which compares with this important situation...in which we have been so helpless." He continued, "Our inabilities to fight the pandemic are a serious reflection upon public health administration, and medical science. It is a shame that we should find ourselves in this position. Many of us have been seeing this epidemic coming for months. Yet, public health officials and scientists both have done nothing to prepare. We ought to have been able to obtain all the scientific information available before this reached us at all. Some did try to sound the alert. People like General William Gorgas, Lieutenant Commander Milton Rosenau, Colonel Victor Vaughn, Major Edward Noble, and Lillian Noble all tried to warn the nation. But, apparently, few were listening."

Biggs finished his opening statement by saying, "Dealing with the pandemic has become the single biggest question in science."

The Influenza Commission, along with other invited guests, began a general discussion. The pathological findings in the disease varied widely from victim to victim. However, all agreed the pulmonary findings were dramatic, and unlike anything they had seen before. The microbiological findings were equally confusing, with multiple strains of pneumococcus, streptococcus, staphylococcus, and other bacteria found in living and dead specimens. The general consensus of the Commission was that these organisms represented secondary infections. The primary agent in influenza remained unknown.

Several investigators described the detection of Pfeiffer's *Bacillus influenza* bacterium in the great majority of pandemic victims. However, Rufus Cole told the group that Oswald Avery found *B. influenza* in thirty percent of healthy people. Since healthy people also carry pneumococcus, streptococcus, and staphylococcus on and in their bodies, all of these findings proved nothing. Avery himself was too shy to discuss his own work.

William Park raised the question that perhaps a filterable virus was the agent in the pandemic. One researcher agreed, and stated, "There can be no question that influenza is a living organism, and may be a virus beyond the range of microscopic vision." Another researcher said, "We may be dealing with an undiscovered virus, and pneumococci and Streptococci may be responsible for the gravity of the secondary pulmonary complications." Both researchers reported that their queries were to be published in the *Journal of the American Medical Association* on November 16th and November 2nd, respectively. Others thought bubonic plague might be responsible, and others thought there may be an entirely new agent involved. One fact was clear: no one was sure what caused influenza.

There were numerous case studies of successful action against the pandemic. A naval facility in San Francisco, located on an island, enforced a strict quarantine and experienced no influenza cases. The New York State Training School for Girls developed a quarantine that allowed no outsiders into the school. No girls developed influenza. The same thing occurred at the New York Trudeau Sanatorium. M.K. Wylder of Albuquerque, New Mexico, discussed a related finding.

"Observations can be very misleading. I used the prophylactic vaccine. I used it in a girls' school in which I immunized, or at least attempted to immunize, the pupils, teachers, and the rest of the staff. At the same time, we established and enforced a complete quarantine. There were eighty people in that institution, and not a single case of influenza developed. One mother insisted on being admitted to visit her daughter. Being refused, she took the girl home. In less than a week that girl was dead of influenza."

The verdict was in: isolation worked.

Clearly, overcrowding made the situation much worse. The mountain of data from the nation's army camps was overwhelming evidence against cramped living conditions in a time of influenza epidemic.

Studies found no correlation whatsoever between atmospheric pressure or weather conditions in areas with, or without, influenza. Some of the best work in this area was performed by the U.S. Public Health Service surgeon, W. H. Frost, in Washington D.C. His epidemiologic studies conclusively showed no correlation between natural weather phenomenon and the severity of influenza. This evidence was the death nail for the miasma theory of this disease.

Victor Vaughn mentioned that there was emerging evidence of immunity to influenza. Some of this data had been generated recently by Edward and Lillian Noble. In the nation's army camps, new recruits from large cities seemed to contract influenza significantly less often than recruits from rural states. Vaughn theorized that city dwellers over time may have come in contact with more influenza, and developed immunity to some strains.

At Camp Shelby, unlike other army camps, troops remained from March 1918 through the fall. Troops from March had very few cases of influenza, while newer recruits had many influenza deaths.

Data also compared civilians who contracted influenza in the spring of 1918 to those who did not contact influenza in the fall. The former suffered fewer deaths than the latter.

C.C. Browning of Los Angeles gave additional supporting data. He told the group, "At Fort McArthur on the Pacific coast early in the pandemic, there were only twenty-four influenza cases among the recruits from more thickly populated districts. And, there were no deaths. One week later, 800 recruits from mountain districts and ranges in the West arrived at the camp. Within three days, 115 of these men were hospitalized with influenza. Forty-seven of these men, or 41%, were dead in just a few days. Could the men from thickly populated areas have had some immunity to the present pandemic because of past exposure to more common infectious organisms?"

Henry Herbert of Iowa City studied results at yet another girl's school. When the spring epidemic arrived, dormitory A was quarantined, and dormitory B was not. There were seventy-six influenza cases in B, and none in A. After the spring infection passed, some girls from each dormitory were relocated in the other. Both dormitories were quarantined during the fall epidemic. However, a teacher left the compound briefly. After returning to the school, she inadvertently exposed both dormitories to influenza. There were eighty-two new cases of influenza among the girls. But, importantly, none of the original seventy-six cases in B developed the disease.

Researchers at the conference wondered if there might be a way to exploit this apparent development of immunity.

Another clear result of epidemiological data showed influenza deaths among twenty to thirty year olds was significantly higher than other groups. There had been a slight increase in women deaths. Those over sixty-five years had fewer deaths than common influenza seasons. Some theorized the older demographic group had developed some immunity during the 1889-1890 pandemic. At present, at least 30% of influenza victims with pneumonia will die.

Lewis Conner of New York compared the two pandemics of 1889 and 1918. He said there were striking similarities. Both had abrupt onsets, severe prostration and myalgias, injected conjunctiva and very painful eye motion, and a notable skin rash. Also, the complication of pneumonia was very similar. However, there also were striking differences. 1918 had a much higher proportion of the population attacked. As mentioned earlier, the associated pneumonia was much more severe and of a different histological type. Finally, and most importantly, 1918 has had an extraordinary mortality rate associated with it.

Conner also mentioned that his epidemiologic studies confirmed the observations first made by Major Noble, of the Army Communicable Disease Division. Local and isolated spring influenza epidemics eventually established in Camp Funston, Kansas, and spread quickly to the rest of the country. By April and May the influenza had spread to Western Europe. By June and July, the infection was spreading through Great Britain, the rest of Europe, China, India, the Philippines, Brazil, etc. The pandemic mutated into a much more lethal form, and returned to the United States through Boston at the beginning of September. It took about four weeks for the infection to spread from Boston to San Francisco.

Conner finished by saying, "Recurrences are characteristic of influenza epidemics. The history of the 1889 pandemic, and previous ones, point to the conclusion this disease has not yet run its full course. It seems probable we may expect at least local recurrences in the near future, with an increase over normal mortality from pneumonia for perhaps several years."

Herman Biggs then introduced Lieutenant Commander Milton Rosenau, who would present his findings on the spread of influenza. Rosenau began, "Thank you, ladies and gentlemen. We obtained one hundred healthy volunteers from the navy, and conducted our five experiments at the Boston Harbor quarantine station at Gallops Island. The subjects were eighteen to twenty-five years of age, and by history and physical examination had not had influenza. In the first experiment, we isolated thirteen different strains of Pfeiffer bacillus from lungs at necropsy, and sprayed them with an atomizer into the eyes, nostrils, and throats of nineteen volunteers. None of the volunteers became ill."

"In the second experiment, we took secretions from people with influenza, mixed it with saline, and sprayed it into the nostrils of ten volunteers. None of the volunteers became ill. In the third experiment, we took blood from infected ill patients, mixed it with 1% sodium nitrate, and injected 10 cc each into ten volunteers. None of the volunteers became ill. In our fourth experiment, we took mucus from ill influenza patients and past it through a Mandler filter. The filter holds back bacteria of ordinary size, but allows ultramicroscopic organisms to pass. 3.5 cc of the filtrate was injected subcutaneously each into ten volunteers. None of the volunteers became ill."

"In our final experiment, we took ten volunteers to the Chelsea Naval Hospital and exposed them to influenza patients on the wards. They sat with the patients, shook their hands, put their faces two inches from the ill patients' mouths, and allowed the patient to sneeze and cough into their faces. None of the volunteers became ill."

Rosenau continued, "I think we must be very careful not to draw any positive conclusions from negative results of this kind. Many factors must be considered. Our volunteers may not have been susceptible. They may have been immune. They may have been exposed as all the rest of the people had been exposed to the disease, although they gave no clinical history of an attack."

"Dr. McCoy did a similar series of experiments on Goat Island, San Francisco, and used volunteers who, so far as known, had not been exposed to the outbreak at all. He also had negative results. Perhaps there are factors, or a factor, in the transmission of influenza that we do not know."

Rosenau finished by stating, "As a matter of fact, we entered the outbreak with a notion that we knew the cause of the disease, and were quite sure we knew how it was transmitted from person to person. Perhaps, if we have learned anything, it is that we are not quite sure what we know about the disease." Following Rosenau's comments, there was much talk among the conference attendees. Rosenau, who was one of the world's leading experimental epidemiologists, had openly admitted medical science really did not know anything about influenza. To say the least, this revelation was unsettling to the entire audience.

Commissioner Biggs then introduced William Park, the Director of the New York Health Department Laboratories, who would speak on his research. Park began, "When the recent outbreak of influenza appeared, it was assumed by all that it was probably due to the same cause as that of 1889. Health official, epidemiologists, and bacteriologists, already overwhelmed by the demands of The War, were called on to investigate and combat the infection. Everyone first sought the Pfeiffer bacillus, since there was an established a relationship between the organism and influenza. But, it became clear this year that the situation was much more complicated. In Europe, some found the bacillus everywhere, while others found it in a small minority of patients. In America, pneumococci, streptococci, and gram negative micrococci were found in several varieties, and often together. In addition, some observations in England and France indicated that a filterable virus was present in at least some of the cases."

"We have tried to follow at least some of Koch's postulates. That is, to identify a microorganism as the cause of a widespread epidemic, the germ must be capable of producing the type of disease under investigation. The organism must be present in the advancing area in all cases at the beginning of the infection, and in any outbreak it must have the same characteristics when freshly isolated from different patients. The microorganism responsible for the epidemic may be either a microbe hitherto unknown to us, or be a new and more virulent strain of some known form. Even if we assume the latter alternative, we will have a difficult problem to obtain the proof. We must discover how to identify it as a new strain."

"The most delicate test we have for identification of microorganism strains is the injection of animals with the microbe, and then to look for the subsequent production of identical antibodies. With the filterable viruses, we have to depend on finding a susceptible animal, or revert to human volunteers. If we are successful in producing infection in animals or humans, we must then test for specific immunity. This is a most difficult and time consuming endeavor."

Park proceeded to use a large number of 4X5 foot cardboard posters on easels to show data from all over the United States. John Keegan from the Chelsea Naval Hospital had found a large number of patients with *B. influenza*. Researchers Spooner, Scott, Heath, Opie, Freeman, Blake, Small, and Rivers had all found substantial numbers of patients with *B. influenza*. All of these scientists believed that the infection sequence occurred as follows: *B. influenza* is introduced in the bronchi. Later, pneumococci may invade the inflamed bronchi, enter the lungs and produce either lobar pneumonia or bronchopneumonia. However, Park believed there was really no proof of this scenario. The fact remained that no one had shown a difference between *B. influenza* isolates in patients and healthy people.

At the same time, Chicago researchers Nuzum, Pilot, Strangl, and Bones thought their results insufficient to indicate the pandemic was due to a filterable virus. Wahl, White, and Lyall from the Yale Army Laboratory School in New Haven had raised the same possibility. They believed pneumococci were the most important early secondary invader.

Park continued, "Therefore, Anna Wessel Williams and I decided to test the immunologic reactions of isolations from more than one hundred cases. In a single infected individual, the great majority of isolations were identical. But, the majority of the isolations from other individuals differed from each other completely."

"These results appear to throw the influenza bacilli clearly into the class of secondary invader. We believe other microorganisms under suspicion, such as certain streptococci and pneumococci, will also not possess necessary characteristics of a primary agent in this epidemic. They, like the influenza bacillus, will be included among the important secondary invaders."

Park concluded, "There is no proof that any one germ is present in all cases of influenza. Our final conclusion is, therefore, that the microorganism causing this epidemic has not yet been determined."

Again, there was much chatter in the conference room after William Park's talk. Many had come to the meeting certain that the pandemic agent would finally be revealed. It now appeared that the microbiologists were as uncertain as the epidemiologists and pathologists. This is not what the clinicians in the room wanted to hear. Still, there was the hope that the immunologists and infectious disease specialists had pleasant surprises in store for the audience.

Henry Stoll of Hartford, Connecticut was then introduced to talk on influenza treatment with convalescent blood and serum. He also used 4x5 foot cardboard posters covered with numbers and percentages. Stoll discussed the production of the agents. "When blood was used, donor and recipient specimens were always typed for agglutinins. This is not necessary with serum. Pooled serum was used in about one half of the cases. We obtained the blood when patient's temperatures had been normal about ten days. When laboratory facilities are at hand, the use of whole blood is simpler and quicker, as it takes only a few minutes to determine the iso-agglutinins. Plasma is obtained by allowing the citrated blood to stand several hours. No grouping of recipient and donor is required, and the serum from several donors can be pooled, which is an advantage."

Stoll continued, "The mortality in the 435 cases of pneumonia, including those patients treated with convalescent serum, was 52 percent. The mortality of the serum-treated patients was approximately 45 percent, but the prognosis was distinctly bad in 70 percent. In the officer's ward, notwithstanding the fact that in 62 percent of the cases the prognosis was unfavorable, 72 percent of the patients showed definite improvement. In the general troop ward only 17 percent benefited from the treatment."

"Lieutenant Reed, in charge of the general pneumonia ward, considered the serum to be without value. Captain

Key, the officer ward surgeon, thought highly of it. Major Randolph, chief of the medical service, felt that in some cases it was of real value. In further analysis, it was found that the officers were given the serum within a few hours, while the pneumonia patients waited twelve to twenty-six hours for the serum."

Stoll said, "In conclusion, convalescent serum is of value when used early. It seems to lower mortality, shorten the course of the disease, and diminish complications. The blood from those vaccinated against pneumococcus Types I, II, and III possesses no advantage."

The audience applauded the results, and there were at last smiles on many faces. Positive results were finally occurring. However, the smiles were short-lived. In the question and answer period that followed, Lillian Noble called to the audience's attention that Stoll's studies had no control groups. There was no distinction made between the officer ward patients who had pneumonia and those who did not. There was no blinding of the physicians who assessed the results. Finally, the clinical descriptions of the assessed patients were so vague that there was no way to know if any of the groups were really comparable. Following her remarks, there was once again a silence of concern in the large room.

Augustus Wadsworth of Albany quickly summarized his experience with a *B. influenza* vaccine used in New York. Out of thirty-three state institutions, twenty-eight had more influenza outbreaks with the vaccine than without. In one particular institution, 203 inmates were equally divided into two groups. There were 166 cases of influenza in vaccinated patients, and thirty seven in non-vaccinated patients. Not only did the vaccine not work. Patients given the vaccine had far more cases of the disease than the non-treated patients.

Anna Wessel Williams joined in the audience floor conversation. "If the pandemic is a true microbial pandemic, starting from one cause and spreading from it, we should be able to prove there is one variety or type of organism responsible. Of course, we have to determine what test we must choose to prove this. Up to the present, we have decided we would accept the serum agglutination test. This is where antibodies clump together with antigens on the organism. In our lab, we have shown that all the *B. influenza* strains we have isolated do not respond to the test. This is where we make a series of assumptions. We assume the test is valid, that we have not missed a pandemic strain, and the strains have not changed in their power to produce the agglutinins. If our assumptions are correct, then *B. influenza* has nothing whatsoever to do with initiating the pandemic."

Edwin Le Count of Chicago commented, "Certain facts stand out in connection with this disease. One of the most astounding facts is the way in which it spreads. It has been compared to other eruptive fevers, such as measles. We need to all recall that measles is caused by a virus."

Le Count continued, "With this influenza, the saturation of the lungs with fluid is remarkable. The way fluid runs into the pleural cavities is astounding. In the early part of the pandemic, a mistake was probably made in its treatment. Withdrawing fluid from the pleural space by thoracentesis amounted to continued severe bleeding. This probably did more harm than good."

At this point, Fredrick Lord of the Massachusetts General Hospital rose to speak. Noble thought highly of him, as he always thought through clinical problems like a true internist does. Lord said, "At Mass General, we had twenty-three patients who were treated with the convalescent serum, and of this number we lost six. At the same time we had twenty-five controls, and we lost three. In a disease so variable in its symptoms as influenza pneumonia, one may readily fall into error in a judgment based on favorable symptoms following the administration of a serum. This is why it is so essential to have a properly chosen control group. There seems to me no ground for the belief that a vaccine in the treatment of disease is of any value whatsoever. Vaccines may be of use in prophylaxis, but they have never been shown to be of value in treatment."

E.C. Rosenow from Rochester, Minnesota, slowly rose from his seat to speak. Noble, Vaughn, and Milton Rosenau all looked at each other as they sat in their seats, and rolled their eyes toward the ceiling. None of them liked Dr. Rosenow, who could always be counted on to give inflated data that no one else could reproduce. E.C. Rosenow stated in his baritone professorial manner, "The vaccine we used in Rochester hospital contained the bacteria isolated in influenza pneumonia patients. This includes *B. influenza* and a type of pneumococci. Subjects were revaccinated with a lower dose from six weeks to two months later. Averaging all results obtained, it appears that the incidence of influenza was about three times as common and the death rate five times as high amoung the uninoculated as amoung the vaccinated persons."

As some applauded in the audience, Noble, Vaughn, and Rosenau could only shake their heads. It was hard to make any sense of Rosenau's presentation. Lillian Noble giggled, and put her hand over her mouth. Noble looked at his wife, grinned, and put his right hand index finger to his mouth as if to say "shhhh".

James B. Herrick from Chicago rose from his chair and was frowning. Vaughn had known Herrick for many years, and always referred to him as a "straight shooter" in research. Herrick stated, "Many general practitioners, deprived of the opportunity to put their patients into a well-managed hospital, have asked what they are to do. I believe general practitioners should try to get hold of their patients as early as possible. They should insist on their patients going to bed, make them stay until they are well, and not over drug them. I have not been very impressed by the harmlessness of many plans of treatment. That is why I have not used the vaccine or serums. I am not in principle opposed to them, but I do not think that as yet we have the proof that they are helpful. They may even be harmful."

E.C. Rosenow began to rise from his chair to debate Herrick, but those around him quietly told him to remain seated.

Herrick concluded, "I believe the general practitioner should, if possible, get his patient early and give him or her some general line of treatment that has at least the virtue of harmlessness. I have seen the following occur many times over the last several weeks: Patients come into the same hospital, the same ward, and are cared for by the same doctors, assistants, and nurses. But, patients admitted on the second, third, and fourth days of the disease died with a mortality which was so large that I hesitate to confess it. However, those admitted on the first day of the disease recovered at a much greater rate."

Some applauded after Herrick's comments. Milton Rosenau leaned over to Noble and whispered, "There seem to be two distinct factions in the audience". Noble nodded in agreement.

Chairmen Biggs adjourned the meeting for lunch. The audience made their way to another meeting room where a buffet was served. All sorts of salads, fruits, casseroles, pastas, and deserts had been placed on long tables for the guests to sample. The conference attendees were not shy about doing just that. For the next hour, two distinct groups could be seen talking in the dining area. In one group could be found the Nobles, Vaughn, Rosenau, Park, Williams, Cole, Lewis, Herrick, Lord, Avery, Wylder, Browning, Herbert, Conner, the Governor of New York, Charles Whitman, and many others. In a separate and somewhat smaller group, guests clustered around E.C. Rosenow while he lectured on the virtues of his vaccine.

The guests were called back to the main conference room for the afternoon session of the Influenza Commission. Chairmen Biggs brought the meeting to order, and then said, "It is my distinct pleasure to introduce to you our next speaker, Lillian Noble. Many of you know she is raising a large family. However, her work in Dr. Milton Rosenau's lab in Boston has brought her to the attention of the epidemiological community. She will speak to us today about the new emerging intellectual discipline of epidemiology, and its application to pandemics like the present one that has ravaged our country. Please greet Mrs. Lillian Noble."

Lillian rose from her seat during applause, and stepped to the podium. Her husband watched her in awe. She was about to speak to the most prestigious group of physicians and medical researchers in the United States. Yet, she appeared so calm and collected that one would think she gave a speech like this every day.

Lillian began, "I want to thank the Influenza Commission, and the New York City Academy of Sciences, for the honor to be with you today. From the Greek *epi*, *demos*, and *logos*, the term epidemiology means "the study of what is upon the people". It has become more than a passive observation of the factors affecting the health and illness of populations. Rather, it has become a meticulous research of outbreak investigation, study design, data collection, analysis, the development of statistical models to test hypotheses, and the proper documentation of results. It combines the disciplines of biology, medicine, chemistry, physics, geography, geology, meteorology, sociology, mathematics, statistics, anthropology, psychology, economics, and political policy into one endeavor."

Lillian described the major statistical tools now being applied in epidemiology. She knew that many in the audience did not yet use these tools, and many still did not understand them. She talked about discovering causal relationships, and that correlation does not imply causation. Lillian described the different types of studies, such as case series, case control studies, prospective studies, and cohort studies. She defined relative risk, odds ratios, and confidence intervals. She spoke of random error, sampling error, systematic error, and the ways to reduce bias in studies. Lillian called bias the "murderer" of well-intentioned research, and how to manage it with internal validity and external validity. She talked of the need to watch for volunteer bias, selection bias, and the concern with study non-respondents.

Lillian continued her lecture. "We must recognize the sources of bias and understand their influence. You are all discussing many clinical trials during these Commission sessions. As you do, you need to be aware of bias and how to reduce it. In industry-sponsored clinical trials, obtaining positive results provides substantial financial benefits to companies. There are also professional benefits for the company's employees. Government research sponsors also have considerable bias toward positive results. Many journal editors also have a preference for publishing articles presenting positive results. Positive results are of integral importance to the professional reputation, timing of promotion, and salary of researchers. The interest in being able to report favorable results is pervasive throughout health care research. It is important to realize that bias need not be intentional. In fact, it is usually introduced into a study unintentionally. However, steps can be taken to address the risk for bias induced by these factors."

Lillian stated, "Although exploring the data in a study is useful, it becomes particularly problematic when exploratory analyses are conducted with the intention to find evidence more favorable than what was provided by the prespecified primary analysis. Problems in the interpretation of data were clearly shown to me when I visited a hospital nursery some years ago."

"At the nursery, I was surprised to see that there were twenty babies of one gender, and only two of the other. I calculated the odds of such an event occurring in an equal gender population. The probability of an imbalance this extreme occurring by chance was 1 in 10,000. So, what could explain this paradox of obtaining compelling evidence against a hypothesis that nevertheless is known to be true? The explanation is that I did not walk into the hospital with the intention to gather prospective data to assess and report on this hypothesis. Rather, the data generated the hypothesis. Had the unusual gender ratio not occurred at that hospital at that time, I would be commenting now on some other equally rare coincidental observation made at some other time. On the other hand, if I had walked into the hospital with the intention of assessing a prespecified primary hypothesis about gender balance in newborns, evidence against such a balance would have been far more persuasive.

"The important insight is that the probability of chance is interpretable only when you understand the sampling context from which it is derived."

Later, Lillian mentioned, "In clinical research, you should not query clinicians about the biological plausibility of a certain event after showing them the data. Clinicians can readily provide biological explanations for why a factor may be a treatment effect by calling on their clinical insights. More reliable insights comes from asking clinicians to predict, before they are shown the results, which factors will be seen."

Lillian continued. "Researchers need to understand the concept of 'random high bias' when many sets of data are used to find benefit. A great example is Major League Baseball. I have to say that my sons would <u>love</u> this example, because they are baseball statistics fanatics. A first-year player with the most outstanding performance is recognized as the *Rookie of the Year*. The career-long performance for the typical player will, on average, improve after his first year. However, there is a paradox: The *Rookie of the Year* does not show such improvement. For the most recent thirty players who were awarded *Rookie of the Year*, 80% regressed or statistically performed less impressively in their careers after the first rookie seasons. This is based on the classical measures of batting average for hitters and earned run average for starting pitchers. This paradox is explained, not by the effect of pressures or distractions due to recognition as being the best, but rather by '<u>random high bias</u>'."

"In the setting of the *Rookie of the Year*, to have the best performance amoung a large number of players, the winner of the award will tend to be someone who overachieved in his rookie year. In other words, the rookie winners usually do better than other rookies by <u>chance</u>. Therefore, such players will tend to regress to their true level of performance over subsequent years.

Medical research can suffer from 'random high bias', just like *Rookie of the Year* can. When exploratory analyses are done with the goal of achieving positive results, analyses that seem to be most favorable will tend to be random overestimates of true treatment effect on those measures. The likelihood of random high bias would be greatly reduced if our goal was the pursuit of truth rather than the achievement of positive results, because our focus would not systematically or preferentially be on the positive outliers."

"The phenomenon of 'regression to the mean' seen with *Rookies of the Year* can also be seen in medicine. When biological measures are particularly variable, such as blood pressure, temperature, pulse, and blood cell counts, the common normalization of extreme values due to natural variation may be misinterpreted as benefit from some treatment."

"Everyone must remember that a hypothesis generated by particular favorable results usually require formal evaluation in subsequent adequate and well-controlled trials. Such studies have been called *confirmatory* trials."

Lillian then said, "Taking care with the principles we have discussed today will help researchers focus their attention and resources on finding the truth. In the situation we find ourselves now, this means solving 'the single biggest question in science' mentioned by Chairman Biggs."

Lillian concluded, "My husband and I have always liked the quote by Charles Farrar Browne, using the *nom de plume* Artemus Ward. He said, 'It isn't so much the things we don't know that get us in trouble. It's the things we know that aren't so'. Thank you again for inviting me to your wonderful conference."

As Lillian stepped from the podium and returned to her chair, she received a very loud and appreciative applause. Noble was so proud of her that he could barely contain himself. After she had sat down, she looked over at her husband. He wore a grin that filled the conference room. He blew a kiss to her, and then formed the "OK!" sign one makes with their thumb and index finger. Vaughn leaned over to Noble and whispered with a smile, "And, what is it that she ever saw in you?" Noble had to bite his lip to avoid laughing out loud.

Chairman Biggs returned to the podium, and said, "Thank you so much, Mrs. Noble, for your extremely relevant and important talk today. It is now my honor to present out next speaker, Dr. Edward Noble. Since 1905, Dr. Noble has been the Director of the Infectious Disease 'South Department' at Boston City Hospital. After his tour of duty in France ended in January, Major Noble has been attached with the Army Communicable Disease Division, and its office at Boston City Hospital. Dr. Noble will speak today on the current immuno-logical treatment of influenza."

Noble walked to the podium during a very warm applause for him. Both he and his father held exceptional reputations in American medicine. Many in the audience were well aware of Noble's tireless attempts to warn of the pandemic, and that he probably had more direct clinical experience with it than anyone else in the room.

Noble was accustomed to public speaking, but not to an audience such as this. His face suddenly felt flushed, and he became hot in his army field uniform. He could feel beads of sweat forming on his forehead and temples, and his hands developed a fine tremor. He had to concentrate on holding his 5X8 inch cards so that he would not drop them. He kept his hands hidden behind the podium so as not to show his slight shaking. Noble was surprised to discover that he was actually suffering from stage fright.

After clearing his throat twice, Noble said, "The Influenza Commission, the New York City Academy of Sciences, Governor Whitman, and honored guests: Thank you for your invitation to speak today."

"It has only been twenty-seven years since Emil von Behring discovered an antitoxin to the toxin produced by *Corynebacterium diphtheriae*. Behring found that animals giv-en *C. diphtheriae* developed an antitoxin. If blood was then taken from the animal, and the solids removed, the remaining serum could be injected into diphtheria patients and have a clinically important effect. This was done over the Christmas holiday in 1891, and became the very first cure of a disease. Our own William Park and Anna Wessel Williams independently produced anti-serum, and found a way to make it in large quantities, and more inexpensively."

"When the horror of the present pandemic breached our shores, the death of family, friends, and countrymen reached a rate not seen before. The dying continues even today. Naturally, healthcare workers desire to do everything possible to save lives. But, American researchers have been inexperienced at producing vaccines, and American physicians have been inexperienced in conducting vaccine trials. In addition, medical and public health facilities have been stretched to the limit by both the pandemic and The War. Serum and vaccine trials have had poor designs, and journal editors have been overly enthusiastic about publishing these studies."

"There has been no shortage of attempts to produce successful influenza vaccines and antisera. Eighteen different vaccines have been produced in Illinois alone. William Park has tested a vaccine in New York City. C.Y. White has made a multivalent vaccine with dead strains of *Bacillus influenza*, two types of pneumococci, and several strains of streptococci. The Army Medical School has produced a vaccine with pneumococcus Types I, II, and III, and distributed two million doses. Rufus Cole and Oswald Avery have worked on an anti-pneumococcus serum against pneumococcus Type I. Tufts Medical School has delivered a huge shipment of vaccine to San Francisco by rapid train. The Mayo Clinic laboratories have produced hundreds of thousands of vaccine doses. Paul Lewis first thought a filterable virus may be to blame for the catastrophe, but has since concentrated on *B. influenza* after finding much of the microbe in necropsy lung specimens. The list of such heroic work goes on and on."

"What have these serum and vaccine trials reportedly found, and how have the studies been conducted? As Mrs. Noble has mentioned, the way a study is conducted is as important as the findings attributed to it. Today I will focus on six of the more prominent studies conducted to date in the United States. I do not discuss these studies simply to find fault. Rather, I discuss these studies in order to help all of us find the truth. We can all agree the involved researchers have performed the best job possible to promote the health of the general public."

Noble continued, "In our first study, Maurice Katzman of Denver injected 980 patients with streptococcus vaccine during the pandemic peak in that area. He furnished a card to each patient so they could report their subsequent course. He published the numbers of cases among those who completed the full course of injections and among those who did not, but he provided no information on cases who received no vaccine. He concluded his vaccine was safe and effective. Important problems with this study involve bias associated with self-reporting, and bias from non-responders to a survey. Obviously, those who died of influenza did not send in their survey cards. If an entire family was ill with influenza, no one might have remembered to send in their cards as well. It is therefore hard to conclude the vaccine was effective."

"The second study was conducted by Charles Duval and William Harris of the Tulane University Department of Pathology and Bacteriology. It used a killed *Bacillus influenza* vaccine produced with care and thoroughness. They gave the vaccine to 3,072 employees of a particular business in New Orleans. They used as controls 866 employees who refused vaccination, and justified them as controls because they worked and lived under the same conditions as the vaccinated. The pandemic was at its peak when the vaccine was administered, with about 40% absentee rates. 1.7% of those who received three vaccine injections developed influenza, and 8% became ill after two injections. 24% fell ill with influenza with only one injection. No one who was vaccinated developed pneumonia. However, 41.6% of the unvaccinated contracted influenza."

"This second Tulane study brings up the problem of choosing a control group. Those who refused vaccination may have had the grippe in the past and feared becoming ill with the vaccine. On the other hand, those who refused vaccination may never have had the grippe in the past and therefore were willing to 'take their chances'. In any case, the controls were not randomly assigned, so they may have had immunity to influenza. Receiving the vaccine had its own risks. In 30% of the vaccinated, side effects from it were deemed severe."

"The third study was conducted at the naval station on Puget Sound, and used a vaccine to streptococcus. Military procedures and war time conditions prohibited the researchers from dividing seven units into experimental and control groups. Vaccinated and unvaccinated men were simultaneously observed in only two units. Among the other five units, four were entirely vaccinated, and one was entirely unvaccinated. Cases of influenza were already breaking out on the station before the vaccine was administered. A navy unit had just arrived from Philadelphia, were the pandemic was raging. Many of these men were already ill on arrival. Nevertheless, it was claimed the vaccine prevented many illnesses and mitigated its severity in many others."

"This Puget Sound study unfortunately had inconsistent results. In the Philadelphia unit, there were influenza incidence rates of 28.2% among the vaccinated, and 19.6% among the unvaccinated. In the Seamen's Barracks, the other divided unit, the proportions were reversed with incidence of 2.03% among the vaccinated and 12.3% among the unvaccinated. It is therefore difficult to draw any conclusions from this vaccine study."

Noble stopped briefly to take a sip of water due to dry lips. His hand tremor was now moderately better. It helped immensely that Lillian smiled at him with wide adoring eyes during his talk.

Noble continued. "The fourth study was performed by George Wallace who was the Superintendent of the Wrentham State School in Massachusetts. He used a vaccine prepared by the Tufts Professor of Pathology and Bacteriology, Timothy Leary. Leary used three strains of heat killed and chemically treated *B. influenza*. The three types of *B. influenza* are called the Carney, Navy, and Devens strains. Eight days into the pandemic, 122 cases had already developed in Wrentham. Wallace reported very favorable results, but gave no indication of how the vaccinated and control groups were selected. He did not even calculate incidence rates. Of the seventy-one employees who were vaccinated, only five contracted influenza. Of the fifty-eight employees who were not vaccinated, thirty-eight became ill. In another building with 156 inmates, there was one influenza case in the twenty-eight people vaccinated. There were sixty-four influenza cases among the 128 unvaccinated inmates. On this basis, Wallace concluded that Leary's vaccine was protective."

"In the Wallace study, with the infection all around Wrentham, there is no way to know who in the control groups were already immune to the disease. This is a serious problem with any vaccine study conducted after an epidemic is already established. Harry Barnes tested the Leary vaccine in a Rhode Island state sanatorium, and found that it offered only slight protection. This conclusion was reached after excluding wards that were not thought to be sufficiently exposed to influenza. If these 'unexposed' wards were included in the study, the vaccine offered no benefit at all."

"The fifth study used a vaccine prepared by William Park at the New York Health Department laboratories. Park theorized that the influenza agent was either a new virulent form of *B. influenza*, or an unknown agent like a filterable virus. This latter agent might be quickly followed by secondary invaders such as streptococci and pneumococci. Current strains of *B. influenza* were injected into animals that produced antibodies to them. Cultures of *B. influenza* were grown, and then heat killed. Park gave subjects three injections of increasingly larger doses of the vaccine. About 300,000 dose of the vaccine were given, and side effects were said to be mild. However, there was no clear evidence that the vaccine worked. It is to Dr. Park's great credit that he can report these negative results as honestly as he would report positive results."

"The sixth and final study was by E.C. Rosenow of the Division of Experimental Bacteriology of the Mayo Foundation in Rochester, Minnesota. Since the cause of influenza is not known, Rosenow decided to attack the question of secondary infections. He believed a vaccine against these secondary microbes needed to represent local bacteria mixtures. Therefore, his vaccine was adjusted to the composition of bacteria in circulation at the time. His first vaccine contained 30% pneumococci Types I, II, and III, 30% pneumococci Type IV and diplostreptococcus, 20% hemolytic streptococci, 10% *Staphylococcus aureus*, and 10% *B. influenza*. The vaccine was distributed to physicians in the upper mid-west, and the doctors were asked to return a survey on the effectiveness of the injections. No one knows the number of doses given by the Mayo Foundation, but Rosenow received 143,000 returned surveys. The Director of the Chicago Health Department laboratories, F.O. Tonney, produced over 500,000 doses of Rosenow's vaccine and distributed it throughout Illinois. Reports were very positive concerning the vaccine."

"George McCoy, Director of the Hygienic Laboratory of the Public Health Service, V.B Murray, a USPHS Assistant Surgeon, and A.L. Teeter of Stanford University Hospital, tested E.C. Rosenow's vaccine with great scientific rigor. Their vaccine came from the Chicago Health Department, and they conducted the trial in a single institution. All their subjects were kept under close observation. They completed the vaccinations eleven days before the first case appeared. They sought to equalize risk by vaccinating on every ward alternative patients under forty-one years of age. This was the cohort they considered most likely to contract influenza. McCoy and associates concluded that Rosenow's vaccine offered no protection whatsoever."

"Scores of bacterial vaccines of numerous types and recipes for therapeutic and prophylactic purposes have been produced during the pandemic. Some have used *B. influenza* exclusively, and others were developed as multivalent vaccines. Sera have been used by live patients, and serum and lung tissues have been harvested from dead victims. Some treatments have been little more than infectious 'soup' taken from victims and injected directly into patients. Regardless of the vaccine tested or the approach used, most researchers who published results concluded their vaccines were effective."

"We know many of the fundamental methodological weaknesses in these studies came from the extreme conditions at the time. Nevertheless, most of the studies this year have had significant problems with selection bias, unequal exposure to risk, no attempt at blinding or double-blinding, and no use of placebos. There was no insistence on randomization, or a discussion about who is a proper subject for experimentation. One finding is for certain: The closer a study was able to equalize risk and obtain complete information, the more likely it was to conclude the vaccine was useless."

"So, ladies and gentlemen, where do we go from here? How do we judge the worthiness of future serum and vaccine trials? I have a number of suggestions for you to ponder. Just four years ago, Major Greenwood and Udny Yule published a landmark article in the *Proceedings of the Royal Society of Medicine* describing the statistics that should be used in planning vaccine trials. George McCoy has obviously learned from this treatise. McCoy has discussed recently the statistical fallacy of vaccination during an epidemic, and including among the controls all illnesses that occurred among the unvaccinated."

"There should be five standards for the endorsement of a vaccine trial to be adequate: First, the numbers of the vaccinated and unvaccinated persons should be equal, and the groups 'in all material respects, alike'. Second, the vaccinated and unvaccinated should be of equal susceptibility as determined by age, gender, prior exposure, and racial composition. Third, the degree of the exposure during the trial should be equal in duration and intensity. Fourth, the vaccinated and unvaccinated should be exposed concurrently to infection during the same phase of the epidemic. Five, the criteria of the fact of inoculation and of the fact of the disease having occurred, must be independent."

Noble began to conclude his remarks. As he did, he noticed that he was no longer sweating, and his tremor was gone. His confidence with the material had given him comfort to deliver it. Noble summarized, "Readers of the medical literature this year have been faced with a remarkable task, while trying to help their patients. Clinicians have had to sift through all of these vaccine trials, regardless of their composition or mode of administration, and decide what to do. The fact is, there is no proof that any antiserum or vaccine has had any effect on the pandemic. Therefore, all of us must attempt to apply the five principles we have discussed this afternoon when assessing future vaccine trials. Above all else, ladies and gentlemen, 'primum non nocere'. I have been honored to speak to you today. Thank you."

Noble walked from the podium, and the applause was even louder than before his talk began. Although clinicians in the audience hoped to hear about "the cure" of influenza, the great majority of them appreciated the voice of reason coming out of the chaos of American immunological research. Noble did notice a few in the audience that were not clapping, and one of them was E.C. Rosenow. Noble sat on his front row chair, and the applause continued. The audience then rose to their feet. Noble sat uncomfortable with the attention, but finally stood and faced the audience smiling. He walked over to Lillian and lifted her arm up with his. The applause grew even louder. The couple knew the applause was for both of them, and their new approaches to the sciences of epidemiology, immunology, and subspecialty infectious disease. Only when the Nobles again took their seats, did the applause cease.

James Herrick of Chicago then gave an important summary of influenza treatments other than vaccines and sera. His concluding remarks forced many to pause and consider their own approaches to the disease. "In regards to influenza, so many ignore the fact of the self-limited nature of the infection and its natural course. So many conclusions are crude, and so many have optimistic credulity that takes the place of the more desirable skepticism. The fact remains that no drug or drugs is known to prevent the occurrence of influenza, and there is no specific treatment for those who contract it."

Herrick continued, "One of the hardest things to do in the treatment of a serious, self-limited, infectious disease is to refrain from prescribing drugs merely because the diagnosis has been made. A physician's good judgment is apt to be smothered in the semihysterical atmosphere of alarm that pervades the community during the pandemic. The doctor forgets that a large proportion of patients with influenza do not need a single dose of medicine. The treatment of influenza is really expectant, symptomatic, and individualized. To have favorite remedies which we talk about too much is to expose ourselves to the danger of believing in them more than is warranted by the facts. One ought not be a nihilist in regards to drug therapy in this disease. But, no apology is needed for being a good deal of a skeptic as to the value of much of the therapy that is prevalent."

Herrick then summarized, "Wholesale and indiscriminate drugging and the giving of huge doses is much too common. There should be a management of influenza as rational and simple as that of a developed case of typhoid fever. In the hands of the intelligent physician, and the enlightened public, drugs in the treatment of typhoid fever play a subordinate role. How much harm may be done by over drugging, no one can estimate. But, the danger is real and not imaginary."

By mid-afternoon, the Influenza Commission had decided on two pathways as it moved forward on research directions and the allocation of available resources. One path was the exploration of the epidemiology of the disease. The other was looking for evidence in the laboratory linking the disease to the cause. Everyone realized what a massive scientific effort was required. In addition to the Influenza Commission, a number of groups pledged their support in the work. This included the American Medical Association, the U.S. Public

Health Service, the U.S. Army and Navy, the Red Cross, the Rockefeller Institute, and the Metropolitan Life Company. Noble thought to himself that today marked the beginning of a coordinated scientific assault on the demon.

During an afternoon break in the conference, the Nobles left for their hotel. The Commission would meet again tomorrow, and would have multiple meetings in the future. However, the Nobles had a family requiring attention, and they needed to return soon. They had an early train to Boston the next morning, and wanted to be rested for the trip.

CHAPTER 23

Manhattan was cold and clear on Thursday morning, October, 31st. The Nobles boarded their train at the cathedral-like Grand Central Station, and again enjoyed a small private Pullman room for their trip back to Boston. They both took naps as the train started up, for they were both still worn from their conformance preparations and talks.

After about forty-five minutes, the Nobles awoke and decided to get something to eat. They made their way to the dining car and were seated at a small table with a white table cloth and a rose in a small vase. They ate croissants, Danish pastries, and drank coffee along with freshly squeezed orange juice.

The Nobles talked about the wonderful reception they received at the Commission, and how much it meant to them. However, it was much more important that physicians and researchers begin to use all the tools of scientific method examined by the Nobles in their talks. Both felt, in some small way, they had helped advance American medical research beyond the era of simple description and expert opinion. If this one concept was carried home with conference attendees, the Nobles could say they were wildly successful.

Edward and Lillian agreed there was no greater tribute to their son Arthur than their discussions the day before. Still, Lillian said Arthur would have made faces at both of them if he had been there. They both laughed at the thought, because they knew it was true.

Both read sections of the *New York Times* for awhile. Then, Noble put down the newspaper and said to Lillian, "Lilly, I have to say that I am fairly upset with the government."

"What do you mean, dear?" said Lillian.

"After what we have seen...after what we have been through...wouldn't you expect the President of the United States to say something? Something about what horror the country is enduring?"

"Of course, Edward," said Lillian. "Of course."

"Well, he hasn't," said Noble. "President Wilson has said nothing about the pandemic whatsoever. It says here on page eleven of the *New York Times* that our devout Presbyterian President has not attended church in October. At all. This is a man who reads the Bible daily, says grace before every meal, and prays on his knees each morning and night. He is an elder of the Central Presbyterian Church in Washington and often attends Wednesday evening prayer meetings. But, he has missed Sunday church this month? So, I guess he knows better than to go out into public. I'm sure his private physician gave him that advice."

"Dear, I know how you feel. But, recall that the churches in Washington have been closed for some time. How could he attend?"

"Well," said Noble, "he hasn't had many visitors at the White House this month, including the traditional big Sunday lunch. He hasn't been seen for more than a few times in public during October. The Vice President, Thomas Marshall, and his family have been quarantined at the Willard Hotel because they all have influenza. So, he knows there is a 'problem' in the country. From his office, he could raise the issue of quarantine to a high and important level. Yet, we hear nothing. Absolutely nothing. And this is not even mentioning the issue of troop ship transports and the lack of their quarantines. The President has made the pandemic so much worse."

Lillian frowned slightly, and resumed work on her crossword puzzle. She had her own issues with President Wilson, and his early hesitation to advocate for women's suffrage. It took America's entry into The War, and his need for women's support of it, to change his mind. Still, he did change his mind, and American women needed his assistance to pass the 19th Amendment to the U.S. Constitution. Perhaps the President's military and civilian public health advisors were to blame for his inattention to the pandemic. Lillian was willing to give him more of the benefit of the doubt than her husband could.

When Lillian finished the puzzle, she watched the passing Connecticut landscape and the many trees that had already lost their leaves. After a time, she sighed deeply, looked over at her husband as he read the *Times* financial section, and said, "Dear, I am still concerned about a few things."

Knowing what was coming, Noble replied, "What's that, Lilly?"

"I don't want to be repetitious, Edward, but you do have a hearing with the Massachusetts Medical Board coming up. To add to all of this, you must now deal with reaction to your national cables warning of the pandemic. You know I am always behind you, Edward. But, I can't help but worry."

Noble placed the newspaper on the table, poured coffee from a small pot on the table, and drank it from his cup. He knew his wife only wanted the best for him. He knew he had to comfort her. He also knew exactly what he was doing.

"Lilly, we both know who lodged the medical board complaint against me. I'm not worried about Cunard, and I stand behind my decisions with the South Department. I know full well what could happen with my cables to the public health services and newspapers throughout the country. I am not only ready to confront those who challenge me, I am eager to do so. They will only bring more attention to my cause. I am ready, and I am confident."

As Noble looked at his wife, tears began to appear in her eyes. He took her hands in his across the small dining car table. He leaned closer to her, and spoke almost in a whisper. "Lilly, when I was little, my father told me of his travails with medical care during the Civil War. When touring the army camps, he found commanding officers who completely ignored the most basic public health directives of The U.S. Sanitary Commission. Some of these officers were even generals. When he took the commanders on, many of them pledged to destroy him. But, my father still prevailed."

"Dad always told me to first be assured that one's chosen mission is the right one. The search for this assurance is truly the most difficult part of any quest. One must look at all sides of the question, and know all the relevant information completely. Dad said one must be able to argue the reasons not to take on the mission just as well as the reasons to move forward. Only after this examination is completed can one make the final commitment toward the goal. At that point, a person must not allow anything to deflect one from that mission. Lilly, this is where I am in the process. I am at the point where I must not be detoured. The health and safety of tens of thousands are at stake."

Lillian knew the determination of Charles Noble ran strong through his son's veins. She understood he had to take full advantage of the opportunity given to him with the A.I. Office. She also knew Edward was challenging very strong forces that could cause much damage to him, his career, his reputation, and to his family. She supported her husband, and knew with all her heart that he was right in his mission. But, that did not stop her worry.

The remainder of the Nobles' return journey to Boston was mostly spent in quiet contemplation. In their Pullman car room they read, napped, and sometimes just held hands as they both watched out the window. They wanted to go home.

Arriving at the Boston and Main train station in the early afternoon, the Nobles were met by Sergeant Campbell as they stepped off the Pullman car. As always, he was right on time. The Sergeant helped them with their luggage, and they set off for Beacon Street in the army staff car. The Nobles immediately noticed that Boston had changed in just the few days they had been away. The city was busy. Cars, carts, buses, and pedestrians were everywhere. There were even some traffic jams along the way. Noble thought Boston seemed even busier than ever before, but knew this was only in comparison to its state over the last six weeks. There did seem to be a lot of trucks and carts hauling garbage. Lillian suggested that people were now able to clean up homes and buildings that had been left unattended.

Sergeant Campbell drove the car to the Noble home, and again helped the couple with their things. He shook Lillian's hand, saluted the Major, and asked him to call any time he needed transportation. Noble asked him to come into the dwelling for a time, but the Sergeant said he needed to return to Devens. Campbell drove away while waving at his favorite officer. The Nobles were finally home.

Akeema and Florence had kept a tight ship while the Nobles had been in New York. Even with seven children, the house was clean, neat, and all chores completed. Somewhat later, Akeema arrived with seven excited children after school. It was Halloween, and there were costumes to put on. It short order, a whole menagerie of characters emerged from the children's bedrooms. Marguerite and Helen were princesses. Bernard, Michael, Brian, and Joseph were all Red Sox baseball players. Mark McCracken wanted to be a ghost with a sheet over his head, but Lillian pointed out how insensitive that would be this year. He decided to be a pirate instead.

Lillian and Edward carved pumpkins as they planned a limited form of trick-or-treat in the Back Bay neighborhood. Influenza was still present in the city, but the Nobles decided to let the children go to a few friends' homes in the early evening. Considering the confinement the children endured for nearly a month, and the unspeakable experiences of the

McCracken children, this outing was something that had to happen. The whole Noble clan walked with the children as they collected candy from nearby homes. There was finally a hint of normalcy in their lives.

On Monday, November 4th, the weather was chilly, but remained clear. The trolley was now fully-functioning, so Noble took it to Boston City Hospital. The Major went directly to the A.I. Office, saluted the sentry, and entered the main office as always. He anticipated an empty office, since this was not a scheduled shift. However, seated at the cordboard was a Second Lieutenant he had never seen before. This new officer was a tall woman with long sandy brown hair tucked under her Signal Corps cap. She was fair in complexion, with large brown eyes and naturally red lips. Noble noticed her long fingers as she plugged and removed circuit cords on the switchboard. Shortly after Noble opened the office door, her head turned toward him and took a double-take. She immediately stood at attention.

"Major Noble, sir!" said the new Lieutenant.

"Uh...yes, Lieutenant," said Noble. "I'm Major Edward Noble."

The Lieutenant saluted, and said, "It's a great pleasure to meet you sir!"

Noble listened to her heavy French accent, and guessed that she was a new immigrant to America. He also estimated she was about six feet tall. "Likewise," said Noble. "Are you our new addition to the Army Intelligance Office team, Lieutenant?"

"Yes, sir! My name is Second Lieutenant Adelina Quellet, sir. I am the new third shift for the A.I. Office. I guarantee I will do my very best at my duties, sir! Lieutenant Pierre-Louis and Lieutenant Lafayette are such great mentors! But, I can assure you that I am fully trained as a manual exchange operator. I am well versed in Morse code, transcontinental telegraph transmissions, and radio. I can type one hundred and twenty words a minute, sir. I am also trained in the library sciences, the Dewey decimal system, and can research a wide range of topics on a moment's notice, sir."

"That's wonderful," said Noble. "We can really use your talents here, for sure. Where are you from, Lieutenant?"

"I was born in Bordeaux, France, sir. My father was French, but my mother was Portuguese. Eight years ago, when I was fifteen, my family came to New York. I did not speak any English then, so please pardon my accent, sir. I was fortunate to be given an opportunity to study at NYU. After graduation last year, I joined the Army Signal Corps in New York. That is where I learned how to work with various forms of electronic communication. I was just transferred to Camp Devens a week ago, sir."

"Sounds like you have been very busy the last few years," said Noble. "By the way, there is no need to make any excuse for your accent, Lieutenant," said Noble. "It is quite delightful."

"I speak French, English, and Portuguese, sir, so I think I can be helpful. I also have a bachelor degree in mathematics. So, I can help in that regard, in any way I can, sir. I must also say, sir, Claudette and Marié speak so highly of you. It is an honor to be under your command, sir!"

Noble sensed that Lieutenant Quellet's enthusiasm was completely sincere. He saluted her, and said, "I'm glad you are on our team, Lieutenant. At some point you'll have to meet my wife, who absolutely adores statistics." Quellet smiled widely. She was pleased with the idea there might be another woman with whom she could discuss her passion for numbers.

"That would be terrific," said the Lieutenant. "I enjoy algebra, geometry, trigonometry, and calculus. I hope to meet her soon." Quellet stood motionless for a moment, just smiling. She then said, "Oh...Major. Claudette and Marié told me how you like to have your messages set out on the big table. I have various cables arranged as they mentioned. If there is anything you need, or if I'm making mistakes, please tell me, sir."

"I'm sure it's all fine, Lieutenant," said Noble. I'll get right to the cables, since I have some catching up to do. Noble walked to the table, and began to read war related messages.

After German Imperial Chancellor Maximilian's October 3rd letter to Washington D.C., President Wilson had sent a series of diplomatic messages to Germany. Wilson demanded Germany's retreat from all occupied territories, and cessation of all submarine activities. He also implied that the Kaiser's abdication was an essential condition for peace, but did not explicitly state as much. Wilson's October 23rd message said, "If the Government of the United States must deal with the military masters and the monarchical autocrats of Germany now, or if it is likely to have to deal with them later in regard to the international obligations of the German Empire, it must demand not peace negotiations but surrender."

The President had actually outlined his plan for an armistice in his "Fourteen Points" speech made in Congress ten months earlier. However, army intelligence had found evidence that the Allies had no intention of accepting the Fourteen Points. France and England considered the "Points" to be clever and effective American propaganda designed to undermine the fighting spirit of the Central Powers. However, in principle, the Allies found them unacceptable. In addition, many in Germany thought the condition of the Kaiser's abdication completely unacceptable. So, the delay in an armistice continued.

Despite the diplomatic stalemate, the situation in Germany was worsening. The economy had collapsed, influenza had taken a horrible toll, and starvation was apparent everywhere. Sailors at the port of Wilhelmshaven revolted on October 29th, and the uprising began to spread throughout the country. A German revolution was underway. Germany had no resources left to combat the Allies. However, America continued to pour 10,000 fresh and well equipped troops every day into the European theater.

On October 30th, the Ottoman Empire signed an armistice in Mudros. The Austrian and Hungarian army disintegrated, which effectively ended the Austro-Hungarian Empire on November 3rd.

Earlier in the day, some metropolitan newspapers in the U.S. reported the signing of a Central Power armistice. Celebrations had started briefly in some cities, but quickly stopped when the news was found to be erroneous. Noble wondered when the madness would finally end.

With great surprise and happiness, Noble found in the personal message pile a cable from Harvey Cushing.

Monday, November 4, 1918
From: Base Hospital #5

Camiers, France

I know that it has been awhile my friend, and for that I am sorry. I am working hard at recovering fully from my debilities, but it is a slow go. My eyesight is now better, but I am still somewhat unsteady with standing, and my legs remain weak. Still, I continue to be optimistic.

We heard today of the assassination of President Wilson, but learned soon after that it was a baseless rumor...thank God. The War plods on, even as it is obvious to everyone that the Central Powers are finished. The news is astounding. Old world dynasties are teetering.

With the very real promise of an end to this war, many American neurosurgeons here in France have begun to think of the future. We are considering the formation of a National Institute of Neurology when we are back in the states. Some think we should ask the government to help fund such a venture. I think not. If Congress has any brains, they don't use them. A Congressman is nothing but lungs and a pants' pocket for others to stuff with cash.

I hope to come home soon, Edward. Please give my love to Lillian, your children, and of course Katherine and the kids.

Sincerely, your friend,
Colonel Harvey Cushing, AEF.

Noble dictated a reply to Cushing with Lieutenant Quellet's assistance, and summarized some of the highlights of the past few weeks. He laughed as he agreed Congressmen are nothing but lungs and pants' pockets. However, he added they also must have stomachs, given their hunger for cash.

After thanking the new Lieutenant, Noble went off to the South Department pavilions. He entered the influenza quarantine ward and found a very different place from a few weeks earlier. About half of the ward beds were occupied, and the patients in them all appeared stable and resting. The small tables at the head of the beds had clean basins, folded linen, and carafes of fresh water upon them. The floors were scrubbed clean. Even the walls had been washed. A number of nurses and aids in clean white uniforms, gowns, and gauze masks, darted about the patients as they tended to their various needs.

In the middle of the ward, Noble spied Dr. David Schafer auscultating an abdomen. Schafer also looked very different. He had put on about ten pounds since their last meeting. His skin had a fresh pink quality, and his cheeks again had the blush of a young man in his twenties. His hair was cleaned and combed, and his clothes and white clinic coat were free of blood, sputum, and vomit stains. As Noble walked toward the young doctor, he called out, "David...Lieutenant Schafer."

Schafer looked up and smiled broadly. "Major! Major Noble! You're back from New York! Gosh it's good to see you, sir!"

Noble patted the young man on the back. "You look great, Lieutenant. I mean really."

"What you mean is that I look normal, right sir?" said Schafer.

Noble chuckled. "Yeah, I guess that is what I mean. The last few weeks you...well..."

"You mean I looked like hell," said Schafer. "It's OK, Major. Everyone has said the same thing. With the work, the food rationing...things were getting tough, Major."

"I have to say," said Noble, "the whole staff looks great. Funny what a little food and rest can do. All of you have also done a spectacular job cleaning up BCH. What a difference in just about a week."

"Thanks, Major," said Schafer. "I swear, the epidemic changed in forty-eight hours. One day there were hundreds of severely ill and dying people lined outside the warehouse satellite hospital. Two days later there are virtually none. Almost all the satellites are now closed, and the residents, medical students, and nursing students are back on their campuses or hospitals. Within a week, we had enough hospital supplies for the greatly reduced number of patients. Along with the help of the army and navy troops and sailors, we had BCH spit-spot clean in just a couple of days."

"It's really quite remarkable, Lieutenant," said Noble.

"The interesting clinical observation is that the patients themselves have changed," said Schafer. "A much milder form of influenza is showing up in the hospital clinics. Almost all of the admitted patients are now Type I. Very few are what we termed the 'pre-dead'...the Type III's. I'm not sure if it is due to better hospital resources, a mutation in the infection, or both, but I would venture an estimate that we are saving 90% of the Type I's. Of course, the patients are coming to us better fed and hydrated to begin with. There is more food in the community now, and healthier people to assist the ill. In an influenza pandemic, it seems the worse things get, the worse things get. Conversely, the better things get, the better things get. And, it all happens pretty fast."

"Well put, Lieutenant," said Noble. "Everything about influenza is exponential, and rapid."

"I hope we somehow made a difference, Major."

"Of course you made a difference, Lieutenant," said Noble. "You <u>all</u> did. You encountered thousands of patients in the critical first days of their illnesses. Those who had any fighting chance to mount a defense against influenza needed your expert help quickly. I know all of you gave that help in the highest measure. Some of you brave and selfless residents and students even lost your own lives in the fight."

Noble paused for a moment and pondered his next statement carefully. "But, Lieutenant, we must remain extremely humble regarding the pandemic. Against the infection itself, we have done nothing. No one is even sure what influenza really is. We did not stop it. It simply ran out of susceptible hosts...and moved on. We have had no more effect on the influenza agent than Europeans did with bubonic plague in 1347. This is not a comforting thought, Lieutenant."

Noble's comments were a sobering reminder that medicine had not "won" the war against influenza. Rather, it was more like a unilateral withdrawal by the victor. True, the eastern United States had seen a substantial reduction in influenza deaths in the last two weeks. But, this was not the case in other parts of the country where the pandemic was still increasing.

Noble again praised the young Schafer for his excellent hard work and leadership. Noble then left the quarantine ward in order to find other residents and nurses he could give similar praise.

On Wednesday, November 6th, Lillian Noble took the trolley with her husband to Boston City Hospital. She wanted to help Milton Rosenau put finishing touches on his manuscript describing results of the Gallops Island experiments. Rosenau was beginning to submit the manuscript for a *Journal of the American Medical Association* editorial review. Late in the morning, both Lillian and Rosenau dropped by the A.I. Office to see if Noble could have lunch with them. They found the Major seated at the large central office table with many stacks of cables before him. He was apparently in the process of categorizing them in some unknown fashion. As the two entered the office, Noble looked up and greeted them.

"Hi, dear," said Lillian. "What are you up to?"

"Well," said Noble, "over the last few weeks many messages transcribed in the A.I. Office have not been sorted, or even read. I have become intrigued by many of them, and want to be sure they are kept safe somewhere."

"What kind of messages do you mean, Edward?" asked Rosenau.

"These multiple stacks before me represent individual descriptions of the pandemic in various parts of America, and at various times. They represent random accounts by common citizens. As I read them, it became clear to me that these accounts are some of the best historical records of our trying times. I want them to be secured for future generations. Once they are properly prepared, I will have the A.I. Office Lieutenants systematically categorize them for inclusion in the National Archive in Washington D.C."

Lillian and Rosenau both sat on the oak coaster chairs near the center table. Lillian asked, "Dear, this is fascinating. Can you share some of the cables with us?"

"If you have a moment, I would love to," said Noble. He began to reach across the table and read random cables out loud. As he read, Lieutenant Lafayette took off her headset and swung her coaster chair around so she could also listen to the Major.

"Let's see," said Noble. Here are some of the cable stories."

'Pennsylvania: The Maffeo family had emigrated from Italy. When the pandemic swept through the Maffeo's small farming community in Pennsylvania, all seven of Constance Maffeo's children fell ill. A separate room in their house was curtained off for the infirmed. She wore a gauze mask when caring for them. Four of the children, Frank, Dominic, and the twins; Nick and Rosa, died. The other three surviving children said later they knew when one of the others was not going to live. Their mother, Constance, would sit with the dying child in the family's creaking rocking chair and sing to him or her. When the rocking chair stopped creaking, they knew their sibling was gone.'

'Wilson, North Carolina: A Methodist clergyman's wife, Mrs. Stanbury, was comatose for several days with influenza.

Her three year old son stayed with her during the family's ordeal. For weeks his mother remained ill, and the boy watched an endless procession of hearses and coffins outside his home. He now cries when he hears any automobile or cart wheels on a street.'

'Cedar Rapids, Nebraska: Thomas Langan had five children, and four of them became seriously ill with influenza. Within four days, three of his children died. Thomas's wife died of influenza less than one month later.'

'Shenandoah, Virginia: Twenty year old Gussie Gordon Bumgardner said about her fight with the grippe, 'I thought I was going to die. In my high fever, I remember lying in the front room and watching hearse after hearse with the influenza dead pass by my window outside. At times, I wished I was one of them'.'

'Bellflower, Missouri: Mary Hensley was a strong farm wife who had eight children. She awoke one morning healthy and ready for her chores, and was dead from influenza by sunset the next day. The small church in that community could not keep up with the funerals, and many stayed away because of fear. In the same town, Amos Brownell was a lively railroad switchman. He too was healthy one day, and died the next day of influenza. His burial was delayed for weeks because gravediggers could not keep up with the demand.'

'Provo, Utah: A family's four sons, Eugene, Knight, Mark, and Joseph, were all ill with influenza and confined to a semienclosed summer porch at their house. This was for 'fresh air treatment' ordered by the family doctor. As the boys lay on the porch, they could hear the horse-drawn hearses going back-and-forth continuously, day and night, taking the dead to the cemetery.'

'Mountain View, Missouri: Evelyn and Gordon Cox had six children. Four of the children; Virgil, Theodore, Myrtle, and Dora, went for a sleigh ride. One of the other children wanted to go on the ride, but could not make it. Within one week, all four of the sleigh ride children were dead from influenza. It was so cold that the family put the bodies outside to await burial. Before he died, one of the boys said, 'Just put me outside. I will join the others in a few days'.'

'Manayunk, Pennsylvania: Winifred Conner wrote about war rationing of heatless Mondays, meatless Tuesdays, no sugar...and then the influenza came. Her daughter, Mary Agnes, was expected to die by the next morning. Somehow, she survived and described the routine outside her house as she lay helpless with the febrile illness. 'Wagons came up the street each morning. Families brought out their dead to load into the wagons without coffins'.'

'Ooltewah, Tennessee: Twenty-one year old Beulah Justice-McAnnally commuted to Chattanooga several times a week to attend art school. Many times she went through the terminal station in Chattanooga and saw coffins that contained the remains of soldiers that had died of influenza and were being sent home for burial. She recalls that the coffins 'were just every place'.'

'Waltham, Massachusetts: A senior in high school, Paul Burke, had a part-time job selling snacks on railroad trains. Sometimes he would work at the station serving Camp Devens. For weeks, the platform at the Devens station was stacked with coffins of recruits who had died of influenza.'

'Swain County, North Carolina: Wade Breedlove's family was overjoyed when he came home on leave from the army. They 'put the big pot in the little pot' for his visit, which means they cooked special meals and everyone came to visit. Only a few days later, Wade's entire family was terribly ill with influenza. Their throats throbbed with pain, and they coughed up huge amounts of sputum...and then blood. One of the women in the household gave birth while she was deathly ill. One night the entire family sounded as though they were drowning. The next morning, Ida and two year old Woodrow were dead. The newborn, Paul, died two days later. It was not immediately clear if Paul had died from influenza, or if he simply starved to death in a household where everyone was just too weak to take care of him.'

'Missouri: The Thompson family lost several members to influenza. They describe the horror of sickness and death everywhere. Coffins were even becoming in short supply.'

'Russell County, Virginia: Many miners and their families were ill and dying from influenza at the Wilder Coal Camp. Mrs. Breeding sewed day and night making the white shrouds for 'laying people out'. Healthy men were kept busy building pine boxes for caskets. Dr. Beckner came to the camp on horseback and asked Mr. Breeding to go to the moonshiners in the area and bring back plenty of moonshine. The moonshine was mixed with honey, sugar, and garlic salves as a remedy for influenza. Many in Russell County believe the concoction saved their lives.'

'New Jersey: A sailor was happy to be assigned to the USS Virginia, because he had a girlfriend named Virginia back home in New Jersey. Later, the ship's name was changed to USS Chatham. The crew saw this as an omen, since they regarded the change of the ship name as bad luck. The sailor later went to the home of his girlfriend, Virginia. Her mother answered the door, and burst into tears. Virginia had died of influenza. The sailor blamed his ship's name change for her death.'

'Alliance, Nebraska: The Red Cloud Indian family earned money periodically by traveling five days to Alliance, Nebraska and picking potatoes. In October the family had a full load of potatoes when they were told of 'a real bad sickness' coming. They decided to leave for home. When they reached Gering, Nebraska, several family members were deathly ill with influenza. It began to rain so hard that the family's wagons could no longer travel. A farmer allowed the family to stay on his property until the rain would stop. The family matriarch, Nancy Poor Elk-Red Cloud, saw that the situation was becoming dire. She instructed everyone to stay in their tents, and she would bring them food and water. In this way, she separated the ill from the healthy. Nancy boiled a big bucket of flat cedar tea and gave it to her family. No one was to use the cups of others. She 'smugged' the tents with sweet grass to help with breathing and to ward-off evil spirits. When severe coughing closed throats, she gave them sugar mixed with kerosene to open them. Nancy helped her family immensely by applying principles of quarantine, prevention of cross-contamination, providing hydration, and giving inhalation therapy. All of the Red Cloud family survived.'

'East Chicago, Indiana: Influenza was ravaging the neighborhoods, where every household had at least one death. The town posted guards on every block to keep people from moving around and transmitting influenza. The guards built fires in the middle of the streets in order to keep warm. The Seggerson family in East Chicago gargled several times a day with Listerine©, and credit their survival to it.'

'North Dakota: The rural North Dakota farming community outside of Bismarck consisted of tiny sod farmhouses. The close-knit community witnessed influenza deaths in every family known for miles around. The epidemic undermined the community's capacity to bury their dead, let alone care for the dependent survivors.'

'East Vineland, New Jersey: The Grillo family emigrated from Palemo, Sicily. Their home was near an intersection with the Mays Landing Highway, and soldiers traveling home from The War often stopped and ask for water. A few days after some soldiers had come by, the entire Grillo family became so ill with influenza that none of them could even get out of bed. An 'American' man (someone who spoke English) came to their house to check on them. He killed several chickens from their coop in order to make chicken soup for the family. He used a spoon to feed each person. The man helped family members to the outhouse, cleaned them up, changed the bed sheets, and cleaned their clothes. After all family members recovered from influenza weeks later, they went to the 'American's' house to thank him. His house was empty, and no one knew what happened to him. The Grillo family credited the man for saving their lives. And, they never even knew his name.'

'Cripple Creek, Colorado: Lorraine Brinton gave birth to her daughter in a hospital full of influenza patients. Four healthy robust high school students helped her home, since her husband was in the navy and stationed in San Diego. Next morning, two of the high school students were dead from influenza.'

'High Coal Camp, West Virginia: Mr. and Mrs. Hubble were both very ill with influenza, and were barely able to care for their baby, Ethyl. One morning Mrs. Hubble went to the kitchen to get something, and left the baby with her husband next to the wood stove for warmth. The baby woke up crying while her father was delirious and confused with fever. Her father thought his daughter was a wild cat attacking his family. He had lifted the baby over his head to throw her into the fire. Just then his wife ran into the room and grabbed the baby away from him.'

'Blackford, Kentucky: Eli Brantley's wife and six children were all extremely ill with influenza, and nearly all the homes in his neighborhood where filled with similar victims. Eli spent every minute of every day, for weeks, making sure his community was warm and dry. He milked neighbors' cows, fed their livestock, and provided them with fresh drinking water. His kindness saved the lives of many dozens of people.'

'Finney Hollow, Virginia: Mr. Sykes developed a cough syrup that was formulated with boiled and strained cherry tree bark and sweetened with honey. He then added a little 'white lightning', or moonshine. Along with the syrup was an adjunctive treatment of an ointment made of hog lard, kerosene, and camphor. The ointment was applied to the chest of the infirmed. Mr. Sykes, and the entire town of Finney Hollow, swear the syrup and ointment will cure the grippe.'

'Erie, Pennsylvania: Two boys, who were four years old, lived next door to each other. Both had been delirious with influenza fever for days. One boy's mother called the family physician who prescribed an experimental medication he called a 'shot'. The boy's mother consented to the treatment, while the parents of the other boy did not. Neither boy was expected to live through the night. The boy who did not receive the shot was dead the next morning, while the boy who received the injection lived. No one, including the doctor, was sure what medication the 'shot' contained.'

'Lusk, Wyoming: A physician in Lusk boasted that he had never lost a patient to influenza. His secret? 'Rotgut' blotto whiskey. The physician poured 'rotgut' into patients to make them cough and produce copious amounts of phlegm. During the pandemic the physician ran out of whiskey, and there was none to be had in the community. The only whiskey in Lusk was locked-up in the sheriff's office as evidence in a bootlegger's trial. The sheriff refused to release the liquor. So, the doctor recruited a few prominent Lusk citizens and formed a vigilante committee. The committee seized the whiskey, depriving the sheriff of his evidence.'

'Rainsville, New Mexico: Amelia Pacheco became deathly ill with influenza, and could not produce milk for her two month old son, Manual. The boy's father, Juan de Jesus, fed the boy coffee with sugar until he could afford to purchase a goat: The goat's milk sustained Manual until his mother was well.'

'Lewisport, Kentucky: Edward Gregory, his wife, and thirteen month old son all came down with influenza. His wife and child recovered, but he worsened. As his fever increased, he treated it by repeatedly ingesting one half-hand full of aspirin. Edward sweated completely through his mattress, and eventually died.'

'North Atlantic: Lloyd Nelson was a farm boy from Boone, Iowa, and was aboard a troop ship bound for France. Lloyd was assigned to help an officer who was ill with influenza. As he lay sick, the officer asked for some oranges and other fruit. After a time, Lloyd was able to find some fruit for the officer, who died before he could eat them. Lloyd ate the fruit himself. While hundreds of men with influenza died aboard ship, Lloyd did not become ill. He believed that his 'fruit therapy' saved his life.'

'Manitowoc, Wisconsin: Dr. Otto Wernecke was a dentist who died of influenza. The doctor was very kind, and performed many dental procedures for people on credit over the years. Many people felt that because the doctor died, they were not obligated to pay the money owed for his dental services. As a result, the doctor's family was thrown into poverty. They lost their home, their property, and became homeless.'

'Perry County, Kentucky: Officers of the U.S. Public Health Service reported huge numbers of influenza deaths in the mountains of Kentucky. Worse yet, many were starving to death even though there was an adequate amount food. Thousands were dying because no one would help them. Many people did not go near the ill for fear of contracting the grippe. Physicians were offered $100 to come to a community for just one hour. Many mountain villages witnessed 30% deaths of their entire populations.'

'Loveland, Colorado: The general hospital in Loveland, like many American cities, was full with influenza patients. An emergency hospital was set up by the Red Cross in the banquet hall of the Elk's Lodge on the second floor of the Community Building on Cleveland Street. All eight members of the Phye family were admitted to the emergency hospital. Within ten days all eight were dead. They were all buried together.'

'Campobello, South Carolina: William Perry had a prosperous taxi service. When soldiers returned home with influenza, William picked them up at the train station. However, as the number of influenza stricken soldiers grew, he stopped charging for his services. William died of influenza, throwing his young wife and son into poverty.'

Noble placed the cable he had just read back onto its specific pile, and leaned back in the oak coaster chair. He clasped his hands behind his head. He sighed deeply. The only other sound in the A.I. Office was the hissing of steam running through the heating system elements in the room. No one spoke for a long time.

Finally, Noble took off his glasses, rubbed his eyes with his fingers, and replaced his glasses on his nose. He said, "I realize that's a lot to hear, since you know it's only a tiny slice of the anguish our countrymen are experiencing. But Lillian, Milton, and Marié, this is only part of the global picture. We are beginning to receive intelligence from the rest of the world. In many parts of the world, the situation is worse, much worse."

"That's hard to imagine, Edward," said Lillian, who hung her head down as she spoke.

"It is, Lilly," said Noble. "This…this demon…is not confined to cities or developed parts of the world. Oh no. It has an absolutely amazing ability to go anywhere and everywhere. It is on every continent. It is in areas with frozen tundra and ice flows. It has reached the densest rainforests on the planet. It has made its way into the most desolate and driest deserts, and the smallest and most obscure islands. The farther it gets from civilization, the more ferociously it feeds on people. And it is still very much at work."

The other three people in the office were riveted to Noble's discussion. Noble reached across the center table and picked up a handful of cables from a new pile. He began to read some of them.

'Labrador: In the village of Cartwright, all the citizens became ill two days after a boat sailed into port, and then left. Entire households were unable to feed themselves or find water. In Hebron, 68% of the entire small village died within a few days. The dead were found in their bedclothes, where their sweat had frozen to them. Army intelligence estimates that one-third of the population of Labrador is dead.'

'Frankfurt, Germany: Army intelligence estimates 27% of hospitalized patients have died of influenza.'

'Paris, France: Death rate with influenza is 10%, with 50% of survivors showing crippling compilations.'

'China: Statistics are not available. However, missionaries have stated that there are huge numbers of influenza deaths throughout China.'

'Gambia, Western Africa: Navy intelligence states that entire villages of three to four hundred are dead.'

'Fiji Islands: Influenza killed 14% of the population in sixteen days.'

'India: Civilian influenza deaths are not available. Missionaries describe bodies stacked in the streets of many cities. U.S. Army intelligence estimates 21.7% of all Indian troops are dead with the grippe.'

'Guam: The USS Logan docked in port with sailors ill with influenza. A few weeks later, about 5% of the entire native population of Guam was dead.'

'Switzerland, Spain, Sierra Leone, Senegal: Army intelligence believes these countries have lost in excess of 10% of their entire populations to the grippe.'

'Japan: Death rates are not known, but it has been reported that 33% of the population is severely ill with influenza.'

'Cape Town, South Africa: Navy intelligence reports 4% of the population dead with influenza in four weeks.'

'Buenos Aires, Argentina: 55% of the population severely ill with influenza.'

'Western Samoa: The steamer Talune brought influenza to the South Pacific island. 22% of the population has died.'

'American Samoa: The island is located just one hundred and ten miles west of Western Samoa. A rigid quarantine has been in effect in American Samoa, and there have been no influenza deaths to date.'

'Alaska: Members of Red Cross teams say that following the arrival of influenza, Eskimos 'could be extinct'.'

'Mexico: The state of Chiapas estimates 10% of its population is dead with influenza. In San Benito, Texas, along the Mexican border, Dr. Ralph Marshal Ward reported seeing the horizon covered with Mexicans fleeing to the U.S. They mistakenly believed that they would be safe in America.'

'Russia and Iran: The U.S. Army calculates that 7% of the entire Russian and Iranian populations are dead from influenza.'

Noble placed the cables from which he was reading onto a much larger stack on the table. He once again sat back in the oak coaster chair as he brushed a lock of white hair from his forehead. He rested his right hand atop his head, with his right elbow bent out in front of him. He tightened the muscles at the corners of his mouth that give a universal expression of dismay. The four people in the room spent the next few minutes simply looking at each other.

Noble then said matter-of-factly, "There are many more cables like the ones I just read. But, I think you get the idea. And, these are all just preliminary intelligence reports. There will be thousands more in the weeks to come."

After a time, Noble turned to Rosenau and said, "Milton, this is why your own work is so important, my friend. When the Influenza Commission picked you to lead many of the battles against this enemy, they picked exactly the right man for the job."

"I hope I'm up to the task, Edward," said Rosenau. "The Gallops Island studies didn't exactly spell out any useful clues about influenza."

"That simply is not true, Milton," said Noble emphatically. "Your studies did the opposite. They told all of us we don't even know, what we don't know, about the infection. The medical science community needed to hear that loud and clear. Many researchers thought the problem could be solved in a few weeks, and with meager resources. You showed the problem to be considerably more complex than most originally thought. The Gallops Island studies will also shake out many institutional and government 'pocket books' to liberate more money for research. Your research gave a needed slap of reality to those who have been working with influenza."

"We certainly gave it our best go," said Rosenau. "At the Harvard lab, and here at BCH, we'll now follow the two avenues of research that the Commission has asked us to tackle. We'll be working as hard as possible to identify the influenza agent using everything from porcelain filters to new culture techniques. We'll be sharing information with

Parks, Williams, Avery, Lewis, and dozens of others working simultaneously on the problem. In addition, we'll perform epidemiological studies to better understand the behavior of influenza. This can help us to make better predictions about other epidemics, and may even help point the way to finding the offensive organism itself. I know that Lillian has many jobs ahead for her in the coming weeks. However, I hope she can eventually help us with the work."

"I'd love to help, Milton," said Lillian. "But, I must first help New England and national social services get back onto their feet and mount an effort to help communities heal themselves. It's still pretty desperate out there."

"Lillian," said Rosenau, "I completely understand. You just let us know when you're ready."

Lillian and Rosenau had come to the A.I. Office simply to ask Noble if he could go to lunch with them. However, they had become enthralled with the intelligence reports telling of the breadth of national and global effects of the pandemic. Lunch time had come and gone. In view of the reports read to them, no one was particularly hungry anymore. Lillian and Rosenau went back to the BCH satellite laboratory, Noble resumed sorting cables, and Lieutenant Lafayette resumed monitoring world communications. All silently wondered if they had seen the end of this unprecedented and unpredictable pandemic.

In the evening of Sunday, November 10th, Noble returned home from a short visit to the A.I. Office. As he entered the house, he relayed to his wife some of the army transmissions he had read that day. "Lilly, things are really heating up in Germany."

"How so, dear?" said Lillian.

"Over the last twelve days, a revolution has been quickly gaining power in the German homeland. With resources depleted, supply lines cut off, advancing Allies, hundreds of thousands of troops incapacitated with influenza, and six million war casualties, Germany has finally moved toward peace."

"Oh, Edward, that is wonderful!" said Lillian. What a blessing!"

"German Chancellor Maximilian has been secretly negotiating with the Allies," said Noble. "Reportedly, German negotiations by cable with President Wilson hoped to offer better terms than the British or French. However, Wilson has reportedly continued to demand the abdication of the Kaiser."

"Has that posed a problem?" asked Lillian.

"Apparently it has, up until now," replied Noble. "Last Tuesday the Allies finally agreed to take up negotiations for a truce. There was no resistance in the country when the social democrat Philipp Scheidemann declared Germany a republic yesterday."

"A republic!" exclaimed Lillian. "This is truly unbelievable!"

"Yes, Lilly, this is monumental. Imperial Germany is now dead. A new Germany has been born, and it is called the Weimar Republic."

The Nobles went to bed knowing that The War could not last much longer. Still, fighting continued in many parts of northern France with the usual associated deaths. They both prayed that it would end soon.

Shortly after 11 PM that evening, the Noble home phone rang. Lillian awoke first and went into the parlor to answer the call. "Hello? [pause] Yes...yes. He's right here. I'll get him." Lillian quickly walked back into the bedroom. "Edward... Edward," she said as she shook her sleeping husband.

"Lilly...eh, what's wrong?"

"Edward, its Lieutenant Pierre-Louis. She says it's important." Noble took his round lens wire rimmed glasses from his night stand, put them on, and walked into the parlor. Lillian followed him.

"Yes, Lieutenant. [long pause] I see. Yes. [long pause] Thank you, Lieutenant. [pause] No, not at all. I'm glad you called. I'll see you at the office in the morning. Bye." Noble put the telephone receiver on its hook, took off his glasses, and rubbed his eyes. He stood motionless and silently in his bed clothes.

"Edward," said Lillian. "Edward. What is going on? Why did Claudette call? Edward. Edward!"

Noble put his glasses back on, and walked over to the parlor sofa. He slowly sat down and stared at the adjoining wall.

CHAPTER 24

"Edward!" said Lillian in a near yell.

"Lilly, on Thursday, acting German commander Paul von Hindenburg requested a meeting with French Supreme Commander of the Allied Armies, Ferdinand Foch. A German delegation headed by Matthias Erzberger crossed the front line in five cars. After driving ten hours through northern France, the delegation boarded Foch's private train car parked on a railway siding in the Compiegne Forest. Over the next three days, the talks between the Allies and the Germans were not negotiations. The Germans are in no position to negotiate much of anything. The discussions were only over the terms of the armistice. An agreement was reached, and signed, at 5 AM Paris time. That would have been 11 PM our time…just a few minutes ago."

Then Noble said," The armistice takes affect at 11 AM Paris time. The eleventh hour, of the eleventh day, of the eleventh month. That will be at 5 AM our time tomorrow. Lilly…in a little less than six hours…The War will be over."

Noble and his wife looked at each other for some time. Then, spontaneously, Noble jumped off the sofa as Lillian lunged toward him. They embraced tightly and kissed each other in an overflow of emotion and affection. The two went to bed with a new sense of optimism. The pandemic was waning, at least in New England. And now, The War...or as many now called it...The First World War...was coming to an end. It now seemed as though the future would be a bright one. That evening, Noble and his wife both experienced the kind of deep and wonderful sleep that comes from the magic of hope.

On the crisp autumn Monday morning, November 11th, Noble boarded an early trolley to Boston City Hospital. There were already hundreds more people in the Boston streets than usual. As the trolley headed south on Massachusetts Avenue, Noble could see the many ways Bostonians were processing the news. Some stood or sat alone in thought. Some formed groups of five to ten people to discuss the situation. Many already carried special editions of the Boston Globe in their hands. People were hugging, and kissing. Some people were dancing, and others just ran for no particular reason.

Noble entered the A.I. Office as Lieutenant Quellet jumped from her chair in attention and saluted. "Isn't it marvelous, Major! The War is over! Isn't it wonderful!"

Noble smiled, saluted back, and said, "It's God's blessing, Lieutenant. A blessing." Noble saw a New York Times front page on the center table. It read "ARMISTICE SIGNED, END OF THE WAR! BERLIN SEIZED BY REVOLUTIONISTS: OUTSTED KAISER FLEES TO HOLLAND." He sat down at one of the roll top desks, placed his right elbow on the oak desk top, and rested his head in his right hand.

"Major," said the Lieutenant, "are you alright?"

Noble took a moment to answer her. "Yes, Lieutenant. I'm fine. But I'm not sure everything else is".

"What do you mean, Major?"

"We now have two new problems," said Noble. "The short term problem is obvious if you look outside."

Lieutenant Quellet looked out of the second floor window. "Major, I see a lot of happy people. Very happy people. It looks like spontaneous victory parades have begun on both Massachusetts Avenue and Albany Street. There's even ticker tape falling from the buildings. Wow! Listen. The crowd outside the pavilion on Mass Ave is singing *Onward Christian Soldiers*. Can you hear it, Major?"

"Yes, I hear it very well, Lieutenant," said Noble. "You are looking at our first problem. Pockets of influenza are still very much with us in Boston. Throwing thousands of strangers into close quarters in the streets…talking, hugging, coughing, kissing…is going to unleash our 'friend' from those confined pockets. We must be ready for the inevitable in Boston, and the nation will have to be prepared as well."

"I see," said the Lieutenant, with a new look of worry on her face. "You said we have another problem?"

"Yes, we do," said Noble. "It is a blessing that The War is over. But, very soon, more than two million American soldiers will begin returning to the homeland from Europe. Massive numbers of men will quickly carry influenza for reintroduction into communities throughout the nation. In addition, no one knows what organism mutations will be on those troop transport ships. While the nation deals with a new immediate epidemiologic nightmare, it must simultaneously deal with a similar new long term problem. Lieutenant, I need your help."

The Lieutenant looked even more worried. "You can count on me, sir. What do you need?"

"Thank you, Lieutenant. The Signal Corps officers have always been a Godsend. First, I need you to transmit urgent cables to Army Surgeon General William Gorgas and Colonel Victor Vaughn. I'll help you draft the messages. But, in essence, I will plead with them to get the War Department to require a seven day minimum quarantine of all troops prior to boarding transport ships. Special quarters will need to be established in France for troops that show any signs of illness during the quarantine."

Noble continued, "Second, I want you to send a broad cable distribution to every U.S. Public Health Service bureau and every major American newspaper. The other Lieutenants have that distribution list for you to use, and the message will be similar to one I sent late last month. The only difference is that I will mention specifically the dangers in armistice celebrations and the return of our troops. Specifically put my name on all these cables, Lieutenant. I am the one responsible for sending them. Not you."

"Consider it done, sir," said the Lieutenant. She immediately went to large three ring binders on the book shelves to help her begin the cable transmissions.

Noble wrote out in long hand what he wanted in the messages. Last summer he had tried to work through the chain of command to warn the nation about influenza. These "channels" had only given him a cruel sense that he was a living example of Apollo's curse on Cassandra. But, unlike Cassandra, Noble refused to live through the endless pain and frustration of knowing the future and not being believed. This time he was going to act, knowing full well the possible consequences.

Noble left the office for the South Department pavilions. Small clusters of both hospital staff and even patients were participating in mini-celebrations. It was a stark, and pleasing, contrast to the mood of the hospital just a few weeks earlier. He found Dr. David Schafer tending to a fractured ankle, and quickly explained the problem. Noble wanted a second influenza quarantine ward set up immediately. He asked Dr. Schafer to instruct the hospital outpatient clinic staff to triage influenza patients into a clinic specifically for them. This time, the hospital would not make things worse by exposing every patient to influenza when they came to the clinics with other medical problems. Noble also asked that the BCH administrative staff warn other New England hospitals of the danger. Dr. Schafer had another resident take over the ankle fracture, as he literally ran off to fulfill the Major's orders.

As Noble travelled home by trolley that evening, there were now tens of thousands of revelers in the streets. Parades of all kinds were occurring on avenues both large and small. Fires in garbage cans were lit at street corners and added to the excitement. Bands all over the city played popular war tunes. There was also consumption of very large volumes of alcohol. Noble knew this would result in numerous brawls, with many subsequent emergency room visits. This would only complicate an already serious emerging situation.

In the second *Boston Globe* addition for the day, Noble read about the armistice terms. There would be an immediate removal of all German troops from France, Belgium, Luxembourg, and Alsace-Lorraine. All German troops would leave territories west of the Rhine River, plus thirty kilometers. All German troops would leave the eastern front, and return to German territory as it existed on August 1, 1914. The treaties with Russia and Romania were renounced. The entire German war ship fleet was to be immediately decommissioned and interned. Germany also had to surrender 5,000 cannons, 25,000 machine guns, 3,000 minenwerfer short range mortars, 1,700 airplanes, 5,000 locomotive engines, and 150,000 railcars.

At 2:30 PM, an official American government communication was published. "In accordance with the terms of the Armistice, hostilities on the fronts of the American armies were suspended at eleven o'clock this morning".

Now would begin the arduous task of crafting a peace treaty between the Allied Powers and the Central Powers.

Later that evening, over the loud protests of the seven children who wanted to participate in the celebrations, all those under the age of fifteen had to go to bed. Noble, Lillian, Florence, and Akeema sat in the parlor and had glasses of Champagne. Noble did not mention the new epidemiologic urgencies. He avoided dampening the high spirits of the others. Instead, everyone spoke of the future and how much better 1919 would be. They also discussed the enormous changes The War had brought to the world.

Army intelligence estimated that 70 million military personnel were mobilized during The War. Over 15 million people died. France lost 10.5% of its male population. Germany lost 15.1% of its men, and Austria-Hungary lost 17.1%. Four major world empires disappeared because of The War: the German, Austro-Hungarian, Ottoman, and Russian empires. Four medieval dynasties ceased to exist: the Hohenzollerns, Habsburg, Romanovs, and the Ottomans. New states emerged, such as Austria, Hungary, Czechoslovakia, Yugoslavia, Estonia, Finland, Latvia, Lithuania, and Poland. The Turkish core of the Ottoman Empire became the Republic of Turkey. The Balfour Declaration by the British government endorsed the creation of a Jewish Homeland in Palestine. Everyone in the Noble household knew these changes would affect generations to come.

On the cold Friday morning of November 15th, Noble entered the newly established second influenza quarantine ward in the South Department. The ward already had about fifty percent of its beds filled. Dressed in the usual white gown, rubber gloves, and gauze mask, Noble walked over to Dr. Schafer. Schafer was speaking with the second year medical resident, Dr. Anna Reed. "Oh, hi Dr. Noble," said Reed. "We were just talking about you."

"Hope there was something half-way good to say," said Noble smiling.

Reed laughed, "Don't worry about that, sir. David and I were just commenting on how you called this one exactly on the mark. Right, David?"

"On the money," said Schafer. "Just as you predicted, we began to see a real spike in influenza about seventy-two hours after the armistice celebrations began. But, because of you, we are pretty much ready for them this time. When the first influenza ward filled yesterday, we were ready with the second one here. Also, we have some of the BU and Harvard medical students outside the hospital outpatient clinics triaging patients. The grippe patients are immediately sent to a segregated influenza clinic. If patients look like they need admission, they are kept apart from the general hospital population during their entire admission. Nevertheless, we did have some deaths yesterday."

"Great job, in any case," said Noble. "Please keep me informed about the numbers of influenza admissions. If necessary, let me know every hour. My wife and I have made some thumbnail calculations on the extent of this pandemic increase. We have tried to incorporate what we know of the epidemiology, the type of public exposures over the last few days, and the numbers involved. The bad news is we had a lot of potential exposures all at once. But, the good news is the cramming of the public together was short lived. Also, we are certain there is a degree of immunity in some of the public now. So, given all of that, Mrs. Noble and I estimate we will need only two or three quarantine wards. When we hit eighty percent capacity in the second ward, let me know and we will have to open a third ward."

"Do we have your permission to open another ward as you have directed, sir?" asked Schafer.

"Absolutely," said Noble. "If anyone disagrees, or tries to stop you, just send them over to me immediately. I take full responsibility for this plan."

Both residents said they would monitor the situation just as Noble had asked. The three spoke of the various logistical matters of opening a third ward, when an army Medical Department Corporal walked up to Noble. "Major Noble?"

"Yes, Corporal. Can I help you?"

"Sir," said the Corporal, "Lieutenant Lafayette at the A.I. Office asks that you come over right away."

Noble thanked the Corporal, and excused himself from Drs. Schafer and Reed. It was unusual for the Signal Corps officers to call him like this, so he walked quickly. As he entered the office, Lieutenant Lafayette said, "Oh, good Major. You're here. Colonel Vaughn is on the telephone, sir. He wants to talk to you right away." Noble told her he would take the call in the small office. He closed the door to the smaller room, sat at his desk, and put the telephone receiver to his ear.

"Colonel…Colonel Vaughn? Are you there, sir?"

The telephone reception was uncharacteristically good today as Vaughn said, "Edward! I am so glad I can get a hold of you. How are you and the family doing?"

"We're doing great, sir," said Noble. "It's been a wild week."

"No kidding!" said Vaughn. Things are really wild here in D.C. You can imagine all the happy military in the city. Congressmen are also happy as hell, and it isn't because of all the alcohol!"

"There has been plenty of ethyl alcohol ingesting here too, sir. And that is saying a lot for Boston!"

Vaughn let out a belly laugh. "Edward, first I want to tell you what a great job you and Lillian did in Manhattan two weeks ago. You knocked the medical establishment's socks off! You two reminded the rest of the profession that it is high-time they actually thought like scientists. Scores of researchers and clinicians returned home with new tools to use in their work. Edward, I can't tell you how proud your father would be with you...and his daughter-in-law."

"Thank you, sir," said Noble. "Coming from you, that is truly a great honor."

"I have a few other items to talk about, Edward," said Vaughn. "First, I have some great news. After General Gorgas received your cable, he personally walked over to the War Department and requested an urgent meeting with Secretary Newton Baker. The Army Surgeon General basically demanded a seven-day troop quarantine in Europe. I'm sure the events of the last two months have changed many points of view. In any case, you got your one week quarantine, Edward!"

"Oh, Colonel!" yelled Noble. "That's...that's...wonderful!"

"As you know," said Vaughn, "General Gorgas is retiring. This is pretty much his last action in a long and very distinguished career. He has always trusted your judgment, Edward, and he wanted you to know that."

"This is a double honor, Colonel," said Noble. "Both you and the General will go down in history as giants in epidemiology and the study of infectious diseases."

"I don't know about that," said Vaughn. "However, I do have another thing to talk to you about."

"What's that?" said Noble, although he knew exactly what the "thing" was.

"Well," replied Vaughn, "yesterday the civilian Surgeon General himself, Rupert Blue, barged into my office and screamed, 'Colonel, who is this Major Noble? He's under your command in Boston, I'm told! Who the hell does he think he is, anyway?' When I got Blue to calm down a bit, I found out what he is all riled up about."

"I know what he is riled up about, sir," said Noble, as he began to grit his teeth.

"Edward, I completely understand your position in this situation, because it exactly mirrors my own. But, you have to understand the political currents here. Surgeon General Blue has many friends in very high places. I understand he is very friendly with the President. He certainly has many friends among the Joint Chiefs of Staff, many high-ranking generals, and a load of politicians in Congress. Many people in the U.S. Public Health Service, which he leads, are beholding to him because he gave them jobs. He's not really someone you want upset with you."

Vaughn continued, "Blue is quoted in nearly every American newspaper saying most citizens have little to fear with influenza. His greatest concern is public hysteria and the harm that could cause. At the same time, you are contacting newspapers and the Public Health Service and saying exactly the opposite. You are an esteemed Internist, and Infectious Disease subspecialist, whose comments carry great weight in the medical community, Edward. It would be one thing if you were a private citizen with an opinion. However, you are a U.S. Army medical officer attached with the Communicable Disease Division. And, you are sending cables from a U.S. Army instillation that Blue finds inflammatory. Can you see the danger here, Edward?"

Noble felt his respiratory rate increase as he bit his lower lip, and closed his eyes tightly. He could feel his face heat as he carefully chose his next words. He took in a deep breath, and let it out slowly.

"Edward?" said Vaughn. "Are you there, Edward?"

Noble stopped biting his lip. "Yes, Colonel. I'm here."

Noble went on, "Colonel, please know I would never want to put you in the middle of something like this. I cannot tell you how much I appreciate your confidence and support. But, Colonel, I cannot sit idly by and watch more of the horror of the last months fall upon the nation. There are things individuals, organizations, and communities can do to lessen the risks. But, they will not act if there is no sense of urgency. We have a lethal pandemic that continues to spread to every square inch of the United States. Americans have grouped themselves closely together in celebration just at a time when they shouldn't. And, a couple million of our favorite sons are about to come home...perhaps with more deadly disease in their bodies. The nation <u>can</u> fight this, if they <u>know</u> about it. And, I am going to tell them. As far as I am concerned, the Surgeon General is a complete fool."

It was now Vaughn who paused for a time. "Edward, I am not going to command you to stop writing your cables. I am also going to defend you in every-and-all ways at my disposal. However, I need to caution you about the forces that may come after you. Profound and powerful forces. I may not be able to stop them, Edward. Do you understand what I am saying?"

"Yes, Colonel, I know exactly what you are saying. I am going into this with my eyes wide open."

"Ya' know what, Edward?"

"What, sir," said Noble.

"The only man I ever met that was more of a stubborn son-of-a-B than you, was Dr. Charles Noble. Gee, you are a chip off the ol' block, Edward!"

Noble chuckled. "I take that as a compliment, Colonel."

"You should," said Vaughn. "Charles was a great man. Your father didn't take any crap from the brass during the Civil War, and you're following right in his footsteps. I gotta' go, Edward. But, we'll be in touch."

Noble put the telephone receiver on its hook. He sat for awhile at his office desk and thought about all "Uncle Victor" had said. He decided he would mention nothing of this to Lillian, who would be beside herself with worry if he did. He then walked back into the main office to monitor progress with his cables to newspapers and USPHS bureaus.

CHAPTER 25

B y Wednesday, November 20th, it was clear the Nobles' epidemiologic projections were correct. The pandemic surge from armistice celebrations was temporary and not sustained. Only two quarantine wards were needed in Boston City Hospital, with a similar proportion in other Boston area hospitals. The number of influenza admissions was already at a steady state with discharges. There was one sobering finding, however. Influenza mortality rates in BCH, and as reported by social services in the communities, was identical to the October rate. The difference was a much smaller overall influenza case rate. This meant to Noble that the responsible agent was just as virulent as ever. The demon was simply having a harder time finding prey.

Since The War was over, many military deployment plans had suddenly changed. Much to the delight of her parents, Ensign Florence Noble was informed that she would not be going to Europe. Instead, given the local need, Boston City Hospital and the Naval Reserves both agreed to allow her to assist the Red Cross in community health outreach. Florence was very pleased to be assigned duty with one of the chapter's senior officers: her mother. And, there was plenty to do.

During a light autumn rain this Wednesday, Florence met her mother at the Commonwealth Avenue Red Cross Center. She was dressed in her navy uniform, and her mother was wearing a tan mid-calf light rain coat with brown knee-high boots. Florence waited for her mother to complete a phone call with a Boston Catholic parish social worker.

"What's the plan today, Mom?" said Florence.

"The first order of business today is the huge orphan issue," said Lillian. "The Red Cross estimates that tens of thousands of New England children are now without parents, or have one or two parents that can no longer care for them. We've organized teams of Red Cross volunteers to help locate orphaned children and bring them into safe environments. Camp Devens has even permitted Sergeant Campbell, with an army staff car, to join in the effort."

Lillian continued, "The Red Cross usually receives orphan referrals from concerned neighborhood citizens. After the referrals, volunteers drive to houses and apartment buildings to locate orphaned children. Sometimes the volunteers encounter homeless children living on the streets. However they are found, all the children needing care are taken to city or county shelters, churches, or even private homes. I was just on the telephone with a parish that is willing to help in this regard. Once they have a place to sleep, warm dry clothes, food, and access to medical care, the job of permanent placement begins."

"And, that is the really hard part, right?" said Florence.

"No kidding," said Lillian. "It's always difficult in a normal economy. But, there are so many more barriers now. Rationing during The War has made child adoption, or the establishment of guardians, much more difficult. The pandemic has left Boston, and much of the country, with a struggling financial system that is far from back on its feet. City, county, and state treasuries have been drained, and projected budgets going into the 1920's are dismal. The mid-west and western segments of the country are still very much nearing their peaks of the pandemic. Therefore, national agricultural production and manufacturing is still decreasing. On top of everything else, we have the other problem."

"What problem is that, Mom?" asked Florence.

"In a single word, Florence, it's poverty. Sudden and profound poverty. Large families may be otherwise intact, but many previously healthy breadwinners are now dead. Many young families are now rock-bottom poor. It's not just an issue over the necessities of food, clothing, and shelter. It is also the nurturing and education of the young...or the lack of it. This will have an enormous impact on the coming generations."

"I didn't think of that, Mom," said Florence. "I doubt many are thinking about pandemic effects in that way."

"Unfortunately, I think you're right," said Lillian. "It's actually worse still. Many countries have lost a huge number of their young men to war. An even larger number of young men and women have now died from the pandemic. This will definitely have colossal social and economic consequences for decades. We can't even predict what those consequences might be."

Lillian continued, "For now, our three biggest social problems are orphaned children, the new poverty, and greatly reduced social services for the aged and infirmed. That is where we come in, my dear."

"I'm ready to do what I can, Mom." Florence paused for a moment, and pursed her lips together as she lowered her eyes. "You know, Mom...just now it was almost like I heard Arthur say those words. 'You can do what you can do.' He always used to say that."

Lillian just smiled the way all people do when they remember how much they loved someone who is gone. Rather than dwell on that, she quickly decided to "do what you can do" and picked up the telephone earpiece. She had several more church parishes and prominent Boston citizens to call and ask for help in the city's orphan crisis. Later, she and Florence would start making calls to Red Cross volunteers about establishing regular and long-term automobile food shuttles. The city government had no more funds for this kind of effort, and it was now up to the citizens themselves to step in. Widows, widowers, the dependent elderly, and the chronically ill might require months or years of intensive assistance. Lillian would need to use all of her local, state, and national contacts to put assistance programs together in New England and in other parts of the country. She was up to the task.

Late in the morning, the two Noble women went on a drive through South Boston with Sergeant Campbell. The Nobles had made these journeys for several days, and Florence called them "orphan patrols". The large Boston population of children living alone, or in the streets, had learned of the "orphan patrols" and began to recognize the volunteers in the automobiles. The army staff car was particularly easy to spot. Scores of children came up to the staff car as it drove through the South Boston neighborhoods. The most Lillian and Florence could do was take down names and addresses of children, or where they could be found, so that other volunteers could return for them. The army staff car always arrived back at the Red Cross Center with a load of the youngest children, or ones that were ill. A frantic attempt of treatment and child placement then commenced.

There was another problem Lillian could not yet completely define in her own mind. It was a subjective feeling she had when talking to many influenza survivors. It was hard to pinpoint, and even harder to describe. But, nevertheless, it was there. The only words she had found to portray this feeling were 'lowered vitality'. Deep and pervasive lowered vitality. And it bothered her.

On the afternoon of Friday, November 22, Major Noble walked over to one of the outpatient Boston City Hospital pavilions to fill in for an ailing attending. Noble agreed to supervise the residents and medical students in the Neurology clinic for a few hours. Right next to the Neurology clinic, in the same pavilion, was the Psychiatric outpatient clinic.

Noble entered the Neurology clinic patient care area. As he walked past an exam room, he saw Dr. David Schafer seated beside a patient lying on her left side on a padded table. The patient was facing away from the young doctor. Schafer's back was to the open exam room door so that he could not see Noble. Noble watched Schafer palpate the patient's spine. He located the space between the lumbar vertebral bodies numbered 4 and 5. He cleaned the area with iodine, and instilled a local anesthetic under the patient's skin with a needle. He then inserted a long thin spinal needle into the chosen area until he felt the needle pass through the dura matter of the spine. He continued to push the needle until it passed through the arachnoid matter and into the spinal subarachnoid space. He then attached a twelve inch long slender column monometer to the needle as fluid filled it. He took a measurement, and then began to collect more of the fluid in glass test tubes.

As Schafer removed the needle from the patient's spine, Noble remembered the first time he had seen a lumbar puncture for the collection of cerebral spinal fluid (CSF). He was a first year medical student at the time. An assistant professor at Harvard, Dr. Arthur Wentworth, had brought the technique from Germany the year before. Wentworth demonstrated a lumbar puncture during a Neurology lecture at Boston University.

Schafer stood up from his stool, turned, and saw Noble. "Dr. Noble! I didn't know you were here. I heard you were going to attend for the day."

"Yes...and good job. I see you have ample CSF for analysis. What's the story with this patient?"

"Dr. Noble, you're <u>really</u> going to find this interesting." Schafer asked the patient to lie on her back for a few minutes. He then said, "This is Mrs. DiGuilio who is thirty-five years old. Do you mind if you tell Dr. Noble what brings you hear today?"

"No, that's fine, Dr. Schafer," said DiGuilio. "For the last few weeks I have been having some trouble walking. And I seem to be dropping things."

Noble noticed that her speech was unusual. It sounded as though her tongue was thick. Her speech rhythm was shortened, the tone high-pitched, and the volume very soft.

"I see," said Noble. "Have you had any head injuries, loss of consciousness, a stiff neck, or one side of your body with difficult movement or sensation?"

"No, not really," said DiGuilio. "I've never had anything like this before."

"Have you had any new medications, or do you drink alcohol?" said Noble.

"Nope," said DiGuilio.

"Have you had any fevers, chills, unexplained weight loss, or excessive sweating?"

"Not now," said DiGuilio. "But, boy was I sick with the grippe a little over a month ago! I was in bed for a week with such a very high fever! I thought I was going to die."

The two doctors excused themselves briefly to examine the CSF under the microscope, and invited the patient to rest after her lumbar puncture. In a nearby clinic laboratory room, Noble noted that the CSF was clear, had no red blood cells, and had a very slight lymphocytic pleocytosis of seven white cells/µL. The opening pressure of the CSF had been a normal 180 mmH2O.

The two men returned to the patient, and Noble performed a physical exam. Most of the exam was completely normal. This included a normal oral, neck, and muscle strength examination. But, in addition to her speech, Noble noted other abnormalities. DiGuilio had a horizontal bilateral eye nystagmus and a fine resting bilateral hand tremor. She also had difficulty maintaining her trunk position. When seated, her body moved side-to-side and back-and-forth. Then, she quickly moved back to an upright position. These seated motions repeated themselves. The finger-to-nose test showed that she over or under-shot touching a finger placed before her. She had difficulty performing rapid alternating hand movements, called dysdiadochokinesia. Her gait was staggering, lurching, unsteady, and wide-based. Interestingly, her sensation to touch and reflexes were all normal.

The two doctors stepped out of the exam room for a moment. Noble said, "Well, the woman has acute cerebellar ataxia. Rarely, this occurs days or weeks after measles or typhoid fever. It can resolve over months, or be permanent. However, because the woman is a pandemic survivor, my guess is that you and the residents have made another connection."

Schafer smiled a mischievous grin. "Awe, yes! The Internal Medicine detective work begins! But, we're getting ahead of the story. Let me have one of the BU medical students tell Mrs. DiGuilio about her prognosis, and then I have some other patients to show you."

Schafer went off into the clinic to speak to some of the other residents. He returned for Noble, and escorted him to another Neurology clinic exam room. There, another resident introduced thirty year old Mr. Tyner, who was an accountant. "Can you tell us again what's bothering you?" asked the resident.

"What's bothering me the most is that I'm forgetting things. My wife says I can't seem to stay attentive to things at home. My boss at work is saying the same thing."

"We've talked about some of your other problems, Mr. Tyner," said the resident. "Can you tell Dr. Noble about them?"

"Sure," said the patient. "I'm having difficulty walking and sleeping. I also seem to sweat all the time, although it hasn't been hot. I've also been pretty depressed since the grippe."

"How long ago did you recover from the grippe?" asked the resident.

"Oh, about a month ago," said the patient. "But, all of this other stuff started about ten days ago."

Noble's physical exam of the patient showed a mild cognitive impairment in recent memory recall. Mr. Tyner had a right hand resting tremor. His limbs had some slight rigidity from increased muscle tone, and there was an accompanying slowness to his movements. This is known as bradykinesia. The patient's performance of sequential and simultaneous movements was hindered. His gait had a forward-flexed posture, was slowed, and he walked with small steps.

The three doctors excused themselves for a moment, and walked into the adjoining clinic hallway. Noble said, "This is getting interesting, gentlemen. Mr. Tyner appears to have paralysis agitans, or Parkinson's disease. However, its onset is so rapid. And, it started only a few weeks after influenza. I've never seen this before. Therefore, I don't think we can tell the patient what his prognosis is. We are either dealing with something very rare, or altogether new." The resident returned to the exam room to explain to the patient what they knew, or didn't know, of his disorder.

Schafer had another patient to show his attending physician. He and Noble walked into another clinic exam room where Dr. Anna Reed was interviewing a twenty-seven year old man. "Sir, this is Dr. Noble," said Reed. "Can you kindly repeat some of the things we have talked about since you arrived?"

"Absolutely," said the patient. "I'm having trouble walking...actually, climbing stairs. When I comb my hair I have to stop and rest my arms. They just feel...heavy. It seems to be getting worse."

Noble then said, "Hello, sir. Are you otherwise in good health? Do you take any medication, or do you drink alcohol?"

"I've been in great health, doctor, and I have been very athletic all my life." said the patient. "That is, until I had the grippe about five weeks ago. I was really sick. I felt better for a few weeks, and then this all started up. Oh, and I don't use any medicines, and I have never used alcohol."

Noble conducted his third neurological examination of the afternoon. Noble asked him to spread his arms out like an airplane, flex his elbows, and then try to resist an attempt to press his arms down. He had the patient sit up from a supine position, and noted that his head lagged behind the rest of his body. The patient was unable to rise from a seated position without the use of his upper extremities. He could not perform a deep knee bend. The rest of his exam was normal. Specifically, there was no marked muscle atrophy or tenderness, his reflexes were normal, and he had no Babinski sign.

Noble, Reed, and Schafer left the exam room briefly to discuss the case. Noble said, "The patient has bilateral deltoid muscle weakness at 3 of 5, neck flexor weakness that is 4 of 5, and bilateral quadriceps muscle weakness at 4 of 5. So, we have a real muscle weakness and not asthenia. By history, his muscle weakness is progressive. This apparent myopathy is symmetric, localized and proximal in distribution. And, it seems to have started weeks after a run with influenza. You might consider asking a surgical resident to obtain a biopsy from an effected muscle. We need to learn more about this myopathy."

Dr. Reed went back to attend to her patient as Noble and Schafer talked further. "Dr. Noble," said Schafer, "I wanted you to see what the residents are now encountering in Neurology clinic. The striking thing is that there are a lot of patients with the same stories. I was able to show you representative cases in short order because there are so many of them, and all day long."

"David," said Noble, "you and the other residents are likely seeing something very new, and extremely important. You all might want to consider carefully documenting your observations and submitting them for publication."

"There's more, Dr. Noble," said Schafer. "Much more. In patients with a history of the grippe this fall, we have seen a full range of neurological signs and symptoms. I believe they are influenza complications. They include difficulty with eye focusing, confusion, peripheral neuropathies, and something the residents are calling the 'wobbly leg syndrome'. The 'wobbly legs' are sometimes due to ataxia, myopathy, or a motor neuron disorder. Some patients come in with muscle twitching of the face and forearms. We think we saw a case of encephalitis lethargica last week, with extreme lethargy that was almost catatonia."

"This is remarkable, David," said Noble, who recalled Harvey Cushing referring to his own "wobbly legs".

Schafer continued, "Of interest are recent comments by the Psychiatric clinic residents. They tell us of a huge range of problems in post-influenza patients. Mental inertia, delirium, severe melancholia, anxiety, dementia, hysteria, restlessness, irritability, fear, slowed cerebration, boisterousness, suicidal ideation, and violence are now seen every day. The psychiatrists are diagnosing post-influenza psychosis and even schizophrenia. It is also worrisome that these psychiatric patients seem to have a very slow and tedious convalescence. Some patients show no evidence of improvement at all."

"The implications here for the health care system, community social services, and even law enforcement, are obvious and quite disturbing," said Noble. "My wife told me something just last night. She has been out in the communities trying to help orphans and those who can't care for themselves. There are lots of them, too. She has used the term 'lowered vitality' to describe what she sees among the citizens. I wonder if her observation is a mild form of what you are seeing here in the neuropsychiatric clinics. This is very, very troubling. It has enormous ramifications for the entire nation now, and for the future."

The attending physician and his third year resident then went off to care for more Neurology clinic patients.

For several weeks, Lillian Noble had been sending letters and cables to people who might be related to the McCracken children. Lillian, Florence, and Akeema had taken careful histories from the four children, looked at the few personal effects they brought with them, and had searched their old apartment for any information they could find. There was not much to go on. The children remembered some vague names and places, but they were not sure who those people were. Lillian had found a few cancelled checks, and envelopes without letters, in a closet shoebox in the apartment. This information provided the only leads they had.

That all changed on Saturday, November 23rd. Early in the afternoon, Lillian went to the Noble mail box and found a letter from Mr. and Mrs. Silveira. The letter explained that a great uncle had forwarded one of Lillian's letters to them. Mrs. Silveira was a first cousin to the children's mother, making the McCracken children her first cousins once removed. The couple lived on a five hundred acre ranch outside of Sedona, Arizona, which was twenty miles south of Flagstaff. The Silveiras bred horses, raised cattle, and also grew peaches and apples. In their late forties, they were without children of their own. However, they were excited about having the McCracken children live with them.

Lillian immediately wrote a letter giving more details about the children, and asked questions about available education in the area. She also asked specific questions about the Silveira home, their per capita income, and said the Nobles would need three personal references. Lillian placed a return special delivery airmail envelope with her letter, and quickly posted her letter special delivery airmail. There was no way to know if there was any airmail service near Sedona, but at least the letter would travel to Arizona as fast as possible by train.

On Monday Lillian went to the County Clerk's office to verify the existence of a Silveira ranch, and to check for any criminal records. She also contacted the Red Cross, the Women's Auxiliary, and the Bureau of Child Hygiene to find out any useful information about the Silveiras. She also asked Edward to send cables to law enforcement agencies in Flagstaff and Phoenix. In a week or two, Lillian promised herself that she would know more about the Silveiras then they knew about themselves.

Noble turned up his army coat collar against the moist cold wind as he sat on the Massachusetts Avenue trolley.

This action reminded him of his walks on the *USS Madawaska* decks, which seemed like such a long time ago. The late autumn Boston weather was living up to its historical reputation. This Thursday morning, November 28th, was overcast, dark, and doubly cold by a marked wind chill. A light snow had fallen the night before, and was already a muddy slush in the streets. At night it would freeze, and create a brown solid irregular ice layer that made Boston streets very hard to navigate. Noble referred again to the four New England months of November through February as "hibernation". It was always a question whether March would count as the fifth month.

The Boston City Hospital pavilions were generally kept comfortably warm during Boston winters. However, the second story A.I. Office on the building corner was usually cold. As Noble entered the office and greeted Lieutenant Pierre-Louis, he did not bother to take off his coat. The Lieutenant also had her army coat on along with a long neck scarf. The recurring hissing of the radiator heating system steam did not make them feel any warmer.

Among the routine communications today was a cable from Colonel Vaughn. He again congratulated the Nobles on their Influenza Commission talks and the positive influence they would have on American medicine. Vaughn's cable was also much more philosophical than his usual messages. He wrote of his sadness over Arthur's passing, and his delight over the signing of the armistice. But, it was his comments about influenza that made the biggest impression.

Colonel Vaughn wrote Noble, "The saddest part of my life was when I witnessed the hundreds of deaths of the soldiers in the Army camps and did not know what to do. At that moment I decided never again to praise the great achievements of medical science, and to humbly admit our dense ignorance in this case." Vaughn then wrote, "In the future, I will not be able to write extensively about the influenza pandemic. I just cannot do that. It is enough to say that it encircled the world, visited the remotest corners, taking toll of the most robust, sparing neither soldier nor civilian, and flaunting its red flag in the face of science."

Noble was interested in U.S. Public Health Service (USPHS) cables praising the efforts of San Francisco, as the pandemic approached the city. Hundreds of volunteers worked within city districts to transport medical personnel and supplies to where they were needed. Health officers immediately quarantined naval installations. Tens of thousands of gauze masks were given to the populace, and restrictions on public gatherings were in place weeks before the pandemic reached the city by the Bay. When schools and businesses closed, everyone flocked to volunteer stations to help. San Francisco was held up as a public health model for the rest of the nation.

Although the pandemic continued in many parts of the country, even the west was now seeing a decrease in overall cases and mortality. All the military and USPHS intelligence agreed in this regard. This is why two cables from USPHS did not raise any particular concern four Noble. The cables described isolated influenza increases in Montana and Alabama that seemed larger than one would expect. However, these isolated reports were within the context of a waning epidemic.

But it was an Army intelligence cable that made Noble's heart rate climb precipitously.

Thursday, November 28, 1918
From: Camp Pike, Arkansas

Approximately eight hundred troops admitted to the hospital with influenza.

Army Intelligence.

Noble slowly placed the telegram sheet on the center table. He suddenly felt beads of sweat appear on his forehead. He began to formulate a series of next steps as his hands trembled. He noticed he was breathing very rapidly, which made him dizzy. He was hyperventilating. He sat briefly in a desk chair until he felt more composed.

Noble stood again, and slowly walked over to Lieutenant Pierre-Louis. She glanced up at him as he approached, and slightly gasped. The Major was very pale, and very diaphoretic. "Major," said the Lieutenant, "Major Noble. Are you alright, sir?"

Noble spoke so quietly that Pierre-Louis could barely hear him. "Lieutenant, the following request is highest priority. I will tell you what to write in a minute. However, send another broad cable distribution to the newspapers and USPHS bureaus. I will need to send urgent messages to Colonel Vaughn and the Naval Quarantine stations in Boston Harbor. I will also want a call made to Lieutenant Commander Milton Rosenau at the Chelsea Naval Hospital.

"Major," said the Lieutenant in a strained voice, and worried expression, "what is the matter, sir?"

Noble stood motionless so long that the Lieutenant repeated herself. "Major, what is the matter?" Noble continued to pause. His slow eventual answer was almost a whisper.

"It's back."

CHAPTER 26

By Monday, December 2nd, Noble had once again sent cables to hundreds of American newspapers and dozens of USPHS bureaus. Colonel Vaughn and the others had also been contacted. In the cables he described the epidemiologic reasons why the Camp Pike influenza spike was not part of the autumn pandemic wave. In fact, this represented an emerging "third wave" of the pandemic. Rather than wait for confirmation that could take weeks, Noble had decided to act decisively now. Public Health Service officers and nurses would be required to travel quickly. Medical and public hygiene supplies, and food, needed to be stockpiled promptly. Preparations for expanding hospital services and facilities were essential. And, most importantly, strict and immediate quarantines needed to be enforced. Noble asked Lillian to increase a sense of urgency among the Red Cross, Women's Auxiliary, and local, state, and federal governments.

Boston City Hospital, and numerous other local hospitals, was already well prepared. Even though the satellite hospitals had been closed, they could be opened and operating within a few hours. The BCH influenza quarantine ward was readied, and there were now contingency plans in place for opening others. Supplies were more ample than before the "second wave", and more would be procured with the advanced warning. The house officers, nurses, aids, and attendings were all now seasoned in the care of critically ill influenza patients.

Noble knew it was always a mistake to believe one was prepared for the demon. Still, he could not help but feel that way this time.

In the A.I. Office, as Noble passed by Lieutenant Quellet, he noticed that she was preparing a cable with the title "Urgent: Boston Harbor Quarantine". He waited for her to complete its transcription, and then asked if he could read it. She handed him the yellow paper telegram.

Monday, December 2, 1918
From: Department of the Navy/U.S. Public Health
   Service/Boston Harbor Authority

Urgent: Boston Harbor Quarantine.

Beginning today, and until such time as the order is lifted, all ships entering Boston Harbor will observe a four day quarantine. Vessel captains will need to report any crew members showing signs of illness during the course of the quarantine. USPHS officers, and/or navy health personnel, will inspect all ship crew members as necessary until the quarantine is lifted. Such personnel have the authority to have any crew members taken to Navy health facilities, or to extend a ship's quarantine, as deemed essential. Please direct all questions and other enquiries to the Boston Harbor Authority.

Sincerely,
Commander Richard Cunard, USPHS.

Noble thought to himself how difficult it must have been, on many levels, for Cunard to send this memorandum. On the other hand, to his credit, the Commander was not making the same mistake twice.

On Monday, December 9th, Lillian accompanied Noble to the A.I. Office in order to begin modeling the incoming epidemiological data. Substantial pandemic increases in case numbers and mortality were now evident in diverse areas. USPHS and military intelligence cables showed the following: Iowa: Important increases. Kentucky: Larger numbers of schoolchildren than in the second wave were being infected in Louisville. Louisiana: Increases seen in New Orleans, Shreveport, and in Lake Charles mortality rates are equal to the second wave. St. Louis, Missouri: 1,700 new cases in three days. Nebraska: Considered serious increase. Ohio: Serious increases in Cincinnati, Cleveland, Columbus, Akron, Ashtabula, Salem, Medina. Pennsylvania: Mortality numbers worse than the second wave in Johnstown, Erie, Newcastle. Washington State: Very serious mortality spike. Arizona: Phoenix seeing worse mortality than in the second wave. Michigan: Mortality worse. Georgia: Quitman closing schools and re-enacting pandemic ordinances. Washington D.C.: Rising death rate.

Just eighteen days earlier, San Francisco had declared it had avoided almost all of the pandemic cases and mortality. But, that was then. Now, the third wave of the influenza pandemic rammed full-force into the city. The city by the Bay, only twelve years earlier, had endured the worst earthquake in U.S. history. Now, it experienced unbridled and unyielding influenza. California was seeing huge increases in mortality, but it was San Francisco that now burned brightest with death in the West.

Noble and his wife again sorted cables, drew upon influenza epidemiologic data, and produced spread sheets with calculations and projections. They concluded the influenza agent had mutated again. Some degree of immunity from the previous two waves seemed maintained. However, the agent was now capable of attacking both new and some previously exposed populations. At present, the third wave was more segregated than wave two. But, one thing was certain: Whatever influenza was caused by, it was now just as lethal.

Among the day's cables was a message from the Surgeon General to U.S newspapers.

Monday, December 9, 1918
From: U.S. Public Health Service

The country need not fear that the influenza epidemic will return. It has come and gone for good.

Surgeon General Rupert Blue

Noble read the telegram, and pounded his fist on the center office table so hard that it caused Lillian's cup of coffee to fall to the hard wood floor. He was red-faced when he rushed over to Lieutenant Lafayette and ordered her to send yet another set of cables to the newspapers and USPHS bureaus. Under his breath, Noble recited a number of things he would like to say to the Surgeon General in private some day.

The weather continued to cool, and snow became more frequent. In response to more uncompromising environmental conditions in the A.I. Office, Noble bought a very expensive new product called an area electric heater. It was a prototype from a new company called Watlow. It consisted of a series of elements that glowed red hot when electricity was sent through them. Noble brought the twenty pound heater to the office on Wednesday, December 11th, and no one ever saw a happier Second Lieutenant than Pierre-Louis. The heater only warmed a small area around it, and the A.I Office generally remained a cold place to work. But, when placed next to the Lieutenant's information post, it provided a measurable degree of comfort that was truly a luxury. The Lieutenant said she was so pleased she wanted to kiss the Major...but "that is something one does not do with a commanding officer". Noble laughed and laughed with the admission.

Early in the afternoon Lillian dropped by BCH between her trips from one Boston relief agency to another. As soon as she entered the room, Noble called her over to one of the office roll top desks. "Lilly, I think you'll get a belly-laugh over this." He handed her a cable to read.

Wednesday, December 11, 1918
From: U.S. Public Health Service

Please be informed that influenza has not passed, and severe epidemic conditions exist in various parts of the country. It is strongly advised that you stockpile necessary community and medical supplies, plan on the use of volunteers and medical personnel if influenza cases increase in your area, decide on appropriate quarantine plans, and exercise caution in large public contacts. Look for more alerts.

Surgeon General Rupert Blue

After reading the cable, Lillian sat down next to her husband and let out a great sigh. "Edward, it looks like your cables on Monday had an immense impact. The Surgeon General has, in effect, completely reversed himself on his assessment of the pandemic and his recommendations...in just two days."

"My guess is that Blue received a blast of negative responses from communities facing the pandemic's third wave. He apparently used my cables in his response. Maybe my attention to public education early on this time has helped." Noble smiled with that thought. "Lilly, have you had a chance to look at the epidemiologic spread of the infection to project when it might significantly affect Boston?"

Lillian frowned slightly. "Well, I've looked at the scant data that intelligence has provided, Edward. The problem with the third wave is that it's emerging from several centers in the country at once. The first and second waves had discernable starting points. This is not the case with the third wave. Of course, I have no idea why the infection is acting this way. Nevertheless, it makes it much harder to predict future influenza geographic involvements. It's simply acting differently this time." Both agreed that there was not enough information on which to draw an accurate epidemiologic model of the third wave.

On Monday, December 16ᵗʰ, Noble learned just how complicated the third wave would be. The first group of American troops returning from Europe was beginning to arrive. Noble came across an intelligence cable describing the USS Leviathan, and its eight thousand troops docking in Hoboken. In spite of the quarantine in France, one hundred fifty cases of influenza were aboard ship. Four soldiers had been buried at sea. Although this was a tiny fraction of the deaths aboard Leviathan in the fall, it was ominous news for two reasons. First, the quarantines set up by General Gorgas were not perfect, by any means. Second, lethal influenza was leaking into the United States at a time when the pandemic was already rising again. Noble realized the demon was attacking humankind this time from all directions, instead of the prior frontal assaults.

The A.I. Office continued to put as much pandemic information together as possible. There was no question that serious outbreaks persisted, and were increasing, in pockets throughout the U.S. Influenza was also increasing in Boston, although gradually. A second influenza ward had now been opened in Boston City Hospital. There was no way to predict its severity or peak, and therefore no way to send resources to particular areas ahead of time.

The U.S. Public Health Service was out of money, and was requesting more funding from Congress. At the same time, USPHS and the Surgeon General were again sending messages to the newspapers requesting calm. And again, Noble had Lieutenant Quellet distributed hundreds of telegrams that essentially rebutted the official statements.

That evening Noble returned home to find Lillian at the residence library desk with a few dozen documents spread out before her. "Hi, dear," she said. Sit with me."

"What's up, Lilly?" said Noble. "You look so serious."

"I'm not really serious," said Lillian. "I'm actually a combination of glad and sad."

"How so?"

"I've pretty much completed my exhaustive investigation of the Silveiras in Arizona," said Lillian.

"Did you find something wrong?" asked Noble.

"I guess that is the problem," replied Lillian. "There's absolutely nothing wrong with them. Everything checks out, including the law enforcement information you obtained for me. It turns out that Mrs. Silveira has a college degree and teaches both elementary and high school students. She appears to be as active in the Red Cross as I am. Mr. Silveira is a war hero from the Spanish-American War, and has made a modest fortune with his ranch and orchards. By every possible source and metric, they're model people."

"I take it that is the 'glad' part you are feeling," said Noble. "And the 'sad' part?"

Lillian did not answer right away while she smiled with just one side of her mouth. "I'm so glad that the McCracken children will have a wonderful life in Arizona. We couldn't have found a better environment for them. Still, I'm going to miss them, Edward. We're packed in here on Beacon Street, for sure. But, they're really good kids. I know they need to be with family and have a new start after the terrible events this fall. I'm just not required to like the fact they must depart. It makes me so sad."

"Lilly," said Noble, "this is one of the reasons everyone loves you so. You care about people to the maximum possible, and you make such a positive impact on the lives of everyone around you. I know this is hard for you. It's very hard for me as well. However, focus on what you are accomplishing here. Not only have you provided a wonderful new chapter in the lives of these four children. Arizona will be gaining four stellar citizens in years to come. And it's all because of your diligence, your strength of character, and your love."

Lillian stood from the library desk and hugged her husband. She was still both glad and sad simultaneously. But, he was always able to calm her troubled heart and bring peace to her. She wondered what she would ever do without him.

Eventually, Lillian and Edward called a family meeting and explained the entire situation to the McCracken children and the rest of the Noble family. Tears ran like the Colorado River, and hugs were countless. The smaller children, Joseph, Helen, and Marguerite needed special attention with the coming transition. They took the idea of separation with great sorrow. The older children, Bernard, Michael, Brian, and Florence spent extra time with the little ones. Lillian, Edward, and Akeema immediately began to plan for various McCracken bon voyage activities, since the children would be leaving by train in less than three weeks. All decided that the first celebration would be at their favorite roller skating rink that Saturday.

The week before Christmas was a very busy one. The Noble family loved the holiday, and their home was thoroughly decked out for it. Noble purchased a tree that was so tall that its top was bent by the parlor ceiling. The family placed large and small glass bulbs of every color imaginable upon its branches. Ample quantities of tinsel were layered onto the tree, and then strings of popcorn were laced upon it. A golden angel adorned the tree top, even though it was slightly bent by the ceiling. A traditional nativity was set up on a parlor table. The parlor, library, and entryway walls were strung with garland, and candles were lit all around the first floor of the house. At night, the rooms glowed with a soft warm orange-yellow light that warmed the soul. The magical scene was completed with a blaze in the parlor fireplace that warmed the body against the cold Boston nights.

Noble would come home in the evenings and wish that time would simply stop. Surrounded by the beauty of his home during this religious season, it was almost possible to forget the hell that had visited Earth this eighteenth year of the 20th century.

Wednesday, Christmas Day, all of the children were up at the crack of dawn to see what was beneath the Christmas tree. Before opening any presents, the children checked their stockings hanging about the fireplace, and found to their delight apples, oranges, pears, and even some grapes. These were treasures in the New England winter. Then came the Noble family frenzy of tearing wrapping paper and ribbons to expose other treasures.

Akeema and Florence received new blouses along with skirts that reached a scandalous four inches below the knee. Lillian was not sure where they could possibly wear them in public. The Noble and McCracken boys screamed when they opened packages with assorted new baseball gloves, baseballs, and caps. Marguerite and Helen were both enchanted with new dolls displaying long flowing hair and billowy dresses with petticoats. Apparently, Marguerite had taught Helen how to hop when excited. There was a lot of hopping that morning. Lillian gave her husband a new portable sphygmomanometer for when he returned to his private practice. Noble gave his wife a yellow gold emerald ring with the names of her family engraved inside the band. Lillian kissed her husband, and whispered something in his ear that made him blush...and smile.

The whole clan then took public transportation to attend Christmas Mass at the Cathedral of the Holy Cross. Returning home, the group all chipped-in to put the finishing touches on the traditional Noble ham dinner. At the urging of the Noble children, a vacant seat was placed at the dinner table for Arthur. Marguerite carefully set a plate, fork, napkin, and a glass for her departed brother. That moment, there was not a dry eye in the Noble home.

Just before the group began to eat, they all held hands as Akeema said grace…five times. She was raised in the ancient religious ways of her Yup`ik Alaskan people, and was also taught the Christian ways by missionaries. She loved both traditions, and had made both of them her own. She recited the same Yup`ik prayer in French, Russian, German, and in Unaliq. Then in English she quietly said, "May God and the ancestors cover this family with goodness, happiness, and the gift of long life. Amen." All then repeated together, "Amen."

It was Noble's first Christmas with his family since 1916. Much had changed since then. But, surely the coming new year held the real promise of better days.

By Monday, December 30th, Noble was becoming concerned. There had been a steady increase in New England influenza cases for over three weeks. The South Department was about to open a fourth influenza ward, and there was no evidence of any slowing of new cases.

The good news was that the city was much better prepared than in the fall. Volunteers in automobiles and horse-drawn carriages were now adept at finding community patients in early stages of compromise. Getting these people to the hospital quickly, and having both the staff and supplies to serve them, was an enormous advantage over the second disease wave. Boston had come together to donate goods, stockpile reserves, and procure enough medicines for the third battle with the pandemic. The citizenry was also much better prepared to help distribute the needed supplies, as well as take over certain community functions if needed. Those functions would include helping public transpiration, police, firefighters, medical personnel, telephone operators, and other essential services.

The bad news was obvious. The infection seemed to be coming from everywhere at once. Even though the city had more supplies than before, another prolonged battle with influenza would wear reserves thin in just a few weeks. They were now in the winter, and movement within the city would be harder than before. The city, state, and federal budgets were still in the red, and the economy was far from fully recovered from the last engagement with the disease. Finally, there was no influenza vaccine, no antiserum, and no cure. No one had any idea what influenza was.

Noble decided to take some preemptive action. He instructed the BCH staff to re-open the shoe warehouse satellite hospital clinic immediately. His intent was to serve as many influenza victims close to their homes as possible. This would make transportation of the ill easier, faster, and would decrease potential influenza exposures. He called other communities, like Brookline, and suggested that they once again raise their hospital tents for the same reason. He called upon Lillian to ask the Red Cross and the Women's Auxiliary to redouble their efforts at collecting food, bottled water, blankets, coats, and linen. He asked the army and navy to spare all the IV bottles, needles, and tubing they could.

Finally, Noble sought to give Boston City Hospital, its residents, nurses, and staff another commodity in very short supply. Hope. He called the South Department staff into one of the empty wards just before it was to be turned into a quarantined area. He thanked them for their selfless service over the last four months, and the many sacrifices they had made. Those sacrifices included many who had lost their lives in the service of others. He asked them to encourage each other, help each other, and be available for each other for difficult times. He told them evidence from past pandemics indicated influenza disappearance would come with the passing of winter.

He told them there was no reason to think differently of this pandemic. Hearing these words from Dr. Noble himself…a man they trusted more than any other physician…went miles to help keep up their spirits. Of course, Noble did not dwell on the fact that he was not sure this pandemic would act like others in the past. In fact, 1918 influenza had not acted like any other pandemic in history.

Tuesday, December 31st finally arrived. As Noble prepared to leave the A.I. Office that evening, Lieutenant Lafayette told him she, Claudette, and Adelina planned to attend a New Years Eve party near their Worcester Square apartment. He bid the Lieutenant a happy New Year, and rushed out into the windy and snowy Boston weather. The trolley ride back to Beacon Street was bitterly cold. Noble slipped once on an ice covered sidewalk and fell squarely on his right hip. With a bit of a limp, he made his way to his house.

New Years Eve was another splendid holiday for the Nobles. The house was decorated with brightly colored ribbons and strips of paper. Music played from the family phonograph. Songs like *After You've Gone, Oh! How I Hate to get Up in the Morning*, and *Till We Meet Again*, reflected the mood of the year. Party hats already adorned the children. Plates filled with potato chips, cheese, fruit, sliced meats, small sandwiches, cookies, brownies, pies, and cakes could be found on most horizontal surfaces in the house. Bottles of Dr. Pepper were in ice containers for the children, and bottles of wine and Champagne were available for adults. Noise makers were ready for the midnight hour. Noble checked to ensure the parlor grandfather clock was up to its midnight obligation.

In addition to the Nobles, Akeema, and the McCracken children, invited guests for the festivities included Milton Rosenau and his wife, Katherine Cushing and her three younger children, and Rose Kennedy and her three children. Rose's husband was on a business trip to Hollywood, California, to look into possible motion picture investments.

In all, twenty-one revelers would bring in the New Year at the Noble house.

Not long after Noble arrived home, he noticed that Bernard and Michael seemed bothered. Both of the boys sat in the parlor with party hats on, but no smiles or excitement. "Boys," said Noble, "why so glum? You both look like you lost your best friend."

"Its kind-of-like we did, Dad," said Michael.

"No kidding," added Bernard.

"What happened?" said Noble.

"You are <u>not</u> going to believe this, Dad," said Michael. "This is just about the worst thing that could possibly happen. Bernard and I just can't believe it's true. It's also the dumbest thing ever."

"So, what is 'it'?" asked Noble again.

"Bernard and I found out that the Boston Red Sox are assigning Babe Ruth to left field next year! That's right, the Babe won't be pitching as much. Can you believe it? It's like if the Allies made General Pershing into a Buck Private, or something like that. They've all 'gone phute'. It's disgusting!"

Noble let his two sons vent for awhile, and assured them the Red Sox would be as good a team next year as they had been in the 1918 season. His sons greatly disagreed, and gave him many baseball statistics as evidence for their positions on the matter.

Later on all the invited guests arrived. Between snacking, the activities between various groups were very predictable. Noble spoke with Rosenau extensively about the rising third wave and all the implications for New England's health care system. They talked about the ongoing work with identifying the influenza agent, and the production of various serums and vaccines, by William Park, Paul Lewis, Oswald Avery, Anna Wessel Williams, and Rosenau himself.

Florence, Akeema, and Mark McCracken talked about new fashions, styles, and movie stars. They discussed recording artists like Marion Harris and Arthur Fields, and talked about the men they knew who would be returning home soon from Europe.

Bernard, Michael, Henry Cushing, and the two McCracken boys, Brian and Joseph, brooded over a recent decision by the Red Sox and went into exquisite statistical detail over the folly of it. However, this did not stop any of them from consuming large amounts of sweets and soda.

Marguerite, Betsey and Barbara Cushing, Helen McCracken, and Joseph and John Kennedy, played with toys and games, and also ate a great deal of party food. The phonograph player was a particular hit. The children did their best to sing along with songs like *Somebody Stole My Gal*.

Lillian, Katherine Cushing, and Rose Kennedy with her infant Rosemary, talked about the blessing of The War's end. Katherine had not seen her husband in nearly a year-and-a-half, and was very worried about his slow convalescence from the Spanish Flu. All three women were active in relief efforts for families devastated by the pandemic. In addition, they were part of local preparations with the new emergence of influenza.

Later in the evening, Marguerite walked up to Rose and said, "Mrs. Kennedy?"

"Yes, dear," said Rose.

"How come you call your boy 'Jack'?" asked Marguerite. "I thought his name was John."

"'Jack' is a nickname for John, dear," said Rose smiling. "His father and I just call him that."

"I think I'll call him John, anyway," said Marguerite. Marguerite and John then ran off to play with toy boats.

Just before the younger children were put to bed, Akeema Ayuluk sang a song of prayer in her native Unaliq. The song asked the ancestors, who are among us in the form of animals, to watch over her family and tribe. She translated into English, and added that the people present were now part of that family and tribe. Akeema had a beautiful singing voice. However, Unaliq sounded odd to speakers of European languages. It consisted of back-of-the-throat guttural utterances that at times were a combination of clicks, coughs, and the sounds one makes when they are about to spit. The strange language made the children laugh. But, that did not bother Akeema. The opportunity to share her song of prayer with new loved ones, and inviting them to be part of her new family, was precious to her. For the adults present, the song was quite moving and emotional.

The young children were put off to bed, and the rest waited for the traditional count-down. All present wished someday to witness, in the warm Pasadena, California weather, the Tournament of Roses Parade. The *Boston Globe* always published pictures of the parade some days after the January 1st extravaganza. Noble and his wife thought they might travel to see the parade when the children were older. Rosenau said he would also like to see a future Tournament East-West Football Game in Pasadena. Rose said her very young boys seemed to like football as well.

The final moments of 1918 arrived. What was strikingly absent in all of the evening's conversations was any remorse over the passing of this year. Without saying so, everyone was glad to see the year leave.

Four, three, two, one... The group spontaneously broke into chores of the old Scottish ballad *Auld Lang Syne*...except for Akeema, who was not sure what the words meant.

It was January 1, 1919. Only the Lord, and the ancestors, knew what was coming.

CHAPTER 27

Over the next three days, the Nobles prepared for the McCracken departure. Lillian took the children shopping for new clothes and luggage for their big one-way trip. Akeema looked up "Arizona" for all the Noble and McCracken children in the home library's *Encyclopedia Britannica*. She wanted the children to have a destination in their minds as the journey began, rather than a sense of traveling to nowhere. They read together other books about the United States containing more information and pictures. There was even a picture of the town of Flagstaff. The children drew pictures to help envision what they had read from the books, and the drawings were pinned around the house. Everyone was trying to make this difficult transition as smooth as possible.

Early in the evening on Friday, January 3rd, the Nobles took both the family truck and a taxi to a nearby nickelodeon. It required two automobiles to cart eleven people around the city. At the nickelodeon they watched a series of Charlie Chaplin comedies. Everyone ate popcorn and laughed with

Chaplin's character The Tramp in *Kid Auto Races in Venice* and *His Prehistoric Past*. After the movies, the clan went to Boston's North End. On Salem Street, across the street from Paul Revere's Old North Church, the group went to a new kind of informal restaurant. It was called a pizza parlor, and it served an Italian baked thin crust pie made of flour, cheese, tomato sauce, and sliced meats. Everyone said pizza parlors were now their favorite restaurants. Noble thought there could be a national interest in these establishments someday.

At the end of the memorable evening, the group returned to Beacon Street. Everyone helped the McCrackens pack for their great adventure, and then retired at eight o'clock.

Early next morning, Saturday, January 4th, Lillian made a pancake breakfast with scrambled eggs, bacon, sausage, orange juice, and coffee. Noble loaded up the Ford, and again drove along with a taxi to assist in the transportation of several people. At the Boston and Main Train Station the reality of the situation set in. Everyone, including Noble, began to sob. The closer the group came to the waiting train, the greater the emotional response became. The conductor helped load the children's luggage into the storage area. Lillian went over the travel documents with the conductor to ensure various train connections were understood. The Silveiras had employed a young woman, Miss Everright, to travel with the children. She would also be their nanny in Sedona. Miss Everright was already on the train when it was time for the McCrackens to board it.

It was now time to go, and the train's whistle blew. Noble, his wife, and Florence, hugged the four McCrackens and told them their home was always open to them. They made sure the children had the Noble address so they could write anytime. Akeema had cared for and taught the children since their arrival in the Noble home. She cried as she gave a list of special items about each child to Miss Everright. Bernard and Michael gave Mark, Joseph, and Brian papers with their handwritten Red Sox projections for the 1919 season. Marguerite cupped her hands to her face and cried loudly. She loved her "little sister" Helen, and could not bear to see her leave. "All aboard!" yelled the conductor. As Helen climbed onto the train car, Marguerite gave her a little pink stuffed rabbit. "My Daddy calls me 'Rabbit'", said Marguerite. "Please keep this so that you can remember me." Marguerite kissed Helen goodbye, and the train began to move. The Nobles and the McCrackens waved at one another until there was no train left to see.

The Ford truck carried a very sad Noble family home that morning.

Monday, January 6th, was the coldest day yet of the winter. The sky was overcast, and it had snowed six or seven inches over the last twelve hours. Under the deceptively white fluffy snow was a thick layer of ice that was the cause of numerous pedestrian falls. To add to the difficulty was a strong freezing wind that helped encourage those falls. Yes, it was winter in New England.

Even considering the difficult weather conditions, Noble noticed fewer vehicles on the streets. He immediately thought of the previous autumn. His fear was given more fuel as the Massachusetts Avenue trolley reached Boston City Hospital and ran along its southwest border. In spite of the weather, there were a large number of people outside the BCH outpatient clinics. A very long line had formed just outside the Adult Medicine Clinic. Noble already knew what was going on, but needed to see it for himself.

The hospital was filling with influenza…again. Noble had staff instructions in place to sequentially open influenza quarantine wards as early areas filled at certain rates. In just forty-eight hours, the hospital had gone from 1½ pavilions quarantined to 2½. This represented five wards that were now full. A sixth ward was being readied.

Noble asked where he could find Dr. Schafer. As always, the third year resident was found in the thick of it on one of the influenza wards. With gown, gloves, and gauze mask on,

Noble walked up to the young doctor. He and a nurse were working with a patient who was likely a Type I influenza victim. She was covered with sweat, and had soaked through her bed linen and blanket. Her long black hair was drenched with sweat, and had been tied into a long braid. She had also vomited on the bed and floor, and was incontinent of urine and feces. A nurse was busily putting on fresh bedding as an aid cleaned the floor. The patient coughed with the hideous particular sound that only this disease produced. Her labored breathing numbered thirty breaths a minute. She was also in a state of server delirium that was common with this influenza. The delirium caused her to yell out names, moan incessantly, scream, and struggle to get out of bed. For this reason, soft restraints had been placed on the patients limbs for her own safety.

On closer inspection, the patient appeared to be in her early twenties. She was extremely flushed about the face and trunk. Her conjunctiva was injected and she had slight epistaxis. Her sputum was the very characteristic frothy yellowish-pink that was another hallmark of this affliction. Both of her tympanic membranes had apparently ruptured, and a serous clear fluid tricked from both ears. Noble noted paralysis of her eye muscles; another common finding. Schafer had placed an oxygen mask to her face. The mask was connected to rubber tubing that led to an O2 tank with an adjustable flow valve.

"David," said Noble who stood behind the capable resident, "things have changed over the weekend."

Schafer looked up and smiled as he saw his favorite attending physician. Jokingly he said, "Ya' think so, Dr. Noble? Good to see you, sir. I know you had the weekend free. Things have really taken off, as you can see." Schafer had re-started an IV and was giving the patient D5N saline at a rate of 300 ml per hour. Judging from the various bottles on the bed stand, the patient had been given morphine, sodium salicylate, epinephrine, sodium bicarbonate, and caffeine.

"What has been the clinical course of this patient, David?" asked Noble.

"Pretty typical Type I, sir," said Schafer. "She was progressively worsening at home over about three days, and came to the outpatient clinic in a fairly severe condition yesterday afternoon. She has been gradually deteriorating ever since. We have found that we need to be more aggressive with rehydration early on. The influenza patients loose a huge amount of fluid in a very short period of time. The losses come from copious amounts of sputum, and diaphoresis with the fevers. It all adds up fast. She has already had blood counts, urinalysis, and sputum and blood obtained for gram stains and cultures. But, given her presentation, we don't expect any new findings. We generally have stopped asking for chest roentgenograms, since they all show bilateral pneumonias that don't follow the severity of the clinical course."

"Those are important learnings that I will pass on to others, David," said Noble.

"Dr. Noble," said Schafer, "your term 'third wave' has really caught on. Everyone knows that you called this one pretty early. I want you to know that this time no one is giving you any grief over your warnings or decisions, sir. No one."

"Thank you, David. Any other new insights? You are a master at them. Your fame in this regard is growing here in Boston."

Schafer blushed. "Our newest insight is not that hard to figure out. If we can get to the Type I patients quickly, and if we have the supplies and drugs, we can cut their mortality by a third or more, sir. That's why we seem to be more successful this time around. We have more to work with...and faster. I can't tell you what a wonderful job the volunteers in the field are doing. In spite of the weather, and extremely ill patients, they're getting the sick to us with incredible speed. This work is saving lives."

"It is so important for all the volunteers to hear that, David," said Noble. "They get pretty discouraged out there. Without this kind of encouragement, it's truly a thankless job. My wife is one of the regional volunteer organizers. I will be sure she passes your praise on to them."

"I know your wife is really involved with the Red Cross relief efforts, sir," said Schafer. "We hear her name from staff, patients, and family members all the time." Schafer paused for a moment, and then continued. "I should mention what we have learned about the administration of oxygen. We had almost no O2 available last fall. However, there is a select group of Type I patients that really benefit from oxygen therapy. This woman here is a good example. For sure, not all Type I patients benefit. If they have not reached a respiratory rate of thirty or so, or if they are Type II or Type III patients, we waste the precious resource of O2 if we use it. Just as before, nothing seems to help the Type IIIs. We are seeing a lot more Type IIIs right now because patients are coming to the hospital faster."

"I know you're busy, David," said Noble, "but can you give me a run down on hospital census and other conditions?"

"Sure, Dr. Noble. At the rate we are seeing new influenza cases, we will need to open the sixth ward today. The shoe warehouse satellite hospital is full. You can get a sense of the patient acuity by looking at this ward. There are over a dozen Type I patients here right now. It looks like there are four Type IIIs, based on their obvious cyanosis and the ID tags on their big toes. Those patients will be at the morgue by evening, or early tomorrow morning. You can see from the overall condition of the ward, the staff is doing a hero's job keeping it clean. It is a far cry from the fall, sir."

"Thank you, David," said Noble. "Be sure a sixth ward is fully readied. We need to prepare two of the previously closed satellite hospitals for re-opening. This time, I want you to stay at BCH and help lead the effort here. I need your clinical skills and leadership in a central position so that we can provide the highest quality care here, and in the satellites. I need to get the word out to city officials that it's again time to close schools, churches, and other public meeting places. As you know, this is a very unpopular request."

Noble continued. "One other thing, David. We need to be the best stewards possible of BCH resources. We need everyone's complete attention to this. No one knows how long the 'third wave' will last, and how much more severe it will get. We don't even know if there might be a 'fourth wave', and if so, when. We do know that two million men are coming home in the next few months. We are already seeing lethal influenza cases aboard the inbound troop transports. There are a lot of unknowns here, David. We need to stay agile, flexible, and we need to preserve all our supplies and drugs for as long as possible. As one of the third year residents, do you think you can keep that thought front-and-center in the minds of the staff?"

"I'll mention it every day at the resident's morning report, at every lunch meeting, and will repeat it constantly to the support staff, sir," said Schafer.

"Great," said Noble. "And one more thing...this is an order, Lieutenant. I order you to eat three square meals a day, and get at least seven hours of sleep every twenty-four hours. I don't want you looking like you did last fall." Noble smiled with these comments, but meant them nevertheless.

Schafer also smiled, and saluted Noble. "Yes sir, Major!"

Noble then walked briskly away toward the A.I. Office in order to send cables to city, state, and U.S. Public Health Service officials. Just before leaving the office, he was saddened to learn former President Theodore Roosevelt had died of a myocardial infarction earlier in the day. Roosevelt remained a popular figure in America, and had been highly critical of the Wilson administration's handling of The War and the pandemic.

By Wednesday, January 8th, disturbing intelligence reports were coming into the A.I. Office. First, in China's Shansi Province, Dr. Percy Watson estimated that eighty percent of those who came in contact with influenza developed the disease. What was more frightening was an estimated one hundred percent morality for those who contracted influenza. Second, parts of the United States that had been relatively spared in the second wave were being ravaged by the third. Such was the case in Cincinnati, Ohio, where hospitals were packed with severely ill and dying victims of the grippe this January. Third, increasing influenza cases and deaths were again being reported in several army cantonments.

Australia had avoided almost all influenza in the second wave by a strictly enforced quarantine of all ships coming to the island. However, U.S. Navy intelligence learned that a troop ship teaming with influenza had docked in Australia in late December. Although the troops stayed aboard the ship, some medical personnel did not. Within only a few weeks, the island nation was experiencing the same dreadful fury the rest of the world knew all too well. To date, no one had any idea what devastation the aboriginal Australian population might experience.

Lillian came by the office in the late morning to complete some calculations she began in December. She had a very serious look on her face as she arrived from a Red Cross food distribution trip to South Boston. Noble noticed her facial expression and asked, "Lilly. Why so troubled?"

Lillian rolled her lower lip against her upper lip, and then spoke as she hung up her coat. She decided not to remove her heavy navy blue sweater. The office remained cold despite steam heating and the area heater parked right next to Lieutenant Quellet. Lillian eventually said, "Edward, I just came from South Boston. Things are not good, dear. There aren't as many long white linen bags on sidewalks as last fall. But, they are reappearing. Also, new crepe had not adorned neighborhood doors for a time. Not so, now. It's also reappearing. Do you have any time to go over some case numbers right now? If there are any projections we can make, we need to go over the available data so that we can make them."

Noble wholeheartedly agreed, and began to pull out ring binders containing recent military and USPHS cables. Much like in October, they began to create spreadsheets and grids, and perform long hand calculations. At times they used slide rules. Lieutenant Quellet, with her degree in mathematics, asked if she could help. She proved to be a wonder. The

Nobles completed their work in half the time with her amazing abilities to complete calculations at breathtaking speed.

After a couple of hours, the Nobles sat back in their chairs and looked at one another. "Well, I think we have some conclusions. Don't you think, Lilly?"

"Looks that way," said Lillian.

"Mrs. Noble," asked Lieutenant Quellet, "may I ask what you conclude from all our calculations?"

"Sure, Adelina," said Lillian. "Without going into details in a given area, the higher the influenza case rate was in the fall, the lower it is presently. The reverse is also true. The lower the fall case rate was in a given area, the higher it is presently. There is emerging a pattern that is most interesting. These ratios hold true at just about every level you look."

"What do you mean, Mrs. Noble?" said the Lieutenant.

"At the national level, the states and counties partially spared by influenza last fall now have some of the highest case rates. The hardest hit states and counties last fall have lighter case rates right now. When we look at Boston, the same findings are evident with different neighborhoods. This is evidence for some partial immunity given to survivors of the second wave. We saw similar phenomenon between the first and second waves."

Noble then said, "Lieutenant, this has practical application. We can now suggest that scarce resources be allocated to areas with less influenza last fall. Moving medical personnel and supplies ahead of the third wave can be done locally, as well as nationally."

Lillian added, "There are some definite caveats, though. First, we do not have enough data yet to know if mortality rates are different from the fall. Second, we're not sure if infection during the first wave conferred any immunity for this most recent wave. Third, we have absolutely no data on gender or racial infection differences yet. Fourth, there's no way to know if this pattern will hold up over time. Finally, none of this gives us any idea how long the third wave will last."

"At least it's a start," said Noble. "I'll summarize these findings and send them out immediately to the Communicable Disease Division and the U.S. Public Health Service. The implications for their work over the next couple of weeks are obvious. Oh, by the way Lieutenant. Thank you so much for all your help. You are truly amazing! I have never seen anyone able to do arithmetic, algebra, and use a slide rule, so fast."

"Thank you, Major. Let me know whenever I can help."

Lillian left for a Red Cross Center as Noble began composing another broad telegram distribution.

Many of the city and state ordinances passed during the previous fall were again in place by Friday, January 10th. Schools, churches, theaters, pubs, and many other public gathering places were closed. There was the usual grumbling by effected businesses. For example, Boston stage and cinema owners felt all businesses should be closed if theirs were ordered to do so. However, Noble noticed there was generally much more cooperation this time around from most quarters. And the speed of needed changes was quintuple what it had been four months earlier. Boston Harbor had a good ship quarantine program in place. The USPHS officers were much quicker at setting up quarantines for effected families, and there were many more social services available for those in need. For what it was worth, the city again required gauze masks to be worn in public. Red Cross volunteers began producing tens of thousands of masks...again.

Noble arrived later than usual to the A.I. Office, because the trolleys were running late. This was partly due to the weather. However, it was clear the numbers of trolley cars in service was reduced from a typical Friday. Noble saw this as an ominous sign. Illness was again beginning to take a toll on the city. Along with fewer trolleys, there were fewer passengers, fewer vehicles, and fewer pedestrians. The socioeconomic downward spiral was starting up again.

Upon entering the office, Noble found Lieutenant Pierre-Louis with her head upon her folded arms. Instead of sitting at her station at the operator cordboard, she was at one of the roll top desks. Noble walked up behind her and heard that she was sobbing softly. Noble pulled up a chair next to her, and put his hand on her shoulder. "Claudette," said Noble. "Claudette. What's the matter?"

The Lieutenant continued to sob, and said nothing. Again Noble asked, "Claudette, what's wrong?"

A few more moments went by, and the Lieutenant finally lifted her head from her arms on the desk. Her large dark brown eyes were reddened from crying. Tears ran down her cheeks and onto her uniform. "I'm...I...I'm sorry, Major," said the Lieutenant. "I'm just...sorry."

"Sorry for what?" said Noble.

"Sorry...sorry for acting this way, sir."

Noble patted her on the shoulder, and asked with a kindly smile, "What's up, Lieutenant?" He handed her a handkerchief, and she used it to dry her face.

"Well," began the Lieutenant, "I received the first letter from home...in Haiti...in nearly three months. My mother wrote me that my younger sister died from the grippe. She died about four weeks ago. Included in the letter was a long list of cousins, uncles, and aunts who also died of the 'Spanish Flu'. My home town cannot bury the dead fast enough. At the time she wrote the letter, my father was also very ill with the grippe." The Lieutenant put her face down on her forearms, and once again began to cry.

Noble again patted her shoulder. He took a long deep breath and let it out slowly. "I am so sorry, Claudette. So very sorry." He stood from the desk, took another handkerchief from a small table, and gave it to the Lieutenant. "Claudette, it's fine with me if you want to go back to your apartment and rest. I can take care of things today here. I really wish you would take some time off."

"No...no, Major," said the Lieutenant. "Please let me stay here. I need to work. I'm better if I am working. Is it OK if I just stay here and keep working, sir?"

"Of course it is, Lieutenant," said Noble. "You are part of the A.I. Office family. You are always welcome here. I just want you to know that you can go anytime if you feel that you need to. Anytime."

The Lieutenant dried her entire face, and wiped her eyes with the second handkerchief. "Thank you, sir,"

A moment later the Lieutenant continued, "Sir, can I ask you a dumb question?"

Noble smiled a little. "Lieutenant, my father used to say the only dumb question is the one you have to ask twice. What's the 'dumb' question?"

"Sir," said the Lieutenant, "I read in the A.I. Office everyday what is happening in the world. Everyone can see what is happening in Boston now. The grippe is back. People are losing their jobs, again. It's only a matter of time before we run out of food, again. Families are putting their dead loved ones out like garbage, again. There's more crepe on the doors, again. From our apartment on Worchester Square, across the street from Boston City Hospital, I see the people lining up, again. A growing number of sick are here, again. The lengthening lines are here, again. Yesterday I saw a steam shovel digging a mass grave...again. Again, again, again!"

The Lieutenant stopped. She sat up straight in her chair and put her hands across her eyes. Several moments went by as Noble listened for her question.

"Major."

"Yes, Lieutenant?" Noble said in a soft voice.

"Major. When is this going to <u>end</u>? You are the smartest doctor in Boston. Everyone says so. I trust you more than anyone else in the United States. Major, do you know when this is going to all end? Or, is this <u>never</u> going to end? Will the grippe just keep coming back for us until we are all dead? Major, do you know?" The Lieutenant began to sob once again.

For a second time, Noble took a long deep breath and let it out slowly. The Lieutenant's question was a simple one. But, it was one of the most profound questions he had ever been asked. It was the question over a billion people on planet Earth were all asking themselves. What is this demon? Why is it killing us? And, most importantly, when and how is it going to stop?

Noble turned the Lieutenant's coaster oak chair around slightly so that she faced him squarely. He waited for her to sit back into the chair, and open her eyes. When she did, he began, "Lieutenant, thank you for your confidence in me. I appreciate it more than you will ever know. But, please know something. I don't know when this is going to stop. Like everyone else in science today, I don't know why it started in the first place. We don't know why it has become the most efficient killer in history. We don't know why it comes, goes, returns, and how it seems to mutate. We don't know how to stop it, beyond keeping people as far away from it as possible. We don't even know what it is."

Noble paused for a moment, took another deep breath, and began again. "However, Lieutenant. I want to tell you something. I want to give you, and everyone that has put trust in me, a solemn promise. I will pursue this disease in every way I can, and for as long as I can. I am going to help throw all the socioeconomic, political, medical, scientific, and psychological weapons at it for as long as I am around. Of this, you can be certain."

With tears still forming in her big eyes, the Lieutenant gave a little smile and hugged Noble. "Thank you, Major. Thank you. If there is anyone that can stop it, it's you."

The Lieutenant seemed to have been given a new measure of optimism. Without any further discussion, she returned to the cordboard and began taking messages as though their conversation had never happened. However, both knew it had. The Lieutenant, at least for now, felt better. But, Noble did not. The demon only stops when it has killed everyone that cannot resist it. Nevertheless, here it is again. It leaves, changes into something new, and returns every bit the killer it was before. Would it never stop?

A foot of snow fell over the following weekend, and the Noble children took full advantage of it. The three younger children, with help from Florence, spent hours outside the front of the Beacon Street residence building a six-foot, four-inch snowman. They named the new member of the Noble family "Dr. Noble". A large carrot was made into a nose, and stones created a wide smiling mouth. Bernard fashioned a pair of wire rim glasses out of a coat hanger, and placed them over two large red buttons used as eyes. Extra snow was used to make parted white hair that draped over the round forehead. To finish the presentation, Michael gave the good doctor a stethoscope made of twigs. Their mother was called out to see the frozen statue, and she hugged the work of art as though it was the real Dr. Noble. All four children laughed and laughed.

After some Akeema imposed homework, Bernard, Michael, and Marguerite drew pictures of their snowman creation. The drawings were placed with letters to the McCracken children, and the envelopes addressed to Sedona, Arizona. The stamped letters were then carefully placed in the mail box. Each Noble child was certain that the McCrackens would miss Boston the moment the letters were opened.

It was too cold later in the afternoon to be outside, so the children decided to play checkers. Marguerite preferred to help her doll "Lucy" stack the checker pieces rather than play the game. Later, their father introduced Bernard and Michael to the game of chess. The two boys, forever competitive, took to the game with a vengeance. Noble wondered if chess would now take the place of baseball as the boy's number one distraction. But then again, this was the winter. Spring would see the rise of the Red Sox. Board games would ultimately give way to gloves, bats, and baseballs.

Continued snowing through the weekend in Boston had left Monday, January 13th to deal with all the white material. Everything moved slower. Walking, trolleys, buses, and just standing on an icy sidewalk, became an ordeal. It was the nature of New England living.

It took twice as long as usual for Noble to reach Boston City Hospital and enter the A.I. Office. He had to chuckle when he entered the large room and found Lieutenant Lafayette with a thick knitted neckerchief wound around her neck, and a red and white wool hat on upon her head. The electric area heater on the floor near her feet was turned on "high". "Lieutenant, you are definitely out of uniform," laughed Noble.

The Lieutenant turned toward the Major and at first looked worried. Then, she saw that he was joking and smiled. "Actually, Major, this is the new uniform of the Army Signal Corps. We're trying to be more stylish now that The War has ended. Besides, it keeps the ice sickles off our ears."

Not to be undone, Noble said, "I think ice sickles would be very attractive on the Signal Corps officers. It could become part of the uniform service devices. Don't you think?"

"Only if the medical officers also have to wear them," joked the Lieutenant.

It was cold enough in the office for Noble to keep his army coat on. His first order of business this chilly morning was to monitor the national influenza data coming from the U.S Public Health Service, the military, and individual clinicians who sent in their own observations. Clearly, the third wave was increasing throughout the country. But, the case increases were not homogeneous. Some areas seemed almost spared of influenza. Others saw a resurgence that was worse than the second wave. In the West, it was sometimes difficult to know if an increase was part of the second or the third waves. Nevertheless, it was increasing throughout the United States.

New England was continuing to experience more influenza and resulting mortalities, and Boston was no exception. The slope of the line for new cases was not logarithmic as it had been in the fall. Rather, the slope was linear and steady. The slower increase rise, plus the experience gained from the fall, was making a difference. Noble was certain that lives were being saved by the city's vastly improved preparation. Still, the big questions remained: How long would the linear influenza increase continue, and how many more times could it leave and return? After studying greater Boston data, Noble asked that another BCH satellite hospital be opened immediately.

Noble went off to check on hospital medical stockpiles at the materials supply pavilion. He was discouraged to find stored supplies in smaller quantities than he was originally told. At the anticipated rate of use, and assuming no significant re-stocking, BCH would be out of most medical supplies in less than ten days.

Noble returned to the A.I. Office just before noon. Entering the office, he was about to joke with Lieutenant Lafayette again about the room's temperature, when the look on her face stopped him.

"Major," the Lieutenant said softly, "your wife called, and said you need to call home urgently."

An icy cold shiver ran down Noble's shoulders to his fingers, and from his hips to his toes. It was as though he lost all feeling and motor control of all his limbs...at once. There is that word again, he screamed to himself. "Urgently". He hated the word "urgently". Horrible things followed those eight letters. It took some time for Noble to walk toward a roll top desk phone. He sat down. He picked up the ear piece, and without asking, the Lieutenant put him through to 468 Beacon Street. The phone rang only once.

"Yes?"

"You called, Lilly?"

"Edward, come home. Come home quickly. Michael and Marguerite are sick." Lillian hung up the phone.

CHAPTER 28

Noble's temples throbbed so hard that he could feel his temporal arteries slamming against the sides of his glasses. He instantly became so lightheaded that he had to steady his torso by holding onto the chair arm. Noble suddenly realized these sensations of periodic terror were becoming commonplace for him. He put his left hand to his forehead, where it seemed to freeze. Think, Edward, think, he said to himself. What do I need? What do I need right now?

The Lieutenant's voice brought Noble back from the timeless place he had been for an instant. "Major. Major. Is everything OK?"

Noble put his left hand back at his side, stood, and turned toward the door. "No," said Noble. "I must go."

Noble nearly ran from the office hallway door. Think, Edward, think. There seemed to be a cerebral fog that would not allow him to think. Edward, stop it, he said to himself. Let Edward the physician take charge instead of Edward the father. With that notion, a different man emerged within Noble. Now, Dr. Noble would be calling the shots. The other man…the father…would now be a bystander for a time. The fog began to lift. The throbbing of Noble's temples decreased.

Noble hurried by one of the pavilion clinical labs, and took up a stack of fresh Petri dishes and blood collection tubes. He placed them in a paper bag, and quickly left the South Department. He had to run to catch a Massachusetts Avenue trolley heading north. Since it was mid-day, it did not take long to reach Beacon Street.

Opening the front door to his house, Noble's eyes darted about to find Lillian. Seeing no one, he ran upstairs. He found Lillian with Michael in his room. "Where's Marguerite?" asked Noble.

"She's in her room, and Akeema is with her. Bernard is in his room and won't come out."

"What's happened?" said Noble very calmly.

"Akeema was giving a lesson in the first floor library when Michael said he wasn't feeling well," said Lillian. "Akeema told him to lie on his bed for awhile. Only about a half-hour later, Marguerite had the same complaint and also asked to lie down. I came home a little before noon and found both of them with fevers. They are both pretty lethargic, Edward."

Noble said nothing, and went to the library to fetch his black medical bag and new portable sphygmomanometer. Returning to Michael's room, he took vital signs: pulse 81, respiratory rate 20, blood pressure 90/51, and temperature 101° F. Michael was diaphoretic and lethargic, but attentive. "Hey, pal," said Noble, "how are you feeling?"

"Not so hot, Dad," said Michael. "Well, I mean I don't feel that great. I do feel hot [cough]. I have a headache."

Noble's exam of Michael showed injected conjunctiva, a dry cough, and very fine bibasilar rales on chest auscultation.

Noble then went into Marguerite's room, where Akeema was sitting next to her bed. "Hi, Rabbit," said Noble. "How are you doing, kiddo?"

Marguerite had been sleeping, but awoke with her father's words. "Daddy!" She sat up for a moment to hug her father.

"How are you doing, Rabbit?" asked Noble.

"Daddy, my arms and legs hurt, and my head hurts [cough]."

"Dr. Noble," said Akeema, "Most of the time since coming to her room, she has been asleep."

Noble proceeded to take Marguerite's vital signs: pulse 75, respiratory rate 18, blood pressure 85/42, and temperature 101.5° F. Her physical exam was identical to her brother's, except that she had a slightly moist cough and modest bilateral limb muscle tenderness. Noble patted her on the head and told her he would be back in a few minutes.

Lillian met her husband in the upstairs hallway with an extremely concerned expression, but said nothing. "Well," said Noble, "this is pretty much the early stage of textbook influenza. Right now the BCH clinics are packed with patients identical to our children. For the moment, they're doing OK. We must keep them orally hydrated, and I'm going to do some tests." Just then, Florence returned home from a community food distribution drive, and her father gave her the details about her siblings. Even with all Florence had seen over the last few months, she still had to sit down with the news.

"Do they have to go to the clinic for the testing?" asked Lillian.

"No, Lilly," said Noble, "I have everything I need hear. We still have the full stock of medical supplies you purchased last fall, and all the medications as well. I just need Florence to help me obtain some specimens."

Noble told the children that he needed to draw some blood, collect some sputum, and also examine their urine. Florence drew tubes of blood from the children's median cubital veins in the fossa anterior to the elbow. The venipuncture brought tears to Marguerite, but she refused to cry overtly. "Don't worry, Daddy," said Marguerite. "I won't cry. I'm going to help you." Noble plated blood on Petri dishes for culture, and made blood smears as well. He also plated sputum for culture and made sputum smears. Both children provided urine for microscopic examination. Florence was instructed to take the plates to the BCH clinic with the Ford, pay the registration fee for children, and have the plates incubated. She departed for the hospital immediately. Noble prepared gram stains in the family's kitchen.

Using the microscope and centrifuge in his library, Noble examined his newly harvested specimens. Both children had the following blood count ranges: WBC 3 to 5 K/μL, HCT 45 to 48%, platelets 210 to 350 K/μL. The urine specimens were clear dark yellow, rare mucus, specific gravity 1.047 to 1.051, pH 6.0 to 6.5, squamous cells 0 to 1/LPF, hyaline casts 0/LPF, WBC 3 TO 4/HPF, RBC 3/HPF, and very rare bacteria. In other words, aside from slight dehydration, the CBCs and UAs were normal. Blood gram stains were negative, and sputum gram stains showed only the usual mixed flora. Noble gave the children aspirin for their fevers, headaches, and for Marguerite's myalgias. Oral liquids were greatly encouraged.

That afternoon, the Noble residence was set up as a mini-quarantine hospital. Noble, Akeema, and Florence would be direct caregivers for the ill children, while exposure to Lillian and Bernard would be minimized. Noble theorized that Akeema and Florence might carry some immunity because of their spring influenza illnesses. There was no scientific evidence that gauze masks prevented the spread of influenza. However, secondary bacterial infections seemed to be a major cause of influenza morbidity and mortality. So, when caring for the ill children, masks, gloves, and gowns would be worn. Hand washing, before and after entering the children's rooms, would be strictly enforced.

In the evening, Michael and Marguerite rested comfortably. Noble kept logs of urinary volumes excreted by the children. Together with calculated increased incidental fluid losses through fever, oral fluid intake goals were established for each child. A rough hydration estimate could be made with urine specific gravities. After awhile, one could look at the color of a specific child's urine and have a sense if he or she was running behind in fluid intake. The children were drinking adequate amounts of fluid. However, in spite of the aspirin, Michael and Marguerite's temperatures rose to 102.5° F and 102° F, respectively. Through the night, Noble checked on the children at least every two hours.

The next morning, Tuesday, January 14th, both children were slightly worse. There vitals remained the same, but each had new, or more severe, symptoms. Both children's cough was more forceful and more frequent, and both had courser bibasilar pulmonary rales. Michael's headache had become "pounding" and made him wince. Marguerite developed a hot turbid appearance to her face, with an erythematosus flushing of the trunk and neck. Both children were given caffeine and benzyl benzoate for coughing, and Michael was given hypodermic morphine for pain. Along with aspirin, the children seemed to be comforted with symptomatic treatments and rested well.

Noble called the A.I. Office and told the Lieutenant on duty he would be away for some days. He dictated a cable to be sent to Colonel Vaughn about the situation, and had the Lieutenant inform the hospital administration of the problem.

Noble began to call various third and second year medical residents on a regular basis. He discussed their cases with them, made suggestions about diagnosis and treatment, and kept abreast of general patient management. He developed a schedule for some of the residents so they would know to be near a particular telephone at a particular time. Noble found he could learn a great deal about the wards in just fifteen minutes. He wondered if this could be a way for attending physicians to keep better tabs on hospital work in the future, and made a note of it.

Noble had seen radio successfully used between field officers and artillery batteries on the front. Perhaps radios could be placed on medical wards and have a similar future function. In fact, Noble had read in Scientific American that a Russian scientist had invented a cathode ray tube attached to a mirror-drum scanner. The device was able to send geometric shapes over telegraph or telephone wires. Maybe pictures could be sent far distances in the future. Could medicine use such an invention in certain ways?

A little after the noon hour Noble checked again on the children, and made a call to the BCH laboratory. He went downstairs and found Lillian eating lunch with Bernard. Lillian had tried to keep some degree of normalcy in the household, and had given lessons to Bernard that morning. All Boston schools remained closed, but instruction went on in the Noble library. While Akeema performed more patient care duties, Lillian filled in as tutor. Noble had not seen his son since the previous morning. "Bernard, how are you, Son?"

"OK."

"Are you worried, Bernard?" asked his father.

Bernard did not answer. He only briefly looked up from his ham and cheese sandwich with an expression of great emotional pain. His father was not going to press the issue, and gave a supporting pat in his shoulder.

"What's happening up stairs, Edward?" asked Lillian.

Noble sat down at the kitchen table. "They're generally about the same, Lilly." Noble knew this was not completely accurate. However, he saw no need to worry his wife over every tiny clinical change he saw. "I called the lab, since the cultures were plated about twenty-four hours ago. The blood cultures are all negative, and the sputum cultures show normal flora. I'll check again at forty-eight and seventy-two hours."

"Is there anything special for us to do at this point?" asked Lillian.

"Not really, Lilly. They are both stable, comfortable, and are showing symptoms and signs of a moderate bronchitis. So far, so good." With that statement, Noble gave a slight kindly smile that was completely acted. He did not feel like smiling, and did it only to help console his wife. It had its desired effect, since Lillian seemed somewhat relieved. Lillian and Bernard went back to the library, while Noble continued to monitor his ill children. Akeema and Florence assisted Noble at times, and at other times cleaned laundry and prepared food for the evening.

That night saw more symptom and sign changes. Both children now had coughing productive of yellow-white sputum, and it was requiring more medication to control it. Both children also had new bothersome pleuritic chest pain, so Marguerite was also given hypodermic morphine. Michael's headache had centered at, and behind, his eyes. Just moving his eyes hurt. Still, the medication was moderately effective at controlling their symptoms, and they remained very well hydrated.

After library lessons finished for the afternoon, Bernard disappeared into his room. He emerged to eat half of his dinner, and then went back to his own calm space. His only comment to his parents was that he was preparing a Red Sox spring training summary for Michael, when he was better. Noble told Michael of his brother's summary that evening, and Michael told his father to thank Bernard for him. Noble read a short story to Marguerite, who did her best to keep her eyes open for it. He brushed her auburn curly hair, and blew her a kiss as he often did. She smiled as only her father's "Rabbit" could.

Wednesday, January 15th came. At mid-morning, Noble found both children to be considerably more obtunded. Both could only be moderately aroused, and both would not drink fluid. Michael's vital signs included a respiratory rate of 22, and a temperature of 104° F, and Marguerite's numbers were 21 and 103.5° F. Coughing had become nearly constant. Chest auscultation reveled course bubbling rales bilaterally, moderate rhonchi, impaired resonance, and suppression of heart sounds. Michael moaned with any movement. Marguerite periodically whispered, "Daddy...Mommy... help me. Daddy...Mommy...help me." But, it appeared her pleas came from delirium since she did not respond to her father's words.

Noble went downstairs and met Lillian at the foot of the staircase. His expression told Lillian everything. Her eyes widened in a manner Noble had never seen before in his wife. Tears immediately pooled at her lower eyelids. She cupped both hands at her chin and cheeks. "Oh my God, Edward. Oh my God."

Noble took her hand and sat with her on the parlor sofa. He continued to hold her hand as he spoke. "Lilly, they're worse. Both now have bilateral pneumonias. They are holding their own, but they're not able to take in the volumes of fluid they need. We will need to start IVs for both of them. As you know, we bought oxygen tanks last fall for just such a situation as this. If their ventilation worsens, we'll have to apply O2. Our tanks are limited, so I'll use that treatment only when we absolutely must. Compressed oxygen is in short supply everywhere."

Lillian hung her head as though she could not continue to live with this insult to her family. "Edward, do you think we should take the children to the hospital?"

"Lilly," said Noble, "There is not a thing any of the Boston hospitals can do that we can't do here. Actually, they would receive a small fraction of the care that we can give ourselves. With the numbers of ill increasing in the city, it's likely they would not see a doctor, nurse, or even an aid for hours at a time. We can do one hundred times better than that. Boston City Hospital's supply of O2 is such that they would be given that treatment later than here at home." Lillian put her elbows on her knees, her hands across her face, and sobbed loudly. Noble put his arm around her back and hugged her. He said softly, "Lilly, the children are getting the best care on Earth. I would not settle for anything less." With that, Noble stood and went to find Florence.

Florence and her father went upstairs, and she proceeded to place IVs in both her siblings. Noble hung normal saline with five percent glucose, and started the rates at 100 ml an hour. The rates would be titrated to calculated fluid needs for each child. He also administered IV sodium bicarbonate. So many other prophylactic remedies were still only anecdotal, such as quinine and camphorated oil. Noble had them available, but was not convinced by the scientific method that they helped. *Primum non nocere* would apply to his children, as it applied to others.

Noble completed this stage of influenza management, and went downstairs to find Lillian still seated in the parlor. He sat with her and explained what he and Florence had done, and that things remained stable. However, Noble noticed Lillian's facial expression had changed while he was upstairs. She now had a look he knew very well. It was her determined look. And, nothing stopped Lillian when she became determined.

"Edward," said Lillian in her resolute voice, "what about Milton Rosenau?"

Noble now understood exactly where his wife was headed in this conversation, but still asked anyway, "What about Milton?"

"Dear," said Lillian, "Milton and John Keegan have been working on an antiserum at the Chelsea Naval Hospital for a couple of months. I know that they are finished with its preparation. Why not call Milton and see where he is with it?"

Of course, Noble already knew all of this. He spoke with Rosenau all the time. Lillian also knew her husband was aware of dozens of different antisera and vaccines under development throughout the United States. In fact, with his access to the A.I. Office, he likely knew more about this research than anyone else in the world. Noble said, "Lilly, I understand the need to look at all options in patient care, all the time. But, Milton's antiserum is in preliminary development. I am well aware..."

Lillian cut into Noble's sentence in a way she rarely ever did. "Edward...I want you to call Milton. It is important to me. Extremely important."

There was no point in arguing with his wife on this point. She wanted her husband to explore the possible use of Rosenau's antiserum. So, that was that.

Late in the morning, Noble called Rosenau in Chelsea. Noble brought him up to date on the situation with the children, and his good friend was shocked and dismayed. Rosenau, as always, asked if there was anything he could do to help. Noble said that there was something, and brought up Rosenau's antiserum.

"Well, Edward, I don't know," said Rosenau. "I know you will remember that the horse antiserum is multivalent, and consists of antibodies to a specific recipe of organisms. These include bacteria found in both live and dead subjects, such as diplostreptococcus, pneumococci Types I, II, III, and VI, *Staphylococcus aureus*, hemolytic streptococci, and *B. influenza*. Agglutination reactions confirmed the presence of antibodies to these organisms. We have successfully completed our animal studies with the antiserum, and we were quite pleased with the results. But, Edward, we have not studied it in any human subjects yet."

"Milton," said Noble, "Lillian wants to know if you feel the antiserum is ready to be tested in humans."

"That's our next step, Edward."

"Would you be opposed to entering Michael and Marguerite in your first trial...now?" Noble did not believe any of the antisera in research or production worked. The question came down to *primum non nocere*, and its application in this case. Of all the antisera and vaccines yet produced, Noble knew his friend and Dr. Keegan were the best at formulating a safe product."

"I'm not opposed to it, Edward. From what you say, both children meet our entrance criteria. We would need access to all your clinical and laboratory data, of course. All you would need to do is give a subcutaneous dose to both kids to ensure no adverse allergic reaction to horse serum. John is actually at the Boston City Hospital satellite Harvard lab right now. We have some of the antiserum there."

"Thank you, Milton," said Noble. "I will provide you with all our data, and we will have meticulous records for their clinical courses. Can Florence pick up two doses of the antiserum now?"

"I'll let John know to expect her very soon."

"Thank you again, my friend," said Noble, as he hung up the earpiece. He told his wife of the plan, and she seemed more relaxed.

Florence drove the Ford to BCH as soon as Noble's telephone conversation ended. In a little over an hour, she returned with the antiserum. Noble drew up a small amount of the clear light-yellow fluid in a small syringe, and injected 1 cc subcutaneously on the forearm of each child. By late in the afternoon, there had been no skin reaction, or any other reaction, to the test doses. Therefore, each child was then given 10 ml IV of the Chelsea Naval Hospital/Harvard influenza antiserum. The protocol called for the administration of 5 ml each successive day, for three days.

At forty-eight hours, the blood and sputum cultures at BCH remained negative and normal.

Next morning, Thursday, January 16th, the children were in two different forms of intense delirium. Delirium had become one of the hallmarks of severe influenza. Michael's mental state was agitation that required soft restraints for his own safety. Marguerite, on the other hand, was now very quiet and rarely spoke. Her only words now were "Daddy... Mommy", which she would repeat over and over again. Her eyes would open occasionally, fix on her father whenever he was in the room, and then close again.

Michael's evaluation by his father included the following: pulse 95, respiratory rate 27, blood pressure 85/50, and temperature 105° F. Marguerite's vitals showed a pulse of 75, respiratory rate 25, blood pressure 80/45, and a temperature 104.5° F. Marguerite had light epistaxis, and Michael now produced slightly blood tinged sputum. Coughing was more frequent, forceful, and interfered with their respirations. The children's lungs now had a matt percussion quality, and the wheezes were audible even without the use of a stethoscope. Both children were incontinent of urine and feces, and needed linen diapers and constant cleaning.

Noble tried to use crushed aspirin tablets to control the rising temperatures, and administered them into the esophagus with a suction bottle. He later switched to cinchonidin salicylate. In addition, Akeema and Florence kept moistened cool towels upon the children's skin. Sweat rolled off the children and soaked their bed sheets. Noble found that he was continually increasing the IV fluid drip rates in order to keep up with their fluid losses. He began to worry about his supply of normal saline for IVs.

Epinephrine IV was given to the patients in order to open up constricted airways. Given the mornings clinical deterioration, it was now clear oxygen would be required by facial masks. The O2 flow was initially set at 2 liters per minute in order to conserve the compressed gas supply. Lillian was sent in the Ford to see if she could find supplemental sources of O2 and IV fluids. She was able to find a few additional bottles of IV fluid, and one additional partially full oxygen tank. However, she had to pay in cash $100 for the former, and $200 for the latter. She gladly paid in full for both items.

After each child received their next maintenance antiserum dose, Noble called the BCH lab for the final time. Again, at seventy-two hours, none of the cultures gave any new clinical clues. This was the rule with influenza. Noble, Florence, and Akeema now took shifts staying with the children continually. Two people watched the Noble family patients as one rested. Lillian and Bernard cleaned laundry and washed fluid basins, which seemed to be an endless job.

It was Noble's turn to rest in the early afternoon. Lillian kept a pot of coffee available at all times for the adults, so Noble poured a cup...black. He sat down at the kitchen table opposite Lillian. Neither spoke. Noble and his wife had barely slept two hours each over the last three days. Dark circles had formed beneath both pairs of their eyes. They were both pale, and drawn. Noble reached across the table with a red checkered table cloth, and held Lillian's hand firmly. In turn, she squeezed his hand back. Their two very ill children were now receiving the maximum therapy known to be efficacious for influenza in 1919. In addition, the children had been entered into a research treatment protocol created by one of the world's best experimental epidemiologists. There was nothing left to do, except more of the same.

At 5:00 PM, after a very short restless nap, Noble took his place watching over Marguerite. He checked her fluid input/output log, calculated her fluid needs for the next one to two hours, and adjusted the IV drip rate. He changed her linen diaper and bed linen, and re-applied cool towels to her hot diaphoretic body. He auscultated her chest, and then administered IV epinephrine and sodium bicarbonate. Her vital signs were pulse 95, respiratory rate 29, blood pressure 75/43, and temperature 105° F. He increased her O2 flow rate to 4 liters, keeping in mind that their supply was very limited. He sat down in a wood chair at bedside near her head. He watched her carefully with his hands folded in his lap. Every now-and-then, Marguerite would speak so softly through her oxygen mask that it was barely audible. "Daddy...Mommy. Daddy...Mommy."

The event at 6:00 PM was so subtle that it would have been missed by anyone who was not cognizant of its meaning. It was so minor that even astute clinicians who were masters of physical diagnosis would have ignored it. Noble was replacing a cold compress on his young daughter's forehead, when he saw it. He halted his motion as though he had suddenly been frozen in a huge block of ice. He put his face close up to the left side of Marguerite's head. He then checked her right side. He double checked. He triple checked. Noble felt all the air in his chest leave in one rapid exhalation. He slumped into the wooden chair. No. No. This could not be. His eyes filled with tears so fast that he could no longer see. He brushed them from his eyes, only to have them fill again. And again.

Ever so faintly, and occupying only one millimeter of skin at the tips of Marguerite's earlobes, was the almost invisible hint of indigo-blue.

CHAPTER 29

Edward the father remained incapacitated in the wooden chair, not sure what it was he should do next. It was not long before Dr. Noble pushed the father aside and took over the situation. Dr. Noble knew vital signs were the first order of business; pulse 99 and irregularly irregular, respiratory rate 31 and labored, blood pressure 72/41, and temperature 105.5° F. He examined Marguerite's airway and found it was patent. A small trickle of blood appeared from the left corner of her mouth. Auscultation of her chest showed dense consolidation bilaterally with worsening wheezes. Heart sounds where nearly silent through her chest. Pulses had normal bilaterally, but were now reduced. Marguerite was no longer responsive.

Noble increased the oxygen mask flow to the maximum 6 liters. He knew this would mean the family would empty the O2 tanks soon, but there was no time to lose. He gave an early dose of epinephrine, and an additional dose of cinchonidin salicylate. He gave an IV dose of digitalis for presumed atrial fibrillation. He quietly went downstairs to the kitchen ice box to retrieve ice cubes. Once upstairs, Noble replaced the moist cool towels upon his daughters little body with towels wrapped around ice. He then increased the IV flow rate for the higher fever.

Noble quickly left Marguerite for Michael's room where Akeema sat sleeping at the bedside chair. He did a very quick observational exam and found no evidence of cyanosis. Vital signs taken just fifteen minutes earlier showed Michael's clinical stability. He ran back to his daughter's room.

Marguerite's father did not remain still for the next hour. He checked logs, re-checked logs, and checked logs three, four, five times, and more. He performed vital signs and detailed physical exams every five minutes. He calculated, and re-calculated, fluid inputs and outputs as fast as he could perform the arithmetic.

At 7:00 PM Marguerite's coughing worsened. Noble's exam revealed that her ears were now a deep blue color. Her face had taken on a cherry-red hue, and her lips had a crimson appearance. Marguerite's coughing was productive of frothy pink sputum that flowed from both corners of her mouth. Blood dripped from her nose, and serous fluid drained from both ears. Her urine now had a pink color. His daughter was beginning to struggle with breaths as her respiratory rate reached 35 a minute. Noble used a suction bottle to remove as much bloody fluid from her laryngopharynx as possible. But, the more he suctioned, the more accumulated.

It was 7:30 PM when the gentle hissing of the oxygen flowing through Marguerite's mask quickly stopped. Her O2 tank was empty. Noble rushed into Michael's room while Akeema continued to sleep, and made a quick clinical assessment of his son's condition. Michael was resting comfortably, and was stable at that movement. Making a choice that Dr. Noble could make, and father Edward could not, he disconnected the Michael's O2 tank and carried it into Marguerite's room. He reconnected the oxygen tubing to his daughter's face mask, and resumed its flow at 6 liters per minute. For the next thirty minutes, each one or two minutes, Noble ran from room-to-room checking on both children.

A little before 8:00 PM, Noble's suctioning could no longer keep up with Marguerite's bloody respiratory secretions. Her entire head had turned a deep indigo-blue, which was in sharp contrast to her curly auburn hair. Now her torso and limbs had become cyanotic. Noble hated the thought, but he needed help.

Noble ran downstairs to his bedroom where Lillian was resting on their bed. He touched her on her arm, and she awoke with a start. Noble did not say anything. He did not have to. Lillian looked into his eyes, and she knew. She burst into tears and loud sobs, but rose off the bed to follow her husband upstairs.

Entering the room, Lillian saw her daughter for the first time in about two and one-half hours. Along with her ghoulish coloring, Marguerite was now arching her back with many of her struggling breath. Fluid gushed from her mouth and nose. A bloody-yellow fluid trickled from both ears. Lillian screamed, and fell to the floor with her fingers buried into her brown hair. Hearing the scream, Akeema and Florence ran into the room. Each woman placed a hand over her mouth with the shock of the scene.

Without words, Noble motioned to Florence who immediately began to suction her sister's secretions. Akeema went downstairs for more ice. Lillian rose to her knees on the floor next to Marguerite's bed and stared at the activity. Noble took another set of vitals: pulse 70 and irregularly irregular, respiratory rate 38 and labored, with marked wheezes and productive coughing, blood pressure 61/35, and temperature 106° F. He administered more epinephrine and increased again the IV rate. Akeema returned with additional ice for cooling the child, and began to sop up the voluminous pink frothy fluid on the floor.

Over the next fifteen minutes, Marguerite's movements gradually decreased as did her respirations. Two adults desperately tried to keep her own secretions from chocking her.

However, Marguerite was suffocating from within. Noble could also see the disease was quickly shutting down one organ system at a time: pulmonary, neurologic, cardiac, and now renal. Her urine output was essentially zero. Another set of vitals were taken: pulse 45, thready, and irregularly irregular, respiratory rate 15 with almost inaudible breath sounds, blood pressure 45/25, and temperature 106° F. Noble raised the IV bottle pole to the ceiling in order to pump as much fluid into his daughter as possible. He gave another dose of epinephrine. This time the drug was intended more for blood pressure than ventilation. Noble sat on the wood chair next to the bed and waited.

A great stillness came over Marguerite. Her room was completely silent. The three adults sat motionless about her bed. After several moments, Noble felt his daughter's bilateral carotid arteries. Then her bilateral brachial arteries. Then her bilateral femoral arteries. He took her blood pressure as almost a habit. He watched the sphygmomanometer gauge as he opened a small valve on the pressure cuff hand pump bulb. Air rushed from the cuff as it deflated. After a time, he removed the blood pressure cuff from the limp slender upper arm.

Lillian was kneeling by her husband. She looked up at him as though expecting good news. Noble slowly turned his head toward Lillian, and in an instant a universe of information was transferred. Lillian fell to the floor with a moan that seemed to come from a place outside this world. The other two women began to weep when they realized that no good news was coming. They went to comfort Lillian as she cried in short gasping breaths. For the moment, Dr. Noble again took over from Edward the father. He removed Marguerite's respiratory mask and unplugged the O2 tank hose from it. He carried the tank into Michael's room and restarted the flow of oxygen to him. Noble checked his son's vitals: pulse 90, full and regular, respiratory rate 24 with moderate rhonchi and rales, unlabored, and a severe cough, blood pressure 92/55, and temperature 104° F.

Noble returned to Marguerite's room. He found Lillian hysterical, and the other two women on the floor nearly so. Noble could hear Bernard crying loudly from his room, and knew his oldest son had also realized what had happened. Noble asked Florence and Akeema to help him take Lillian to their bedroom. It was necessary to almost carry her because of the severity of her grief. For the next three hours, Lillian did not stop crying. Noble held her hand, rubbed her shoulders, and brushed her hair from her face wet with tears. Florence disappeared behind the door of her room, and tried to comprehend the reduction of her siblings from four to two. Akeema went upstairs to watch over the other patient who was far from well.

By midnight, Lillian had fallen into a restless sleep. Noble went upstairs to relieve Akeema from watching Michael. Akeema was exhausted, and went off to her room whimpering. Noble set about updating Michael's fluid input/output log, checking IV flow, slightly lowering O2 administration to conserve the gas, applying fresh cool cloths, and giving more doses of epinephrine, caffeine, benzyl benzoate, sodium bicarbonate, and cinchonidin salicylate. For now, his son was at least stable.

At 2:00 AM, Friday, January 17th, Noble walked across the hallway to Marguerite's room. Akeema had lit a single candle on the left bed stand. It was the only light in the room. In the ways of the Yup`ik, Akeema had carefully cleaned Marguerite and dressed her in a fresh ironed nightdress. She lay on her bed, eyes closed, and with her hands folded across her abdomen. Akeema had placed the favorite doll "Lucy" next to Marguerite. On the right bed stand she had also set Marguerite's roller-skates, her stereo picture viewer, and several family photographs. Aside from her deep blue color, Marguerite looked as though nothing unusual had transpired over the last several days. Noble pulled a rocking chair to the side of the bed and sat down. He remembered the times he read books to his daughter on his lap while rocking her to sleep in that very chair.

Noble quietly rocked as he viewed his daughter's body. "Rabbit" was so still. So very very still. It was so unlike her. He thought about the things that his "Rabbit" would never again experience: Family parties. Skating. Red Sox games. Playing with her dolls and 3-D pictures. Hugs from her parents and siblings. Noble also thought about the things "Rabbit" would never experience: School football games. Graduation from high school and college. Being shy with a special boy on a first date. The first kiss. Marriage. Her own children.

Noble could not find a measure to his own grief; a grief which made it hard for him to even breathe.

In three and one-half days, Noble had slept only a few hours. In his exhaustion, reality was becoming harder to define. The flickering of the room's candle created shapes that seemed to move on their own. At times, Noble could see a form in the shadows that came together, parted, and came together again. If he looked hard enough, he could make out breathing of the shape. Maybe there were facial expressions as well. "I'm...I'm...so tired," Noble said quietly.

After a time, Noble became certain the shape was actually the demon. It sat calmly across the room in the darkness, just beyond the full candlelight. As Noble's fatigue overpowered him, the demon became more real with every passing minute. It was therefore not unexpected when the demon spoke to Noble.

"Edward," said the demon.

Noble was having difficulty keeping his eyes open, but quickly answered back, "What?"

"That was quite a speech you gave to Lieutenant Pierre-Louis a few days ago, Edward," said the demon. "Very touching."

"What speech was that?" asked Noble, who was irritated by the conversation.

"Come on, Edward," said the demon. "You remember. 'I will pursue this disease in every way I can, and for as long as I can.' Very courageous, Edward."

"I remember," said Noble.

"You are such a 'noble' opponent, Edward." The demon laughed at its own pun.

"Why are you here?" asked Noble impatiently. "Now that you have succeeded in your work, why don't you just go away?"

"I'm here to give you a little message, Edward."

"What's that?" asked Noble.

Noble thought he saw the demon smile, but was not sure. Its demeanor was tranquil, and almost soothing. "You cannot beat me, Edward," the demon said confidently. "Go ahead and pursue me with your stupid science and maudlin medicine. You will never even know who I am, let alone catch me. However, my little message to you is that I am not content to just win. I seek to completely destroy you in the process. I will pick off the members of your family, one at a time. I will do it when I want, how I want, and where I want."

"What are you after?" Noble interrupted, almost shouting.

The demon giggled with the question. "What am I after, Edward, my old friend? I desire to make you a shell of a man, as I take everything you love from you. Everything." The demon paused for a time, then said cheerfully, "Oh yes, Edward. Always remember that I am both nowhere and everywhere. My trademark is arriving when one least expects me. And, I can take many forms. Here is a kind warning. You have only seen one of my many forms...Dr. Noble."

Putting both hands to his eyes, Noble lowered his head. He was at the end of his emotional rope, and could banter no more with his enemy. Everything gradually became very quiet.

There was a noise in the house that startled Noble as he found himself slumped in the rocking chair. The single candle on the bed stand had burned out. The room was dark, except for soft moonlight coming through the bedroom window. Noble checked his wristwatch. It was 6:00 AM. I've been asleep for four hours, he thought.

Noble walked across the hallway to Michael's room and found Florence sitting quietly with him. Quick vitals revealed a sick, but stable, boy: pulse 85, full and regular, respiratory rate 23 with moderate rhonchi and rales, unlabored, and still with a severe cough, blood pressure 93/56, and temperature 104° F. This morning Michael could be aroused slightly. The O2 tank was empty, so Noble removed the oxygen face mask. He medicated his son to treat his ongoing bronchospasm, cough, and fever.

Noble sat down next to Florence. She told her father she was going to make all the arrangements now required. Florence did not feel her mother was capable of that. She had just called a mortuary in Brookline, and they would be sending a hearse over within two hours. Mortuaries were well beyond busy this January. But, the owners of this particular mortuary were good friends of the Nobles and would "work them in." Later in the day she made calls for various other services, and to friends and family. Her father thanked her for taking charge at this horrible time.

By 8:00 AM the hearse came and collected Marguerite's little body. Her mother did not want to be present for the transfer, and instead remained in bed. Except for eating a little soup prepared by Akeema, and using the bathroom, Lillian stayed in bed for the next two days.

Noble tried to help Florence with the duties at hand. However, he was not very effective. The loss of Arthur, and now "Rabbit", had left him in a dead world from which there seemed to be no escape. Lillian would not talk, or even get out of bed. Bernard could rarely be coaxed from his bedroom. Florence wrapped her grief in the industry of funeral arrangements. Akeema threw herself into all the family duties Lillian had abdicated. The family that was the center of Noble's life was disintegrating in more ways than one.

Every day, Noble went alone to the Cathedral of the Holy Cross. Since Boston public meetings were restricted, there was no Mass to attend. Only small numbers of people were allowed in the church at a time, and most of them were attending small memorial services. Noble was desperately trying to make sense of his children's deaths. He sought some peaceful resolution to the madness that sprang from a Kansas prairie. Haskell County seemed like a million years ago, even though he had been there less than twelve months earlier. With all his efforts, and the work of thousands of dedicated professionals, it appeared they were all simply wrestling with thin air.

Five days later, on the icy morning of Wednesday, January 22nd, Noble, Lillian, Florence, and Bernard attended a fifteen minute memorial at the Holy Cross Cathedral. Akeema stayed at home with Michael who was slowly recovering. A number of small gatherings were being conducted at the same time, just as had occurred during Karen Pecknold's memorial months earlier. The only difference was the degree of efficiency with the simultaneous services. The church was now well-practiced in the art of brief and rapid memorials.

The attending priest read some versus from scripture, and said a few prayers. He talked about a little auburn-haired six year old girl who bounced through life, and loved every moment she had on Earth. Marguerite's family was so taken with anguish that they could not respond during the Kyrie, or even say a few words about her at the end of the short memorial.

The Noble family left the cathedral in heavy coats, put blankets around them in the Ford truck, and drove to the Brookline Chestnut Hill Cemetery. Three inches of snow covered the ground, and a moderate wind sank a chill through the warmest of clothing. Blue sky was interspersed between billowy clouds, allowing intermittent sunlight to briefly warm cemetery visitors.

As the Nobles walked up the hill to the grave site, they were astounded to find over four hundred people waiting for them. Large groups were bared from gathering indoors, but there were no restrictions for outside meetings. People from a wide variety of groups came to pay their respects to the Noble family. Boston City Hospital residents, nurses, and staff, Red Cross volunteers, Women's Auxiliary, city, state, and federal officials, a large number of patients, and common Boston citizens came to give their respects. Milton Rosenau, William Park, Paul Lewis, Oswald Avery, Anna Wessel Williams, William Welch, and Victor Vaughn were some of the physicians and scientists present. Old and new friends, such as Katherine Cushing and Rose Kennedy, were also in the large group of mourners. They all came for Marguerite, of course. However, they also came for Arthur, who never had a fitting funeral. Finally, people came out of respect for a Boston family that had come to mean so much to so many.

Holy Cross could not spare a priest that morning, so Florence led a short ceremony for both Marguerite and Arthur. She read Bible passages the family had read when Arthur was buried, and two that Marguerite's father used to read to her. Luke 18:16:

"But Jesus called the children to him and said, 'Let the little children come to me, and do not hinder them, for the kingdom of God belongs to such as these. I tell you the truth; anyone who will not receive the kingdom of God like a little child will never enter it.'"

Also, Proverbs 20:7:

"The righteous man leads a blameless life; blessed are his children after him"

Over the years, Noble dramatized the "righteous man" and "blessed are his children" phrases when he read it to his family. Marguerite had always laughed when her father read the passage that way.

As people filed past the little coffin next to the fresh grave, dozens of flowers and small stuffed animals were placed upon it. Bernard walked by the scene with his head hung down. Earlier, he had given the mortuary a Babe Ruth baseball card to place in the coffin. Noble had placed a tiny stuffed toy rabbit for burial with his daughter. Akeema had the necklace of fish bones, from the spring Providence trip, set next to Marguerites body. Florence had written a note to be interred with her sister, but would not say its contents. Lillian could not bear to look at the coffin at all.

Near the grave were two new granite headstones. One headstone was for Marguerite, and the other was to replace the wood branch cross on Arthur's grave.

Marguerite's grave site gathering was the largest that morning, but it was not the only one at Chestnut Hill. Dozens of ceremonies were going on simultaneously for victims of influenza. At the same time, far in the distance, mourners could hear children chanting a rhyme. The Nobles, and everyone else, had heard it many times before:

I had a little bird,
Its name was Enza.
I opened the window,
And in-flu-enza.

CHAPTER 30

Following Marguerite's burial, the world of the Noble family could only be described as gray. The sky was perpetually gray. The ground was gray. The snow in Boston was always a grayish version of white. During the long winter nights and short days, even colors were muted into gray pastels. There seemed no end to any of it.

For several days, Noble stayed home with his shattered family. He cared for Michael as he slowly recovered from influenza pneumonia. He also tried to care for Bernard and his severe reactive depression. His oldest living son wanted to know how God permitted such things to occur. These were questions for which Dr. Noble, the evidence-based Internist subspecialist, had no answers.

While Bernard seemed lost, his sister underwent a transformation. Boston City Hospital continued to allow Florence to work with relief agencies as the influenza third wave swelled. Finding within herself a new level of maturity and determination, Florence began to assume many of the community roles her mother had always performed. She mobilized government services, coordinated Women's Auxiliary and Red Cross aid projects, and assisted in procuring resources for influenza quarantines. Noble watched her voluntarily take on huge new responsibilities. He thought he could see the best of both her parents blooming in his daughter.

Akeema maintained Noble household operations. She made sure there were meals to eat, clean dishes, clean clothes, and a clean house. Without her devotion to the Noble family, the situation would have been much more dismal than it already was. Akeema spent much of her personal time in Unaliq prayer. Her industry for those she loved, and her faith, were the ways she dealt with her own deep loss.

Lillian, however, was the most profoundly affected Noble family member. She became emotionally absent, and never left the house. She participated in no activities beyond essential life functions, and even those were minimally performed. Lillian slept twelve to fourteen hours per day and ate very little. She was losing a substantial amount of weight. Dresses, skirts, and blouses drooped on her frame as though she was a mannequin.

Lillian rarely spoke. When she did speak, it was only in response to questions posed to her. She gave only one word answers to those questions. Questions requiring more complexes responses were ignored. Lillian spent hours silently sitting on her bed looking out the bedroom window, or sitting in one of her departed children's bedrooms. Her husband worried about her mental and physical health more with each passing day. He asked Katherine Cushing and Rose Kennedy to come by the house to speak to her. But, Lillian would not receive them. To Noble, his dear wife, and his best friend... was vanishing.

By the end of January, Michael was able to sit in a chair and walk short distances within the house. His strength and resilience grew each day. He had moderate difficulties with balance, which forced him to have a slow and rather wide-based gait. Nevertheless, this neurologic sequela to influenza appeared to be gradually improving. Michael was eventually able to spend increasing amounts of time with his brother, Bernard. Their jovial interactions improved both their spirits immensely. Before long, both boys were reappraising their earlier estimates for the Red Sox 1919 season with numerous statistics and theories. Since Boston schools remained closed, Akeema restarted her Noble library tutorials for her two remaining students.

Michael was on the mend. Bernard was recovering from depression. Akeema remained the rock of the household. And Florence was becoming a new vibrant force within nursing and community health. What was left for Noble was to find a way to coax his wife back from the depths of severe clinical depression. There was no time to lose. It was apparent to everyone that Lillian's mental condition worsened with every new day.

Noble met with a psychiatric colleague at BCH and spent two hours going over recent and past familial history. Dr. Piero Garzaro agreed to begin treating Lillian on a regular basis. Florence would drive Lillian three times per week to the BCH Psychiatric pavilion for visits with Dr. Garzaro. The sessions were to begin immediately. Lillian did not resist the first trip to her psychiatrist on Friday, January 31st, but did not help in the endeavor either. Noble was not heartened by Dr. Garzaro's guarded overall prognosis following the first visit. He spoke to the psychiatrist by telephone after Lillian was brought home by Florence. "So, Piero, how does it look?"

"First, Edward, your wife does not appear to have any underlying medical disorders," said Garzaro. "It takes considerable effort to get her do speak, but she did supply me with an adequate history. She has been having intermittent headaches, dyspepsia, difficulty in taking pleasure in normal activities and making decisions, intermittent insomnia linked with intermittent hypersomnia, very significant weight loss, and persistent anxiety and emptiness. In addition, she has severe pessimism, hopelessness, loss of energy, and very significant guilt over the loss of her children."

"Guilt?" asked Noble.

"Yes, Edward," said Garzaro. "Guilt. She feels as though she should have been able to protect her children better from the grippe, or at least save them somehow."

"Piero, there is nothing more she could have possibly done."

"Edward, this is not rational, of course. But, it is very real to her. She developed extreme chronic stress as she dealt with the epidemic. Two sudden changes in her environment have been superimposed on that stress, and that was the death of her two children. Clearly, she is suffering from a severe form of reactive depression from chronic stress and bereavement."

"Piero, what can be done for her?" asked Noble. "She has lost about fifteen pounds, and that hasn't stopped. She is beginning to look skeletal."

"Yes, Edward, I'm glad you sought help when you did. Some wait much too long. She most certainly is on the extreme end of the reactive depression scale. But, there are some positives here. First, I find in her no ideation of suicide. Second, she has an excellent support system around her. Third, she is otherwise in good health. Finally, during most of her life, she has maintained very adequate coping strategies. These are all positive prognostic indicators. We will start on a course of interpersonal therapy. There is also a new approach called behavior therapy that actually has roots with the Stoic philosophers. There have been positive results recently reported in the psychiatric literature regarding to reactive depression and behavior therapy."

"Piero," said Noble, "I have known you for a long time. There is no one else I trust more in psychiatry. But, I hear some concern in your voice. Piero, what is it?"

"I keep forgetting, Edward, that you learn things about people before they know it themselves. You should have been a psychiatrist. Edward, most patients are able to be cured of reactive depression in about six months. However, there is an exception to the rule. Not all depressive individuals are capable of moving on easily. There are depression suffers whose condition continues over a much longer period of time."

"Do you think that applies to Lilly?" said Noble.

"I don't have a crystal ball, Edward. But, in my opinion, your wife may be in the subset of patients who have severe lingering symptoms for the long-term. In any case, we'll start therapy at her very next visit."

Noble thanked his psychiatrist friend. He was glad Lillian's psychiatric therapy would begin soon, and that she was in the best of hands. In the meantime, Noble would ensure for Lillian's adequate nutrition and safety. He would provide as comforting a home for her as possible. Noble would also make himself available anytime to talk with Lillian. But, he would not force the issue. He had individual conversations with Florence, Bernard, Michael, and Akeema, so they all knew Lillian's situation. They all had a new patient to care for.

Noble had kept in touch with Boston City Hospital residents by telephone since the beginning of Michael and Marguerite's illnesses. He found a considerable amount of clinical work could be conducted in this manner. The critical factor was the degree of trust an attending physician had in his or her residents. For Noble, this was the easiest part of the equation. He was blessed with a superb resident staff at BCH. Still, Noble had been mostly away for three weeks. He needed to return to the hospital, to the A.I. Office, and to the battle with influenza.

On Monday, February 3rd, Noble arrived at the A.I. Office early in the morning. The office sentry saluted the Major, and told him how sorry he was for his daughter's passing. Noble thanked him, and received the same comments from Lieutenant Pierre-Louis once inside. A mountain of cables and other messages were stacked on the central table, the roll top desks, and on the floor. Noble did not know how he could ever catch up with them. He also thought of a time when Lillian might have helped sort through the data to find critical pieces for them to study and discuss. At least for now, such collaboration was impossible. Stringing all her single words and phrases together, Noble's wife had barely said a full paragraph to him since the middle of January. He stood for some time and simply stared at the hundreds of unread messages.

"Sort-of overwhelming, isn't it, Major?" said the Lieutenant.

Noble shifted his weight onto one leg, put his left hand on his hip, and scratched his head with his right hand. "No kidding, Lieutenant. I don't know where to begin."

"Well, sir, the three of us have been trying to help you," said the Lieutenant. "I hope you don't mind, sir, but we have been writing a running summary for you. I'm sure we haven't done that good of a job, but we have tried to focus on the things you like to read most."

Noble smiled for the first time in weeks. He did not have to see the summary to know it would be a very good job indeed. The Lieutenant handed him a thick stack of paper in a three-ring binder with the title *A.I. Office Summary*. On each page were typed single-spaced cable summaries. The pages were organized in the same manner that cable stacks had always been placed on the center table. Noble quickly thumbed through the papers. He removed his glasses briefly to conceal his tearing eyes. Noble had not cried since the death of Marguerite, and he did not want to start now. Still, he was very moved by the extra work it had taken the Signal Corps Second Lieutenants to prepare this summary for him.

"Thank...thank you, Lieutenant. I can't tell you what this means to me...how much I appreciate all of you." The Lieutenant smiled, and said nothing. All three Signal Corps officers felt privileged to give the Major, who they admired so much, their additional efforts. It had not been a duty for them. It had been a pleasure.

The Lieutenant went back to work at her cordboard, and Noble began to read through his summary. The officers had put together an excellent synopsis. The summary painted a broad picture of the state of the pandemic both locally and nationally.

The numbers of new influenza cases and mortally were increasing. There was no hint the pandemic was abating. New cases were more clustered in more discrete areas than had been seen in the second wave. Also, pandemic disruption to industrial production and distribution was not as profound as before. However, since economic sectors are interrelated, only a few areas along the continuum could substantially slow the movement of goods and services. For example, medical supplies and drugs had been produced and packaged in adequate quantities in many parts of the country. But, these essential products were sitting on loading dock pallets because trains were not running regularly. Consumer goods were becoming scarce once again.

The international pandemic situation mirrored the United States. The third wave was effecting some world areas as much as the second, and yet not others. Influenza continued to roll over the planet, leaving misery and death wherever it came to call.

Teams of the greatest minds, in the greatest scientific institutions, around the world struggled to find the cause of the pandemic. Vaccines, antisera, and other drug therapies proliferated on both sides of the Atlantic and Pacific Oceans. Still, there was no evidence that anyone really knew what influenza was, or had the vaguest real notion how to stop it once it infected a victim.

There was one brilliant star in the blackness of the pandemic. Quarantine remained the only weapon humanity had against the infection. Given all the difficulties in starting and maintaining quarantine, it worked when strictly applied. If there was anything that could bring any happiness and fulfillment to Noble and his broken heart, it was one realization: Noble's cables to newspapers and the U.S. Public Health

Service had prepared many communities for the coming third wave. There was a clear and demonstrative effect for those who took the warnings seriously and planned ahead of the wave. Those who relied on the overly positive pandemic assessments, and the wishful thinking of certain government officials, were now paying the dreadful price.

Even though many in high places ignored it, there was an irrefutable and conclusive fact: Noble and the A.I. Office Signal Corps officers had been more successful in the fight against influenza than just about anyone else on Earth.

That week Lillian attended all her psychiatry visits. Dr. Garzaro told Noble that progress was very slow. However, his wife had opened up more verbally and emotionally during successive interviews. Lillian was not gaining weight, but was no longer loosing it. Akeema tried to prepare meals for her that would be appealing, and she seemed to be moderately successful in that endeavor. Lillian now smiled when Noble returned from work or entered the room. Occasionally she would put her hand on her husband's knee at dinner, or hold her husband's hand in the parlor at night. Once she asked Florence to take her to the Holy Cross Cathedral where she knelt and said a brief prayer. She still rarely spoke at home, and spent much of her time sleeping in her room or sitting in her deceased children's rooms.

Noble had his hands full at home. But, he was also being challenged at Boston City Hospital. The facility was overflowing with influenza patients, and the outpatient clinics were jammed with even more. Long lines formed each day outside the hospital gates. A constant procession of hearses on Massachusetts and Harrison Avenues, and on Albany Street, picked up the hospital dead each day. Most hearses went to funeral homes, but some deposited their cargo at the growing mass grave sites about the city. Carts continued to collect some of the dead wrapped in sheets and left on sidewalks, as they had in the fall.

BCH opened up the last satellite facility it could afford to equip and staff. Several more physician and nurse deaths had actually left the hospital with fewer staff than it had during the second wave. Supply rationing had begun again. The volunteer relief agencies were working twenty-four hours a day, and the army and navy brought the city all the medical supplies they could. Nevertheless, the New England medical care system was on the verge of collapse...again.

Early on the morning of Friday, February 7th, Noble did not go directly to the A.I. Office.   Instead, he went to the medical resident morning report. Each morning, along with one or more attending physicians, the residents presented patient cases who had been admitted in the last twenty-four hours. The histories, physicals, labs, and roentgenograms were discussed in detail. Residents were quizzed on their differential diagnoses as well as their treatment plans. The residents saw the exercise as a form of torture. The on-call residents stayed up all night making various critical and complex decisions. Then, they were severely challenged on those sleep-deprived decisions by well-rested attendings. It was the "no pain, no gain; trial by fire" approach to clinical Internal Medicine training.

Some attendings could be tyrants at morning report, and could bring a resident to tears. However, the residents loved to see Dr. Noble at their morning report. He had a way of teaching that did not dress-down the residents. He could be critical of decisions made by residents, but remain supportive of them at the same time. All the residents believed he was the best clinical teacher in Boston.

After morning report, Noble joined one of the resident ward teams on their morning rounds. The team's second year resident, Dr. Anna Reed, turned to Noble as they walked to a nearby bed and said, "We need your help with a case, Dr. Noble."

"Fire away, Anna," said Noble.

"Mr. Fakhouri is a thirty-five year old man who has been admitted to Boston City Hospital many times. Four or five times per year, he has the onset of severe global abdominal pain. He usually has a fever to about 100.0° F when he is admitted. His white cell counts are usually slightly elevated during attacks, to a level of about 14K/μL, but are normal when the attacks stop. Blood cultures, urine cultures, electrolytes, and Roentgenograms are always negative."

Dr. Noble walked over to the patient, and put his hand on his shoulder. "Hi, Mr. Fakhouri. How are things today?" Noble pulled up the man's hospital gown slightly to see a healed scar in the right lower abdominal quadrant. He also gently palpated the man's abdomen and listened to it with his stethoscope.

"I'm feeling better today, Doctor. It usually takes about ten to twelve hours for the pain to decrease."

"I see," said Noble. "How old where you when you started to have these attacks, and what did your doctor tell you after your appendix was removed?"

"I was fourteen, Doctor. My doctor told me that there was nothing wrong with my appendix after he took it out."

Noble asked, "Where were you born? Oh, yes, do you ever have any joint pains, chest pain, or skin rashes?"

Mr. Fakhouri answered, "I was born in Armenia, Doctor. Come to think of it, I often have right knee pain that really hurts when I have the stomach pains. I sometimes have a lot of pain if I take a deep breath, but only during my attacks. I don't think I have any rashes, Doctor."

"Tell me about your immediate family, Mr. Fakhouri," asked Noble.

"Well, my parents, my two sisters, and my brother, are all in good health. They don't have attacks, if that is what you mean."

Dr. Noble turned to the residents and students, and began to speak so that the patient could also hear him. "There have been reports at Internal Medicine meetings of a disorder afflicting Mediterranean peoples that involve cyclic severe abdominal pain and fevers. It seems to run in families in an autosomal recessive pattern of inheritance. My guess is that people with similar ethnic backgrounds living around the Mediterranean Sea have known of this malady for centuries. Solitary joint pain, and pleurisy, is common in this group. Many times physicians rightly believe these patients have appendicitis. This appears to be the case with Mr. Fakhouri. Appendectomies almost always show a histological normal appendix in these patients."

"What can we do, Dr. Noble?" asked one of the residents.

"As yet, there is no known treatment. Aspirin definitely helps, as do opiates, when the pain is most severe. There have been a few cases of renal failure in these patients, so that is something to keep in mind. Hopefully, someday we'll better understand this fascinating and debilitating disorder."

Noble finished the team's initial rounding at about 10:30 AM, and returned to the A.I. Office. As always, the sentry saluted him as he entered the facility. Lieutenant Lafayette was taking new cables off the Buckingham Machine Telegraph as Noble entered. "Good morning, Major. Were you on rounds this morning?"

"Good morning, Lieutenant," said Noble. "Yes, I've missed a lot of morning reports recently, and thought I should get back into the habit of attending some of them." Noble then went to the new cables and telephone transcriptions on the center table, and began to review the most up to date pandemic information.

About thirty minutes later, the Lieutenant turned around to Noble, who was standing behind her. She was wearing her earphones. With a confused expression, she said, "Major, the sentry is on the office intercom. He says there are several men here to see you."

Noble's expression showed the same confusion as did the Lieutenant. "Who are they, Lieutenant?"

"The sentry says they are Military Police," said the Lieutenant, whose expression had turned from confusion to concern. Noble told her to allow the men entrance.

Seconds later, six men entered the A.I. Office. Noble's clinical observation abilities quickly determined who the men were. Two of the men wore "MP" armbands for Military Police. A third man had a bronze "IP" service device on his left collar that stood for Intelligance Police. Two men had "CID Agent" badges that stood for the Army Criminal Investigation Division. CID had been created by General Pershing just a few years earlier. The sixth man was a Captain with a bronze collar "sword and quill" service device on olive branches. He was from the Army Judge Advocate Department. The Captain looked as though he was not a day over eighteen. Noble knew that could not be the case, because he was a lawyer.

"Major Edward Noble?" asked the Captain, as he walked within a foot of Noble.

"Yes," said Noble. "What can I do for you, gentlemen?"

"Sir," stated the Captain, "you are under arrest."

CHAPTER 31

The mammalian "fight or flight" fear reaction in the body's peripheral vascular system can cause transient dizziness, or even fainting, before the blood pressure is sufficiently high enough to compensate. After hearing the Captain's words, Noble experienced this dizziness along with a brief darkening of his vision. Adrenalin then suddenly poured into his arteries causing his heart to pound at 130 beats per minute, his respiratory rate to climb, and his face to redden. Already knowing the answer, he calmly asked, "What's the charge, Captain?"

"Major Noble," answered the Captain, "you are charged with the unauthorized use and distribution of classified government documents, breaking of the peace, and wrongful disposition of military property...sir." Noble stood straight and motionless as the MPs walked up to him. One MP put his hand on Noble's shoulder as the other placed Noble's hands behind him and applied handcuffs. The IP Sergeant, and the CID Agents, began taking three ring binders off the office shelves and cables off the center desk. The A.I. Office sentry walked into the room to find out what was transpiring.

The Captain turned to a frightened Lieutenant Lafayette and said, "Lieutenant, you are to stand down immediately, and return to your place of residence until further orders. The other Signal Corps officers are to do the same. Please collect your things and leave this office…now." The Lieutenant, with tears running down her cheeks, took off her headset, put on her army coat, and quickly left. The Captain then turned to the sentry and said, "Sergeant, this U.S. Army facility is hereby sealed for a criminal investigation. No one without specific authorization from CID is to enter it. Do you understand, Sergeant?" The sentry nodded in disbelief.

The Captain then turned to Noble and said, "Major, we have orders to take you into custody and transport you to the army camp at Devens. Please come with us." With that, the MPs put Noble's coat around his shoulders, put on his cap, and led him out of the A.I. Office.

Noble's heart rate was still racing as he was taken from the South Department to a pair of Military Police automobiles parked on Albany Street. Two back doors were opened on one of the cars marked "MP". Noble was instructed to enter through the doors and sit on one of two benches that faced each other. He was barely seated before both cars quickly started up and drove away.

No one spoke as they drove to Devens. Noble felt his heart return to a normal resting pace, his breathing relax, and the skin on his face cool. He was surprised how tranquil he had become, and in such a short period of time. All the way to the camp he thought about the words Colonel Vaughn had spoken weeks earlier. "…I need to caution you about the forces that may come after you. Profound and powerful forces. I may not be able to stop them, Edward. Do you understand what I am saying?" Noble expected some reaction to his memos warning of the pandemic. He had hoped it would not take this form, but it was not a complete surprise in any case.

Noble worried much more about Lillian, and how her present fragile constitution would handle all of this. His arrest might be the final straw that pushed her into a permanent and disastrous melancholia. He thought about what the loss of three children, and her husband, did to the intelligent Mary Todd Lincoln.

Two hours after his arrest, Noble arrived at the Camp Devens stockade. The stockade was a very large gray concrete building in the near-center of the camp, with adjoining clapboard offices. Noble was taken to a stockade receiving area where the contents of his pockets were taken and placed in paper bags. He was given a plain field uniform without insignias to wear. He was then allowed to make one ten minute telephone call. Not wanting to shock his family, he chose to call his good friend Milton Rosenau in Chelsea. If Milton already knew what this was all about, he would be able to break the news to others in the least traumatic way possible. If there was such a way.

Noble was then led by two guards down a long dark corridor lined with thick locked steel doors. The door to his cell, No. A-66, was opened and Noble was unceremoniously deposited inside. His handcuffs were removed, and the heavy black door was slammed shut and locked.

Noble's cell was ten by ten feet, and had a ceiling that was also ten feet high. The floor, walls, and ceiling were all concrete, and painted gray. The door had a small window that was closed from the outside, and a thin horizontal slat at the bottom where food trays were slid into the cell. On the opposite wall from the door was a simple cot with a very thin mattress. On the mattress were folded sheets, olive colored blankets, towels, and a thin pillow. The wall to the right of the door had a small sink with a bar of soap and a tooth brush. There was also a toilet with a roll of paper nearby. Hanging from the ceiling was a short electric cord with a single bare light bulb turned on. Almost at the ceiling was a single small horizontal window that was also closed. The cell was dark, cold, and damp. It had the musty smell of fungi.

Two hours earlier, Dr. Noble had been teaching admiring medical residents in one of Boston's best hospitals. Now, he was inmate No. 121-A-66, with nothing to do.

Since there was no clock in his cell, his wrist watch had been taken from him, and there was no direct sunlight, Noble had no sense of time. He guessed some number of hours elapsed before the door opened, and two guards escorted him handcuffed out of his cell. Without speaking, the MPs led him down a number of dark corridors until they came to a thick steel door painted olive green. On the door was a stenciled sign that read "Consultation Room". The door was unlocked and his handcuffs were again removed. Noble was directed into a twenty by twenty foot concrete room that was also painted olive green. He was told to sit on a gray metal chair next to a large wooden table located in the center of the room. Once seated on the chair, the steel door was shut.

Noble sat alone at the table with his hands folded in front of him. On the opposite side of the table was another metal chair. Two bare light bulbs hanging from short ceiling cords lit the windowless room. The wall to the left of the green steel door displayed a six by four foot screen made of a very fine mesh. Noble thought the screen was likely used to observe inmates from another room without detection. The only sound Noble could hear was his own breathing. He thought the room walls must be extremely thick to block out that much ambient noise.

Another long period of silent time went by. Then, suddenly, the steel door was opened by a guard. A Captain, who appeared to be in his late twenties, walked in the room and sat down opposite Noble. He had a pleasant open face and light brown hair fashioned in a crew cut. He stood about 5 feet 7 inches. Based on his thick neck and chest, Noble guessed that he had been a wrestler at some point. The Captain also had a bronze collar "sword and quill" service device. Another lawyer, thought Noble. The Captain placed a large file on the desk, along with pencils and two pads of paper. He then asked, "How are you holding up, Major Noble?"

"Depends on who you are," said Noble with a wryly smile.

The Captain laughed. "They told me you were witty, and used dry sarcasm as a probing tool with people. Forgive me, Major. I'm Captain George York from the Office of the Staff Judge Advocate. I'm your defense counsel."

Noble relaxed a bit. One of the "good guys", he thought. "I'm OK, I guess. I have a ton of questions, but I suppose you do too."

The Captain laughed again. "Both of us have questions, and our job is to get some answers. I know a lot about you, doctor. But, just so we're even... I graduated from the University of Pennsylvania Law School, and was a defense attorney for three years before joining the Army a year ago. Patriotism, you know."

"Yes," said Noble, "I know. Been there."

"I think you heard the charges at your arrest this morning," said York. "But, just so that we are all on the same page. The Filing of Information has three counts. First count: Unauthorized use and distribution of classified government documents. Second count: Breaking of the peace. Third count: Wrongful disposition of military property. By far, the first count is the most serious. But, if found guilty on all counts, you're looking at twenty to twenty five years hard labor with confinement, a $10,000 fine, and a dishonorable discharge."

Noble thought the only thing worse than hearing about a possible bad prison sentence is the realization the sentence is for you. "Is there extra credit for good behavior, like in college?" Noble did not want to be too flippant about this, but he could not resist.

"Sure," said York. "If you're a good boy, you might get off in fifteen years." Noble thought that was not exactly the type of extra credit he was accustomed to in school.

"Major, all joking aside," said York. "You have a problem. You're scheduled for a general court-martial that is on the court calendar for February 13th. That's just six days from now. And, that includes the discovery phase. I have almost no time to prepare this case. In addition, I'm told this will only be a one or two day court-martial. Major, I have never seen anything like this before. I don't know who you pissed-off, but it is someone important. And, they want you out of the way, fast, and permanently."

"So, I'm 'Mr. Collegiality', Captain?" said Noble.

"Someone doesn't think so," said York. "Anyway, we have a lot of work to do, Major. I have already started some of it on your behalf. I tried to have the jurisdiction of the court-martial changed, since you are attached to the Communicable Disease Division and not the infantry. But, the general courts-martial convening authority is the post commander at Devens, and he decides jurisdiction. The motion to challenge jurisdiction was denied. So, we're staying here. I suspect that anyone who has any knowledge of infectious disease is not supposed to hear your case, Major."

York continued. "Your plea is crucial. I think you will agree it is impossible to make the case that you did not divulge some classified government documents. You did, right?"

"Like you said, it's going to be hard to argue otherwise," said Noble.

"The government will try this case on the unauthorized use of those materials, and not on the outcome," said York. "The trial counsel will attempt to have the court ignore the circumstances surrounding the use of the military assets, and also ignore the intent of their use. The government will argue the ends did not justify the means in this case. Also, regardless of the reason, you distributed a wide range of U.S. Public Health Service information. We must remember that the USPHS is part of the military."

"There is another extremely important point here, Major, and it is political," said York. "President Wilson appointed the Judge Advocate General, or 'TJAG', as he is called. Wilson has had no problem abridging freedom of speech over the last year-and-a-half. In other words, this case will be tried by people who ultimately report to TJAG, and are sympathetic to Wilson's policies. Freedom of speech, even when it was exercised in the public's best interest, will not be a sacred item in this court-martial."

"So, Captain, how should I plead?" said Noble.

"My advice," said York, "is to plead according to section II-108 of the U.S. Manual for Courts-Martial. That is, a plea of *affirmative defense*. This plea does not deny that the accused committed the objective acts constituting the offense charged. Rather, it denies criminal responsibility for those acts."

"OK," said Noble. "Let's go for an *affirmative defense* plea."

"So be it," said York. "Now, onto the next order of business. The government has already put on the table a plea bargain. Do you want to hear it?"

"Talk is cheap, Captain," said Noble.

"They offer eight years confinement only, probation for five years, a $5,000 fine, and a dishonorable discharge," stated York.

"No," said Noble.

"Didn't think so," said York. "Another important decision that you need to make right now is the type of court-martial you want."

"I have a choice?" asked Noble. "Well, I choose not to have one at all."

"Major," said York, "your personality profile said you often deflect stressful situations with humor. This situation definitely qualifies as stressful for you. But, I need you to stay on-task here. We have very little time. Now, you may choose between a panel or judge court-martial. The former consists of five officers of equal or greater rank than yourself who would decide the verdict in your case. They would be chosen much as any jury in civilian courts would be. The other option is to have a judge decide the verdict. Before you choose, let me tell you a little about the judge who will preside over your court-martial."

York continued. "Your judge is Major General Harry Parker who is fifty-eight years old. He is considered legendary in the Army JAG Office. At sixteen years old, he joined the army. He was underage, and normally would not have been allowed to enlist. But, the U.S Army was involved in the Great Sioux Wars at the time, and was in need of many soldiers. So, someone turned a blind eye when Parker joined. Within a few weeks, Private Parker was riding with the Seventh Calvary in Montana chasing Lakota and Cheyenne Indians. Parker would have been with Colonel George Armstrong Custer at the battle of the Little Big Horn. However, the day before the battle, Parker was thrown from his horse and suffered a severe concussion with seizures. Of course, Custer and five companies of the Seventh Calvary were annihilated the next day. People started to talk of 'Parker's Luck', which is a term that has stuck with him."

"A very colorful character, it seems," said Noble.

"Later, Parker applied to West Point while still an enlisted soldier. He graduated at the top of his class. While an officer, he went to the Ohio Northern University School of Law where he also graduated at the top of his class. His law career just took off from there. He has a reputation as a fair judge, but a very tough one. He conducts his court by the book, and that is what concerns me. I don't think you have a 'by the book' type of case, Major. My advice is you choose a court-martial by a panel."

"From what you say, Captain, I completely agree," said Noble.

"One other piece of history," said York. "The trial counsel in this court-martial, who would be called the 'prosecuting attorney' in a civilian court, is Colonel Jason Perry. He is a graduate of Harvard Law School and is a twenty-five year veteran of the Staff Judge Advocate Office. He is considered one of the most gifted army trial counsels in the Eastern U.S. Major, the bad news is that he is perhaps the last choice I would make as an opposing attorney, if it were up to me."

"Captain, you say that as though there is some good news as well?" said a hopeful Noble.

"The good news is," said York, "I think I'm pretty good, too. I was in the top ten percent of my law school class. And, I am dedicated to the zealous pursuit of your cause, Major.

For what it's worth, I believe your actions deserve a medal instead of a court-martial. I only wish I were the one to make that call."

Noble gave a brief smile. "All joking aside, Captain, I very much appreciate that. Your comment is the nicest thing I've heard all day."

York smiled back. His client was a good man. He wanted to do all he could to keep this physician contributing to the health and welfare of the people, and out of a military penitentiary jail cell for decades. "The preliminary hearing is on Monday. I am going to give you several documents to study over the weekend, as well as lists of questions and answers I want you to start contemplating. I already filed a motion to discover. We'll find out on Monday if there will be stipulations when trial counsel and I have an issue conference with the judge. The government already sent out subpoenas to various witnesses, and we'll have to see what CID and the Intelligence Police dig up at the A.I. Office. Can you begin looking over this file?" York handed Noble a thick folder file, along with a pencil and pad of paper.

Noble again smiled. "Looks like my weekend is free, Captain. I'll have plenty of time."

The two men saluted, and York knocked on the door. Two guards entered the room, handcuffed Noble while he was still holding the thick file of papers and paper pad, and everyone departed. Noble was led back to his cell where the handcuffs were again removed. One of the guards quickly informed Noble of the stockade schedule: Revelry at 5 AM. Communal shower at 5:30 AM. Meals are delivered to the cells at 6:30 AM, Noon, and 5 PM. One hour of exercise per day at 2 PM. Inmates awaiting trial are allowed thirty minutes of visitor time per day, with no more than three visitors present during those thirty minutes. Cell lights are turned out at 9 PM. A number of other rules, and punishments for breaking the rules, were also stated unambiguously.

As the cell door slammed shut, Noble went to work reading the file given to him.

Noble had a terrible night. The damp cell carried a chill to his skin no matter how well he wrapped himself in blankets. He slept in increments of fifteen to twenty minutes punctuated by long periods of starring into the pitch black cell. He had numerous unpleasant disjointed dreams that usually made no sense whatsoever. However, a few of them did.

In one dream, Noble was twenty-five years in the future. It was 1944, and there was mayhem and death around the globe. Entire cities were destroyed with single explosions. He was seventy-one years old as he completed his prison sentence. He was discharged from prison into a destroyed world where he had no family or friends. In another dream, Noble was standing on the Chestnut Hill cemetery knoll where his parents and children were buried. Shockingly, there were now four more graves added to the four already present. He could not read the names on three of the new headstones. However, the fourth headstone said "Lillian Noble". He woke up from this dream drenched in sweat.

Noble was already awake when revelry was called at 5 AM, Saturday, February 8th. He had a towel and bar of soap ready when he was led to the stockade showers in only his shorts. It was bitterly cold, and the shower water was freezing. Twenty-five men showered together at a time. When he returned to his cell, a clean uniform without insignias was on his cot, along with a coat. Promptly at 6:30 AM, his breakfast tray was slide into his cell through the locked door. His first meal as inmate No. 121-A-66 consisted of cold scrambled eggs, cold sausage, and cold toast with a frozen slice of butter. Lukewarm black coffee in a steel cup finished off the menu. Noble had not eaten in twenty-four hours, and therefore finished eating all the food on his meal tin. Noble then began to study his defense file and make copious notes.

Just before 11 AM, Noble's door swung open and he was summoned by two guards. "You have visitors," one guard said quietly. Noble was handcuffed and led down many corridors to an olive green door that had "Visitor Room" stenciled on it. Noble was brought into a room that was about forty feet long and fifteen feet wide. A guard was seated at each end. Along one of the long walls was a counter that stretched the entire length of the room. Six small windows, covered with the same small net found in the "Consultation Room", were located along the counter. Each window was numbered, one through six. A wooden chair faced each window at the counter. Four bare light bulbs hung from the ceiling, and the room was painted in the ubiquitous olive green. Noble could see partially through the small net windows because there was adequate lighting on the other side. It appeared that an identical room was located beyond the windows. Three men were already seated and speaking to people on the other side of the net. Noble was told to sit at the empty chair before window No. 3, while still handcuffed.

Several minutes went by as Noble waited for unknown visitors. All of a sudden, Florence and Bernard sat down upon wooden chairs on the other side of the net covered window.

"Florence...Bernard...I'm so glad to see you!" shouted Noble at the top of his lungs. "Quiet!" yelled back one of the guards at the end of the room. Noble lowered his voice, but his delight could not be contained. "Oh...gee...thank you for coming! I'm so glad you're here! I mean...I'm so sorry you have to be here!"

"Daddy, please know that we love you!" Florence said quietly. "Yes, Dad, we all love you," said Bernard. Florence continued, "Daddy, Dr. Rosenau came over to the house last night and explained everything to us. We know that you didn't do anything wrong! We know you're innocent! The idea that you would betray your country is...is...a damn lie!"

"I'm so fortunate to have such wonderful children as you all, and such a wonderful friend like Milton!" said Noble. "Please...please know that I did not do anything to harm our country! On the contrary, I tried to help save it."

"Daddy," said Florence, "the telephone has not stopped ringing since your arrest. Dozens of people came over to the house last night. No one can believe any of this, and everyone is behind you, Daddy. The hospital residents, nurses, support staff, and attending physicians have started a petition demanding your release. Professors at the Boston University School of Medicine, Harvard, and Tufts want to sign it. Even the *Boston Globe* sent reporters over to the house this morning!"

"How is Michael?" asked Noble.

"He's doing really well, Dad," said Bernard. "He's not staggering around as bad as last week. He even wanted to go out and play in the snow this morning. But, Akeema wouldn't let him because he's still a little weak."

Noble paused for a moment, and actually dreaded the next question. "Kids...how is your mother?"

Florence and Bernard both looked at one another. Bernard whispered something to Florence that Noble could not hear. "Daddy," said Florence, "Mom won't come out of her room. She locked the door to her room after Dr. Rosenau left last night, and she won't open it. Both Akeema and I pleaded with her to come out, but she won't. She wouldn't come out for Bernard or Michael either."

Noble felt a wave of nausea that always came to him at times of great despair. He put both of his hands across his eyes, pursed his lips, and swore under his breath. He thought that he could not take one more indignity imposed on his life. Not one more. He put his forehead on the counter before him.

"Daddy," said Florence. "Daddy. Are you OK?"

"Listen, both of you," Noble said sternly, raising his head of the counter. "I want you to call Milton Rosenau when you get home. Tell him that you have talked to me. Tell him that if your mother has not opened the bedroom door by this afternoon, I want him to come to the house and break it down! Do not let her stay in that room all alone. Also, call Dr. Piero Garzaro at BCH and tell him all that is going on. I fear that if she is left alone too long, something awful is going to happen."

"OK, Daddy," said Florence. "We will call as soon as we get home." Noble asked Florence to write down some items that would need attention. Bills needed to be paid along with other financial duties, and it did not appear that Lillian was capable of performing them. It would be up to Florence to take charge of family affairs for now. Noble knew his daughter was up to the task.

Only a few minutes had seemed to pass when the allowed thirty minutes were exhausted. A guard walked over to Noble, tapped him on the shoulder, and led him out of the Visitor Room.

Lunch was as unappealing as breakfast. At 2 PM, inmates were given one hour of exercise time in a large asphalt covered area adjoining the stockade. A fifteen foot steel chain link fence with barbed wire enclosed the exercise area, where men performed calisthenics, played basketball, jogged, or just walked in large circles near the fence. Noble was just happy to be out of his ten by ten foot cell, and was one of the men who simply walked for the entire hour.

Noble was barely back in his cell at 3 PM when he was taken again to the Consultation Room. There he met with Captain York for an hour to go over his defense. York said that CID agents and the IP Warrant Officer did not find any additional seditious evidence in the A.I. Office. The government's entire case would be built on cables sent to newspapers and the USPHS, and a few unrevealing notes written by Noble himself. However, York cautioned Noble about dismissing this evidence. His cables contained information that was classified. And someone, or some people, in the government did not like that at all. York told Noble they would meet every day until the day of the trial.

Dinner was cold, and included a thin stew known as "slum" by soldiers. Nevertheless, Noble again ate all of it. He read documents and wrote notes until just before 9 PM. As he was getting ready for bed, he thought about his first full day in jail and the routine that was already in place. He hoped there would not be many more days like this one. The single light bulb in his cell went dark promptly at 9 PM.

Sunday, February 9th was exactly like Saturday, except for the visitor half-hour. Inmates were never told in advance who was visiting them. So, it was the only surprise in the otherwise dull and repetitious day of prison life. Noble sat at Visitor Room window No. 3 awaiting his visitor, when his good friend Milton Rosenau sat down in front of him. "Milton! I can't...I just can't tell you how great it is to see you!"

Rosenau smiled his usual broad smile. "Edward, you never do anything little, do you! How are you doing, old friend?"

"Enjoying the food immensely, and looking forward to my daily walks in the stockade exercise area!" joked Noble. The only true statement by Noble was the second one.

"Edward, there is a firestorm of controversy over your arrest," said Rosenau. "All of New England is shocked, and the Infectious Disease/Epidemiology communities all over the country are outraged."

Although interesting to Noble, he wanted to talk about something else. "Milton, how is Lilly?"

Milton's smile faded to concern. "Well, Florence called me yesterday and told me of your worries. I came over to the house and was able to convince Lillian to unlock her bedroom door. She didn't want to talk at all, so I called Dr. Garzaro who immediately came over to the house. He gave her 60 mg of phenobarbital to help her rest."

"How does she seem to you, Milton?"

"Edward, her affect is completely blank. Her brief words are mechanical. She seems...she seems completely disconnected from everything. Since your arrest, it's like she has... 'turned off'."

"She can't be left alone, Milton. I'm very troubled over her worsening condition."

"Please don't worry, Edward. You have enough on your plate right now. I'll see if my wife, Katherine Cushing, and maybe Rose Kennedy can take turns staying with her. She doesn't resist company, Edward. She just doesn't interact with it." Rosenau went on to tell Noble about the continued rise in Boston influenza cases and how most hospitals were now out of supplies. Just as in the fall, many extremely ill patients were not receiving the care they needed. The situation was again dire. Noble asked Rosenau to contact the third year resident, Dr. David Schafer, and make a few operational suggestions for Boston City Hospital. However, given Schafer's competence, he was likely running the place already.

At 8 AM the next morning, Monday, February 10th, Noble was taken to his scheduled pre-trial court appearance. In court, defendants were to wear their usual uniforms with ranks and other insignias. So, after his ultra-cold shower, Noble put on his regular uniform.

The pre-trial appearance was in a small room near the stockade, and only lasted a brief time. Noble entered the room with Captain York and a guard. Seated at a small desk at one end of the sunlit room was the famous Major General Harry Parker. The judge had a kindly face with salt-and-pepper hair parted on his right side. His eyes turned slightly down on the distal ends, which gave him an almost sad expression. He had a bushy graying mustache and matching eyebrows. Noble guessed his height to be about 5 feet 7 inches, even though he was not standing.

Seated to the left of the judge, and facing his desk, was the trial counsel. Colonel Jason Perry was very thin, and completely bald. His zygomatic processes jutted out from his cheeks. His eyes were a searing light blue that seemed to protrude from their sockets. Noble wondered if his exophthalmos might be due to hyperthyroidism. Noble estimated the seated man was at least 6 feet 2 inches tall. Neither Parker nor Perry changed their expressionless faces when the defendant entered the room.

Noble and his counsel sat to the right of the judge as he matter-of-factly started the hearing. The defense had previously waved the arraignment reading. Parker looked directly at Noble as though he were an inanimate object, and began to explain the charges and their penalties to the defendant.

The judge's voice had a smooth low quality that seemed too gentle for a magistrate. "Do you understand these charges and what they mean, Major?" said Parker. "Yes, your honor," said Noble. The judge then addressed the defense motion to grant military bail. "Due to the defendant's flight risk...bail is denied," said Parker. The judge set the preliminary trial hearing for the next day, and adjourned the morning's session.

As Noble, York, and a guard left the pre-trial room, York leaned over to his client and whispered, "Flight risk, my ass."

The late morning visitors for Noble this day were Lieutenants Pierre-Louis, Quellet, and Lafayette. The Visitor Room guards had to quiet the women down a number of times as they all attempted to talk at once. However, Noble loved the excitement in their voices, and their loyalty to him. Each told the Major how sorry they were for all of this, how much they admired him, and what he had done for America. They couldn't wait to get "back to work" at the A.I. Office. Since the office was sealed by CID, the three Lieutenants had been helping out in the South Department in any way they could. As always, the thirty minutes ended way too soon.

The 8 AM preliminary hearing on Tuesday, February 11th was very different from what Noble had expected. It was held in the place where the court-martial would be conducted. Noble was driven in a Military Police automobile to a completely vacated barrack that was 150 feet long, 75 feet wide, and had rafters 35 feet high. Since the end of The War, the numbers of troops at Devens was decreasing. This left a lot of unused space for things like court-martials. Light from the outside easily lit the huge room, although large electric lamps hanging from the ceiling also added light. Sounds echoed through the barrack and its concrete floor, and it reminded Noble of the Cathedral of the Holy Cross in that regard.

At one end of the barrack was a large judicial bench that had steps up to it. The judge's seat was at least three feet higher than the other chairs in the room. On either side of the bench were the U.S. and Massachusetts flags on poles. The focal point of the entire building was a twenty foot long U.S. flag that hung on the wall behind the judicial bench. It gave the scene a commanding and formal decorum. Next to the bench on the right, and sitting on a two foot high pedestal, was a wooden chair.

Facing the bench were two long tables with two chairs on the right, and one chair on the left. To the extreme right of the bench were five chairs that faced the two long tables in front of them. Well behind the two long tables, and facing the bench, were a few dozen chairs. All together, the seating accommodated the principal players of the court-martial: the judge, the stand for a witness, seats for the defendant, the defense counsel, the trial counsel, and the panel.

Noble and Captain York walked over to the long table on the right, and took their seats. Off to the left of the judicial bench was a seated court reporter who would take short hand of all proceedings, and a chair for the court bailiff. A number of Military Police were seated in chairs along the barrack walls. A few minutes later, Colonel Perry entered the room and took his chair at the long table to the left of the judicial bench.

Not long afterward, the bailiff ordered, "All rise", and the people in the room stood for the entering Judge Parker. The bailiff then asked everyone to be seated. Positioned at his high bench seat, Parker used his hammer to open the preliminary hearing. He asked the government, represented by the trial counsel, to demonstrate probable cause for each of the three charges. Perry rose and stated that the government had evidence the defendant had committed the stated crimes, and showed an A.I. Office cable to the judge. Parker listened carefully to the trial counsel, and then said, "The government has shown probable cause. The defendant is bound over to court-martial."

The judge asked if the defendant was prepared to offer a plea. York said, "Yes, your honor. The defendant pleads not guilty with an affirmative defense." Parker said, "Duly noted."

The judge asked that five potential panelists be sent into the room. Five officers were led by the bailiff to the five seats to the right of the bench. Then began the laborious process of *voir dire*, when prospective panelists are questioned about their backgrounds and potential biases. Their interrogations by the judge went on for a few hours. One officer was removed for cause because he had been involved in a 1914 national security case. A second officer was removed because he was a Captain, and therefore a lower rank than the defendant. There was only one peremptory challenge made by the government. It removed an officer in the Medical Corps. What was left to be seated as panelists were a Brigadier General, two Colonels, a Lieutenant Colonel, and one Major. The highest ranking panelist became the President of the court-martial, who would be called the presiding juror in a civilian court room.

The judge gave the panelists some basic conduct instructions during the court-martial. He set the court-martial to begin at 8 AM, on Thursday. He then hit his gavel upon a sound block and said, "This session is adjourned." All rose as Parker left the room.

As Noble was about to be led back to his cell, York whispered to him, "Thus begins the shortest, and likely the weirdest, court-martial in American military history."

At the visiting half-hour, Noble was overjoyed to see his son Michael accompanied by Akeema. Michael was bundled up against the February cold, with a knit hat, a thick coat, and a long red scarf. Not forgetting her heritage as a Yup`ik Eskimo, Akeema always referred to Boston as a "warm place", and usually wore light coats. Michael told his father that he loved him, and that he missed Marguerite. He and his brother, Bernard, were counting the weeks until baseball season. When Noble asked about his mother, he said she was seeing her doctor almost every day, and that friends were staying with her constantly. At the end of the visiting time, Akeema asked to say a Unaliq prayer for Noble and his wife. Noble fought back tears when it was time to return to his cold, damp, and lonely cell.

Wednesday, February 12th was especially cold in the stockade. Noble put blankets around his coat after the morning shower, but he still remained cold. He figured his breakfast had been left out for some time before it arrived at his cell, because the scrambled eggs were frozen. The coffee could not have been colder if there had been an ice cube in the cup. Aside from an afternoon meeting with Captain York, the day had nothing else in it. Noble set out to finish his study of various documents, and review his notes, before the court-martial the next morning.

Just before 11 AM, two guards came for Noble. One said without expression, "You have a visitor". Handcuffed as usual, Noble was taken to the Visitor Room. As he sat down at window No. 3, he tried to guess who might be visiting today. He thought it likely Rosenau would come, or perhaps one or a few of the Boston City Hospital residents. Florence might visit, but she had many competing responsibilities right now.

Noble could just barely see a small clock on the wall of the room beyond the net window. It was the first timepiece he had seen since his arrest. As he waited for his visitor, he watched the second hand move around and around the clock face. Five minutes went by. Ten minutes went by. Fifteen minutes went by. Noble began to think a mistake had been made. Someone erroneously thought he had a visitor. Probably a mistaken identity, or some other military snafu, he thought.

Twenty minutes into his half-hour visiting time, Noble was about to ask the guards to take him back to his cell. All of a sudden a human form rushed to window No. 3 and sat down. At first Noble could not see who it was, since there was a thick scarf over the entire face...except the eyes.

The eyes. My God, thought Noble; the eyes. It was her. Could it really be? Oh, was it really her? The scarf was lifted from the face...and it was Lillian.

"Lilly!" yelled Noble. "Shhhh!" yelled the guard. "Oh, Lilly!" Noble said with a lowered voice. "It's you! Oh, God, it's you!"

Lillian smiled broadly. Her eyes glistened, and Noble thought they actually twinkled. After a few moments as the two just gazed at one another through the net window, Lillian said softly, "Daring...I'm back." A few moments later she added, "Florence drove me here".

Tears rolled down Nobles face. Between his sobs, he could only say, "Oh, Lilly! Oh, Lilly, I love you!"

"Edward, darling," said Lillian, "I'm back. I'm back for you. Do you remember what you said to me after Arthur's death, Edward?" Noble could only nod his head. "You said to me in our kitchen, 'Lilly, I will not abandon you. I will not abandon our children, or medicine. And, I will do <u>everything</u> to honor the memory of Arthur. Arthur would say to me, 'Dad...come on! Fight this thing! You can't do everything, but you can do what you can do!' Well, I'm here now to take a dose of my own medicine, Edward. It's my turn to honor Arthur, Marguerite, and you. And, you need me, and I want you to know that I'm here. We'll get through this, Darling."

Noble brushed away copious tears and said, "Lilly, do you remember what you then said to me in the kitchen?" Lillian also nodded. "You said, 'That's my doctor!' Not to sound ridiculous, Lilly, but let me say, that's my epidemiologist!" Both Lillian and her husband laughed so loud that the guard again said, "Shhhh!"

A guard stepped over to Noble and tapped him on the shoulder. As he stood from his chair to leave, Noble whispered "I love you" to Lillian. In turn, Lillian blew her husband a kiss. Noble was then led out of the room and back to his cell.

Noble was elated. His wife had come to see him. She said she "was back". And, her eyes stated that she really was. The ten minute visit gave Noble a burst of new energy to face the next day.

The cell light bulb went off a 9 PM, and Noble began to drift off to sleep. The day had been emotionally exhausting, and more was soon coming. However, just as he became very relaxed, Noble thought he heard a voice. "Edward."

After a few moments, Noble said quietly into the cell darkness, "What? What now?"

"Remember that I take many forms." Before he could contemplate the voice further, he slipped into the deepest sleep he had experienced in weeks.

CHAPTER 32

Immediately after breakfast on Thursday, February 13th, Noble was taken from his cell to a waiting Military Police car. He was scheduled to have a pre-trial meeting with Captain York. As they approached the barrack where the trial was to be held, Noble saw something unusual at Camp Devens. Hundreds of people in civilian clothes were standing about the front of the trial barrack. Two guards escorted Noble into the building through a side door, and into a small room where York was seated at a table. York stood, saluted, and said, "Big day, right Major?"

"I'd say," said Noble. "And it's a considerably bigger day for me than you. Say, what's with the crowd outside? Who are they here for?"

York laughed. "They're here for you, Major". Noble looked quizzical. York continued, "This morning when the sentries opened up the camp road gates, there were hundreds of people waiting to attend your court-martial. For these trials, we usually have a few dozen people ask to see the sessions, so this is…extraordinary. They just kept arriving at the gate until the sentries stopped letting them in the camp. So, only a fraction of those who showed up are here now. I'll bet that over a thousand people came to witness your trial today, Major. Several newspapers even sent reporters and photographers. Nevertheless, a maximum of seventy-five people can be admitted to observe the trial. I guess the rest will be escorted off the camp by Military Police."

Noble and York went over some last-minute strategy discussions and procedural issues. Just before 8 AM, two guards escorted Noble and York to their defense table. Colonel Perry was already seated at the trial counsel table, along with several stacks of documents with numbers on them.

Every seat in the public gallery was filled. Familiar faces from Boston City Hospital, many other New England hospitals, and all three Boston medical schools were in the crowd. In the front row, Noble could see a number of men and women with "Press" tags on their clothing. Also present were Katherine Cushing, Rose Kennedy, Florence...and Lillian. Lillian gave a small wave from a slightly raised hand, and her husband gave her a thumbs-up sign.

The bailiff escorted the panel officers to their seats, and motioned for everyone to rise. Judge Parker entered the huge room with a file of papers, climbed up to the bench, motioned for everyone to be seated, and hit his gavel while stating, "This general court-martial is in session; the *United States vs. Major Edward Noble*". The judge put on a pair of reading glasses. Parker asked the defendant to stand, and read three charges against him: First count: Unauthorized use and distribution of classified government documents. Second count: Breaking of the peace. Third count: Wrongful disposition of military property.

Parker stated in no uncertain terms that any noise from the public gallery would not be tolerated. He turned to the panelists and reiterated that only evidence presented in this trial could be considered in any judgment. Parker also reminded the panelists that the government had the burden of proof in the case. The defendant did not have to prove his innocence. He then said, "The court is ready for counsels' opening statements."

Colonel Jason Perry rose from his chair, and walked over to the panelists. He had a loud staccato cadence that matched his military appearance. He told the panelists that the government would prove beyond a reasonable doubt that the defendant willfully disseminated classified documents, and had no authority to do so. The defendant's actions also caused harm to communities where the information was unlawfully published. Finally, and conclusively, the defendant ordered military property to be used for his own personal needs. In a theatrical gesture, Perry bowed to the panel as he completed his statement.

Captain George York rose from his chair and also walked over to the panelists. His public speaking voice had a friendly youthful quality to it. He repeated the directions of the judge: the government had the burden of proof, and the defendant did not have to prove his innocence. The defense would demonstrate Major Noble neither meant harm, nor committed harm, against the country he loves. Rather, as a nationally renowned infectious disease subspecialist, Noble sought only to save tens of thousands of lives. Only good came from his actions; not injury. Finally, the Major did not profit from any orders given to subordinates that involved military property. York smiled, and went back to his seat. Now would come the presentation of the evidence. The judge stated, "The trial counsel will now open the argument".

Colonel Perry rose from his chair and said, "The government calls Second Lieutenant Marié Lafayette to the stand." Lafayette walked from the public gallery, was sworn in by the bailiff, and was asked to state her name, rank, and unit in which she served. She briefly mentioned what the A.I. Office was and what work was performed there. She took her seat on the raised witness stand. Perry walked over to the witness, stood only inches from Lafayette, and while smiling said, "Lieutenant, could you identify this document for the court?" He handed Lafayette several typed pages stapled together, and she took a moment to study them. She instinctively moved slightly away from Perry, who was standing very close to her.

The Lieutenant was very nervous as her eyes darted back and forth from Perry to Noble. However, in her distinctive New Orleans dialect, Lafayette said, "Uh...uh...yes. It is one of the cables I sent from the A.I. Office."

"Who wrote the text for the cable, who asked you to wire it, and to whom did you send it?" said Perry.

"Major Noble dictated the cable, and asked me to send it to several dozen newspapers and U.S. Public Health Service offices throughout the country." Perry then asked that the document be added into the register of action.

"Could you please point out Major Edward Noble for the court?" asked Perry. The Lieutenant complied. Perry then asked her to read for the court excerpts from the transcription. She read from the document that stated government agencies were not correctly portraying the risks of the pandemic in America. Government authorities were greatly under reporting mortalities, and were overly optimistic in their pandemic projections. "Do you think this document caused fear in the population?" asked Perry. "Objection, your honor," said Captain York. "Counsel is asking for an opinion." "Sustained," said the judge.

"Lieutenant," said Perry, "could you read these sentences for the court?" Lafayette read, "'Numerous influenza deaths have occurred in military facilities, and they are increasing. The infection in these facilities poses a threat to...'" Perry interrupted, "That's fine, Lieutenant. How do you think those sentences might be interpreted by an enemy of the United States?" "Objection, your honor," said York. "Counsel is asking for an opinion and conclusion." "Sustained," said the judge.

Perry went on to use the same sequence of questioning for two other cables dictated by Noble. Each was included as an exhibit, and entered into the trial record.

Perry then asked Lafayette, "Lieutenant, did you ever hear the defendant make disparaging remarks about the U.S.

Government?" "Objection, your honor," said York. "Counsel is leading the witness." "Overruled," said the judge. "The witness will answer the question. And Lieutenant, please remember that you are under oath."

Lafayette replied, "Well, the Major said on a number of occasions that he felt the government was controlling information too tightly. He wondered if it would ever stop, even after The War ended."

"Did the defendant ever want more information available to the enemy?" said Perry. "Objection, your honor," said York. "Counsel is fishing for a conclusion." "Sustained," said the judge. "No further questions, your honor," said Perry.

The defense began its cross-examination of the witness. York rose from his seat and walked over to the witness stand. He asked, "Lieutenant, could you please finish the sentence you were reading when the trial counsel cut you off?" "Sure," said Lafayette. "'The infection in these facilities poses a threat to…the civil population, unless strict and meticulous quarantines are put in place early.'"

"Lieutenant," said York, "why would the defendant include that sentence in the cable?" "Objection, your honor," said Perry. "Counsel seeks a medical opinion when she is not an expert witness." "Sustained," said the judge. York continued, "Lieutenant, did you ever think you were doing something wrong by sending any of these cables?" "Objection, your honor," said Perry. "Counsel is asking for an opinion." "Overruled," said the judge.

Lafayette answered, "I thought the Major was just correcting a misunderstanding many authorities had about the grippe." "No further questions, your honor," said York.

The government went on to call Second Lieutenant Claudette Pierre-Louis and Second Lieutenant Adelina Quellet as witnesses. The questions and objections by the government and the defense were similar for all three A.I. Office Lieutenants. The answers given by the three Signal Corps officers were also very much the same.

The trial counsel then introduced affidavits from numerous newspapers and U.S. Public Health Service offices around the country stating they had received the cables offered as evidence. The judge allowed all these affidavits entered into the register of action. The government provided a number of newspaper copies containing articles and commentaries on the cables sent to them by the A.I. Office. There were no objections from the defense, and all of these items were entered as evidence exhibits.

"The government now calls Colonel Victor Vaughn to the witness stand," said Perry. From the back of the public gallery walked Vaughn. Weighing nearly three-hundred pounds, the Colonel continued to look out-of-place in an army officer's field uniform. Vaughn was given the oath, and he took the seat on the stand.

"Good morning, Colonel," said Perry, who was leaning against the small railing that enclosed the witness box. "Could you please tell us your military unit, sir?" Vaughn said, "I'm Chief of the Army Communicable Disease Division, with headquarters in Washington DC." Perry then went on to outline Vaughn's long history with the defendant, and how he knew him even as a child. The long and friendly relationship with the defendant's father was also detailed for the court. "Colonel," said Perry, "would you say my summary of your interactions with the Noble Family is accurate?" "Yes," said Vaughn.

Perry then asked, "Colonel, were you aware that the defendant sent the cables in question?" "Yes," said Vaughn. "Did you read all of the cables, sir?" asked Perry. "No, I read parts of them," said Vaughn. "Did you know about the cable's depiction of U.S. military facilities being devastated by disease?" "Objection, your honor," said York. "Counsel is using language not found in the cables." "Overruled," said the judge. Vaughn paused for a moment. "Please answer the question, Colonel," said Perry.

"No," said Vaughn, "I didn't see anything written like that in the cables." Perry asked, "Did you ever give direct permission for the defendant to send these cables?" "No," said Vaughn, "but I..." "Just answer the question, Colonel," said Perry.

Perry put his right hand thumb and index finger to his chin, walked several feet from the witness stand, and then returned to it. As he watched Perry, Noble thought to himself that these mannerisms were likely meant for effect. "Isn't it true," said Perry, "that your relationship with the defendant clouded your judgment, Colonel?" "Objection, your honor," said York. "Colonel Vaughn is not on trial here." "Sustained," said the judge.

Perry again walked several feet from the witness stand. This time he turned, put his right hand on his right hip, and asked, "Colonel, have you ever heard the defendant disagree with government conduct during or immediately after The War?" Vaughn replied, "Yes, and I guess one could say the same thing of the late former President Theodore Roosevelt." There was laughter around the court room, to which the judge struck his gavel and said "Order!"

"The government has no further questions, your honor," said Perry.

York walked over to the witness stand and began the defense cross-examination. He initiated a discussion of the numerous academic positions held by Vaughn, his past research, and the volumes of papers he had published. He added, "Colonel, no one has ever questioned your patriotism, and your loyalty as an American." He then asked the court to accept the Colonel as an expert witness in the field of communicable diseases. There was no objection by the government, and the judge ruled it so.

York asked, "Given your position as an expert in the field of infectious diseases, Colonel, what is your opinion concerning the actions of Major Noble?"

Vaughn replied, "The Major tried to use regular channels to warn the military and the nation of the infectious threat before them. Sadly, few listened. We need not belabor what transpired next. We are all still living through that. Therefore,

Major Noble decided to do the work other military services, and leaders of the USPHS, would not. Noble did not steal any classified documents for subversion or to give to the enemy. Rather, he gave to the public information commonly known in the medical community in order to stop an enemy. In this case, the true enemy was a highly infectious lethal disease. This disease has most certainly threatened the national security of the entire nation."

"Objection, your honor," said Perry. "The Colonel is an expert in microorganisms, and not in national security." "Sustained," said the judge. "The panel will disregard the Colonel's comments about classified documents, enemies, and national security."

York could be seen gritting his teeth. He was notably upset by the last pronouncement by the bench. Noble realized that Colonel Vaughn had succinctly summarized the entire defense position, and the panel had been told to ignore it. Noble developed a sudden dyspeptic churning and twisting in his mesogastrum. It was accompanied by a sinking feeling that made it difficult for him to stay upright in his chair. He wanted to rest his head on the table before him, but resisted the temptation.

York recomposed himself, stood up straighter, pushed his shoulders back, and asked, "Do quarantines work against the grippe, Colonel?" "Yes," said Vaughn, "the literature has proven quarantines work against influenza." "Therefore," continued York, "advocating their use is scientifically sound, and therefore good public policy?" "Most certainly, yes," answered Vaughn. "Colonel," asked York, "what if the public doesn't know the risk of disease even exists?"

"Objection, your honor," said Perry. "Pejorative." "Sustained," said the judge. "The panel will ignore the comment."

York drew a deep breath, and said, "Colonel, if quarantines work so well, why have tens of thousands died of the grippe?"

"Because," said Vaughn, "the quarantines were put in place too late, were not strictly enforced, and/or were not used at all."

"Thank you, Colonel," said York. "No further questions, your honor.

Judge Parker gave the court a ninety minute recess. Noble was taken by Military Police to a small holding room near the court. He was given coffee and water, and was offered a sandwich that he could not eat. Captain York came by and spoke to him for about fifteen minutes in preparation for the next court session. Noble could see in York's face a degree of concern that was not there before the trial began. This did not inspire additional confidence in the progress of the proceedings. Since the pace of the trial was even faster than York had predicted, Noble wondered if presentation of evidence might actually end today. Developing a headache, Noble rested on a cot located in the holding room. He began to doze off, when he was tapped on the shoulder by a Military Policeman. Ninety minutes had already elapsed, and it was time to reconvene the court.

Noble was escorted into the enormous court room where every seat was again filled by the public and court officials. Lillian waved at her husband, and Noble faked a thumbs-up gesture. He was not all together certain things were going that well, but he surely was not going to display that to Lillian. The court again stood for the entrance of the judge, who immediately used his gavel to call for order.

Colonel Perry looked rested, and even rather pleased. As he stood at his table, he stated, "The government calls Lieutenant Commander Milton Rosenau to the stand." Perry walked to the witness stand and waited for Rosenau, who was seated at the back of the public gallery. A natural athlete, Noble always thought his muscular friend walked like a cat. In his usual manner, Rosenau moved with confidence toward the judicial bench. The oath was administered by the bailiff, and Rosenau took the witness seat.

"Good afternoon, Lieutenant Commander," said Perry with a smile that he put on for every witness. "Could you tell the court your service and unit?" "Of course," said Rosenau. "I am with the Navy Medial Corps, and am presently stationed at the Chelsea Naval Hospital." Perry continued, "You are also on the Harvard Medical School faculty, and conduct epidemiological and microbiological research at both Harvard and Boston City Hospital. Correct?" "Yes, that is correct," said Rosenau. Perry went on to describe Rosenau's long friendship with the defendant, and also his research relationship with the defendant's wife.

Perry asked, "Did the defendant tell you he was sending the cables in question to newspapers and USPHS offices throughout America?" Rosenau answered, "Yes, because he..." Perry interrupted, "Just answer the question, Lieutenant Commander."

Noble could see that his friend was becoming noticeably irritated with Perry's questioning. He knew Rosenau had a slow-to-boil temper with limits. He hoped his friend could keep his irritation within those limits today.

Perry then asked, "Has the defendant ever expressed dismay over military handling of classified information? Remember, Lieutenant Commander, you are under oath." "Yes, he has," said Rosenau. "Did the defendant say he was going to 'fix the problem'?" "Objection, your honor," said York. "Counsel is leading the witness." "Overruled," said the judge. "Please answer the question." "Yes," said Rosenau.

"Do you think it was a good idea to let the enemy know there was a substantial reduction in our troop capacity to fight?" asked Perry. "Objection, your honor," said York. "Counsel is asking for personal opinion." "Sustained," said the judge.

"No more government questions," said Perry.

Rosenau had set his jaw and was leaning forward in the witness stand. Noble could see that his respiratory rate was slightly increased, and he knew his friend was doing his best to control his temper. As York reached the witness to begin the defense cross-examination, Rosenau sat back in the chair and began to breathe more easily.

York started his examination of the witness by detailing his exemplary work as a physician, researcher, and in the service of his country as a naval officer. He then asked, "Lieutenant Commander, did the defendant do all he could to establish a quarantine in Boston Harbor at the beginning of the pandemic?" "Objection, your honor," said Perry. "The question is really not relevant at all to this case. The government accepts the fact that the defendant is against lethal disease." "Sustained," said the judge.

Rosenau's calmed appearance began to change again. York ushered in another question. "Lieutenant Commander, do you think the defendant's actions, in regards to the cables in question, saved many American lives?" "Objection," said Perry. "An irrelevant line of questioning in this case, your honor." "Sustained," said the judge. "The defense counsel will restrict his questions to issues directly concerning the charges."

York put his right thumb and the side of his index finger to his forehead, and bent his head downward. It was a look of both contemplation and desperation. He took a deep breath, looked up to the judge, and said, "May the counsel approach the bench?" The judge peered at York from the top of his reading glasses and said, "The defense and trial counsels may approach the bench." York waited for his court adversary to reach him.

When the judge and two counsels were huddled close together, they each conversed in a whisper. York began, "Your honor, with all due respect, the defendant pled not guilty with an affirmative defense. The defense must therefore be able to show why there was no criminal activity, or intent, with actions we all know took place. Those actions are the transmission of the cables in question."

Perry jumped into the conversation immediately. "Your honor, the government is not refuting some good may have come from the defendant's public health disagreements with a few authorities. The government has taken the position that these disagreements don't matter in this case. The government, very simply, wants to establish the defendant's guilt in the unauthorized use of classified information. Why he did it is irrelevant."

Judge Parker took off his reading glasses, rubbed his eyes, and looked down at his bench papers for a time. Then, he put his glasses back on and looked at York. "Captain, your client knew full well what an affirmative defense plea is, and is not. The defense will restrict its comments and questions to the court-martial charges."

York backed away from the bench and said quietly, "The defense has no further questions, your honor." Noble saw the expression on his defense counsel's face as he slowly walked back to his table seat next to him. The conference at the bench had obviously not gone well. It had not gone well at all. Noble felt increasingly disheartened.

Parker was heading back to his table seat when the defense chose not to continue Rosenau's cross-examination. With that statement, Parker quickly made a quick about-face to the witness stand. He was smiling widely, and almost jubilant. Noble knew Perry's positive affect was not a good sign. The government counsel was feeling new trial vitality with concessions from the bench.

"The government calls Second Lieutenant Clyde Dronner to the stand," said Perry, who was standing very straight. From the middle of the public gallery walked a man of about twenty-five years, with a slight build and long sideburns. Noble could tell the young officer, who stood only about 5 feet 5 inches, appeared extremely apprehensive as he quickly moved toward the witness seat. After being sworn in, Dronner sat down.

Perry started the direct examination by saying, "Thank you, Lieutenant, for coming such a long way, in such short notice. Can you please tell the court the unit to which you are attached, and where?"

"Ye...ye...yes, Colonel," said Dronner. "I am an officer with the U.S. Public Health Service in Beatrice, Nebraska. Beatrice is about forty miles south of Lincoln."

"Thank you again, Lieutenant," said Perry. "I know the train ride over the last few winter days was difficult, and we appreciate your efforts. Are you familiar with this article from your local newspaper, the *Beatrice Sentinel*?" Perry showed the witness a copy of the *Sentinel*, and had it entered as an exhibit. "Yes, sir," said Dronner, "I'm very familiar with it."

"What did you see just before this article appeared in the newspaper, Lieutenant?" asked Perry.

Dronner sat up in his chair and stated, "We received nearly an identical cable at the USPHS office in Beatrice one day before the article was printed, sir. It's nearly word-for-word. There's no question the paper published the contents of the cable as an article."

Perry showed the newspaper copy, along with a Noble cable transcript, to the judge and the panel. All six men nodded their heads as they compared the two. They were nearly identical. Perry continued, "Lieutenant, can you tell the court what you saw happen next in Beatrice, Nebraska?"

"Well, sir," said Dronner, "when the newspaper article came out, the whole town panicked as though they were incited by, or inspired by, the article."

"What happened then?" said Perry.

"As crowds rushed to leave the town, six people were seriously injured," said Dronner. "Two suffered broken arms, two had broken legs, one had a concussion, and one man developed a heart attack. The man with the heart attack died."

"I hope the five surviving injured people are recovering from their terrible ordeal," said Perry. "The government has no further questions, your honor."

Perry and York crossed paths as the former sat confidently down, and the latter began the defense cross-examination. It was clear there was growing hostility between the two attorneys.

Reaching the witness stand, York leaned against its rail and said calmly, "I want to also thank you, Lieutenant, for making your long trip to New England. I'm sure it was trying." Dronner smiled and nodded. York continued, "Lieutenant, I have here lists of death announcements from your local newspaper, the *Sentinel*. They were all published a couple of weeks prior to the article that the government showed you. Do you remember seeing these?"

York held several newspaper copies that he showed the Lieutenant. "I think I saw some of these," said Dronner. York showed them to the judge and panel, and had them entered as evidence.

"Lieutenant," said York, "the population of Beatrice was about 8,000 people as of last summer. Isn't that about correct?" Dronner said, "Yes, I think that's right." "Well," said York, "there are about 640 names on these newspaper death announcement lists. And, they are all from influenza. That's about 8% of the entire population of Beatrice. All of them died in just a few weeks, and please look at their ages. Could you read just a few of the ages of the dead for the court?" Dronner read some of the ages of the dead from the list: 24, 3, 17, 30, 28, 2, 21, 29... "Those seem to be mostly young adults, Lieutenant." "Yes," said Dronner, "a lot of young people have died in Beatrice from the grippe."

York then showed Dronner another newspaper article from the *Sentinel*. "Lieutenant, here is an article stating that over 240 people died in Beatrice from the grippe in just the 'previous week'. Could you read for the court when this article was printed, Lieutenant?" Dronner looked at the article, and then said, "This article was printed the day before the newspaper article copied from our USPHS cable was published."

"Thank you, Lieutenant," said York. "Therefore, about 3% of the entire population of the town died the week before your USPHS office received one of the cables in question. Isn't it much more likely Beatrice citizens were panicking over the grippe itself, rather than the cable sent to the newspaper and your USPHS office by the defendant in this case?"

"Well," said Dronner, "I...I suppose that's possible."

York had the mentioned article also placed as an exhibit. "The defense has no further questions, your honor."

As Second Lieutenant Dronner stepped down from the witness stand, Noble glanced to his left in order to catch a glimpse of Perry. The trial counsel was frowning and shuffling papers at his table. Noble took an ounce of pleasure in the under-performance of the government's previous witness.

Perry stood slowly, and announced, "The government calls Staff Sergeant Raymond Campbell to the stand." Even though the court room was gigantic, it was not hard to see Sergeant Campbell in the public gallery. His 6 foot 4 inch height, and broad shoulders, made him a stand out. Noble was slightly amused to see numerous women in the gallery careening their necks to see the handsome young Sergeant as he walked toward the bench. As Campbell passed the defense table, he winked at the Major he so admired.

When Campbell was seated on the witness stand and was sworn in, Perry walked over to him. The government's counsel had a growing air of confidence that Noble found unnerving. "Good afternoon, Sergeant," said Perry. "Could you please tell the court your unit?" "Yes, sir," said Campbell. "I'm a Wagoner at Camp Devens, sir. I drive army staff automobiles for officers, and I'm also a mechanic. When I'm not driving, I repair army motor cars and trucks."

"Sergeant," said Perry, "you have been the defendant's driver many times over the past year. Is that not true?" "Yes, sir," said Campbell. "I was specifically assigned to Major Noble's official transportation needs, when he has them." "I see," said Perry.

Perry went to his table and took out a sheet of paper. Walking back to the witness stand, he said, "Sergeant, do you remember certain occurrences on September 26, 1918? That was a Thursday."

Campbell took on a very sad expression. After a moment he said, "Oh yes, sir. I'll never forget that day. It was the day that Major Noble's son died at Devens. His son was First Lieutenant Arthur Noble, sir."

"What happened after the defendant's son died, Sergeant?" said Perry. "Let me remind you that you are under oath."

"Well," said Campbell, "the Major...the defendant... asked me to drive his son's body in an army staff car back to Boston. The Major drove with his wife in his own truck. We first drove to the Noble home in Boston. From there I drove Lieutenant Arthur's body to a Brookline cemetery. I helped the Major bury his son." Campbell very discretely wiped tears from his eyes.

"I see," said Perry. "So, the defendant arranged for a Devens Wagoner to transport his son's body in a government property vehicle. Then, he had an enlisted soldier help dig a grave for his family. Is that what happened, Sergeant?"

Well, sort of, sir," said Campbell. "Actually, I..." "That's all, Sergeant," said Perry. "Thank you so much. No further government direct examination questions, your honor."

York quickly moved to the witness stand to cross-examine Campbell. "Sergeant, thank you for appearing today. Did the defendant order you to drive his son's body to Boston, and to the cemetery, and then to help bury the Lieutenant who died of the grippe?"

"No, sir," said Campbell. "The Major asked me to. I wanted to help him, sir." "Thank you again, Sergeant," said York. "No further defense questions, your honor."

Perry quickly stood at his table and asked, "Your honor, the government requests a re-direct examination of the witness." "Trial counsel has permission for re-direct questioning of the witness," said the judge.

"Sergeant," said Perry, "the defendant is your superior officer, is that not correct? "Yes, sir," said Campbell. "You have orders to respond to his command for transportation with an army staff car when he wants one, is that not also correct, Sergeant?" said Perry. "Yes sir," said Campbell.

"Sergeant," said Perry, "don't you feel a bit intimidated by a superior officer asking you to do something? In this case, isn't 'asking' a lot like ordering, Sergeant?"

"Well," started Campbell, "I guess...I guess that some might think of it in that way, but in this case I..."

"No further questions, your honor," said Perry. "And, the government rests its case."

It was now early afternoon. Parker removed his reading glasses, checked some papers in a file before him on the bench, and asked the court reporter for clarification on an item. He suddenly hit his gavel upon his sound block and ordered, "This court-martial is adjourned until 8 AM tomorrow". The bailiff then said abruptly, "All rise", and the judge quickly left the court room.

There was immediate talking heard about the public gallery as people began to leave the converted barrack. Noble looked over his shoulder to see Lillian smiling while she blew him another kiss, and Florence waving enthusiastically at him. He flashed another thumbs-up sign because he knew he was supposed to. But, Noble was not feeling enthusiastic. Noble was feeling extremely depressed. He only hoped he didn't betray his emotional state to his wife and daughter. Deeper into the crowed were two former witnesses also waving at him: Vaughn and Rosenau. Noble waved back in an obligatory fashion. Then, two MPs came to escort Noble out of the court room.

By prior arrangement, if the trial did not end that day, Noble was taken directly to the stockade Consultation Room. He sat for some time before his attorney arrived for a very brief post-court session discussion. York hurriedly came into the room with several files under his arm. He sat down, and stared at his client. Noble stared back for a time, and then said, "Well, Captain?"

York took some moments to reply. "Well, Major, this was a difficult day." "What do you think, Captain?" said Noble.

York took out a handkerchief to dry off his forehead and upper lip. He was still breathing quickly from a rushed trip to the Consultation Room. "Major, it's hard to make our case if we can't talk about <u>why</u> you sent the cables. It's just that simple. Bench rulings today really tied our hands in making our case." York stopped to catch his breath, and then continued. "Nevertheless, before court begins tomorrow, I will ask the judge to allow the introduction of critical defense evidence. That evidence, in the form of USPHS notifications and other government comments in the press, will show authorities were not depicting the pandemic correctly to the public for some time. I believe all our arguments at that point will be far easier to make."

"I cannot tell you how much I look forward to those arguments," said Noble. "What about the other charges?"

York said, "The government knows they have no case whatsoever in the 'breach of the peace' complaint. That is a nuisance charge, and they know it. However, so far, they have made a good case for the unauthorized classified document use, and for the wrongful disposition of military property. Our job is to substantially whittle away at the first charge, and hope the panel doesn't focuses on the third and less important charge. Don't forget that the third military property charge could still give you five years in jail. I will meet with the judge and the trial counsel early tomorrow morning. Please try and get a good night's sleep, Major."

With that, MPs took Noble back to his cell. He asked not to attend what was left of the exercise hour, since he wanted to concentrate on the next day's court session.

A little after 3 PM, a guard came by Noble's cell and asked him if he wanted to see a visitor. As always, no mention was made who the visitor was. Noble was curious, and was taken in handcuffs to the Visitor Room. He sat at window No. 3 for only a moment, when three men came scurrying into the visitor area. They wore brown and dark blue suits, and two wore tweed newsboy caps while the third had a teardrop fedora. They jostled each other for the two chairs at window No. 3, such that one had to stand. "Major Noble, Major Noble!" they shouted as a guard told them to be quiet. "Do you have a statement, Major?" "How are they treating you?" "What's your prediction for tomorrow?" "Did you do it?"

Noble listened to their barrage of questions for only a fraction of a minute, before he said under his breath, "Reporters". He finally put up his right palm and said, "Gentlemen, I'm sorry, but I have no comment." Noble then motioned to a guard and asked to be taken back to his cell.

Later in the evening, Noble tried to read his legal summaries and notes. But, he had difficulty concentrating. The same thoughts came back to him again and again. In about sixteen hours, a court hearing would begin that would result in one of two very different future paths. One path was a return to his wife, family, friends, and profession that he dearly loved. The other path was a dark and cold journey to oblivion, essentially forever. That second path would likely never allow him again to touch his wife, go to a ballgame, or ponder the differential diagnosis of a real patient. The second unthinkable sojourn would be an endless stream of days doing nothing, planning nothing, and going nowhere.

However, Noble had to remind himself that he made a conscious decision to put himself potentially in this awful position. The strangest fact of all, Noble thought, was that if he had to do it all over again...he would. It was the right thing to do. That is what he was thinking when the cell light went off at 9 PM.

CHAPTER 33

E arly on the morning of Friday, February 14th, Noble was
actually glad to have an ice cold shower. He had not slept
well the night before, and felt as though he was walking
about in a mental fog. Later, he was amazed at how quickly a
human being can become accustomed to frightful food if they
are hungry enough. He ate breakfast with that in mind.

At 7 AM, guards took Noble to the Consultation Room for
an attorney-client discussion. York was sitting at the room's
table, and Noble immediately noticed that his attorney looked
solemn. As Noble sat down at the opposite side of the conference table, York tossed the morning edition of the *Boston
Globe* in front of him. The front page headline read "GRIPPE
EXPERT SILENCED BY GOV". Noble stared at the paper and
did not attempt to read it further.

"You've become quite a folk-hero, Major," said York. "In
New England, and in many other parts of the country, your
court-martial is being followed very closely by the press and
their readers. You are being portrayed as one man who stood

up to forces that were not attentive to the coming pandemic. It's a real 'David and Goliath' story."

"Captain" replied Noble, "people want to believe there was a reason for the horror that fell upon humanity. Like many things in print, a quarter of this story is likely accurate, and seventy-five percent of it is probably not."

"In any case, Major," said York, "you are a sensation."

Wanting to talk about other things, Noble said, "So, how did the conference with Judge Parker go?"

York looked down at the table and folded his hands upon it. His jaw moved to the left as he clinched his teeth. As he looked back up, he said, "The judge denied our request to introduce any written evidence of government pandemic notifications given to the public. Interestingly, this was done on the grounds that the material is 'completely irrelevant' to the charges. Obviously, we disagree. Nevertheless, there will be no court introduction of U.S. Public Health Service, Surgeon General, or newspaper articles or commentaries on government public pandemic instructions. We will address this in your testimony. But, Major, your version of events will not have the impact that written government evidence would have. Perhaps we can introduce the evidence on appeal."

York's last sentence made Noble sink in his chair and catch his breath. It appeared that his own attorney thought the situation hopeless. Noble paused for a moment, and then said, "In the present day 'David and Goliath' tale you mentioned, it appears David will be the one slain this time." York did not comment on Noble's attempt at dark humor. He stood up and prepared to go to court with his client.

Outside the converted barrack were more civilians than Noble had seen the previous morning. According to York, more than double the number of people tried to enter the Camp in order to have a chance to see the trial. Noble saw in the crowd many men with tweed newsboy caps, and he muttered again, "Reporters."

York and Noble sat at the right hand court table. The trial counsel was already seated on the left and pouring over documents. All other chairs in the mammoth room were filled with public gallery citizens, Military Police, or court officials. Noble smiled at Lillian and Florence, who sat in the same seats as the previous day. Noble also waved at Rosenau in the back row. The five member panel, led by the bailiff, sat down at their designated chairs. All rose for Judge Parker who brought the court to order. "This general court-martial is in session; the *United States vs. Major Edward Noble*". "We will now hear the presentation of evidence by the defense".

York rose to his feet and said, "The defense calls Major Edward Noble to the stand." Many hushed voices began to speak in the public gallery, and the judge pounded his gavel, "Order in this court!" Noble rested his left hand on a black Bible and raised his right hand. The bailiff asked, "Do you swear to tell the truth, the whole truth, and nothing but the truth, so help you God?" "I do," said Noble, who then sat on the witness chair.

York walked to the witness stand and smiled at Noble. He began a lengthy discussion of the Major's life, accomplishments, credentials, and his willingness to join the army right after America's declaration of war. He talked about his service in France, and the fact that he was hand-chosen to direct the Army Intelligence Cable Office work. He talked about Noble's firsthand look at the effects of influenza, and his tireless work with the ill in Boston. York spoke for forty-five minutes without hesitation.

Then, suddenly, York stopped his dissertation, walked several feet from the witness stand, and said loudly, "Major, why did you write the cables that the government is so upset about?"

Noble's heart raced as he immediately broke into a heavy sweat. As he began to speak, he thought to himself 'lights, camera, action'. "Why did I send the cables?" Noble said rhetorically. "The USPHS, the military, the Surgeon General, and many other government officials were not being direct enough with the American people, Captain. For many weeks I read official statements in newspapers regarding the pandemic terror. They said things that were just not true, like 'no reason to fear', 'no reason for unusual alarm', and 'the pandemic has passed'. These comments were made just as influenza mortality figures were soaring and the disease was spreading in logrhythmic fashion."

Noble continued, "There needed to be public awareness of the real dangers ahead of them. Only with this awareness could they prepare for the pandemic quickly and collectively. Without preparation there would be no volunteers, medical personnel, or supplies ready for the infectious wave. There would also be no preemptive quarantines. Why did I send the cables? I did it for the good of the people. I did it for the good of the nation."

"No further defense questions, your honor," said York.

Perry walked to the witness stand, and also smiled at Noble as he prepared his cross-examination. "Two questions, Major. First, is it true that you have been very critical of government domestic policies since America entered The War? And second, is it true you perceived the government's abridgment of free speech was not warranted?" "Objection, your Honor," said York. The Constitution allows Americans to disagree with the government." "Overruled," said the judge. "Freedom of speech is not guaranteed to those in military service. Answer the questions, Major." "Yes, to both" said Noble.

Perry asked again, "Is it true that you tried to embarrass the government by sending your cables in question?" "Objection, your honor," said York. "The defendant has already explained why he sent the cables." "Overruled," said the judge. "No," said Noble. "I sent the cables to properly warn, and therefore prepare, America for an extremely lethal disease."

Perry stepped away from the stand, put his fingers to his chin, and then walked back to Noble. As Perry leaned against the stand rail, he developed a thin smile while his eyes squinted. Noble thought it was the expression chess players make when they know they have their opponent in checkmate. "Major, aren't you scheduled to appear before the Massachusetts Medical Board in just four days…February 18th?" "Objection, your honor," said York. "The question has no relevance to this court's charges." "Overruled," said the judge.

"Yes," said Noble. Perry then asked, "Is it true that you have been asked to appear before the Medical Board for the following reason: 'The improper allocation and use of a Commonwealth city and county hospital ward facility'?" "Yes," said Noble, who was now feeling extremely nauseous. "No further questions, your honor," said Perry…smiling.

"Your honor, the defense asks for re-direct examination of the witness," said York. "Proceed, Captain," said the judge.

"Major," asked York as he walked toward Noble, "of course, the Medical Board hearing has not been held, and there is yet no resolution to the issue. Nevertheless, what is your alleged improper allocation of city and county medical resources?"

Noble said matter-of-factly, "For opening up an influenza quarantine ward, just as the first pandemic cases arrived in Boston."

"No further questions, your honor," said York. "The defense rests its case."

Everyone expected the judge to move directly to government and defense summations. However, the judge put on his reading glasses and began to read. Several minutes went by. Whispering could be heard in the public gallery, to which the judge slammed his gavel and said "Order!" The court fell silent again. Four minutes went by, then five, then six.

After nearly ten minutes elapsed, the judge began to speak. "According to the U.S. Manual for Courts-marital, II-122, section (c) 3, Rules of Evidence Relaxed, the presiding judge can introduce evidence at his discretion. I hereby exercise discretionary introduction of evidence.

Noble looked to his left and right, and saw both attorneys with open mouths and wide eyes. Obviously, no one expected this turn events, and no one would ever expect it from Major General Parker. No one had any idea what was to happen now.

"Yesterday afternoon," said Parker, "I received the following letter in the U.S. Mail. I will now read it in its entirety."

"'Dear General Parker;'

'I write this letter in order to give you some thoughts about the man whose court-martial you now oversee. Please pardon my written thoughts, since no one has yet asked my opinion.'

'Mankind has been grappling with the following question for millennia: Does the end justify the means? Are the means the solitary test of the human soul? Or is it the ends?'

'Examples of the moral dilemmas circling around 'mean' and 'ends' are numerous. There are those that say lying is wrong because of the negative consequences produced by lying. Some believe certain foreseeable consequences might make lying acceptable. Others believe lying is <u>always</u> wrong, regardless of any potential good that might come from lying. Immanuel Kant argued that we have a moral duty to always tell the truth, even to a murderer who asks where the would-be victim is. Another example of a moral dilemma would be stealing, and then giving the stolen items to the poor. How many would condone ignoring a street stop sign in order to speed a gravely ill child to a hospital?'

'These are difficult questions for the ages.'

'Philosophers, theologians, and even students of the law have toiled long and hard to help humanity tackle such questions. They have told us conflicts and tensions between different states of 'good' are to be expected. Ultimately, it is the goodness of the <u>intention</u> that reflects the balance of the good and evil of consequences.'

'Many have theorized about the existence of certain universal moral rules. However, some have wondered if these rules may be violated if strict adherence to the rules would lead to much more undesirable consequences. In this regard, the right action is the action that will bring about the best consequences from the perspective of an <u>ideal neutral observer</u>.

An ideal observer would see the whole situation completely, would understand for whom the consequences are really intended, and would entirely see the <u>responsibility</u> of the agent in question. Was there a <u>right motive</u>? Was the agent showing high <u>character</u>? Did the agent show a moral imperative to inform himself or herself as much a possible about the consequences? Were consequences intended for oneself, an individual, or a group? Were the consequences intended to reduce suffering, or to increase pleasure and luxury? All of these means-and-ends factors must be placed into the complex computation that may equal goodness, evil, or nothing at all.'

'In the end, we mortals must judge <u>both</u> the means and ends to determine the good, the right, the moral, and the ethical. In our daily lives we look at both. We weigh both. We succeed or fail with both.'

'Major Edward Noble felt the struggle between the different states of 'good' as he read cables of the coming horror. He saw the violation of some rules would lead to infinitely more desirable outcomes. An ideal observer would have determined his actions were intended for the good of the masses, and not for himself. The observer would have noted the motive correct and his character golden. Noble's knowledge of the consequences would have been obvious, and the goal of suffering reduction manifest. There was no personnel gain involved in the Major's actions whatsoever. Information was not passed to foreign or subversive groups. The information was passed to the people in an attempt to defeat an invisible enemy threatening America in ways the Central Powers never could.'

'If other people, and groups, in places of authority had done their jobs and shown the courage and intelligence of Edward Noble, he would not have had to risk himself to do the right thing.'

'Major Edward Noble is the <u>best</u> man I have ever had the privilege to know. All of the rest of us can only hope to hold one-tenth the character that lives within him.'"

"That is the end of the letter," said Parker. "Please enter it into the register of action."

There was complete silence in the gigantic court room, and the silence was maintained for a very long time. Finally, Colonel Perry spoke. "Excuse me, your honor. Could you please tell us who wrote the letter you have just read?"

"Oh, yes, of course," said Parker. "The letter was written by Commander Richard Cunard, U.S. Public Health Service, Boston City Hospital."

"Cunard", thought Noble. His adversarial medical school classmate, courter of his wife, and cause of Medial Board enquiries, had now sought to help him in ways he never thought possible. Noble was utterly speechless.

"I have already contacted Commander Cunard, and confirmed his authorship of the letter," said Parker. "I realize the government and defense have not interviewed the Commander, deposed him, nor obtained an affidavit from him. Do the trial or defense counsels choose to perform any of these investigations with this individual?"

"No, your honor," said York. "No, your honor," said Perry.

"Then, we are ready for summations," said Parker. "Will the government please proceed?"

Perry slowly rose from his chair and walked over to the court-martial panel. He had a very serious look as he began. "During these proceedings, the government has shown conclusively the following: First, the defendant sent summaries of classified government documents to the newspapers. Second, the defendant had no direct permission to send public cables created from these classified documents. His job was to analyze the document information for the military only. Third, the defendant was critical of the government for its secrecy and restriction of free speech...even as the government was conducting a war. The government has a legal right under the Constitution to keep potentially damaging information out of the hands of the enemy. Fourth, the defendant promoted fear unnecessarily in the nation, which caused chaos, and breached the peace. <u>Finally</u>, the defendant used government property for his private use. Gentlemen of the panel, with these facts in the case, you must find the defendant guilty on all three court-martial charges. Thank you very much for your careful attention." Perry slowly walked back to his seat.

York walked to a point directly in front of the panel, took a deep breath, and began his summation. "What does a citizen do when his government is wrong, and tens-of-thousands of lives are in jeopardy over days or weeks? And, what if the risk of huge numbers of deaths is not from a traditional enemy? In fact, the enemy is not even human. Instead, it's a disease. A disease that threatens the vitality of the nation, and therefore will <u>directly</u> affect national security. What would you do? Gentlemen, you need to ask yourselves that question."

York continued. "Major Noble, a talented and caring physician, saw the government irresponsibly informing the nation there was 'nothing to fear' from influenza. Nothing to fear? Can anyone alive these last five-and-one-half months say that was prudent advice?"

"The government alleges that trying to better prepare people for a lethal pandemic will cause panic, even when the disease is already all around them," said York. This allegation is ridiculous and requires no further comment."

"Major Noble," said York, "needed help burying his son when there was no one else to assist him. What was the result? Two soldiers dug a grave, with dignity, for a fellow soldier who died while on duty."

York concluded, "Gentlemen of the panel. Do the right thing. Find this good man, Major Noble, innocent of all charges. Thank you for listening." York turned and walked back to his seat. His shoulders were slumped with fatigue, and a degree of relief that his part in this trial was over.

Judge Parker gave his charge to the panel. He talked about the standard of proof required in this criminal case, which is "beyond reasonable doubt". The panelists were also to base their conclusions solely on the evidence presented during the trial. Instructions on panel deliberations were given, and Parker adjourned the session.

Noble was taken to the small meeting room where he had been on the first day of the trial. He and York would have a short debriefing. "Thank you, Captain," said Noble, "for all your help. No matter what happens now, I have been honored to have you as my defense counsel." York just smiled and patted Noble's back. Noble continued, "So, what's the theory on the length of time it takes for a jury to reach a verdict?"

York laughed. "Major, there are as many theories on jury deliberations as there are attorneys. But, I can give you my theory. First, one must consider if the defense had difficulty proving its case. I think we both agree this was an uphill battle for us. If the defense had difficulty, then a shorter deliberation time is indicative of a guilty verdict. This means the jury had already made up its collective mind when they left the court room. On the other hand, a longer deliberation indicates that they are not so sure. They are still considering alternatives offered by the defense."

"So," said Noble laughing, "we want a deliberation that lasts months."

"Always the joker," laughed York. "Not months, for sure. But, not minutes, either."

Two Military Police handcuffed Noble and took him to the waiting MP automobile. He was led back to his cell, handcuffs removed, and the door slammed shut. Noble rested on his cot and mentally prepared for a long panel deliberation. He had been in his cell less than five minutes, when the cell door reopened.

Two Military Police stood at the door. One said, "Come on Major. The panel has reached a verdict."

Noble's heart rate suddenly skyrocked, and his abdomen churned with an aching discomfort. The ubiquitous nausea followed. He thought to himself 'Oh my God, it took them less than thirty minutes'. His legs felt weak, and he had to use his arms to help himself to a standing position. The handcuffs removed just minutes before were reapplied. Back to the MP

automobile they went. Outside the barrack-turned-court-
room, a large crowed of civilians was reforming. People were
running, pushing, and shoving one another. Their scurrying
feet were stirring up fluffy snow that had fallen that morning. Noble said quietly, referring to one of his court-martial
charges, "Now, that is real chaos."

Perry and York were in their seats, and people were rushing to take public gallery chairs. Eventually, Noble saw
Lillian and Florence run into the court room. They had also
not expected to be back so soon. Only minutes later, Rosenau
took his seat.

Noble leaned over to York and said, "So much for a long
deliberation." York replied, looking surprised, "No kidding."

It took Judge Parker quite some time to return to the
bench. When he finally returned, Parker directed the court
room to be seated, and to be quiet. He whispered something
to the bailiff, who quickly left the room. Several minutes later,
the bailiff reentered the court while escorting the five member panel to their seats. Parker then asked, "Has the panel
reached a verdict?"

The President of the panel, the Brigadier General, replied
while standing, "We have, your honor."

"Please hand the verdict to the bailiff," instructed Parker.
The panel President did so, and the bailiff walked the folded
piece of paper to the judge. Parker read the verdict silently,
and then gave it back to the bailiff. The paper was returned
to the President.

Noble was not sure that he could actually live through
the next few minutes. The nausea he often felt when emotionally upset was now severe. He regurgitated some stomach contents into his mouth, but did not frankly vomit. He
wanted to turn around and look at Lillian without a barrier
between them...perhaps for the last time. But, instead, he
looked at the floor. He could not bear to look at Lillian at all.
His head throbbed with an extremely high pulse rate. He
placed his forearms on the table before him to brace his torso
from falling. Noble was about to faint.

Parker stated, "The defendant will please rise." Noble stood slowly, but had to steady himself with all ten fingers against the table before him. York stood with his client. Parker then asked, "What is the verdict on the first count of unauthorized use of classified military documents?"

"Not guilty, your honor," said the President. Yelling and clapping broke out spontaneously throughout the public gallery. "Order in this court!" demanded Parker, while slamming his gavel. "I will jail the next person who makes such an outburst." The court fell perfectly silent. York, smiling from ear-to-ear, looked at Noble, who remained expressionless.

Parker continued. "What is the verdict on the second count of breaching the peace?"

"Not guilty, your honor."

"What is the verdict on the third count of wrongful disposition of military property?"

"Guilty, your honor,"

There was a pause in the court room, and absolutely no sound could be heard. Then, the panel President said, "Your honor, the panel has an exceptional suggestion...or request."

Looking up from his bench, peering from the top of his reading glasses, and looking somewhat surprised, Parker asked, "What is the panel's request?"

"Your honor," said the President, "the panel would like to make the following unusual request. We believe sentencing on the third count should be handed down now. In addition, we have a suggestion concerning what that sentence should be."

"OK," said Parker as he took off his glasses, "what does the panel feel the sentence should be?"

"Your honor, we do not want to cause any further discomfort to this fine man. We have calculated what we believe are the costs of the use of an Army automobile, and an enlisted soldier, for the time Major Noble used them."

"What do you think that cost is?" asked Parker.

"Well, your honor, we believe it is $18.26. We also request that the Major's Army record be expunged of the third count guilty verdict once he has paid the sum."

Parker put on his glasses, wrote something on a piece of paper, read another document, and scratched his head. He put his right hand to the side of his face as though he was thinking in a very focused way. "This court has considered the request by the panel. Does either the trial or defense counsel object to this extraordinary sentencing?

Perry and York looked at each other, and said in unison, "No, your honor."

"Therefore, the panel request is granted. The defendant is sentenced to pay $18.26, and is free to go once the sum has been given to the bailiff. With the payment, Major Noble's Army record is expunged of the guilty verdict and the sentence. This court-martial is adjourned." The judicial gavel hit the sound block with a crisp cracking noise.

CHAPTER 34

Loud yelling and clapping resumed in the court room.
People rushed up to Noble and York. Some saluted, some
shook hands, and some tried to hug both of them. However,
one person ran up to Noble and grabbed him so hard that
he nearly fell over. It was Lillian, who pulled Noble's head
to hers and kissed him until he could not breathe. Clasped
in her hand was a check she had hastily written for $18.26.
She quickly ran over to the bailiff, handed him the check, and
ran back to her husband. By now, Florence was hugging her
father. Flash bulbs went off by the score. Noble saw Rosenau
many yards away put his arms up over his head with clasped
hands. There were just too many people around Noble and
his attorney to reach his friend.

Noble looked over his shoulder and saw that Colonel
Perry, and Judge Parker, had already left the courtroom.

In any case, Noble was now a free man.

The Military Policemen offered to drive Noble, without
handcuffs, to the stockade in order to pick up some of his personal effects. Lillian went with him, holding her husband's

hand and resting her head on his shoulder. York also came along, with Lillian sitting between him and Noble. Florence went to drive the family Ford to the stockade.

On their way, Noble asked York, "So, why did Parker introduce Richard Cunard's letter, Captain?"

York put his right elbow against the backseat window of the car, and rested his head on his right hand. "My guess... and it's just a guess...is that Parker was under intense pressure from somewhere to conduct the court-martial solely on the question of government leaks to the newspapers. Although he felt he could not challenge that pressure directly, he saw his opportunity to challenge it indirectly when the letter arrived. In my mind, there is no question the letter was the deciding argument for the panelists. In essence, the letter gave the panel permission to include in their deliberations the horrors of the pandemic. And, these were the same horrors you went to singular lengths to stop. In the end, the panelists agreed with those lengths you took."

"Thank you again, Captain, for everything," said Noble. "You have saved my life, and the life of my family." Lillian smiled broadly, and kissed York on the check.

"I'll save your lives more often, if that is the thanks I get!" York giggled. "However, Major, you need to thank that Cunard chap as well. Who exactly is he, anyway?" Noble and Lillian looked at each other, and just smiled. They did not even try to answer York's question.

Florence drove home from Camp Devens, while her father fell fast asleep on the second Ford bench seat with his head in Lillian's lap. When the Beacon Street home was reached, Noble went promptly to bed. The death of Marguerite, and the court-martial, had worn him to the end of his endurance. He slept, without interruption, for twenty-four hours.

On Sunday, February 16th, Lillian found her husband in the late morning sitting in the parlor and staring at Beacon Street through the window. She prepared for him his favorite breakfast of scrambled eggs, pancakes, maple syrup, an English muffin with butter and a preserve, sausage, and black coffee. He nearly absorbed the food through his skin, he ate so quickly. On the kitchen table was the Saturday morning *Boston Globe*. The *Globe* front page headline read "BCH FLU DOCTOR AQUITTED". There was an accompanying photograph taken at the time of the court verdict. Noble did not even look at the newspaper.

When he was finished, Noble asked Lillian to sit on his lap. Then, he cried for the first time since his daughter's passing. Noble sobbed deeply while placing his face on Lillian's chest. She brushed his gray hair and kissed his forehead as he let out a universe of emotion. The couple felt closer than they ever had before.

Later in the day, Rosenau came to call on his old friend. Rosenau said he wanted to meet "the most famous Internist in the United States". Noble had become quite a celebrity, be it an unwilling one.

On Monday morning, February 17th, Lillian drove her husband to Boston City Hospital. Noble walked directly to the hospital Rotunda. He wanted to thank Cunard in person for the letter that had such an influence on his court-martial. However, when he reached the second story Rotunda door to Cunard's office, he noticed the name plate upon it was gone. He opened the door to find a nearly vacant office. Gone were the paintings, photographs, and ship models that previously adorned the room. Cunard's secretary was working behind her desk as Noble entered the office. "Dr. Noble!" said the secretary. "My, it's an honor to see you, sir! What can I do for you?"

Noble's eyes looked about the empty room. "Hello. I was wondering if Commander Cunard was in today?"

The secretary looked surprised. "Oh, Dr. Noble. You haven't heard?"

"I guess not," said Noble. "What haven't I heard, Miss?"

"The Commander resigned his position with Boston City Hospital," said the secretary. "He had all his things removed and taken to storage last Friday."

Now it was Noble that was surprised. "Do you know where he went, Miss?"

"The Commander took a position as a U.S. Public Health Service officer at the Wind River Indian Reservation in western central Wyoming. I guess the pandemic has been brutal to the Eastern Shoshone and Northern Arapaho Indians that live on the reservation. Dr. Cunard will be working to establish and maintain adequate primary care for those Indians."

"Thank you, Miss," said Noble. "You have been most helpful." Noble left the office. As he returned to Lillian waiting in the Ford, Noble believed he understood what Cunard had done and why. Cunard realized that his own pride and arrogance had likely contributed to the unnecessary deaths of many people. He was atoning for his error in judgment by helping his old foe in the best way he could. His letter to General Parker was, in essence, a sincere apology to Noble. To further help redeem himself, Cunard left his privileged position in Boston in order to assist a group of people devastated by the pandemic. Cunard was bringing his life full circle.

Returning home, Noble wrote a letter of thanks to Cunard and sent it to the USPHS station at the Wind River Indian Reservation. The Noble family then drove to the Chestnut Hill Cemetery for the first time since Marguerite's burial. They placed flowers on the graves and said prayers. When it was time to leave, Noble asked the others to return to the car while he took a few minutes alone with his departed family members. He was comforted by the time he spent on the hill.

Early afternoon the next day, Tuesday, February 18th, Noble drove to the Department of Public Health at 250 Washington Street in Boston. He was there to attend his 2:30 PM hearing with the Massachusetts Medical Board. Noble sat for some time on the 2nd Floor waiting area. Dozens of people were also waiting for their own hearings. The Medical Board was obviously a very busy place.

Noble was finally brought into the Board chamber two hours late. The seven member Board sat at a curved table in the form of an open "C". In front of the Board table was a smaller table for hearing attendees. Noble took his seat.

The chair of the Board said, "Good afternoon, Dr. Noble. You are certainly the most famous physician we have on our calendar today." The other Board members laughed. The chair then read the allegation against Noble. Then, Noble read a brief response to the allegation. He summarized why he had established an influenza quarantine ward when he did. He stated that he had information about the pandemic before many others in New England, and he used that information in making his decisions. Noble also carried letters of reference from Victor Vaughn, Milton Rosenau, William Welch, and retired Army Surgeon General William Gorgas. As each member of the Board saw the author names of the letters, and read them, their eyes grew wide with astonishment. Noble was then asked to briefly step out of the chamber while the Board discussed the allegation against him.

After only ten minutes, Noble was asked back into the Board Chamber. "Dr. Edward Noble," said the chair. "It is the opinion of the Massachusetts Medical Board that the stated allegation against you is completely groundless. The Board finds no inappropriate professional behavior on your part, whatsoever."

"Thank you, gentlemen," said Noble, as he gathered his documents together in preparation for his departure.

"One more thing, Dr. Noble," said the chair. "The Medical Board would like to thank you for the difficult decisions you have made on behalf of the people of Boston, and the nation. We want to state for the public record that the five physicians on this Board are honored to be your colleagues, Dr. Noble."

Noble found it difficult to talk as a wave of emotion came over him. He said in almost a whisper, "Thank you,

gentlemen. Thank you very much. But, the honor is all mine."
He turned and left the room.

Wednesday, February 19th was Noble's first day back to
work since his arrest. The sentry at the A.I. Office saluted
as Noble opened the office door, and told him it was great
to have him back. As he entered the large office, loud applause greeted him. Spread out on the far office wall was a
large hand-drawn banner that said "Welcome Home Major
Noble". All three Signal Corps Second Lieutenants were in
the office at the same time. There was a large chocolate cake
on the central table.

Lieutenant Pierre-Louis said smiling, "Welcome home,
Major! Your wife told us you were coming back to work today. So, the three of us baked a cake in celebration of your return to us!" Noble smiled at all of them, and shook his head.

Lieutenant Lafayette then said, "Sir, permission to hug the
commanding officer!"

Noble laughed, and said, "Permission granted." All three
women hugged their Major. Noble then said, "Gee, what
more could a guy want? Three pretty girls hugging him all
at once! You better not tell Lillian how much I enjoyed it!"
Everyone laughed until their sides ached.

While they ate slices of cake, Noble remarked about one
office wall covered with stacks of cables wrapped in bundles
with rubber bands. "What's all this, ladies?" while pointing
to the stacks.

Lieutenant Quellet answered, "Major, those are several
thousand well-wishing telegrams from all over the country. We
thought you might want to read some of them, sometime. There's
even one from the famous actors John and Lionel Barrymore!"
Noble told his officers that he would have his family help transfer the cables to their house sometime soon. But, right now, he
wanted to go to the wards and catch up on clinical news.

It was difficult for Noble to simply walk around Boston
City Hospital. Wherever he went, crowds of people gathered

around him to shake hands, salute, and just to say "great to see you back". This was true for the entire hospital staff, and patients as well. As Noble walked on various wards, patients in hospital beds reached out to touch him. Some patients climbed out of beds to see him. Noble realized that some of this attention was due to his new celebrity status. However, most of the frenzy about him was a true outpouring of joy over his return from jail. There was now a public awareness of the personal risks he took for the good of the nation. Everyone knew Noble was a fine physician. But now, he was also a national hero.

Noble continued to excuse himself from enlarging groups of people, only to be engulfed in other enlarging groups. He finally saw Dr. David Schafer reading a patient medical record, and motioned him to go into one of the small ward lab rooms. With a trail of people following him, Noble slipped into the lab room and closed the door.

"Major, looks like you have quite a following, sir," said Schafer with a chuckle.

"Exactly, David," said Noble. "I'll be walking on water, and feeding the five thousand, very shortly."

"We're all <u>so</u> glad your back, Major, seriously," said Schafer. "All of us were worried sick about you."

"I was pretty worried about me too," joked Noble. "Perhaps we can talk about that experience another time. I would rather hear about the hospital, and what you are seeing with influenza."

Noble had his fill with the whole court-martial escapade, and Schafer perceived that. "Well, Major, a lot has happened since you...a...left. We've seen a dramatic, and sudden, drop in influenza cases. This is both in the clinics, and in the acuity of patients admitted to the wards. We've closed all the satellite hospitals except one, and it is only about one-quarter full as we speak. We'll probably close that facility in one or two days. It looks like your third wave is vanishing, and quickly." Noble gave a thin smile with his lips pressed together. It was wonderful that the

demon was disappearing again. But, he thought to himself, why did it have to take his daughter before it left?
Noble refused to entertain that notion again, because it was
too painful.

"Major," continued Schafer, "do you think it's gone for
good this time? There still seem to be sporadic pockets of it
that come and go about the city."

Noble slowly shook his head. "David, I just don't know.
We have no precedent for a pandemic like this. My epidemiologist extraordinaire...my wife...and I, have been 'preoccu-
pied'. We haven't seen any of the latest data from around the
country and world. It will take some time to synthesize all of
that. For now, I just don't know."

Noble caught up on many important hospital issues, such
as the full complement of supplies it now had in its store-
rooms. He went back to the A.I. Office, where Lieutenant
Quellet handed him a number of messages and cables. One
telegram was from his old friend Colonel Harvey Cushing,
who said he believed he would be coming home within the
next four to five weeks. Another message came from commonwealth local officials who were lifting the ban on public
gatherings, and reopening the schools. A cable from the navy
was informative.

Friday, February 14, 1919
From: USS George Washington

President Wilson left Brest, France today to return to the
United States. The President plans to lobby Congress for
the establishment of a League of Nations when he returns
to Washington DC.

U.S. Navy Intelligence.

But, another cable was much more ominous.

Tuesday, February 18, 1919
From: Paris, France, American Diplomatic Corps

Over the previous two weeks, the number of influenza related deaths in Paris has doubled. Several members of the American Delegation are ill with influenza, or have died of it recently. General Pershing's personal aid-de-camp, William Borland, who had been a Congressman, died. Colonel Carl Boyd died. The aid-de-camp to the commander of the American Atlantic Fleet, Commander Edward Blakeslee, also has died. Colonel Edward House, representative for the Supreme War Counsel, and close aide to the President, is very ill with influenza. Government intelligence is concerned that Colonel House's absence from the Versailles negotiations may significantly impede America's interests in those talks.

U.S. Army Intelligence.

Apparently, it was not yet time to hold a requiem for the demon.

On Friday, February 21ˢᵗ, Noble dropped by Dr. Piero Garzaro's office. Garzaro told Noble how happy he was with the court outcome, and how all the attendings at BCH were so glad to have him on staff. Noble then asked, "Piero, can you give me some idea about where you think Lillian is in her treatment?"

"Edward, how does she seem to you?"

"Piero, frankly, she now seems completely normal in every respect. If I didn't know better, I would say she never had any melancholia at all."

"It is quite amazing," said Piero. "She was making a slow but steady recovery...until your arrest. There were a few days when she greatly regressed after you went to the stockade. That is when she locked herself in the bedroom. But, a little later, she came to one of our sessions and said bluntly, 'Dr. Garzaro, I'm better now'. It was like psychological daylight for her after a long black night."

"So," said Noble, "you saw it too."

"Absolutely, Edward. It was the realization that <u>you</u> were in danger that brought her promptly back to us. I liken it to a female lion who suddenly realizes her den is under attack. Lillian has always shown very strong mental adjustment and coping strategies. Some of that is just her psychological makeup, but much of it is the fact that she is so darn smart. To some degree, she reasoned herself out of severe depression. I can't say I have seen anything like it before."

"Is she cured, Piero?"

"Let me say, Edward, that I believe she has an excellent prognosis for a quick and full recovery. I hope you don't mind if I continue to see her once a week for a time. I think additional sessions will help solidify her remarkable recovery. She is very willing to continue therapy, by the way."

"By all means," said Noble. He then grinned and said, "You're the doctor!"

By Thursday, February 27th, the Noble family was trying still to reach a more stable and calmer routine. Since all Boston facilities of learning were open again, Bernard was back at school. Akeema continued to hold home classes for Michael, who remained weak with a staggering gait. However, Michael was making steady progress. He had scheduled exercise periods each day, took walks with his family about Back Bay, and practiced negotiating the home staircase. It was hoped he could return to school in a few weeks. Florence attended her nursing studies at Boston City Hospital, but continued her increasingly active role in public health agencies.

Dozens of letters arrived every day from around the country, and now the world, at the Beacon Street house for Dr.

Noble. The letters dealt with everything from well wishers, to invitations to speak at various conferences. Many letters offered Noble faculty positions in universities.

Noble came to the A.I. Office in the morning and tried to pretend nothing of interest had happened recently. This was made more difficult with increasing number of cables and letters stacked along the walls for Noble. "Major," said Lieutenant Pierre-Louis, "we've been keeping new and separate stacks of letters and cables for you. They're in that corner, over there. Most of them are messages from people asking you to be their doctor, or the doctor for a loved one. They're very sad, sir. They describe all kinds of ailments. I think that some of them think you have special healing powers."

Noble put his hand to the side of his face. "Obviously, I can't answer each one of these letters individually. I certainly can't address any of their clinical problems. On the other hand, I don't want the letters to go completely unanswered. Can we send a form letter to them? The letter might offer some general advice when seeking help with medical issues."

"Sure, Major," said the Lieutenant. "We can create a form letter and make copies using our Roneo mimeograph single drum machine. Just tell us what you would like the letter to say. Oh, one more thing, Major. You are getting a fair number of letters with offers of...marriage."

Noble gave a boyish grin. "Lieutenant...mimeograph a short letter that tells my suitors that I'm taken." Pierre-Louis grinned back.

Just then, Lillian entered the A.I. Office. "Hi, Claudette. What are you so smiley about?"

Pierre-Louis giggled, and said, "Hi, Mrs. Noble. I was just telling the Major that we are getting a lot of letters from women offering their hands to him in marriage."

Lillian looked at her husband lovingly, and laughed. "Aw...the problems one encounters when one is married to a superstar. Tell all those ladies they will have to fight me for him first." All three laughed, as Noble came over to his wife, grabbed her about the waist, and kissed her passionately.

The Lieutenant asked, "Mrs. Noble, what brings you to the office today?"

"Well," said Lillian, "Edward asked me to help organize the A.I. Office records. We haven't gone through any official cables in weeks. What has recently arrived isn't in any form we can use for study. So, for the next few days I'll be working on improving organization."

"Do you need any help, Mrs. Noble?" asked the Lieutenant.

"No, that's OK Claudette. You have enough to do. There's more than a year's worth of cables stored in the office, and space is getting pretty tight here. I'm going to first pack up the office records received before August, 1918, and have them sent to the National Archive in Washington DC. This will ensure the records are available for future researchers. Then, I'm going to categorize the cables sitting in stacks. When that is finished, I'm going to perform an epidemiological influenza update for Edward. One more thing. This weekend we'll bring the Ford truck around to load up all of the personal messages our 'superstar' has received. I guess we'll keep them in our garage for now."

"How about all the marriage proposals, Lilly?" Noble said, still grinning.

"Very funny," said Lillian.

On Wednesday, March 5th, Noble dropped by the Boston City Hospital Harvard satellite laboratory to check on any progress Milton Rosenau and John Keegan could report on their influenza antiserum. This was the same antiserum administered to Marguerite and Michael. Unfortunately, results were still too preliminary. So far, all that could be stated with certainty was the antiserum was not toxic.

Noble spent much of the day with his residents in the care of hospital patients. Aside from his family life, this was the activity he loved most. Like all clinicians, he spent much time thinking about the patients he saw on the wards. He thought about them at breakfast, lunch, and dinner, on the weekends, and even after retiring for bed. It was not unusual for Noble to get out of bed at night and read from his textbooks and journals on some clinical point he had seen that day. Noble knew all physicians do this kind of study during their careers. It comes with the territory; along with the worry physicians always carry for their ill patients.

Later, second-year resident Anna Reed, her intern, and two fourth year medical students were rounding on their patients in the South Department. Reed saw Noble reading a medical record at the other end of the ward, and walked over to him. "Dr. Noble, do you have a minute?"

"Sure, Anna. What do you need?"

"We have a patient that is a bit of a conundrum. He's on this ward, toward the end window." Reed and her group walked down the center room isle with rows of patients on either side. Dr. Noble followed. Reed picked up the patient's chart on a clip board hanging from the end of the hospital bed.

"Dr. Noble, this is Mr. Fallen. He was admitted to Boston City just a few hours ago. He's a 51 years old man who works in a South End factory. He's been having some progressive pain along his left anterior leg which he describes as tingling. We think he has degenerative disk disease, but wonder if he might have early Herpes Zoster that is symptomatic prior to the typical rash. What do you think?'

Dr. Noble motioned for the clip board, and studied it for a moment. "Hello, Mr. Fallen. How long have you been having this pain?"

"Since about 8 o'clock last night, doc."

"About eighteen hours, then. What was it like when it started?"

"Well, I started to have some left hip pain after dinner, and then later some 'electric' shocks down the front of my leg. It's getting worse."

"Do you have any numbness in your leg?" asked Noble.

"Well, eh, ya. My left big toe is numb."

"May I take a closer look at you, sir?" asked Noble.

"Sure, doc."

Noble looked at the patient's skin. He percussed the patient's back and found an area of severe tenderness along his lower spine. He asked one of the residents for a needle, and tested the patient's skin sensation. Noble noted decreased sensation from the patient's low back, along his anterior front left leg, and to his great toe. He noted there was also decreased pinprick sensation on the web of the left great toe. He asked the patient to raise his knee up to his chest while Noble pressed down on his thigh. He then asked the patient to stand and walk on his heels. Mr. Fallen had no problem walking on his right heel, but was clearly having trouble performing the maneuver on the left.

"Sir, how long have you been having trouble walking?" asked Noble.

"Funny you should ask that, doc. That is what really brought me to the hospital a couple of hours ago."

Dr. Noble turned to Reed and said sternly, "This man must go to surgery immediately."

Looking puzzled, Reed asked, "Dr. Noble, what is the problem?"

"The patient has a spinal epidural abscess on the left lateral side of L3 and L4."

"But, the patient doesn't have a fever," remarked Reed.

"Many don't." said Noble. "The patient has had symptoms for less than 24 hours, and that is a good prognostic sign. His symptoms suggest that the abscess is progressing along the true epidural space that is present below the foramen magnum. It likely started between L3 and L4, and has extended to L4 and L5. This is a common area for spinal epidural abscesses because of the larger amount of infection-prone fat there. His only hope for avoiding a potentially disastrous complication is drainage of the abscess as soon as possible. He has progressing weakness of the left quadriceps muscle, as well as the flexor muscles of the left foot."

"But, Dr. Noble," asked the service intern. "The patient's white blood cell count is normal. What tipped you off to the diagnosis?"

"Two things," said Noble. "First, I see form his history that the patient has diabetes and is also an alcoholic. These are risk factors for this type of abscess. Second, look at the patient's left shoulder."

While the others looked on, Reed lifted up the sleeve of the patient's left hospital gown and saw a small tattoo.

"Do any of you notice something about the tattoo?" said Noble.

"Yes." said one of the medical students. "It's slightly erythemic."

"Right you are." said Noble. "This is a new tattoo, right Mr. Fallen?"

"Yes sir. Got it just a couple of days ago. A beaut, eh?" The tattoo was a small waving American flag.

"Everyone, the tattoo is likely the portal of entry for the *Staphylococcus aureus* that entered his blood stream and has colonized his spinal epidural space. Time is of the utmost. Please call the surgical service and let them know about our conversation as early as possible."

"Should we order a Roentgenogram, Dr. Noble?" asked the intern.

"No. Roentgenograms don't show any changes in the early stages of these abscesses. Please. Get in touch with surgery quickly. You have less than 6 hours to save this man's ability to walk, or perhaps his life." Noble was careful to say this softly, and away from earshot of the patient. Noble was always sensitive to patients' feelings. Still in hushed tones, he said, "He's going to have a rough time of it. We have probably diagnosed the problem early enough for him to regain most, if not all, of his neurological function. But, the death rate from septic infection after surgery is unfortunately very high. Keep him in your prayers, everyone, and keep his postoperative dressings clean." Noble walked away from the bedside slowly, with his hands held behind his back and his head lowered. The residents and medical students wondered if Noble was, in fact, praying.

Lillian worked in the A.I. Office that afternoon, and went home that evening with her husband in the Ford. "You seem to be in an uplifted mood today, Lilly," said Noble, as they drove north on Massachusetts Avenue.

Lillian turned to Noble and said, "Thank you for noticing, darling. I really am."

"Any particular reason?" asked Noble.

"Not really," answered Lillian. "Since your court-martial, I've thought a lot about you, our marriage, our family, Boston, and a lot about my own life. My sessions with Dr. Garzaro have also been very revealing."

"Any conclusions that you can share?" asked Noble.

Lillian smiled. "I can share everything with you, darling. I hope you know that I love you so much." Lillian paused for a moment, and then continued. "After little Marguerite died, and so soon after Arthurs's death, I felt as though my life had come to an end. I couldn't stand living in my own skin anymore. Being awake was a form of unbearable torture, but sleeping was impossible. Talking, thinking, eating, and even breathing became a chore. Edward, I didn't tell Dr. Garzaro this, but at one point I briefly thought about killing myself."

Noble was both shocked, and yet not surprised, by his wife's revelation. In some ways, Lillian was admitting feelings that he himself had. However, Noble could not admit to anyone that he had held those same dark emotions at one time. He could not even admit this to Lillian. "I didn't know that, Lilly," said Noble.

"I haven't told that to anyone else, Edward," Lillian said softly. "Nevertheless, you are the one that came to my rescue."

"But, Lilly," said Noble, "I was in jail."

"Exactly," explained Lillian. "Two of my children were dead. Another child was deathly ill. My husband was facing twenty-five years in prison for doing the right thing. And, my community continued to be ravaged by a disease that seemingly had no end in the suffering it inflicts. As I thought about these insults to <u>my</u> life, I became exceedingly angry. 'How can these injustices continue?' I thought. 'Who is going to stop all of this evil?' It then dawned on me."

"What was that, Lilly?" said Noble.

"Who is going to stop all of this evil?" said Lillian. "It must start with <u>me</u>. I have to begin to stop it. I can't cure influenza. But, I do know how to slow its spread, and I know how to begin to heal its aftermath. I couldn't stop your court-martial. However, I could help support you through the process to its conclusion. And, none of this can happen while hiding in one's room. It comes back to Arthur's old favorite saying: 'You can't do everything. But, you can do what you can do.'"

The Ford neared its right turn onto Beacon Street. The couple remained silent for a time. Lillian placed her hand on her husband's right knee as they whisked along in the cold late winter evening. She finally turned her head back to him and said, "The other thing that has helped me immensely, Edward, has been my faith."

"I know how important that is to you," said Noble.

Lillian continued, "The times Akeema and Florence took me to the Cathedral of the Holy Cross were defining moments for me, Edward. My times in prayer were a true blessing. It was during one of my cathedral visits that I believe I actually heard the Holy Mother request that I continue my service to others. My time for turning inward, she said, was over. It was now my charge to turn outward, and turn my personal grief into God's work. That is when I received my mission."

"What is the mission?" asked Noble, knowing that his wife was sharing her most intimate thoughts.

"I am creating a large charitable fund that will comfort those who have been hurt by influenza," said Lillian. "I have named it the 'A & M Charitable Fund', after Arthur and Marguerite. I have already contacted a number of wealthy potential benefactors, as well as church, philanthropic, city, county, state, and federal sources for initial donations. I have received a number of large pledges and have begun to deposit money in a charitable New England bank account. The fund will spend only the interest, and will never touch the principal. In this way it will best serve those who carry the neuropsychiatric scars from the pandemic, and those who have been thrown into hopeless poverty."

Noble was always amazed at his wife's ability to make big and important things happen. She was telling him about this wonderful huge project underway, and it was the first he had heard of it. "You are an incredible person, Lilly. How long have you been planning this fund?"

"I began the project a few hours before I came to visit you at the Devens stockade," said Lillian. "Edward, two successive generations will be forced to deal with the health and financial debilities created by the pandemic. It will take everyone pulling together to find accommodations for tens of thousands of its living victims. I will do my part in the ways I am able. It is my mission."

The Ford neared the Noble house. After a moment of contemplation, Lillian then said, "Of course, I have another more immediate mission."

"What could that be, Lilly?" said Noble.

Lillian gave a sly smile, and looked at her husband from the corner of her eyes. "I can't tell you that, Edward. But, I'll show you when we get up to our bedroom."

Noble suddenly felt extremely flushed. He could not wait to get into the house.

CHAPTER 35

Saturday, March 8th, was a long awaited day for Akeema. Several weeks earlier she had read in the *Boston Globe* that an Arctic Studies exhibition touring the United States would arrive briefly at the Peabody Museum in Cambridge. The exhibit featured artifacts from the Alaskan Yup`ik people, and Akeema dearly wanted the Noble family to go with her to see it. So, off the Nobles drove on a very cold and snowing morning to the museum near Harvard University.

Whenever Noble was off duty, and was in public, he tried to disguise himself to avoid the "Major Noble" notoriety. Today he wore brown loafers, khaki slacks, a light blue soft collared shirt, a heavy black overcoat, and a wide-brimmed tan fedora hat. Noble did not like hats. But, the fedora was partially successful in covering his white hair that had become famous in Boston. Even when it was overcast, Noble wore aviator sunglasses outside.

Noble parked the Ford on Divinity Avenue, and the group of six entered the large red brick Peabody Museum. The entire first floor contained the Alaskan culture exhibit. Noble had never seen Akeema so animated and utterly happy. As she showed her Boston family various artifacts, she sometimes spoke so fast that English, Russian, French, German, and Unaliq words all ran together. This often made the explanations a challenge to understand. Nevertheless, the Noble family enjoyed their opportunity to experience Akeema's cultural so thoroughly.

The Peabody exhibit wove a rich story of an ancient intelligent people living in harsh conditions. Groups of about three hundred Yup'ik usually maintained permanent settlements during the very cold winters. Just as Akeema had previously told the Nobles, men lived in a communal *qasgiq*, while women and children lived in groups of four to twelve in *ena*. A life-size *ena* was part of the exhibit. It was made of sod, and was partially subterranean in construction. Akeema told how she and the other children were taught in these dwellings how to cook, sew, and hunt. Various survival techniques needed for life in the near-Arctic Circle were also part of the curriculum. Since recording family histories was a major part of Yup'ik life, scholarship in general was honored among them. This is why Akeema's village encouraged her dream of studying in Boston.

The ancient religion of the Yup'ik was Shamanism. However, Russian explorers and trappers had introduced Christianity to Alaska during the early 19th century. The Yup'ik were free to incorporate Christianity into their own beliefs in any way they personally chose. Therefore, many varied combinations of Shamanism and Christianity were found among the Yup'ik. Akeema explained that her village at Golovin tended to emphasize Christianity.

Golovin still had many Shaman beliefs and rituals. Akeema showed the Nobles a display of the "Bladder Festival" which she vividly remembered as a child. The Yup'ik believe souls of the dead are cycled into future generations. This belief extends to animals, and was the basis of Akeema's respect for the striped bass she caught in Providence the year before. Souls of killed animals must be cared for so they may be reborn.

The souls of seals were thought to reside in the animals' bladders after death. For the Bladder Festival, bladders of killed seals were inflated and hung for five days in the *qasgiq*. Then, village families took the bladders and pushed them through holes cut in the ice in order to release the souls for rebirth.

In the summers, Yup`ik communities usually traveled to temporary sealing and fishing camps. The Yup`ik caught walrus, whales, bear, salmon, trout, and caribou. Every part of these animals was used for food, or to make clothing and tools. The more moderate summer temperatures allowed the gathering of vegetable, berries, and eggs which helped feed the village during the winters. Akeema showed the Nobles her people's spears, arrows, knives, bowls, cups, that she herself could make. Fur clothing that completely covered the body, except the face, were on display. Beautiful baskets woven from indigenous grasses and dyed with bright colors adorned the exhibit. Noble thought to himself how much better Akeema could survive in Arctic weather than just about anyone else in Boston. He knew the name Yup`ik means "real people". He thought about how these "real people" were superbly adapted to one of Earth's most challenging places.

Of all the artifacts, Akeema and the Nobles enjoyed the ceremonial masks the most. Akeema's stories, along with the masks, made the artifacts come alive for the family. For thousands of years, the Yup`ik have created graceful expressive masks for traditional dances and festivities. Much like the Cherokee, feathered hand-held fans often accompanied the masks. Over the long winter darkness, storytelling took place in the *qasgiq*. The shaman, using a wood red, white, and black *Nepcetaq* triangular mask with feathers, usually moderated the stories.

Sometimes a mask of a strange creature with a wrinkled forehead, one eye partially closed, and a bent face with a sideways mouth, would come to the *qasgiq* with odd tales for the tribe. Akeema showed another mask from the well-known and terrifying story that still made her shiver. The mask was of a child with a smile from ear-to-ear who ate his mother, and then went from house-to-house eating people. As children, Akeema and her friends sometimes played a game called *Ap´apaa* in which they pretended they were that child.

One of the masks was of a small bird. This mask, explained Akeema, told the story of a famous shaman who was on an ice flow one early morning. Suddenly, a small bird landed in front of him and began to sing. The shaman understood the bird's singing to say, "It's going to get stormy! Don't stay here! Go up to the land!" The shaman obeyed, and soon a storm caused the ice flow on which he was standing to float out to sea. The shaman believed the bird had been his little *tuunraq*, or "helping spirit". Akeema said the story tells us we must listen to the helping spirits in nature in order to avoid disaster.

The group stayed at the Peabody exhibit for several hours. When it was time to leave, everyone understood what a remarkable people the Yup`ik are. The group talked all the way home with Akeema about what they had seen, and had dozens more questions for her. However, Noble remained contemplative as he drove back toward Boston. How had the shaman dealt with the pandemic, thought Noble? How did they try to arm the villages against the demon? Surely, Noble's weapons against influenza were no more effective than the ones shaman used. The only difference, thought Noble, was that he did not think he had a *tuunraq* to protect him.

All next week, Lillian labored in the A.I. Office. Scores of binders containing cables and letters dating from January to August, 1918, were loaded into an Army Military Police truck for transport to Washington DC. This made room for the cataloging and indexing of office records from August to the present. Lillian then went about studying the national and international pandemic data that could now be properly researched.

On Wednesday, March 12th, Noble returned to the A.I. Office in the late morning after hospital rounds. He greeted

Lieutenant Quellet, as she assisted Lillian in various calculations. As he took off his army overcoat, Noble noticed that
Lillian, who was seated at the center office table, had a frown
on her face. "Lieutenant," asked Noble, "how come Mrs.
Noble is scowling?"

"I'm not scowling," insisted Lillian.

"Yes you are," said Noble smiling, as he saw an opportunity to tease his wife.

Quellet looked up from her paper and pencil and remarked, "Hi, Major. Mrs. Noble was just telling me she's still
upset about the vote."

Noble instantly knew what this was about, and knew that
his wife was not in a teasing mood over it. "Lilly, the most recent Senate vote was February 10th. It's been almost a month.
Are you still upset over it?"

"Of course I'm 'still upset over it', Edward," said Lillian.
"The two-thirds majority needed for passage of the Nineteenth
Amendment was defeated in the Senate...again. Only this
time it lost by one vote. One vote! I just can't believe it. It
is an outrage to all American women and the sacrifices they
make for this country every day. One vote!"

Noble knew where this discussion was going, and tried
to diffuse his wife's fury. "Well, Lilly, the President is rein-
troducing a suffrage bill which will hopefully come up for
a Senate vote this spring. Since 1920 is a presidential election year, and both parties don't want sizzling condemnation
from the nation's women, I think it will have a good chance
of passing this time. I also suspect both parties hope they will
benefit from ballots cast by the fairer gender." Noble sought
to change the subject and put his wife in a better mood. "How
is the research going, Lilly?"

Lillian immediately switched from the mode of an activist, to one of a scientist. "I now have some firm conclusions
based on available data, Edward. There remain isolated small
outbreaks of influenza in New England and the rest of the
Atlantic seaboard. However, the 'third wave' has definitely
ended in our area of the country. Still, various cities in the U.S.,

like San Francisco, continue to have serious lethal outbreaks. States that continue to have large numbers of new cases include Pennsylvania, Nebraska, Ohio, Missouri, Louisiana, Kentucky, Michigan, Georgia, Washington, and California."

"Internationally," said Lillian, "the situation is very similar. Right now, most continents are going through a 'third wave'. Europe has its own wave three, and France seems to be particularly active with influenza right now."

Lillian continued, "We suspected a few months ago that there was evidence of immunity when comparing the second and third waves. My analysis shows this evidence is now even stronger. The third wave of influenza is filling in the areas it missed with the second wave. But, the third wave has not been as large as the second, even though it is just as lethal. This likely means wave three represented the same disease as wave two. The pandemic simply had fewer susceptible hosts the third time around. Edward, you originally hypothesized all of this, and you were completely right."

"This really gives us room for hope, Lilly," said Noble. "There is a vulnerability within influenza, and it involves our own immune systems. If we can learn more about that weakness, then we may be able to manipulate the human immune system to resist or temporize the influenza infection. This means the work of William Park, Anna Wessel Williams, Milton Rosenau, and Oswald Avery is on the right track. We're just not there yet. We can have the Signal Corps Lieutenants cable off your results to the Influenza Commission and Colonel Vaughn today."

Lillian was wrapping up her most recent A.I. Office data analysis. She now planned to spend most of her non-family time with private and government welfare projects for pandemic victims. This included donation solicitations for her new A & M Charitable Fund.

Before Noble left the A.I. Office that evening, he placed a call to pathologist Dr. Timothy Caron at Camp Devens. During his visit to the camp the previous fall, Noble remembered seeing numerous histologic pathology slides prepared from necropsy material. He asked what was to be done with the material, and Caron thought the thousands of specimens would likely be destroyed. Noble pleaded passionately for the material to be archived for future study. He also suggested similar pathology material at all other containments needed preservation. Caron agreed, and said he would pass the request up the chain of command. After the call, Noble cabled a corresponding request to Colonel Vaughn. He proposed that pathological influenza specimens should be archived at the Army Medical Museum, in Washington DC. Vaughn's return cable completely agreed with Noble's excellent idea. He would pass on the suggestion to Dr. James Ewing at the museum's "Old Red Brick" building.

Early in the afternoon on Friday, March 14th, Noble was the attending physician for a number of resident rounding teams on the wards. As he was walking through one of the pavilion floors, Noble noticed a medical intern looking quizzical. He had seen this particular expression on the faces of so many residents over the past fourteen years that he knew exactly what it meant. He remembered displaying the same look himself more than once as a resident. It was the facial expression of complete bafflement, dismay, and sheer terror. The intern was not sure what to do next.

Noble walked over to the intern, gave a friendly smile, and said, "John, can I help you?"

The intern turned toward Noble, did a fast double-take, and looked as though someone had just thrown him a life preserver. "Dr. Noble! Ah...yes, I...well, yes. I could use some help, sir." Noble invited him to tell him the problem.

"Sir, I have a patient here who is a 41 year old woman who came to Boston City Hospital about an hour ago. She complains of a few hours of progressive abdominal pain and bloating, after one week of watery diarrhea without bleeding. She has no remarkable medical history, other than a Caesarian section six years ago."

Noble looked at the patient's name on the bed stand and asked, "May I take a look at you, Mrs. Write?"

"Yes," replied the patient. "Doctor, I'm not feeling very well."

Dr. Noble noticed the patient was modestly uncomfortable in her hospital bed. She shifted from side-to-side as though she could not find a satisfactory position. She was also mildly diaphoretic. Noble performed abdominal auscultation with his stethoscope. Bowel sounds were hypoactive. The abdomen was slightly distended, and tympanic to percussion. He elicited moderate diffuse tenderness with light-to-moderate palpation, but there was no guarding, rebound tenderness, or rigidity. There was also no organomegaly, and no masses were appreciated. Noble then asked the intern, "John, do you have any other clinical data available?"

"Well," John replied, "She has a normal temperature, heart rate, respiratory rate, and blood pressure. Her white-cell count is 10 K/μL, with a differential of 25% bands, 46% segmented neutrophils, 3% eosinophils, 1% basophils, and 25% lymphocytes."

Noble stated, "I see there is a Roentgenogram at the end of the bed. Has a Roentgenologist seen the film?"

"No sir," said the intern. "The film was taken just as the patient was taken from the emergency room to the ward."

Noble took the large brown envelope hanging from the end of the bed, removed the Roentgenogram of the abdomen, and held it up to the light in the room. After briefly studying the film, Noble said, "John, let's look at the abdominal plane film. If you look at the subphrenic area and the ventral surface of the liver, you will see darkened areas. There is also a longitudinal linear density on the ventral surface of the liver, which is known as the falciform-ligament sign. There is a linear density running along the inferior edge of the falciform ligament, which is called the ligamentum teres sign. Finally, there are darkened spaces on both sides of the bowel wall, known as the Rigler's sign. All these signs indicate pneumperitomeum, or free air within the abdominal cavity. This patient has had a perforation of the intestine, and requires an exploratory laperotomy at the earliest convenience. Could you please call our surgical colleagues? Please be sure to let me know what is found."

"Thank you, Dr. Noble," said John. "I most certainly will." The medical intern ran so fast from the ward that he dropped his clip board, and had to rush back to pick it up.

Noble thought to himself that the patient's presentation was slightly atypical. She had no vital sign changes, and a normal leukocyte count. Still, her WBC was considerably shifted to the left, and her physical examination was notably abnormal. Nevertheless, very smart residents can sometimes be clinically blinded by the flurry of incoming information and the tensions of the moment. The situation can be complicated by fatigue and numerous patients to see in a short period of time. Noble was also aware the traditional medical school curriculum was not keeping pace with changes in medical technology. For example, Roentgenogram interpretation was not yet taught concurrently with physical diagnosis in many medical schools. These were issues doctors of Internal Medicine would need to address nationally.

At about 2 PM, Noble made his way back to the A.I. Office. He saluted the sentry as always, and opened the small office door. To his surprise, Colonel Victor Vaughn was sitting on the office couch reading the latest issue of *The Boston Medical and Surgical Journal*. It took a moment for Noble to realize who he was. Then Noble saluted, and Vaughn smiled and saluted back. "At ease, soldier," said Vaughn. Noble sat down at his desk chair.

"Colonel...I'm so surprised," said Noble. "I had no idea you were in Boston, sir."

"I just arrived by train," said Vaughn. "The Lieutenant said you would be here soon, so I decided to wait. You had a copy of the *Journal* on your desk, so I thought I would catch up on the latest in Internal Medicine. With my administrative duties, I don't get a chance to read as much as I would like to." Vaughn went on to say how sorry he was about Marguerite, and the numbers of people at her burial prohibited him from talking with Noble. Noble told him he completely understood. Noble then thanked his old friend for his comments at the court-martial. Vaughn said he thought he had not helped at all, but could not contain his glee with the acquittal. The two then caught up on family events, some of the influenza research going at the Rockefeller Institute and other places, and the news about Richard Cunard.

After a half-hour discussion on numerous topics, Noble finally exclaimed, "Colonel, I know that you didn't come here from Washington to simply socialize. Don't get me wrong, sir. It's great to see you. But, you're here for another reason... aren't you?"

Vaughn had been slouching in the couch. But, with Noble's question, he sat up straight. His demeanor suddenly changed from one of a friend, to one of an army officer. "Gee, you're so much like your father, Edward. Both of you could only take so much chit-chat before you had to get down to business. Yes, I'm here for a reason."

There was a pause that seemed almost theatrical to Noble. It was the pause that occurs when someone has practiced a speech, and is about to deliver it to the intended audience. After a time, Noble said, "What would that be, Colonel?"

There was yet another brief pause. Vaughn's face took on a very serious expression. "Edward, there is a lot going on right now. When I say a lot, I mean all things political, social, economic, and medical. And I also mean nationally, and internationally."

"Do you mean the post-war negotiations in Europe?" asked Noble.

"Yes," said Vaughn, "that includes the Paris Peace Conference. Edward, the world is being carved up in very different ways, now that The War is over. Exactly how that's going to look when all is said and done, is not yet known. How the Allies will work, or not, with the former Central Powers is uncertain. There are those who want to be lenient with Germany, and those who want to punish her maximally for The War. Europe itself is in shambles. The only world powers that remain strong right now are the United States and Japan. And, those two countries are beginning to be suspicious of each other's ambitions."

Vaughn went on, "In addition to all of this, the President has a grand design for the post-war world. He feels there needs to be a structure in place that will make future world wars impossible. That structure is the League of Nations."

"It's the major news in the papers these days, Colonel," said Noble. "The President has been darting back and forth across the Atlantic to help design the 'new' post-war world, and to make his case for the League of Nations in Congress. He's also been traveling around the country discussing the League with Americans directly."

"That's completely accurate, Edward," said Vaughn. "Superimposed on all of this is the pandemic. By the way, Lillian's epidemiologic summary of world influenza was brilliant. I read it the moment I received it two days ago, and re-read it on the train today. Tell her if she ever wants a university appointment anywhere, she can name her position."

"I'll be sure to tell her," said Noble with a large degree of pride. "This is all very interesting, Colonel, and I really enjoy the geo-political insights. However, what does any of that have to do with me?"

Vaughn became even more serious. "Edward, Lillian's summary has crystallized concern in the government for the President's safety. The attempted assassination last month of George Clemenceau, the French Prime Minister, has made everyone very worried. But, there is the other danger that might be even more ominous."

Noble was starting to see what was coming. Still, he asked, "What is that danger, Colonel?"

"That danger is influenza," said Vaughn, who was now intermittently gritting his teeth. "Lillian's summary clearly shows France to be a focal point for the pandemic in Europe right now. To make matters worse, the area around Paris is the focal point in France. Dozens of diplomatic personnel from several nations have died from influenza in Paris in the last few months. We couldn't ask for a more dire situation."

Noble sat listening to Vaughn, and leaned back in his desk chair. His all-too-often experienced subtle nausea made itself known again as he anticipated Vaughn's next statements. Vaughn then said, "Edward, just after I read Lillian's paper on the 12th, I had a long conversation with the President's personal physician."

"You mean Rear Admiral Cary Grayson...himself?" said Noble.

"The very one," said Vaughn. "The Admiral is the President's closest friend. He even introduced Wilson to his second wife, Edith. They often play golf and take long automobile rides together. The Wilsons and the Graysons go to the theater all the time. Grayson is a good man, Edward, but he knows the pandemic is way above his areas of expertise. He only had one year of internship at the Columbia Hospital for Women in Washington DC, and is not proficient in caring for critically ill patients. He asked my opinion on the matter, and I showed him Lillian's findings."

"So, what did you tell him, Colonel?" asked Noble, who already knew the answer to the question.

"Edward," said Vaughn, "I can already see in your face that you are upset. I remember that same look at the age of five when your father would tell you it was bed time. Edward, the Admiral wants to have an Internist along on the coming trip to Paris. He specially wants an infectious disease specialist who understands influenza complications. And, he wants the best. I made my suggestion, and Grayson has even discussed it with the President himself. Edward, the President has specifically asked for you."

Noble suddenly developed his usual crampy abdominal pain that came on when he was emotionally distraught. He removed his glasses, put both hands to his eyes, bent back his head over the desk chair, and took a deep breath. He pursed his lips together, and rubbed his eyes. He felt like running from the room, but knew that would accomplish nothing.

"Colonel, this is really not a very good time for this. I take it this is an order?"

"Edward, the President of the United States has specifically asked for you to go with him to France. I know you have been through a lot over the last few months. I'm certain that your family needs you. But, your President needs you, too. Your country needs you. Perhaps the world needs you, Edward."

Patriotism, with the "country needs you" speech, had sent Noble through two continents over the last year-and-a-half. He was tired of the army, and tired of "you're the best" compliments that always had unpleasant new jobs attached to them. He worried that his departure would cause Lillian to relapse into serious melancholia, and that his boys would suffer even more without their father. He worried about Boston City Hospital and its devoted residents. And, he worried about himself. He was no longer sure he could give his all for these recurring trips. "When is this all happening, Colonel?"

Vaughn also took a deep breath. "The President's ship, USS George Washington, sails from Hoboken on the 18th; just four days from now. You'll need to leave for New Jersey on Monday, the 17th." Noble simply stared blankly at Vaughn. "Edward, I know that you have requested a removal from active army duty. I can guarantee that will happen when you return from Paris. You only need to be gone a few weeks. As you know, all military physicians leaving active duty must enter the Medical Reserve. However, except for a few weeks per year, you'll be done with the army."

Vaughn's last sentence was the best thing Noble had heard in a long time. Noble thought about a return to civilian life, and his old infectious disease consultative practice. He thought about spring walks with Lillian, and Red Sox baseball games with his children in the summer. He thought how nice leaving the army would be. He thought how nice being normal again would be. "Colonel," said Noble, "you must admit there is more than a little irony here. Just a few weeks ago, I was under court-martial for trying to subvert the government. Now, the President asks me to go along with him to Europe and be his personal Internist. In addition, Lillian's wonderful work helps send me away. Odd turn of events, wouldn't you say?"

Vaughn laughed, and agreed. He also told Noble that he could keep in constant contact with the A.I. Office, and his home, with the use of the U.S. Embassy cable system. Vaughn said he had to catch a train back to Washington in an hour. He shook Noble's hand, wished him luck, saluted, and promptly departed.

Noble stood alone in the small office for quite some time. He finally collected his thoughts, walked into the large office, and saluted Lieutenant Lafayette. On the center table was a cable that caught Noble's eye immediately.

Friday, March 14, 1919
From: Base Hospital #5

Camiers, France

Happy day, Old bean! I'm leaving Brest for home on Sunday! I'm 'napoo' with Europe! Should be back in Boston by the 25th! Look forward to seeing you and the family soon!

Your good friend,
Colonel Harvey Cushing, AEF.

Edward Noble, and Harvey Cushing, would pass each other in the middle of the Atlantic Ocean, going in opposite directions. Another irony, thought Noble.

CHAPTER 36

I t was 4 AM on Monday, March 17th, and the Noble
household was not a joyful place. Everyone had elected to
get up early and see the Major off on his third transatlantic
crossing, but no one was happy about his leaving Boston
again. Lillian, Florence, and Akeema made Noble his favorite
breakfast with extra flare. There were even flowers on the
kitchen table to cheer up a dreary event. During breakfast,
Bernard and Michael complained bitterly, but not about
their fathers departure. According to their calculation, the
upcoming Red Sox season did not show as much promise as
1918. They definitely did not agree with the conversion of
Babe Ruth from primarily a pitcher to a left fielder. The boys
were already calling the team the "1919 Black Sox", and the
ball club was "conked-out". Their father reminded them they
would have to "get over it".

The ladies packed sandwiches, fruit, brownies, cookies,
and chocolate bars for Noble's trip, and made a Thermos of
hot black coffee for the train ride. The night before, Noble had
retrieved his old duffle bag from the garage and prepared it for

the voyage. He remembered putting it away and thinking at the time he would never need it again. Florence and Akeema said it would be exciting to sail with the President. This, however, was a sentiment not shared by the two older adults.

Noble's old friend, Sergeant Campbell, arrived in an army staff car, and it was suddenly time to go. Noble bid his children and Akeema goodbye, and he and Lillian walked out into the dark overcast morning. Lillian hugged her husband tightly, and told him to "be careful". Always trying to use humor to ease anxious moments, Noble said to his wife, "At least there's one bright spot in this trip."

"Whatever could that be, darling?" asked Lillian.

"During this third voyage," said Noble, "there won't be any U-boats." Lillian pretended to hit her husband, but he kissed her first before she landed a punch. He then climbed into the staff car, and zoomed away.

As Colonel Vaughn had arranged in the past, Noble had a private compartment on the train to Hoboken. He slept most of the way. But, the train made numerous slow-downs and stops for snow on the tracks which interrupted his naps.

Noble kept his officer hat on, and the collar of his coat turned up, in order to avoid recognition on the train. However, once a porter came to call on him in his compartment and asked excitedly, "Are you Major Noble?" Noble answered, "No. But, I get asked that a lot." The porter then said, "You sure do look like him!"

Noble drank all the hot coffee from his Thermos later in the trip in an attempt to stay alert. With no desire to do much of anything else, he timed the click-clack sound of the train wheels on the track. He calculated that each train click-clack took him twenty-four yards farther away from Lillian.

The trip to Hoboken took longer than usual because of the weather. It was mid-evening when Noble arrived at the train station. He caught a bus to the same hotel where he stayed a year earlier, and promptly prepared for a very early morning departure. However, before retiring, he enjoyed several of the brownies his wife had made for him.

Noble left the hotel at 4 AM on Tuesday, March 18th. He was amazed at the huge number of military personnel walking around at that hour. Tens of thousands of troops were returning home from Europe every day, and the Hoboken port seemed even busier than it had been fourteen months earlier. It took some time for Noble to make his way to the long finger dock building leading to his point of departure on the Hudson River.

Unlike the other docks at Hoboken, the dock building Noble entered was nearly empty. The army had provided him with documents to present at the numerous security areas he encountered. Noble went through several military checkpoints, and was interrogated twice by Secret Service agents from the U.S. Treasury Department. Near the end of the nine hundred foot long dock building, he walked out of a twenty foot high double door to a staging dock running alongside the building. And there she was.

USS *George Washington* was the largest ship Noble had ever personally seen. She was 214 feet longer than the *Madawaska*, and was two-and-one-half times larger by displaced weight. Painted gray, she had two smoke funnels and four tall masts. Her coal fired boilers had been converted to oil fired steam turbines, and she could cruise at a respectable nineteen knots. Like so many naval transport ships, the *Washington* had been built by the Germans as a passenger liner and seized by the United States at the beginning of The War. The liner had been named by the Germans *George Washington* as a way to make the ship more appealing for those immigrating to America. Immigrants made up the majority of transatlantic passengers in the first decade of the 20th century. The US government decided to keep the name.

The *Washington* was famous for three reasons. First, she was a very big ship. Second, she was "sumptuously appointed", which was the likely reason President Wilson chose her for transatlantic travel. Third, she was indirectly involved in one of history's greatest maritime disasters.

While heading to New York on the morning of April 14, 1912, the *Washington* crew observed a large iceberg as the ship passed south of the Grand Banks of Newfoundland. The *Washington* sailed within a half-mile of the iceberg, which was estimated to be 112 feet above the waterline and 410 feet long. The crew recorded the iceberg's position and radioed a warning to all ships in the area. The White Star steamship *RMS Titanic*, some 250 miles away, acknowledged receipt of the message. On April 15th, the *George Washington* received a garbled transmission stating the *Titanic* had struck an iceberg less than twelve hours after the *Washington* warning. *Titanic* struck the iceberg at nearly the same position as reported by *Washington* the day before. History would forever lament; if only *Titanic* had been more vigilant after *Washington's* radio warning.

Carrying his duffle bag, Noble went through two more check points as he was scrutinized by Secret Service and military personnel. On more than one occasion, he was recognized as "that flu doctor". Finally, Noble was permitted to walk up one of the long steep gangways leading to the ship's stern.

Once aboard, Noble noticed how different this voyage would be compared to his previous Atlantic crossings. On the stern portside, he could see a military band practicing with some sheet music. Along with numerous sailors, soldiers, and marines, there were many young men and women in civilian suits. Noble knew these must be the aides to the many executive branch, congressional, and diplomatic officials on board.

A young Petty Officer Third Class asked Noble for his name, found it on a long passenger manifest on his clipboard, and gave him a stack of documents and a map of the ship. Soon, a Seaman came by and escorted the Major to a room on the port side of the ship's superstructure. Noble was surprised to find a "posh" cabin three times larger than his *Madawaska* room. The cabin included its own bathroom, a double bed, a table with chairs, and an icebox with bottles of sodas, wine, and other spirits. Noble thought to himself that the executive branch of government travels well.

After Noble unpacked, the recent early mornings caught up with him. He put his head upon the bed pillow for "just a minute", and promptly fell sound asleep.

Noble awoke to the low rumbling sound of ship engines. He looked at his watch and saw it was noon. He quickly peered out the berth porthole and saw they were underway. In fact, the ship was already beyond the Hudson River and heading east, off the Long Island coast. Several naval destroyers could be seen off the portside. Because there was such a large contingent of the American government aboard, the *Washington* was accompanied by ten such vessels on this voyage. Noble washed his hands and face, and decided to take a self-guided tour of the ship using a booklet given to him that morning.

The tour began by observing the walls on first class meeting rooms. The German fresco artist, Otto Bollhagen, had painted murals in many of the public rooms depicting the life of George Washington. There was a two-story smoking room which Noble avoided completely, and a gymnasium with machines for "Swedish exercises". Noble loved the novelty of two electric elevators on the ship, and traveled up and down in them several times. On the awning deck was an open air café for after-dinner coffee. But, the café was too cold to use this time of year. There was a beautiful seventy-by-fifty foot solarium decorated with green and gold tapestry, palms, and many species of flowers.

Noble particularly liked the huge two-story ship library with its own librarian. Adjoining the library was a luxurious reading room with extremely comfortable red leather wingback chairs. He looked forward to visiting the library often during the nine day voyage.

It was lunch time, so Noble sought out the officer's dining room. He found that it spanned the width of the ship and could easily seat three hundred and fifty officers at small tables. The walls were decorated with floral designs against a deep blue background. Above was a gilded high dome ceiling with hundreds of small light bulbs that looked like stars. On one of the room's end walls hung two large paintings of George and Martha Washington. Noble wished Lillian could see this wonderful place, and that he could dine with her. However, the thought only saddened him. After ordering a cheese sandwich with coffee, he avoided any recognition by sitting alone at a corner table.

After lunch, Noble went below to look for sickbay. His underlying desire to be clinically involved was already nagging at him. He thought he would volunteer his services as he had done aboard *Madawaska*. However, there were no patients in any of the ship's sickbays. Navy medical officers on duty were reading, playing cards, or napping. The ranking officer thanked Noble for his enquiry, and said he would definitely let him know if medical patients appeared. But, there was no work presently. Nevertheless, upon learning who was visiting their sickbay, several officers invited Noble to talk to them about the pandemic and the court-martial. Noble was in no mood to discuss any of that, and graciously declined the offer.

Noble returned to his cabin and prepared to read a few medical journals he had brought with him. To his surprise, he found an envelope on his bed with his name on it. He opened the envelope containing a message that read, "Rear Admiral Cary Travers Grayson respectfully requests your presence at dinner. 8 PM." Directions to the Admiral's dining room were included. Noble knew this would be a most interesting meal, and looked forward to meeting the President's closest friend. On the room's desk was yet another envelope written with his name. Noble found it was a cable from the Boston A.I. Office, and that it was a simple transcription of a phone message from Lillian. Right now, the message was the dearest thing in the world to Noble. He read it out loud several times.

That afternoon, at Noble's request, a Seaman pressed a fresh uniform and delivered it to the Major's berth. Noble was also sent a choice of dishes for the evening's meal. For a man that truly enjoyed cheese sandwiches, the menu posed a challenge. Nevertheless, he finally settled on Supreme of Grape Fruits, Crème of Celery Soup, Troute Meuniere, Parslied Potatoes, California Asparagus with Hollandaise Sauce, Roasted Squab, Caesar Salad, Plombiere a l' Ananas, and Lemon chiffon Cake. It helped that Noble was very hungry.

At 7:45 PM, an Ensign came to escort Noble to the Admiral's cabin at the top of the ship's superstructure. He was led into a very large sitting room with overstuffed cloth sofas and matching chairs. The view of the sky from the numerous portholes was magnificent, as the moon shown a silvery light on periodic clouds above the horizon. Walls in the room featured a fresco depicting George Washington's crossing of the Delaware River on December 25, 1776, and a large painting of the *USS Constitution* during its battle with the *HMS Java* in 1812. The hard wood floor was covered with a thick maroon carpet and the room's lighting came from several matching brass lamps on end tables. The Ensign invited Noble to be seated until the Admiral arrived.

Exactly at 8 PM, Rear Admiral Cary Grayson entered the sitting room from one of several doors leading to it. He was five years younger than Noble, but looked younger still. He had a very pleasant face and smile, thick dark eyebrows, and wavy brown hair beneath a Navy cap he removed as he entered the room. Noble stood from the sofa as the Admiral approached him with an outstretched hand. "Major Noble!" said Grayson. "It is an honor to finally meet you, sir!"

"The honor is all mine, Admiral," said Noble, as his hand was vigorously shaken.

"Please, please, have a seat," said Grayson, as he sat in a chair opposite to Noble. "I've heard so much about you from Colonel Vaughn! I feel as though we are already the best of friends!" Grayson asked Noble all about his childhood, education, family, military duty, and his practice in Boston. He could tell that Grayson was a genuine man. Noble appreciated people who paid close attention to the answers when they posed questions. He also noted Grayson had a quick mind.

However, beneath his affable ways, Noble could tell Grayson was sizing up his new colleague. A man who was promoted from a navy Lieutenant to Rear Admiral, in one step, knew a lot about politics and how to judge men.

Noble also had the ability to learn much about a person quickly. He learned Grayson had earned a second MD degree from the Naval Medical School in Virginia. He served as the Navy Surgeon on the *Mayflower*, which was President Theodore Roosevelt's Presidential yacht. He continued in that role through the William Taft Administration. While attending a dinner party in 1913, Grayson treated President Woodrow Wilson's sister who suffered a minor injury from a fall. He quickly became Wilson's confidant. Grayson was perhaps the person closest to the President. He enjoyed a unique position in Wilson's life as both his personal physician, and a personal friend. Grayson married Alice Gordon in 1916, and the President attended his wedding. Noble was surprised to learn Grayson and his wife presently lived in the White House.

A Petty Officer Third Class, and Culinary Specialist, announced dinner was ready. Grayson and Noble walked into an adjoining room with a small dinner table in the center. The table had a white table cloth and a center candle on a brass holder. The two place settings were Wedgwood bone china with small navy blue anchors around the borders. Noble once again wished Lillian could be with him for this meal. He also remembered something that Lieutenant Commander John Mullen had told him on the *Madawaska*. "The navy always eats well". Tonight that comment was hard to refute.

The meal was wonderful, even for a basic eater like Noble. Well into the third course, and after a Seaman poured Noble another glass of Chardonnay from a Napa-Solano California vineyard, Noble thought he would find out more about his new patient. "Admiral, I know that I'm on board the *Washington* as consultant, and that I might not even be needed during this trip. But, I wonder if you might be able to give some basic medical history concerning the President, if I am consulted at some point?"

Grayson finished swallowing a spoonful of Crème of Celery Soup. "Of course, Major. But, I have to tell you that the President has not made his medical history completely available…even to me. He is a private man who only lets out personal information when it is essential to be known. He has not always sought medical attention, even when he should have. So, his medical history is incomplete, at best."

Grayson took another helping of soup, and began again. "The President had some difficulties as a child. He didn't learn the alphabet until he was nine years old, and didn't learn to read until he was twelve. However, that slow start didn't stop his overall academic achievement. He went on to earn a PhD from Johns Hopkins, and became President of Princeton."

Noble wondered if Wilson had suffered with a learning disability as a child. While in France, Noble had read a new book called *Congenital Word Blindness*. The author, James Hinshelwood, discussed a disorder known as dyslexia where children reversed written words, and had difficulties with spelling and reading. Even if the President suffered from dyslexia, he had conquered the debility to become an obvious high-achiever.

Grayson drank from his wine glass. "The President has had a number of bouts of neuritis over the years."

"Really?" asked Noble. "Tell me about them."

"At various times, he has had right hand or arm weakness. The first time it happened in 1896, he was unable to write normally for almost a year. With that deficit came a decrease in sensation in his right fingers for a time. During another episode in 1904, weakness in his right upper arm lasted several months."

Noble listened carefully, and put his right thumb and index finger to his chin. "Interesting, Admiral. Has he had any other sensory deficits, aphasia, apraxia, fevers, mental status changes, or visual defects?"

"Not that I know of." said Grayson, "Although, as I said, his medical history is sketchy. The President did have a temporary sudden loss of vision in his left eye in 1906. I don't know if that was associated with any other symptoms at the time."

"How many times has this weakness occurred, Admiral?" said Noble. "Does the President have any motor weakness or sensory deficits now?"

"As far as I can tell, his right arm or hand weakness has occurred at least eight times. The last episode was in September of 1915," said Grayson. "He doesn't have any neurologic deficits now, that I can see."

"Does he have diabetes mellitus or hypertension?" asked Noble. "Any ocular problems, or other symptoms?"

"No diabetes," said Grayson, "but his blood pressure can be moderately elevated. When an ophthalmologist examined him in 1904, slight retinal vascular narrowings were mentioned in the examination. The President can also have some awful headaches."

Noble did not want to go into a long differential diagnosis with his new general practice colleague. He wanted to continue the pleasant and relaxed atmosphere of the dinner, and not begin to question the President's past medical care. However, he thought about the President's diagnosis of neuritis. Could Wilson have had a noxious exposure? Toxic upper extremity neuropathies, as can be seen with lead poisoning, would not have such an intermittent clinical presentation. The same could be said for mononeuropathies of the median nerve, as seen in diabetes, myxedema, carpel compression, and rheumatoid arthritis. Median nerve disorders tend to have more sensory deficits anyway. Damage to the ulnar nerve is predominantly motor in nature. However, ulnar dysfunction gives a "claw hand" extensor deformity of the fourth and fifth fingers that is hard to miss. Radial nerve abnormalities could make it very difficult to write, but are usually traumatic in origin. The President does not likely have much of a traumatic history that would support such a diagnosis.

But, there was a more likely diagnosis given the episodic symptoms over years, headaches, a history of hypertension, and a vascular retinopathy. The neurologic literature had recently described a transient form of stroke that was ischemic in etiology. The source of the stroke was thought to be a narrowed carotid artery. This type of stroke was often associated with amaurosis fugax, or transient unilateral blindness. Motor or sensory symptoms in a single extremity could be seen. In the upper extremity, the weakness was often described by patients as a "clumsy" hand.

Another form of stroke, studied over the previous two decades, could cause the prolonged symptoms experienced by the President. These were known as lacunar strokes produced by the occlusion of small arteries penetrating deep into the brain.

Noble hoped to eventually meet the President and establish the level of his hypertension. This raised the issue of treatment, which was an entirely different problem. Sodium thiocyanate was wrought with serious side effects, and was now rarely used. Surgical ablation of certain parts of the sympathetic nervous system was infrequently performed because of the maladies associated with it. Pyrogen therapy, with the injection of substances that induced fever, indirectly lowered blood pressure by causing profound peripheral vasodilatation. But, pyrogenic therapy had a short duration of action and left patients unable to function normally. The only therapy with relatively few side effects was a profound dietary salt restriction. Perhaps the President would consider reducing his salt intake. However, in Noble's experience, it was nearly impossible for patients to follow this diet for very long.

At the end of the meal, the two men were served Brazilian coffee. Noble usually avoided coffee in the evenings because of the insomnia it caused. However, this time he made an exception because the brew had such a deep and rich aroma.

During conversation, Admiral Grayson mentioned an odd situation concerning the President. The previous summer, Grayson had removed several polyps from Wilson's nose in order to improve his breathing. It apparently left the President bedridden for several days. Grayson reminded Noble that

The War was raging at the time, and America's advisories would take advantage of any perceived weakness. Therefore, both Grayson and the President's wife, Edith, decided to keep the President's incapacity hidden from practically everyone. Aside from a nurse, and a White House usher, no one else knew the convalescing President was unable to lead the government. Noble concluded on his own that executive branch decisions at that time were made solely by Mrs. Wilson and Dr. Grayson.

After dinner, the two men discussed the state of the nation following The War and the pandemic. They talked about various new ideas in medicine, and traded old medical school stories. It was nearly midnight when Noble thanked Grayson for the fine meal and conversation. On his way back to his berth, Noble reflected on the man he had met this evening. He liked the Admiral, and was certain he truly wanted the best for his country. The medical care he provided the President was within excepted standards. However, Noble wondered if Grayson's close personal relationship with Wilson might cloud sound medical judgment at times. Grayson honestly believed his "number one patient", President Wilson, was the key to a more peaceful and prosperous world.

Just before retiring, Noble read the telegram from Lillian several more times. He fell asleep thinking of her, despite the Brazilian coffee.

CHAPTER 37

Over the next six days, Noble tried to make the best of his idle time aboard the *Washington*. Every day he went to the sickbays to see if he could help in some way. But, there were ample numbers of navy doctors, and very few patients. Noble assisted in the diagnosis of appendicitis, set a simple radial fracture, cleaned and dressed various small lacerations and burns, and treated a few cases of classical migraine headache. In addition, there were eight cases of true influenza. These patients were promptly diagnosed and placed in strict quarantine. All eight cases were minor, and each patient was recovering quickly.

Noble spent much of the rest of his time in the huge ship library. There was a large medical section with brand new additions covering all branches of medicine, and Noble made a comprehensive reading list for the nine day voyage. Even though he knew it was not proper etiquette, he often wore his army hat indoors. This seemed to decrease the number of people who recognized him. Noble also made himself available to all the good food in the officer's mess hall. It was not long before he felt his pants getting tighter, and therefore decided a strict diet was in order. He began to clock his walks around the ship, and strived to break his time record with each deck circuit.

Noble received two or three telegrams a day from his family, via the A.I. Office. Lillian continued to pressure government and private relief agencies for the resources needed to care for pandemic victims. Her A & M Charitable Fund was growing quickly, and now had over one million dollars in it. Florence was doing extremely well with her nursing studies, had become a mentor for more junior students, and was overseeing some of the interest distribution from the fund named for her departed siblings. Akeema had begun to file applications for nursing school in the fall. Michael was back at school, and playing catch with his brother on warmer days. Bernard and Michael wrote that they were not happy with the telegram word limit imposed on them. They had much to say about the upcoming 1919 baseball season, and did not feel it was fair to restrict discussions with their father. The Boston Red Sox would start the season on April 23rd against the Yankees in New York. The first Boston home game would be on May 1st against New York, and Noble dreamed of attending that game with his family.

Noble even received a brief telegram from Harvey Cushing as he sailed home aboard the *USS President Grant*. Cushing commented that he was also packing away the superior navy food, and that it was a far cry from British "maconochie" army rations.

Eventually, *USS Washington* would be too distant to receive radio transmissions from Boston. At that point, the A.I. Office would send messages via the transatlantic cable to an AEF intelligence center in France. The French AEF center would in turn radio messages to the approaching *Washington*.

On Monday, March 24th, Noble received another Grayson invitation to dinner. The two men were again treated to a delicious meal with a Medley of Garden and Field Greens with Ranch dressing, old Fashioned German Lentil Soup, V Spinach and Ricotta Cheese Ravioli, Pan Fried Fillet of Idaho Rainbow Trout Almondine, and Apple Hollander for dessert. The wine was a fruity Zinfandel from Lodi, California that Noble had never tasted before. He made note of it so he could buy some for Lillian.

The two men talked on a wide range of topics, as they had done six evenings earlier. However, this time conversation eventually turned to world events. Noble became very cautious with his words. He knew Grayson was aware of his critical views of the government and the present administration. He did not want to offend his host, and his new friend. On the other hand, Noble was having dinner with the confidant of the principal leader of the post-Great War world. This was a fascinating and rare opportunity to learn about a new emerging age in human history.

"It is hard to overemphasize the importance of this trip, Major," said Grayson. "Generations yet unborn will live with the agreements made, and not made, at the Paris Peace Conference. Empires are being broken up. Whole new countries are being created. And, the leadership of the President will hopefully bring about a more peaceful and diplomatic world."

"That is very interesting, Admiral," said Noble, seizing the chance to broaden the dialogue. "What exactly is the President's vision of such a world?"

"Well, the President outlined his vision over a year ago when he spoke to Congress about his now famous Fourteen Points," said Grayson, finishing a bite of ravioli. "The first five points deal with broad international concerns which include open diplomacy, freedom of the seas, removal of economic barriers, reduction of armaments, and adjustments to colonial claims. The next eight points refer to territorial questions over conquered territories in Russia, preservation of Belgian sovereignty, restoration of French territory, redrawing Italian frontiers, division of Austria-Hungary, redrawing Balkan boundaries, limitations on Turkey, and the establishment of an independent Poland."

"You know those by heart, Admiral," said Noble, with recognition of the doctor's keen mind. "But, that is only thirteen points."

"You're pretty quick, Major," responded Grayson with a grin. "The fourteenth point stands alone as the President's favorite, and is the most important on the list. In fact, the President feels it was his destiny to present this particular issue before the world community. Point number fourteen suggests that a general association of nations must be formed as a world covenant guaranteeing political independence and territorial integrity to all states."

"Of course," said Noble nodding. "The League of Nations."

"Absolutely," said Grayson. "And the League has many critics."

"I have been reading about opposition to the League," said Noble. "Senator Henry Cabot Lodge, from Massachusetts, stated the treaty creating the League will be 'dead on arrival' in Congress."

"There is stiffer opposition to the League than Senator Lodge," said Grayson. "The President's Fourteen Points set out principles of world respect for democracy, sovereignty, liberty, and self-determination. However, France and Britain already control empires that wield power over subjects around the globe. They both aspire to be dominant colonial powers in the 20th century. These two countries supported the Fourteen Points when they saw them as ingenious propaganda tools against the Central Powers. But, now that The War is over, they view the points very differently. The President knows he has his work cut out for him during this French diplomatic visit."

A Seaman entered the room and poured more Zinfandel wine for the men. Emptied dishes were removed, and the Idaho Rainbow Trout course was placed before them. Its aroma made Noble's salivary glands work overtime.

Finishing a forkful of the newly arrived dish, Grayson said, "Paris will be teaming with international life when we arrive, Major. Thirty-two countries are represented at the conferences. You will see kings, prime ministers, foreign ministers, and crowds of advisors practicing the highest art of world diplomacy. Thousands of journalists will be fighting for every story and piece of news for their papers. And then there are the lobbyists. An army of lobbyists in Paris are promoting hundreds of causes, ranging from independence for the South Caucasus to women's rights. It's quite a sight to behold, Major, and you'll be right in the middle of it."

Noble actually looked forward to walking down Paris streets and not being recognized. "I'll hardly be in the middle of it all, Admiral. However, seeing some of the people making these monumental historical decisions will be absorbing."

"That's for certain, Major," said Grayson. "You might get a glimpse of 'The Big Four'; David Lloyd George of Great Britain, Vittorio Orlando of Italy, Georges Clemenceau of France, and of course, President Wilson. They are by far the dominant figures at the conference, and they will have the most say about the disposition of the defeated countries."

Noble did not want to pry into confidential diplomatic details, but he could not contain his curiosity either. "What do the British want from the talks, Admiral?"

"They seek maintenance of British Empire unity, and promotion of its holdings and global interests," said Grayson. "Specifically, they have the goals of ensuring the security of France, removing the threat of the German High Seas Fleet, and settling numerous territorial contentions. They will add support for the President's Fourteen Points, but everyone knows that is only for public consumption."

Grayson continued, "The newly-proclaimed Irish Republic is making its case in Paris for self-determination, diplomatic recognition, and membership in the League of Nations. But, don't expect Britain to help that process along. On the other hand, Britain supports the Australian desire for steep war reparations and annexation of German New Guinea. This would extend Australia's sovereignty as far north as the equator."

"What about the French?" asked Noble.

"Aw, now, that is really intriguing," said Grayson. "France has seen Germany attack French soil twice in the last forty years, and they insist the German military be weakened. Prime Minister Clemenceau wants an American and British guarantee of French security if Germany ever attacks again. But, at the same time, French diplomat Rene´ Massigli has been in Berlin making some very provocative statements. He told the Germans that France believes the 'Anglo-Saxon powers', the U.S and Britain, to be the major threat in the postwar era. He argued both France and Germany have strategic interests opposing 'Anglo-Saxon domination' of the world. Oddly, there was a hint of a French-German alliance. Hard to believe, don't you think?"

Noble wondered if he was hearing more than he should. Still, he asked the question anyway, "What did the Germans think of that idea?"

"The Germans have rejected this French theory," said Grayson. "Recall that the Versailles treaty is being drafted as we speak. The Germans felt the French overture was a thinly guised trap to accept the treaty prematurely. The German foreign minister believes the United States is more likely to reduce the severity of peace terms than France ever would. Therefore, Germany has no interest in upsetting its relationship with America at this point."

Grayson took another sip of Zinfandel. "Anyone who believes 'The Big Four' are all pals needs to think again. Prime Minister Clemenceau recently ridiculed President Wilson. He said, 'Mr. Wilson bores me with his Fourteen Points. Why, God Almighty has only ten!'"

"Where are the Italians in this process?" asked Noble, not wanting to press his luck with the Admiral.

"The Italians lost 700,000 of its citizens in The War, and have a budget deficit of twelve billion Lire," said Grayson.

"Italy feels entitled to a number of conquered territories, including a protectorate over Albania, Antalya in Turkey, and a good share of the Turkish and German Empires in Africa. But, France, Britain, and the United States are concerned about Italy's own imperial ambitions. Don't count on Italy to come away from the Paris conference with much."

Noble was savoring every mouthful of the main course. However, he forced himself to stop eating occasionally so he could bring up ideas that intrigued him. "Needless to say, there is much debate about the penalties Germany should pay."

"That is the big question, isn't it?" said Grayson. What to do with Germany? With thirty-two participating countries in the conference, there are as many views on Germany. Several diplomats are drawing up drafts of the Versailles treaty dealing with this issue, including Norman Davis and John Foster Dulles. France, Britain, and Italy want severe reparations imposed on Germany, while the Americans want a more moderate approach. I've heard one treaty draft has a so-called 'Guilt Clause' that declares Germany and its allies responsible for all losses and damages suffered by the Allies. Rumors have floated around Paris that the proposed Versailles treaty may require Germany to pay $64 billion, in U.S. gold standard dollars."

Noble's mouth fell open, and he paused. "$64 billion? Wow."

"No kidding," said Grayson. "I can tell you the President believes that sum is excessive. Germany's economy is in ruin, and much of its industrial and agricultural capacity will be meager for some time. However, there is another growing concern among American strategists who study European politics. The German public has not accepted the German army's defeat in The War. Many in the military, government, and newspapers offer an alternative theory that blames Socialists, Communists, and Jews for Germany's downfall. Germans are reading about planned Allied reparations and they are becoming highly resentful. This public resentment could be potent fuel for present and future German politicians to exploit. Major, more than one intelligence analyst has told me the most important policy America could propose is one of moderation with Germany. I know the President plans to follow that course."

Noble had differed with the Wilson administration on many political positions in the past. However, in this case, he completely agreed with the assessment summarized by the Admiral. The quickest and most complete way to bring Germany back into the world community was to do what President Lincoln had suggested in his second inaugural address. Referring to the American South, Lincoln said on March 4, 1865:

"With malice toward none, with charity for all, with firmness in the right, as God gives us to see the right, let us strive on to finish the work we are in; to bind up the nation's wounds; to care for him who shall have borne the battle, and for his widow, and orphan—to do all which may achieve and cherish a just and lasting peace among ourselves, and with all nations."

Noble's father had been in the audience that day to hear President Lincoln's words of reconciliation toward the south. "With malice toward none; with charity for all..." The elder Noble repeated those words to his son many times during his childhood. They were words he now prayed might be whispered in the ears of Paris diplomats each night as they slept.

Dinner had reached the dessert course. Although the two men were full from the previous courses, they both looked forward to the meal's sweet conclusion. As they dug into the Apple Hollander, Noble raised another question about the Paris Peace Conference. "What do the Asian diplomats hope to accomplish in Paris, Admiral?"

Grayson took a moment as he enjoyed his first bite of dessert. "China has demanded Japan return Shandong, and has called for an end to imperialist institutions on its soil, such as military outposts and foreign lease holds. In the spirit of self-determination, the U.S. supports these demands. But, again, the other three major powers with colonial interests will ultimately not allow them."

Grayson went on, "Japan is a different story. She wants the German held islands north of the equator that include the Marshall Islands, Micronesia, the Mariana Islands, and the Carolines. Rumor has it that the Japanese have made a deal that will allow Britain to annex the German held islands south of the equator. I hear this deal has already been completed."

Grayson took a folded telegram from his uniform pocket. "A much more complex issue is the Japanese proposed amendment to Article 21 in the Covenant of the League of Nations. In part, the amendment says, '...to all alien nationals of states, members of the League, [agree to accord] equal and just treatment in every respect making no distinction, either in law or in fact, on account of their race or nationality.' This is known as the 'racial equality clause', and is opposed by many because it creates completely unregulated immigration among League members. This has absolutely no chance of passing the commission forming the Covenant of the League of Nations. I've heard naval strategists theorize that this could end Japan's cooperation with the West. I guess we shall see."

"Another big question is Russia," said Grayson. "The United States supports a strong and united Russia as a counterpoise to Japan. But, the British fear a Russian threat to India, and many in Great Britain would like to see a dismembered Russia. Russia has always wanted control of Constantinople and its port, but there are few who believe that will happen. To make things even more interesting, the Vatican has recognized Ukrainian independence."

Noble and Grayson finished their superb meal, and walked into the sitting room for coffee. Once seated in wingback chairs, each with a small coffee table off to the side, Noble asked another question. "Admiral, what other work does President Wilson hope to accomplish during this Paris trip?"

Grayson eased back into the chair, sipping Turkish coffee. "The President's leadership, and his Fourteen Points, essentially established the framework for the armistices that ended The War. He feels it is now his duty and obligation to the people of the world to lead the peace negotiations. He is enormously popular amoung Europeans, and this includes Germany."

"There are many at home who think the President should not be taking trips to Europe at this time," said Noble. "Numerous Americans believe Wilson is leading the country toward an interventionist foreign policy, and many strongly oppose this approach."

"Quite true, Major," said Grayson. "There is mounting opposition to many of the President's views. The President does not encourage nor believe the responsibility for the war should be placed so harshly on Germany. He does not see this as fair or warranted. He will try to sway the direction the French and British delegations are taking with Germany. There are so many rivalries and conflicting claims that the President must confront."

And then there are the territories of the former Ottoman Empire in the Middle East," said Grayson.

"Oh my, yes," said Noble.

"President Wilson has proposed that an international commission ascertain the wishes of the local inhabitants, as new countries are created from the old Ottoman Empire," said Grayson. However, there are competing Zionist and Arab claims in the area of Palestine. The Conference decided in January that the Arab provinces should be wholly separated from the Ottoman Empire. However, the Faisal's Arab delegation insists that the Arab state include Palestine. The Arabs also disagree with the creation of a mandate that entrusts Britain with administration of the area. Arab foreign ministers site previous Ally promises of independence for the whole Arab Asia."

"Just last month," said Grayson, "the Zionist delegation presented its case to the Conference. The Zionists support the creation of a mandate entrusted to Britain. Their impassioned statement spoke of the Jewish historical connection with Palestine, and they even brought with them a map of the proposed British mandate. They feel they have a right to reconstitute their National Home in Palestine. They would like to see the sovereign possession of Palestine vested in the League of Nations, with the government entrusted to Great Britain as a Mandatory of the League."

Noble stated, "It seems that the new world map creates a number of critical conflict-prone international areas. One wonders if these areas could be the source of serious future battles."

"Well Major, the President seeks to establish a world system that makes such battles less likely, or at least less lethal. Only time will tell, I guess. Only time will tell."

The two physicians talked again until after midnight about world current events, history, medicine, and family. Noble thanked his host for another memorable meal and discussions like no other in his experience. In turn, Grayson was thankful the Major joined the voyage and had lent his renowned expertise to the care of the President. Noble told the Admiral he looked forward to seeing him in Paris.

Noble had an urge to send a cable to Lillian and tell her all about his conversations with Rear Admiral Grayson. However, he was certain much of what he heard was confidential diplomatic information. Instead, he walked by the ships radio room and left a message to be sent by Morse code to the Noble home, by way of the Boston A. I. Office. In the message he told Lillian all about the evening meal menu, and that he loved her. He also said when he came home he was going to buy her a case of California Zinfandel.

As *USS Washington* slipped through the North Atlantic over the next two days, Noble could feel a palpable change in the passengers' collective mood. The diplomats and government officials aboard became increasingly serious, and spoke in more hushed tones. The task before them was to create a new 20th century world from the ashes of dynasties that had existed for hundreds of years. If they were successful, humanity might enjoy a new age of peace and prosperity. If they failed, world conflicts might be even more likely in the new century. The diplomats had their work cut out for them in Paris. None of it would be easy. And, the leader of this new vision for the world was the American President.

Noble watched a flurry of activity begin on board *Washington*. Sailors scrubbed down her decks, fresh paint was applied to worn areas, carpets were vacuumed and cleaned, and numerous red, white, and blue banners were placed about the ship. The military band practiced martial music during the last days of the voyage. Similar activities could be seen aboard the ten escort naval destroyers. It was clear America was coming to the Paris Peace Conference in a big way. The United States had emerged from The War as the most powerful nation on earth, and the President wanted everyone to know it.

On Tuesday, March 25th, Noble received a telegram from Lillian letting him know Colonel Harvey Cushing had arrived safely home in Brookline. It was the first time he had seen his wife and children in eighteen months. Cushing had phoned Lillian to tell her of his homecoming, and to give his best to his good friend sailing to France.

Wednesday, March 26th, was the final full day at sea for this *USS Washington* voyage. Right after lunch, Noble followed his routine of reading new medical texts in the ship's library. He had just opened a book on neuroanatomy when an Ensign walked up to him with a sealed envelope. Noble opened the message which read: "Hello, Major. The President would like to meet you this afternoon. Be in your cabin at 2 PM, and an escort will come for you. I'll also be there. See you soon. Sincerely, Rear Admiral Cary Grayson".

Noble had not felt a similar splash of anxiety since his Board exam at the completion of his Internal Medicine residency. His heart rate zoomed and goose bumps coursed across his limbs. He didn't even remember scurrying off to his cabin. He showered a second time that day, and asked a Seaman if he could have a uniform pressed as soon as possible. He spent some time making sure his uniform's collar service devices, bronze buttons, and gold officer's shoulder loop insignias were shinned and in exactly the correct positions. Noble had not brought along a ceremonial dress Army officer's uniform, so his field uniform would have to do.

It is not every day that a citizen meets the President of the United States.

Noble was ready an hour ahead of time, and tried to keep his mind off the coming meeting. He tried to write a message to Lillian, but found a slight hand tremor made that too difficult. He ended up staring out his room's porthole, tapping his foot, and whistling the popular Hart and Rodgers tune, *Any Old Place with You.*

At exactly 2 PM, a young Marine Lieutenant came to escort Noble to his meeting. They made their way to an upper deck in the forward superstructure area that was crammed with security. Crowds of people in dark suits, along with army, navy, and marine officers, were busy speaking to each other throughout this part of the ship. Noble was taken into a room with many chairs and sofas lined up against the walls. Small tables were arranged in front of the chairs with glasses and pitchers of ice water. Standing in the middle of the room was Admiral Grayson.

"Major!" said Grayson. "Good to see you again! The President can see you now." In some ways, Noble was relieved to learn there would now be an end to his anxious state. However, in other ways, he wished Grayson would say it was all a mistake and he had to leave. Grayson opened a mahogany door and motioned for Noble to walk in.

Noble and Grayson entered a very large wood paneled room with a fifteen foot ceiling and four large crystal chandeliers. The room must have been used for conferences when the ship was a German ocean liner. Several book cases filled with legal storage boxes and other books spanned the floor to the ceiling. The room also had many chairs, sofas, and small tables, just like the smaller receiving room had. Numerous portholes let in the afternoon sunlight along one room wall. At one end of the room was a twenty foot long table with chairs situated around it. At the other end of the room was a grand oak desk with piles of documents. Seated at the desk was the President of the United States.

As the President wrote upon a sheet of paper, Noble quickly studied him as Internists do. Thomas Woodrow Wilson had a long drawn face with neatly combed brown hair and a high forehead. He had a thrusting jaw, large ears, and wire spectacles that fastened to the bridge of his straight nose. From his previous Grayson discussions, Noble knew the President had worn glasses since the age of eight, and had poor right vision due to a retinal hemorrhage. Wilson was engrossed in what he was doing, and had not noticed that the two men who had entered the room. After a brief moment, Grayson said, "Mr. President? Mr. President, sir?" Wilson looked up from his desk. "Mr. President, I would like to introduce you to Major Edward Noble of the Army Communicable Disease Division."

Wilson squinted his eyes slightly, and then a broad toothy grin came over his face. As he rose from his chair, he said loudly, "Aw, Major Noble! The famous Major Noble! It's a pleasure to meet you. Cary and Victor Vaughn speak so highly of you." Wilson walked around his desk, and Noble guessed he stood five feet eleven inches tall, and weighed about 180 pounds. He was dressed in a dark suit with a vest, and had a high white collar shirt with rounded corners. Noble thought his dark blue silk tie looked very Presidential. Wilson walked over to the two men and shook the Major's hand. Noble felt his very firm handshake, but noticed the President had rather poor dentition.

"It's my great pleasure to meet you, Mr. President," said Noble. Wilson walked over to the side of the room where there was a small round table and three wood chairs with green leather seats. He motioned for the two men to sit with him.

"I read in the newspapers that you are the best Internist in America." said Wilson.

"Well," said Noble, "one can't believe everything one reads in the newspapers."

Wilson through back his head and laughed. "How true, Major. Especially when it concerns something the Republicans say!" Wilson laughed again. He took a drink of water, and looked at Noble from the top of his spectacles with a knowing smile. Noble could tell the President liked his depreciatory approach to his new fame. "I also have read that you have been very critical of my administration, and its domestic management of The War effort."

The last thing Noble wanted to do was engage the President of the United States in a political debate, in his office, and on his ship. So, using his usual dry sense of humor, Noble said, "Well Mr. President, you know Americans. We always have differing opinions on something, and aren't shy in the slightest about saying so."

Wilson's smile widened as he said, "Right again, Major." Noble watched Wilson carefully. He could tell the President already liked him. Rather than take the bait, Noble had deflected Wilson's provocation. Noble knew Wilson was testing him to see if he could be trusted as his physician.

Wilson began to polish his glasses, as he often did when he spoke to individuals. Noble thought this was probably a nervous habit. In large crowds Wilson could be an expansive, gifted, and a moving orator who appeared extremely self-confident. However, Noble could tell that in small groups the President could seem shy and even a little awkward.

Noble dearly wanted to have a pleasant conversation with his ultra-famous new patient. He knew Wilson, who greatly valued loyalty, would be skeptical of this Major who the newspapers portrayed as a radical activist. Physicians often know how to turn a negative interaction into something positive. Therefore, Noble used his interview skills to aid him in this situation. "Mr. President, I commend you on your support of the Child Labor Reform Act, your creation of the

Public Health Service Reserve Corps, and your leadership in creating a League of Nations. My wife is also a great fan of yours because of your support of the 19th Amendment."

Wilson sat back in his chair as he began to relax with Noble. "Thank you, Major," said Wilson, as he continually polished his glasses. "I'm also very proud of those accomplishments and future plans. Also, please tell your wife that we will get the 19th Amendment ratified by the Senate. Of that I am certain."

Wanting no further political discussions, Noble quickly changed the subject to health related issues. "Mr. President, do you think we could take your blood pressure at some point?"

"I suppose, at some point," said Wilson in a way that made Noble believe he would not.

"Admiral Grayson has kindly relayed to me some of your medical history, sir. I think a discussion about a low sodium diet would be important."

The President took on the expression people have when they say they will do something, and have absolutely no intention of actually doing any of it. "Maybe we can talk about it in Paris," said Wilson, looking again from the top of his spectacles.

Just then, a man in his mid-forties with a husky build and a dark suit entered the President's office. Noble recognized him as Herbert Hoover, who had been the U.S. food administrator during The War. Hoover had promoted voluntary wheatless and meatless days each week as a way to conserve food for American troops. He was now an economic advisor to the President at the Paris Peace Conference. Hoover was also director of the American Relief Administration that was delivering millions of tons of food to war-ravaged Europe. "Mr. President," said Hoover. "The European economic planning meeting is about to begin."

"Thank you, Bert," said Wilson. "Bert, this is Major Noble, who will be helping Cary look after me during our trip. Make sure the staff knows who he is."

Hoover walked over to Noble, shook his hand strongly, and said, "Welcome aboard, Major. Mr. President, I think everyone knows who the Major is."

The President thanked Noble for his time, and said he looked forward to speaking with him again soon. Grayson and Noble left the office, and Grayson excused himself to work on various naval administrative duties.

On his way back to his cabin, Noble reflected on his extraordinary afternoon meeting. He had just met, arguably, the most important, influential, and politically powerful man on the planet. But, as he planned to send a message to Lillian with a second-by-second accounting of his meeting, one thought greatly bothered him. At no point did the President even acknowledge the existence of the real reason Noble was invited on this voyage: the pandemic.

CHAPTER 38

Early morning activity on the *USS George Washington,*
Thursday, March 27th, was at a fever pitch. Noble had
packed the night before, and after breakfast watched
portside for the first sign of French soil. Thousands of
Americans aboard the ship prepared for a grand European
arrival, and several people running along her decks nearly
plowed Noble over. Scores of international flags had been
strung along *Washington's* four masts and fluttered in the
wind high over her two funnels. A huge Stars and Stripes
flag flew from the tallest of her forward masts. All of her
convoy escorts also had flags strung in the same manner, and
it made for a glorious parade of naval vessels.

A great roar was heard from passengers at the first sight-
ing of the lighthouse located just south of the little French
town of Saint-Mathieu. The American naval convoy continued sailing along the rocky southern granite cliffs that line the
peninsula west of Brest, France. The weather was crisp and
clear with a gentle breeze. The green grass along the coast,
the gray and white cliffs, and the blue-green waves crashing

upon them, made for a spectacular panorama. Soon, the ships cruised through the mouth of Biscay Bay and east on to Brest.

Breast had been used as a significant port since the 17th century. She was chosen as the major European Allied naval base during The War for three main reasons. First, the sheltered Biscay Bay was landlocked and could easily be defended. Second, Brest was the first French port accessible from the Americas. Third, her deep waters could accommodate dozens of large naval ships simultaneously. As a testament to her fitness as a port, millions of Allied troops had safely passed through Brest since 1914.

Washington and her escort destroyers turned north onto the river Penfeld which flowed through the center of Brest. Tugs immediately nudged the large ships along both the east and west riverside docks as thousands watched and cheered from the banks. The navy band aboard *Washington* struck up *Hail to the Chief* when President Wilson and his entourage walked down the starboard bow gangway. The President was met by French Prime Minster Georges Clemenceau and numerous members of his government. Clemenceau still carried a bullet in his shoulder from an assassination attempt five weeks earlier. Several dozen motor cars were lined up and waiting to take the high dignitaries to the awaiting trains.

Noble was among the thousands who departed the ship with far less fanfare. Lines of U.S. Marines checked and re-checked credentials as large buses loaded with Americans left the docks. Noble sat on a bus with his duffle bag on his lap, which made it difficult to look out the window. As the long caravan of buses traveled northeast on the city's Rue de Chateau, many more thousands of well wishers cheered and waved American flags.

At the immense Gare de Brest, a number of trains set out for Paris. The first train carried President Wilson and the most important passengers. With each successive train, less important government personnel were to board. Noble was certain he would occupy the caboose of the last train as his credentials were checked for the tenth time. However, as

Noble handed his documents for scrutiny at a final marine checkpoint, a flurry of hushed discussions followed. A Naval Commander appeared from nowhere and asked Noble to follow him. After a long walk amoung several train tracks, the Commander asked Noble to climb aboard a train with red, white, and blue banners on many of the cars. Once on the train, a marine officer asked that he be seated and wait for further instructions. Noble had no idea why he was on this particular train, or for whom he was to wait.

Noble sat patiently as he listened to dozens of people explain why they needed to be on "Train Number One". Marines with clipboards informed many of these would-be passengers that their names did not appear on Train Number One's roster. This was upsetting to some, which resulted in many loud animated discussions. Since so many felt they deserved to be on this particular train, Noble concluded he was on the President's train.

"There you are," said a familiar voice from behind Noble. "We thought we had lost you at the docks." Noble looked around to see Rear Admiral Grayson grinning at him.

"I'm really glad to see you Admiral," said Noble. "I was beginning to think I would have to hitchhike to Paris."

Grayson laughed. "Maybe on your next trip, Major. Give your bag to the Ensign over by the door. You are to travel in my compartment in the next car." Noble was glad to hand over his duffle, and followed Grayson to the forward car where they would spend the six hour trip to Paris. A porter came by to serve croissants, butter, a choice of berry preserves, and coffee. Not long thereafter, Noble heard the train engine building up steam. With a loud shrill whistle, Train Number One slowly started east.

The west-to-east journey from Brest to Paris took Train Number One through highly agricultural Northern France. From the train window, Noble saw countless squares and rectangles that were usually full of wheat, sugar beets, corn, barley, and potatoes. The tens of thousands of square miles of farm land were very flat, and only slightly above sea level.

Noble could tell much of the land had not been cultivated for some years. This highly productive "bread basket" of France had been neglected during four years of war. Much of Europe, and other parts of the world, suffered starvation because of this land's underutilization.

Grayson and Noble discussed their mutual patient and his reluctance to have his blood pressure checked. Both physicians promised to nag the patient until he did. Noble talked of his family, the loss of his two children to influenza, and his desire to return to civilian life. Grayson mentioned he had a son who was one year old. Noble was surprised to learn Grayson's second son, Cary Jr., was born just six days earlier. In addition, Grayson's wife, Alice, was a distant granddaughter of Pocahontas.

At about 4 PM, Train Number One ran through the northern sections of Paris, and came into the Gare de l'Es. This time, passenger transfers to motor cars were much more orderly. Grayson, Noble, and three other U.S. Department of State officials shared a car that took them south on the Boulevard de Sebastopol, and then west on Rue de Rivoli. One car after another dropped off passengers at Le Crillon Hotel, which was the headquarters for the American Delegation to the Paris Peace Conference. Right next to Le Crillon was the United States Embassy.

Le Crillon was a grand hotel that took up a city block. On either end of the hotel were Romanesque facades that resembled a scaled down version of the Pantheon. Between these structures was a long row of Roman columns against the side of the stone building. The Eiffel Tower was easily seen beyond the River Seine, southwest of the hotel. Noble, Grayson, and the other three dignitaries entered the building and found a beautiful lobby with Roman era statues, wall carvings, and paintings. If only Lillian could be here, thought Noble.

Noble took an elevator to his third floor suite overlooking Rue de Royale. He watched from the room window as long lines of motor cars deposited diplomats at Le Crillon, and then drove away. He put his things in drawers and closets, and sat on the king sized bed for a very long time. It was then he realized just how much he did not want to be there.

The problem was that Major Noble did not have much to do. The reason he was in Paris was to act as a medical consultant for a VIP who did not really want a consultant. The city was in the midst of a serious resurgence of lethal influenza. However, Dr. Noble, the Internist and infectious disease subspecialist, would not be permitted to treat patients outside of the American delegation or the U.S. Embassy. Very ill patients would be taken to nearby French hospitals anyway. There would be little or no opportunity for him to practice his craft.

Noble enjoyed the company of Admiral Grayson. Nevertheless, his new friend had numerous naval items that needed attention. Also, Grayson spent a great deal of time with his best friend, the President. Many would argue Noble was in one of the best sightseeing cities in the world, and that he should enjoy it. But, Noble was not in the mood to sightsee. He missed Boston City Hospital. He missed his practice of medicine. He missed Boston. He missed his children, both here and passed. And, he desperately missed Lillian. Noble recognized all the typical symptoms in himself. He was profoundly depressed.

Noble decided to treat his depression by attempting to plan every second of every day. This is difficult when one is in a foreign country without any particular work to do. Still, he tried to send cables to the Boston A.I. Office as often as the Naval Signal Corps Lieutenants in the U.S. Embassy would permit. The Embassy women officers quickly became long distance "cable pals" with Lieutenants Pierre-Louis, Quellet, and Lafayette. This friendly relationship allowed Noble to send home three and four messages a day. He received at least that number back. Lillian always playfully let him know that his "world touring" was going to cost him when he returned home. She expected his full attention when he was back in Boston. Noble always cabled back that he was more than willing to oblige.

On the morning of Friday, March 28th, Colonel Vaughn asked Noble to look in on a new U.S. Public Health Service partnership in France. The Office International d´ Hygiene Public was a joint venture with the USPHS, and so Noble visited them. He reported back to Colonel Vaughn that the office had a terrific young staff that was eager to replicate USPHS services in France.

Late morning the next day, Noble received a message from a porter asking for his assistance at the U.S. Embassy. Admiral Grayson had requested that he examine three Americans with fevers. Noble found a man and a woman in their early twenties from the State Department, and a marine Sergeant also in his early twenties, in a small embassy infirmary. The infirmary was staffed by one navy nurse who seemed very competent and knowledgeable. Noble diagnosed influenza in all three young adults, but their cases were mild. The usual quarantine protocols were put into place, and Noble told the nurse he would stop by frequently to monitor the patients' progress. The nurse said she would call if there was a negative clinical change in their conditions, but no such change occurred.

On Monday, March 31st, Noble took a bus to the Pasteur Institute south of the River Seine, near Boulevard Pasteur. He was greatly honored to meet three giants in the fields of microbiology and hematology. Felix d´ Herelle was the first to isolate bacteriophages, which are viruses that infect bacteria. Karl Landsteiner had isolated the polio virus, and had also developed the modern system of blood group classification (A, B, O). Based on his work, the first successful blood transfusion was performed in 1907 by Reuben Ottenberg, at Mount Sinai Hospital in New York. Ilya Llyich Mechnikov discovered phagocytosis by white blood cells, and had won the Nobel Prize in 1908. Major Noble would have spent the rest of his Paris tour of duty at the institute, if that had been possible.

Admiral Grayson had a free afternoon on Wednesday, April 2nd. So, he and Noble decided to see for themselves the northeast area of France. The German built Hindenburg Line, nicknamed "No Man's Land", stretched for some four hundred miles in Northeast France, from Verdun in the south, to Lens in the north. The most intense war area extended west from the German boarder to within twenty-five miles of Paris. The two physicians boarded a train at the Gare de I´Es and took a two hour northeast rail ride to Soissons. An arc of total destruction ran right through this devastated city.

Grayson and Noble were saddened to find most of Soissons annihilated. Many of the city streets had been cleared of debris. But even these unobstructed roads were lined with bricks piled one and two stories high. Many other streets were not negotiable due to tons of bricks, stones, and wood littering the thoroughfares. Thousands of three story town homes were simply shells with no roofs. There were too many destroyed military vehicles to count, and skeletons of farm animals could be found everywhere. Bridges across the River Aisne had been blown up. It was safe to assume that the gross domestic product of Soissons was at present zero.

The pride of the city was the classic Gothic style Soissons Cathedral. It was erected in the 12th century, and had taken two hundred years to build. It too was now a shell without a roof, and many of its walls were now pieces within the ruin itself. Noble hoped the people of Soissons could someday repair this beautiful church. But, he wondered if it was even possible.

During their rail trip home, Grayson and Noble contemplated their visit to Soissons. They had been to "ground zero" of humanity's First World War, and it had been a very unsettling experience. Neither man talked about it, but silently they wondered if it was possible for this to happen again. Each man concluded that repetition of this level of war was remote, because the conflict most certainly was the War to End All Wars.

Thursday, April 3rd showed evidence of a waning winter in Paris. The morning was warmer than it had been since the President's arrival, and tiny leaves were beginning to sprout on the city's trees. A blue sky with a few billowy white clouds shown over Paris, and Parisians were beginning to enjoy the first spring-like day since the signing of the armistice. Moods were elevated, and optimism higher than at any time since 1914.

Noble had breakfast in the Le Crillon dining room. Groups of diplomats who ate meals in the hotel usually spoke in whispers, and stopped talking altogether when other people approached their tables. Therefore, unless Admiral Grayson was available, Noble usually ate alone. After breakfast he walked about the Jardin des Tuileries to the east of Le Crillon. After lunch he took a one-and-a-half mile walk to the Parc du Champs de Mars that spreads southeast from the Eiffel Tower. He enjoyed the flowers and song birds, and thought about the similar environmental changes occurring simultaneously in New England.

After dinner, Noble went to his suite to read a few chapters from Sir William Osler's text book. It was slightly after 6 PM when a great pounding came from the door. Startled, Noble's eyes broadened and his hearing sharpened. He wondered who would might pound on his door? He stood from a small reading desk and opened the suite door. Two marines stood at the doorway with drawn handguns. "Major, come with us immediately! There is an emergency!"

Noble was rushed to another part of the hotel by the two marines. They gave him no idea about the nature of the stated emergency, or who it concerned. Noble was led through large French doors that opened to an expansive hotel suite. Standing in the middle of the room containing several couches and small tables was Admiral Grayson. Noble could hear loud paroxysms of coughing from beyond another set of French doors. He knew that sound all-to-well, and thought to himself "Devens".

"Thank God you're still in the building, Major!" said Grayson. "It started only ten or fifteen minutes ago."

"Admiral," said Noble, "what's going on?"

"It's the President," said Grayson. "I saw him at 3 PM this afternoon, and he was fine. However, I was reading here in the Presidential Suite conference room at about 6 PM, when it started."

"Is that him coughing?" asked Noble, referring to the horrible noise behind the French doors.

"Yes…yes, it is," said Grayson, who was visibly shaking. "Please take a look at him."

The physicians entered the next room, which was the President's bedroom. The President was lying on the bed with his necktie off and his collar unbuttoned. His wife, Edith, was sitting at his side, but stepped away from the bed as the two men approached. Noble immediately began to accumulate clinical data. The President was very diaphoretic. His dry hacking cough was so forceful that he was having difficulty breathing. With each cough he winced with pain, giving it a pronounced pleuritic component. Noble put his hand on the President's forehead, which was very turbid. A quick survey showed his pulses to be normal, and his heart rate to be 90 beats per minute and very regular.

Just then, a navy Medical Corpsman and nurse entered the room with one small black bag and a second much larger black bag. Noble recognized the bags as field military medical equipment and supplies. He quickly opened both and took out a stethoscope. The President's heart sounds were normal, as were his bowel sounds. However, there were fine crackling rales across both lung fields with courser rhonchi in the upper segments. His abdomen was soft and flat, and he was moving all extremities. He opened his eyes to questions, but then quickly shut them with a furrowed forehead. Noble guessed the President was experiencing a severe headache, eye pain, photophobia, or all three. The skin was erythemic with decreased turgor, but otherwise pink and without rashes. His conjunctiva were dry, but otherwise normal.

Noble said, "He has a partial upper airway obstruction… likely sputum. Help me turn him to his right side." Grayson and Edith turned the President as Noble cupped his right hand and moderately struck him between his scapula a few times. The President coughed, and produced a large quantity of slightly pink gelatinous sputum. Although his breathing remained labored, it was improved. With the patient now on his right side, Noble could see the President had slightly soiled his pants.

"Is that diarrhea?" asked Grayson.

"I don't think so, Admiral," said Noble. "I think he has a degree of fecal incontinence. Nurse, could you start an IV for me, please?" Noble noticed the nurse was the same woman who staffed the U.S. Embassy infirmary. She quickly and efficiently began to gather a needle and tubing.

"Doctor, what kind of fluid do you want me to hang?" asked the nurse.

"Just half-normal saline, with a bolus of 250cc. We'll follow that with a rate of 100cc an hour, for now. Thank you," answered Noble. He opened the President's mouth to find dry bucal mucosa that was otherwise normal. The pharynx was also normal. He placed a thermometer under the President's tongue. In the meantime, he used a sphygmomanometer to find a blood pressure of 155/92. Noble thought to himself that it took an acute illness to get a blood pressure from the President. He was moderately dehydrated, so his usual pressure was likely higher. Noble removed the thermometer which showed a temperature of 103° F.

"It came on so fast...I wonder if the President has been poisoned?" asked Grayson.

"Influenza," side Noble matter-of-factly.

Everyone in the bedroom froze, except Noble who continued to exam his patient. The navy Corpsman took gauze face masks from the large bag and distributed them to all about the President. With a functioning IV in place, Noble added sodium bicarbonate to the bottle and gave a dose of epinephrine. He also added morphine. He used a mortar and pedestal to grind sodium salicylate into a powder, and mixed it with benzyl benzoate. He asked the President's wife to coax him to drink the solution, which he did.

Within a few minutes, the President's coughing decreased, and he seemed much more comfortable. Noble asked the nurse to begin a careful fluid intake and output chart, as well as a vital sign log. The nurse and Corpsman cleaned up the patient and helped his wife change him into pajamas. Grayson and Noble walked ten feet from the President's bed. "He seems somewhat better, now, Major," said Grayson.

"Well, we will adequately hydrate him and better control his fever, coughing, pain, and bronchospasm. His respiratory symptoms are mostly due to acute bronchitis, but I can't exclude an early progressing bilateral pneumonia at this point. By no means are we out of the woods yet. It's hard to know right now which way his condition will go. It's just too early to say."

"Should we consider any experimental treatments, Major?" asked Grayson.

Noble frowned, and pursed his lips at the corners, in a slight expression of disgust. "Admiral, I don't know how many times this discussion has come up over the last six months. We physicians always do all we can for our patients, and the President of the United States is obviously no exception. However, the cold hard fact is this: nothing works against influenza. <u>Nothing</u>. My advice, in the strongest of terms, is to treat conservatively the President's symptoms. We will also treat conservatively any complications that may arise. But, the various vaccines, sera, drugs, and chemicals used during this pandemic do not work. At best they do nothing, and at worst they put patients in grave danger. Anyway, this is my advice, Admiral."

"I completely understand, Major," said Grayson. "*Primum non nocere.*" Both men smiled knowingly. This was the concept and language all physicians could speak to, and agree upon.

Two more navy nurses were brought from the U.S. Embassy to assist in the care of the President. Three additional army nurses were ordered to travel immediately from Reims to Paris for the same purpose. Two nurses would attend the President with eight hour shifts, at all times. Grayson and Noble would attend to the President, at least initially, in twelve hour shifts. Both physicians would remain in Le Crillon until their patient improved.

Admiral Grayson, and Edith Wilson, insisted on extraordinary secrecy concerning the President's illness. Knowledge of the event was to be on a need-to-know basis only. Therefore, the Cabinet, Secretary of State Robert Lansing, and even Vice President Thomas Marshall, were not to know of the President's debility. Noble did not think this was a good idea. However, a commanding officer had given these orders, and he would obey them. Grayson wanted to minimize any chance that enemies of the United States, and even some allies, might try to take advantage of the situation in view of the sensitive peace conference underway. Noble completely understood that point of view, and wholeheartedly agreed with it. A combination of excuses would be used to cover the President's absence from the conference, including requirements for rest and consultations concerning domestic U.S. issues. Only military personnel would be allowed to clean the hotel Presidential suite or serve him in any way.

The same day the President took ill, a young man on the U.S. diplomatic peace delegation contracted influenza. However, he immediately took a precipitous downhill course which exceeded the Embassy infirmary's capacity to care for him. Noble recommended that he be transferred to a French hospital.

Noble had taken the first shift with the President, and it had not been an easy night. The patient's fever reached 104° F, and he required continuing medication to suppress a relentless cough so awful that it caused some cartilage to separate from a few anterior ribs. This gave excruciating pain that required higher doses of morphine. The President developed marked chills, limb pain on only slight palpation, and moderate epistaxis. There was moderate pink sputum production that occasionally required aspiration with a rubber suction bulb. Now and again, the President seemed to suffer with delirium. He would move his head and arms as if defending himself from an unseen foe. Still, he did not speak.

Eating a light breakfast the following morning, Noble went to bed at 7 AM and slept for nine straight hours. He awoke, took a shower, ate a light dinner, and reported for his second shift at 6 PM. Grayson relayed that the President was no worse, but neither was he any better. The Admiral left the bedroom to send a secure cable to Wilson's Chief of Staff in Washington DC, and Noble did a quick assessment of his patient. There were no substantive changes, but this was actually a positive development. There was still no clinical evidence of frank pneumonia, or ventilation compromise. The President had survived into day two of influenza.

Forty-eight hours after the acute disease onset, President Wilson showed no signs of improvement or decomposition. Both Grayson and Edith Wilson were spending larger amounts of time explaining to impatient dignitaries why the President could not attend various meetings. One of Wilson's friends, Edward House, was filling in for the President. France's Clemenceau and Brittan's George were applying increasing pressure on the U.S. to back down on its moderate approach to German war reparations. House was trying to hold fast to Wilson's position while not actually making policy. This was becoming harder and harder to do. Late that night, Noble had a long conversation with the First Lady in an attempt to be guardedly optimistic. However, Noble did not tell her the next forty-eight hours were critical. By then, no improvement would be a bad prognostic sign.

Four days into the President's influenza, on Monday, April 7th, Noble began his shift at 6 PM. Grayson had reported no important clinical changes, and Noble's own assessment agreed. At 7 PM the army and navy nurses on duty chatted while seated in chairs across the room. Noble was seated next to the President's bed reading a recent issue of *The Boston Medical and Surgical Journal*. Suddenly, the President sat up in bed. "I'm in my bedroom at the Le Crillon, correct?" asked Wilson.

Noble nearly fell off his chair with surprise, and one of the nurses gasped. "Yes...why, yes, Mr. President," said Noble. "You have been very ill, sir. You have been in bed for four days with influenza."

Wilson put his hand to his head, winced, and put his head back on the pillow. He appeared very weak and complained of a splitting headache. He continued to intermittently cough, but his breathing was unlabored. Noble quickly reexamined the President, and found a temperature of 100° F, no rhonchi, and far fewer rales. Mr. Wilson had turned the corner.

Although the President showed gradual improvement over the next several days, he remained too weak to leave his bed. Nevertheless, Wilson pushed his physical endurance to the maximum by holding meetings in his bedroom. On Tuesday, April 8th, Georges Clemenceau and David George actually came to Wilson's bedroom to discuss extremely pressing peace conference issues. Clemenceau was furious about a Wilson threat, made a week earlier, to leave Paris without a peace treaty rather than yield on his principles. However, both Clemenceau and George left perplexed when Wilson did not remember making that threat.

Noble continued to make himself available to help the President in any way he could. His new proximity to the President gave him an opportunity to speak with several people close to Mr. Wilson. This is why Noble, and Admiral Grayson, become increasingly concerned about their world famous patient.

True, the President was physically getting stronger. But, those who knew him well were beginning to notice subtle changes in his personality. Gilbert Close, Wilson's secretary, mentioned to Noble that he had never known the President to be in such a "difficult frame of mind" as now. "Even while lying in bed he manifests peculiarities". One afternoon, Colonel Starling of the Secret Service told Noble and Grayson that the President now lacked the former quickness of mind for which he was famous. Wilson seemed less interested, or even concerned, about the terms of peace between the Allies and

Germany. Oddly, Wilson had now become obsessed with an accounting of persons using official U.S. diplomatic motorcars. The differences in him were apparent to everyone.

By Monday, April 14th, the President was still convalescing in bed. He was walking more, but was still sleeping a great deal after minimal physical activity. Chief White House Usher, Irwin Hoover, had travelled with the President to France a couple of times, and spent nearly as much time around him as did Edith Wilson. In the afternoon, Irwin Hoover asked to speak to Grayson and Noble outside the Presidential suite. "What did you want to say to us?" said Grayson, while sipping a soda.

"Dr. Grayson, and Dr. Noble," answered the usher, "I wanted to tell you that President Wilson…well, the President has some new and strange ideas…sir."

"Can you tell us about it?" asked Grayson.

"Well…you know…President Wilson is a very smart man," said the usher. "He's just about the smartest man I have ever known. We're lucky he's our President. Well, Mr. Wilson told me that he is certain his suite here at the Le Crillon is filled with French spies."

"French spies?" said Noble. "The only people who enter his quarters are Americans."

"Yes," said the usher. "Nothing any of us can say dissuades him from this notion. He also perseverates on the idea that he is responsible for all the furnishings in his suite. We try to tell him the hotel owns all of the furniture, carpets, paintings, and all of that. But, he can't let the idea go. He goes on and on about it. One thing is certain, though. He is not the same since the grippe. This is not like him. You are both doctors, and I thought you would want to know this. Something queer has happened to his mind…I think."

Grayson and Noble were very concerned about these observations, but their next conversation on the topic was even more distressing. On Wednesday, April 16th, the two physicians joined Wilson's economic advisor, Herbert Hoover, for lunch in the grand Le Crillon dining room. After a general discussion about the state of post-war France and Europe, Hoover leaned closer to Grayson and Noble. In a lowered voice he said, "Gentlemen, I have the greatest respect for the President. Whenever I have dealt with him in the past, he has been incisive, quick to grasp essentials, and able to draw conclusions without hesitation. He has always been most willing to take advice from men and women he trusts."

Noble knew that Hoover was a very intelligent and accomplished man. Lillian had recently said in a message that Hoover was mentioned in the *Boston Globe* as a potential contender in the upcoming 1920 Presidential election. His opinion's therefore carried extra weight. "Have you seen some recent change in Mr. Wilson?" asked Noble, without trying to lead the answer.

"I most certainly have," said Hoover, "and I'm not the only one. Others, as well as myself, find we must now push against an unwilling Presidential mind. In addition, when I must have decisions from Mr. Wilson, I suffer as much from having to mentally push as he did in coming to conclusions. It's beginning to hinder progress here in Paris at a most critical point in the negotiations."

Hoover excused himself in order to attend a meeting. After he left, Grayson asked Noble, "Major, what do you think is going on with the President? I have to agree with many of the comments we have heard about him since his recovery from influenza."

Noble thought for a moment. "Admiral, after the first and second influenza waves in Boston, we have seen a significant number of patients with moderate to severe acute and chronic neuropsychiatric disorders. In fact, my wife is desperately trying to raise money for these people who can be markedly debilitated."

"Do you think the President is suffering with one of these disorders?" said Grayson.

"First," said Noble, "let's go through the differential diagnosis. The acute nature of the behavioral change narrows the differential considerably. Without a history of exotic travel or other exposures, and an otherwise completely unchanged neurologic examination, the differential becomes very small. Finally, with a normal CBC, blood sugar, serum electrolytes, calcium, phosphate, and magnesium, we pretty much have our working diagnosis."

"Based on what I see, and what others have noticed, I would have to say 'yes' to your question," said Noble. "The hospitals in Boston are seeing frequent cases of post-influenza secondary psychosis."

"How is that malady manifesting clinically?" said Grayson.

"In view of the many statements we have heard over the last week," said Noble, "tell me if the following description sounds familiar: Patients with secondary psychosis can display delusional beliefs, including degrees of paranoia. An element of this form of paranoia is suspicion...or mistrust without sure proof. At the same time, they often display a striking lack of energy; a sort-of intellectual inertia. Sounds like anyone you know, Admiral?"

Grayson closed his eyes and put his hand to his forehead. He took several moments to speak, although Noble already knew what he was having difficulty saying. "Fits the President perfectly, Major. Is there anything we can do?"

"Choices are limited, Admiral. In a caring and non-adversarial way, those around the President must continually present to him the facts around his suspicions. His advisors must be patient when he takes longer to come to important decisions. At some opportune time, you must tell his wife about this and enlist her help. I can tell he trusts her without question. We do not have enough experience with influenza sequela to know how profound they can be, or how long they last." Grayson began to formulate a plan to protect his patient and help him with his heavy workload. This task would be made considerably more difficult because it had to have the highest level of secrecy.

The next day, as Noble sat in the expansive and sunny Le Crillon lobby reading, a porter walked up to him and gave him an envelope. It was a message from Grayson asking

Noble to come to the Presidential suite as soon as possible. He briskly set out for that part of the building.

Passing numerous marine sentries, Noble found Grayson in one of the hallways outside the suite. "Admiral," said Noble, somewhat out of breath, "is there a problem?"

Grayson looked very nervous and was perspiring. "Major, we do have a problem." Grayson put his hand on Noble's back and led him to a hallway area far from listening ears. "Do you remember when the President threatened to leave Paris if his demands for the German peace treaty were not met?"

"Of course," said Noble. "The President even asked the navy to fuel the *Washington* up for an early trip back home."

"Well," said Grayson, "this morning the President issued a new statement...and he's still in bed recovering. The statement says, essentially, that he is capitulating to Clemenceau's demands for the planned Treaty of Versailles."

Noble caught his breath, and his eyes widened. He gasped, and placed his right hand against the side of his face. "This is unbelievable," said Noble. "The President has fought against Clemenceau's and George's heavy-handed approach to Germany since the armistice. He's giving in to them now?"

"Completely," said Grayson. "The President is yielding to everything of significance Clemenceau has demanded. What is truly shocking is that Wilson has virtually opposed all of these demands...until today."

"So, France's version of the treaty will be the final one?" asked Noble.

"Now, there is no one standing in their way," said Grayson, with obvious regret. "Germany will be compelled to pay huge war reparations, and will be forced to accept full responsibility for The War. The Rhineland will cease to be administered by Germany, and France will get the rich Saar coal fields to mine. The Alsace and Lorraine provinces will go back to France, and Poland will get West Prussia and Posen. Most of Germany's colonies will be redistributed to the victorious powers."

"How about Italy and Japan?" said Noble.

"Almost all of Italy's demands will be met," said Grayson. "Japan will take over Germany's holdings in China."

"From what you have said, Admiral, this is more damaging to the German psyche than it is economically. And economically, this is disastrous for Germany."

"Absolutely," said Grayson, "and there will be far-reaching implications. I can't help but remember what you said yesterday about post-influenza 'intellectual inertia'."

"The President's decision here is of historical importance," said Noble, with trepidation in his voice.

"This is obvious to everyone, Major," said Grayson. "In fact, there is a group of young American diplomats, including John Foster Dulles, who met this morning to talk about 'this disgusting turn of event', as they put it. Some of them have threatened to resign."

Grayson and Noble went to the first floor Le Crillon dining room to discuss further how to help their patient with neuropsychiatric symptoms. They had just ordered coffee when Adolf Berle, one of the "disgusted young diplomats" came by the table and sat down. "Good morning, doctors," said Berle. "I was told by the marine sentries I could find you here."

"What can we do for you, Mr. Berle," asked Grayson, who found the visit very unusual.

"Admiral Grayson," said Berle, "I have just come from a meeting with other U.S. diplomats, and I have decided to resign my position with the State Department. The decision to meet the French treaty demands is not consistent with my views on the matter."

"I'm very sorry to hear that," said Grayson, who knew Berle was a talented and advancing young man in government, and that he was very idealistic.

"I wonder if you could give the President a letter of resignation I just completed?" asked Berle.

"Of course," said Grayson.

"I am <u>very</u> angry, and I need to express it," stated Berle with determination. Opening the unsealed envelope he carried, Berle said, "I want to read the last paragraph of the letter to both of you. 'Mr. President, I am sorry that you did not fight our fight to the finish and that you had so little faith in the millions of men, like myself, in every nation who had faith in you. Our government has consented now to deliver the suffering peoples of the world to new oppressions, subjections, and dismemberments --- a new century of war'." Berle placed the letter back in the envelope, handed it to Grayson, and promptly left.

Both Grayson and Noble said nothing for a long time after Berle's departure. They thought of the young man's condemnation of the President's decision. They wondered if the end of The War had only set the stage for another future world catastrophe. Noble pondered if the dark "gifts" of influenza would continue for many decades to come. Noble also recalled what the demon had told him one night in his stockade cell: "Here is a kind warning. You have only seen one of my many forms…Dr. Noble."

CHAPTER 39

The next morning, Friday, April 18th, Noble rose early and planned a visit to the Musee du Louvre. However, before he could leave his room, Grayson paid him a call. "Admiral," said Noble as he opened the door, "for what do I deserve this honor?"

Grayson smiled, walked through the door, sat down on the sitting room sofa, and said, "Major, I have a surprise for you."

Noble's eyebrows rose with anticipation and some hesitation. One learns early that "surprises" in the military are not always pleasant. "What would that be, Admiral?"

"Last night," said Grayson, "I had a long conversation with the President. We talked about his health, the conference, his recent controversial decisions...and we talked about you." Noble sat down on an overstuffed chair, crossed his legs, placed his elbow on the chair arm, and rested his head on his hand. Grayson continued. "The President wanted to know a little about your life outside of medicine and the army, and I told him a lot about you. I spoke of your family, and the loss of your two children over just a few months. He then told me that he would like you to go home."

Noble could not contain himself, as a wide smile broke out across his face. "I knew that would really break your heart," said Grayson. The President asked that a cable be sent to Colonel Vaughn last night. He requested that you return to the Boston A.I. Office as soon as it can be arranged. Colonel Vaughn has made those arrangements, and you are to sail from Brest tomorrow. That means you must pack now, and catch a train in just a couple of hours. Oh, and by the way Major, that's an order."

Noble was quick to tell Grayson that he would be sure to comply with this order completely, and quickly. He thanked Grayson for his hospitality, kindness, and great company. Noble also asked that he thank President Wilson for letting him return home. In turn, Grayson thanked Noble for everything, and hoped that the two men and their families could meet someday, either in Washington or Boston. Grayson shared that the President credited Noble for saving his life. Noble was not so sure the credit belonged to him, but Grayson said Wilson believed it so. The two men shook hands, saluted, and Grayson left the suite.

Noble packed his duffle, and called for a diplomatic car to take him to the Gare de I'Es, in less than thirty minutes. He contacted a Signal Corps Lieutenant at the U.S. Embassy and asked her to send a cable to Boston about his expedited departure. Although his train did not leave for three hours, he wanted to be the first one on it. Noble was able to secure a seat on the train while many did not. The train was packed beyond capacity with American troops traveling to Brest, and many stood hours for lack of seats.

Troops required quarantine prior to boarding transport ships for the U.S. However, Admiral Grayson had given Noble a Presidential attestation of health document before he left Paris. He would be able to leave the next morning. That evening in Brest, Noble stayed in a crowded hotel and shared a room with four other army officers. But, he did not care in the least. He was going home.

Very early on Saturday, April 19th, Noble showered before the other four officers and took a bus to the docks along the river Penfeld. He did not know which transport ship he would be boarding. Instead, he had only been given a dock number: Dock No. 16. He had to walk a long distance to his departure dock, but when he reached it he developed a kindly smile. There before him was the *USS Madawaska*. It was almost like arriving home early.

Noble presented his departure documents to the marine and navy officers at the *Madawaska* gangway. Both his name, and his health attestation document, caused a great commotion among the military personnel. Noble overheard one officer whisper into a dock telephone, "Yes...it's him. The Major Noble. Right...he's got an attestation signed by Wilson. No... President Wilson."

All departing Atlantic Fleet Cruiser and Transport vessels were crammed with troops. Because every corner of the ship would be full of soldiers, this journey would be very different than the previous voyage aboard *Madawaska* fifteen months earlier. Noble was given a cabin with three other officers, so his personal space for the next ten days would be a berth six feet by two feet. However, Noble believed his biggest problem would be avoiding recognition.

Madawaska filled up with her passengers quickly. Unceremoniously, she set sail down the river Penfeld, through the Bay of Biscay, and west out onto the North Atlantic.

Shortly after departure, Noble decided to pay sickbay a visit. As he walked along her familiar decks, he noted *Madawaska* was a different ship than he remembered. She bore the wear of tens of thousands of troops that had crossed the Atlantic with her. Her plank decks were worn smooth, and her walls showed chipped paint and grease marks from countless hands. *Madawaska* had survived hurricanes, avoided

U-boats, and most certainly showed her age. Nevertheless, she had successfully carried a multitude of Americans safely home.

Turning into Sickbay No. 2, the off-white rooms that smelled of alcohol and iodine brought back a host of memories. The bay was filled with patients, and even had extra cots placed on the floor. At the far end of the first room, examining a leg, was a very familiar face. Noble instantly recognized the man, in spite of a new short light brown beard. Noble came up behind the naval officer, and said, "Lieutenant Commander, do you know where an army officer could get a decent meal on this bucket of bolts?" John Mullen turned around with a quizzical look, saw it was his old friend Major Noble, laughed, and both men hugged each other.

"No decent meals for old army officers aboard this ship, buddy!" joked Mullen. "Gee, it's good to see you, Edward! It's just great! Did you just come aboard?"

"Just a few hours ago," said Noble. "It's wonderful to see you too, my friend!"

Noble once again volunteered his medical services, and was put right to work. Most of the infirmed aboard ship had chronic war injuries, so much of the work involved changing dressings and dealing with superficial infections. In spite of the quarantine, there was already one diagnosed case of influenza aboard. So far, the patient was quite stable.

During dinner in the officer's mess, Captain Richard Baker came by to pay his respects to Major Noble. Noble appreciated the Captain's recollection of him, and that he did not mention the court martial.

After dinner, Noble and Mullen caught up on the past fifteen months. Mullen talked about the hundreds who died of influenza aboard *Madawaska*, and the resulting chaos on the ship. If it had not been for the forthright leadership of Captain Baker, there might have been a mutiny during one particular Atlantic crossing. Noble spoke of the terror in Boston, and his unusual position at the A.I. Office that allowed him to witness the unfolding of the pandemic. However, Noble did not mention the passing of Arthur and Marguerite, nor did he mention his reason for being in France. Mullen also did not once ask about the court martial. Noble knew his friend would only enquire if he brought it up first. And, Noble did not.

Over the next ten days, Noble worked alongside his friend during ten and twelve hour shifts. A shortage of navy doctors ensured there was plenty to do. Each day, a small number of new influenza cases were taken to the quarantine bay. Thankfully, none of the cases was serious. There was a sprinkling of acute medical cases during the voyage, and Noble always enjoyed both the variety and challenge. Still, most of the work was routine.

Noble always made time to give emotional comfort to the men who were finally coming home from The War. Most certainly, they had not had the opportunity to stay at Le Crillon as Noble had.

On the night of Monday, April 28th, the ship prepared for its Hoboken arrival early the next morning. Noble and Mullen finished their shifts in Sickbay No. 2, and went to the officer's mess for a beer. After a time, Mullen took a drink of Pabst Blue Ribbon lager, sat in his chair, and raised his bottle. "Edward, I want to propose a toast." Noble raised his bottle of Miller Genuine Draft. "I want to toast to my last voyage upon the good ship *USS Madawaska*," said Mullen.

Noble tapped Mullen's bottle, and they both took long drinks. "That's the first time you've mentioned that, John," said Noble. "Is this really it?"

"Sure thing, Edward. In fact, this is my last voyage in the navy...period. Well, actually, I'll still be in the reserves, of course. But, my active duty ends with this crossing. Ya' know, Edward, I have been a 'Jackie' aboard this ship for nearly a year-and-a-half. The most time I've spent on land during my duty was ten days in Paris once. I can't wait to get back to Spokane, take walks about the pines and volcanic formations, and start a surgical practice. Can't wait. In fact, my train to the Pacific Northwest leaves tomorrow afternoon." Both men finished their beers, and ordered a second round. "How about you, Edward?"

Noble took another drink, and exhaled loudly as men often due when imbibing beer. "Well, John, I'm hoping to join you in 'reservist land' soon. I suppose I'll be assigned to the A.I. Office for a short time more. But, I also can't wait to resume my private practice in Boston, and my position as Director of the South Department at Boston City Hospital. And, I want to take holidays at Cape Cod and go to as many Red Sox home games as possible! There are six home games between May 1st and the 8th, and maybe my family can catch one of them." With that, both men tapped their bottles again, and toasted to "reservist land".

It was a crystal clear morning as *Madawaska* docked at Hoboken on Tuesday, April 29th. The temperature was cool, but Noble could tell the spring day would be a warm one. Noble and Mullen walked down the gangway. When they reached the bottom, they turned around to glance for a moment at *USS Madawaska* one last time. Among the thousands of soldiers and sailors on the dock, Major Noble and Lieutenant Commander Mullen bid each other farewell. With a salute of mutual respect and admiration, the two men went their separate ways.

If the voyage from Brest had been different, the train trip from Hoboken was even more unique. The two million U.S. service men returning from Europe were all going east to west. This meant trains leaving Hoboken were constantly filled to the brim with military personnel. Some soldiers actually tried hanging on to the outside windows of train cars, until conductors shooed them away. Inside the cars, troops jammed every inhabitable space. Noble could not find a seat, and was forced to stand as his train left the Hoboken station. This trip to Boston would not be a restful one.

There were many more stops during the journey than Noble remembered from his previous trip from Hoboken. He endured nine hours of standing, jostling, and short naps spent upright. Since he rarely had a clear view out a window, the trip to Boston was spent looking directly into the face, or at the back, of a fellow soldier. Rank did not have its privileges on trains from New Jersey. Even with some train car windows rolled partially down, the heat generated by close humanity added to the challenges of the forbidding excursion.

The train arrived at the Boston and Main Railroad Station at 4:30 PM, and Noble felt disembarking was like pealing an onion. A layer of soldiers had to leave the train before the next layer could. This process went on for some time.

Noble was exhausted from the arduous trip. He had to use a combination of carrying and dragging his duffle beyond the train terminal. But, near the street curb Noble heard the familiar voice that made him almost gleeful. "Major! Major Noble! Over here!" Of course, it was Sergeant Campbell with his army staff car. Campbell walked over to Noble and, thankfully, took his duffel from him. "It's great to see you again, sir!" said Campbell. "How long have you been gone this time? I've forgotten."

"It's great to see you too, Sergeant," saluted Noble. "I've been gone six weeks and one day. But, who's counting?" said Noble, with a grin.

"What did you do in France, Major?" asked Campbell.

Noble slightly smiled, raised one eyebrow a little, and said, "Oh, just some army business, Sergeant."

Campbell quickly drove from the train terminal. As they travelled along Commonwealth Avenue, Noble noticed a marked difference in Boston. She had been cleaned, repaired, and renewed. Weeds had been pulled, trees trimmed, and buildings had been washed, scrubbed, and painted. There were more cars, buses, trucks, and horse drawn carts than ever on her streets. Along with the spring leafing-out of trees and blooming flowers, Boston herself was back. Back from a very dark time that nearly destroyed her only a few months earlier. Noble was truly home.

The army staff car pulled up to 468 Beacon Street, parked while idling, and Campbell took Noble's duffle from the trunk. "Need some help with this, sir?" said Campbell.

"Thanks, Sergeant, but I'm fine. Guess I'll see you next time."

"I'll be here if you need me, sir," said Campbell. "One more thing, Major. It is great to have you home, sir." The Sergeant saluted, and then drove off toward Camp Devens.

Noble slung his duffle over his right shoulder and unlocked the front door to his house. He set the duffle on the entryway floor, closed the door behind him, and said, "Anybody home?" There was no response. "Anyone here?" asked Noble. Again, no response.

Noble walked a few steps to the right and looked through the French doors of the library. He then glanced down the hall to the bedroom on the first floor. He could see no one. Walking back to the entryway, he looked up the stairs to the floors above and saw no one. He walked a few steps to the left and looked into the parlor. No one was there either. Noble walked into the parlor where he could see into the kitchen. At the kitchen table were seated Lillian, Florence, and Akeema. Lillian had her right hand on Akeema's left forearm. Akeema was looking straight forward and was expressionless. Florence was sitting across from Akeema, and was crying into a handkerchief. Aside from Florence's sobs, the house was perfectly quiet.

As Noble began to walk through the parlor toward the kitchen door, Lillian looked up and saw her husband. She quickly stood, and walked around the table toward the door leading into the parlor. Noble opened his mouth and was about to say, "Lilly, I..." Lillian put her two right hand fingers to his lips as though to say "shhhh". She threw both her arms around her husband, hugged him tightly, and kissed him. Noble began to speak again. "Lilly, what is..." She again put two fingers to his mouth, took his hand, and led him to the parlor sofa. She sat, and motioned for him to sit as well.

Lillian spoke in hushed tones. Noble could see from her red moist eyes that she had also been crying. "Dear, it is so wonderful to have you home. We received the cable from the 19th that you were coming, and all of us just couldn't wait." Lillian kissed her husband's cheek and held both his hands with hers.

"Lilly...Lilly, what's the matter?" said Noble. "What' happening. What's going on?"

Lillian's eyes began to tear. She took a handkerchief from her skirt pocket and put it to her nose. Lillian's voice broke as she spoke. She put the handkerchief to her eyes. "Edward, Akeema received the letter only forty-five minutes ago." Lillian stopped talking and sobbed.

"What letter, Lilly? Who sent her a letter?"

Lillian recomposed herself and looked into her husband's very worried eyes. After several moments, she said quietly, "Edward, Akeema received a letter from a group of Catholic missionaries that serve the Alaskan southern Bering Strait. They work out of Nome, which is nearly one hundred miles west of Akeema's village of Golovin. It's very hard country, as you know. Travel, and communication, are difficult, to say the least."

"Yes, I recall," said Noble. "The Yup`ik speak highly of the 'Catholic People', as they call them. Lilly, what happened? What did they say?"

Again, Lillian dabbed tears from her eyes as she hung her head in a sign of despair. Looking up, her eyes darted back-and-forth from her husband's right and left eye. She was trying to find the right words to use. "Edward. Edward...they are all gone."

The area between Noble's eyes furrowed, and his head tipped to one side, as he tried to understand what his wife meant. Seconds went by. "Lilly. Lilly...what do you mean 'they are all gone'?

"They are all...gone," said Lillian. "All of them."

"Who is gone, Lilly," asked Noble again. "Who is all gone?"

Lillian began to sob again, and then sat straight up. "The Yup`ik," said Lillian, fighting back tears. All of the Yup`ik in Golovin. All three hundred of them."

"You mean...they're dead?" said Noble, hoping his question was thought ridiculous. "They are all dead?"

"Dead," said Lillian, now in a matter-of-fact tone. "They are all dead. The entire village. They all died of influenza."

Noble could again barely tolerate the churning abdominal sensation and nausea that he experienced so many times over these last many months. He put his right hand over his eyes, bit the inside of his mouth, and gave a short moan. He wanted to say something, but did not know what. All that came out was, "Oh my God...not the Yup`ik. Not those wonderful, generous, kind, gentle, and intelligent people. Not the Yup`ik."

For a split instant, Noble was certain he heard laughing in the house. Far away and cruel laughing. The demon, he thought.

The Nobles sat on the sofa silently holding each other's hands for quite some time. Each sought words of comfort for their dear friend who had lost her entire family and community. The loss was beyond any average person's comprehension.

Nearly fifteen minutes passed before the Nobles looked again at one another and realized they must return to the kitchen. Noble asked where the boys were, and Lillian mentioned she had sent them to a friend's house to play catch. Lillian said quietly, "She hasn't spoken much since the letter arrived, Edward. But, she seems to want us to be with her." The couple arose from the sofa and left the parlor. Lillian resumed her previous seat at the kitchen table, and Noble sat at the remaining forth chair. Akeema looked like a bronze statue; frozen, serine, and expressionless. She peered forward as she sat with an upright posture and squared shoulders. Before her on the kitchen table were several handwritten letter pages and a worn and creased envelope.

Florence sat across from Akeema occasionally sobbing, with her head bent toward the table. Lillian once again placed her hand on Akeema's arm. Noble sat with his forearms flat on the table and his hands folded in front of him. The room was quiet, and Noble was not sure what to say or do next. Without moving any part of her body, except her head, Akeema turned to Noble and said, "It is good to see you, Dr. Noble. I am glad that you arrived safely." Her head returned to the previous straight forward position, as though she was a machine that had just completed a purely mechanical task.

Noble gave a very small closed-lipped smile as the far corners of his eyes drooped down slightly. It was that peculiar smile of great sadness that all cultures understand. "Thank you, Akeema," said Noble. "It's...nice being back." Noble tripped over his words, since "nice" was really not the best descriptive word for the moment.

A long time passed as the three members of the Noble family at the kitchen table sat silently with their friend. Then, Akeema began to speak. She did not speak to any specific individual. Rather, it seemed as though she was reciting items from the letter so she could actually believe the news was true. Her words were only slightly louder than a whisper. Still, her speech was as calm and as void of expression as her body appeared.

"The weather had been very cold for several months in Western Alaska," said Akeema. "So, it was not unusual for little word to come from the Yup`ik villages along the north coast of Norton Sound. Nevertheless, by mid-November, some in Nome became concerned when Russian fur trappers brought rumors of terrible disease among the Eskimos. Groups of the Catholic People and the Red Cross could not use ships to navigate the frozen waters of the sound and Golovin Bay. They had to travel over land, which meant moving through the White Mountains north of Golovin Lagoon. Hundreds of rivers extending south from the mountains, and create a delta that flows into the lagoon. I remember as a child walking to the delta during the summers and helping our village catch game. It was difficult terrain even during the warm months."

"When the Catholic People and the others reached our village in Golovin, they saw and heard no one," said Akeema. This worried them greatly since the Yup`ik stay close to their villages as the winter approaches. They entered the *qasgiq* and the *ena* houses. There, they found the bodies of my people frozen. All of them. They could tell many young adults died in their sleeping furs. Many of them were the color blue, with frozen blood and vomit around them. Young children, now orphans, had huddled with their dead parents until they froze to death. The elderly, who could not help themselves, also froze in their homes."

The Nobles listened as a picture of utter horror was painted for them. Except for quiet sobbing by Florence, the room was completely still.

"The village sled dogs had nothing to eat," said Akeema. "Groups of the huskies broke into some of the *ena* lodges and ate the Yup`ik bodies of women and children. Some of the *ena* contained only the bones of my people. However, it was not long before the dogs also froze to death."

"The Catholic People and the Red Cross traveled by land to ten Yup`ik villages along the southern Seward Peninsula coast," said Akeema. "In all but three of the villages, every inhabitant was dead. In those remaining three villages, including the one at Council west of the Golovin Lagoon, between fifty and eighty-five percent of the Yup`ik were dead."

Akeema paused for a time. She picked up the letter pages, read for a few minutes, and then said, "This letter was written to me by a doctor who came along with the Catholic People. The doctor wrote, 'In Golovin, we found letters you had written your family from Boston. We are so relieved to learn there are Yup`ik living elsewhere. From the devastation here in Western Alaska, we thought Eskimos would soon be an extinct people.' It took months for the letter to arrive here in Massachusetts. All this time my parents, my sisters, my brothers, and my whole village were gone. I did not even know. The ancestors gave me no warning...not even in my dreams."

"The ancestors are surely testing me now," said Akeema. Noble was about to say something in response to Akeema's comment, but Lillian slightly moved her head back-and-forth as if to say "not now, Edward". "Mrs. Noble, Dr. Noble, Florence...please know there are contrasts in the way my people view death compared to others. When we have been to the Cathedral, I have seen the customs of Boston people at funerals for the dead. But, the Yup`ik are different. We have certain ways we must honor the ancestors who are observing us from beyond the vault of the sky. This honor includes the way we express our grief over death."

Noble now recalled how Akeema had seemed after both Arthur and Marguerite's deaths. Her posture, movements, and words were all as they were today.

"Akeema," said Lillian, "we all love you so much, dear. We are so...so, sorry."

"Yes...yes," said Noble. "We are all so very saddened. We are privileged to know a member of the Yup`ik people. Through you, I feel as though I know each and every Yup`ik. There are no peoples on Earth that I admire more." Noble wiped a small tear from his right eye. "Akeema, if there is anything that we can do for you, please let us know. Is there anything you need? Do you need some time to your-self? Would you like Lillian, Florence, or I to drive you to the Cathedral of the Holy Cross?"

Akeema continued to stare forward. But, she developed a slight furrowing of her forehead. She was thinking of dif-ficult things. After a few moments, Akeema turned her head slightly toward Noble and said softly, "Yes. There is some-thing you all can do."

"What is that?" said Lillian. "Anything...we will do any-thing for you."

Akeema took a few seconds to answer. "Let me go, please. Let me go home."

Lillian and Noble both looked at each other with some surprise. "Why...of course, dear," said Lillian. "If that is what you need to do. Of course."

"Mrs. and Dr. Noble, you have all been so kind to me," said Akeema. "I have been so happy here in Boston with all of you. I am the one who is privileged to know you. I love you all. You have become part of my family. And, now you are the only family I have. But, I must go to Golovin. I must go home. I am the last of my clan. The ancestors will require me to travel to Golovin and bury my people in our ways. Ways with honor. The ways of the Yup`ik."

"I have saved a substantial amount of money while in your service," said Akeema. "The money has been for my dream of nursing school. However, I must now use this money to take me home. I know it will take months by train, bus, car, and boat, horse, and on foot. But I must. I must go. I must go now." Lillian and Florence looked over at Noble, who was listening intently to Akeema. Noble sat straight up in his chair, folded his arms across his chest, and set his jaw. He then spoke firmly.

"No."

Lillian and Florence were startled by Noble's deliberate statement, and were about to protest when he spoke again.

"No," said Noble. "I will not let you spend all of your hard earned money like this. A land trip to Alaska will take you many months. I will not have a young woman who is a member of our family traveling alone for that long." Noble's wife and daughter sat back in their chairs when they heard the reason for Noble's forceful comments.

Every day, ships depart Boston Harbor for voyages through the Panama Canal," said Noble. "Akeema, we will arrange for you to board one of those ships as soon as possible."

Akeema's head slumped down for the first time since Noble had entered the room. "Dr. Noble, with all due respect and gratitude, I cannot allow you to do this thing. This is my responsibility, and the ancestors must have me see this through myself."

"Akeema," said Noble, "Would not the ancestors expect you to care for a member of your family in need?"

"Of course," said Akeema strongly.

"Well," said Noble, "a member of my family is in need... you. My responsibility is to ensure that you are able to fulfill yours. I insist on this. We will help you do what you must in Golovin, and at the same time help you maintain your dreams. There will be no more discussion on this matter."

Both Lillian and Florence smiled and nodded in approval of the outlined plan. Without saying another word, Florence went to the telephone and began placing calls to the Boston Port Authority. Akeema folded the letter pages before her, put them in their envelope, and carefully placed it in her skirt pocket.

After about fifteen minutes, Florence returned excitedly to the kitchen holding a sheet of note paper. "Well, I have some positive news, everyone. The SS Alaska leaves Boston Harbor tomorrow at 8 AM. She is an ocean liner that will fuel in Kingston, Jamaica, and then make her way through the Panama Canal. Her ports of call include Puerto Vallarta, Mexico, San Diego, Seattle, Anchorage, and then Nome. I reserved one of the last remaining cabins for Akeema. I think we're set."

There was now a flurry of activity in the Noble household. Florence went upstairs to help Akeema pack for her long voyage. Lillian first placed a call to the home where Bernard and Michael were playing, and asked that they start back to Beacon Street. She then set about making lunches that Akeema could use in her first few days at sea. Noble checked on the family Ford truck to be sure she was road-worthy. He also brought out various items that Akeema might need, such as boots, an army knife, flashlight, a waterproof poncho, etc. That evening, Lillian asked the departing world traveler for her dinner request. It seemed that Akeema had gained a special taste for a particular type of American cuisine. So, the Nobles had cheeseburgers, French fries, potato chips, and Coca Cola for a bon voyage feast. Akeema appreciated not only the meal, but the temporary distraction from her grief.

It was still dark on the cool clear morning of Wednesday, April 30th, when the Noble truck sped off for Boston Harbor. Noble turned from Summer Street to Black Falcon Avenue, and parked the Ford. All six passengers walked to the dock terminal. Bernard and Michael helped carry the Major's army duffle that had been donated for the effort. Noble and his wife both carried a small trunk to accompany Akeema on her long journey. Noble purchased a ticket, and dropped off the luggage that would be taken to Akeema's cabin. The group then walked off to the docks.

SS Alaska was a relatively small ocean liner with the traditional black hull, white superstructure, two masts, and a single funnel. She carried a modest number of passengers, but was mostly used to carry various types of cargo. She had been converted from burning coal to oil, and was generally a faster liner than many. A mixture of passengers and crates were loading as the Nobles approached the stern gangway.

Akeema was dressed in a white blouse, a navy blue mid-calf skirt, and a matching jacket. She wore comfortable low heeled shoes, and carried a small carpet bag. Her long black hair was tied into her usual pony tail. Noble was amused that his family suddenly felt compelled to shower Akeema with a barrage of small talk. He knew this was an unconscious attempt to keep Akeema with them as long as possible. In some irrational way, maybe the chatter would stop her from leaving at all. Any such wishes were shattered by a blast from a loud shrill ship fog horn, and the words, "All aboard!" from a blow horn.

All six people began to cry. Bernard, Michael, and Florence were uncontrollable in their sobbing, and Lillian was not much better. Noble, with tears flowing down both cheeks, tried to contain his mournful emotions. Every Noble family member said many times, "I'm going to miss you! We're going to miss you! My brother is going to miss you! My sister is going to miss you!" Numerous similar sentence combinations were heard over and over again.

"Thank you for everything!" whispered Lillian to Akeema.

"Study your nursing books on board!" said Florence, trying in vain to smile.

"Read about the Red Sox when you can, Akeema!" said Bernard and Michael.

Tears were in Akeema's eyes as well. She hugged Lillian and the Noble children. She put her arms above her head and said something only Noble could hear. "To my two bright stars beyond the vault; Arthur and Marguerite." Akeema opened her bag and took out a carved stone amulet of a walrus head. She handed the amulet to Lillian and said, "This is for the Noble family's protection, Mrs. Noble. Keep it in your house at all times, and think of me when you see it." Lillian clutched the amulet tightly to her chest and tried to smile.

Noble stepped forward and handed an envelope to Akeema. "What is this?" she asked.

"Akeema, this is some additional money for your journey. There is also money for a return trip through the canal. Please come back to us, Akeema."

Akeema looked at all five Nobles standing before her. She wiped away tears as she said, "I go to honor my people, and to give them a proper place with the ancestors. However, please know that I love all of you very much. I will leave you letters from every port."

"I do not know when…but, I will return," said Akeema. "I will return, my Noble family!" She hugged each family member one last time, and kissed each one on the cheek. With that, Akeema turned, quickly walked up the gangway, and disappeared into the ship.

Almost immediately, the gangways were pulled away from the hull, and the huge mooring ropes removed. Tugs began to push *Alaska* from the dock, stern end first. The Nobles viewed the tugs maneuver the liner southward. They watched until *Alaska* was gone from sight.

The Nobles blew their noses and dried their eyes all the way back to the Ford. No one spoke on the trip to Back Bay, as they thought of a thousand Akeema memories. Each found it hard to think of a time when they did not know Akeema.

Noble was drained. He had not slept well during his last night aboard USS *Madawaska*, was weary from the laborious Hoboken train trip, and had not slept much the previous night. The highly emotional issues surrounding Akeema and her sudden departure added to his mounting fatigue. He was glad he only had four miles to drive home, because he could barely keep his eyes open. He parked the truck in the Beacon Street garage, and helped family members into the house. As Noble closed the front door to the house, he turned to Lillian and said, "Lilly, I'm really tired. I hope you don't mind if I take a short nap."

"Daring," said Lillian, "I can't imagine how you have been able to push yourself as hard as you have the last few days. Anyone would be completely exhausted in your place. In addition, we are all certainly wrung out from Akeema's unexpected absence from our family. Please take as long a rest as you need. I'll get the boys off to school, even though they missed the morning session. After that, I need to drop by the bank to do some work with the A & M Charitable Fund. Get some rest! Later, when you are up to it, you can tell me all about the trip from France!" She kissed her husband, and then went off to round up her sons for school. Florence left to catch a trolley for Boston City Hospital.

Noble decided to rest upon the comfortable sofa in the library. He took off his shoes, put a throw pillow beneath his head, and laid down on his back. His tensions began to abate as his muscles relaxed from the trials of the past few days.

However, it was at exactly 10:31 AM when Major Edward Noble felt it.

CHAPTER 40

The first sensation was a tiny, nearly imperceptible, discomfort behind Noble's left eye when he looked from side-to-side. Initially, he thought this was simple eye fatigue. But, the unilateral sensation quickly grew in intensity. It was not long before his left eye was moderately photophobic. Noble therefore drew closed the louvered windows in the library. "Yes," he thought to himself. "That's better". But, it was not really. Soon, his right eye felt the same as the left.

Noble thought the spring day was going to be warmer than forecasted because the library was unusually hot for that hour of the day. He took off the light coat he had worn to Boston Harbor, lay down on the library couch, and placed the coat over his eyes. Perhaps that would help his eye fatigue. It did not.

Standing for hours on the Hoboken train must have been harder on him than he realized. Noble's bilateral trapezius, deltoid, sternocleidomastoideus, rectus femoris, and gastocnemius muscles began to ache with an odd rolling sensation beneath his skin. It was a combination of myalgias and muscle spasm he had not experienced before. It was good that he had a chance to rest, because he surely needed it.

But, resting was not helping. Noble stood from the sofa with some difficulty, walked into the kitchen, and took two aspirin tablets with a tall glass of water. He was sure this would help his myalgias from his torturous train ride.

On his way back to the sofa, Noble checked a thermometer hanging on the library wall. He was certain that Lillian had inadvertently left the oil heater on. "Strange," he said to himself. "It's only 65° F. It feels much warmer than that." Noble even began to experience chilling. He was therefore surprised when he rested back on the sofa and found his shirt to be damp with sweat. "Maybe the thermometer is broken," thought Noble. "I'll get a new one later this week."

Noble's eye pain was now very uncomfortable, and had taken on a throbbing quality. He decided to take two more aspirin tablets, but found that he was very unsteady on his feet. He used the walls to help him ambulate to the kitchen and back. He chuckled slightly, and thought to himself how out of shape he was. "I'm winded just walking to the kitchen," Noble thought. "I wonder if Harvey will be up for a few tennis matches this next weekend. I surely need the exercise."

As he lay down on the sofa once again, he noticed some slight chest pain with each inspiration. "That tiny berth onboard *Madawaska* really was tough on me," thought Noble. "I wonder how sailors can spend months sleeping on them." However, the chest pain worsened. In addition, Noble began to experience a feeling deep in his chest that was difficult to describe. It was something like a twitch, yet painful. He thought that if he voluntarily coughed, the twitch might go away. But, it did not. Soon, the coughing ceased being voluntary. The twitch began to force a non-productive cough. And his coughing was getting worse.

Noble was having difficulty thinking clearly. "If I could just get some sleep, I could...think," he judged. "I could get out of this haze in my head...my head would stop hurting.

If only I could just sleep." However, it was not just thinking that was now a challenge. Noble was now having difficulty breathing as well. He had not noticed how profound his shortness of breath was until he arose again for another glass of water. This time he barely made it back to the library sofa.

Noble's nose began to run, and he used a handkerchief to dry it. When he looked at the handkerchief he finally knew.

There was almost no mucous on the handkerchief. Instead, it was covered with blood.

"I've got it," Noble said out loud.

The pain, the coughing, and now the heat were making it hard for Noble to formulate plans. He tried to let the Internist within him take over, but he no longer could access that part of his mind. "I...I, need help," Noble said as he choked on blood running from his nasopharynx and down his throat. "Help...I need help." It took all of his will to run through in his mind where all four members of his family were. "They're all away. There's no one here." Noble now could not think beyond single words. "Telephone," he thought. However, Noble was frightened to learn he could no longer lift himself from the sofa. His arms and legs felt as though they weighed tons, and the pain associated with their movement was unbearable. Noble was now a prisoner within his own body, and there was no escape.

After dropping off two very sad boys at school, Lillian drove to the First Bank of Boston to sign documents concerning her growing A & M Charitable Fund. With a principle of over three million dollars, she was beginning to disperse interest to the non-profit organizations seeking to help pandemic victims. Completing that work, Lillian drove the Ford back to Beacon Street. She parked the truck at about noon, and entered the kitchen from the garage. She knew her husband was resting from his travels and tried to be especially quiet for him.

Lillian set about preparing for the family dinner that evening. She and Florence would need to assume many of the household tasks previously performed by Akeema. As she worked, she thought of Akeema's journey to Alaska that would take many weeks. She thought how much she missed Arthur and Marguerite. She thought about her gradually healing depression, and her now infrequent sessions with Dr. Garzaro. And, she thought about how happy she was that her husband was now home. Perhaps, finally, the Noble family had reached a stable place from which it could heal its various wounds.

As Lillian cracked an egg into a bowl, she thought she heard a sound from the other side of the house. It was a strange sound that was barely audible. She listened for a moment, heard nothing, and resumed cracking eggs.

A few minutes later Lillian heard the sound again. There had been a coughing noise, and then something else. A second time she stopped her work to listen, but heard nothing further. Again she resumed her preparation of the evening meal.

Then Lillian heard the noise a third time, only it was now clearly coming from the library. It was a cough, followed by a low gurgling sound. She thought the noise was similar to percolating coffee.

Lillian decided to investigate. She put down the bowl with the egg whites and yolks, and started out for the library. Entering through the library French doors, she suddenly stopped, stood silently for a split-second, and then screamed.

On the library sofa was her husband lying on his back, with his eyes open and staring at the ceiling. Blood dripped from his nose. He had begun coughing violently as he struggled to clear his airway. A frothy red fluid ran from his mouth and onto the floor. A small trickle of blood came from his right ear causing a red puddle on the sofa. Between coughing paroxysms, Noble moaned and arched his back as though he was in great pain. But, he said nothing and his eyes did not move. His forehead dripped with sweet, and his clothes were drenched in it.

Lillian had seen firsthand the horrors at Camp Devens. She knew what this was.

"<u>Edward</u>!" screamed Lillian. "My God, <u>Edward</u>!" She recalled enough first aid to see that her husband was drowning in his own secretions. She ran to the sofa and turned Noble onto his right side. Frothy red fluid gushed out onto the hardwood floor. "My God, my God!" screamed Lillian. She used throw pillows to prop up her husband on his side, and ran to the parlor telephone. She dialed the A.I. Office and immediately asked Lieutenant Quellet to try reaching Milton Rosenau at the Chelsea Naval Hospital. A few minutes later, the Noble phone rang. It was Lieutenant Commander Rosenau.

"Milton," yelled Lillian, "its Edward! He has influenza, and he's very sick!"

Rosenau gave some brief instructions, told Lillian he would be there as soon as possible, and also said, "You need to see if that third year resident...David Schafer...can come to the house. From what Edward has said, Dr. Schafer may have more experience treating pandemic influenza than anyone else...on Earth." Lillian agreed, hung up the phone, and called the A.I. Office again. After relaying the message, Quellet said she would get a hold of Dr. Schafer, and Florence as well.

Lillian ran to check on her husband, who was not responsive to her. He was blistering hot to the touch, but seemed to breathe somewhat better on his side. She ran back to the telephone and called Harvey Cushing's home in Brookline. Cushing was not there, but Katherine Cushing told Lillian she would call him at the Peter Bent Brigham Hospital. Lillian ran back to her husband, and did all she could to keep his airway clear. Occasionally, she would pound on his back and facilitate the flowing of frothy fluid from his lungs. A thick slippery pink-red layer of pulmonary secretions now covered the library hardwood floor.

For an hour, Lillian tried to keep the voluminous secretions from impeding her husband's breathing. Finally, Florence arrived from Boston City Hospital along with Dr.

Schafer. Without any discussion, and with the precision of a timepiece, Florence immediately began tending to her father's pulmonary secretions, and Schafer began to examine his new patient. Lillian sat on a chair nearby her husband.

Schafer's exam revealed the emerging clinical picture: pulse 105, respiratory rate 22, blood pressure 95/50, temperature 105° F. Noble was very flushed and diaphoretic. His skin displayed decreased skin turgor, and was not responsive to questions. However, Noble mumbled unintelligible words as he moved all four limbs. His pulses were normal and symmetric, and heart sounds were normal, but suppressed. There were loud rhonchi, wheezes, and course bubbling rales throughout both lung fields. Impaired resonance was also noted throughout both lungs, along with a matt quality noted with percussion. Noble's coughing paroxysms were begging to interfere with breathing. There was some slight use of the extra-thoracic musculature during respirations. Copious amounts of blood tinged frothy fluid gushed from Nobles mouth, and there was also epistaxis. Schafer's otoscope showed a perforated right tympanic membrane along with blood in the right ear. The rest of the physical examination was normal.

Lillian heard a car pull up and stop quickly just outside the Noble home. She looked out the library window to see a navy staff car at the curb, and Milton Rosenau stepping out of it. Moments later Lillian let Rosenau into the house. "How is he?" asked Rosenau.

Fighting back tears, Lillian said, "I...I...I don't know, Milton. I don't know."

"Dr. Rosenau," said Schafer, "I'm glad to see you, sir."

"What's the status, David?" asked Rosenau calmly, as experienced clinicians do.

"From what Florence told me," said Schafer, "Dr. Noble was fine when he was left alone at home at about 10 PM. Mrs. Noble found him like this at about noon. So, the onset is extremely rapid. He has severe dehydration, delirium, a fever of 105° F, a severe bilateral pneumonia, a ruptured right tympanic membrane, severe oronasal-pulmonary bleeding, and it's hard to keep up with his pulmonary toilet." Schafer extended his arm with an open hand to show the secretions about the library."

"Lillian," said Rosenau, "I know Edward keeps some medications and medical supplies here at home. Can you get what you have?" Lillian quickly took on the task without a word. She returned with a large black bag and an oxygen tank. The group put on gauze face masks. Rosenau then said, "Everyone, we need to move Edward into the bedroom down the hall so we have more room to work." Rosenau and Schafer lifted Noble at the shoulders, as Florence and Lillian lifted his legs. They carried the very sick patient into Arthur's old bedroom, and placed him on the bed. Rosenau removed his friend's blood stained uniform, and dressed him in cooler pajamas.

Schafer walked over to Lillian and asked, "Mrs. Noble, do you want us to take him to Boston City?"

Lillian put her right hand over her eyes. Once again, she was forced to entertain the question of hospitalizing a critically ill member of her family. "Dr. Schafer, if at all possible, I would rather that he be treated here."

"Then, that is what we will do, Mrs. Noble," said Schafer with authority. Schafer turned to Florence and asked, "Could you start an IV as soon as you can, Florence? Your father is way behind in his fluids, and we need to correct that immediately." Florence went to the black bag and began assembling the IV tubing. Schafer and Rosenau then made an accounting of available medical supplies, and Schafer began writing a list.

Lillian stood at her husband's bedside, and remembered the times she read stories to Arthur at that exact same spot. "Is there anything I can do?" she asked.

"Actually, Mrs. Noble," said Schafer, "there is." Schafer wrote something on the list he had just created. "Mrs. Noble, we need some additional drugs and supplies. I want you to take this list to Dr. Anna Reed at Boston City Hospital as fast as you can. Tell her what is going on, and give her this list of things we need. This will include more O2, since your tank has less than an hour left in it. The note also asks her to establish a rotation of residents to help out here. As soon as everyone finds out about Dr. Noble, I guarantee they will be waiting in lines to help." Schafer had barely handed the list to Lillian, when she ran out the door to the garage. Lillian had done this before.

After Lillian had departed for BCH, Rosenau took Schafer aside for further discussion away from Florence. "David," said Rosenau, "Edward told me you have just about as much experience with influenza as anyone. What do you think?"

It was difficult for Schafer, a third year medical resident, to answer the question. Rosenau was one of them most famous clinical epidemiologists in the world. And, he was asking for Schafer's opinion. "Well, sir. I have two main concerns at this point. First, the rapid disease onset, and the severity of the pneumonia, point to a much poorer overall prognosis. Second, Dr. Noble was in respiratory distress when his wife found him, which may have been two hours after his symptoms began."

The two physicians looked at one another with the expression that every clinician understands. The expression is a combination of great worry and dismay. "Anoxia," said Rosenau.

"Right," said Schafer. "Ischemic brain damage."

Rosenau put his hand to the side of his face. "We just can't know until we can observe his mentation. And, that may take a very long time. I don't think we need to mention this to his family right now."

"I agree," said Schafer. "What we should do now is get his temperature down, rehydrate him, keep his airway free, and do something about his coughing."

After Florence had established a functioning IV, Schafer began to aggressively rehydrate his mentor. Of all the therapeutic interventions he had used for influenza over the past seven months, this was most crucial. Crushed acetylsalicylic acid, benzyl benzoate, and caffeine were administered orally, while morphine sulfate, epinephrine, and sodium bicarbonate were given IV. Ice packs were placed on Noble's hot erythemic skin. Oxygen was given by face mask. It was a full time job for Florence to just suction secretions from her father's mouth. The oxygen mask made this yet more challenging.

Lillian returned from BCH so fast that Schafer, at first, thought she had not completed the trip. However, Lillian not only returned with boxes of medical supplies. She also brought with her the second year resident, Anna Reed.

"David," said Reed, "I already have several dozen resident volunteers to assist us. There are also scores of nurses and nursing students that have volunteered. I'll put together a rotation schedule right away. Everyone wants to help."

Just then, there was a knock on the house front door. Lillian walked to the door and opened it. At first, Lillian did not recognize the man at the doorway. He was older appearing, with thinning gray hair and pale skin. The man was very gaunt, with his cheek bones protruding below sunken eyes. He stood with a slightly stooped posture, and had a cane. The man said, "Lillian...I came as fast as I could."

Lillian hesitated for some time as she tried to place the man's face. Finally, a smile came to her as she said, "Harvey! Oh, Harvey! Thank you for coming! It is so good to see you!" Cushing slowly entered the house with a modest shuffling gait. Lillian had not seen him in over a year-and-a-half. Gone were his boyish good looks and energetic persona. Cushing not only appeared older than his age. He now looked, to a degree, frail. Lillian hugged him, but worried about knocking him over.

"It's wonderful to see you too, Lillian," said Cushing. "How is he?"

Lillian's smile instantly vanished. "I don't...know, Harvey. You better ask the professionals."

Rosenau walked over to Cushing, saluted him, and said, "Colonel, glad you're back!"

"Thanks, Milton," said Cushing. "But, I'm in the Army Medical Reserve Corps now."

Schafer and Reed stood motionless. From nowhere had walked in the most famous neurosurgeon in the world. They looked at one another wide-eyed. Harvey Cushing, Milton Rosenau, and Edward Noble were all in the same room...at the same time. Schafer leaned over to Reed and whispered, "Now all we need is William Welch, Victor Vaughn, and William Osler to walk in."

Cushing asked for an update, and a hesitant Dr. Schafer gave a succinct summary of events. Cushing had seen his share of severe influenza cases in France, and still carried many of its chronic debilities himself. His expression was of great concern for his friend. From his estimation, everything that could be done for Noble was being done.

Cushing motioned for Lillian to sit with him in the parlor. He smiled as he passed his drawing of Lillian on the parlor wall. He remembered how pleased Noble was when he received it as a gift. It also reminded him of happier and simpler times. "How are _you_ doing, Lillian?" asked Cushing, as the two sat on the parlor sofa.

Lillian began to weep loudly, with short catches in her breaths. Cushing put his arm around her shoulders as he sought to console her in some way. He knew all about Arthur and Marguerite. He knew the hell Boston had been through since the previous fall. However, that hell was now squarely attacking her husband; the man who had spent much of 1918 trying to warn America of its dangers. "Lillian, Edward has some of the best people around to help him right now. In addition, he's just about the most stubborn man I have ever met. He'll beat this on stubbornness alone."

Lillian cracked a faint smile, pulled out a handkerchief from her pocket, and dried her eyes. "He is pretty stubborn, isn't he?"

"Yeah," said Cushing. "Stubborn, hard-boiled, and sarcastic. I guess that's why we all love him so much." Lillian and Cushing both laughed, and knew it was all true. "Lillian, whenever Edward wrote from France, or from his Boston City Hospital office, every other word was always about you. No man on earth loves his wife more than he does. This is another reason he won't let this thing keep him down." Lillian again smiled slightly. She also knew that was true, but needed to hear it once again.

Lillian told Cushing about Akeema and her departure. She then said, "On our way home from Boston Harbor this morning, Edward sounded so sad. He told me all he wanted was his 'life back'. He wanted no more trips to war zones, and no more trips without his family. He wanted to reestablish his medical practice, and to be with his family when he isn't 'fighting microbes', as he calls it. Now, instead of his 'life back', maybe his very life will be taken away." Lillian began to cry again, and Cushing just sat with her and held her hand. He had the same real concern.

Over the next several hours, Noble's overall clinical status improved in some ways, and deteriorated in others. His hypotension resolved with rehydration, and his reduced forceful coughing paroxysms with medication eased his labored breathing. But, Noble's lung consolidation worsened, and his pulmonary fluid output increased. His delirium had deepened. And, there was another troubling problem. In spite of all attempts to lower it, his temperature remained at 105° F. Blood, sputum, and urine samples were sent to the BCH laboratory for further evaluation.

By that evening, a Beacon Street routine had already been devised for the care of Dr. Noble. Residents volunteered four hour shifts at the Noble home, in addition to their Boston City Hospital rotations. Nurses and nursing students also volunteered four hour shifts that overlapped with the physician shifts. This increased continuity of care. Florence would act as "head nurse" when student nurses were assisting. At the completion of their shifts, each physician and nurse signed out clinical information to the incoming volunteer. Rosenau and Cushing would spend as much time as possible at Noble's bedside, and other attendings would be available at the house or by phone twenty-four hours a day. When Schafer was not with Noble, he made sure everyone knew a telephone number where he could be reached.

Lillian kept a constant supply of food and hot coffee for everyone who was at the house. She also cleaned Arthur's room frequently, and also washed her husband every few hours. With the increasing quantities of pulmonary secretions, there was a constant flow of blood soaked linen to clean. Bernard and William were recruited to assist in that regard. When Lillian needed to rest, Katherine Cushing and Rose Kennedy aided their friend whenever they could.

At 9 PM, Lillian was napping on the parlor sofa. Florence was watching a nursing student suction her father with a rubber bulb. This suctioning occurred every few minutes throughout a nursing shift. A medical resident had finished taking vitals and was recording them on the clinical log. He began to adjust the IV fluid rate, when suddenly there was a very loud banging at the front door. Lillian was jolted awake, and took a moment to fully embrace her faculties. When she realized what the noise was, she ran to the front of the house. Opening the door, she was immediately confronted with at least a dozen shouting men and women with note pads. "We understand that Major Edward Noble has the grippe!" yelled one man. "Do you care to comment, Miss?"

"Reporters," thought Lillian to herself. "No comment, ladies and gentlemen," Lillian said out loud. "And, by the way, it's 'Mrs.'." She slammed the front door so hard that the front of the house shook.

The next morning, Thursday, May 1st, Rosenau came to the house to check on his friend. As he was about to knock on the door, he picked up a copy of the *Boston Globe* on the Noble front porch. Lillian answered the door, and Rosenau walked in. "Did you see this yet?" asked Rosenau, as he handed her the morning newspaper. Lillian opened the *Globe* to the front page. The headline read, "ARMY FLU DOC GETS THE FLU".

"No, I hadn't seen that," said Lillian.

"It seems the newspapers are interviewing every BCH resident and nurse who will talk to them. There's a full description of Edward's illness, you, the children, this house... everything. It goes on for several columns. It looks like it's in every newspaper in the country this morning. Also, there's a bunch of reporter-like people all along Beacon Street today."

Lillian was in no mood for any of this, and looked as though she had not listened to Rosenau's newspaper description at all. "Milton, Dr. Schafer wanted to talk to you as soon as you arrived." Rosenau walked into Arthur's old bedroom where he found Schafer with his famous patient. Noble's respirations were more labored than they had been the night before. "Yes, David?"

Schafer picked up the clinical log. "Good morning, Dr. Rosenau. Things aren't looking all that great, sir. Here are the vitals: pulse 81, respiratory rate 26, blood pressure 110/70, temperature 105° F. As you can see, in spite of eight liters per minute of O2, and bronchodilator therapy, his respiratory effort has increased. His bilateral pulmonary consolidation continues to worsen. He's just not moving air as well as yesterday. I have to say his nursing care, and attention to his airway, has been the best I've seen. But, that can't help his worsening influenza pneumonia."

Rosenau took a stethoscope and quickly made his own physical examination. He also looked at the clinical log. "Well, we can't blame this on fluid overload, David. You and the other residents have done a great job managing that. Do we have the lab results from this morning yet?"

"Not yet," said Schafer. "Florence, could you call the lab and see if we have those chemistries and blood counts?" Florence immediately went to the telephone. A few minutes later, she returned with a piece of paper and handed it to Rosenau.

"Well, here's one possibility," said Rosenau, who handed the paper to Schafer.

"No kidding," said Schafer. His hemoglobin is 5.5 g/dl. Even with hemodilution, that's quite a drop from yesterday."

Lillian had been listening to the conversation. "Milton, what exactly does that mean?"

"It means that Edward has had a substantial blood loss and may not have enough hemoglobin onboard to oxygenate his blood. He needs a blood transfusion."

Schafer asked Florence to call BCH hematology and request them to type and cross four units of blood. Florence also volunteered to pick up the blood when it was ready.

After some hours, four sequential units of blood had been hung at Noble's bed side for transfusion. By then, Harvey Cushing had again arrived to monitor his friend's progress. With completion of the transfusions, Noble's less labored respiratory rate was back down to 22 per minute. At least part of his clinical picture had stabilized. Still, Schafer expressed his concern to his well known attendings. "Dr. Rosenau, and Dr. Cushing, it's been about twenty-four hours since the first vital signs were taken. Dr. Noble's temperature is still 105° F, even with all our therapeutic measures."

"What have you seen in the past with similar clinical presentations?" asked Cushing.

"At Boston City we have noticed two early prognostic points with temperatures," said Schafer. "The first is the height of the initial temperature, and the second is the slope of temperature decline with therapy. The lower the initial temperature, the better the prognosis. The faster the decline of the initial temperature with treatment, the better the prognosis. The reverse is also true with poorer prognoses in both cases. Therefore, we have a poorer prognosis for both points: a very high initial temperature, and no fall at all with maximum therapy."

Cushing put his thumb and index finger to his chin. "With all of us to help, let's place Edward in a tepid bath and try to lower his temperature in that way. It often helps with surgical patients with hyperthermia." All three physicians agreed it was worth a try. With the assistance of Lillian, Florence, another nurse, and the three doctors, Noble was carried to the nearest bathtub and immersed in water slightly below normal body temperature. After thirty minutes his temperature was 104.6° F. He was carried back to his bed, where his temperature was found to be 105° F.

That evening, Noble's clinical condition had gradually declined. His vitals were unchanged, but his lung consolidation by clinical exam had worsened. Higher doses of medication were required to control his coughing. His bleeding from his nose, ear, and mouth had not slowed, so more blood was typed and crossed for the morning. Most worrisome was Noble's delirium. He was now moving his extremities less, and was no longer responsive to sternal applied pain.

At 10 PM, Rosenau and Cushing asked Lillian to sit with them in the parlor. Florence was very much aware of the situation, and asked her mother to be present during the consultation. In an unusual additional request, Bernard and William petitioned for an opportunity to listen in. The boys argued they have also lost family to the pandemic, and are no less members of the Noble family. Lillian allowed all three of her children to sit with her.

With his most serious expression, Rosenau began the discussion. "Lillian, we wanted to let you know about Edward's present condition." Lillian sat up straight, and folded her hands upon her lap. She knew the worst was coming, and braced for it. "Milton and Harvey, please," she said, "I just want to know the truth." Tears ran down her face, and she thought to herself how many times she had cried over the previous three days...and, over the previous seven months.

"Edward is gradually worsening in his battle with influenza," said Milton. "Primarily, his pneumonia is beginning to seriously impair his breathing. Every known measure to help his respiration is underway. But, there is another factor that Dr. Cushing and Dr. Schafer want to discuss."

Lillian's eyes darted back and forth, from Cushing to Schafer. "What factor is that?"

Cushing was the physician sitting closest to Lillian in the room. He edged in his chair closer to her as he spoke softly. "Lillian, I am told Edward may have been without adequate ventilation up to two hours before you discovered him ill in the library. At this point, we cannot definitely sort out influenza induced delirium from other neurological insults."

"What sort of other insults, Harvey?" asked Lillian, although her expression betrayed her understanding of the problem.

"Well," said Cushing, with a long pause, "we have a concern about...anoxic brain damage."

The four members of the Noble family looked at each other as they all began to sob heavily. They had heard their father talk many times about hospital patients with anoxic or ischemic brain damage, and Florence had cared for such patients as well. They all knew what that meant. Lillian put her arms around all three of her children, and rested her head upon the familial mass within her arms.

The Nobles were coming together with the new realization given to them. Lillian decided that her family needed to hear the cold hard medical prognosis. She lifted her head toward the doctors and said, "He is dying, isn't he?"

Schafer wanted to answer the question, and the other two doctors nodded with approval to proceed. "Mrs. Noble...his overall prognosis is very poor. If we add the issue of anoxic brain damage to the clinical picture, it becomes dismal."

"Hopeless?" asked Lillian, her eyes red and filled with tears.

"Mrs. Noble," said Schafer, "when your husband rounds with residents on the wards, he frequently uses a phrase to help put things into perspective. He states it when a resident is describing a patient with a particularly bad outcome: 'Even when the prognosis is poor, hope is always rich.' Dr. Noble has said this so often that the whole hospital repeats it."

All four Nobles again looked at each other through their tears...and sadly smiled. Without a word, they all agreed the saying sounded just like their father and husband.

One hour later, Cushing, Rosenau, and Schafer took stock of their patient's clinical situation: pulse 112, respiratory rate 30 and labored, blood pressure 85/45, temperature 106° F. Noble no longer moved his extremities. He had begun to arch his back with each breath, as the organism stained to get enough oxygen. The reflex of coughing was worse, and interrupted the already tenuous respirations. The frothy pink pulmonary secretions that continued to pore from him were now turning frankly bloody. More blood flowed from his nose and right ear. Heart and breath sounds were now barely audible through the highly consolidated lungs. The doctors had seen such lungs at necropsy, and knew how little reserve function was left in them.

IV fluids and units of blood were flowing into Noble's veins as fast as the team knew how to administer them. They could no longer increase the doses of his medications. A delicate balance must be achieved in the treatment of complicated influenza. On the left side of the equation is worsening bronchospasm with coughing, and subsequent decreased ventilation and respiration. On the right side of the equation is drug induced tachycardia with decreased cardiac output, and a reduction in ventilatory drive. Any more attempts to affect the left side of the equation would increase the right side. Noble's cardiovascular and pulmonary systems were on the verge of collapse.

It was Dr. Schafer who saw it first.

It was very faint initially. Only those who had seen it before would have noticed it now. Schafer was assisting the nurse with suctioning fluid from Noble's mouth, when he saw it. Over Noble's bilateral zygomatic processes was a delicate lavender hue. Schafer quickly motioned for Cushing and Rosenau to step up to bedside. "Do you see it over his cheek bones?" said Schafer quietly. Both men slowly nodded. Between the three of them, this particular fatal sign had been seen many times on both sides of the Atlantic.

The cyanosis unique to this disease was like an expanding lake. As it deepened in color, it made a confluent spread on the surface of the victim. It was only a matter of minutes before Noble's cheek bones were a deep indigo-blue, with an expanding pale lavender margin. The pale margins moved about his entire cheeks. As the minutes passed, his cheeks also deepened in color, and the margins marched along to his ears and neck. His lips became a crimson color, as the pale margin flowed onto his chest. In less than thirty minutes, Noble's entire head was an unearthly dark bluish purple.

Cushing noticed a soft puffy quality to the base of Noble's neck and about his clavicles. He palpated the area, and said very softly; "crepitus". The doctors looked at one another as Schafer shook his head. Rosenau then said, "Subcutaneous emphysema. There must be a pulmonary hilar rupture into the mediastinum." The three clinicians knew this was an extraordinarily ominous physical sign. It carried with it a near one hundred percent mortality.

Just then Lillian passed by her husband's bed as she went to pick up some soiled linen. She glanced over at Noble's face, and screamed so loud that all in the room covered their ears. "No! No! No! No! No! No! No! No! No! No! No! No!" she yelled at the top of her voice, over and over. Cushing and Rosenau each put an arm around her in order to escort her out of the room. She began to resist, and the muscular Rosenau had to restrain her arms from hitting him. Hearing the commotion, Bernard and William rushed from the parlor and into the bedroom. Seeing their father in a ghoulish blue cast, they also began to scream uncontrollably. Florence, who was crying herself, took the boys to their upstairs rooms. Someone knocked at the front door, and Schafer ran to open it. A reporter outside had heard the noise from the house, and decided to investigate. Schafer grabbed the man by his lapels and through him off the front door stairs. With chaos all around, Schafer then had the composure to run back to his patient and do whatever he could.

Cushing, Rosenau, and Schafer knew the end was now very near.

CHAPTER 41

Beyond the perimeter it was dark. Actually, dark did not accurately describe it. It was black. Even black did not describe it. It was more than black. It was thick. A thick black. A thick black as one sees with tar, if tar was an atmosphere. And it was sticky. Things stuck to it. Light stuck to it. In fact, it seemed to be the negative of light; the antithesis of light. It sucked light.

Things did seem to stick to the black. It looked as though one might be able to enter the black. One could enter it as one would dive into the ocean, if the ocean were thick and black. But, the ocean gives back things. The black would not. The black held on to things. The black would not give back anything. It held onto everything. One could go into the black. However, one could never return from the black. The best simple term for it was "The Black".

From all estimations, The Black started at a thirty foot perimeter. Feet? Was that even a relevant measurement? Well, it was the best unit available at the time. Yes, about thirty feet. Thirty feet from where? Thirty feet from here. Here.

The point where one is. Is not the beginning of all points from here? The point where one is? Yes. One must be here to have a there. Why was this even a question anyway? If one is not there, one must be here. Right?

The perimeter. There was a real perimeter. Yes, there was, in fact, a here and there. There was The Black, and it was definitely there. Here was, well...here was here. Here was not black. Here was gray. Actually, here was made of gray shades. Dark gray. There were no other colors, as colors were remembered, anyway. The gray within the perimeter was like a silent moving picture. But, the gray perimeter was almost too dim to see. Dim like a cloudy night without the moon.

The perimeter was definitely a place. It had a floor. But, it did not have walls and a ceiling, as walls and ceilings are known to be. Rather, the perimeter was apart from The Black, but set into it. The Black formed a type of dome over the perimeter that was eight feet high, at its highest point. However, it was difficult to tell where the perimeter ended, and The Black started.

The perimeter did have items within it. There was a cabinet, a chair, and a floor lamp. There was also a throw rug. All these things were of gray shades. The perimeter was so dim that the objects within it were more like outlines. If one were to walk about the perimeter, one would have to feel the way with hands.

Edward Noble looked down at his legs and saw he was sitting on a single bed. The bed was situated near the edge of the perimeter. He looked up and thought he might be able to reach over his head and touch The Black, as it arched down toward the perimeter. He decided against touching it when he noticed a slight seething quality to The Black. There was no sound. Noble looked at his hands, which were gray. He looked at his army uniform, which was gray. He unbuttoned one button to his shirt, saw his chest was gray, and quickly buttoned it again.

Noble sat on the bed and observed the perimeter. At the far end of the perimeter, from where the bed was situated, was another outline. It was very difficult to discern, but it looked like it might be a rocking chair. And it was rocking. Sitting on the rocking chair was a silhouette. There were no details within the silhouette. It was so dark. But, there was something familiar about the silhouette. A long time passed as the rocking chair rocked back and forth.

Noble thought that in order to have time, one must have events. Does time cause events to happen, or do events create time? He was not sure. He felt "a long time passed", but without events, what did that mean? There was no relevance to minutes, hours, days, or years in the perimeter. The Black made the concept of time meaningless.

"Edward."

Noble heard his name called from the silhouette, but did not answer.

"Edward Noble."

Another meaningless large amount of time passed. "What?" said Noble with impatience.

"Is that any way to be with an old friend?" said the silhouette, with a slight giggle. "We have been through so much together, wouldn't you agree? Edward, you do know who I am, don't you?"

"I know who you are," Noble said with disgust.

"Now, now, Edward. I detect just a hint of hostility in your voice. You know how it bothers me when we don't get along." Noble heard a playful, or even joyful, tone from the silhouette that was greatly irritating. The silhouette continued, "The last time we chatted, I was on your side. Now, you are on mine."

"What is this place?" asked Noble.

The silhouette laughed loudly. "Come now, Edward, you know this place. It goes by many names."

"Where am I now?" Noble demanded.

"Where do you think you are?" asked the silhouette.

"What has happened to me?" asked Noble.

"What do you think has happened to you, Edward?"

"Why am I here?" asked Noble.

"Why do you think you are here?" said the silhouette.

"Where is my family?" asked Noble.

The silhouette began to speak, "Where do you...," when Noble interrupted. "Stop it!" yelled Noble. "Just stop it!"

Pretending to be hurt, the silhouette said sadly, "Edward, my boy. After our long relationship, this is how you treat me?" Noble could see the silhouette lean back in the rocking chair. It seemed as though it positioned itself into a more relaxed posture. The silhouette then said, "I always get so many questions from you, Edward. But, that is one of the things I like most about you. You are so...so...inquisitive, and so predictable!"

"I know what you are doing," said Noble, with new confidence. "You're using an old debate technique. We used it on our college debate team at Boston University. One tries to confuse and frustrate an opponent by following their questions with your own. Well, I'm not falling for it."

"I've been around a lot longer than Boston University, or debate teams, Edward," said the silhouette, who sounded slightly irritated.

Noble was well aware that the silhouette loved to banter. And, it loved to feign a friendship with him. But, Noble knew this was a form of ridicule. What the silhouette really sought was to demean him, devalue him, and ultimately to destroy him. Therefore, Noble decided to fight back. He would fight in a manner the silhouette would hate the most. He simply would not interact with it anymore. Noble was finished.

Another long pause in conversation occurred that seemed like hours, days, and years, all at the same time. "So, Edward," said the silhouette, "you didn't ask me 'why' you think you are here." Noble did not answer. "Edward, did you hear me?" Still no answer from Noble. "Edward," said the silhouette with growing displeasure. Noble laid down on the single bed, put his arms over his abdomen, and folded his hands. "Edward, I am speaking to you!" said the silhouette with indignation. Noble closed his eyes, and said nothing. The silhouette then went into a rage. "Edward, you had better not ignore me! I've been easy on you, and your sorry excuse for a family, up until now! I can be less benevolent in the very near future, if that is the way you want it!"

Noble actually smiled at the last comment. Any sentence used by the silhouette with the word "benevolent" was a non-sequitur. Noble also knew he was finally upsetting the silhouette, and this pleased him greatly.

As Noble lay quietly on the bed, the silhouette began to throw a mountain of insults and profanity at him. The longer Noble stayed quiet, the louder and fiercer the attacks became. Noble had to put his hand to his mouth to stop from openly laughing. "Finally, it's showing its true colors," thought Noble.

Suddenly, the very dark perimeter became even darker. Noble could no longer see the silhouette, even as it screamed scorning remarks and threats at him. Noble looked up and saw an increasing churning quality to The Black. He could see eddies and whirlpools forming in The Black, and even actual waves. Noble became increasingly concerned as The Black began to pulsate. And, the perimeter was shrinking. "Maybe I went too far with it," thought Noble. But, there was no going back now. The Black was definitely reducing the size of the perimeter. It began to swallow the furniture in the perimeter, and began to collapse onto Noble himself. It reached his feet first, and then quickly enveloped his body up to his head. Noble felt the shearing cold tarry quality of The Black hit his face, and ooze into his mouth, nose, ears, and eyes. He was smothered as the heavy Black filled his lungs. Then The Black filled his abdomen, and finally entered his brain. Then...there was nothing.

CHAPTER 42

T he first perception was light sensed through closed eyelids. Then, there was a soft warm breeze felt upon the right cheek. And, there was a very familiar repeating sound nearby. A mild splashing noise, followed by a gentle hissing. Then, the splashing again.

Noble felt as though he was awakening from the most restful sleep he had ever experienced. He was lying on his back, with his eyes closed, and was enjoying the warm fresh air around him. The ground beneath him was also warm, as it formed to the contours of his body. "What is that smell?" thought Noble. Above him he heard another very familiar repeating sound. "Seagulls," he thought. "There are seagulls over head! And that smell. It's the sea!"

Noble gradually opened his eyes. Above was the most brilliant clear blue sky he had ever seen. Sure enough, there were seagulls flying overhead. He propped up his torso with his elbows, and noticed that he was lying on white sand. The sand was so clean that it seemed laced with tiny points of light refracted through silicon crystals. As Noble moved his head, the sand sparkled with yellows, reds, oranges, blues, greens, and violets. He looked a few yards beyond his feet and realized what the hissing noise was. It was the sound seawater makes as a wave hits the sand and creates a thin layer of foam.

Looking to his left and right, Noble saw the expanse of a pristine beach along an emerald blue-green ocean. "I know this place!" said Noble, out loud. "This is the beach just north of Provincetown, on Cape Cod!" The beach gently curved south on both sides of him. He knew he was lying on the most northern point of the Cape. From this vantage, Noble could see nearly two thousand yards of open beach to the east and west.

Relishing the beauty of the Cape, Noble thought to himself, "The weather is so wonderful today! It must be late spring, or early summer." But, there was something odd about the Cape. With such a wonderful day, where are all the people? "How unusual. I don't see anyone else on the entire beach."

Noble sat up, brought his knees up toward his chest, and wrapped his arms about them. He looked down and saw he was wearing a white shirt with an open collar, and khaki trousers. He was barefoot. Noble moved his toes in the warm glimmering white sand. "I wonder where I put my shoes," he thought.

A very long time went by as Noble watched the small waves lapping up on the beach. He remembered playing in the surf as a child at this same exact spot. For many many seasons he built sand castles, played with sand crabs, and flew kites right here. Right at this place. It was truly a wonderful day.

Noble didn't notice it at first. It was too far away. But, there was movement on the beach a few thousand yards to the west. And it was slowly approaching.

From the corner of his left eye, Noble finally became aware of the movement. Over a thousand yards away, it looked like a light-colored dot that occasionally jumped. He was curious about the dot, but decided to wait for it to get closer before investigating further. Noble wanted to time the dot's approach, but noted that he was not wearing his wrist-watch. So, he began to count to himself as the dot passed points along the beach he knew. He calculated that the dot was moving at about two miles per hour. "Sort of like slow walking," thought Noble.

Closer came the dot. At about six or seven hundred yards, Noble said to himself, "Its people. The dot is people...walk-ing. Walking here." At two hundred yards, it was clear that four people were walking east along the beach. But, it was at fifty yards that Noble's curiosity greatly heightened.

Yes, there were four people. There were three adults, and a child. There was an older man with gray hair, and older woman with graying red hair, a young man, and a young girl. Noble now understood why the distant dot had seemed to jump: the child was hopping and skipping.

The older man had on a white shirt and khaki pants, just like Noble's. The woman had on a pale blue long dress with open neck line. The young man was obviously in the army, given his uniform. And, the young girl was wearing a light red sundress.

But, there was something that was both so familiar about the four people, and yet unsettling. Noble could not put his finger on it. "I am certain I know these people," thought Noble. "But, again, I'm not certain." The sand sparkled be-neath the people' bare feet as they walked closer. And Noble heard the repeating call of the gulls, and the waves on the Cape sand.

When the group reached a distance of thirty yards, Noble knew.

Noble ran as fast as he could to the group. He strained his arms to get them around all of the people at once. All four people laughed and put their arms around Noble as well. Noble tripped, fell onto the sand, and stood up again laugh-ing so hard that his chest hurt. He then began to cry uncon-trollably. The older man put his arm around him, the woman hugged him, the young man patted him on the back, and the young girl clung to his leg.

"It's OK, Son," said Charles Noble.

"You are so handsome, Edward!" said Elizabeth Noble.

"Hi, Dad," said Arthur Noble, smiling.

"Hi, Daddy!" yelled Marguerite Noble.

Edward Noble was speechless, and could barely see through the voluminous tears that were dripping from his eyes. At one point he was so out of breath that he thought he would fall back onto the sand. He tried to speak. "Dad! Mom! Arthur! Rabbit! I...I...I..."

"Take your time, Son," said Charles.

"You always used to tell me that, Dad!" said Noble, trying to regain his composure.

"Charles laughed. "You were always in such a hurry, Son. I just wanted you to see the forest for the trees, from time-to-time."

"And, Mom," said Noble, "you are so...so beautiful! Now I can see why Marguerite was so pretty. She looked just like you!"

"You were always such a kind boy, Edward," said Elizabeth. "Of course, you were always so handsome...and that came from your father."

Noble turned to his son and said, "That is one nicely pressed uniform, Arthur! I also see you are wearing your First Lieutenant silver bars!"

"You bet, Dad," said Arthur. "I worked hard for them. As you know, my plan was to make Captain before I left Devens."

"Yes," said Noble, "if only you hadn't..." Noble caught himself before finishing the sentence. Did Arthur know what had happened? Did he know why he did not have the chance to make Captain?

"Daddy, Daddy!" yelled Marguerite, as she hopped on one foot. "Do you remember this?" She held up to her father a tiny stuffed toy rabbit.

Noble took the toy and studied it. Yes. Now he remembered. It was the toy rabbit he placed in his young daughter's coffin. He handed the toy back to her, but noticed a familiar necklace around Marguerite's neck. He picked up part of the necklace to more closely study it.

"Remember, Daddy?" said Marguerite. "Akeema gave it to me."

Again, Noble remembered. It was a necklace fashioned from the bones of the fish Akeema caught from the Cape. Akeema had also placed it in Marguerite's coffin.

Noble's expression changed from one of effervescent happiness, to one of concern. It took some time for him to formulate the words he wanted to express. He turned back to Charles and said, "Dad. Dad. Do you know that you are dead? Do the four of you know that you are dead?"

Charles again smiled and put his hand on Noble's shoulder. "Yes, Son. That is one way to describe it."

Noble looked down at his bare feet, took a very deep breath, and said, "I see, dad. I see." Elizabeth put her arm around her son's arm in a show of support. Arthur pretended to hit his father in the shoulder, as he had done as a boy. Marguerite again hugged her father's leg, while hopping as she always did.

Looking up again at his father, Noble asked, "Why am I here, dad?"

"Because you want to be, Son," said Charles.

"Why are you here, dad, and why are the four of you here?" asked Noble.

"Because you want us to be, Son," said Charles. "Right now, you actually need us to be here."

"Why is that, dad," asked Noble. "Why do I need you here...now?"

"Son," said Charles, "there is quite a battle going on for you. Do you remember what happened immediately before you came here?"

Noble strained to remember. There was something. Something terrible. Something horrible. Something evil. And, it was cold, and dark, and smothering.

"Call it what you like, Son," said Charles. "Call it protection. Call it a defense. Call it a shield. Call it a shelter. Call it a sanctuary. It is all about security. Your security."

As he looked again down at the ground, Noble said, "I see, dad. I see."

"Edward," said Charles, "We are finished, for now, Son. It's time for us to go."

"Must you?" asked Noble, with tears forming again. "Must you leave...so soon?"

Charles grinned. "You never liked it when I went on trips. You would say those same words to me every time. Yes, Son. We must go now."

"Will I see you again...all of you?" asked Noble.

"You can count on it, Son," said Charles. "We'll be back!"

"Tell Lillian, and the children, that we love them," said Elizabeth.

"Hey, Dad," said Arthur. "Tell Mom, Bernard, Michael, and Florence that I love them too. I'll see ya' around, Dad!"

"Daddy, I love you," said Marguerite. "I'll whisper 'I love you' to mom, the boys, and my sister, in their dreams! You too, Daddy! I'll keep the rabbit for the next time!"

Each of the four hugged Noble, and they had to pull themselves from him in order to leave. Elizabeth and Marguerite kissed him, and the group began walking west along the beach. They waved again from about one hundred yards. Noble stood waving until they were completely out of sight. After a time, Noble remarked out loud, "...and all four of them died of influenza."

Those words were barely out of his mouth when a fantastic change in the weather occurred. Dark gray clouds began to stream across the sky as they blocked out the sunlight. A fierce wind drew up from nowhere and began to whip at Nobles clothes. The temperature became very cold, and the ocean began to churn as it changed to a blue-black color. The waves began to pound on the beach, and Noble had to move to avoid being drawn out to sea. The wind was so strong that it knocked him to the sand. The last thought Noble had as his head hit a large rock was "now the demon wins".

CHAPTER 43

I t started very gradually. It went from imperceptible, to something akin to a weight. No, it was more like a heaviness. A heaviness, as if Earth's gravity was somehow slowing gaining strength. It was first apparent in both arms. Then the legs. Then the shoulders. Finally the back and neck joined in. The heaviness made it hard to move the body, but it also was associated with an ache. Aching...everywhere.

Noble tried accessing the part of his mind that had eluded him only moments earlier: his clinical mind. Yes! It was there. He now knew what he was feeling. Myalgias. Very severe, profound, and global, myalgias.

His eyes had been closed during the discovery of his muscle pain. He slowly opened them and saw a ceiling. "Which ceiling is this?" Noble thought. "Oh yes, it's the ceiling in Arthur's room. But, why am I in here?" He looked at the room's louvered window. From the light coming between the wood louvers, Noble guessed it was very early. 6:00 or 6:30 in the morning, maybe? This is when he discovered yet another sensation. He was having a lot of difficulty focusing his eyes.

With much effort, Noble lifted his right arm. Not only was it very weak, and painful to move, but he was surprised at its size. He could see the outline of the carpel bones of his wrist, and thought he might be able to count all eight of them. The styloid processes of both the radial and ulnar bones were easy to see, and the radius and ulna themselves were prominent. The medial and lateral epicondyles of the humerus stuck out from the elbow. Why was this so? Noble lifted his left arm which appeared exactly like the right, except for an IV inserted in it.

Noble tried to lift his head, but it was too heavy. His head was propped up on pillows, so he was able to look about the room. But, "look" did not equate to "see". His eyes did not focus well enough for him to discern detail. However, there were two other people in the room. On the left, asleep in a chair, was an older man with a cane on his lap. Noble did not recognize him. To the right, on a small couch, was Lillian who was also asleep.

Noble tried to speak, and said, "Lilly." But, he now felt a third change to his body. It was very hard for him to take a deep breath. In fact, anything beyond a resting tidal volume breath was difficult. The word "Lilly" came out as a breathy whisper. "Lilly," he said again, but with no greater voice than before. Noble took as deep a breath as he possibly could, and forced it through his vocal cords as fast and hard as he knew how to do. "Lilly!" Even Noble found his own voice barely audible, but this time he saw his wife move. She stretched her right arm, yawned, and opened her blue eyes. It took her a few seconds to realize that Nobles eyes were also open.

"Edward!" Lillian shouted. "Oh my God, Edward!" Lillian lunged toward her husband's bed. Lillian had awakened the older man, who was now struggling to get out of his chair. Lillian dropped to her knees at the bedside, through her arms around the startled Noble, and began to kiss his face repeatedly. Lillian was already crying, and saying over and over again, "Oh, Edward! Oh, Edward! Oh, Edward! The older man moved his chair next to the bed, sat in it, and also began to say many times, "Edward!"

All the commotion in the household brought people from the upper floors rushing downstairs. Florence ran in, knelt to her knees, and flung herself onto her father. "Oh, Daddy! Oh, Daddy!" It was not long before Bernard and Michael joined in the chant about "oh, Daddy!" Moments later, Dr. David Schafer ran into the room, smiled, and said, "Welcome home, Dr. Noble!" Noble wondered where exactly he had been.

Hugging, kissing, patting, rubbing, and hugging again, went on for some time. It was Lillian that finally actually asked Noble a question. "Oh, Edward! How do you feel? My dear sweet Edward!"

In no more than a whisper, Noble said, "I'm...I'm...fine... Lilly. I just have a lot of myalgias...and I'm a bit short of breath." He had to stop frequently to take deep enough breaths to speak.

When the older man spoke, Noble instantly recognized the voice. "Edward...gee it's great to see you again, my friend!"

Noble knew the voice, but still could not believe the man was actually him. "Harvey? Is that you, Harvey?"

Smiling, Harvey Cushing said, "Yeah, I know. No one says anything, because they don't want to hurt my feelings. But, I know I look like an old man. Well, I'm back in the ol' U.S.A. And, now you are too!" Florence went to the telephone to call Milton Rosenau, who said he would be right over.

"Lilly," asked Noble, "what is going on? What has happened? Why am I in Arthurs' room? And, why do I look like...this?" Noble raised his right arm to show his wife.

"Dear," said Lillian, "what was the last thing you remember?"

Noble thought a moment before answering. He did not want to mention his most recent conversations. He would save those for some other day. "Well, I remember not feeling well after we came home from Boston Harbor. I laid down on the library sofa to rest. When I awoke, I was in here."

Lillian looked both at Schafer and Cushing. She looked back at her husband and said, "Edward, my dear dear Edward. You have had influenza. The severe form, with bilateral pneumonia, bleeding, and cyanosis. You almost died, Edward. In fact, we were not sure if you would ever regain consciousness."

"Well," said Noble, "unconscious? I've been unconscious? How long have I been this way? What day is it?"

Lillian gently kissed her husband's cheek. "Edward, you have been unconscious for twelve days. Today is Monday, May 12th. Dr. Schafer said he has never seen anyone survive with the most severe complications of influenza. You had a fever of 106° F for many hours. We all expected you would die in only a day or so. Miraculously, the cyanosis cleared the day after it started. But, you remained completely unresponsive…until now. The doctors feared you had suffered severe anoxic brain damage."

Now the pieces were coming together for Noble. His twelve days of protein deprivation had caused severe muscle wasting and weakness. His dyspnea was a consequence of marked bilateral hemorrhagic pneumonia. The myalgias, and his difficulty with ocular focusing, were sequela of influenza. Noble was already beginning to estimate the chances of full recovery, verse chronic residual disabilities.

"So, I was completely unresponsive these last twelve days?" asked Noble.

"Well, actually," said Cushing, "you were responsive to pain only intermittently. And, occasionally you displayed pronounced delirium; rarely saying single words or phrases. Much of the rest of the time you were not even responsive to deep pain."

"What did I say?" asked Noble.

"You spoke the names of Charles, Elizabeth, Arthur, and Marguerite…over and over," said Lillian. "You also said something about 'The Black' many times. Do you remember any of that, dear?"

Noble did not want to talk about those things, at least not now. He replied, "Not really. When did I say those words?"

"It was not long after you became ill," said Lillian. "Perhaps ten or eleven days ago."

To Noble, it seemed as though he had used those words, or thought them, only a few moments ago. Someday he would tell Lillian about them. However, he needed to thoroughly contemplate his experiences first. Noble motioned with his right index finger for Lillian to come close to him. When she did, he kissed on the cheek and whispered in her ear, "Thanks for helping me back, Lilly. I love you." She smiled, kissed him, and replied, "Welcome back, Edward. I love you too."

Eventually, Milton Rosenau arrived and greeted his old friend. Like Cushing and Schafer, he had spent numerous rotations caring for Noble during the ordeal. The three physicians set about examining their fully conscious patient. Global muscle wasting and weakness was readily apparent. The lungs were clear. Still, they estimated that pneumonia had significantly reduced Noble's total lung capacity by reducing both tidal volume and vital capacity. Remarkably, Noble's short and long term memory was perfect, except for the past twelve days. However, moderate eye muscle weakness made focusing difficult. Noble was unable to stand, but that was likely due to severe lower extremity muscle wasting. A more precise neurologic motor assessment would await improved muscle tone. There were no apparent sensory deficits, problems with finger-to-nose or heal-to-shin pointing, and no dysdiadochokinesia. All three physicians said his condition, given the severity of the infection, was miraculous.

Noble assisted the other doctors in planning a rehabilitation program for him. Several times per day, Lillian, the three children, or any one of several hospital volunteers would put Noble through range-of-motion exercises to improve joint mobility. Static and dynamic muscle exercises would also be performed frequently during the coming days. These exercises would include gradually longer attempts at walking with an aid. A wheel chair was brought to the home to allow Noble some movement autonomy on the household first floor. He would be encouraged to blow up rubber balloons as a way to improve vital pulmonary capacity. Noble was given a high protein diet with increased kilocalories. The diet was Noble's favorite part of his program. He was now hungry all the time.

The next day, Tuesday, May 13th, Cushing came to the Noble house to visit his old friend. Cushing tossed the morning *Boston Globe* into Noble's lap and said, "Look at this, Edward." The front page headline read, "ARMY FLU DOC SURVIVES". Noble simply smiled.

Noble and Cushing spent much of the morning catching up on a year-and-a-half of life's experiences. They talked about the army, France, Boston, and of course medicine. Noble reiterated his desire to return to his previous Internal Medicine practice, and reopen his office. He was receiving offers to join faculties at dozens of universities. He was seriously considering clinical associate professorships at both Boston and Harvard Universities. However, he would take such positions only if he could remain the Director of the South Department at Boston City Hospital. The Boston academic positions allowed a private practice and the BCH directorship.

Cushing had already resumed his faculty position at Harvard, and had performed some neurosurgery since coming home. He was restarting his studies of hemorrhage control during cranial surgery. He also began compiling notes for a book he wanted to write someday about his war experiences. He asked if he could include some of Noble's cables sent to him, and Noble heartily agreed. Cushing also continued his drawing and illustrating. The only thing he had not yet resumed was tennis. Cushing had a persistent moderate gait disturbance, and marked lower extremity cluadication, since he contracted influenza. With no real improvement in either debility for months, he doubted he would ever play tennis again.

Rosenau also dropped by with the same *Boston Globe* edition that Cushing brought to the house. He told Noble and Cushing that Harvard was considering implementing a school of public health. This was very exciting for Rosenau, who wanted to direct an epidemiology program in such a school. Lillian listened intently to the conversation. Finally, Rosenau said, "Lillian, I am certain this new Harvard school will come to pass within the next few years. When it does, I am going to make two recommendations to the dean: First, you should be offered a position as an instructor in the school. Second, you must be the first student to enroll in the school's PhD program." Noble hugged his wife from his wheelchair as she beamed with joy. She did not have to say yes to either proposal for her to give her approval. Noble whispered to Lillian, "Do you think the world can handle two Dr. Nobles?" Lillian just chuckled.

Later in the day, Bernard and Michael spoke at length with their father about the 1919 Red Sox season. They were not very pleased. True, the Red Sox had played eleven games, and had won seven of them. However, there had been six home games, and the Sox had won only three. The boys saw this as a bad omen, given the enthusiasm of Fenway fans. The next home game was not until June 5th against Detroit, but the brothers asked if they might be excused from school on that Thursday. Noble said he would do all he could to be in shape for a Red Sox game that day. Bernard and Michael could not have been happier.

The next day, Wednesday, May 14th, Dr. David Schafer and Dr. Anna Reed dropped by Beacon Street to check on Boston's most famous patient. Both residents remarked on how well Noble looked, and how fast he was responding to his rehabilitation program. After awhile, Schafer asked, "Dr. Noble, can I speak to you about a few things?"

"Sure, David," said Noble, "what's on your mind?"

"First, Dr. Noble," said Schafer, "I want to thank you for recommending me for the Chief Resident position for this next year. While you were ill, I was honored to be offered that position."

"Congratulations, David!" said Noble. "That is wonderful! But, why do I get the impression that there is more to the story here?"

"Well, sir," said Schafer. "Don't get me wrong. I am very honored, sir. However, as you know, I complete my third and final year of Internal Medicine residency in just six weeks. I was hoping to ask you if...if...if I might apply to be your Infectious Disease fellow this next year? Being the Chief Medical Resident at Boston City Hospital would be great. But, I don't want to miss an opportunity to be one of your fellows."

Noble smiled, and looked up above the top rims of his round lens glasses. "David, take my advice. Accept the Chief Resident position. It is truly a feather in your medical bonnet, and you have earned it. You are a terrific physician. I promise that if you take this position, there will be an Infectious Disease fellowship waiting for you in the 1920-1921 BCH program."

David was overjoyed, and said he would take the Chief position. "Sir, I have one other small request," said Schafer. "Anna and I are going to be married this summer. Anna's father died many years ago, and she would be very honored if you would 'give the bride away' at our wedding." Noble congratulated the fiancés, and said that he would be happy to be part of the wedding. Lillian immediately began to plan her gown for the event, and went off with Anna to discuss her wedding plans.

Over the next few days, scores of people requested an opportunity to visit Noble. Lillian teased her husband about "holding court" in the parlor for well-wishers, while in his wheelchair. Lillian screened requests to see Noble, and would only show him the requests from people of which she approved. Newspaper reporters were strictly banned from the Noble home.

On Friday, May 16th, Lillian received a morning visit request from a favorite guest. Sergeant Raymond Campbell came to call, and Noble greatly looked forward to seeing him.

"I'll never forget my surprise when you came to pick me up the first time at Boston and Main Railroad Station," said Noble. "I thought it was all a huge mistake."

"You looked pretty confused, Major," said Campbell, with a cackle. I wondered at the time if you would be like so many other officers who treat us enlisted men...well...poorly. You turned out to be the nicest officer in Boston, sir."

"I want to thank you for all your help, Sergeant, over the last fifteen months. We will never be able to repay the kindness you showed my family when my son died. And, Lillian and I will never forget you." Noble used a handkerchief to dry the corner of one of his eyes. Changing subjects, Noble asked, "So, what is in store for you now, Sergeant?"

"Well, sir," said Campbell, "that is one of the things I wanted to talk to you about. I will be discharged from the army this weekend, sir. I'm going home to Billings, Montana, next week. My father owns a very successful hardware store there, and he is retiring soon. I'm going to take over the family business when I get home."

"That's wonderful, Sergeant!" replied Noble. Send us a note from time-to-time, will you?"

"Will do, sir," said Campbell. "One last thing. I will always miss Karen, sir...always. She became the end-all for me, and I have never loved anyone as much as I loved her, sir. But, since she died, a high school girl friend has been writing me almost every day. I'm very anxious to look her up when I get home. Do you think that is disrespectful of Karen, sir?"

Noble thought for a moment before he answered Campbell. He recalled his most recent encounters on the north beach of Cape Cod. "Sergeant, as you know, Karen Pecknold was the first person I spoke to when I returned to Boston City Hospital last year. I have known no other more gracious or generous person at that facility. If she cared about you the way her friends say she did, Karen would be pleased if you found happiness when you returned to Billings."

Campbell seemed genuinely comforted by Noble's comments. With great mutual respect, the two saluted one another as they had many times before. Noble watched from the parlor window as the Sergeant drove away in the familiar army staff car for the final time.

Later in the morning, Florence came to speak to her father in the parlor, or "throne room", as Lillian now called it. "Dad, I really have to talk to you," said Florence.

"You sound rattled, Florence," said Noble. "What's up?"

"While you were ill, Dad, we received thousands of letters and telegrams from all over the country wishing you well. We also have many messages from the rest of North America, Europe, Asia, Africa, Australia, and Central and South America. Since you have started your recovery, the letters and telegrams have increased. We have sort of a problem, Dad."

"What's that?" said Noble, who was playing this whole conversation naively, but his snickering gave him away.

"Dad, I'm serious," said Florence. "The A.I. Office is packed with messages, and we are now overflowing with them here at home. We have pretty much filled the garage, and now the Ford is overflowing with them. If we don't do something today, I'll have to move the Ford out onto Beacon Street."

The number of messages surprised Noble. "Have you read any of them, Florence? What sort of things do they say?"

"Well, I have read a tiny fraction of them," said Florence. "While you were sick, dad, the letters mostly wished for your recovery. You see, all over the world you are viewed as someone who fought against uncaring establishments on behalf of the people. Successful or not, you saw what was right and pursued the moral and ethical thing to do. And, you did this in spite of personal danger to yourself. You are an incredibly popular world figure, Dad. Every day I am asked what it's like to be 'the daughter of Dr. Edward Noble'.

"Must be quite a burden," joked Noble.

"Dad, I'm serious!" said Florence. "We all get that all the time. We know you're just a guy who likes cheese sandwiches. But, that's a different story. In any case, since your recovery, the letters say how happy people are that you are better. Of course, there are some odd letters."

"Like what," asked Noble, who was enjoying all of this.

"Like, people who want you to be there doctor, or cure their loved ones...even dogs. Mom doesn't like the ones written by ladies who propose marriage to you. There are a lot of those. But, I can show you a very interesting group of telegrams from Washington DC. A fairly large group of U.S. senators and congressmen...Republican and Democrat...want you to consider running for President in 1920."

Noble threw his head back and laughed louder than he had in many months. He just shook his head, and finally said, "Florence, hire some men to carry the messages away. They are all very kind, but we need to keep the garage for the Ford."

"Thanks, Dad. That really helps." Florence continued to stand in one place, as she looked at her shoes.

Noble knew his daughter's body language. She had something else to say. "Florence, do you have more on your mind?" said Noble.

There was a long pause, as Florence stood in one place and held her hands behind her back. Noble was reminded of the times as a child when Florence would practice a school speech for him, and stood this same way. "Well...dad...there is something." More moments passed. "Dad, I want you to know that I am going to finish my upcoming second year of nursing school at Boston City."

"That's great, dear," said Noble, knowing there was more coming.

"Hmm...well...I've kind of made some decisions, Dad," said Florence. "If I finish my second year, I can still get my RN degree. I know that you and I counted on me taking a third year at BCH. But, dad, I really think that I have a new plan."

Noble was listening intently, and knew his daughter was trying to tell him of a whole new life direction. "OK, Florence," said Noble. "What's your new plan?"

"Dad, instead of taking a third year of nursing, I have decided to apply to business school in the fall of 1920." Noble sat and continued to listen carefully. "As you know, I have been working a lot with local, state, and national philanthropic groups and welfare agencies. I have also been helping Mom with her A & M Charitable Fund, and the multiple banks that are involved. Everyone says that I have a knack for finances, and I really enjoy it. I think I could combine my nursing education with a business degree, and really contribute to the betterment of those in need. I know I wasn't a mathematics whiz in high school, dad, but I really get economics." She waited again for a moment, and then said quietly, "Are you mad at me...Dad?"

Noble waved for his daughter to come closer to his wheelchair. He picked up her hand and held it. Looking up at Florence, Noble said, "Honey, ever since you kids were old enough to stand up, I have insisted on only two criteria as you considered your futures. First, your work must, in some way, improve the lives of others. And second, you need to like what you do. Listening to you, it would seem your new plan accomplishes both criteria famously. I would only add to it now by saying 'go to it, girl!'"

Florence developed a huge smile, kissed her father's cheek, and left for Boston City Hospital. With her father's blessing, she was ready tackle the great new challenge she had set for herself.

After lunch, Noble took an early afternoon nap. He tired quickly and could only sit for a few hours at a time before resting. Noble had just rolled himself into the parlor, when Lillian entered the room. "Edward, you have three visitors who are pleading to see you. Are you up to it?"

"Sure," said Noble. He knew Lillian simply turned away those he did not really need to see. A few moments later, the three Second Lieutenants from the Army Intelligence Cable Office bounded into the parlor. They all hugged him so hard that he nearly fell out of his wheelchair. Then, all three sat on the floor around Noble as though he were their guru. In a way, he was.

The three Lieutenants caught Noble up on gossip at Camp Devens and BCH. They spoke so fast that he became vertiginous as his head turned from one to the other. Finally, Lieutenant Adelina Quellet said, "Major, of course you've heard the news."

Noble looked at Quellet with one eyebrow lifted. "What news is that?"

"Oh boy!" said Quellet. "He doesn't know, does he? Well, Major, the army is <u>closing</u> the A.I. Office! In fact, today was our last day of regular office duty. On Monday, May 19th, Devens Signal Corps soldiers are coming to take away all the communication equipment and furniture. With The War over, and the pandemic on the wane, the army no longer has a need for the office. I guess Boston City is going to turn it into a nursing department office."

Noble explained that he had so many emotions tied up with the A.I. Office it would take time to sort them all out. There was no question, however, that the high points were working with the Signal Corps Lieutenants, and working with Lillian while analyzing data generated by the staff. Nevertheless, Noble secretly wondered what he would be assigned to do after his convalescence. "So, what are you all going to be doing now?" asked Noble.

Lieutenant Claudette Pierre-Louis was the first to speak, and was very excited. "Major, I don't think you saw my shoulders!" Noble looked at her shoulder loops. Sure enough, each shoulder now sported a silver bar. "Congratulations, First Lieutenant Pierre-Louis! Excellent job!" Noble knew that the advancement of woman officers was rare. This was quite an accomplishment.

"I was so excited!" exclaimed Pierre-Louis. "I'm going to re-up for another stint with the army, Major. I'm going to remain with the Signal Corps at Devens for now. But, I have my eye on Captain's silver bars!"

"And I'm confident you'll make it," said Noble. "What about you, Lieutenant Quellet?"

"Major, I'll be leaving the service in just a couple of weeks. I've already been accepted into the Masters program in mathematics at the University of California, Berkeley. So, I'll be moving out west to San Francisco pretty soon. I hope there won't be any earthquakes!"

"Lieutenant," said Noble, "you made it through Boston's awful fall and winter of '18. I think you can make it through anything now." Noble then turned to Marié Lafayette. "And, what about you, Lieutenant?"

Lafayette smiled and said, "I'm also leaving the army in a few weeks, Major. I'm really looking forward to my new job!"

"What's that?" asked Noble.

"Major," said Lafayette, have you ever heard of Edward Willis Scripps...E. W. Scripps?"

"Is he the man who helped start the Scripps Institute of Oceanography in San Diego, California?" asked Noble.

"Yes he is, Major," said Lafayette. "Well, Mr. Scripps is planning to build a public radio station in Detroit sometime next year. It will be called 'WBL Radio'...or something like that. He has hired some people with experience in radio, and I am one of them! Just think of it! Being able to receive radio broadcasts...while just sitting in your own home! Isn't that wonderful?"

All four agreed the prospects were incredible. Noble thought of Arthur's radio dream, and that Lafayette was realizing the very same dream.

As a memento, the Lieutenant's gave Noble the last cable received by the A.I. Office. It was from the Cincinnati's public health department and detailed the natural histories of 7,058 influenza survivors. Months after recovering from influenza, 5,264 of these survivors still needed some form of medical assistance. There were also a large number of 1918 pandemic survivors who suddenly died in 1919. The causes of many of these deaths were still in question. In any case, it was obvious that effects of the pandemic were to be felt for a very long time.

The Major and the Signal Corps officers talked for hours until Noble could talk no more. He bid each Lieutenant a tearful and heartfelt goodbye, and all promised to write. Noble knew this was a promise he would most certainly keep. These women were like close family to him.

By 8 AM the next morning, on Saturday, May 17th, it was clear, sunny, and already warm in Boston. Lillian helped her husband go through his morning exercises, and then the Nobles sat down to a pancake and scrambled egg breakfast. Bernard and Michael went to the park to play baseball, and Florence went to help distribute food to people with influenza induced chronic complications. In the afternoon, Lillian planned to take Noble for a drive to Boston Common. In the beautiful spring Massachusetts weather, Noble was looking forward to the trip as the highlight of the entire day. He wanted to briefly practice walking, with the wheelchair as a support, along the Boston Common paths.

At 10 AM, Noble was sitting in his wheelchair in the kitchen preparing a picnic lunch, when there was a loud knock at the front door. Lillian answered the hail to find Colonel Victor Vaughn calling. "Hello, Lillian," said Vaughn. "Can I come in?" Lillian gave Vaughn a hug and escorted him into the entryway. By now, Noble had wheeled himself into the parlor. Vaughn quickly walked over to his long-time friend, saluted him, and then grabbed both of his hands.

"I heard about your illness, Edward, at the same time I heard about your recovery," said Vaughn. "I came here from Washington as fast as I could." Vaughn pulled up a chair right next to Noble.

"It's so good to see you, Colonel!" shouted Noble. He lunged forward in his wheelchair in order to hug Vaughn.

"You've lost some weight, Major," said Vaughn smiling. "Lillian, are you going to fatten this boy up?"

"I'm working on it, Victor," said a laughing Lillian. "I will say that he is eating me out of house and home!"

"I've heard you have some neurological sequela, Edward," said Vaughn.

"Well...you know, Colonel," replied Noble, "I've got the 'wobbly leg' syndrome and some diplopia. But, with my rigorous exercise program, I'm already improving." Noble described the onset of his symptomatic infection, and Lillian filled him in on the rest. Noble went on to debrief Vaughn on his tour of duty in France.

"Edward, I can't tell you how appreciative the President and Admiral Grayson are with your help in Paris. They have commented on it by cable from Europe several times. By the way, they both are overjoyed with your recovery." Lillian patted Noble on the arm and straightened his white hair. "I'm kind of overjoyed myself," joked Lillian.

"I guess you heard about the A.I. Office, Edward?" said Vaughn.

"Yeah, the Signal Corps Lieutenants told me," said Noble.

"The War has left the government strapped for cash right now," said Vaughn. "The Congress is significantly reducing War Department budgets, so the army is decreasing its size pretty quickly. Besides, the A.I. Office completed its mission."

Noble hung his head for a moment, lifted it, and said, "Colonel, the Office may have seen its mission halted, but I don't think it completed its mission, sir. Or said another way, it was fairly unsuccessful in its mission. Fifty one percent of American casualties in The War were due to disease. That rate was most certainly higher than the average for civilian men of the same age. We did not avoid General William Gorgas' *nightmare*, which was our charge sixteen months ago."

Vaughn put his elbow on the arm to his chair, and rested the side of his head on his hand. "You're right, Edward," said Vaughn. "The percentage speaks for itself. However, I think you need to give the office, and yourself, more credit. First of all, The War had the smallest percentage of disease mortality of any American conflict to date. Second, army mortality percentages due to measles, dysentery, typhus, and typhoid where considerably reduced compared to any previous American war. If it had not been for the pandemic, overall casualties would have been radically less then it turned out to be."

"But, Colonel," lamented Noble, "look at the pandemic outcome. How can anyone take 'credit' for anything in the face of it?"

Vaughn lifted his head off his hand and sat straight in his chair, as if to state something with resolve. "The A.I. Office provided you, and Lillian, a breadth of information that essentially no one else had. If that data were simply filed away without study, we could all say the mission was a failure. But that is not what happened. Your efforts, Edward, enormously affected public awareness about the pandemic. That level of awareness, as slow as it seemed to come, would not have occurred had you not acted on your conscience."

Vaughn paused for a long time. His eyes glistened slightly with tears, and his voice cracked with emotion. "The number can never be known, Edward. But, I believe…and the public believes…that you saved tens of thousands of American lives with your courage. Even though the personal consequences were clear, your refusal to ignore the truth made a difference. I will go even farther, and say your actions may have saved millions of lives around the globe. So, you see, Edward, I must respectfully disagree. I am certain the A.I. Office was successful, even if that success was obviously not perfect."

Noble was honored to know he may have played some important role during the pandemic. The honor was magnified several fold by the fact his father's best friend thought it so.

Vaughn dabbed his eyes with an army issue handkerchief, smiled, and changed the subject. "Edward, I have something for you." He took from his tunic an envelope, and handed it to Noble.

Noble noted the envelope's bold letters that read "War Department" on it. He opened the letter and turned to Vaughn. "Colonel, I'm sorry, but I'm having some difficulty reading right now. I am hoping bifocals will help in that regard, and will be fitted with them this next week. Lilly, can you read this for me?" He handed the envelope to his wife.

Lillian took out a typed sheet of paper, and began to read from it. "'War Department. Department of the Army. Washington DC. Dear Major Edward Noble, Camp Devens, Massachusetts. In view of your service to the army, and the United States of America, you are hereby promoted to the rank of Lieutenant Colonel. Congratulations. Newton B. Baker, Secretary of War.'"

Seeing an opportunity to tease her husband, Lillian opened her right hand and swung it back and forth as though the letter was too hot to hold. "Wow!" exclaimed Lillian. "Lieutenant Colonel Edward Noble! How much bigger can his head get, Victor?"

"I even have these for you, Edward," Victor handed Noble two new silver leafs to replace his gold Major insignias. Noble did not speak, but had the expression people give when they are sarcastically thinking "big deal". Noble was certain that Admiral Grayson, or perhaps even the President, had something to do with this promotion.

Victor laughed and knew exactly what Noble was thinking. "Edward, I have something else for you." Again, he took an envelope from his tunic and handed it to Lillian.

Lillian opened the envelope while joking, "Are they now going to make you a full Colonel?" She began to read. "'War Department. Department of the Army. Washington DC. Dear Lieutenant Colonel Edward Noble, Camp Devens, Massachusetts. With the convenience of the government of the United States of America, and using its secretarial authority to draw down military forces, you are hereby transferred to individual ready reserve. You have served your country with honor. Newton B. Baker, Secretary of War.' Victor, what exactly does this mean?"

"Lillian," said Victor, "it means Edward has been discharged from active army duty with honor. He has been transferred to the Army Medical Corps as a reservist, who does not need to drill."

"Yes!" yelled Noble as loud as he could, while raising both arms in a praising gesture. "Lilly, kiss your civilian husband!"

Lillian did just that, and whispered in Noble's ear she would like more of the same...later.

"Well, Colonel," said Noble, "as just ol' Dr. Noble, I guess I can call you 'Victor' now."

"'Uncle Victor' to you," laughed Vaughn.

Vaughn spoke with the Nobles for some time before mentioning that he had a train to catch back to Washington. He said he would come by again soon and see the Noble children.

Noble rolled his wheelchair up to the parlor bay window. Lillian pulled up a small wood chair, and set it immediately to Noble's left. She put her right arm around her husband's shoulders, and rested her head on his left shoulder. Both watched and waved as Vaughn closed the back door to his army staff car, and drove away.

Noble and his wife were ready for their excursion to the Boston Common. But, they sat silently together for some time. They thought about the poor state of the world. The devastation left by four years of world war, and the horror inflicted by influenza. The lowered vitality of pandemic survivors. The widows and widowers. The huge number of orphans. The swelling ranks of dependent elderly and infirmed. The psychosocial ruin of many. The families left in poverty. And, they thought of their own immeasurable losses. They sought to find the kernels of hope and optimism that would be needed in the months and years ahead. However, they could never forget the events that changed the world forever in 1918.

EPILOGUE

During the winter of 1919-1920, the world witnessed the second largest number of influenza deaths in the 20th century. This was the "fourth wave" of the pandemic, since the pathogen was likely the same as the 1918 strain. The fourth wave lasted only twelve weeks, compared to the thirty-one weeks that began in 1918. The pathogen was so efficient at human-to-human transmission that it simply ran out of susceptible hosts.

Among the pandemic victims was Sir William Osler, who died of influenza pneumonia on December 29, 1919. Dr. Harvey Cushing never fully recovered from debilities he developed from his influenza infection.

The breadth of the pandemic was documented by Dr. Victor Vaughn in his publication *Epidemiology and Public Health*, and volume No. 9 of the *Medical Department of the United States in the World War*. The *Annual Report of the Secretary of the Navy, 1919 – Miscellaneous Reports* also describes pandemic results in detail.

In the United States, 20 million people were infected with influenza in 1918-1919. There were 2 to 3 million influenza pneumonias. During the pandemic, 47% of all deaths in the United States were due to influenza. There were so many additional deaths that the actuarial life expectancy for those born in 1918 was reduced by ten years, compared to 1917. There were quadruple the number of influenza deaths in ages 20 to 40 years, compared to 41 to 60 years. The largest number of deaths was in the 25 to 29 year range, followed by 30 to 34, and 20 to 24 years, respectively. The most vulnerable people were pregnant women, who had a 23-71% influenza death rate. Of the pregnant women who survived, 26% lost their babies. Because so many women in their child bearing years died, along with young fathers, huge numbers of children were orphaned in America.

The calculated economic loss in the United States due to the pandemic was 3 to 4 trillion dollars, in 1918 dollars.

It is estimated that 675,000 people in the United States died of influenza during the pandemic. This estimate may be very low, since many of the states with army containments did not have military deaths counted. It is believed that 50 to 100 million people died of influenza worldwide during the 1918 pandemic. Not only was it the worst epidemic/pandemic in history. The 1918 pandemic was also the worst natural disaster in human history.

Influenza remained the "biggest question in science" through the 1920's. Initially, William Park and Anna Wessels Williams of the laboratory division of the New York City Health Department believed *Bacillus influenzae* was the responsible agent. However, they both changed their minds in 1919. Anna Wessels Williams wrote, "More and more, evidence points to a filterable virus being the cause." William Welch, president of the Board of Scientific Directors of the Rockefeller Institute for Medical Research, said at a 1929 conference, "The fact has always appealed to me that influenza is possibly an infection due to an unknown virus". Milton Rosenau of Harvard University also continued to believe a virus was responsible.

Then began a series of scientific breakthroughs.

Thomas Milton Rivers, Director of the Rockefeller Hospital, made an important discovery in 1926. He summarized his conclusions by saying, "Viruses appear to be obligate parasites in the sense their reproduction is dependent on living cells". Rivers was able to differentiate bacteria from viruses beyond the fact that the later can pass through porcelain filters and the former cannot.

River's work laid the foundation for research conducted by Richard Edwin Shope, a virologist at the Rockefeller Institute for Medical Research. During the 1918 pandemic, a very similar illness killed tens of thousands of pigs in the Midwestern U.S. Most felt the porcine disease was due to a bacterium. Shope began to study *Hemophilus influenzae suis*, which was a bacteria found in many of these cases. This organism is a close cousin to *Bacillus influenzae*, or Pfeiffer's bacillus, which had been renamed *Hemophilus influenzae*. However, Shope found that *Hemophilus influenzae suis* did not cause influenza when injected into pigs. There had to be more to the story. In 1931 Shope detected a virus in the tissues of pigs with influenza. Not only did the virus cause influenza when injected into healthy pigs, but the disease was made worse if the virus was injected along with *Hemophilus influenzae suis*. Shope later found survivors of the 1918 pandemic harbored antibodies to this same pig influenza. People born after 1920 did not have these antibodies. Therefore, the pig influenza virus was at least very similar to the 1918 disease.

Also in 1931, Ernest Goodpasture grew several viruses, including influenza, in fertilized chicken eggs. That same year, Ernst Ruska and Max Knoll took the first images of viruses using a new invention called an electron microscope.

Richard Shope was the first to isolate an influenza virus, and to vaccinate animals against influenza. Using his methods in 1933, Christopher Andrews, Patrick Laidlaw, and

Wilson Smith at the British National Institute for Medical Research studied humans infected with influenza. They finally isolated the human influenza pathogen, and found it to be a filterable virus that was very similar to Shope's pig influenza. They also found that ferrets could be infected with human influenza.

Frank Horsfall and Alice Chenoweth created the first live influenza vaccine in 1936. Thomas Frances and Thomas Magill made the first killed whole virus influenza vaccine, also that year. However, Anatol Smorodintev is credited with the first efficacious live influenza virus human vaccine in 1937.

Thomas Frances discovered a virus in 1940 with distinctly different antigens from the Andrews/Laidlaw/Smith virus. The Frances virus came to be known as influenza B, and the Andrews/Laidlaw/Smith virus was named influenza A.

In 1941, George Hirst found that influenza agglutinated, or clumped, red blood cells. This led to an extremely important discovery: the description of influenza surface proteins known as hemagglutinin (HA) and neuraminidase (NA). These surface proteins provided accessible markers for the study of the pathogen's behavior. Also that year, Heinz Fraenkel-Conrat and Robley Williams showed that tobacco mosaic virus ribonucleic acid (RNA) can assemble itself with coat protein to form functioning virus. They had discovered how viruses are created within host cells.

Large quantity annual production of influenza vaccines began in the 1960's. Now, each year, the dominant influenza A and B strains have vaccines produced against them. In a given year, a recipient of these vaccines has an 85% percent chance of not manifesting symptoms from the represented influenza strains.

Influenza viruses usually have a round shape, but can also be shaped like a capsule, or even take a filamentous form. They are tiny. About one hundred average sized influenza A viruses (or virons) could line up along the diameter of one human lymphocyte. The outside shell of the viron is made of lipoprotein, and has about five hundred protein spikes protruding from it. These spikes are the protein hemagglutinin (HA). The shell also has on its surface about one hundred box-shaped proteins called neuraminidase (NA). There are sixteen subtypes (or shapes) of HA (H1 to H16), and nine different subtypes of NA (N1 to N9).

HA and NA surface proteins are now part of the nomenclature for influenza. Here is an example: A/Johannesburg/33/94 (H3N2). From left-to-right, this signifies the influenza type, the town where it was first isolated, the number of isolates found, the year of isolation (1994), and the major type of HA and NA proteins. Of interest, avian species are the reservoir for all known antigenic subtypes of influenza viruses.

Inside the viron shell is ribonucleic acid (RNA) which the virus uses to reproduce itself. The virus has only eight genes (compared to about 23,000 genes in humans). These eight genes code for only eleven different proteins. Obviously, influenza is a very simple life form.

Influenza is unique in that it does not have its genes in a single strand of RNA. Rather, its genes are separate within the viron shell. This genetic arrangement gives influenza two distinct advantages over the human immune system. First, viral genes coding for HA and NA surface proteins mutate extremely fast. Human antibodies, memory T-cells, and dendritic cells have difficulty recognizing these rapidly changing proteins. Second, the influenza segmented genes allow two or more viruses infecting a mammalian cell to exchange whole genes with each other. This is called reassortment. Reassortment can create an entirely new influenza type very quickly.

Avian influenza usually does not infect humans. However, this infrequently occurs in two different ways. First, avian influenza can infect a species that can accommodate both avian and human influenza viruses. Pigs have sialic-acid receptors on their cells onto which avian and human influenza strains can attach. Therefore, reassortment can occur in pigs and allow avian influenza to acquire genes that permit human infection. Second, avian influenza can spontaneously mutate and develop characteristics permitting infection in human populations.

Every two or three years, gene mutations can cause slightly more changes than usual in influenza HA or NA surface proteins. These changes may be more difficult for the human immune system to recognize. These mutations are called "antigen drift", and can cause an influenza epidemic. However, every fifteen to thirty years, extremely new influenza gene mutations can occur. These genes can code for radically different molecular shapes of HA, NA, or both. When these surface proteins change this much this fast, few if any humans have antibodies to the novel viral strain. This phenomenon is known as "antigen shift" and a pandemic can result.

There were at least four influenza pandemics in the 19th century, including the 1889-1890 pandemic. There were three pandemics in the 20th century: 1918 (H1N1), 1957 (H2N2), and 1968 (H3N2). A pandemic does not necessarily result in a high mortality rate. However, in 1918, there was something very special about that particular pandemic. The 1918 influenza virus became ultra-lethal, and the reasons why remained a mystery for a very long time.

Influenza A is rapidly spread via aerial droplets and fomites (inanimate objects or substances) with inhalation into the pharynx and upper respiratory tract. Its incubation is only 24-72 hours. The viron HA surface proteins can combine with specific receptors on a variety of mammalian cells, such as red blood cells and bronchial epithelial cells. Once inside the host cell, the virus releases its RNA, which is taken to the cell nucleus. The RNA codes for messenger RNA (mRNA) which is sent to the cytoplasm to begin directing the host cell to build viral proteins. Newly replicated RNA is transported to the cytoplasm, and wrapped in new HA and

NA shell proteins. The complete daughter virons then bud out the cell wall, travel into the extracellular spaces, and are ready to infect other cells. One infected mammalian cell can produce 1,000 to 10,000 new virons. One can see how fast an unprepared human immune system can be overwhelmed by influenza.

During an influenza infection, the human immune system has several lines of defense. The first defense is a layer of mucous covering tiny hairs, called cilia, residing on respiratory epithelial cells. The second line of defense are antibodies produced to recognize specific antigens on a pathogen. Third, macrophages and natural killer cells seek out and destroy any kind of microscopic invader. Fourth, anti-bacterial and viral enzymes are secreted directly by respiratory cells. Fifth, a substance called interferon is released by white cells specifically against viruses. Finally, a sixth line of defense are chemicals called cytokines secreted by T-cells and macrophages. Cytokines summon more T-cells and macrophages to fight the intruders.

It was obvious to everyone that the 1918 influenza virus acted very differently compared with other human influenzas. It not only infected the upper respiratory tract, but was able to reach all the way down to the tiniest air sacks of the lungs; the alveoli. Capillaries surrounding alveoli greatly dilated and poured large quantities of fluid into the air sacks. There followed profound necrosis (premature death of tissue) of the epithelial cells lining the entire bronchial tree. The body began to produce fiber-like connective tissue in an attempt to protect itself from the insult. However, the body's defensive measure had terrible unintended consequences. Alveoli became engorged with collagen, fibrin, cell debris, protein, and copious amounts of fluid. This process is known as severe viral pneumonia, which can result in acute respiratory distress syndrome (ARDS). Victims simply drowned or suffocated in fluid produced by their own destroyed lungs. Even if victims survived viral pneumonia, they now had greatly weakened immune systems as well as lungs ripe for secondary bacterial infections. Secondary bacterial pneumonias with *Hemophilus influenzae*, *Staphylococcus aureus*, and *Streptococcus pneumoniae*, were equally as lethal.

In 1918, young adults were uncharacteristically and substantially at increased risk with influenza. Here is why. Cytokines were mentioned earlier as chemical signals that recruit T-cells and macrophages to a site of infection. Cells arriving at that site, in turn, release more cytokines. If too many immune cells are activated at a single site in the body too quickly, the reaction can become uncontrolled. This is why healthy and robust immune systems in vigorous young 1918 adults may have been a liability rather than an asset. The resulting phenomenon is known as a "cytokine storm", where a sudden and massive release of over 150 known mediators of inflammation occurs. (Such mediators include tumor necrosis factor alpha, interleukin-1, interleukin-6, oxygen free radicals, coagulation factors, etc.) If a cytokine storm occurs in the lungs following ARDS and/or influenza, fluid and immune cells flood into the airways. Death would be sudden and horrifying.

No one knows for sure where the pandemic of 1918 began. Some have theorized it came from China. Others have pointed to a British Army post in Étaples, France, during 1916. But, the strongest epidemiological evidence points to Haskell County, Kansas. There is no obvious documented transmission of the virus to Haskell County. However, there is a precise trial of influenza that spread from that county to Camp Funston, and on to other military installations. The pandemic can then be traced to Europe, where an even more lethal viral mutation occurred.

There is also molecular evidence from the U.S. Armed Forces Institute of Pathology (AFIP). (The AFIP was originally called the Army Medical Museum.) Based on viral genomic mutation rates, researchers have determined the virus jumped to humans in the winter of 1917-1918. This timeframe fits perfectly with the Haskell County theory. There is also evidence from the Centers for Disease Control and Prevention (CDC) pointing to a mutation that allowed the 1918 virus to jump directly from birds to humans. Others still hold to the idea that reassortment,

perhaps in pigs, resulted in the lethal virus. Reassortment definitely was responsible for the 1957 and 1968 pandemics. But, the 1918 pandemic behaved differently. Very differently.

Two separate circumstances promoted the creation of the worst disaster in human history. An exceedingly deadly virus emerged just as its transmission was facilitated by millions of densely grouped military personnel. Both nature, and human beings, helped unleash an unequalled pandemic "perfect storm".

In February, 1998, John Hultan traveled to Brevig Mission, Alaska, which lost 85% of its population during the 1918 pandemic. Brevig Mission is only one hundred miles west of Golovin, Alaska. Hultan recovered preserved lung tissue from an Inuit woman who died of influenza in 1918, and was buried in the Alaskan permafrost. He gave the lung specimens to Jeff Taubenberger of the AFIP. The AFIP housed an immense collection of archived tissue samples.

Taubenberger found in the AFIP collection autopsy lung samples fixed in formalin from two U.S. Army soldiers who were victims of the 1918 influenza. The Brevig Mission samples, and the two archival AFIP specimens, were used to sequence the viral HA and NA genes in 1999. All eight 1918 influenza genes were sequenced in 2005.

In 2005, Adolfo Garcia-Sastre of Mount Sinai School of Medicine spliced all eight of the 1918 influenza genes into tiny circular pieces of free-standing DNA, called plasmids. The plasmids were then sent to the CDC in Atlanta, Georgia, where high-containment bio-safety Level 4 enhanced laboratories reside. These laboratories have multiple airlocks that are electronically secured to prevent two doors from opening at the same time. Entrances and exits to the labs have multiple showers, vacuum rooms, and ultraviolet light rooms designed to destroy all traces of a biohazard. Air and water used in the labs are also placed through multiple decontamination procedures. All researchers who worked with the plasmids were given antiviral prophylaxis, and wore positive pressure suits with self-contained oxygen supplies.

At the CDC, Terrence Tumpey and his team inserted the plasmids with 1918 viral genes into kidney cells. The spliced viral genes began to produce influenza RNA, and code for mRNA. The mRNA directed the formation of influenza proteins right on schedule. The new RNA, and new proteins, combined to create fully functioning virons. In just seventy-two hours, the actual 1918 influenza that killed up to 100 million people…was back.

Much has been learned about the reconstructed 1918 influenza virus, as it was compared to a contemporary influenza strain called Texas virus. Designated an H1N1 influenza, 1918 virus is exceptionally lethal. All mice died within six days of infection with 1918 virus, while none died from Texas virus. This high lethality in mice is not shared by any other primary isolate of human influenza virus. This characteristic also highlights the superb virulence of this virus for mammalian species.

Mice lost 13% of body weight two days after 1918 virus infection, whereas weight loss was minimal and transient with Texas virus. There was 39,000 times more virons found in mouse lung tissue four days after 1918 virus infection, compared with Texas virus. Fifty times as many virons were released from human lung tissue cells one day after 1918 virus infection, as compared with Texas virus.

Further experiments by Tumpey, Taubenberger, and others have shown the extreme virulence of 1918 virus came from genes coding for HA, NA, and polymerase proteins (PA, PB1, and PB2). The 1918 virus HA gene, when introduced into a contemporary influenza virus, conferred the same virulence in mice. 1918 virus HA protein had a duel molecular receptor that could bind to both avian and human receptors. The virus genome codes for 13,588 amino acids. However, only a single amino acid mutation can change the binding preference of the HA protein. Therefore, only a handful of mutations can turn avian influenza into a pandemic killer, like 1918 virus.

The 1918 viral gene coding for NA protein allowed it to activate HA protein in culture. This mutation allowed the virus to grow potentially in any cell type, unlike other influenza strains.

Researchers at the CDC found that 1918 viral polymerase permitted the virus to replicate much faster in human respiratory epithelial cells compared to other H1N1 viruses. Genes coding for polymerase reduced the viral dose needed to kill mice by one hundred times.

Experiments have shown 1918 virus contained HA and NA proteins that induce a profound mouse immune response. This response is completely unlike the mild immune response following most other influenza infections. Mice infected with 1918 virus showed severe lung damage from alveolar macrophages, cytokines, and neutrophils. Resulting pulmonary edema, hemorrhage, acute bronchiolitis, aveolitis, and bronchopneumonia was strikingly similar to 1918 human autopsy specimens. In fact, no other human influenza virus has shown a similar pathogenicity for mice three and four days after infection.

A series of other experiments gave fascinating results. Researchers took three groups of mice. One group received no influenza vaccine, one received the usual seasonal influenza vaccine, and one received a specific H1N1 influenza vaccine. Thirty-one days later, all groups were given lethal doses of 1918 virus. Only the mouse group that received the H1N1 vaccine survived.

In another experiment, a group of mice was injected with serum from humans given H1N1 influenza vaccine. A second group of mice did not receive the serum. Both groups were then given lethal 1918 viral doses. The antibodies in the H1N1 vaccine group protected the mice. Therefore, the H1N1 vaccine used in these experiments is effective against 1918 virus.

Further experiments with mice have shown the antiviral drugs oseltamivir and amantadine are effective against 1918 virus. It is interesting that mutations in later viral generations have made these drugs inactive against some strains of influenza.

Reconstruction of 1918 virus has given researchers new insights into "chinks in the armor" of influenza. The world is better prepared for the next lethal influenza pandemic because of their work. However, we will need all the weapons we can create against influenza. Many disadvantages and difficult challenges remain in humanity's battle with the virus. There are now many more humans on Earth than in 1918, and this provides a more densely packed population on which to prey. Vaccines still take many months to produce in large quantity. Administering tens of millions of antiviral drug doses in a very short period of time is problematic. And, the virus itself can mutate very quickly. Influenza is able to find ways to evade our immune systems, and develop resistance to our drugs, with incredible speed.

Locked away deep inside the CDC in Atlanta are ten sealed vials. These vials contain the reconstructed 1918 influenza virus; the cause of the worst epidemic in history. 1918 virus is imprisoned in bio-safety Level 4 laboratory vaults along with other killers of humanity, such as smallpox variola virus.

Jeff Taubenberger has worked extensively with the 1918 viral gene sequence and the reconstructed virus. Taubenberger said this of the virus:

"All influenza A pandemics since [the 1918 pandemic], and indeed all cases of influenza A worldwide (excepting human infections from avian viruses such as H5N1 and N7N7), have been caused by descendants of the 1918 virus, including "drifted" H1N1 viruses and reasserted

H2N2 and N3N2 viruses. The latter are composed of key genes from the 1918 virus, updated by subsequently incorporated avian influenza genes that code for novel surface proteins, making the 1918 virus indeed the 'mother' of all pandemics".

CPSIA information can be obtained
at www.ICGtesting.com
Printed in the USA
LVOW13s1759151216

517424LV00010B/1354/P